Cas[illegible]
Challenge

∞ ∞ ∞ ∞ ∞

M.K. Eidem

The Imperial Series

Cassandra's Challenge

Victoria's Challenge

Jacinda's Challenge

Tornians

Grim

A Grim Holiday

Wray

Oryon

Ynyr

CASSANDRA'S CHALLENGE

Published by M.K. Eidem

Cover Design by Judy Bullard

Edited by: www.A-Z_Media@outlook.com

∞ ∞ ∞ ∞ ∞

I'd like to thank my family for all their support all my friends that have been there for me, answering questions and helping guide me, Judy, Reese, Sally, Julie, Fern, Beth, Susan and Narelle; Thanks, ladies!

∞ ∞ ∞ ∞ ∞

Chapter One

"Admiral, sensors in the Relinquished Zone are tracking a Regulian battle fleet. They've stopped in an uncharted solar system approximately 5000 light years away," Senior Chief Delondra Falco reported.

Admiral William Hale Zafar turned from his Command Center. At 50 cycles, he is the youngest Admiral ever in the Carinian Fleet and currently in command of the Battle Star Retribution with an accompaniment of five battleships as they patrolled their border. He is 7'1" and 325 pounds of solid Carinian male, his lush dark hair just starting to gray at the temples and while not long, was not cut militarily short. His startling violet eyes looked to Falco.

"What Intel do we have on that system?" he demanded.

"Only what the remote sensors scanned, Sir. It seems to be a tiny system with nine planets and one sun. If the Regulians' warp signature hadn't led us to it, it would easily have been missed," Falco replied.

"Our systems aren't supposed to miss anything, Falco!" the Admiral stared her down. "Are you getting any data on the planets with our sensors? The Regulians must be there for some reason."

"No, Sir. Sorry, Sir, we are too far away."

The Admiral turned, "What do you think, Quinn?"

Colonel Quinn Tar was Second-in-Command on the Retribution and one of his oldest friends. At 52, he had some wear and tear on him. He was shorter than his commander by 3 inches but weighed the same. "I agree there has to be a reason they are there. We should get closer and gather more Intel."

The Admiral reached his decision. "Falco, set a course to get us into detail-scan range, warp six. I want to know what the Regulians are up to. Communications, contact High Command and relay that we are going into the Relinquished Zone then connect me to the other Commanders."

"Yes, Sir."

"Set the fleet to Alert Status Two. I want all eyes and ears open while we are in the Relinquished Zone."

"Yes, Sir."

∞ ∞ ∞ ∞ ∞

The Retribution traveled through the Relinquished Zone at warp six for over two days before finally getting within long-range scanning distance.

"Status, Falco."

"Sir, nine planets, one sun. Only one considered habitable, the third from the sun. Scans show abundant life signs; the majority seems to be humanoid, large mineral deposits, large cities."

"Can you ascertain the level of advancement?"

"They have satellites orbiting the planet…probably communications…all defenses seem to be terrestrial. Sir!!! The Regulians have just initiated an attack on the planet targeting the major cities!"

"Fuck!!! How soon can we intercede?"

"Sir, at current speed 23 hours."

"Increase speed to warp nine point six. Inform the Fleet. I want us there yesterday! What the fuck are they doing, Quinn? What's on that planet they want so badly?"

"I don't know, but we'd better find out."

"Falco, how many inhabitants are on that planet?"

"Sir, if the scan is correct just under seven billion."

"Damn! Go to Alert Status One!"

Two and a half hours later the Retribution was closing in on the solar system. The Admiral stood in the Command Center studying monitors. He remembered another time when the Regulians had attacked a planet and help hadn't arrived in time. His past wife had died in that attack.

"How long until we're in range to launch fighters?"

"Fifteen minutes, Sir."

"Have all fighters in the launchers. Reduce speed to warp six. Get us in range to launch, Falco."

"Yes, Sir."

The Admiral waited impatiently.

"We're in range, Commander."

"Launch all fighters," the Admiral ordered.

"Launch all fighters! I say again, Launch all fighters!" was heard throughout the ship.

William looked at Quinn, "I hope there's something left to save."

∞ ∞ ∞ ∞ ∞

Lt. Lucas Zafar, call sign Hawk, was a seven cycle fighter pilot in the Carinian Fleet currently engaged with the enemy in the atmosphere of a previously unknown planet. He and his wingman were closing in on four Regulian Strikers.

"Shit, Hotdog, what are they looking for out here?" He looked out of his Blade at the remote mountainous terrain. Suddenly, the Strikers opened fire on a small town. "Fuck, let's get in there and take them out."

"I'm all over that, Hawk."

The two pilots methodically took out the first three Strikers then chased the fourth into an even more unpopulated area. Hawk lined up and took his shot. Before the Striker exploded it got off a shot of its own, clipping Hawk's wing.

"SHIT!!! Hotdog, I'm going down. I've lost all controls."

"Eject! Eject!" his comm told him.

As Hawk ejected from his crippled aircraft, Hotdog circled to get his location. The Blades they flew only held one, he couldn't pick him up, and he had to watch helplessly as Hawk's parachute disappeared in the trees.

"Retribution…Hotdog! Retribution…Hotdog!"

"Go ahead, Hotdog…"

"Hawk's down. I repeat Hawk's down…"

The Admiral went still and the Bridge went quiet. Picking up the headset, he demanded, "What's Hawk's status?"

"He was able to eject, Sir. He landed in a heavily-wooded area. I lost visual but have his last coordinates."

"Any danger detected?"

"No, Sir, all four Strikers were taken out before he went down."

"Affirmative, get back to base, Hotdog."

"Sir…"

"Back to base!"

"Yes, Sir!"

The Admiral ripped off his headset, "Quinn, you have the command."

"Will, where are you going?" But he already knew.

"I'm going to get my son back."

"Admiral…"

"Colonel, you have your orders."

"Yes, Sir."

The Admiral headed to the Flight Deck. "Chief, I'm going on the recovery mission."

"Admiral."

"I need a flight suit."

"Yes, Sir, you'll be with Dodge and Scratch."

∞ ∞ ∞ ∞ ∞

Hawk awoke to find he was lying on a couch and staring into the most incredible green eyes he'd ever seen. Blinking, he realized they belonged to a young girl. A young girl with flaming red hair. As he moved to sit up, he gasped at the sharp pain. He looked down and saw his right leg had been treated.

"Easy, you'll tear it open."

Hawk assessed the man as he moved the girl aside. He was not very tall, only 6'3". But he appeared solid, fit, and older, somewhere in his sixties, his eyes perceptive.

"Where am I? Who are you?" Hawk demanded.

Cassandra watched her father talk to the large man. She'd witnessed the dogfight, seen the two strange aircraft destroy the four that had been attacking the town of Chester, and watched one eject. He'd landed not far from her in a heavily wooded area.

The branches that caught him had injured his leg. By the time she'd gotten to him, he'd been barely conscious. Getting him to his feet had been an experience. She'd never seen a 6'8" man before, and even with her 6'1" frame had trouble getting him back to the family cabin.

"I'm Jacob Chamberlain," he touched his chest. "My son, Peter; his wife, Cyndy; their daughter, Tori; and my daughter, Cassandra." He pointed to each of the people in the room and watched to see if he understood. "Who are you?"

Lucas tried to understand the language the older man spoke. It seemed similar to his own language…everyone waited… "I'm Lieutenant Lucas Zafar of the Battle Star Retribution…Do you understand what I'm saying?"

The five of them looked at him. The woman, the man called Cassandra, stepped up and put her hand on the older man's arm.

"Some…Your name is Lucas?"

"Yes."

"You have a leg injury," she put a hand on his leg, "do you understand?"

Lucas looked at her, "Yes."

"Why are we being attacked?" Jacob demanded.

"I was hoping you could tell me. The Regulians…"

"Who?"

"The Regulians, the race that is attacking your planet..."

"Earth," the woman interrupted him.

"What?"

"We call it Earth."

"Okay, the Regulians are attacking the Earth. Why? They were here at least several days before they attacked."

"They showed up a week ago, talked to the world leaders...then all of a sudden they attacked. How do you know this?" Jacob asked him.

Lucas sat up straighter, "Two and a half days ago, on a routine patrol we discovered the Regulians' warp signature in the Relinquished Zone and decided to investigate. We were still almost three hours away when they started the attack."

Cassandra stared at him very seriously, "Warp..."

"What do they want?" the man called Peter demanded.

"I don't know especially out here. The cities I understand, but here? They're looking for something."

Jacob jerked and abruptly walked away.

"Dad," Cassandra got up to follow him. Lucas was watching the pair when the communicator on his flight suit went off and all eyes turned to him.

"Hawk-Dodge...Hawk-Dodge..."

"Dodge-Hawk," Lucas replied.

"No, they'll be able to track the signal!" Jacob shouted.

"Give us coordinates and we'll pick you up."

Lucas pushed himself off the couch and saw five sets of eyes watching him. "It's a rescue ship, I need to get to an open area so they can land and pick me up," he tried to take a few steps and stumbled.

Cassandra walked toward him, "There is a meadow about a quarter mile southwest of here. I'll help you get to it." Lucas relayed the message.

"Cassandra!!"

"Dad, someone has to. Peter can't with his shoulder and leg like that. The sooner they're out of here, the sooner the," she looked at the large man called Lucas and continued, "Regulians will leave too." Lucas said nothing.

"Bend your arm and put it on this shoulder," she instructed him as she took his large right arm and put it on her left shoulder.

"This isn't going to work, you're too small."

"It's what got you here so it should get you back," Cassandra replied testily. "I won't be long, Dad. Let's go."

"Cassandra," she turned around looking at her father. "I love you," he said and she smiled.

"I love you too, Dad. Don't burn any more pancakes." The large man and small woman worked their way out the door.

As they entered the forest, his communicator went off again. "Hawk, this is Falcon. Respond."

"Shit," huffed Lucas.

"Problem?" Cassandra asked as he stopped to remove his communicator. They'd only gone a hundred and fifty yards.

"My father is on the rescue craft."

"And..."

"He's a fucking Admiral, excuse me. He's supposed to stay on his Battle Star! Falcon, this is Hawk." Cassandra raised an eyebrow at his apology.

"Where the hell are you?!!" demanded the Admiral.

"I'm a little gimped up, Sir, should be there in ten."

"You're hurt?"

"Not severely, Sir, just slowing me down. I'll be there in ten, over and out."

"Ten minutes, really?" Cassandra raised an eyebrow. "It's taken you ten minutes to go a hundred and fifty yards. Try another thirty at this rate."

"Then let's pick up the pace. The old man will boil over if it's much longer than that."

"Fine by me," Cassandra set a quicker pace, but it wasn't easy when you had a 6'8" man and a 6'1" woman being the helper. "Come on, Lucas, just pretend I'm a crutch. Lean on me and swing your leg." She wasn't sure if he understood what she said, but they seemed to be moving faster. Finally, they got to the edge of the meadow.

"So where's your rescue ship?"

"Falcon, this is Hawk at location ready for pick up."

"Affirmative, Hawk, ten seconds."

Cassandra watched in amazement as a ship came out of the clouds. As the ship landed, Cassandra helped Lucas hobble to the middle of the meadow. To her amazement, a door on the side of the craft slid open and an even larger man got out. He stared at Cassandra with an astonishing pair of brilliant violet eyes before he took his son's weight.

"Dad, Cassandra."

"Do we look like we're at some fucking party?!?" the Admiral demanded as he helped his son up the steps of the Raptor. The time waiting for Lucas had used up all his patience. "Next time you want to stroll through a meadow with some pretty girl, make sure it's not a war zone; we've got Strikers inbound!"

Cassandra grabbed the big man's arm and to his surprise pulled him around, "Strikers?! Are those the planes you shot down?" She looked at Lucas for confirmation. He nodded. Her brilliant sapphire blue eyes locked with the Admiral's, "Where are they heading?"

"Here."

Cassandra stared at him in horror and realized that her father had been right. They'd picked up on the communications between Lucas and the rescue ship. They'd just been waiting to see where to attack.

"Oh shit!!" Dropping his arm, she turned to run across the meadow when it exploded in front of her, throwing her backward. The Admiral grabbed her and tossed her into the Raptor.

"TAKE OFF!!" he ordered. As he reached to pull the door closed, Cassandra scrambled to get up and in doing so saw Victoria running across the burning meadow.

"NO!!! Victoria's down there!!" The Admiral's massive size blocked the door she was trying to get to. Lucas jumped up from his seat.

"DAD!" William saw the terrified child trapped by the flames.

"Dodge, get us over there quick. We're only going to get one shot at this." He turned to the woman, "I'm going to reach down and grab her, and then we're gone!"

"No, she won't come to you. Look at her she's scared out of her mind!" Cassandra pushed her way past him.

"What the HELL do you think you're doing?" She stared him directly in the eye, "GETTING MY NIECE!!"

With the aircraft still moving, she stepped out on the narrow running board of the vessel, took a deep breath, and sat down facing the Admiral.

He was stunned, what the hell was she doing?

Cassandra looked him in the eye, "I hope you're good at holding on." With that as a warning, she let herself fall backward off the running board, and her feet caught the underside of the step.

William dove for her legs, wrapped his massive arms around them, and was about to pull her up when he realized she had added almost five more feet to what he could have reached. He looked down and saw the child looking desperately for a way out of the flames.

"Victoria!!" Cassandra yelled, "Victoria, look up!!" As she did, Victoria saw her aunt hanging upside down out of some strange aircraft. "Victoria, you have to jump up! I'll catch you!"

"I can't!"

"Victoria Lynn Chamberlain, you will jump!! Jump now!!!" And as the little girl jumped, Cassandra stretched out even farther which caused the Admiral to curse as she started to slip out of his grasp. But the extra stretch allowed her to grab Victoria just below her wrists.

Lucas looked over his father's shoulder. "How the fuck do we get them up?"

"Do I fucking look like I know?" The Raptor started to pull away from the growing flames.

"Victoria, listen to me. Remember that game we always played at the park where I flip you around to grab my legs? We're going to do that now."

"No!"

"Yes, listen to me, Victoria, you can do this! Lucas is up there. He's not going to let you fall!!! I promise!!! Here we go! One!" Cassandra began to swing her arms, "Two! Three!" and swung her up as she prayed it would work.

In the Raptor, the two men stared at each other in disbelief as they heard Cassandra's plan. Then Victoria was wrapped around Cassandra's thighs. Lucas reached down and grabbed her wrists.

"Come on, Tori, I've got you. Let go of your aunt, I've got you." And the same green eyes that he'd seen when he awoke in the cabin, now stared up trustingly at him as he pulled her into the Raptor. "It's okay. You're safe now."

"Aunt Cassie!"

Lucas looked over at his father.

With Victoria safe, Cassandra needed to get herself inside. The Admiral had managed to pull her up enough so that he could grip her knees with one arm while he reached down with the other.

"Grab it!!" he ordered, "I won't let go!" Cassandra swung herself up and gripped his outstretched hand with both of hers. He pulled her the rest of the way up into the Raptor and slammed the door closed.

"Go!" he ordered as he pulled her down into a seat with him. Cassandra, breathing hard, looked up at him.

"You're good at hanging on. Thanks."

The Admiral stared down at her, "A little more warning next time would be nice."

"Let's hope I won't have to."

"Agreed." The ship started heading up.

"Wait, you need to drop us off at the cabin. The rest of our family's there." Suddenly an alarm went off in the cockpit. The Admiral and Lucas exchanged glances.

"What? What is it?" Cassandra demanded.

"Nuclear alarm," the Admiral told her.

"Nuclear…" she whispered.

"Dodge, get us out of here!!!!! Get your visors down!!!" the Admiral ordered.

"Victoria!"

"I've got her, she's okay." Lucas pulled Victoria's face into his chest, "Close your eyes, honey. Keep them closed until I say so. Okay?" Victoria nodded and hung on to Lucas.

The Admiral did the same with Cassandra. As he ducked his head, she brought her hands up to shield his eyes. As the Raptor sped skyward, there was a massive explosion behind them. As they rode out the turbulence, the Admiral felt this courageous woman's tears on his hands.

When the ship stabilized he eased her away. She quickly wiped her cheeks before turning to find the girl. She stood and walked over to Lucas. As the child looked up, she all but flew into the woman's arms. When the Raptor made an evasive maneuver, she lost her balance and fell back into the Admiral.

"Sit down before you fall down!" he roughly pushed her into the seat he'd just vacated. He looked at the two for just a second longer then turned his attention to his son.

"How badly are you hurt?" He moved over to look at the leg.

"Just a deep gash. Bliant shouldn't have any trouble with it."

"What happened?"

"Got clipped by a tree on the way down and landed hard." Lucas nodded over toward the woman. "She found me unconscious, somehow got me to their home and fixed me up, then helped me to the field." Lucas looked up at his father. "I owe her, especially now."

"Why?"

"Their family was down there, Dad."

The Admiral looked back at the woman trying to console the sobbing child. Her black hair had come loose from its restraint at the back of her neck, partially shielding her face. She'd called the girl her niece, not her child, but her love was apparent. As if hanging upside down outside a Raptor wasn't enough.

"We'll need to get them back on the planet as soon as possible. But first we've got to get you to Medical."

When the Raptor landed on the Flight Deck of the Retribution, the Admiral opened the hatch. He stepped out first and helped Lucas onto a waiting stretcher. He turned and saw the woman as she stood in the hatch, protectively holding the child, her eyes rapidly scanning the scene before her.

Having been able to calm Victoria down inside the smaller ship, Cassandra now had to contend with where they'd landed. People hustled around what she considered to be a hangar doing unknown jobs. Lucas was helped onto a stretcher while what appeared to be a team of medical personnel attended him. Her eyes came to rest on the large man Lucas called his father, the Admiral. He took a step toward her, put a hand on her elbow, and helped her out of the Raptor. When she stepped down, he discovered she barely came up to his shoulder. He reached for the child and her eyes hardened.

"No," her voice was surprisingly forceful for someone in a strange new place.

"You'll both go to Medical with Lucas."

"Aunt Cassie..."

"It's okay," Cassandra rubbed her back. "We're fine. Just get us on another one of those things," Cassandra nodded to the Raptor, "and get us back on the planet."

The Admiral raised an eyebrow at this small woman's order. "I can't spare a crew right now. Once this battle is over, we'll get you back. But for now you go to Medical." There was no doubt it was an order this time, the Admiral's violet eyes clashed with her sapphire ones.

"Cassandra," Lucas intervened, "it'll just be for a little bit. Set Victoria down here." He moved his uninjured leg and made room on the stretcher. "It's a ways to Medical. Bliant's just going to make sure we haven't been exposed to any radiation from the blast."

Cassandra looked away from the Admiral to Lucas. In a voice hoarse from crying, Victoria asked, "Aunt Cassie? Where are Mom and Dad?"

The Admiral saw the stricken look that came into the woman's eyes before it was gone so that she could look down at the child called Victoria.

"They're back on Earth, baby," she told her, not lying but unable to say the rest.

The child's green eyes stared into Cassandra's before moving to the Admiral, then Lucas, finally returning to Cassandra.

"Can I sit next to Lucas?"

The Admiral saw the indecision in the woman's eyes. "She'll be okay," he told her in a low voice as her eyes met his. He could see she was trying to decide if she could trust him. It stung after her trust on the Raptor. Slowly, she walked over to the stretcher and set Victoria down next to Lucas.

"Get them out of here!" the Admiral ordered in a gruff voice then headed to the Bridge. He had more important things to do than wonder if some woman trusted him or not.

∞ ∞ ∞ ∞ ∞

As they entered Medical, Cassandra saw it was not that different than any emergency room on Earth. As they wheeled Victoria and Lucas in, a man approached.

"What's wrong with you, Lieutenant?" Dr. Bliant demanded in an impatient voice.

"A leg gash."

As Lucas was moved over to a different cot, Cassandra picked Victoria up. Her eyes widened as she looked around. "It's okay, honey," Cassandra whispered to her, "I'm here."

"And who do we have here?" the impatient voice of the large man became very soft when he spoke to the child.

"Victoria," she said in a quiet voice.

"Hello, Victoria," he held out his large hand. After a moment and to Cassandra's amazement, Victoria put hers in it. As they shook hands Bliant said, "Nice to meet you. Are you okay?" He took in the soot on both their faces.

"Yes," Victoria responded.

Bliant looked at Cassandra. "Yes, we're both okay."

"Gabor!" A woman turned to the Doctor, "Show these two where they can clean up."

Nodding, he turned back to Lucas, "Well, let's have a look."

Cassandra and Victoria followed the woman into a smaller room.

"There's cleanser here," she pointed to a pump, "towels here," she opened a drawer, "and if you need anything else let me know." Then she exited the room.

Cassandra put Victoria down. "Well, sweetie, what do think?" Pulling out a small towel she looked at what she thought was a sink. "So how do you think we get water?"

Victoria walked up to the sink, looked it over, and turned a dial. Water started to flow. Tori gave her aunt a smile that quickly faded.

"Very nice, let's get you cleaned up." Wetting the cloth, Cassandra started on Victoria's face, cleaning off the soot and tear marks. Working her way down to her hands she finished. "There, good as new," she smiled at her.

"You're still a mess, Aunt Cassie."

"Well thank you very much, young lady," and as she looked in the small mirror, Cassandra saw Victoria wasn't exaggerating. Her hair was loose and singed; she had soot streaked across her face from wiping her tears so that she looked like an ancient warrior. "Nice," was all she thought. She worked quickly doing what she could to get clean.

∞ ∞ ∞ ∞ ∞

The wound had effectively been cleaned and sealed. Bliant looked up at Lucas, "You closed this in the field?"

"No, Cassandra closed it," Lucas gestured toward the washroom.

Bliant thought about the small woman, "She did a good job. I'm going to give you the standard booster, but I don't think you'll need it. Anything else I need to know?" Bliant looked at Lucas.

"Like what?"

"You seemed pretty attached," Bliant nodded toward the washroom.

Lucas felt his anger rise, "They just saved my life. Oh, and the Regulians nuked their family for it, but besides that..."

"Take it easy, just asking, it's not regulation to bring unknowns on board."

Lucas didn't reply as he saw Cassandra and Victoria approach. Bliant moved on to his next patient, nodded to the two but gave a second look at the woman. There was something about her.

"Should we get out of here?" Lucas asked limping over to them.

"How long until we can get back?" Cassandra demanded. Lucas motioned that they should walk as they talked.

"Look, the Regulians are still attacking the cities. It's safer here." Lucas gave a pointed look to Tori. "Once they're gone, we'll get you back. But for now, let's see if we can find you some food."

Leading them to the mess hall, Cassandra heard the Admiral's voice booming out of a room, "What the fuck are they doing?"

Lucas looked down at Victoria and saw she'd heard his father. "That's the Bridge."

Cassandra walked toward the hatch.

"That's not the best idea."

She ignored him and entered the room. She gazed around and was astounded.

The room was filled with the crew, each apparently with a specific duty. There were screens showing locations of ships, movements, and the Earth. The one the Admiral was swearing at showed the Regulians firing at the Earth's moon.

Watching in horror, she saw a large chunk of the moon being blown out into space, only to be caught by the Earth's gravitational pull. Not realizing she'd moved, she found herself at the Admiral's side. "How big is that?" she asked staring at the screen.

The Admiral's head whipped around. How the hell had she gotten on to his Bridge? Looking up he saw his son at the hatch with a hand on the little girl's shoulder. Lucas shrugged in apology.

"What the fuck are you doing here?!!" the Admiral's voice was frozen fury and caused even the Colonel, who'd come to his side, to cringe. The woman was unfazed.

"How big?" she asked again, pulling her eyes away from the screen to look into his.

What he saw confounded him. There was pain, fear, sorrow, anger, knowledge, and understanding all flashing at once in her eyes.

"One-hundred thousand cubits," he told her.

"It will decimate the planet."

"Yes," turning he ordered, "I want all aircraft back on board! Combat landings! Now! Falco, I want us out of here at warp eight as soon as all aircraft are accounted for. Is that clear?"

"Yes, Admiral!"

He gripped Cassandra's arm as he removed her from the Bridge, past Lucas, and into the corridor. "I don't know what you think you're doing," the anger in his voice a living thing.

"I believe it's called watching everyone on my planet die," she interrupted her voice as dead as Earth would shortly be, and killed the Admiral's anger. He hadn't known this woman long, but the utter lack of emotion in her voice cut at him.

"Aunt Cassie?" The sound of the small voice had her closing her eyes for just a second before she looked down at Victoria.

"Mommy, Daddy, and Grandpa are dead, aren't they?" The pain the Admiral saw in Cassandra's eyes made him wish they hadn't changed.

Cassandra dropped down to her knees and told Victoria the truth. "Yes, baby, they are," and she pulled her into her arms.

Knowing there was nothing he could do, the Admiral turned to his son. "Get them some quarters. They're going to be with us for a while." As he walked back on to the Bridge, he found it difficult to put them out of his mind.

Chapter Two

Over the next few days, Lucas stayed close to the two refugees from Earth. He secured them quarters on G Deck that while small, did have a couch and private bathing facilities. He showed them the Mess Hall on their deck and supplied them with changes of clothing while trying to explain things to them.

"Lucas," Cassandra started one night after Victoria was asleep, "don't think we don't appreciate what you've done for us. But why are you?"

Lucas looked from Cassandra to Victoria. He wasn't about to tell her that there was something about her niece that pulled at him. What he was thinking wasn't possible. Looking back to Cassandra he said, "I think I owe you, both of you."

She just looked at him, "As much as I'd like to blame you, this wasn't your fault. If anything we owe you, we'd be dead too if you hadn't crashed."

"So maybe we're even," Lucas gave her a slight smile.

"Maybe," but she couldn't bring herself to smile back. Over the last few days, Cassandra had been trying to figure out what to do. How were they going to adjust, find their way in this new place? Nearly everything they'd ever learned was irrelevant here. They needed knowledge if they were going to survive, especially Victoria.

"Lucas, you said that Tori isn't the only child on board. There are families?"

"Yes."

"So what do they do? How do they learn?"

"They go to class on E Deck. There's an Educator."

"Would Tori be allowed to go?"

"I don't see why not," he said but was concerned. "Don't you think it's too soon?"

"She needs something to focus on. To keep her mind occupied. On Earth, she was considered a very intelligent little girl. Here, she'll have to start over, find her way. I need to get her into some kind of routine. She needs things as close to normal as I can give her."

"Not only Tori," Lucas looked at her.

"No, not only Tori. Can you look into it for me?"

"Yeah, I will."

He left their quarters and headed to his father's. Entering the Admiral's Ready Room, he found him at his desk reading reports. He took a seat and waited.

Finished with the report, the Admiral leaned back to look at his son. While he seemed to be recovering from his injuries, he still wasn't back on the Flight Schedule.

"What's up?"

"What do I need to do to get Victoria into the class?"

"Victoria?"

"The little girl from Earth," Lucas said impatiently.

"I know who she is, Lucas," the Admiral replied in the same tone. "Why would you think she could handle our classes?"

"I don't know if she can, but Cassie does. She wants to get her into some kind of routine."

"And she thinks throwing her into something she isn't going to understand will help?"

"She says by Earth standards, Victoria is considered very intelligent," Lucas held up a hand to stop his father. "I know. But they have been adjusting very quickly, understanding the differences. That our languages are similar, as unusual as that is, seems to be helping." Lucas looked at his father, "She's going to have to learn it eventually."

"You seem to have gotten pretty involved," William watched his son. The woman named Cassandra kept intruding in his mind at odd times. Knowing his son was spending time with her irritated him.

"I'm just trying to help make it right, Dad."

"It wasn't your fault."

"That's what Cassie says too."

"What?" William couldn't keep the surprise out of his voice.

"She said I don't owe them anything, that if anything they owe me. If I hadn't crashed, they'd be dead too."

The Admiral was silent, the thought bothering him for some reason.

"They helped me when I needed it, now I need to help them."

"Have her in the classroom tomorrow. I'll arrange it with the Educator."

"Thanks, Dad," Lucas got up to leave. "Did you ever find out why the Regulians destroyed the planet?"

"No."

∞ ∞ ∞ ∞ ∞

"Are you sure I can do this, Aunt Cassie?" Victoria asked before they left their quarters.

"Of course I'm sure. You're not going to know or understand everything right away. It's going to take some time but after a while you'll get it."

Victoria looked up at Cassandra with trusting eyes, "Okay."

"And besides, we're Chamberlain women, aren't we?" Cassandra put her fist out for a bump, and Tori gave her one.

"Yes."

Opening the hatch, they found Lucas about to knock. "Ready to go?" he looked at them.

"Yes," they said in unison.

As they approached the classroom, Cassandra saw the Admiral coming out of the room followed by an attractive woman.

"Hello, Victoria," the woman said as if she was talking to a slow child. Cassandra frowned.

"I'm Madam Reese, your Educator."

Victoria stared at the woman. "Hello, Madam Reese. I'm Victoria Chamberlain."

Cassandra stepped forward, "I'm Cassandra Chamberlain, Tori's aunt," she held out her hand. The woman looked at the Admiral then shook Cassandra's hand.

"Well, Victoria, let's go in and get you situated."

"What time is class over?" Cassandra interrupted.

"1600," Reese told her.

"I'll see you then, Tori," Cassandra told her as she crouched down to look into Victoria's nervous green eyes. Lifting her fist she waited. The nerves left Tori's eyes as she gave her aunt a fist bump. Turning, she followed the Educator. Rising, Cassandra found herself under the scrutiny of the Admiral.

"Admiral," she nodded to him and turning she found Lucas behind her. "Thanks, Lucas. I'm going to head back to quarters." Turning she left before her tears fell.

The Admiral watched her retreating back having caught just the glimmer of the tears before she blinked them away. That told him she was more upset than she had let on.

Lucas looked at the hatch Victoria had just walked through. The two men started to walk down the corridor.

"I'm going to head to Medical and see if I can't get Bliant to clear me so I can get back on the Flight Schedule," Lucas told the Admiral.

"Good, let me know what he says."

∞ ∞ ∞ ∞ ∞

Once secured in her quarters, Cassandra began to strip and headed straight for the shower. With the water running, she slid down the wall and hugged herself as she wept, for her father, her brother and her sister-in-law, for all the senseless loss of life on Earth.

Why?

She had no answers.

All the fears and doubts she wouldn't let Victoria see came pouring out as she cried where no one could hear…or care. After what seemed a lifetime, she leaned her head back against the wall. What was she going to do? On Earth, she'd been considered extremely intelligent. She'd been nominated for the Magellan Award.

She had graduated from Harvard at 15 with three majors, by 19 she was teaching at MIT. Now, she felt like a three-year-old trying to relearn everything. If only there were books she could read. She had a photographic memory and once she read something she never forgot it. But unlike some with this skill, she could actually apply and connect the information in an incredibly rapid fashion. Her mother always told her she was the brightest light. Now she didn't know what to do.

"Sitting here in the shower isn't going to help anything," she berated herself. She stood, got out of the shower and dried off. Touching the ring she wore around her neck, she took it off. As she looked at the ancient ring, she kissed the stone then hung it on a hook. It was time for her to find her place in this new world, to make a life for herself and Victoria.

∞ ∞ ∞ ∞ ∞

Leaving her quarters, Cassandra started to explore this ship called the Retribution that was, at least for now, their home. Wandering around on the ship, she received a few looks but was mostly just ignored, something she was not used to. She was over 6 feet tall and on Earth that drew attention. Here, she was short. Tori was the only one she'd seen shorter.

She found herself in Engineering. She was amazed by the technology. There were panels and screens everywhere. Different systems controlled speed, navigation, life support, and defenses. Her mind was racing trying to make sense of it all, wanting to know how it all worked.

"Who the fuck are you?!? How'd you get in here?!?" Cassandra turned to find a large, hell they were all large here, blonde man behind her.

"I'm Cassandra, Cassandra Chamberlain and I walked in through that hatch," she pointed to the hatchway. "Who are you?"

The blonde man started to sputter, "I'm Chief Engineer Leander Michelakakis! What are you doing here?" The chief gripped her arm and led her into what seemed to be an office.

"I'm just looking. I didn't touch anything." Cassandra knew how she was about her equipment. "Your technology exceeds what we had on Earth. Do you have some manuals or books I can read on it? What type of lasers are you using? How are you…?"

"Stop!" the Chief looked at her. While her questions were valid, he wasn't allowed to discuss them with her, not without the Admiral's approval. "Sit," he told her pointing to a chair. Walking over to his communications console, he picked up a headset.

Connecting to the Bridge, he waited.

On the Bridge, the Admiral picked up a headset, "What is it, Chief?" When the Chief explained the situation, the Admiral went still, "I'm on my way."

"Colonel, you have the Bridge," Quinn watched the Admiral leave.

Going directly to Michelakakis' office, the Admiral entered to find Cassandra and the Chief standing next to a screen arguing.

"Chief!" he slammed the door. The Chief immediately turned to the Admiral.

"Sir!"

Cassandra turned a little slower saying nothing.

"What's going on here, Chief?" The Admiral glared first at him then moved to Cassandra.

"Sir, sorry, Sir. We were discussing the pros and cons of the carbonite cooling system in relation to a crystal laser."

"What?"

"Sorry, Sir."

"What are you doing in my Engineering section?" the Admiral demanded of Cassandra.

Cassandra bit her tongue at the response she wanted to give. With a father and brother both having served she knew the rules, and it didn't seem that different here.

"I was looking around the ship, getting my bearings. The hatch was open and I came in," Cassandra decided less was more.

"Chief?"

"I found her looking at the laser targeting system. She didn't touch anything," he said quickly. "She just started asking questions."

"Since when are questions a bad thing?" Cassandra demanded.

"It's part of our defense system."

"I was asking about the laser, not the targeting system," her eyes started to blaze into the Admiral's. "Hell, it's not like I don't have the clearance…" suddenly Cassandra stopped, realizing she didn't have any clearance, not here, the fire in her eyes quickly died. Looking away she said nothing. The room was silent.

"Admiral," the Chief risked his fury, "what we were arguing about was the same thing any second-year cadet would argue about; nothing specific to the Retribution." Leander looked over at Cassandra, she intrigued him. "She has knowledge."

The Admiral looked at the Chief. He'd known the man since he was a boy, had served with his father. He trusted his judgment.

"You have what you need and the time?"

"Yes, Sir." They both looked at Cassandra, who was frowning at them trying to figure out what was going on.

"Nothing that's not common knowledge, Chief."

"No, Sir."

"Then carry on. Keep me informed." With one last look at Cassandra the Admiral left.

"Would you mind telling me what just happened?"

The Chief looked at the small woman, wondering if he'd done the right thing. "You're going to school," he told her in his best intimidating voice and was surprised by her reaction.

"Really?!!" she gave him a blinding smile, "When and where do we start?"

For the rest of the day, the Chief worked between his engineering duties and Cassandra giving her volumes of information, mostly in digital format on his comm center. He was somewhat surprised at the rate she was digesting the material. When she had a question, it was direct and to the point. Looking at the time, he interrupted her.

"That's enough for today. I need to get my daughter from class," Leander shut down the screen. Cassandra was about to protest when what he said penetrated.

"Class? What time is it?"

"1545."

"Crap! I need to get Tori." She looked at the Chief, "Can you send this to my comm center? I'd like to work on it later."

"Where are you at?"

"G 43."

The chief pushed a few buttons and the information was sent. "Now I need to go."

"Thanks."

Leaving Engineering, Cassandra discovered that the Chief's daughter was in the same class as Victoria. They arrived just as class was getting out. Leander's daughter ran up into his arms.

"Daddy!" With a quick hug, he put her down and together they walked off.

Cassandra saw Victoria coming out of class and could tell that she was not happy.

"Bad day?" Cassandra asked quietly and just got 'the look.'

"Hey! How'd it go?" Lucas came up all smiles. The faces that turned to him had the smile fading.

"I think it's been a long day. Let's head back to quarters. What do you say?" Cassandra looked down to Tori, who just nodded and took her aunt's hand. "We'll see you later, Lucas," and turning she led Victoria away.

∞ ∞ ∞ ∞ ∞

Sitting on the couch, Cassandra turned to Victoria, "So what happened?"

Victoria raised miserable eyes to her, "This teacher…Educator is acting like I'm stupid or something!"

"Did she give you any homework?" Tori handed her a sheet. "That's it?"

"See, she thinks I'm stupid!"

"What were the other kids doing?"

"They were working on their screens."

"Okay, how about this. Tomorrow we will go in early and I'll talk to the…Educator. See what can be done. Did you make any friends?" Cassandra asked changing the subject.

"Not really, there was this one girl. She's my age, her name is Amina. She smiled at me a couple times."

"Well, that's a start at least."

∞ ∞ ∞ ∞ ∞

As she walked to Engineering the next day, Cassandra felt confident about Tori's day after she spoke with the Educator. She seemed honestly interested in helping Tori to adjust to her new setting and was willing to teach her at the same level as the other kids to see where she was in their learning process. The girl called Amina happened to be the Chief's daughter. When she'd gotten to class, she'd come over to talk to Tori. It was a good sign.

Passing through Engineering, Cassandra entered the Chief's office impatient to get started. She didn't see the Admiral until she literally ran into him. He gripped her arms to keep her from falling and Cassandra's surprised eyes shot to annoyed ones.

"Admiral," she took a quick step back as his hands released her. The Admiral moved past her and left Engineering.

That woman was going to drive him to distraction, the Admiral thought as he headed to the Bridge. Here he was, checking in with the Chief on her progress personally when a call would have been enough. But he'd wanted to see her. Her running into him had caught him off guard. He hadn't touched her since he'd brought her onto the Retribution. It annoyed him that he'd wanted to pull her closer instead of releasing her. Entering the Bridge, the Admiral pushed thoughts of her aside.

"So what have you got for me today?" Cassandra turned from the Admiral's retreating back to the Chief. The Admiral's obvious annoyance caused her heart to ache for some reason.

Not sure what he had just witnessed, the Chief looked at Cassandra. For the Admiral to personally come down to see how far they'd gotten yesterday was unusual, for him to not verbally acknowledge her, even more so.

"You can start up where you stopped yesterday. I'll be out in Engineering," he rose from his chair.

"I got through the rest of that last night, but I have some questions."

"You finished…the entire file?" the Chief sat back down. There'd been over a thousand pages remaining in that file, detailed pages.

Cassandra sat down across from him, pushing the Admiral out of her mind. "I have a few questions regarding the configuration of the Kryer system in relation to the crystal." As the Chief answered her questions and they discussed differing options, the day flew by.

∞ ∞ ∞ ∞ ∞

Victoria was all smiles as she came out of class that afternoon. Seeing it, some of Cassandra's concerns eased.

"Aunt Cassie, this is Amina," Tori grinned at a girl standing next to her. She was just a little taller than Victoria with long, blonde hair and brown eyes.

"Hi Amina, I'm Cassandra," she smiled down at the girl.

"Hi!" Amina's voice was sparkly. "Mama! Come meet Cassandra and Victoria." Cassandra turned as Amina's mother approached. While her hair was brown, she and Amina shared the same eyes.

"Hello," the woman said in a polite, if somewhat reserved voice, "I'm Javiera Michelakakis."

"Cassandra Chamberlain," Cassandra held out her hand and the other woman shook it firmly. "You're Chief Michelakakis' wife."

So this was the woman her husband had told her about last night. "Yes," the woman said, "come on, honey, we need to go."

"But, Mama, I want Tori to come with us." Javiera looked from her daughter to the little girl.

"Not tonight," Javiera looked at Cassandra, "maybe another time?" Cassandra could take a hint.

"Not a problem, we need to..."

"Hey!" Lucas interrupted with a big smile on his face. "Oh, hi, Javiera. So how was it today?" Lucas asked looking down at Victoria.

"Good! This is Amina, my new friend."

"Well hello, Amina," Lucas turned smiling at her. "Any friend of Victoria's is a friend of mine." Amina giggled.

"So do you ladies have plans?" Lucas looked from Victoria to Cassandra.

"Looks like we do now," Cassandra replied. "It was very nice meeting both of you," she told the Michelakakis' as they walked away.

Walking toward their quarters Cassandra asked, "So what's got you in such a good mood?"

"I'm back on the Flight Schedule," Lucas grinned.

"What's that mean?" Victoria asked.

"That means I can fly missions again."

"But…" Victoria looked at Cassandra.

Cassandra knew where this was going and quickly opened their hatch. "Let's go inside," she gave Lucas a pointed look.

"Sure," he gave her a confused look.

Once the hatch was secured Victoria started, "You can't fly again, Lucas!"

"Victoria, that's what I do."

"No!" Running to Cassandra she buried her face in her stomach. Cassandra shot him an angry look.

"What!" Lucas looked on helpless.

"Can you really not figure it out?" she knelt down to console Victoria.

"Hush now. Victoria, hush," but she was inconsolable.

"Lucas, you need to leave. Now!"

Confused he left, not sure what had just happened.

"Tori, calm down, it's okay."

"No! What if he gets hurt again? We won't be there to help him!"

"Shhh…Victoria, you know who the Admiral is right?" Cassandra was grasping at straws.

"Yes, he's Lucas' dad."

"That's right. Do you think he'd let Lucas fly if he weren't good at his job?"

"But he crashed."

Cassandra had known that was coming. "I know, baby, but he didn't die, did he? He knew what to do to stay alive. You have to trust him to know what he's doing now. Trust that the Admiral knows what he's doing."

"But what if he dies, Aunt Cassie?"

"That's not going to happen," she prayed she wasn't lying. "Trust him, Victoria." Exhausted even though it wasn't even 1800, Victoria fell asleep in her aunt's arms.

∞ ∞ ∞ ∞ ∞

Lucas couldn't figure out what just happened. Victoria had a good day, she'd been all smiles and laughter, had made a new friend. What went wrong? Looking down the corridor he saw his father approaching.

"Lucas, what's wrong?" the Admiral knew his son.

"Are you heading to quarters?"

"Yes."

Lucas followed him into his Ready Room. "I don't understand women," Lucas burst out.

The Admiral stilled knowing he was talking about Cassandra. "No man really does."

"I mean, what's the big deal. I'm back on the Flight Schedule. That should be a good thing… right?"

"I take it that didn't go over so well." The Admiral tried not to visualize Cassandra upset about his son.

"That's an understatement. First, she was all happy telling me about her new friend then she's all upset. Cassie's trying to calm her down, telling me I should be able to figure it out and then ordered me to leave."

The Admiral stared at his son, "Who was upset?"

"Victoria! She was crying and hugging Cassie," Lucas looked at his father. "What did I do?"

William turned away, looking at the painting of the setting suns of Carina and found he was relieved that Cassandra wasn't the one his son was talking about. Piecing together what had happened he turned.

"She's scared, Lucas. Victoria's afraid. She's in a new place, with new people. You're someone she's come to depend on. You were on Earth, on the Raptor, now here. It makes sense that knowing you're flying again would scare her. She's scared to lose anyone else."

Lucas looked at his father, "What do I do? Shit, I don't want her upset."

"You do your job," the Admiral told him forcefully. "She has to understand that this is what you do. And you come back, every time."

∞ ∞ ∞ ∞ ∞

In the middle of the night, Victoria sat up screaming.

"NO! NO!"

"Victoria! It's okay! I'm here!"

"Fire! Fire!"

"Shhh, open your eyes, there's no fire here. Victoria! Open your eyes!" As the frightened child did, she saw her aunt and the room beyond her.

"You're safe, Victoria, there is no fire."

"Aunt Cassie…."

"Shhh…it's okay, I've got you." Cassandra rocked the weeping child. Every night it had been the same, nightmares of being trapped in the fire. But tonight it was worse. Cassandra knew it was her fear of losing Lucas. When Victoria finally fell back into a fitful sleep, Cassandra tried too, knowing it was going to be a very long night.

Over the next week, Cassandra and Victoria developed a routine. Tori adapted quickly and developed a close friendship with Amina. While she still had nightmares, they had started to lessen in severity. Lucas stopped over every couple of days to check on them and that helped.

Cassandra learned all the 'common' knowledge of the laser system. The Chief, with the Admiral's permission, was moving on to the areas more specialized for the Retribution. And while there had been no more 'run-ins' with the Admiral, Cassandra did occasionally see him in the corridors. He would give her a quick glance then ignore her.

"But you can turn it into a backup system by just changing out the chips here, here, and here," Cassandra pointed on the schematic to the Chief.

"Well yeah, it's possible, but look where they're at. It would take a good hour to get the casings off to get to it. In an emergency, that's too long. Besides, we have a backup system," the Chief argued.

"Then what's this access hatch and ladder for?" Cassandra argued back.

"Once the casings are removed, you're little enough you might fit but otherwise…"

"Ha, ha, very funny. You know I used to be considered big," Cassandra and the Chief had started to become good friends.

"Only around a bunch of kids," he joked back. "Speaking of kids, I'm supposed to ask you if Victoria can come for a sleepover next week. Amina is having a couple of classmates over."

Cassandra hesitated as she looked at Leander. While it was true that Amina and Victoria were close friends, Cassandra wasn't sure Javiera was thrilled with it. "Let me talk to Tori, see how she feels. Nights are pretty hard on her."

"She's having problems?" Leander asked concerned. It was the first he'd heard of it.

"It's just…"

Suddenly the Alert sounded across the ship. "Alert Status One. Repeat Alert Status One. We are tracking Regulian ships inbound!"

"Stay in my office," the Chief ordered Cassandra as she hadn't been trained in combat operations. As Cassandra got out of the way, the Engineering crew jumped into their assigned positions. Across the Fleet, hatches were secured and fighters were launched. The sound of the Retribution's guns reverberated throughout the ship. Cassandra closed her eyes and prayed that Victoria was all right, that Lucas and the Admiral were safe, and her heart ached at the thought of any of them being hurt.

Suddenly the Retribution shuddered violently. Something had gotten through the defenses. In Engineering, system alarms started going off.

"Fuck! Get the backup system running!" the Chief hollered at Ensign Truple. "Do it manually!" Cassandra looked into Engineering to see that the laser system had been compromised and that the backup hadn't automatically kicked in.

"Chief! What the fuck is going on down there?!! I need my lasers!" the Admiral's voice boomed through the comms.

"Working on it, Sir! That was a direct hit on the system. We're working on the backup now."

Cassandra could tell from the readouts that the backup wasn't going to come up. It was too close to the hit. Thinking about the conversation she'd just had with the Chief, she turned to get what she needed. Leaving the office, she tried to find him.

"Damn it, Michelakakis, I need those lasers. Now!" the Admiral's voice demanded. Deciding she couldn't wait, Cassandra headed to the hatch on the upper level of Engineering and opened it. A hand spun her around.

"What do you think you're doing?" Leander demanded.

"Your backup system is fried! You know that! There's another option," she looked him in the eye.

"You want to go into the array, while it's active and reroute the lasers?!?" Leander didn't know if she was the bravest or the craziest woman he'd ever met.

"How long can the ship last without those lasers?" Leander didn't respond. "That's what I thought." She climbed in feet first and started down the ladder. Leander was right, your average Carinian wouldn't fit. Bringing the schematic into her mind's eye, Cassandra located the first chip she needed to change. Moving further down the ladder, the second changed just as quickly. The third she found was a little more stubborn. With sweat running down her back, she finally replaced the last chip.

"Hustle up, Chamberlain!" Leander yelled.

"Done! On my way up!"

As the Retribution took another hit, Cassandra slipped slamming her cheek into the ladder, "Shit!"

"Admiral! Lasers are restored!" the Chief reported to the Bridge.

"Fire them!" the Admiral ordered.

Back in Engineering, Leander pulled Cassandra out of the array. She was sweaty, dirty, and a bruise was forming on her cheek, but otherwise she was fine. Closing the hatch they heard the lasers firing.

"Nice work, Chamberlain." Leander didn't want to think about what might have happened if she hadn't been there.

"You would have found a way," Cassandra said not realizing his thoughts. "Do you think the girls are okay? I'm not sure how Victoria is going to handle this." Worried eyes met his.

"Reese knows what to do. Once the fighting has stopped, they'll release the kids. Javiera will go pick up Amina, I can call her and have her get Tori too."

"No, I'd better go."

"You need to clean up first."

"What?"

"You're a mess, Chamberlain. After we're done here you head to quarters, Javiera will pick up both girls and drop Tori off. That will give you time to clean up."

"You're sure she won't mind?"

"It will be okay. Why don't you go see if you can figure out how to fix the primary laser system?" Walking away, the Chief didn't see Cassandra's jaw drop. Closing it she headed to the laser control station.

∞ ∞ ∞ ∞ ∞

On the Bridge, the battle was winding down with the Regulians taking heavy losses.

"It doesn't make any sense, Quinn. They're attacking as if we've stolen something."

"I agree, this wasn't some border skirmish."

"I want damage reports on all vessels. And get Michelakakis up here. I want to know what happened to my lasers!"

"Yes, Sir."

∞ ∞ ∞ ∞ ∞

"Chamberlain!" the Chief called out. Seeing her slide out from under a control panel, he walked over shaking his head. She had a nasty bruise growing on her cheek. "I'm heading to the Bridge. Finish up there and head to quarters. Javiera will be by with Tori in about an hour."

"Okay, Chief. Thanks." She slid back under the panel.

Still shaking his head, Michelakakis headed to the Bridge.

∞ ∞ ∞ ∞ ∞

In his Command Center, the Admiral was reading damage reports. The Sentinel had received the most damage as if it were being targeted. While the Retribution, even with its lasers down, was basically left alone. The Chief approached the Command Center.

"Sir."

"What happened to my lasers, Chief?"

"Admiral, it shouldn't have been able to happen. One of the Regulian hits sent a Buric shock through Engineering. It basically fried the laser system."

"But it didn't affect the backup?"

"Actually, Sir, it fried that too."

"What! So how did you get my lasers back online?" The Chief looked the Admiral in the eye.

"I didn't, Sir. Chamberlain did."

"Chamberlain?" the Admiral questioned quietly.

"Yes, Sir. I've been bringing her up to speed on the Retribution's specifics, as you authorized." Leander thought it might be good to remind the Admiral. "We've been discussing this other potential back-up, but because of its location I considered it unfeasible.

"Why?"

"Admiral, it involved replacing three circuits in the array. To get to it you have to remove the casing and that alone takes at least an hour. In a situation like we just had it's too long."

"How did you manage it then?"

"Chamberlain was able to fit in the array with the casing on."

"With the array active?" the Admiral's voice was icy.

"Yes, Sir. She was able to replace the circuits thus reestablishing the laser system."

"Her status?"

"Admiral?"

"Was she hurt, Chief," the Admiral's voice was deadly.

"Sir, a couple bumps and bruises. She's currently working on the primary laser system trying to bring it back online." At the Admiral's look, he hastened to add, "She knows the system, Admiral. She'll get it back up faster than anyone on the ship, including me. By now she should be heading to quarters. She wanted to clean up before Javiera brought Tori home."

"Dismissed, Chief." The Admiral turned back to his damage reports. Cassandra fixed the laser system. She entered an active array. She was injured. With his mind racing, he pretended to read his reports. She'd found a champion in the Chief Engineer. He hadn't touched her in seven days. She was hurt. The Chief said bumps and bruises. He needed to see for himself.

"Colonel, you have the Bridge." The Admiral left to find out for himself.

Knocking on Cassandra's hatch, he discovered it was not secured. Entering, he secured the hatch and heard the shower shut off. Moments later Cassandra came out of the bathroom wearing nothing but a towel.

∞ ∞ ∞ ∞ ∞

Getting back late to quarters, Cassandra knew she needed to move. Victoria couldn't see her like this. Pulling a towel around her she walked into their living area, freezing when she saw she wasn't alone.

"Admiral…" was all she could get out. How had he gotten in? She could tell he was assessing her.

Looking at her, he saw that while she was okay she had a major bruise forming on her right cheek.

"Is there something I can do for you?" she hitched the towel up.

"You left your hatch open."

"Oh," looking behind him she saw the hatch was now closed. As he approached, she stiffened.

"You're hurt."

"Just a bruise."

Cupping her jaw, he gently rubbed his thumb across her cheek.

"Admiral…"

"Shhh…" Seeing the confusion in her eyes he was relieved he wasn't the only one.

"I don't understand."

"I think it should be self-explanatory. Especially to someone who can fix the Retribution's laser system."

Looking up at him she stated the truth, "You don't like me."

"You are wrong." Putting an arm around her waist he pulled her close, letting her feel how much he liked her. "Does that feel like I don't like you?"

"I…"

"Let me explain it this way." Leaning down, he gently kissed first her bruised cheek and then her lips. Changing the angle of the kiss, he increased the pressure, fully aware of the difference in their sizes.

Momentarily stunned, Cassandra quickly found herself responding. At her response, William lifted her by the waist so their bodies were more aligned. When the towel began to slip, he groaned and eased her feet back to the floor while still looking at her.

"You need time to adjust to all these changes, but never think I don't like you." He ran his thumb across her slightly swollen lips, never breaking eye contact. "We need to..." he didn't get to finish as the hatch opened. He quickly turned, shielding her only to find Victoria entering the quarters. Cassandra quickly readjusted her towel.

"What are you doing here?" Victoria demanded walking toward him.

"Checking on Cassandra," the Admiral replied.

"Why?" As she stepped around the Admiral, she saw Cassandra's bruise. "What did you do to her?" she turned accusingly to the Admiral.

"Victoria! Stop! The Admiral would never hurt me. You will apologize! Now!" The two Chamberlain women stared each other down.

"You didn't hurt her?" Victoria looked at the Admiral.

"Never," he replied. "Men don't hurt women."

"They can," Victoria persisted.

"Not Carinian men," he insisted. There was something more behind this.

Victoria stared intently into his eyes. "I'm sorry then. It was wrong for me to accuse you."

The Admiral raised an eyebrow.

Victoria turned back to Cassandra, "What happened?"

"I fell down during the attack. You know me and my big feet," Cassandra looked up at the Admiral and he realized she didn't want him to say anything.

"Then why is he here?" she jerked her head at the Admiral.

"To make sure she's okay," replied William.

Tori stared at him very seriously. "You worry about her too?"

Cassandra rolled her eyes. The Admiral squatted down so he was at eye level with Tori.

"Yes, I do."

"Good."

Standing he turned back to Cassandra, "We'll talk later."

Cassandra said nothing as he left.

Chapter Three

Over the next few days, the Admiral made a point of stopping by Engineering to check on the laser status. Looking in his eyes, Cassandra saw…something but she was just not sure what to make of it. How different are relationships between men and women on Carina than Earth? She didn't know and had no one to ask.

Amina's sleepover arrived and while Victoria was excited, Cassandra was concerned.

"You're sure you want to do this?" she asked one last time as they walked to the Michelakakis' quarters.

"It's going to be fun, Aunt Cassie!" Tori's eyes sparkled.

"Okay then."

Arriving at their quarters, the hatch opened to an excited Amina. "You're here! Come on, I want to show you my room!" Victoria turned, gave Cassandra a quick hug, and was gone.

Cassandra looked to Javiera, "If you have any problems I'll either be in Engineering or my quarters."

"Everything will be fine," Javiera reassured her. "You go enjoy the time to yourself." Javiera hesitated, "Cassandra, Leander told me what you did with the laser system." Cassandra waited saying nothing. "Thank you."

"For what?"

"A ship without lasers is unprotected. My husband and daughter are on this ship. So thank you. You didn't have to go into that array."

"It needed to be done." With that, she left feeling Javiera's eyes on her. Nearing Engineering, she met up with Ensign Truple. As they talked, Cassandra laughed.

∞ ∞ ∞ ∞ ∞

In Engineering, the Chief was talking to the Admiral about the possibility of allowing Cassandra to work on the laser tracking system.

"It won't take her long to get up to speed. She sees our systems differently. I think she'll find ways of improving it like she did with the lasers."

"What does she say about it?"

"I brought it to you first, Admiral."

"Get her in here. Let's see if she thinks she can handle it," the Admiral demanded impatiently while inside he was glad for a reason to talk to her.

"She's not here, Sir. Amina's having a sleepover. Cassandra took Tori to it."

"So that's why you're still here," the Admiral grinned and Leander grinned back.

"Five little girls," Leander shook his head, "I think it will be quieter in a launch port."

"You might be right. Bring it up to her, let me know." Rising, the Admiral left, disappointed that he wouldn't see her. Thinking about Cassandra alone tonight the Admiral walked down the corridor to find her laughing with Ensign Truple. His face turned to stone.

"Ensign Truple! Nothing to do?" his tone was harsh.

"Admiral, Sir, um... I'm on my way," Truple made a hasty retreat leaving Cassandra with the Admiral.

"Cassandra, I need to speak with you in my Ready Room." As they walked to the Admiral's quarters neither spoke. William was wondering how he could become so jealous so quickly all because she was laughing with another man. This woman pulled at him in a very basic way, stretching his renowned control. Cassandra entered the room first, moving toward his desk while the Admiral secured the door.

"I'm not sure what..." turning she found him right behind her. For a large man, he moved quietly. The Admiral put an arm around her waist, a hand behind her head and lifted her up for a passionate kiss.

Cassandra was stunned. Would she ever understand him? With her senses reeling all she could do was grip his powerful biceps and hang on.

Walking her backward, he sat her on his desk to slip between her thighs pressing his erection against her stomach. When he changed the angle of the kiss, she started to understand the passion hidden in him and found herself responding. She hooked her ankles around his thighs as she pulled him closer.

Breaking off the kiss, William buried his face in her neck. He hadn't meant to move this fast, but seeing her laughing with Truple made him feel the need to mark his territory.

"William..." she groaned.

Going still, he captured her face in his hands. She'd never said his name before. "Again," he demanded looking her in the eye, "say it again!"

"William..." she whispered as she gazed up at him with passion-drenched eyes.

His control snapped, the sound of his name on her lips had him needing to touch her, all of her, to join with her. He stripped off her shirt as she undid his jacket. Shrugging it off, he ripped his t-shirt over his head. Pulling her off the desk, his mouth descended. The feel of skin against skin caused Cassandra's thighs to tighten trying to bring him even closer. Never breaking the kiss, William entered his private chambers going directly to his bed.

Cassandra was on fire, she'd never felt like this. Her entire life, her intellect had ruled her actions. Everything was thought out and calculated. Her emotions were always controlled. Only her family penetrated the barrier she maintained. But here, with William, her emotions overwhelmed her. She couldn't control them. She needed more and William was the only one who could give it to her.

Slowly lowering her onto the bed, William worked on her pants slipping them down slim hips that reminded him just how small she was. He needed to regain some control. Breaking off the kiss, he eased back looking at her lying naked on his bed. His bed! Running large, rough hands up her quivering body he realized he had wanted her since he'd first felt this strong woman's tears on his hands. Standing, he watched her as he removed his remaining clothes.

Cassandra was in awe that his size and girth matched the rest of the man. The thought of them together started a trembling deep inside. Kneeling on the bed, William braced a massive arm on either side of her head sinking down for another passionate kiss.

"Cassandra," he groaned as he rolled pulling her up and over him. His hands moved down kneading her thighs, spreading them wide so she straddled him. Gripping her hips, he lifted her then watched her beautiful blue eyes as he slowly lowered her, pressing against her entrance demanding entry. Entering her, he found she was even smaller and tighter than he had thought, but oh so hot, so wet, his massive arms started to quiver. He didn't want to hurt her.

As he continued to enter her, Cassandra groaned. Nothing in her life had prepared her for him. He was heated steel covered in velvet. Her sapphire eyes blazed into his before they began to glaze over. Her hips circled wanting more.

"Easy," he groaned, sweat beginning to slick his chest from the strain of holding back. "We need to go slow. I don't want to hurt you."

But Cassandra was past all thought only need ruled. "William," putting her hands behind his head she pulled him up into a wild kiss that had her wrapping her tongue around his.

His hips jerked thrusting deep. He closed his eyes as her tightness surrounded his thick shaft. Cassandra threw her head back with a stunned cry. Freezing, he held her still, fearing he'd hurt her.

"It's all right," his voice was strained as sweat broke out on his face. Hearing her low moan, he gripped her hips tighter. "Shhh, it's all right, Cassandra, we'll stop," he started to lift her.

Bringing her head forward, she locked passion-filled eyes to his and in an urgent voice said only one word, "More!" She demanded more while trying to grind her hips into his. "Oh, God, please more!"

William was stunned. Carinian women were larger than Cassandra and many of them were unable to accept a fully-erect Carinian male.

"William," her passion-drenched voice jerked him back. Easing his grip, he allowed her to set the rhythm. Gripping his shoulders, she circled her hips grinding against him, building the tension to an unbearable level. Pulling her to his chest, his teeth scraped along her lower jaw on his way to her swollen mouth. Once there, his kiss imitated their bodies. Cassandra's nails dug into his shoulders.

"Let go, Cassandra!" he ground out, "I've got you! I won't let go!"

Cassandra screamed as the unbearable tension finally snapped, sending waves of pleasure coursing through her body. Going limp in William's arms, her head dropped onto his shoulder.

William held the trembling woman running a soothing hand up and down her spine. Brushing back her damp hair, he kissed the delicate neck he'd exposed. She amazed him, so small, so delicate, yet so passionate and strong.

As minutes passed, Cassandra's breathing finally started to settle. Lifting her head, she looked at him with dazed eyes. Moving to kiss his lips, she realized he had yet to find his own release.

"William," she whispered moving her hips slightly. She ran her hands up his sweat-drenched chest and eased herself back. The small movement had him groaning.

Putting her hands on either side of his face, she looked deep into his wild violet eyes, "Let go, William, I've got you." As she kissed him, his control finally broke.

Twisting her under him, he set a frantic pace then with one final thrust emptied himself into her only holding his body off of her at the last second to keep from crushing her. He rested his forehead on hers as he tried to regain his breath. He'd never experienced a release like that and feared his lack of control had harmed her.

"Cassandra," gently he kissed her lips, "look at me, please." Slowly she opened her eyes revealing a dazed but fully satisfied woman, "You're all right?"

"I believe that would be an understatement."

Releasing a deep breath, he bowed his head.

"William," as her brain started to re-engage she realized he'd truly been afraid. "Look at me, please." He raised his head revealing turbulent eyes. "I would let you know if you hurt me," she framed his face with her hands looking directly into his eyes, "I won't lie to you. I may be sore, but that is due to my undesirability, not you. Believe me."

He said nothing as he moved to her side, but she sensed his anger. On Earth, except by her family, she'd been desired only for her intellect. Her 6'1", 165-pound frame wasn't something men desired. She should have realized it was the same here. It was only as she started closing herself off that she realized how much of her true self she'd revealed. Hoping he hadn't noticed it, she moved away only to have William grab her.

"You will explain!" he demanded.

Cassandra just stared at him.

"What do you mean?" Cassandra asked as he felt her try to pull away and again his grip tightened.

"I demand an answer!" his voice was harsher than he'd intended as he discovered he couldn't take her pulling away from him.

"I'm not one of your crew! You can demand nothing of me!" Pushing against his chest, she tried to get loose. "Damn it let go!"

Switching his grip to her forearms, he pulled her up until she was eye-to-eye with an outraged Carinian male. "I'm not letting go! What do you mean undesirable," he felt her stiffen but didn't back down.

"You have no right!"

"You gave me that right! Here in this bed!"

"What do you want to know?" she shot back angrily. "That there's only been one before you?" He felt her trembling in his hands. "And that he had to be paid?" The words tumbled out before she could stop them. Shock had him loosening his grip.

Twisting away, all she could think was that she had to get away before she humiliated herself further. But she'd forgotten how fast he moved. One moment she was on her feet and the next she was in his arms.

"You were taken advantage of?" William's voice was very still, very controlled.

"No," suddenly weary she closed her eyes. "William…" she felt the tears build behind her eyelids, "Let it go, it was years ago, he doesn't matter."

"No," tipping her chin up he tried to get her to look at him but only managed to make her tears seep out. Tears that told him all he needed to know.

"Cassandra, tell me. Let me in." Startled eyes met his. "Did you think I couldn't feel you pulling away, shutting me out?" his voice was gentle.

"Why do you need to know?"

Her shivering caused William to realize they were both naked. Reaching behind him he pulled the blanket off the bed. Wrapping it around her, he lifted her into his arms. Comfortable with his own nakedness, he carried her over to the couch. Cradling her, he sat, his thumb gently wiping away her tears.

"Talk to me."

Cassandra found she could do nothing but lay her head on his shoulder in confusion. Who was this man? She'd seen him in battle commanding thousands, knew he wasn't afraid of making the tough decisions. He could be impatient and short. His presence intimidated, his anger terrified. And here he was wiping her tears, waiting for her to talk to him. Something shifted deep inside her.

"I was in my second year of teaching at MIT. Because of my age and credentials there was some friction between myself, the other staff and students. A group of students and faculty nicknamed me the 'Ice Bitch.' I didn't socialize with them, I didn't play favorites or let people slide. Eventually, they decided that if I got 'laid,' I'd take it easier on them." She looked to see if he understood what she was telling him. She still hadn't entirely grasped all the terms in their language.

William followed her story, generally understanding, his jaw tightened at the term 'Ice Bitch,' realizing what it meant. "What does 'laid' mean?"

Cassandra took a deep breath, "Sex."

He continued to look at her.

"What's your word for what we just did?" asked Cassandra.

"Mating."

Her eyes widened slightly, "Is that what you call it when it's a one-night-stand?"

"One-night-stand?" he frowned.

Cassandra's frustration was growing, "One-night-stand, when you and a woman meet up, mate, and then go on as if it never happened."

William's arms tightened around her, his eyes turned fierce. "That's not what we did!"

"Then what's your term for what I described."

Looking at her, he realized she needed this knowledge so she could understand what was happening with them.

"Slamming."

Cassandra looked away. "Okay, so if I was slammed that maybe I'd ease up on them. But their problem wasn't only finding a man willing to be the other half, but one that I might be interested in."

William's jaw tensed, but he said nothing, knowing he needed to let her finish.

"So anyway there was this one student on campus, he'd been in my class the previous year, he was extremely intelligent. We'd have coffee sometimes and discuss theory. He was attractive in that blonde, beach boy sort of way. Never mind, I'm not explaining that," she told him as he opened his mouth. "He was having money problems so the group got together and came up with a thousand dollars. All he had to do was get me in bed." At his look she corrected, "Slam me. So he asked me to his apartment to see a research paper he was working on. Anyway, he made some advances, they were pretty good; so I thought why not, I was nearly 20. So we did it and that was that. End of story." Taking a deep breath, she looked at him.

"There's more."

"No."

"If there wasn't, it wouldn't still bother you." When she tried to look away, he gripped her chin. "What happened the next day?"

"It wasn't the next day. It was the rest of the semester. One-by-one, everyone involved asked me if I could stop by their apartment to look at a research paper."

William could see it still hurt her. "It was your first time," he whispered.

She lowered her eyes.

"I'm sorry."

The eyes she raised to him had a wicked gleam. "Don't be, I fully believe in payback." He raised an eyebrow. "I gave them the mother of all finals. Not one of them passed it."

William tipped his head back letting out a deep rumbling laugh. When she smiled at him, his heart stuttered. Swooping down he captured her mouth. "I desire you, Cassandra," the laughter left his eyes. He wanted to make sure she understood him. "This," he said as he ran a hand down her back, "was not a one-night-stand!"

"Then what was it?" The question was out before she could stop it. "Wait! Forget I asked that."

"You can ask me anything. Cassandra, I realize this is all new for you. Not just us, but the Retribution, the Regulians. You need time to adjust, to learn what is the same and different between our worlds. I'll help you all I can."

"Why?"

"You'll eventually figure that out." Before she could question him more, his intercom went off. Capturing her lips in a quick kiss, he stood putting her down on the couch. Still naked, he went to his communication console and pressed a button.

"Zafar."

"Admiral, we have the translation on some Regulian chatter we've picked up that you need to hear," Colonel Tar informed him.

William watched Cassandra get up to retrieve her pants. "I'll be there in thirty."

"Yes, Sir. See you in Communications at 1830."

Cassandra's mind was churning as she tried to come to grips with everything that had transpired in the last sixty minutes. God, had it really only been sixty minutes? It seemed like a lifetime. She'd revealed more to William than she had to anyone in her life. No one knew about John. Struggling with her pants while trying to stay covered, William came up behind her resting his hands on her shoulders.

"What are you doing?"

Finished with her pants she stepped away from his hands. "Getting dressed. You need to go."

Seeing she was looking for her shirt, William pulled on his pants and said, "It's in the other room, Cassandra." Following her out of his private chambers, he watched as she went directly to the pile of discarded clothes and hesitated.

Knowing she was trying to figure out how to get her shirt on without dropping the blanket, he removed the problem by pulling the blanket away. He lifted her onto his desk, moved between her legs, and pulled her against him skin-to-skin. "We're back where we started," he murmured as he nuzzled her neck.

"William," her desire was instantaneous as she wrapped herself around him and pulled him in closer. As he worked his way up her neck, she groaned letting her head fall back. Pulling her head forward, he scorched her mouth.

"Cassandra," as he broke off the kiss, he rested his forehead against hers. Heavy eyes met his barely-controlled ones, "I need to leave for a while."

She immediately loosened her grip trying to regain control of herself, "Of course, you do. I'll just finish getting dressed…"

He cut her off, "Stay."

"What?"

"Victoria is gone for the night. Stay with me. Let me hold you while you sleep."

"How do you know Victoria is gone?"

"I'm the Admiral," he smiled. Cassandra stared at him. "Stay. When I get back, we'll eat. This shouldn't take that long."

"That's a crock of shit."

"Excuse me!" William was stunned. No one had the nerve to talk to him like that.

"You get a call from your Second-in-Command, telling you they've decoded transmissions from the Regulians that they think you need to hear. And you really expect me to believe that you won't give it as much time as it needs? Do I look stupid?"

He gave her a considering look, "I believe you are a very intelligent and astute woman. Please stay. I want to know you'll be here when I'm done. I want to come home to you," he said it out loud, knowing she didn't understand the commitment he was making to her.

"William, I need to be in my quarters. It's Victoria's first night away, I don't know how it's going to go. If Leander calls, I need to be able to answer." Her eyes pleaded for understanding.

He stepped back and helped her off his desk. "Is that what it will take for you to stay? For Victoria to be able to contact you if she needs to?"

"Yes," Cassandra answered, watching as he walked around the desk moving to his communications console. Suddenly she realized she was still naked from the waist up. Picking up her shirt, she turned it right-side out to pull it on.

"Communications, this is Admiral Zafar." She watched him with questioning eyes.

"Yes, Admiral."

"I want to reroute all transmissions from G 43 to my secondary line with the selected ring attached. It is to ring in both locations and is to take effect immediately. Is this understood?" he saw Cassandra's eyes widen.

"Yes, Admiral."

"I want a test call initiated. One minute." Disconnecting, he waited. The console lit up with a different tone. Answering it, he responded, "That'll be all." Walking around his desk he rested his hands on her shoulders. "Will that do?"

She looked at him in amazement.

"Why would you do this?"

"I will do whatever it takes for you to be here." Lifting a hand, he gently caressed her healed cheek, "Cassandra, I need you here tonight."

"I want to be here," she wrapped her arms around his still bare waist and tilted her head up. "You've got 15 minutes, Admiral."

Putting an arm around her, he walked with her back into his private quarters leading her to his library, "These are books that I've treasured all of my life. Read any of them you want."

She stared first at the books, then at him. Her eyes shining as if he'd just given her the universe.

"Really?"

"Really. Now I need to get dressed." He left her staring at the books. In the bathroom, he splashed water on his face and gave himself a serious look in the mirror. Books… He should have realized how important they would be to her, such a small thing.

Drying his face, he went to his closet for a fresh shirt. Cassandra was already curled up in a chair, engrossed in a book. His jacket was lying next to her, the blanket folded on the couch. The small acts touched him deeply. Pulling on the shirt, he walked over for his jacket and Cassandra looked up.

"What did you decide on?" he asked pulling on his jacket.

"I decided I'd just start at the bottom and work my way up," she told him sheepishly.

Putting an arm on either side of her, he leaned in to kiss her goodbye. "Sounds like a good plan. I'll see you in a little while. Make yourself at home." Turning, he fastened his jacket on his way through his Ready Room. Entering the corridor he was in full Admiral-mode.

∞ ∞ ∞ ∞ ∞

Back in his quarters, Cassandra lowered her book. What the hell had she done? She looked around his private chambers. How did she get here?

Too agitated to sit, she walked into William's Ready Room and stopped. She hadn't gotten a clear look at it earlier…they'd been a little busy. He had an over-sized desk, even for him, which faced the hatch letting all who entered know who was in charge. It seemed to be made of wood. Moving to run her fingers over the top she found it had a very smooth, silky feel. On the corners, there were a variety of boxes and what she considered photos. Looking closer she smiled, discovering they were of William's sons at different stages in their lives. There were several chairs in front of the desk but a large space in between, an area for those not offered a seat. She was sure many a man had trembled in that spot. Tables in the far corners held charts, reports, and correspondence.

While the walls in her and Victoria's quarters were the drab color of the rest of the ship, William's had the warmth of paneling. On those walls, he'd displayed several pieces of framed artwork. Scenes she'd never seen before. The one catching her eye seemed to be of a sunset, but it had three suns of differing colors, all setting at the same time. She'd have to ask.

Turning back around, Cassandra looked at the room. It was a reflection of the man she knew as the Admiral, over-sized, strong, confident, intimidating and sometimes formidable, but there was warmth there too.

Reentering his private chambers, she realized there was another door. As she opened it she discovered a storage room containing unused furniture. She closed it and continued on and found a kitchen area with what looked to be a cold unit under the counter. Opening it, she found several bottles of what appeared to be wine. The couch William had held her on was against his office wall with his library housed in the corner, two over-sized chairs were in front of it. Well, over-sized for her. There was a built-in closet, a private bathroom and, of course, the bed.

Staring at the bed she judged that it was easily 8-foot long and 7-foot wide and right now looked well used. Blushing at what she'd done in that bed she walked over touching the spot where they'd 'mated' as William called it. She couldn't believe the passion this man brought out in her. She'd never had her body control her like that, had never not been able to control herself, or unaware of what she was revealing to another person. She got up and put the bed back in order. Finished, she heard the Ready Room's hatch open and close. He had finished quickly.

"You're a big girl, Cassandra, you can handle this," she whispered to herself as she walked to the door separating the rooms.

Chapter Four

In Communications, the Admiral was reading the transcript Quinn called him about. "This has been rechecked?"

"Yes."

`'Imperial Light still shining. Believed being protected. Will continue the search, if unable to obtain, will destroy. Agreement will then be honored.'`

The Admiral reread it aloud.

"It makes no sense, Will," Quinn was one of the few who could address the Admiral by his given name.

"They're searching for something. That's what Earth was about. Something they desperately want but couldn't find before we got there. Something they don't want us to have." William stood, "'Imperial Light?' Regulus is ruled by a military council. There's nothing 'Imperial' there. 'Being protected.' Protected by who and where?"

"We'd need to know what it is before we can answer that," Quinn replied.

"Wouldn't that be helpful, but it's pretty clear they don't have it. It was either taken from Earth before it was destroyed or was never there in the first place. How did we get this transmission?"

"The Sentinel recorded it after the attack a couple of weeks ago. They sent it to us for translation at 1200 today."

"What the fuck was the delay?"

"I don't know, Admiral," Quinn addressed him formally. He knew the Admiral well.

"Find out! Find out NOW! Two fucking weeks, Quinn, they had this for two fucking weeks! Get me Captain Procne on the Sentinel. Now!"

The Communications Specialist cowered behind the Admiral as he contacted the Sentinel. The Admiral's wrath was legendary and he didn't want it directed at him.

"Admiral, I have Captain Procne on the comm."

"Admiral, this is Procne."

"What the fuck are you doing over there, Procne? It takes you two fucking weeks to send over Regulian traffic for translation?!!"

"Admiral, I can explain."

"It'd better be good!"

"Admiral, the transmission was recorded after the battle, but it wasn't on any of the regular Regulian channels. As you know, we took a severe hit during the attack and lost one of our Communications Specialists."

"Stop making fucking excuses!"

"Sir, I'm not. But with that loss, all remaining specialists made reviewing the Regulian channel tapes top priority. This transmission was only found after they started reviewing Carinian channels."

"You're telling me you found a Regulian transmission, in Regulian, on a Carinian channel?"

"Yes, Sir, at 1130 today."

The Admiral looked at Quinn, "Were you able to track the signal?"

"Sir, using available data the source was the Regulian battleship, Cimex. We were unable to track the destination."

"General area?"

"Deep in Carinian space, Sir."

"Good work, Captain. Tell your Communications crew well done."

"Thank you, Sir!" It was high praise from the Admiral. William turned to Quinn and in a low voice stated, "We have a traitor."

"So it would seem, but what do they need this 'Light' for?" Quinn ignored a ringing line.

"We need to start monitoring all Carinian traffic in this sector."

"Agreed."

"Commander," the Communications Specialist interrupted.

The Admiral turned to him impatiently.

"Sir, I have Senior Chief Falco on the secure line requesting to speak with you. She said it was urgent, Sir." The Admiral took the headset the officer held out.

"What is it, Falco?"

∞ ∞ ∞ ∞ ∞

Cassandra entered the Ready Room expecting to see William. Instead, there was a 6'5" woman in military garb behind William's desk. She was running her hands, in what could only be described as lovingly, up and down the chair. "Can I help you?" she asked.

The woman's head snapped up. She immediately removed her hands from the chair like a child with her fingers caught in the cookie jar. "What are you doing in here?" she demanded.

Cassandra walked further into the room, "That's my question to you."

"I'm Senior Chief Falco! I'm dropping off a report for the Admiral. No one is allowed in his quarters when he's not here!" Falco stood tall trying to intimidate the smaller woman.

"Then what are you doing here?" Cassandra demanded. She'd be damned if this woman would make her feel like an unwanted guest.

"You're that refugee from Earth," Falco sneered, "I'm calling security."

"Go ahead. Do that," Cassandra sneered back, "but before you do, you'd better think about who was here first. You also might want to consider calling the Admiral to report your 'intruder.' He might have something to say about it. Oh, and I'd do it on a secure line unless you want the entire ship to find out you entered the Admiral's quarters without permission!" Cassandra's temper was starting to get the better of her. Here this woman was, acting like she owned the place like she had some prior claim on William. She'd be damned if she gave up without a fight.

The woman named Falco turned to the Admiral's communications console.

"By the way, he's in Communications." Falco shot her a furious look. Cassandra just smiled in return.

"Vasa, this is Falco, is the Admiral there?" she demanded keeping her eyes on Cassandra, the first shadow of doubt flickered through her eyes when she got an affirmative. "I need to speak to him on a secure line, it's urgent," she waited for the Admiral with a sinking feeling.

"What is it, Falco?"

"Admiral, I'm informing you that I've discovered an intruder in your quarters."

Silence greeted her comment, "Would you repeat that, please?"

"Admiral, I'm in your quarters and have discovered an intruder."

"Why are you there?" William asked in a quiet voice, so full of fury that Quinn raised an eyebrow.

"Sir, I was dropping off a report."

"Are you on a secure line?"

"Yes, Sir," Falco started to feel more confident and added, "I wanted to inform you before calling security, Sir."

"Put me on the intercom, Falco."

"Sir?"

"DO IT!"

"Yes, Sir!" Pushing a button she removed the headset.

"Am I on the intercom?"

"Yes," Falco replied.

"Yes," Cassandra stared down Falco.

"Now listen very carefully, Falco. Are you listening?

"Yes, Sir."

"You will leave immediately. If everything isn't in the same condition I left it, I will knock you back down to Private. Is that understood?"

Falco swallowed hard, "Yes, Sir!"

∞ ∞ ∞ ∞ ∞

William disconnected throwing his headset down.

"Problem?" Quinn inquired. He'd known William for over thirty cycles and knew his moods, but this was something new.

"There'd better not be." Damn, he wanted to make sure Cassandra hadn't spooked. But she had been right, he wasn't leaving this until this was finished.

"Set up extra shifts on all ships. I want all transmissions monitored, recorded, and analyzed."

"I'll take care of it, Admiral," Quinn replied.

"Send that transmission to my Ready Room comm. I'll be in my quarters."

"Yes, Sir." *'And I hope it's the way you left it,'* Quinn thought to himself.

∞ ∞ ∞ ∞ ∞

Falco disconnected, sent Cassandra a hate-filled look, walked to the hatch and left. There was no report in her hands or on the Admiral's desk. Cassandra remained where she was. She tried to figure out what shocked her more; the jealousy she was feeling knowing that this other woman felt she had a claim on William or the utter hatred that was in her eyes as she left.

Moving back into William's private chambers, she tried to rationalize her feelings. What was going on with her? Jealousy? Really? That meant she cared about him. He'd have to matter.

"It's just physical," as she said it out loud she could hear the lie in her own voice. Running her hands through her hair, she paced the room. Hearing the hatch open and close, she froze.

"If that bitch is back again...," she muttered storming through the connecting door ready for a fight and straight into William's arms.

He instantly realized he was holding an outraged woman in his arms. Still he couldn't help but be relieved that she was still here. Tipping her chin up, he kissed her as her arms tightened around him.

"Where were you rushing off to?"

Cassandra's hazy eyes sharpened, "I thought I heard an intruder."

He let out a deep sigh, "I'm sorry, that never should have happened. No one just walks into my Ready Room."

"How would you know?"

"What?"

"If you're not here and the door isn't secured, how would you know if someone had been in your Ready Room?"

William had no answer.

There was a knock on the hatch and the door opened. "Admiral?" Cassandra gave him an I-told-you-so look as she turned and walked deeper into his private chambers.

"It's just Hutu bringing dinner," William said in exasperation.

"Admiral, do you want me to bring it back?"

William walked back into his Ready Room, "No, Hutu, just put it on the table over here. That'll be all."

"Yes, Sir." Hutu left.

Walking to the hatch, William secured it. Picking up the tray, he headed back to Cassandra and found her sitting on the couch her head in her hands.

"Cassandra..." Lifting her head she looked at him. He couldn't read her expression as he set the tray of food down. "Come on, you haven't eaten."

He took the lids off two plates of food. Looking at them she didn't recognize a single thing. One more thing to prove she was completely out of her element here.

"Who was she?" she asked lifting her eyes from the plates to his.

"Her name is Senior Chief Delondra Falco. She is the Navigations Specialist on board the Retribution," he replied, handing her eating utensils.

"Who is she to you?" Cassandra narrowed the question ignoring the utensils.

"I just told you."

Cassandra looked him in the eye for a few more moments waiting. "So she was never anything else?" She knew she was not wrong.

William went still. Carefully, he put the utensils down. "Nothing important," he finally admitted. He didn't want to discuss this, especially with her. No one who came before mattered to him including his past wife. Didn't she understand that?

"I think she would disagree." She'd be damned if she would let him off the hook. "Earlier you asked me not to shut you out, I'm asking the same."

William's eyes settled on hers.

"I may not have been in many relationships, but I know what I want in one."

"What do you want, Cassandra," he was almost afraid to ask.

"Honesty. Even if I don't like the answer, I need the truth." As she started to stand, he gripped her hand stopping her.

"It was nearly eight cycles ago," he began. "I wasn't even an Admiral yet. I was in command of the Battleship Babirusa. We'd just come back from a one-year tour, we'd taken heavy fire," William watched her face. "We put in, orbiting Diomede for repairs. I took a five-day leave. I met Falco. She was on leave from the Battleship Talaria. Things…happened."

"It wasn't a one-night-stand."

"No."

She waited.

"It was three days," he said through clenched teeth.

"So a fling?" William raised an eyebrow at her term. "Something you enjoy for a while then forget about?"

"That would fit. I didn't even realize she was assigned to the Retribution until after we were underway."

"Would you have reassigned her?"

"No. There was no reason to."

"So what is your term for the three days?" She needed to know.

"Leave," he told her bluntly.

Cassandra looked at his face, realizing he wasn't used to being questioned, and that he was tolerating it from her. She turned her hand over in his.

"Okay," she squeezed his hand. "But there are a couple of things you should be aware of."

William laced his fingers into hers. "What?"

"Falco doesn't consider it 'leave' and she's been in your quarters before." She had to put it out there.

"Why do you believe that?"

"First, because of the way she looked at me after you ordered her out. And second, where's the report she was bringing you?"

"What?"

"Did you see one on your desk because she sure didn't leave with one?"

Standing, he entered his Ready Room and went to his desk. Everything was exactly as he'd left it. There was no report. Turning he found Cassandra in the doorway.

"So what's the stuff on the plates?" she asked letting the subject drop. This was Admiral Territory. He'd decide what he was going to do.

Walking her back to the couch they sat, "It's called Zebu."

"How does it taste?"

He looked at her and then chuckled. "I'll let you decide," he picked up a piece with his forc and put it to her lips. "Open up."

Trusting him, she opened her mouth letting him feed her. "Not bad," she finally said after she swallowed.

Swooping in for a quick kiss, he handed her a forc, then ordered, "Eat."

They ate together in a comfortable silence with Cassandra all but licking her plate clean. She found him watching her and gave him a sheepish look.

"I didn't realize I was so hungry."

"You needed it. Do you want more?"

"No. Where do I put these?" she gestured to the now empty dishes.

"I'll take care of them," he said as he picked up the empty plates.

Returning he found her in the middle of a big yawn. Seeing him she grinned, "Sorry, it's not the company."

"You need sleep, come on."

"William, it's only 2130."

"And you're tired. You need sleep."

Cassandra looked at him as he led her to the bed. "William…" she wasn't sure what to do.

"Cassandra, get undressed, get into bed, go to sleep. I have paperwork to do. I'll be in later." He pulled the blanket and sheets down on the bed, realizing she'd restored it.

"But, I thought…" she stuttered to a stop.

"Thought what?" Realizing what she had thought, he found he wanted to hear her say it.

"That we'd…" confusion filled her eyes as she looked up at him.

"Cassandra, don't think I don't want to mate with you again," he rubbed his hands up and down her arms. "Your body needs time to recover. We have time. Get into bed, get some sleep." Pulling her up, he kissed her then walked into his Ready Room.

Standing by the bed she watched him leave. Was she ever going to figure him out? She expected a repeat of this afternoon and found she was disappointed. She couldn't stop the next yawn that hit her. Maybe she'd just take a short nap. Undressing, she put her clothes on the chest at the foot of the bed then climbed in. She was almost instantly asleep.

∞ ∞ ∞ ∞ ∞

In his Ready Room, William was replaying his day. Cassandra. The transmission. Falco. All in all an eventful day. While she'd brought up some good points concerning Falco, he thought she was reading them wrong. Leaning back in his chair he remembered how responsive she'd been. That she'd been able to accept his entire length. He'd never experienced that before, she truly was his life mate. Now he just had to make her understand what that meant.

Turning his attention to his desk he thought about Falco's missing report. That was something to deal with tomorrow. At the comm center he brought up the Regulian transmission to study again.

∞ ∞ ∞ ∞ ∞

The nightmare had Cassandra sitting straight up in bed looking frantically around. Where was she?!! Where was Victoria?!! Heart pounding, she tried to get her bearings. There was a light, but it seemed so far away. It was the scent that finally calmed her.

"William," she whispered. But he was not here. Picking up the pillow that carried his scent, the nightmare came back to her, and she lowered her head to the pillow.

She'd been having the nightmare since the Regulians attacked Earth. There was supposed to be a light, but all she saw was death and destruction. Every time she tried for the light someone she loved died. It was all her fault…if she'd just been smarter she could have saved them all. But tonight the nightmare changed; for the last seventeen days it had always had her dropping Victoria, and falling after her, something that even now made her shudder. But tonight it included William, William falling out of the Raptor after both of them. What did it mean?

Her maternal Grandmother had always told her to listen to her dreams to learn from them. They would reveal things that she needed to know. She had always believed her, but she didn't know what this meant.

What she did know was that she wanted William. He scared her, not with his size or passion, but with what he made her feel. She could lose herself to him, trusting he would take care of her. How did she know that? It wasn't her mind telling her, it was her heart. She had never trusted it to anyone other than family, but her heart said she could trust him. Did she have the courage? There were so many things they didn't know about each other.

In the latter part of his life, her father had been a carpenter. And while he'd loved to build things, he'd gotten his greatest pleasure out of restoring pieces that had been either forgotten or neglected. He'd tell her that sometimes you just needed to strip away the outer layers to see the true beauty. That it was what's underneath that really matters. She could hear his voice in her head telling her this was such a time.

So, if she stripped way all the crap that had been going on since the Regulians attacked, stripped back the layers, what was really important to her? Her first thought was, 'William.' Could she let herself trust that? Could she not?

Staying in bed was no longer an option. Getting up she wrapped the blanket around her. There was only one place she wanted to be. There was the light and she moved to it. Standing in the doorway she saw him. He was her Light, just him. He sat at his desk with his back to her, she walked over and touched his back.

William was so deep in thought that he didn't realize Cassandra was behind him until he picked up her scent a moment before she touched him.

He turned in his chair and was floored. She stood in front of him wrapped in a drooping blanket that exposed her bare shoulders. She moved between his legs and sat. He pulled her closer and she nestled into him, the blanket falling away.

"You should be sleeping," he caressed a bare thigh.

"Bad dream," she rested her head on his shoulder.

He should have realized. With everything she'd been through; the attack, the destruction of Earth, not only saving but caring for her niece, trying to find her way in a new world, and then him on top of it. How much was one small woman able to take. He put a hand on her cheek and tucked her in close.

"Cassandra," sighing her name, he kissed the top of her head.

"Just hold me for a minute. I'll be okay, and then you can get back to work."

William wasn't getting any further than he had before in figuring out the translation. His mate needed him and that took priority. Shutting down the comm center he cradled her in his arms as he moved into his private chambers.

"You still have work," she mumbled.

"No, I don't." Laying her on the far side of the bed he quickly disrobed and pulled her close. "Sleep, Cassandra, I've got you." Without hesitation, she wrapped herself around him. Her utter trust humbled him. Together they fell asleep.

∞ ∞ ∞ ∞ ∞

Hours later his secondary line rang, instinctively he picked it up.

"Zafar."

"Admiral?" Leander quizzed, "I'm looking for Cassandra."

"Hold on," realizing this had to be about Victoria, he nudged her. "Cassandra, it's Leander." She was instantly awake reaching across him for the headset.

"Leander, what's wrong?" her voice was panicky.

"Victoria had a nightmare. We've tried to calm her down, but..."

"I'll be right there!" she told him sliding across William dropping the headset as her feet hit the floor. "Shit, I should have known better," she muttered pulling on clothes.

William followed her, pulling on his clothes as he listened to Cassandra berate herself.

"Stop, Cassandra, stop!" he grabbed her arm. "You couldn't have known."

"I should have!" Sitting, she pulled on her boots. "She's been having nightmares ever since the attack. They haven't been as severe lately but still."

"You aren't going to be any help to her beating yourself up."

Looking up she realized he was fully dressed. "What are you doing?"

"Going with you."

She just stood and looked at him and then sighing she nodded, "Okay."

∞ ∞ ∞ ∞ ∞

At the Michelakakis' hatch with William at her side, she knocked. Leander opened the door almost immediately.

"Cassandra, she's in here."

Stepping back he let her in. "Admiral." William nodded as he watched Cassandra rush over to the softly, sobbing child lying on the couch. Javiera moved to the side.

Sitting down, Cassandra put a gentle hand on Victoria's back as she softly whispered, "Tori, it's all right. I'm here." Tori opened red-rimmed eyes and was instantly in her arms, her sobbing increased.

"Shhh. It's okay, baby, it's okay. I've got you. You're safe. Come on stop crying," Cassandra cooed to her and rubbed a hand up and down her back as she held her tightly. "Look at me, Tori." Cassandra tucked her hair behind her ear, "Come on, look at me."

As Tori raised tear-filled eyes, Cassandra framed her face with her hands and looked directly into her eyes. "You are safe!" Her voice was her urgent voice. "It was just a bad dream. I won't let anything happen to you."

"Fire," Victoria whispered in a pitiful voice. "I couldn't get out of the fire, Aunt Cassie."

Pulling her close with a fierce hug she told her, "We got you out, Victoria, remember? We got you out."

Victoria looked up, "You, the Admiral, and Lucas."

"Yes, you're safe."

"Promise?"

"I promise. Now let's get out of here so the Michelakakis' can get some sleep." Victoria nodded, closed her eyes, and laid her head on Cassandra's shoulder. As she went to stand, William stepped up.

"Let me take her," William said softly as he knelt down and reached for Victoria. "She's too heavy for you."

"I'm not sure she'll let you." Victoria opened her eyes to look at him.

"Victoria, is it okay if I carry you?" He waited for her answer.

She watched him with unblinking eyes and slowly let go of Cassandra's neck and held her arms out to him. Standing, William pulled the small body close, feeling her arms wrap around his neck.

"Leander," Cassandra started...

"It's okay, we'll talk later." She nodded as she followed William.

∞ ∞ ∞ ∞ ∞

Opening the hatch to their quarters, Cassandra secured it once William was inside. She stepped around him, went to the bed and pulled back the covers.

"Lay her down over here," she whispered. Victoria had fallen into an exhausted sleep on the walk over. Gently laying her down, William removed her arms from around his neck. When he eased back, Cassandra pulled the covers up around her. Victoria opened exhausted eyes. "The Glitter Man was there," she whispered and Cassandra froze.

"What? Where?"

"In the dream. He was there, watching. He's trying to find me, Aunt Cassie." Frightened eyes looked into hers.

"No, Tori, no. He's not coming for you, you're safe! It was just a dream. A bad dream."

"It's the Glitter Man."

"He'll never find you, Victoria."

"He said he'd always be able to find me."

"When Tori? When did he say that?" Cassandra's voice was urgent.

"Back when he took me," she replied a single tear falling from one eye. Cassandra didn't know what to say.

William silently listened and then spoke up, "I wasn't there last time, Victoria. Neither was the Retribution nor Lucas. He won't be able to take you from us. You're safe here." Cassandra and Victoria both looked at him. "You're safe. I promise."

Cassandra swallowed hard as she turned back to Victoria. "You see, you're safe. The Admiral promised you. Now sleep. I'll be here." Victoria closed her eyes and was instantly asleep.

William stood and pulled her quietly across the room and into his arms. She rested her head on his chest.

"Who's this Glitter Man she's talking about?" Cassandra put a hand over his mouth, her eyes darting back toward the bed.

"Shhh…not here. If she wakes up and hears us talking about it…" her eyes pleaded with his.

"But he's real. Not something she's made up?"

"He's real."

"Okay," he put a hand under her chin so she looked at him. "We'll talk about it tomorrow. You need to get more sleep." He quickly looked around the quarters they'd been assigned. "Where do you sleep?"

"With Tori."

He let out an enormous sigh, "We really haven't been taking very good care of you, have we?"

"We're fine. The bed is huge. It's more than enough for the two of us."

He let it drop because if he had his way, which he damn sure planned on having, they wouldn't be here for long.

"Tomorrow, come to my quarters. We'll have third meal and talk."

"William, I need to stay with Victoria."

"Both of you, 1800, I'll have Lucas join us. Then you'll tell me what happened to Victoria."

Cassandra nodded. She knew he was right. He needed to know. "Okay."

He leaned down and gave her an urgent kiss.

"Secure the door behind me," he ordered. In the corridor, he waited until he heard the locks engage before turning.

Chapter Five

The next morning Falco was standing at attention in the Admiral's Ready Room. Leaning back in his chair, William's gaze bored into hers, "Explain."

"Admiral, last night at 1900 hours I entered your Ready Room with what I considered vital information on the Retribution's navigational system. Once inside I encountered what I considered unauthorized personnel. I identified myself, stated my business, demanded to know hers, she refused. I informed her I was calling security."

"What makes you think you have the right to demand anything from someone in my Ready Room?"

"William," Falco started.

"It's Admiral, Senior Chief!" he cut her off. Falco stiffened, her face turning red.

"Yes, Sir! Sorry, Sir!"

"Finish," he ordered.

"Sir, the woman was coming out of your private quarters which is off limits to all personnel. I believed she was possibly there to cause harm, being who she is."

"And who would that be, Senior Chief?" the Admiral asked leaning forward with a deceptively quiet voice.

"Sir, she's that refugee from Earth. She couldn't possibly have any business in your private quarters! When she refused to disclose her reason for being there, I informed her I was calling security."

"Then why didn't you?"

"What?" Falco was thrown off.

"You didn't call security. You called me in Communications. How did you come by that information?" the Admiral fired at her. Falco didn't respond. "Answer, Senior Chief!"

"Sir, I was informed of your location by the woman."

"Did that tell you anything, Senior Chief?" he demanded.

"Sir, I didn't know that's where you were until I confirmed it, Sir," Falco was starting to sweat.

"Why the secure line?"

"Sir, I was protecting the Admiral's reputation."

He leaned back in his chair waiting.

"Sir, a refugee was able to gain access to the Admiral's private chambers. I knew you didn't want that to be common knowledge on the ship."

"Now you know what I want my crew to know? Is that what you're telling me, Senior Chief?"

Falco realized she was sinking herself.

"No, Sir."

"What did you discover as a result of the call, Senior Chief?" William demanded drilling the point home. Falco's attitude toward Cassandra rubbed him wrong.

Falco swallowed not wanting to say it out loud, "That the refugee had permission to be there, Sir."

"And you didn't," he finished for her. "Understand this, Senior Chief, Cassandra has permission to be in my quarters at any time. You do not. Is that clear?"

"Yes, Sir!" Her hatred for Cassandra grew.

"You have no reason to be in my Ready Room unless ordered here. Is that understood, Senior Chief?!?"

"Yes, Sir!"

"Dismissed!"

"Sir!" Falco saluted the Admiral and turned to escape.

"Senior Chief," the Admiral's words caused Falco to turn back slowly. "Where is that vital information?" he asked raising an eyebrow at her.

"Sir?"

"The report you said was the reason you were in my Ready Room."

"Sir, I left it on your desk."

He spread his hands across his desk, "Where?"

"Sir, I left it right in the middle. The refugee must have taken it," Falco couldn't bring herself to say the name.

"Really, why would Cassandra do that?" William asked in a neutral voice making sure he emphasized her name.

Falco's jaw tightened as the name left William's lips. "Sir, I'm sure it was to throw suspicion in my direction; to discredit me in your eyes."

"Why would Cassandra want to do that?"

"For having access to your Ready Room, Sir."

"YOU DON'T!!" the Admiral erupted, and as he stood, his legs sent his chair into the wall, "DO YOU UNDERSTAND, SENIOR CHIEF?"

Falco cringed under his rage, "Yes, Sir!" she finally got out.

"Have a copy of that report sent to the Bridge by 0900! DISMISSED!"

Falco hustled out of the Ready Room.

∞ ∞ ∞ ∞ ∞

Cassandra was trying to give Victoria a normal morning or at least as normal as mornings were on the Retribution.

"So now that we're done with breakfast, what do you want to do?"

"Can we go to the play room? It's an area on the ship in the family section that kids can go and hang out. Amina said they were going there today."

"Sure, if you want."

As soon as they arrived, Victoria saw her new friends.

"Is it okay if I go?" she asked.

"Go," she told her.

Seeing Javiera, she walked over to sit by her. "I have to thank you for last night…" she began.

Javiera waved a hand at her. "No, you don't. I'm just sorry she had such a terrible dream. I didn't even think about it. She seemed to have adjusted so well to all the changes this last month. But it has to have taken a toll on her, you too."

"Yeah, we're working on it."

"She slept okay the rest of the night?"

"Yeah, she only remembered bits and pieces this morning."

"Makes it easier for her, harder on you."

Cassandra said nothing.

"Look, Cassandra," Javiera glanced over to see that the kids were occupied then turned to her. "I've been an officer's wife for close to ten cycles. Before that, I was on several ships following my father. So I know my way around. If you have any questions about procedures, who's who, or why things are done certain ways you can ask me," she looked her in the eye. "And I don't gossip. What you ask or tell me stays between us."

Cassandra remained quiet.

"I realize I should have offered sooner, but to be honest I wasn't sure I was going to like you." She shrugged her shoulders, "Leander thinks you're great and normally I'd just trust that but…"

"It's another woman he's talking about," Cassandra finished for her, "and not a Carinian woman who knows what's allowed and what's not."

"Exactly!" Javiera smiled at her seeing she understood. "But I've gotten to know you, seen you with Victoria, and understand more. I think we could be great friends."

Cassandra was a little amazed, "That would be nice, but really I thought after last night…"

"Please, all kids have nightmares. Victoria's are unfortunately based in reality."

"Yes."

"So some night soon we'll try another sleepover."

"She'd like that."

"So would Amina. Victoria's her 'bestest' friend."

∞ ∞ ∞ ∞ ∞

Back in their quarters, Cassandra sat Victoria down on the couch, "Tori, we need to talk about last night."

"I'm sorry, Aunt Cassie," her sad voice broke Cassandra's heart.

"No! No, Victoria, you have nothing to be sorry for. Look at me, Victoria." She raised her eyes, "Nothing." She watched to make sure Toni believed her then Cassandra went on. "I need to know what you meant about the Glitter Man looking for you."

"He said he'd always be able to find me," she whispered digging at her right arm, something she'd always done when talking about her kidnapping.

"When?"

"When he had me."

"Tori, you've never said that before," Cassandra looked at her seriously.

"I just remembered it, Aunt Cassie," she started to cry softly.

"Shhh, it's okay, honey." Gathering Tori in her arms, Cassandra stopped her from digging into her arm. "Shhh, is there anything else you've remembered?" Victoria shook her head. "Okay, but if you do remember anything, Victoria, you need to tell me, okay?"

"Okay."

Time to change the subject, "Guess what we're doing tonight."

"What?"

"We are going to eat third meal with the Admiral."

"Where?"

"In his quarters."

"What are we having?"

"I don't know. We'll have to be surprised."

"We're surprised a lot," Tori said with a rueful grin.

Cassandra laughed, "Yes we are. Why don't you go get cleaned up so we're ready when it's time to go."

"Okay." Giving Cassandra a quick kiss she jumped down.

∞ ∞ ∞ ∞ ∞

William's day continued at a somewhat less confrontational rate. The report delivered didn't really say anything. Before he confronted Falco again, he wanted to think about it. He contacted High Command on secure channels relaying the information they'd obtained and his suspicions. He made contact with Lucas and told him about supper, then he notified Hutu of the number for supper and that one was a child.

∞ ∞ ∞ ∞ ∞

Cassandra and Victoria arrived outside the Admiral's quarters. "So who's going to knock? You or me?" Cassandra was suddenly nervous.

"I will," Victoria smiled and knocked on the hatch. The hatch opened almost immediately. "Lucas!" Victoria squealed jumping at him. Catching her, he swung her up. Cassandra smiled entering behind them.

∞ ∞ ∞ ∞ ∞

At the end of the corridor, Falco watched as the hatch opened and the two refugees entered the Admiral's quarters. The woman was smiling. Jealousy was raging through her. Who did this person think she was coming between her and the Admiral? He was hers! She would have to pay! Falco turned and walked away.

∞ ∞ ∞ ∞ ∞

Inside the Ready Room, Victoria chattered away to Lucas giving Cassandra a chance to see a table was missing.

"Where have you been, Lucas? I haven't seen you in forever!"

"I've been busy on patrol," he told her walking into the Admiral's private chambers. "What have you been up to?"

She proceeded to tell him all about school and Amina.

Following them she found William coming toward her. The look in his eyes told her she was about to be kissed. Her nerves calmed as she gave him a half smile reaching up for him as his mouth swooped down to capture hers. It was a thorough kiss leaving them both breathless.

The buzzing at the hatch separated them. "It's Hutu with third meal. I want you to meet him."

Several men entered the room carrying covered trays. "Take them to the table in the back," the Admiral told them. A large, golden-skinned man with golden eyes directed them, "We'll be out of here in a few minutes, Admiral."

"That's fine. Hutu, I'd like you to meet Cassandra. Cassandra, this is Hutu. He's been my personal chef for five cycles now. If there's something you want just ask him, he can probably make it. He's a genius in the kitchen."

"Thank you, Admiral. Out you two, get out!" He made shooing motions to his staff. "It's nice to meet you, ma'am." He held out his hand, not sure if she'd take it. Cassandra shook the man's hand firmly and without hesitation. Hutu was impressed.

Victoria stepped into the room. "And this," the Admiral said motioning Victoria forward, "is Victoria, Cassandra's niece."

Hutu leaned down to the child again holding out his hand. Victoria put her much smaller one in his and shook. "Nice to meet you," she said, melting the large man's heart.

"You too," he straightened. "Will there be anything else, Admiral?"

"No thanks, Hutu."

"Goodnight then," Hutu nodded to Lucas, who had entered the room.

"Goodnight."

After Hutu had left, William walked over to secure the door.

Lucas raised an eyebrow, "So are we going to eat or what?"

Entering the private chamber, Cassandra discovered the missing table with two chairs on both sides of it and the trays of food sitting on it. A sit-down family meal. Her breath caught in her throat stopping her in her tracks.

William put his hands on her waist and leaned down to whisper, "It's all right?"

"Better than all right," she whispered back as she put a hand over one of his and squeezed. She walked to the table.

Lucas witnessed the exchange and looked from his father to Cassandra then back. William met his son's gaze straight on.

"Lucas," Victoria said grabbing his hand, "Where are you going to sit?"

Lucas looked down at her, "Why next to you of course." Victoria grinned and chose her seat while Lucas waited until Cassandra sat then the two Zafar men pulled the covers off the plates and joined them. Cassandra and Victoria looked at their plates. Three of them were the same, one different, the one in front of William.

"Here," he said, "I think this one is for you, Victoria. It's called cnaipini sicin. Hutu said all the children on the ship like it."

"Okay," she said in a brave voice.

"So what are we having?" Cassandra asked trying to draw attention away from her.

"It's called Rhea. You liked the Zebu, you'll like this."

"You had Zebu?" Lucas demanded looking at his father.

"Last night," William grinned at him, "Hutu cooked it perfectly."

"And you didn't invite me?" he demanded.

"No, I had someone much prettier to share it with," William looked at Cassandra who felt her face get warm. Thankfully it all went over Victoria's head as she bravely tried her first bite. Slowly she chewed and then her face lit up.

"Aunt Cassie! It's chicken nuggets!"

Cassandra grinned at her as she quickly took another bite. "Awesome, what do you say?"

"Thanks, Admiral!" Victoria said, her mouth full, a large grin on her face.

"Victoria Lynn!" Cassandra scolded.

"Sorry," Victoria covered her mouth, her eyes still grinning. "But it's the best 'surprise' we've had since we got here."

"Surprise?" Lucas asked starting to eat.

"It's just what we call meals on the Retribution," Cassandra watched to see how to eat what was in front of her.

"Why?" he persisted, missing his father's look.

Looking to see Victoria was engrossed in her meal, she answered quietly, "It's just unfamiliar."

"Patrol went well?" William asked already knowing the answer.

Looking at his father, Lucas let the matter drop. "Went fine."

Cassandra chewed her food, "You're right, William, I like this." Immediately she realized she'd addressed him by his first name in front of Lucas.

"Of course I was right," he joked, trying to put her at ease. Lucas continued to eat saying nothing.

Tori turned to Lucas, "Lucas, do you ever go to the play area?"

"The what?" he gave Tori a confused look.

"The play area. It's really fun!"

"Deck F," Cassandra told him, "It's an open area for kids to run."

"Oh no, Victoria, I don't really get down there much."

"Oh."

Cassandra knew William wanted to talk about what happened last night, but she couldn't with Victoria listening. As they finished their meals, he caught Lucas' eye.

"Victoria, Lucas and I need to do some work in my Ready Room. Would you and Cassandra put the dishes over there?"

"Guy talk?" Both men just looked at Victoria.

"Daddy and Grampa Jacob used to do that a lot. Mommy always said they did it when they thought it would upset her." Her look was older than her years.

"Or it could just be work," Cassandra interjected. "Let's clear the table and we'll get started on homework."

Victoria just shrugged, "Okay."

William shut the adjoining door as they entered his Ready Room. Once Lucas got to his father's desk, he turned demanding to know. "What the fuck is going on? You secured your outer door? You and Cassandra have obviously been intimate, she called you William. You're having private dinners. Who the fuck is taking care of Victoria?"

William stood toe-to-toe with his son. "Don't you dare question her commitment to that child! She hung upside down out of a Raptor, flames all around her! She's been there every night since dealing with the nightmares!" William turned taking a deep breath.

Lucas was amazed by his father's emotion. He was normally very reserved except for family. "Dad, what's going on between you and Cassandra? Don't bite my head off!" he said quickly as his father turned. "I think I have the right to know."

William wasn't sure how to explain to his son that his mother wasn't his life mate so he decided to just say it, "She's my life mate."

Lucas' jaw dropped, "What? How? You're sure? You have no doubts? It hasn't been long enough," he stuttered.

William just looked at him, "I know the difference. I'm sorry."

"For what?"

"That is wasn't your mother."

"Dad, it was perfectly clear that you and Mom weren't life mates."

William was surprised at his comment.

"If you tell me she's your life mate then I believe you. I know she's committed to Victoria. But what the hell is going on. What nightmares? Dad…" Lucas hesitated.

"What son?"

"Victoria…" he looked at his father, "She's my life mate," Lucas let it stand.

William didn't say anything at first, assessing his son. "You're sure?"

"Just as sure as you are," Lucas replied.

"You have a long road ahead of you then."

Nodding, "I know. What nightmares?" At William's hesitation, Lucas continued, "She's mine to protect whether she's nine or nineteen. I can't do that if I don't know what's going on!"

William walked to sit behind his desk. "Last night Victoria was having a sleepover at Amina's. I'd convinced Cassandra to stay with me. Leander called and said Victoria was having a nightmare. We went to get her." He looked at Lucas judging what he thought he could handle then realized that it wasn't up to him. His son had found his life mate. He couldn't interfere in that by withholding information. "I've never seen a child so distraught," William told his son. "She was petrified but trying to control it. She dreamed she was trapped in the fire."

"Shit!"

"There's more." Lucas looked at him. "She told Cassandra the Glitter Man was there." Lucas was confused.

"I don't know everything yet. Cassandra wouldn't talk about it with Victoria in the room. But this Glitter Man did something to Victoria. He's real and she's dreaming he's trying to find her, can find her…anywhere."

Lucas paled, "What are we going to do?"

"We find out the truth and protect our life mates."

∞ ∞ ∞ ∞ ∞

Back in William's private quarters, Cassandra was wondering what was going on in the other room.

"Aunt Cassie?"

"Yeah, baby?"

"I'm tired. Can I lie down?" Cassandra looked sharply at her.

"You're feeling okay?"

"Yeah, just tired."

Cassandra got up and took a pillow and blanket off the bed. "Here you go, lie down on the couch."

"Will you tell Lucas goodnight for me?"

"Yes," and in minutes she was asleep.

∞ ∞ ∞ ∞ ∞

The men looked up as Cassandra entered the room, quietly closing the connecting door.

"She's asleep," she said as she crossed the room. She sat back in a chair, suddenly as tired as Victoria.

"Is she normally asleep this early?" Lucas asked.

"No."

"Cassandra, I decided that Lucas needed to know what's going on with Victoria."

"You decided?" Cassandra's voice was sharp as she sat up, tiredness forgotten. "That's not your decision to make, Admiral. She's my niece!"

"It concerns the safety of my ship and crew. That makes it my decision!" William's tone was the one his crew feared. However, it had no effect on her.

"That's bullshit!" Cassandra started, cutting herself off when Lucas began to chuckle.

He'd been following the heated exchange with keen interest. When his father told him this small woman was his life mate, he'd been concerned she would be unable to handle the demands of a Carinian male. Seeing her go toe-to-toe with the Admiral, his doubts faded away.

"What's so funny!" she demanded pinning Lucas to his chair with angry blue eyes.

He held up his hands in a universal sign of surrender, "Just glad to see there's someone not afraid to stand up to the old man." Still chuckling he looked at his father, "Should keep things interesting."

"What?" Shocked eyes turned to William.

"Lucas, that's enough," William watched her.

"I'm just saying that as unusual as it is, the two of you seem to work…" Lucas trailed off at his father's furious look. As he turned to look at Cassandra, he finally realized his blunder.

Cassandra paled. William had told his son about their intimacy. Just like at MIT. What else had he told him? Had she made a mistake being with William?

"Cassandra," William watched her eyes take on that shuttered look he was coming to hate.

"You need to know about Victoria's kidnapping," her voice was brisk, flat. Unable to sit, she walked across the room staring at the painting of setting suns.

"When Victoria was two, she, her mother and my grandmother took a trip to meet me in Kayseri. I was finishing up my doctorate on ancient Sumerian. I was eighteen. Dad thought it would be a perfect girls trip, so he stayed behind. Peter was gone. I'd rented a two-bedroom house with a private courtyard once I knew they were coming. Victoria and I were sharing a room. That morning, I left earlier than normal. I had to present my dissertation. She was in bed sleeping when I left." She turned away from the picture looking at the avidly listening men but not moving toward them.

"I'd barely been gone thirty minutes when Cyndy, Victoria's mom, called frantic. They couldn't find Victoria. The doors were all locked, but she wasn't there. Her robe and slippers weren't in the bedroom. We searched the area again and we found one of her slippers in a bush. The other was on the roof, the fucking roof! We called the police, but they didn't have any more to go on than we did."

"We couldn't find her. No one had seen anything. God, what a helpless feeling. My grandmother just kept saying, *'it was them, it had to be them.'* Eighteen hours after she was taken she was back. She was lying in the courtyard crying. A house full of people had been trying to help find her and then she was just there." Cassandra ran a hand through her hair. "We couldn't get her to stop crying. She was terrified. We took her to a doctor, but one look at him and she went crazy. It took four of us to hold her down so they could give her a sedative. While she was out, we had the doctor examine her," Cassandra finally met William's eyes and saw he understood.

"She hadn't been sexually assaulted." William released the breath he hadn't realized he'd been holding. "There wasn't a mark on her. Not a hair, not a fiber, not a piece of dust," she sat back down and watched William.

"Nothing?" William asked.

Cassandra shook her head.

"She wasn't physically hurt?" Lucas demanded of Cassandra.

Cassandra looked at him totally confused by what she saw on his face. It was like he'd been sucker-punched, but his eyes were raging.

"We couldn't find anything physically wrong with her, but she couldn't remember anything. Not even getting out of bed. Only what she called the Glitter Man. She said he was huge and his eyes seemed to 'glitter' at her. Until last night, that's all she'd ever remembered."

"What did your grandmother mean?" William asked replaying what she'd said in his mind.

"Back when my grandmother was a young girl, she lived in Kayseri. She was 'abducted;' her word. She was gone a week. When she was 'returned;' again her word, the man she was supposed to marry refused her. He believed she'd been with another. No one believed her except my grandfather. They married leaving the 'homeland,' as they called Kayseri, behind. The 'girls trip' was the only time my grandmother went back. It's amazing, though," she looked at William, "she described the Regulians perfectly."

"You believe the Regulians abducted your grandmother cycles ago?"

"I believe my grandmother. I believe Victoria. That's it," she stood. "That's what I know."

"The nightmares?" Lucas asked.

Cassandra looked at him. "Every night for the first year, after that they tapered off to almost none. Then the Regulians attacked Earth. After we got here, she has had them every night but only about being trapped in the fire. It was getting better until last night. It's the first time the Glitter Man has shown back up. Hopefully, the last. Excuse me, I need to check on Tori."

"I will," Lucas was on his way to the door before Cassandra could say anything. There was something there that needed to be explained.

Lucas needed to make sure Victoria was okay. Cassandra's story of what she'd been through had shaken him. She'd been unprotected. That wouldn't happen again.

She looked at William.

"He'll make sure she's all right," he walked around the desk and leaned against it watching her, "are you?"

"Am I what?"

"All right?"

"I'm all right. I need to get Tori back."

William reached for her, pulling her into his arms for a blazing kiss that melted any defenses she sought to build in her anger with him. When she finally responded, some of the fear loosened in him. The fear she would shut him out. Breaking off the kiss, he rested his forehead against hers.

"I didn't tell Lucas anything about what is happening between us." Cassandra snapped out of the haze William's kiss had put her into. Her eyes shot to his. "I didn't have to, all he had to do was see us together. My son knows me, Cassandra. He knows I don't do this on a tour."

"What exactly is the 'this' you're talking about?" Before he could answer there was a scream from the other room.

∞ ∞ ∞ ∞ ∞

"NO! NO! GO AWAY!" Victoria screamed. As Lucas tried to comfort her, Cassandra raced to her side.

"Move!" she told Lucas but he wouldn't budge.

"Lucas!" William gripped his son's arm and pulled him away. "Let Cassandra handle this. You're scaring Tori."

"Victoria! It's Aunt Cassie!" Her voice was firm pulling the struggling child into her arms. "You're safe!"

"He's here! The Glitter Man is here!!!" she cried.

"No! No, he's not! William, switch the lights on!" she ordered. William immediately turned the lights up.

"Look, baby. Look it's just you, me, Lucas, and William! No Glitter Man!"

Lucas got his first look at Victoria's face. He thought he understood, between what his father and Cassandra had said. But nothing prepared him for the terror he saw in Victoria's eyes. It ripped his guts out knowing he'd scared her, that he couldn't comfort her, his life mate.

William still had his arm, "Easy, Lucas, this isn't about you. Don't take it that way."

"How am I supposed to take it?"

"As a nine-cycle girl who's had a nightmare."

Victoria's eyes started to clear. She looked at Cassandra then turned her head and saw William and Lucas.

"He found me, Aunt Cassie," she whispered urgently as she rubbed her right arm. "He found me."

"No, baby, no."

"Set Alert Status One throughout the ship! Repeat Alert Status ONE! Regulian ships approaching, two minutes to contact!"

"Fuck!" The men said in unison.

"Stay here!" the Admiral ordered. "It's the safest place on the ship." He and Lucas headed for the door. In the corridor, William grabbed his son's arm.

"Get your head on straight. You're no help to her," the Admiral gestured back to Victoria, "if you're dead!" Lucas nodded and both men headed in different directions.

∞ ∞ ∞ ∞ ∞

"It's the Glitter Man, he's trying to get me," Tori cried in Cassandra's arms.

"No baby, no, it's the Regulians. You said the Glitter Man was a man, a big man."

Tori looked up at her, "There were others there I couldn't see, but I could hear them."

"Tori! When did you remember this? Tori!" Cassandra gave her a little shake, "when?"

"Back on Earth when the Regulians first arrived."

"Why didn't you say something?"

"If I talk about what happened they'll hear me. They'll get me again."

"Who told you that, Victoria?"

"The Glitter Man!" she wailed, "I'm sorry, Aunt Cassie, I'm sorry."

Cassandra gripped the little girl tightly to her chest, "Shhh... It's okay, baby, it's okay. It isn't your fault. Shhh... calm down." Cassandra heard the guns of the Retribution firing, repelling the Regulians. The Retribution shook as it took fire.

"Aunt Cassie?" Tori's voice was shaking for a different reason.

"It will be okay, baby. Lucas and the Admiral are out there." Cassandra tried to ignore the stab of fear in her heart, "They're making it safe. So the Regulians can't hurt us. That's what they do. Trust the Admiral, Tori, I do."

"Aunt Cassie, can I tell you a secret?" Cassandra looked down at her worried.

"Of course you can."

"Lucas is my life mate."

Cassandra pulled her head back to look at Tori, "Your what?!?"

"Life mate. That's what they call a soul mate up here. Like Mommy and Daddy, and Grandpa and Grandma, and…"

"I get the idea, Tori. Who told you this?"

"Amina, when we had the sleepover. She really likes Jules, she thinks he might be her life mate."

"Who told you Lucas was yours?"

"No one, I just know. Like you know the Admiral is yours."

The raging battle faded into the background. Cassandra was shocked and it was as if a light went on. "Why would you think that, Tori?" she whispered.

"Because," Tori answered, "he didn't let go, did he? He held on, on the Raptor. He's a really big man but he's not mean, not like…" she trailed off, "And Lucas is his son," she finished.

Oh to be able to think like a nine-year-old.

"You won't tell him, will you?"

"What?" Cassandra was trying to keep up.

"You won't tell Lucas, will you? I'm too little to be his life mate yet, but when I'm eighteen, he'd better watch out!"

Cassandra stared at her niece wondering who was the wiser.

"Why eighteen?" she was curious to know.

"That's when Carinian women are considered 'of age.' So you won't tell him?" Tori was nothing if not persistent.

"No, I won't. You know what? Sometimes you give me a headache." Tori giggled. "Let's just be quiet for a little bit, okay?"

"Okay."

Cassandra held her niece close as the sounds of the battle echoed throughout the ship. Closing her eyes, she prayed.

Chapter Six

The Admiral surged onto the Bridge just as the first guns started to fire.

"Two minutes, Quinn?!! What the fuck is TWO MINUTES! Why weren't they picked up sooner?!!"

"At this point I don't know, Admiral. All I could do was respond. The Sentinel picked them up first. They're taking the hardest hits. They only had a forty-second warning."

"Are our fighters launched?"

"Working on it, Sir."

"Get them up! Get them up now!"

∞ ∞ ∞ ∞ ∞

Lucas was in his Blade ready to launch, "You ready to kick some Regulian ass, Hotdog?" Lucas asked.

"All over that, Hawk!"

"Then let's do it!" Lucas launched. In seconds, they were in the fray.

∞ ∞ ∞ ∞ ∞

After nearly an hour of heavy fighting, the Regulians were driven back into the Relinquished Zone. While all ships received some damage, the Sentinel was again targeted. Crews were sent to assist.

"We may need to send it back to Carina for repairs, Admiral."

"We'll see, maybe a stop at Rodham will do the trick."

"What's our damage?"

"All reports indicate light damage, Sir. We were the farthest away, we had the most time."

"Since when is two minutes time? What happened? Falco! Report!"

Falco looked at the Admiral for the first time since her dressing down in his Ready Room earlier that morning. "Sir, it appears the Regulians came in at warp 9.9, reduced their speed only when they were ready to launch fighters. That's when the Sentinel picked them up, when we all picked them up, Sir."

"How the fuck did they know where we were without scanning, Quinn?"

"Someone would need to have transmitted our location to them, Admiral," Falco replied.

The Admiral shot her a frigid look, "Was I speaking to you, Senior Chief?"

"No, Sir!"

Quinn leaned over to him, "But it's a thought, especially with the translation. Could be they received a signal from the general area we're in but not an exact location. That would explain how they could come in so hot."

The Admiral examined that explanation. "How far have we gotten on monitoring transmissions?"

"Started at 0600 today. All ships have extra ears."

"Can we go back 36 hours?"

"Yes, Sir. You sniffing something, Will?"

"Maybe. You got this under control?"

"Yes."

"I'll be in my quarters. You find anything let me know."

"Yes, Sir."

∞ ∞ ∞ ∞ ∞

As William approached his quarters, Lucas met him coming from the opposite direction.

"Nice hunting," the Admiral told him.

"Yeah, felt really good," Lucas replied causing the Admiral to raise an eyebrow. "I kept my head."

Entering the Ready Room they continued back to the private quarters finding lights blazing and two sleeping females. As they approached, Lucas hesitated. He didn't want to scare Victoria again. Walking around him, William squatted down to gently rub Cassandra's leg.

Her unguarded eyes opened slowly revealing relief when she saw he was unharmed. She blinked and it was gone. She started to shift and realized she was holding Tori. Looking up she saw Lucas.

"You're both okay?"

"Yes," William answered squeezing her leg, "You two?" He received a serious look.

"We need to talk, all of us. Tori," Cassandra gave her a little shake. "Wake up, baby."

"Let her sleep."

Cassandra stared Lucas down. "No. Come on, baby. Lucas and the Admiral are back. Wake up."

"Lucas is back?" Tori asked drowsily.

"Yes, open your eyes and see." Lucas wasn't sure this was a good idea.

"Maybe..." he started then met Victoria's green eyes, she smiled at him. Leaving the safety she had found with Cassandra, she walked over to him and lifted her arms. Leaning down he picked her up and pulled her close. She put her arms around his neck and settled in. Lucas was humbled by the simple act and closed his eyes.

That's when Cassandra realized that it wasn't just Victoria who believed they'd found their life mate. She looked to William.

"It will be okay," he told her quietly.

"Victoria," Cassandra said firmly, "you need to tell the Admiral what you told me."

Lucas felt Victoria stiffen in his arms. His protective instincts kicked in.

"Aunt Cassie..." she whispered.

"We need to figure this out, Tori. You're the only one who can help us."

"He'll hear!" Tori whimpered.

"Who, Tori?" William asked.

Scared eyes looked at him then up at Lucas.

"Who, Tori?" Lucas repeated.

"The Glitter Man," she whispered rubbing her right arm.

William frowned as he turned to Cassandra, "How long has she been doing that?"

"What? Rubbing her arm? Since she was taken. Whenever she talks about the Glitter Man, it's a reflex."

"Maybe, maybe not," William looked at Lucas.

"Tell me what you remember, Tori," William sat next to Cassandra motioning Lucas to sit with her.

"I remember getting up, Aunt Cassie was gone. I put on my new robe and slippers, we bought them especially for the trip," Tori looked at Cassandra.

"I remember, baby. Go on."

"I went into the courtyard to the orange tree. I wanted an orange," she looked up at Lucas, "He was just there."

"Who, Tori? What did he look like?" Lucas asked gently.

"He was big, really big. He reached the top of the tree," William heard Cassandra suck in a breath. "He picked me up, my slippers fell off, and then it got really dark," Victoria shivered causing Lucas to hug her closer.

"Do you know where he took you?" William quizzed her.

"No, it was really bright but really dark. It hurt my eyes. There was this humming sound, and…."

"And what, Tori?"

"It sounded like voices, but I couldn't understand them. Then he was standing there, looking at me, looking at my feet, my hands."

"He touched you?" Lucas asked in a very controlled voice.

"Some. He said something to someone, I couldn't understand it. Then he told me he'd find me no matter where I went. He'd hear me and find me, I wouldn't take his light."

William went very still watching Victoria rub her right arm again.

"You said you had a doctor check her after she was returned?" he turned to Cassandra.

"Yes."

"Did they do a body scan?"

"A what?"

The Admiral's comm center rang. William got up to answer. "Zafar."

"Admiral, Quinn. You were right. There was a low-frequency transmission made at 0230 this morning."

"From…"

"The Retribution, Sir. Can't pinpoint it any further than that."

"Good work, Quinn." He looked at Cassandra. "We need to get Victoria to Medical."

"Why, what's going on?"

"We need to do a body scan on her."

"What?"

"Aunt Cassie," Tori started to squirm in Lucas' arms.

"It's okay, Tori," Lucas told her. "Look at me," he tipped her face up to his. "It won't hurt, there's nothing to be scared of. I'll be there with you."

"You will?"

"Yes."

"Aunt Cassie too?" she looked at her aunt.

"You couldn't keep me away, baby," Cassandra glared at the two men.

"Let's get this done." William notified Dr. Bliant to be available.

∞ ∞ ∞ ∞ ∞

Arriving in Medical, the four were ushered into Bliant's office.

"So what's up?" he smiled at Victoria.

"I want a body scan done on Victoria for Regulian technology."

"What?" Bliant was stunned.

"Primarily her right arm."

"Why would you think..."

The Admiral cut him off. His patience was gone. "Just do it!" he ordered.

Victoria shrunk in Lucas' arms.

It was Cassandra who responded. "That's enough, Admiral! You're scaring her! And until you explain to me just what the hell is going on nothing will be done!"

Bliant watched the drama unfolding, glad they were in his office.

"This is a military decision," the Admiral began.

"She's not military! The truth or we're out of here."

Remembering what Cassandra wanted most in a relationship, honesty even if she didn't like it, he told her.

"At 0230 this morning, a low-frequency transmission was sent from the Retribution to the Regulian fleet allowing them to pinpoint our location to make a high-speed attack. We have to find the source of that transmission."

"Why would you think..." things started to fall into place for Cassandra. "You think...?"

"We need to know."

"Cassie," Lucas drew her gaze, "the scan won't hurt her." She looked at Victoria.

"What's going on, Aunt Cassie?"

"Have you been listening?" Tori nodded. "Do you understand what the Admiral's worried about?"

"That the Glitter Man can find me because he put something in my arm." All three men sucked in a sharp breath, amazed such a young child would understand.

"Do you think he did?" she never broke eye contact with Tori. Slowly Tori nodded yes. "So we'll let them do the scan to see."

Tori looked to Lucas, "It won't hurt?"

"No, sweetheart, it won't. I'll be right here."

Tori looked the Admiral in the eye, "Okay."

"Do it!" the Admiral ordered Bliant.

Turning on a scanner the size of Cassandra's hand, Bliant ran it up and down Tori's left arm then her right arm. It started beeping over the spot Tori always rubbed. Cassandra closed her eyes. He quickly went over the rest of her body with no more signals.

"Now what?" Cassandra asked.

"We remove it." Dr. Bliant walked up to Victoria still in Lucas' arms. "This is what we're going to do, young lady," he said. "You are going to sit right where you are. I'm going to wrap this," he showed her what looked like a white bandage, "around your arm here." He touched the spot. "It will slowly get tighter. It might be uncomfortable but shouldn't hurt at all. It's going to get that nasty little thread out of you."

"Thread?" Tori asked.

"That's what it's called. Should be done in five minutes tops!"

Tori allowed him to put on the device and sat very still in Lucas' arms. A few minutes later Bliant took the device off, immediately putting it in a container.

"See that wasn't so bad, was it?" Bliant asked.

Tori rubbed her arm then beamed up at him. "Thanks!"

"You're welcome, young lady."

"Lucas, why don't you walk them back to quarters? I'll be right behind you." After they had left, the Admiral turned to Bliant.

"It's actually relatively low grade, Admiral, at least seven cycles old; I don't know why they'd use it.

"Unless it was top of the line seven cycles ago."

"But the thing is it's basically Carinian technology with a few Regulian additions. Without those additions, the scanner wouldn't have picked it up."

"I want it secured; no one is to know about it, is that clear?"

"Clear, Sir. And Sir, Victoria shouldn't have any side effects from the removal."

"Understood."

∞ ∞ ∞ ∞ ∞

In the corridor, Lucas stopped as Cassandra turned toward their quarters.

"What are you doing?" he asked still carrying Tori.

"Going to our quarters."

"That's not what he meant, Cassie."

Cassandra had reached the end of her rope. "I could really care less what he meant, Lucas. It's late, Victoria needs to get some sleep, real sleep in her own bed. I'm her aunt. I make the decisions concerning her well-being, not you, not the Admiral. If you can't deal with that, then give her to me," she held out her arms.

"I've got her, go," he nodded toward their quarters. Once inside he reluctantly put a drowsy Victoria down.

"Tori, why don't you go to the bathroom and get ready for bed."

"Okay." Once the door shut, Cassandra turned to Lucas ready to tear into him but instead let out a tired sigh. "Look, Lucas, I don't know exactly what this thing is between you and my niece. To be honest right now I'm too tired to argue about it," she looked him directly in the eye, "but we will be discussing it."

Lucas could see Cassandra was exhausted and tried to help ease some of her worries. "I'd never hurt her, Cassie, she's important to me."

"She's nine!"

"I know that! But that doesn't mean I'm not going to watch out for her now! Maybe if I'd been there seven cycles ago none of this would have happened."

Cassandra was shocked at his passionate response. "You couldn't have done anything, Lucas."

"I could have held her when she was scared."

"She had her parents for that." Lucas looked at her. "I'm all she has left, I'm her parent now. Do you understand me?"

Lucas gave her a level look and in a voice eerily like the Admiral's said, "I understand what you mean but now she has me too."

"Fine, just as long as you understand there are limits."

The bathroom door opened and Tori came out in her night clothes, hair brushed, face washed.

"Tell Lucas goodnight, Tori, he has to leave."

She walked over to him, lifting her arms.

Lifting her up, she wrapped her arms around his neck giving him a big hug, "Goodnight, Lucas, I love you."

He held her for a moment then lowered her to the floor and in a tight voice replied, "Night, Tori, I love you too." He was rewarded with a big smile before she turned to the bed.

Cassandra silently witnessed the scene before she walked him to the hatch. "Goodnight, Lucas, thanks for the help," she said as she opened the door.

"Anytime," as he walked through he heard it secure behind him.

∞ ∞ ∞ ∞ ∞

William approached his Ready Room knowing he still had dozens of things he needed to take care of, but his priority was Cassandra. Things happened tonight that she misunderstood. They needed to talk, to straighten this out. He needed her if only to hold. Entering he found his quarters empty. Hearing the hatch open he saw Lucas enter, alone.

"Where are Cassandra and Victoria?"

"In their quarters," Lucas shut the hatch.

"You knew I meant for you to bring them here!" William's patience was gone.

"I know, but Cassie wanted Tori in her own bed." Lucas didn't have to wait for the explosion.

"That's not where I wanted them!"

"It really isn't up to you, is it?"

"The fuck it isn't! There are still things to settle!" He headed for the hatch.

"Dad! They're both exhausted! It'll keep until tomorrow. Shit, it's almost tomorrow now." Lucas blocked his path. "What are you going to do? Kidnap them?"

That stopped William from just moving him aside. He turned rubbing the back of his neck, "They're okay?"

"As well as can be expected. I actually think Tori is handling it better than Cassie," Lucas knew the storm had passed.

"Cassie! Why the hell are you calling her 'Cassie'?" William demanded.

"I guess I picked it up from Tori," Lucas shrugged. Walking over to his father's desk, he opened a drawer and took out the bottle containing Carinian ale and two glasses. Opening it, he poured some into each glass before walking over to his father as he handed him one. William raised an eyebrow as he tapped his glass to Lucas'. "It's been a hell of a day."

William looked at his son, proud of the man he'd grown into. "I'll second that." As he took a drink, he walked over to his desk and sat.

"Anything I can help with?"

"No, mostly reports to write." William knew how much his son liked reports.

"Then I'm going to catch some shut eye." Lucas finished his drink and put the glass on the desk. "You find anything I need to know you'll call?"

"I'll let you know."

As Lucas left, William leaned back in his chair thinking about the Regulian transmission they'd decoded. The Glitter Man told Tori she wouldn't 'take' his Light. But the Regulian transmission said they were 'looking' for the Light; something they were going to use to get what they wanted.

Otherwise they would destroy it. Whoever the Carinian traitor was, they wanted it bad enough to give the Regulians Carinian technology to track a little girl. A little girl on a planet that wasn't on any Carinian star chart. Earth was closer to Regulian territory than Carinian. How would he have found out about her? What made her so special? Light. Imperial Light.

William wrote up his report then decided Lucas was right. It was enough for one day. Getting into his bed alone he lifted the pillow that carried Cassandra's scent, laid his head on it, and went to sleep.

∞ ∞ ∞ ∞ ∞

Turning the corner from the classroom, Cassandra ran straight into Lucas.

"Whoa," he gripped her arms to keep her from falling, "you okay?"

When she looked up at him, he was startled at what he saw. She looked even more exhausted than the night before.

"Cassie, what's wrong?" He pulled her aside lowering his voice. "Did Victoria have another nightmare?" He'd hoped the removal of the thread would end them.

"No, no nightmares, she had a great night's sleep. She couldn't wait to get to class to see her friends." Cassandra nodded toward the hatchway. "I just dropped her off."

Lucas released the breath he hadn't realized he'd been holding. Stepping back they started walking.

"Limits, Lucas," she muttered.

"Understood," he replied. "So if she had a good night why do you look like crap?"

Cassandra stopped in the middle of the corridor. There was no way she was telling him that after one night, she couldn't sleep without his father's arms around her.

"Why, Lucas Zafar, I didn't realize you were such a sweet talker."

Lucas stopped, realized what he just said and started to turn red, "Look, I didn't mean… it's just…" he stuttered.

"Yes?" she stared at him and tried not to grin.

"You just look tired and if it was a good night…Oh hell, I'm just digging myself deeper." Cassandra started to laugh, he looked at her grinning. Turning they saw the Admiral standing several feet away.

William hadn't slept well. Her scent wasn't enough now that he had held her. This morning he'd decided they would talk, he'd cleared time. Going to her quarters he discovered them gone. That hadn't been a good start. Now he found her laughing in a corridor with his son. She should be laughing with him! As Cassandra looked at him, she stopped laughing.

"Admiral," Lucas spoke first noticing his father's stillness.

"Lucas, you on patrol today?" his eyes never left Cassandra.

"Yes, Sir."

"Shouldn't you be preparing then?"

He knew when he'd been dismissed. Lucas looked at Cassie seeing her eyes locked with his father's.

"Yes, Sir."

Cassandra turned to look at Lucas, "Thanks for the compliment."

Lucas gave her a quick grin and left the two of them in the corridor.

Turning back to the Admiral, Cassandra discovered she was ready for a fight. "Something I can do for you, Admiral?" she asked walking toward him, her eyes unreadable.

William fell into step beside her, "We didn't finish last night. I've cleared time this morning."

"Cleared time? How nice," she replied testily.

The Admiral gave her a frigid look that she ignored. Others in the corridor didn't and hastily got out of their way.

Within minutes, they were in the Admiral's Ready Room. As soon as the door was secured, Cassandra turned ready to tell him what she thought about him 'clearing time' for her, only to find herself crushed between his massive chest and the bulkhead.

William could no longer control his desire. Before she could speak her mouth was ravished, the fight she was ready for changed into passion.

Groaning into his mouth, she struggled to get her hands free to grip his back, matching his desire.

Releasing her mouth, he attacked all the sensitive points on her neck he'd discovered earlier. Cassandra went wild in his arms, she had to have him.

"William!" she pleaded wrapping her legs around his waist.

Turbulent violet eyes blazed into uncontrolled blue and what he saw had him ripping her pants down and loosening his.

"Please, William! Now!" she begged and with one thrust he entered her to the hilt.

"Yes..." she groaned throwing her head back pumping her hips against his.

William knew he was out of control, but he couldn't stop. The look in Cassandra's eyes, her desire for him, his need for her, had driven him to this point. He returned to her mouth ravaging it, taking the last of her breath. Her entire body tensed, imploded around him, and her scream was captured by his mouth. Seconds later he followed her, emptying everything he was into her.

Cassandra was a quivering mess, relying on William to hold her up. Breathing heavily, he pushed off the wall and carried her to the closest chair.

Sitting with her in his lap, he gently caressed her bare left leg. Turning, she kissed his neck. The simple act caused him to lose the breath he'd just caught.

"Cassandra..." he whispered in her ear.

She nestled in closer, "William, I'm not sure what just happened but..."

He stopped her with a kiss. He needed to be honest. Easing her back he looked her in the eye, "Cassandra, you are my life mate. That's what this is. It's not leave, not a one-night stand." Her eyes widened. "I don't know what you call it on Earth, or if you had something like it."

"Soul mates," Cassandra's voice was quiet, not breaking eye contact, Victoria had been right. "It was a rare thing on Earth."

"It's rare on Carina too." Framing her face with his large hands he continued, "I wasn't looking for this, but now that I've found you I'm not letting go." His kiss was possessive.

Cassandra reached a hand behind his head returning the kiss. His words touched that place deep inside her she kept guarded. Here was the one who could leave her defenseless while still protecting her. Her heart had recognized him from the first moment on the Raptor. It was her head that'd been trying to catch up.

William ended the kiss trying to read all the emotions in her eyes. "Tell me what you're thinking."

"William…I…" she broke eye contact.

"Honesty, even if I don't like it. It works both ways, Cassandra," he reminded her of what she had asked for in a relationship.

Looking at him, she saw the flicker of uncertainty in his eyes. She was stunned to think she could cause any uncertainty in this confident man. "William, I don't know what to say or even how to say it." He stiffened beneath her. "I can't get my thoughts organized," and for her that was unheard of.

"Just say what you're thinking," he insisted in a stilted voice, his hand stilled.

"I can't, it won't come out right." She needed to get up, she couldn't think straight in his arms. As she tried, he put a restraining hand on her still naked hip. "I need to get up, William." When he didn't move his hand, she looked at him with pleading in her eyes. "Please." Slowly he removed his hand.

He watched silently as she fought with her pant leg getting dressed. He fixed his own clothing but remained where he was. When she started to walk away, he gripped the armrests to stop himself from pulling her back.

She turned back to face him, frustration causing her to run both hands through her hair. What she saw on his face stopped her cold. With the distance between them her mind was clearing and she realized she could hurt this man, that her lack of response had hurt him. She needed to give him what he'd given her. Truth.

"William, I want this. I want this with you. Whether we call it life mates or soul mates it doesn't matter. It's real. It also scares me."

William, in the process of getting up, froze, "I scare you?" A fist tightened around his heart.

"No! Don't be an idiot. Why would you even think that?" Her immediate and vehement denial released the grip on his heart.

"I am a bit larger than you," he said walking toward her.

"No, you stay right where you are," she said putting up a hand. "I can't think straight when you touch me."

Ignoring her, he grabbed her outstretched hand pulling her into his arms. Grinning he said, "Don't think," and proceeded to kiss her senseless. When he finally let her up for air, she could only lean on him.

"William, we need to talk," she said softly, "please."

The comm center rang and had Cassandra easing out of his arms. He walked to his desk and picked up the headset.

"Zafar." She watched his eyes change becoming the Admiral.

"Tell them to do what they can until we get to Rodham for more extensive repairs," he put down the headset.

"Looks like you're out of 'cleared' time."

He walked around to lean on his desk watching her, "Not quite."

"I'm not something to be 'fit in,' William," her temper over the whole thing was coming back.

"I never meant to give you that impression," his own temper was starting to rise.

"Really, well you did. Between you and Lucas I'm not sure which one's insulted me more," she flung back.

"Lucas?" William said quietly, but Cassandra didn't hear him.

"No, I am sure. It's you since it's your fault in the first place," she gave him a simmering look, finally noticing his stillness. Standing he moved toward her.

"What did Lucas say to you?" he demanded gripping her arms pulling her up on her toes, she watched his eyes go icy.

"Oh calm down, it wasn't anything major. He just wanted to know why I looked like 'crap,' okay?" William's eyes didn't change. "And it's your fault!" she poked him in the chest with her finger. "So don't be going off on Lucas for stating the obvious. I already reamed him for it."

"What did I do?" he asked confused, trying to calm down.

"You made it so I can't sleep without you!" her eyes shot flames at him. "Victoria finally sleeps the whole night without a nightmare and I'm the one awake. I missed you, damn it," she thumped him on his chest.

William swooped down silencing her with a kiss, her fiery response instantaneous. "We'll take care of that tonight," he told her releasing her mouth trying to catch his breath as he eased her back down.

Cassandra rested her forehead on his chest trying to find her voice. "That's one of the things we need to talk about," she tipped her head up. "William, I can't stay here." Seeing his eyes flare she put a hand on the side of his face. "I won't leave Tori alone. You know that. She can't sleep on your couch." With his eyes calming she finished, "You know I'm right."

"Yes, you're right," he replied, kissing her palm. When his comm center rang again, she slowly pulled her hand away letting him move around his desk to answer.

"Zafar," he picked up the headset, watching her walk away, "I'll be there shortly."

"You need to get going, Admiral," turning she found him still behind his desk.

"Come here," he held out his hand, walking over she took it. Pulling her in front of his comm center, he put her thumb on what Cassandra had come to know was a security panel. He entered a code.

"Say your full name."

"Cassandra Qwes Chamberlain."

William raised his eyebrow he hadn't known her full name. The console beeped at him.

"William?"

"You now have access to my quarters, our quarters. You only have to put your thumb on the security pad at the door. Say one of your names, it will be recognized."

"Why?"

"I know we have things to work out, Cassandra, but I want you here. I need you here, you and Victoria. I want you to feel secure. These quarters will be secured when no one is here, the only time they will be unsecured is if I'm having a meeting. You will be able to tell by the light on the security pad. This is your home. You'll both be safe here."

"Okay," was all she could say.

"I want you to come back tonight, you and Tori. We'll eat, talk, figure things out," he waited for her to nod. "So what are you doing today?"

"I need to get back down to Engineering to work with the Chief on your defense system. I've been busy for the last few days."

"Yes you have, and you will continue to be," he allowed himself one more kiss. "I need to get to the Bridge. Tonight, you'll both be here?"

"Yes," she agreed as they walked to the hatch. As the Admiral opened the door, Cassandra stepped away. With one last look, she stepped through the hatch heading to Engineering. The Admiral watched her go then turned to the Bridge. Neither saw Falco standing in the shadows.

Chapter Seven

Cassandra's day was productive in Engineering. Leander had studied her ideas for speeding up the defense system's response time agreeing it was possible. It would take some time to implement but would be highly effective.

Leaving Engineering, she headed to the classroom to get Tori. Down the corridor from the room, Falco stepped out confronting her.

"I know what you're doing!" she hissed, "I'm going to stop you! Then he'll see what you really are!"

"Cassandra? Is everything all right?" Javiera asked. Falco looked at her then walked away.

"It's fine, Javiera."

"What did Falco want?"

"Nothing." She walked to the classroom. As the two women approached, the door opened and children came spilling out. Victoria and Amina were laughing.

"Aunt Cassie! Can we go to the play room? Everyone's going!"

"Oh really? What about homework?"

"Later… please???" Cassandra looked at Javiera and saw her smile and agreed.

"Okay, but after dinner, it's homework."

"Okay." The two girls skipped ahead as the women followed.

"You look tired," Javiera said.

"You know I've heard that a couple times today."

"Is she okay?" she nodded to Victoria.

"She slept really well last night. I'd say the best since…well since."

"How are you doing?"

"What?"

"I've been thinking about it ever since we talked yesterday. I don't know how I would cope if Carina were suddenly destroyed along with nearly my entire family. I know I wouldn't handle it as well as you. As similar as our cultures seem to be there are differences, those have to be hard."

"We're working on them."

"I'm sorry, I'm not helping am I?"

"You're trying, that's something. Can I ask you something?"

"Sure."

"Where do you eat?"

"What?" Javiera gave her a confused look.

"I'm having trouble getting Victoria to eat enough. The food is different enough. Last night we had cnaipini sicin which she loved. But I didn't see any this morning."

"Where were you eating?"

"Deck G."

"Well, there's your problem you need to bring her to Deck F. She'll love the food and will get to see Amina."

"Okay, we'll try it tomorrow."

"What about tonight?"

Cassandra looked at her. "We have dinner plans."

"Really?" Javiera let the subject drop.

∞ ∞ ∞ ∞ ∞

Back in quarters, Cassandra told Victoria they were going to eat in the Admiral's quarters again. She looked up at her, "Is it going to be like last night?"

"I don't see why it would be. He might ask some questions, but there shouldn't be much else."

"Will Lucas be there?"

"I don't know. So go clean up and we'll go."

∞ ∞ ∞ ∞ ∞

Approaching the Admiral's quarters, Cassandra could see the red light on the security pad. Walking up she put her thumb on it and said her name. The door unlocked, Cassandra pushed it open. They entered to find the Ready Room empty, the lights on low.

"Let's go back to the private quarters, Tori. We'll get started on your homework."

On the Bridge, the Admiral sat at his command post dealing with his routine duties while coordinating repairs for the damaged battleship. Looking at the time he realized he hadn't informed Hutu that Cassandra and Victoria would be there again tonight. He picked up a headset and contacted his chef.

"Hutu, there will be three for tonight," the Admiral informed him. "Yes, like last night. At 1800." He disconnected not realizing he'd been overheard and went back to the communications report. As 1800 drew near, Quinn approached the Admiral.

"What is it, Quinn?"

"Communications picked up a transmission heading into Regulian space, same channel as before, in Regulian."

"Origin?"

"Unable to determine."

"Fuck!"

"Yeah."

"What did it say?"

"Should be here any minute."

William looked at the clock, picked up his headset and called Hutu. "I'm going to be late, go ahead and deliver it, though. I'll call when I want mine." The Admiral listened, "That would be fine." He hung up.

Quinn looked at him, "Dinner plans?"

"Yeah."

"Look, Will, we go back a long way," his voice was low.

The Admiral looked at him, "What's up, Quinn?"

"That's what I want to know. There's been something going on with you ever since Earth."

William stared at his friend and Second-in-Command. They'd been through many a battle together, but he wasn't ready to share Cassandra with him yet.

"Nothing I'm ready to discuss with you."

"You're having meals in your quarters."

"I've always had meals in my quarters."

"Usually for one."

"My business, Colonel," the Admiral's eyes went hard.

"Yes, Sir," Quinn let it drop as the Regulian translation was delivered. It was short and to the point.

"No agreement until no Light."

"That's it?" Quinn asked.

"That's it. Whoever the traitor is knew we were going to be attacked; and now knows we were able to repel it. They have access to our reports at command."

"That's not possible, that would make it…"

"Someone very high up, someone with a lot to lose," William finished. Looking at Quinn he made a decision. Opening a drawer he handed him the report he'd written up on everything he'd learned last night. "That's why I didn't send this to command." Leaning back in his chair he waited.

Quinn's face revealed nothing as he read the report. "You trust this information?"

"Yes."

"It would explain the Regulian attack. But why would they want the child?"

"Victoria."

"What?"

"Her name is Victoria, she's nine, extremely smart and has been through hell."

"Okay, so why Victoria? What makes her so special?" Quinn asked.

"It has something to do with this Light. It's a threat to someone," the Admiral looked at the clock; he'd only be an hour late.

"Tell Communications I want to know as soon as they receive the reply to this." He held out his hand for the report. "This stays between us for now, Quinn. There's something big going on. I want this traitor." Leaving the Bridge, he headed for his quarters.

∞ ∞ ∞ ∞ ∞

Cassandra raised her head from the book she was reading at the buzzing at the hatch. Victoria looked at her. They hadn't discussed if she should answer his door. There were lots of things they hadn't discussed. Getting up she went into the Ready Room. The buzzing sounded again.

"Ma'am, it's Hutu with dinner." Cassandra opened the door. "Hello," Hutu greeted her carrying two covered plates on a tray. He waited while she secured the door. "The Admiral asked me to inform you he is going to be late and to not wait on him. Can I take this back to his quarters?"

"Yes, thank you, Hutu."

"It's nothing. Hello there, little one, how are you today?"

"Good. Finishing my homework. Is it cnaipini sicin again?" she asked in a hopeful voice.

Hutu took a cover off, "It certainly is by the Admiral's request."

"Yes!" Victoria said with a fist pump.

Cassandra smiled at Hutu, "You've made her night. Thank you."

"Anytime. I'll secure the door on the way out. Have a good night." Cassandra waited until she heard the locks secure then turned to Tori.

"So should we eat?" Sitting down Cassandra took the cover off her plate, smiling that hers was something she recognized. William had thought of both of them.

"Hey, you've got Ranch!" Tori exclaimed as she reached for the small bowl on Cassandra's plate. There hadn't been one last night. Quickly dipping her nugget into it, she took a bite.

"Don't you think you should ask first?" Cassandra laughed at her. Victoria used to dip everything in Ranch. Tori just grinned then made a nasty face.

"What?" Cassandra asked. Swallowing Tori shoved the bowl back at Cassandra.

"That's not Ranch! It's really nasty!" Tori let go of the bowl and reached for her glass before Cassandra could grab it. As it fell it flipped over and splattered across the table.

"Tori!"

"Sorry, Aunt Cassie," Tori said still drinking her water. "But that was bad!" Getting a towel Cassandra cleaned up the spill.

"Let's see if we can eat without any more spills. What do you say?"

Eating, Cassandra looked at the time. 1830; she wondered how long William would be or if they should stay. Looking at Tori she saw she'd cleaned her plate.

"That was fast. Did you even chew?"

Tori grinned at her, "It was good."

"You know I talked to Amina's mom today. She said the food on Deck F is much better than on G. Want to try that tomorrow?"

"Sure."

"All right we'll try it. Do you want some of mine?" she gestured to her plate.

"No, I'm full."

"Okay, let's clean up these dishes then I want to talk to you about something."

"Okay."

Once the table was cleared, Cassandra sat on the couch facing Tori. "You know how you said last night that you could hear voices but didn't know what they were saying?"

"Yes," Tori whispered.

"What if there was a way for you to understand them?"

"What?" her eyes widened.

"Well, I was thinking. You are so good at learning other languages. How many do you speak now?" she waited knowing the answer.

"Nine."

"That's right nine. How about you learn a new one?"

"What one?"

"Regulian."

Tori just looked at her, "You know lots of languages."

"Yes, but I didn't hear what you did. Do you want to know what they said?"

"What if it's bad?"

"Then you'd at least know but, Tori, what if it's not? What if they were saying something that they didn't want you to know? If you knew it, then it would be like beating them," Cassandra watched Tori think.

"So it would be like me finding out secrets they didn't want me to know?" Her eyes took on a fierce look.

"Yes."

"How do I learn Regulian?"

"I'll ask the Admiral," Cassandra started to get up when Tori stopped her.

"Aunt Cassie…I don't feel good."

Cassandra started to laugh then really looked at her. She began to look green. Grabbing her she made it to the bathroom just in time.

"Oh, baby, you shouldn't have eaten so fast," she held her forehead as another spasm hit her, stronger than the last. She got a wash cloth to wipe her sweaty brow.

"Aunt Cassie, make it stop," she pleaded as she was racked by another spasm. Cassandra was beginning to realize this wasn't eating too fast. Something was wrong.

"Come on, baby, we're going to get you some help." Lifting the now limp child, she rushed out of the bathroom straight into William.

"What's going on?" he looked into Cassandra's frantic eyes, then down to Victoria.

"She's sick. All of a sudden she just started throwing up." William took the unconscious Tori from her and could immediately tell there was something seriously wrong.

"Get the hatch! We're taking her to Medical."

∞ ∞ ∞ ∞ ∞

Dr. Bliant was just getting ready to leave Medical when the Admiral burst into the room, carrying a very pale, limp child.

"Put her over here. What happened?" He immediately demanded.

"We don't know," William replied.

"How long has she been like this?" he looked at Cassandra.

"She started vomiting maybe fifteen minutes ago, she was fine before. We'd just finished eating."

"What'd she eat?" he demanded.

"Cnaipini sicin, some water."

"Nothing else?"

"No! Wait, there was some type of side sauce on my plate, she thought it was Ranch tried it and thought it was nasty."

"How much did she ingest?"

"She dipped part of a nugget in it, ate that bite, that's all."

William went very still beside her. "Did you have any?"

"Me? No. Tori spilled it giving it back. I just cleaned it up."

"Where did you put it?" William demanded.

Cassandra looked up at him, "I cleaned it up with a towel on the counter then put it on the food tray. Why?"

"Stay here," he looked at Bliant.

Cassandra watched William leave, her mind trying to catch up. Bliant started hooking all sorts of machines up to Victoria.

"This isn't just food poisoning is it?"

"It's some type of poison. I need to find out what!" As Bliant left to get more equipment, Cassandra moved to Tori's side. She picked up her hand, leaned down to kiss her forehead, and whispered, "You hang on, Victoria Lynn, I'm here, and I'm not leaving. Fight!"

Bliant returned moving to the other side of the bed.

"You should wait outside," he told her.

"You and what army is going to make me?" she replied in a lethal voice, causing Bliant to look at her. What he saw in her eyes gave him pause. There was anguish and fear, but also steel. He'd seen enough in his cycles of medicine to know who would stand and who would crumble in a crisis, she would stand.

"Fine."

William returned with the clear bag containing the towel and remaining sauce. Bliant immediately took it to analyze. Cassandra was still at Tori's side holding her hand. She looked at William but didn't speak.

The look in Cassandra's eyes tightened William's throat. He knew there was nothing he could do for her right now.

"It's Xyphrine! At about 1000 times the lethal limit!" he stated as he rushed to Tori's arm giving her an injection.

"Xyphrine," William repeated looking first at Tori, then Cassandra. While Cassandra didn't know what Xyphrine was she could tell by William's eyes, it wasn't good.

"That's the antidote?" she finally asked Bliant.

"Yes, if we're in time."

She looked at him. "Tell me," she demanded looking at Victoria so still on the bed. Bliant looked to the Admiral, who nodded.

"Xyphrine is a level D drug," he started but at Cassandra's furious look stopped. "It's a nasty drug. At low dosages, it helps with some attachment issues but at these levels…Its fast-acting when ingested, causing seizures, coma, and death."

"She didn't have any seizures. Within 15 minutes of eating she was vomiting. There couldn't have been much absorbed with the little amount she had."

Bliant looked at her, "That may be, but she's also little."

"When will you know?" Cassandra forced herself to ask.

"Know?"

Cassandra took a deep breath looking up at him, "If the antidote's working?" William walked up behind her putting a hand on her lower back.

"I honestly don't know. As little as she is and with such a high concentration, I gave her double the amount of antidote to try and compensate, but I honestly don't know." Then Bliant left them alone.

William pulled a chair to the side of the bed, "Sit," he told her putting his hands on her shoulders to ease her down.

"Who would do this, William?" she asked still looking at Tori's face. "Who would do this to a child?" William realized she hadn't thought it through. The dish was on her plate, not Tori's.

"I don't know, but I'll find out. I promise." Cassandra lifted a hand to squeeze his. William leaned down kissing the top of her head. They waited. Dr. Bliant was in and out several times checking the machines. Tori didn't move.

"Admiral," Colonel Quinn drew his attention. He'd been standing in the doorway long enough to observe his longtime friend with the woman from Earth. There was some type of connection there. It would explain the Admiral's behavior over the last few weeks. "Interviews have been completed."

"Report." Quinn looked at Cassandra.

"She has the right to hear it."

"Yes, Sir. As ordered, all kitchen personnel were interviewed to see who had access to the plates of food. It was narrowed down to four with only one having the opportunity to poison the sauce. Hutu, sir."

"That ridiculous," Cassandra replied flatly before William could.

"Excuse me?" Quinn responded in a sharp voice.

"Hutu would never hurt Victoria. You need to do a better investigation if that's all you can come up with," Cassandra's eyes clashed with Quinn's.

"Who do...?" Quinn started only to have the Admiral cut him off.

"Enough! Both of you," William looked at Quinn. "She's right. Hutu wouldn't do this. Not to Victoria, not anyone. Something's been missed."

"Would you like to re-interview yourself, Admiral?" Quinn said stiffly.

"Maybe, I know I want to talk to Hutu," he looked down at Cassandra. "I'll be out in a minute, Quinn."

"Yes, Sir."

"Cassandra, I need to leave for a while."

"I know. It's okay." She stood turning to William. Still holding Tori's hand with one of hers, she reached up and touched his cheek. "Time to be the Admiral. We'll be fine."

William leaned down to kiss her gently. "There will be a guard posted at the door. No one gets in."

She nodded. "William," Cassandra took a deep breath, "you need to let Lucas know."

He realized he'd forgotten all about his son and his connection to Tori. "I'll let him know."

"Okay." She sat back down and gave all her attention, all her strength to Tori.

∞ ∞ ∞ ∞ ∞

Neither man said a word as they walked the corridors of the Retribution to the Admiral's quarters. Once inside, William went to his comm center.

"Close the door. Communications, I need to locate Lt. Lucas Zafar immediately! I'll hold while he's located," the Admiral impatiently tapped his thumb on his desk as he waited.

"Zafar here," Lucas came on the line.

"Where are you?"

"Dad? I'm on G Deck. What's happened?"

"Get to Medical. Victoria's been poisoned with Xyphrine. Cassandra's there. It's not looking good, Lucas," William needed to prepare his son.

"What?"

William could hear the break in his son's voice. "Lucas, keep it together. You're no help to either of them otherwise."

"Yes, Sir," Lucas disconnected. Quinn waited until the Admiral put down his headset.

"What the fuck is going on here, Will! Planetary destruction, Regulian threads, traitors in Carina. Now poisoning a child? Then there's you cozying up with some woman while we're on tour!

"Be careful, Quinn, be very careful," William's voice revealed his barely contained fury.

"Shit, it's not like she's your life mate or..." Quinn trailed off, "is she? No she can't be. She's not from Carina."

"Is there some rule about that?" Will raised an eyebrow.

"Well no, but...Will...You're sure?" William just looked at Quinn. "Of course, you're sure. You wouldn't have gotten involved on tour otherwise. What a mess." He sat down. William reached down into the same drawer his son had the night before and pulled out two glasses and the bottle. Pouring, he handed one to Quinn.

"What are you going to do?" Quinn asked taking a sip.

"I'm going to protect what's mine while finding out who's betraying the Coalition."

"You realize they're part of it. The thread was in Victoria. She's been poisoned."

"I don't believe the poison was meant for Victoria, and once Cassandra's head clears she won't either," William took a drink.

"She's the target? Why?"

"I don't know, but she's right, Quinn. Hutu wouldn't hurt Victoria. He has a soft spot for her."

"And Cassandra?"

"He has no reason. There was a reason for this," it pissed him off that he couldn't see it.

"Your instincts are rarely wrong, Will, but are you too involved this time?"

"I'm fully involved, Quinn. That's going to be to my advantage."

"Okay, can I see your report again?"

"What are you sniffing?" William asked pulling the original out of a drawer.

"Something's been bothering me." Quinn scanned the report, "Here. If we assume this Glitter Man, who she said is really big, is Carinian, why not just take her then?"

It was a thought that had crossed William's mind before. He didn't like his conclusion. "What if they weren't sure? If they were waiting to see?" William posed the question.

"Weren't sure they needed her or that she was the one they wanted?"

"Maybe both, but there is something there. Cassandra said her grandmother had been abducted when she was young. She described them, they were Regulian."

"Two in one family?" Quinn questioned.

"Yeah, I know. One Regulian, one Carinian." It seemed farfetched, but William believed Cassandra. "Quinn, I need you to find out what happened here tonight. I know it wasn't Hutu. Same as I know it wasn't you."

"Okay, I'll dig further," Quinn raised an eyebrow. "Why aren't you spearheading this?"

"Because if I'm right, someone just tried to kill my life mate. If I get to them first…" William trailed off as Quinn watched the rage in his friend's eyes.

"Understood. You don't think she has realized it yet?" he asked.

"No, if she did she'd be racking herself with guilt." William picked up his headset, "Hutu, report to my Ready Room."

∞ ∞ ∞ ∞ ∞

The friends finished their drinks in silence. Quinn opened the hatch at Hutu's knock. Hutu stood in front of the Admiral's desk.

"Sir, how is she?" his voice was urgent.

"Stable for now," the Admiral gave him a hard look. "Did you put the bowl of sauce on the plate, Hutu?"

"Sir, no! I took the cover off Victoria's plate myself. She'd asked what she was having so I showed her. She was so excited. There wasn't a bowl of sauce on her plate."

"And Cassandra's plate?"

"Sir?" Hutu gave him a confused look.

"Was there one on Cassandra's plate?" William repeated.

"Sir, I never removed her cover. It was on her plate? There would be no reason for it. She had Rhea. If I'd removed the cover, I would have known something was wrong, Sir." Hutu looked at the Admiral with earnest eyes, "I'm sorry, Sir."

"I know you are, Hutu. I also want you to know that I don't believe you did this."

"Thank you, Admiral!" Hutu replied in a relieved voice.

"Neither does Cassandra."

Hutu closed his eyes, "Thank you, Sir."

"But still someone got to those plates. I need you to think. When were they left unattended?"

"I've thought of nothing else, Sir. I personally prepared the food. Plated and covered them. The tray was…" Hutu paused.

"What!" the Admiral demanded.

"The tray, it wasn't where it normally is. I had to go back to the storage area to find it," Hutu said remorsefully. "I'm sorry, Sir. I left the plates. When I came back, I just put them on the tray. I didn't recheck the food."

"There was no reason for you to, Hutu."

"Sir, I brought it to her," Hutu's distress was easily seen by both men.

"Who else was in the kitchen? Anyone not normally there?"

"Sir, no one stands out. I don't remember anyone unusual."

"Keep thinking about it, Hutu. If you remember anything report to Colonel Quinn immediately."

"Yes, Sir."

"Dismissed." Hutu left.

William got up from his desk, "If you need me I'll be in Medical," he told Quinn.

Chapter Eight

Lucas headed to Medical; the look on his face moved everyone out of his path. Anyone seeing him had no doubt he was the Admiral's son. Entering Medical he didn't see Victoria then he saw the guards. Heading for the room a guard stopped him.

"Let him through Paa, that's Zafar."

Entering the room, he got his first look at Victoria and his heart dropped. She was so small lying in the bed with machines hooked up to her. She was pale with dark circles under her eyes and so eerily still. Cassandra was sitting in a chair on the far side of the bed holding her hand to her cheek talking softly to her.

"Cassandra..." Lucas quietly approached the bed. Still holding Victoria's hand to her cheek she turned agonized eyes to Lucas.

"Tori, Lucas is here. Why don't you open your eyes and see?" Cassandra tried to get a response from her niece.

"Take her hand, Lucas. She needs to know you're here."

Lucas gently picked up Victoria's other hand, so small in his and rubbed his thumb across the top.

"Tori, I'm here, baby. Come on, open your eyes." He got no more response than Cassandra had for the last two hours.

"We need to keep talking to her, keep her with us."

Bliant entered to check Tori's stats. He met Cassandra's look.

"No change."

"Okay."

"What's that mean?" Lucas demanded.

"She's not getting any worse," Dr. Bliant informed him. He gave Cassandra one last look then left the room. Outside he saw the Admiral approaching.

"There's been no change, Admiral, no better, no worse. It's a waiting game now."

"Thank you, Bliant." Entering the room he saw his son on one side of the bed, Cassandra on the other. It didn't look like she'd moved since he left. Walking over he put a hand on her shoulder. Tipping her head to the side she leaned into his touch.

"You need to take a break, Cassandra," he rubbed his thumb against her cheek.

"No, I'm good," her voice was firm as she lifted her head. Knowing she wasn't going to leave he pulled over a chair and sat beside her.

Cassandra didn't notice the passing hours; Victoria had her complete focus. She'd been talking to her almost non-stop. William and Lucas had to leave several times but always returned. She knew they both had other responsibilities but Victoria was her only one. Alone in the room she rose from the chair and climbed onto the bed to hold her niece in her arms.

"Come on, baby," she whispered in her ear, her voice rough. "I've got you. You're safe. Wake up, baby." Softly she began to sing in her ear, an old song she knew Cyndy sang to her when she'd been sick or scared. She was so focused on Victoria she didn't hear the door open.

"Come on, sweetheart, you know I need help here. You need to sing your part or I sound stupid. You know how I hate that." Starting the song again she was part way through when Tori's lips began to move, Cassandra's voice caught. As she continued to sing, Tori was whispering her part when she finished she opened her eyes.

"Hi, baby," Cassandra whispered blinking back tears.

Dr. Bliant, who'd entered with Lucas and the Admiral, moved quickly to the bed, "Hello there, young lady."

Tori looked at him with confused eyes, "Aunt Cassie?"

"It's okay, baby, you got sick. Dr. Bliant's been making you better," she slid off the bed still holding her hand.

Tori watched Bliant until she saw Lucas at the foot of the bed. She gave him a little smile, "Lucas, you're here too?"

"I had to come see my best girl, didn't I?" he told her in a strained voice that made the smile grow. Cassandra stepped back holding Victoria's hand out to Lucas. He walked up to take it, giving her a grateful look.

"Tori, I need to steal your aunt away for just a few minutes okay?" William asked her.

"You'll be back?" Fear entered her eyes.

"You bet. Lucas will stay until then okay?" Cassandra's voice trembled.

"Okay," Tori turned her eyes to Lucas.

Leading her into Bliant's office, William pulled her into his arms as the door closed. Wrapping her arms around his waist, Cassandra burst into tears. Holding her close he knew she had finally released her fear. He'd seen her instant reaction to a crisis, with the rescue of Tori from the fire. But what he'd witnessed here was the underlying strength, her total commitment, without reservation, to someone she loved. She would give until she broke. William wondered what it would feel like to have her feel that way about him.

As he continued to rub her back, she calmed. Lifting her head she looked up at him. "I soaked your jacket," her voice was hoarse.

"It'll dry," William took a visual inventory of her, seeing the pale skin, red-rimmed eyes, the dark circles underneath, tears still threatening to overflow, her exhausted body trembling slightly.

"You need sleep. You've been up for forty-eight hours."

"I know, but Tori needs me." As she stepped away, she wiped her remaining tears away. Putting a hand on his cheek she looked into his concerned eyes, "Thank you."

"For what?"

"Being here."

"I'll always be here for you." Cradling her head he tipped her head back, "I'm not letting go." Gently he kissed her lips, and with a sigh she sank into him drawing on his strength.

"I need to get back to her."

"I know." Opening the door he let her exit first. Victoria's eyes were closed when they reentered the room. Cassandra's eyes flew to Bliant.

"She's just resting. All her signs are looking good she just needs some food and rest now." Cassandra looked at her niece as she listened, nodding at what Bliant was saying.

"Does she need to stay here?"

"I'd like to keep her overnight making sure she's keeping her food down, but after that she can go home." Tori opened her eyes looking at her aunt.

"Aunt Cassie…you look terrible," she said in a stronger voice. Cassandra raised an eyebrow at her niece. Lucas tried not to chuckle.

"Really…" she eyed Lucas.

"Hey, innocent here."

William saw his opportunity and took it. "Victoria, would it be okay if Cassandra left for a while to get some sleep? That might help her." Cassandra looked at him, but before she could speak Victoria chimed in.

"You'll make sure she sleeps?" Tori demanded.

"Yes."

"But you'll come back later, Aunt Cassie?"

"Tori, I'm not leaving you here alone."

"I'll stay with her," Lucas interrupted. With three pairs of eyes watching her, Cassandra could do nothing but give in. Moving to her niece she leaned down and gave her a kiss.

"I'll be back in a little while." Tori nodded as Cassandra and the Admiral walked out the door.

Cassandra was nearly asleep on her feet by the time they got to William's quarters, her extreme exhaustion making her unaware of where he was leading her until they got there.

"Why are we here?"

"You'll sleep better," he led her back to his private quarters.

"But..."

"Cassandra," he'd been patient as long as he could. Watching her exhaust herself, being unable to help had ripped at him. There was something he could do now and he'd be damned if she'd stop him, "Shut up and get into bed." Cassandra tried to be upset at his tone but found she was just too tired.

"We'll fight about this later," she mumbled as she all but collapsed on his bed.

"Come on, baby," William kept her upright, "let's get these clothes off. You'll sleep better." Sliding her pants over her narrow hips he realized her boots were still on. Impatiently he pulled them off, then finished with the pants.

"I'd sleep better if you were with me," she mumbled. William looked up at her, seeing she was already half asleep as he tucked her legs under the blankets.

"I will be later, count on it," he pulled off her shirt.

"Promise?" she asked in a sleep-filled voice her unfocused eyes trying to stay open.

"Promise," William gave her a hard kiss as he pulled the blankets over her. She was asleep before the kiss ended. Watching her sleep for a moment he turned to his Ready Room. He had work to do.

∞ ∞ ∞ ∞ ∞

Several hours later, William put down the final report he received from Quinn. There was no new information on where the Xyphrine came from. No one remembered anyone out of the ordinary in the kitchen. Whoever did this had blended in. Rubbing his eyes, William headed into his private quarters.

His life mate slept in his bed. Someone on his ship wanted to harm her. But why? William pondered it as he removed his clothes. Getting into bed he gently pulled her to him. In her sleep, she wrapped an arm around him. Closing his eyes, he let sleep come.

∞ ∞ ∞ ∞ ∞

Waking, she knew she was alone. Seeing the closed adjoining door, she realized the Admiral was already in a meeting. It was only 0730. Sliding out of the bed, she headed to the bathroom for a shower.

In his Ready Room, the Admiral was reading the translation of the Regulian response to the earlier translation.

"Light will be extinguished."

William looked at Quinn, "They're getting testy with each other."

"Yeah," Quinn agreed.

Hearing the shower running, he picked up his headset calling Hutu. "Twenty minutes," was all he said.

"Were we able to get any closer to finding who received the transmission?" William asked turning back to Quinn.

"No."

"Okay, tell Communications to keep up the good work."

Knowing he was being dismissed Quinn stood, "How's she doing, Will?"

William looked up at his friend, "She slept like the dead. Getting some food into her should help."

"She stands, Will. I had my doubts. But she stands." Turning he left the Ready Room. Getting up William secured the hatch then headed to Cassandra.

He found her sitting in a chair pulling on her boots. He walked over, squatted down, and rested his hands on her knees. He was relieved by what he saw. Her thick, black hair was damp on her shoulders, the dark circles under her eyes had faded and there was color in her cheeks.

"Tori?"

"Still sleeping, kept her supper down. You look better," he said looking into sharply focused blue eyes.

"I feel better," she covered his hands. "You were right, I needed the sleep."

"Now, you need to eat." He pulled her to her feet. "Hutu is on his way." Her stomach rumbled at the thought.

She grinned at him, "Yeah, I could eat."

∞ ∞ ∞ ∞ ∞

Hutu put the tray down on the table, removed both covers, the smell made her mouth water.

"Smells great, Hutu, thank you," Cassandra smiled at him.

"Ma'am, I just want to say how sorry I am that my negligence caused Victoria to be harmed," he started...

"Hutu," Cassandra interrupted him, "I don't think you were negligent. I know you'd never hurt Tori. This wasn't your fault."

"Thank you, ma'am," he was shocked at the generosity of this woman.

"So what's for first meal?"

"It's loblolly with thimbleberries. It will fill you up."

"Thank you, Hutu," the Admiral told him. Leaving them in the Admiral's private chambers, Hutu secured the hatch. Cassandra sat down picking up a spoon to try a bite.

"Tastes like oatmeal."

"It's good for you," William told her as he started in on his, enjoying watching her eat. She didn't speak until she'd finished the bowl.

"You're right again, I needed that." Sitting back she watched him.

William finished his then leaned back. He could tell there was something on her mind. "What?"

Picking up the bowls, she took them to the tray gathering her thoughts. "The other night, before Victoria got sick, we were talking about her kidnapping."

"Did she remember anything else?"

"No. But there might be a way she can." William waited. "Victoria is an incredibly smart and gifted little girl. She can read, write and speak nine languages, well Earth languages."

"How many do you know?" he asked.

"What?" Cassandra asked distracted, "Oh, twenty-two."

William raised his eyebrow.

"But the point I'm trying to make is she learns languages quickly. She could learn Regulian."

William gave her a serious look, "It's a difficult language."

"Please... she can handle that." She waved her hand dismissing the difficulty. "The problem is how do you teach it? Is there someone on the Retribution, a learning device? What?"

"We have a program that teaches it. Why would she want to?"

"In her nightmares she can hear voices. She knows they're talking about her. If she knew their language, she would know what they were saying. Knowing what they were saying when they don't think she could means she's not helpless. That knowledge may shed some light onto why she was taken. She needs to know. We all need to know."

He stood up walking over to her, "When do you want to start?"

"As soon as you can get the program. It will give her something to do while she's recovering. Keep her mind busy."

"So you're going to learn it with her," he stopped in front of her.

"Yes."

"I'll order the program up, have it relayed to the comm center in your quarters."

She put her arms around his waist giving him a grateful hug, "Thank you."

William put a finger under her chin tipping her head up, "You haven't kissed me yet today." As he bent down, Cassandra went up on her toes to meet him. The kiss started out soft and grew demanding before William finally broke it off leaving her breathless.

"I'll go with you to make sure Tori's settled," he led her to the hatch.

Cassandra nodded, "I need to stop by our quarters to get her a change of clothes.

∞ ∞ ∞ ∞ ∞

In Medical, they found Victoria and Lucas finishing first meal.

"You look better, Aunt Cassie," Tori told her as they entered.

"So do you," she replied approaching the bed, relieved to see color in the little girl's cheeks and her eyes bright. Lucas, on the other hand, looked a little ragged.

"So you slept okay?" Cassandra inquired.

"Yes, she did," Bliant answered as he entered the room. "So how are you feeling this morning, young lady?"

"Good, can I go home?"

Bliant checked several machines then disconnected them. "Not feeling sick to your stomach?" he quizzed.

"No."

"Then I don't see why you can't return to your quarters. Provided you take it easy for the next three or four days." He looked at Cassandra. "If she has any nausea I want her back here right away."

"Understood."

"Three or four days!" Victoria exclaimed, "That's forever!" Cassandra and Bliant shared a smile. She was on the mend.

"Okay, let's get you dressed then we're out of here."

Moving toward the door the three men left the room. "So how was the night really?" William asked Lucas.

"She slept well, but that chair is hideous. I don't know how Cassie stood it!"

"Go get some shut-eye."

"I need to get Tori settled first."

William gave him a hard look, "Cassandra and I will handle that."

Lucas realized the line was back, "Tell her I'll stop in later to see her."

"Give them a few days. Let things settle."

Sighing, Lucas nodded and headed for his quarters.

∞ ∞ ∞ ∞ ∞

"So are you ready to go?" Cassandra asked looking at Tori.

"Yes."

"Let's go then," she held out her arms.

"Aunt Cassie, I'm not a baby. I can walk."

"I know you're not, but you've been sick. It's a long way to our quarters."

"Is that where we're going?"

"Where else?" she asked confused.

"The Admiral's?"

"Tori…" Cassandra trailed off.

"I'm not a baby, Aunt Cassie. He's your life mate. You love him. You should be together like Mom and Dad. He needs you." Cassandra didn't know what to say. "If it were me, you couldn't keep me from Lucas."

"This is my decision. We go to our quarters."

"But you love the Admiral, right?"

"Yes, Tori, I do. Now, let's get you out of here."

Jumping off the bed she took Cassandra's hand and walked out the door. The Admiral was waiting for them.

"Ready to go?" he looked from one to the other.

"Yes," Tori replied. "We're going to walk to our quarters," he was informed.

"Really?" was all he said as he turned and walked with them out of Medical.

"Where's Lucas?" Tori asked walking beside the Admiral.

"He needed to get some sleep before his next patrol. He said to tell you he'll see you later."

"Oh."

Cassandra looked at William and realized he'd understood. The walk from Medical to their quarters wasn't all that far, but for a little girl just recovering it seemed to take forever.

"Tori?"

"I'm fine." When they finally reached their quarters, Tori headed straight for the bed.

"Damn!" Cassandra whispered. "I should have made her let me carry her."

"I believe she has too much of her aunt in her to allow that." Putting a hand behind her neck he tipped her head up pulling her close. "I'll get the program sent so you can keep her occupied."

She flashed him a grateful smile.

"You will sleep when she does," he ordered quietly, "or I will be moving you both into my quarters. Don't fight me on this, Cassandra!" he ordered as she opened her mouth. "You know I'm right! Hutu will be providing all your meals, call when you're ready for them. If she's up to it, come to my quarters tonight," he paused, "Otherwise let Hutu know." Pulling her close he kissed her deeply.

"Secure the door," he said walking through it. Cassandra secured the door then climbed in next to Tori, pulled her close and she was asleep too.

∞ ∞ ∞ ∞ ∞

Entering the Bridge, the Admiral went to his console and sent the Regulian language to Cassandra's quarters. That completed, he turned to Quinn.

"So, what's on the agenda for today?"

Chapter Nine

Waking, Cassandra found Tori already up and sitting on the couch.

"Aunt Cassie?"

"Yeah?" she rolled out of bed.

"What am I supposed to do for four whole days?"

Smiling, Cassandra rubbed her face. "Well, I guess I could make you scrub the floors!"

"Aunt Cassie! I'm serious! I'll die of boredom!"

Knowing just how close Victoria had come to dying wiped the smile off Cassandra's face. "Tori, do you remember what we were talking about before you got sick? About learning Regulian?"

"Yeah," Tori leaned forward excited.

"Well, I talked to the Admiral. He thought it was a good idea. So he's going to send their learning program to our console here so you can study it while you're recovering."

"Really?" She loved learning different languages.

"Yes." She walked over to the comm center and saw there was something there from the Admiral. She smiled at Tori. "Looks like it's already here. Ready to get started kicking some Regulian butt?"

"Yes!"

∞ ∞ ∞ ∞ ∞

Several hours later they were interrupted by a call.

"Yes?" Cassandra asked distracted.

"Ma'am, this is Hutu. Are you ready for second meal?" Looking at the clock Cassandra realized it was past time for Tori to eat.

"Yes, Hutu, I'm sorry I didn't call sooner."

"That's not a problem, ma'am. I will bring it directly."

Putting the headset down Cassandra looked at Tori. "Tori?"

"Yeah," she replied as distracted as Cassandra had been.

"Hutu's on his way with lunch. There's something you need to know."

"What?" Her eyes moved away from the screen.

"When you got sick the other night, it was from the sauce you dipped your nugget in."

"The sauce made me sick?" Tori gave her a confused look.

"Yes," Cassandra wasn't going to tell her someone tried to kill her. "Hutu blamed himself."

"Why? It wasn't his fault. He didn't do it on purpose."

"No, he didn't. You might want to let him know you don't think it's his fault."

"Okay," Tori nodded and jumped up at the knock on their hatch. Opening it, she let Hutu in.

"Hi, Hutu!" Tori smiled at him.

"Hello, little one."

"Is it nuggets?"

"Not today. Dr. Bliant said you should have soup. So…" he took the cover off revealing 'nugget soup.'

Tori giggled.

He then removed Cassandra's cover. Cassandra watched as he quickly checked the plates making sure there were no 'additions.'

"It looks good, Hutu, thank you."

"Yeah thanks, Hutu," Tori walked up to the big man, crooked her finger for him to lean down to her.

Hutu looked at Cassandra then squatted down so they were at eye level.

Putting her small hands on his cheeks she stared into his eyes, "I know you didn't make me sick. So stop blaming yourself," she gave him a quick kiss then turned to her food.

Rising slowly, Hutu found he couldn't speak. With a nod to Cassandra, he turned and left. After the meal, Tori's eyes began to droop.

"Hey, kiddo, why don't you lie down here on the couch and take a little rest?"

"Aunt Cassie, I'm not a baby. I don't need to take naps," she said huffily.

"I didn't say you were a baby. But you've been sick and your body needs extra rest. If you want to get back to class, you need to rest." Cassandra grabbed a pillow and blanket off the bed.

"But the Regulian…" Tori protested.

"It will be there when you wake up." She dropped the pillow on the couch. "Come on, put your head on it." As she lay down, Cassandra covered her. Teary eyes looked at her. Cassandra dropped to the floor. "Oh, honey, what's wrong? Does your stomach hurt?" Fear gripped her heart.

"No," she whispered as tears started to fall.

"What then?" Cassandra pleaded.

"I miss Mommy and Daddy," she whispered, tears quietly falling.

"Oh, baby!" Cassandra pulled her into her arms rocking her, "so do I."

"I'm sorry I'm not braver," Tori whispered.

"What?"

"Brave like you."

"Tori…" Cassandra's throat tightened.

"Lucas and the Admiral are brave too."

Cassandra had to close her eyes, "Sweetheart, you are brave," she looked into Tori's drenched green eyes. "You are. Who jumped out of that fire? You swung up into the Raptor. You've faced the Glitter Man and now you're learning a strange language so we can stop him. You're the bravest little girl I know!"

"But I still miss Mommy and Daddy and Grandpa," she whispered as tears fell from Victoria's eyes.

"So do I. We'll miss them for the rest of our lives, baby. That's what happens when you love someone. When they're not here, you miss them."

"But it hurts, Aunt Cassie, in my heart."

Pulling her closer, Cassandra let her tears fall. Something she hadn't been letting Victoria see. That had been a mistake. How many others was she making?

"I hurt too, baby. I miss them all too." Tori wrapped her arms around her. As they cried, they found comfort in each other.

"Tori," Cassandra pulled back a little not bothering to dry her eyes. Tori needed to see them. "We will always miss them. We love them. They loved us. But we need to remember all the good times we had together. We were a family. They would want us to continue living, to be happy. It's what you would want for them, isn't it?"

"Yes," she whispered.

"So we remember them. We talk about them, all the fun times we had. But we go on. Just living, Tori, *that's* brave."

"But Lucas and the Admiral, they fight the Regulians," Tori persisted.

"So are you. You're learning their language so you can know what they are doing. That's fighting. The Admiral said it's a difficult language. There are all kinds of brave, Victoria," Cassandra informed her.

"Really?"

"Really. Now, why don't you take that rest?" She laid her back onto the couch.

"Okay." Drained, she was asleep in moments.

∞ ∞ ∞ ∞ ∞

Later while she was studying the Regulian program, the comm center rang. Looking over to make sure it hadn't woken Tori, she picked up the headset to answer.

"Chamberlain," she said in a quiet voice.

"She's sleeping?" William asked on the other end as a warm feeling filled Cassandra.

"Yeah, fell asleep after lunch," William looked at the clock it was 1500.

"She's doing okay?"

"We've had our ups and downs. But she will be," Cassandra's voice was firm.

"What happened?"

"I screwed up," she replied before she thought about what she said. Looking at the couch she saw Tori had started to wake. "Look, William, she's waking up. I need to go. Everything's being handled." As she disconnected, she moved to Victoria.

∞ ∞ ∞ ∞ ∞

Removing his headset, William looked at it. What was it about this woman? Something had happened. It had upset her. He heard it in her voice. But did she ask him for help, her life mate? No, she said she'd handle it and hung up on him. Tossing the headset aside, he stood.

Quinn watched him. Unknown to both of them so was Falco from her navigation station.

"Falco, how long until we reach Rodham? Falco!" The Admiral demanded his temper showing.

"Sir, at current speed, just over five days," she replied. The Admiral wasn't happy. That woman was making him unhappy. She'd have to pay for that.

"Quinn. How are repairs coming on the Sentinel? Can we increase speed?" He walked over studying a chart.

"No, Sir. All repairs that can be completed en route have been. This is their max speed until they get to Rodham for more extensive repairs."

"Rodham's been notified so they're prepared? I want these repairs expedited. We need that ship back."

"Yes, Admiral, they've received copies of all the damage. They say two days until it is battle ready."

"Fine, we'll put the Fleet in for two days."

"I'll let Medical know they'll be having a run on Ollali juice," Quinn joked, missing the Admiral's startled look.

"Admiral, I have a communication for you from Carina," the Communications Specialist on duty told him. The Admiral went to his desk picking up his headset.

∞ ∞ ∞ ∞ ∞

"Hey there, did you have a good rest?" Cassandra walked over to the couch.

"Pretty good," mumbled Tori as she leaned into her. Cassandra rubbed her back, giving her time to fully wake up. After a couple minutes, Tori lifted her head.

"Can I have a drink?"

"Sure, let me get you some water." Filling a glass in the bathroom she returned. Tori drank thirstily.

"You okay? You want to talk?"

"I'm okay. I want to work on the program some more," there was a gleam in her eye.

"All right, but you're not going to overdo it. Is that understood?"

"Aunt Cassie…"

"I mean it, young lady."

"Okay, okay." Together they headed back to the console. Several hours later Cassandra leaned back from the console rubbing her neck. Glancing at the clock she realized it was already 1745.

"Tori, time to stop."

"What? No, just a little longer!" she beseeched.

"Tori, we need to give it a rest. Let it soak in. Now," Cassandra raised a finger, "you know I'm right. We can start again tomorrow."

"But what if I have the dream tonight?" she demanded.

"Well, then it will be a good test. So mark where we're at and shut it down."

"Okay, but what are we going to do for the rest of the night?"

"Well, the Admiral has invited us to dinner in his quarters. Are you up for it? Or would you rather stay here?" Tori looked at her then away.

"What?"

"Nothing."

"Victoria Lynn. What?"

"It's just, what if something bad happens again?"

"You mean getting sick? That won't happen again."

"And the other?"

"Your arm?" Tori nodded. "But that was a good thing. We found the thread, got it out, now you're safe."

"Yeah, I guess I didn't think about it that way." Victoria watched puzzled as her aunt went into the bathroom. Returning, Cassandra squatted down in front of her. Opening her hand, she let Victoria see what was in it then put the chain around Victoria's neck. Touching it, Victoria looked at her.

"It's your lucky ring," Tori's eyes widened.

"You wear it," Cassandra smiled at her.

"Really?" her green eyes hopeful.

"Really. So what's your choice, here or the Admiral's?"

Tori looked around their quarters. It would be nice to get out for a while. And the Admiral's was bigger and better. Then there was the chance that Lucas might be there. "Let's go to the Admiral's," Tori grinned at her aunt.

"Sure you can walk that far?"

"Yes."

"All right, go brush your hair then we'll go."

"Okay."

∞ ∞ ∞ ∞ ∞

William couldn't believe he'd been so irresponsible. What was he, some cadet with his first girl? On Carina, contraception was the man's responsibility. Ollali juice caused the male to become infertile within twenty-four hours and the effects wore off within twenty-four hours after use. How could he have forgotten? Cassandra could already have conceived.

William hesitated, would that really be so bad? The thought of her carrying his child was taking root, his desire for the child surprisingly strong. Entering his Ready Room he heard laughter. Securing the door, he followed it into his private quarters. Walking back he saw Cassandra on the floor tickling her niece.

"Hi, Admiral!" Victoria giggled seeing him first.

Cassandra twisted around, her face full of mischief, those beautiful blue eyes sparkling. "Hi, Admiral," she mimicked but she saw the serious look in his eyes before it was gone.

"Looks like you're feeling better," he made himself smile at Victoria.

"I am," Tori got up from the floor. Walking over, William helped Cassandra up and pulled her close. Could she be carrying his child? He wondered. She raised an eyebrow at his serious look, her smile dimming. Leaning down he kissed her gently.

"Hi."

Cassandra put a hand on the side of his face, "What's wrong?"

"Nothing's wrong, just glad to see you, both of you," he turned to smile at Tori. "I wasn't sure you'd be up to it."

"I'm good," she said as a thought crossed her mind, "really good." With a gleam in her eye, she walked up to hold his hand. "Maybe you could order Aunt Cassie to let me go back to class tomorrow."

William had been watching the little girl's eyes as the idea came to her. She was going to be a handful.

"Victoria Lynn! You are not going to school tomorrow!"

"But he's the Admiral. He gets to order people around. Don't you?" Tori asked still holding his hand.

"Well, let's see," William wondered how he was going to get out from between two females. "No. Yes. I'll go see where Hutu is."

"What?" Tori looked at her aunt as the Admiral made a hasty retreat to his Ready Room.

"No, he's not going to order me. Yes, he gets to order people around. And what you just witnessed was a man not wanting to be in the middle of an argument between two women."

"Oh," Tori looked at the door, "is he coming back?"

"Oh eventually. Why don't I go check to see when Hutu's going to be here, okay?"

"Sure."

Entering the Ready Room, she found William leaning back in his chair. "We kind of chased you out of your quarters, Admiral." William watched as she crossed the room to him. His eyes were serious again.

"What's wrong? What don't I know?"

William was continually amazed at his life mate's intuition. Pulling her into his lap he kissed her. "There's nothing wrong, just something we need to discuss." A knock at the hatch interrupted him. "But not right now." Releasing her, he opened it to Hutu.

"How is the Regulian going?" William asked as they sat down to eat. Tori gave him a pained look.

"It's okay, it would be better if Aunt Cassie wouldn't go so slowly," she complained.

"It's a difficult language, Tori, don't feel bad if you didn't get very far today."

"Yeah, we only got a third of the way," Tori took a bite of her dinner.

William looked at Cassandra, "A third?!?"

"I know!" Victoria agreed. "If Aunt Cassie didn't make us go so slow, we could have gotten a lot farther."

"You'll remember more if you take it in smaller chunks. You know I'm right," Cassandra stopped Tori from arguing with her.

"A third?" William looked at Cassandra to see if he'd heard right.

"Yeah." She wasn't sure what he was asking.

"The two of you made it through a third of the program in..."

"I don't know, five, six hours? Wouldn't you say, Tori?"

"Yeah, slow!" Tori looked at Cassandra hopefully, "I could do some more when I get done eating."

"No, but if you wanted to practice the writing for what we've done so far you can."

Tori shot her a disappointed look, "Okay."

William was trying to decide if the two of them were joking with him. He'd known Cassandra was 'smart' and that Victoria was very 'intelligent' for her age but this... "So just how smart are the two of you?"

Two pairs of eyes turned to him.

"I guess it depends on your point of reference."

"Aunt Cassie was the smartest person on the planet!" Tori exclaimed proudly.

"Victoria!"

"What? That's what Great Grams always said. She said you were the brightest light!"

"She was just a little biased," Cassandra informed her.

"But you were up for the Magellan Award!" Tori persisted.

"Victoria, enough! Give it a rest, please!" Hearing the strain in her aunt's voice, Tori stopped.

"I'm full. Can I go study?" Cassandra looked at her nearly empty plate.

"You're sure?" Tori nodded. "Okay for a little while." As Tori moved around the table, Cassandra pulled her in for a hug, "I love you, Victoria Lynn." Drawing back she continued, "never doubt it."

Tori smiled at her, "I don't." She moved to the couch.

William's mind was whirling as he tried to follow this conversation. It typically took a good six months to a year for an exceptionally bright Carinian to get through the program he'd given Cassandra.

How had these two gotten so far?

Victoria said the 'brightest light.'

The Regulians were looking for 'the Light.'

What was this Magellan Award Cassandra didn't want to talk about? She said she'd screwed up earlier today. What was that about?

"Sorry," Cassandra brought his attention back to her, "not quite the dinner conversation you expected when you invited us over."

He turned in his chair to look at her. "It doesn't matter, as long as you're here. Eat." He pointed to her nearly full plate. Once they were both done, William picked up all three plates and took the tray back into the Ready Room while Cassandra checked on Victoria.

"So how's it going?"

"Not too bad," Tori looked up at her aunt. "You were right. I need to know this better before we go on."

"So you study it and tomorrow we'll see. Okay?"

"Okay. Are you going to go talk to the Admiral?"

"Why?"

"I think he has some questions."

Cassandra looked toward the connecting door. "I'm sure he does."

"I'm sorry."

"For what, sweetie?"

"For arguing with you."

"Oh please, families argue. Didn't your dad and I argue all the time?"

"Yeah," Tori smiled remembering, "You always won. It used to make him so mad!"

Cassandra smiled at her niece, "I didn't always win. Your dad was one tough cookie."

"Yeah, he was," Tori turned back to her writing. After a quick kiss on her head, Cassandra went to find William.

He was standing in front of the painting of the three setting suns when she closed the connecting door. She didn't think this was a conversation for Tori's ears. Turning when he heard the door close, he raised an eyebrow.

"You said we needed to talk."

Walking over he pulled her close, feeling her arms go around him. "What did you think you screwed up today?"

"What?"

William put a hand under her chin so she looked at him. "When I called, you were upset. You thought you'd screwed up. What happened?"

"I just should have realized something, that's all, given Tori more attention."

"I'm not sure that would be possible. Cassandra, you give her everything. You think about what she needs before she does. What didn't you do?"

"I didn't let her know that I missed her parents too, that I missed my father. I was so damn busy trying to be strong and brave for her that I didn't let her know that it was okay for her to cry for them, to miss them. I'm smarter than that!" Putting her hands on his chest she tried to push away.

Holding her upper arms, he gave her a shake. "Stop that!" He wasn't going to let her do this to herself. "You haven't screwed anything up! You can't think of everything, be everything, all the time!"

"Why not?!?" she demanded. "She needed me to be! God, she's just a little girl! She shouldn't have to go through something like this. To lose everyone she loves!"

"She didn't! She has you!" William tightened his grip bringing her to her toes. "You shouldn't have had to go through this either! But you have! Give yourself a break, you lost too!" The eyes that met his broke his heart.

"How do I make this right for her?" she whispered.

"You can't," he needed to use the truth to get through to her. "You can't bring her parents back, Cassandra. You can't get the Earth back for her. All you can do is be there for her while she adjusts to the world she's in now. That's what you've been doing, damn well too." Resting his forehead against hers, he finished, "I'm here. You don't have to do this alone. Hang on to me. I'm not letting go." Pulling back a little, "What can I do?"

Cassandra put her arms back around his waist and hung on.

"Just what you're doing." Leaning back she looked at him with sad eyes. "She thought if she cried it would mean she wasn't brave. Brave like me, because I never let her see me cry. Brave like you and Lucas for fighting the Regulians. If she missed my father or her parents and cried, then she was letting us down."

William's throat tightened at the thought of any nine-cycle thinking they needed to be that strong. Not knowing what to say he leaned down to kiss her. "We'll figure something out together, because we are together, Cassandra, never doubt that."

"I'm working on it," she replied. William's earnest eyes reminded her that he'd had something on his mind earlier.

"So what is it that I need to know?"

"What?"

"This isn't the conversation you had in mind when you came in tonight. There is something you need to tell me. What?" The connecting door opened before William could reply.

"Aunt Cassie?" He let her slip out of his arms.

"Hey, what's up?"

"I'm tired." Cassandra shot a look to William.

"Well, then I'd say it's time we get you home and into bed."

"Okay, I already picked up my work."

"Wow, without me telling you to?" That got a tired grin out of her. William walked over and squatted down.

"Do you mind if I carry you to your quarters?" He couldn't call it their home. Tori shook her head and stepped trustingly into his arms.

"I'll go get her things."

By the time they arrived at their quarters, she was fast asleep. William put her in the bed as Cassandra secured the door. Removing her shoes, she covered her and lowered the lights. Turning to William she took his hand leading him to the couch.

"So, Admiral, what did you need to tell me?"

William hadn't had time to decide how to tell her. Should it be the straight out truth that he'd been irresponsible? Would she ever trust him again? Would she be upset?

"William?" she started to get nervous.

"Did I ever tell you about Salish?" his voice quiet enough not to wake Victoria.

"Your wife?" Cassandra was taken by surprise.

"Past wife," he corrected.

"There's a difference?"

"Definitely! We had concluded our union ten cycles before she was killed."

"Oh."

"I've never talked about this, Cassandra. No one knows about it, not my sons, not even Quinn."

"William, you don't need to tell me."

"You're my life mate. You have the right to know why I had a union with another."

Not sure what to say, she remained silent.

"We met when I was stationed at Annam on Carina. Her father owned the Rathskeller next to the base. I was twenty-five and full of myself. I'd just come off my first three-cycle tour and thought I was invincible. She was twenty-four and the most beautiful woman I'd ever seen. Every man wanted her. I was the one she gave herself to." William was caught up in the past and didn't notice how still Cassandra had become.

"We were together whenever I was off duty. After a month, she told me she had conceived. It crossed my mind that she shouldn't have as I'd been taking the Ollali juice. We united within the week. Then I had to leave for six weeks. When I got back, I didn't worry about the Ollali juice since she'd already conceived. Five weeks later she told me she was with child." At Cassandra's shocked breath, he finally looked at her, noticing her intense blue eyes and still body.

"She lied to you."

"I allowed myself to be lied to. There's a difference. I knew I was on the Ollali juice but didn't question her. By that time, she told me she'd conceived Lucas and it didn't matter. She was still having my child."

"So you stayed."

"Yes."

"I take it this Ollali juice is some type of birth control."

"Birth control?"

"So you can't get or, in this case, cause someone else to conceive."

"Yes, it is the male's responsibility."

"Really? On Earth, it was mostly the woman's since she's the one that gets pregnant…conceives."

"Where's the man?"

"There if he wants to be."

"Doesn't sound like much of a man."

"Sometimes you're right. But it's the woman's body. She has the right to say what happens inside it."

William looked at her, "That's what you believe?"

"Yes. You have control over your body with the Ollali juice. Why shouldn't a woman have the same?"

William just looked at her and then continued. "Not long after Lucas we had Kyle. Salish stayed on Carina with the boys. She wanted to be near her family."

"They didn't go on tour with you?"

"No, after one extended tour, I came home and discovered that there was nothing left of our union except our sons. So we concluded it."

"I'm sorry, William."

That startled him. "Why are you sorry?"

"Because it still hurts you," she leaned in to put a hand on his cheek. "You think you failed. You don't like to fail. But you didn't. She lied to you, but you did the honorable thing. You didn't fail."

"Most life mates wouldn't see it that way."

"I'm not most life mates now am I," she gave him a slight smile. "What she did was wrong. But what I know is this. If she hadn't tricked you into a union, then you'd never have had Lucas. If you hadn't had Lucas, then he wouldn't have crashed on Earth. If he hadn't crashed, then you wouldn't have come to save Victoria and me. If you hadn't done that, then I wouldn't have found you. So while I think what she did was entirely wrong, I'm thankful she did," Cassandra leaned in to finish her little speech with a gentle kiss.

A stunned William pulled her closer.

"So why did you want me to know this?" she leaned back as she looked at him. Taking a deep breath, William was ready to tell her when her comm center rang.

Jumping out of his arms, Cassandra moved to silence the ring before it woke Victoria. Picking up the headset she answered.

"Chamberlain. Just a minute," she turned her head to William, "It's Quinn for you." She handed him the headset as she stepped away.

"Zafar." He watched Cassandra. "I'll be right there. I need to leave."

"I gathered that," she walked him to the hatch.

"Cassandra, we need to finish this. There are things you still need to understand."

"But not now. Now you need to be the Admiral. We'll talk later." She opened the hatch and secured it as he walked away. William was halfway down the corridor before he realized he hadn't kissed her goodbye.

Turning from the door, Cassandra's mind was racing. What's really going on here? Why did William want her to know about Salish? Just to know? Or was there something else? He was an honorable man, she'd always known that. This just reinforced it. Unable to come to a satisfactory conclusion, Cassandra changed and climbed in next to Tori. Tomorrow would be here soon enough. Maybe she'd find the answers then.

Chapter Ten

During breakfast, Cassandra answered her comm center to find Javiera on the other end.

"How are things going there?"

"Pretty good, we're just finishing first meal."

"Well Amina has been begging me to call to see if Victoria would be up for a visitor this afternoon," Cassandra looked at Tori.

"I think that would be a great idea. She's starting to climb the walls here."

"Great! It's a date then. We'll see you around 1500." Cassandra turned to Tori.

"Well, it looks like we're having company this afternoon."

"Yes!"

"So we'll study for a while, then after lunch see how you're feeling."

"Aunt Cassie, I'm fine."

"We'll see. Done?"

"Yes."

"Then let's get started."

Before they knew it, Hutu was at the door with second meal. After they had eaten, it was Cassandra that was feeling tired. She did some quick math and realized it was time for her cycle.

"Crap!" she muttered. How was she supposed to handle this? She knew her body. She was going to be in for a lousy day and a half. Most women had a five-day cycle every twenty-eight days. While Cassandra was lucky to only have hers every forty-five days, she paid the price by having the five days condensed down into just thirty-six hours. On Earth, she had all the supplies she needed. Here...

"Is something wrong, Aunt Cassie?" Victoria looked at her.

"No, honey, nothing's wrong. So you want to take a rest before Amina comes or work a little longer?"

"Let's work a little longer."

At 1500, Javiera was knocking at their door. When Cassandra opened the hatch, Amina went rushing by to find Tori.

"Amina, manners!"

"Sorry! Hi, Cassie," Amina said as she hugged Tori. Javiera smiled an apology to Cassandra as she came into the room.

"She all but ran here."

"That's okay, Tori's been the same. She's pretty sure I'm taking Dr. Bliant too seriously."

"But you're not," Javiera said in a knowing mother's voice. Cassandra gave her a grateful smile. "Are you okay? You're not looking very good."

Cassandra looked to see that the girls were chattering away on the bed. Dare she confide in Javiera? Could she not?

"Javiera, what do Carinian women do when they have their menstrual cycle?"

"Their what?"

Cassandra was trying to figure out how to explain.

"When you conceived Amina, you knew because..."

"Well my first clue was I missed my flow...oh...so which is it?" she asked.

"Which?"

"Have you conceived or..."

"No!"

The girls looked over then returned to their conversation.

"No," Cassandra said in a lower voice. "My 'flow' is starting. I don't have anything to..."

"Understood. Why don't I just run back to our quarters and get you what you need." Cassandra gave her a grateful look.

Surprisingly, what Javiera brought back wasn't that different from what she was used to. Carinian and Earth woman seemed to have very similar biology.

After the girls had played for a couple of hours, Javiera and Amina got up to leave.

"Thank you again, Javiera. You're a life saver," Cassandra said as she opened the hatch.

"Please, we women have to stick together. I'll show you where you can get your own supplies sometime when we're out. Now you get some rest. You've been through a lot lately." Securing the hatch, Cassandra looked at Tori. The little girl was starting to fade.

"What do you say we eat dinner here tonight? I'll let Hutu know, then we can have an early night."

"What about the Admiral?"

"I'm sure Hutu will let him know."

"Shouldn't we?" Tori persisted.

"Tori, if I knew how to get in touch with him I would. I can't just call the Bridge asking for him."

"Why not?"

"Because he's the Admiral and that's not something you do. Please, enough."

"Okay."

A little while later Hutu arrived with their meals. Cassandra looked ill enough for Hutu to notice.

"Are you all right?" he asked as Cassandra walked him to the hatch.

"I'm fine," she insisted as she secured the door. Picking up her forc she found she really had no appetite.

"Aunt Cassie? What's wrong?" Cassandra looked at her niece. Did she tell her the truth? Had Cyndy ever talked to her about these things?

"Aunt Cassie, are you sick?" Tori's voice wavered.

"No, honey, no." She had to calm her fears. Setting down her forc she looked at Tori. "I don't know if your mom ever told you about what happens to your body when you become a woman."

"You mean your menstrual cycle?"

"Yes," she closed her eyes relieved.

"Yeah, we had this whole talk about it last year. Mom showed me all the 'stuff.' It was weird. So that's why you don't feel good? Your cycle?"

"That's about it."

"Wow. I didn't know it could do that. I hope I never get it."

"Sorry, kid, you will but not for a while. Now you eat. I'm going to take a shower."

∞ ∞ ∞ ∞ ∞

In the Admiral's quarters, Hutu delivered a single meal. William looked at the solitary plate and realized that less than a week ago he wouldn't have noticed. Now it seemed wrong.

"I took the ladies their dinner at 1800, Sir," Hutu hesitated.

"What is it, Hutu?"

"Cassie looked ill, Sir. She said she was fine but…I thought you should know."

"Thank you, Hutu," William's gut clenched. Was she already having conception side effects? Why hadn't she called him? Going to his comm center he rang their quarters.

"Hello," Victoria answered.

"Victoria, this is the Admiral."

"Hi, Admiral."

"I need to talk to Cassandra," he realized he needed to hear her voice.

"She's in the shower, she's not feeling good." The shower shut off. "Sounds like she's done, you want me to get her?"

"Yeah," it took several minutes but he could hear Cassandra telling Tori to get in. Finally, she picked up the headset.

"Hi."

"What's wrong?"

"Wrong? There's nothing wrong here."

"You're not feeling well."

"How could you possibly know…" she broke off turning to look at the bathroom.

"Hutu, then Tori. What's wrong?" he repeated.

"William, it's really nothing. I'm just tired. Everything's catching up with me."

"Why didn't you let me know? I'll call Bliant and be right over."

"No. William, no! I don't need Bliant. Honestly. I just want to get some sleep."

"I'll come get Victoria then."

"No. She's had a full day. We got through another chunk of the program then Amina came over for a couple of hours. She's worn out too. We're just going to call it a night." He was silent on the other end.

"William?"

"If that's what you want," his voice was stiff at her rejection.

"It's not what I want, but I think it's what I need to do."

He ran a frustrated hand through his hair. "Okay, you'll call if you need anything."

"William…"

"Damn it, Cassandra!" William's temper was getting the better of him. She was shutting him out! He could feel it.

"Don't you swear at me, William Zafar!" Cassandra's own temper rose. "I'm tired! I'm irritable, and I don't need you making me feel stupid for not knowing how to get hold of you!" Suddenly she was close to tears. She took a deep breath. Hearing it made William's temper disappear.

"Cassandra..."

"I'll talk to you tomorrow," she disconnected.

∞ ∞ ∞ ∞ ∞

William slowly took off his headset as he sat back in his chair. His life mate just hung up on him.

She was sick and he'd let his temper get the better of him. She stood toe-to-toe with him then hung up on him.

What the hell was the matter with him! How could he not have realized no one had shown her how to work everything on the comm console in her quarters? That he hadn't shown her.

She could learn Regulian but not know how to get in touch with him if she needed to or just wanted to. She was upset with him. He couldn't say he blamed her. This not knowing if she had conceived or not was making him stupid, it ended tonight.

∞ ∞ ∞ ∞ ∞

"Come on, Tori, finish up and we'll get some sleep," Cassandra said standing in the doorway of the bathroom.

"Okay," was the watery response.

Cassandra sat down on the couch to wait. She hated feeling this exhausted. It had always been this way for her. Grams always told her that someday it would get better. God, she wished it was today.

Coming out in her jammies carrying a towel and brush, Tori sat between her legs. After drying her hair, Cassandra started to brush.

"So what was your favorite part of the day?" she asked as if she didn't know.

"Amina coming over! Aunt Cassie, did you know that in a few days we're going to be stopping at Rodham. It's a space station. A real, *in space,* space station! Amina said we would be able to leave the ship and go on to it!"

"Really?"

"Yeah, so can we?"

"Can we what?"

"Go on the Rodham Space Station?"

"Well, I..." Cassandra trailed off as someone knocked on their hatch door. Opening it, she wasn't surprised by who was outside. Stepping back she let him in.

"Hi, Admiral!" Tori said from the couch.

"Hi," William took everything in at once. Tori in her jammies with damp hair, Cassandra's tired eyes shooting sparks at him, a plate of uneaten food on the table, Cassandra's plate. Putting a hand behind her head, he leaned down and kissed her until she responded, "I missed you."

Cassandra leaned against him for a second then straightened. "I need to finish Tori's hair." Stepping around him she moved back to the couch.

He understood she was still mad at him. Good, he was too. Following, he sat down next to her. "So, Tori, I hear you had company today."

"Yeah, Amina. She says we're going to be stopping at Rodham. It's a space station!"

"Yes, it is."

"We can go on it.?"

"Yes."

Cassandra finished brushing Tori's hair as she talked William's ear off. She had to give him credit, he took the bombardment well. "That's it, kiddo, all done. Time for bed."

"But the Admiral's here."

"Well okay, but then I guess you won't be able to go for a half day of class tomorrow."

"What? Really?" Tori quizzed excitedly.

"Half a day."

"Yes!" she jumped up and gave the Admiral a quick hug, "Night, Admiral!" Running across the room she dove into bed. Shaking her head, Cassandra walked over to tuck her in.

"Love you, kiddo. Sleep well."

"Love you, Aunt Cassie." Rolling onto her tummy she was asleep. Dimming the lights she turned to face William.

William watched her walk back to him. Seeing her fatigue and saying nothing he pulled her down into his lap.

"William..."

"Shhh, just relax, I need to hold you for a bit." Pulling her closer, he leaned back. She wanted to be mad at him, but just didn't have the energy. It felt so good just to curl up into his arms. Letting herself relax, sleep took her.

He'd meant to have it out with her, but her obvious exhaustion had him letting her sleep. Content, he closed his eyes.

∞ ∞ ∞ ∞ ∞

Groaning in her sleep, Cassandra tried to move to relieve some of the discomfort. Finding she couldn't she opened her eyes to discover she was being held by a sleeping William. With the cramping getting worse, she moved. William's arms tightened around her.

"William," she whispered not wanting to wake Tori. "William, I need to get up." She shook his arm. Waking he found Cassandra struggling to get out of his arms.

"What's wrong?"

"I need the bathroom. Let me up," her tone almost frantic, he immediately released her. Rushing to the bathroom, she closed the door. Waiting impatiently, William finally stood ready to pound on the door when it suddenly opened. She came out looking pale and sweaty. Walking by him, she lay back down on the couch.

"Cassandra," sitting on the edge of the couch he tucked a piece of hair behind her ear, "tell me what's wrong so I can help." He found her skin was clammy.

"You can't help with this," she whispered and pulled her legs up to her chest. William was indeed starting to fear for her.

"Cassandra?" when she said nothing he stood, "I'm calling Bliant."

"No!" she grabbed his arm, "he can't do anything either."

"Cassandra, you're scaring me."

Stretching her legs out, she swung them over the side of the couch. "William," she started then quickly headed back to the bathroom. This time he wasn't letting her shut the door.

"Damn it, William, get out!" she hissed trying to shut the door.

"No."

"I need some privacy!"

"Not until you tell me what's going on!"

"I have my cycle, all right? Now get out!"

"Cycle?"

"God, William, you were married! Figure it out! Now get out!" Shoving him out, she closed the door.

Standing on the other side of the door he was trying to make sense of what she'd said. What the hell was a cycle? He'd told her he'd been 'married' as she called it. What does that have to do with her obvious cramping? Did she mean flow? She has her flow? That would mean she hadn't conceived. Salish never had this problem…Had she? William realized he didn't know.

Walking away from the door, he sat down trying to sort out his thoughts. There was no child. He wasn't sure if he was relieved or upset. When the door opened, he watched her cross the room.

"Cassandra…"

"Are you happy!" she demanded in a fierce whisper. "Now that you know you can leave!"

"I'm not leaving!"

"There is nothing you can do here, except leave me some pride."

"You should have told me."

"Really? How many Carinian women have talked to you about their cycle?"

She had him there. "Sit down. Please," he added. Cassandra sat easing herself back closing her eyes.

"I need to explain, Cassandra. I'm not very good at it."

"At what?" she asked tiredly.

"Explaining myself. I don't do it very often."

"I noticed."

William gave a little smile she didn't see. "Cassandra," he picked up her hand. He needed to touch her. "I forgot to kiss you goodbye last night." She opened her eyes to look at him. "How could I forget that?" He looked up and saw that she watched him.

"Today I didn't hear from you. You're not in our quarters for dinner. Hutu tells me you're ill. Tori tells me you're sick. You tell me you're okay." She can hear the impatience growing again in his voice. "I missed you. I needed to see you, make sure you were okay. You tend to get stubborn when it's about you."

"I get stubborn?"

"Yes, you do," he caressed her cheek. "Cassandra, I'm as new to this life mate thing as you are. I'm trying to find my way too. When you're obviously ill, I'm going to be concerned."

"I'm not ill. Fine, you want to know? This is what my cycle is like, for thirty-six hours every six weeks like clockwork. Are you satisfied, anything else you want to know?"

"Thirty-six hours?" he looked at her.

"Yes."

Realizing she was being brutally honest, he had to do the same. "I thought you'd conceived." Never breaking eye contact, he saw the confusion enter her eyes.

"Why would you think that?"

"I didn't start taking the Ollali juice until last night."

"What?"

"I have no excuse. I just didn't think of it. It was irresponsible of me."

"You thought I was pregnant; that's why you told me about your wife."

"Past wife."

"Whatever. You thought I'd lie to you."

"No!" Urgently he framed her face. "I wanted you to know I'd accept the child."

"You would accept a child from me," she pulled her face away, "because you'd forgotten to take the Ollali juice?" Her tone was as icy as her eyes had become.

William commanded a Battle Star, five battleships, and seven thousand men. He was known for his sharp mind and level-headedness. But a six-foot woman had him tripping over his words.

"No!" he looked to make sure Tori was still sleeping. "Damn it, Cassandra, I haven't been able to think of anything else since I realized my mistake."

"Mistake," she repeated quietly.

He shook his head, ran his fingers through his hair, "Shut up and let me finish. When I first realized you might have conceived I was angry, at myself, not you. It's my responsibility to protect you. Mine. And I didn't, you're my life mate and I didn't protect you. Then I realized I wanted the child. I wanted you to have conceived, for you to have my child, our child." He framed her face. "I know this is fast, especially for you where everything is new. I'm sorry I forced you to tell me what was wrong. I thought it might have been because I didn't protect you. I couldn't handle that, Cassandra. I just found you," he gently kissed the tears running down her cheeks, "Don't cry, please don't cry."

Cassandra found his mouth, sinking into a kiss. This man, she thought, continually amazed her. "William," she broke off the kiss, "I'd accept your child, proudly, willingly." She met his dark violet eyes. "But I'm glad I haven't conceived. Can you understand that?"

"Yes," he rested his forehead on hers. "It's too soon, there's too much going on. Our time will come, Cassandra. We'll take our time."

"Really, you can be patient?" she smiled at him.

"If I work really hard at it."

Cassandra rushed to the bathroom for a third time, causing William's heart to ache. Getting up he went to her comm center to program in some lines. He was still there when she came back out.

"Come here," he held out his hand. Taking it he pulled her into his lap. "I've programmed in my private lines. This," he pointed, "will get my private line in both the Ready Room and our quarters." At her look he repeated, "It's our quarters, Cassandra, that's how I think of them. And this," he indicated another button, "is my private line on the Bridge."

"William, you don't… "

The angry look he gave her effectively stopped her. "Yes, I do. It should have been done long ago." Cassandra's tired body relaxed against his. "Now that you can get in touch, I need to leave so you can rest." Walking to the hatch he asked one more time, "Are you sure there's nothing I can do to help?"

She raised tired eyes to him, "I just need time."

"I will see you tomorrow." Giving her one last kiss he opened the hatch, "Secure the door," he ordered.

∞ ∞ ∞ ∞ ∞

"So what do you think? Do we need to go over anything again?" Cassandra asked Tori as she sat back from the console.

"No, I think I've got it."

"You're sure?"

"Yeah, can I get ready for school now?"

"Sure, Javiera is going to walk you. Is that okay?"

"You're still not feeling good are you, Aunt Cassie?" Tori looked at her.

"By tonight I'll be fine, don't worry. I've been going through this for years now, sweetie," Cassandra reassured her niece. "You'd better hurry. Hutu will be here soon with lunch then Javiera will pick you up."

As Tori hustled off, Cassandra shut down the Regulian language program. All in all, it had been a good morning. While she wasn't feeling great, she wasn't quite as fatigued as last night. Once Tori left she was going to have to sit down and give some serious thought to what William said last night. Rising to answer the door, Cassandra called Tori.

"Hutu's here."

Opening the hatch Cassandra found he was not alone. Backing up she let William and Hutu enter. Hutu placed the plates on the low table in front of the couch removing the covers he checked the dishes then left. Tori skipped out of the bathroom.

"Hi, Admiral."

"Hi, Tori, you look ready for class."

"Yeah," she smiled at him. "Javiera is going to walk me." Sitting on the floor across from the couch she started to eat. "Is she going to walk me back too, Aunt Cassie?"

"I'll come get you," Cassandra told her as she and William sat on the couch.

"Eat," William told her as he started on his.

"We finished the program, Admiral," Tori informed him.

"Really?"

"Yeah! Now when I have the dream, I'll know what they're saying and can tell you."

"That's good."

"Yeah," hearing the knocking at the hatch Tori jumped up, "that's Javiera." Cassandra walked to the hatch with Tori, opened it to a smiling Javiera.

"Well, you look a little better today." Turning her attention to Tori she asked, "Ready to go?"

"Yes."

"Then let's go. Do you want me to bring her back?"

"No, I think by then the walk will do me good."

"Okay, bye."

"Bye, Aunt Cassie."

"Bye, Tori." Securing the hatch she returned to sit sideways on the couch watching William. He looked at her.

"I didn't think I'd see you until tonight."

"I wanted to see how you were doing." Tucking a piece of hair behind her ear, he rested his hand on her leg. "You seem better. How'd you sleep?"

"Pretty good. I slept on the couch so I wouldn't wake up Tori." She saw his eyes harden. "I'd have done the same if I were in your quarters."

"Our quarters," he corrected.

"How long until you need to get back?" she changed the subject. He looked at his wrist unit.

"I have some time."

"Good." Holding his hand, she stood leading him to the bed. "I was going to take advantage of Tori being gone by sneaking in a nap." She kicked off her shoes and knelt on the bed to face him, "But since you're here, I'll just take advantage of you instead."

Putting her arms around his neck she stretched up to kiss him. His response was instantaneous, gripping her waist he found only bare skin causing him to groan against her lips.

"Cassandra, you're killing me here," running his hands up her back he pulled her close caressing her skin.

"Sorry," kissing his neck she smiled.

Tipping her face up he saw the smile, "I don't think you are."

With a small squeal, she found herself on her back, her hands above her head caught by one of his. With a devilish gleam in his eyes, he ran his fingers along her side causing her to giggle.

"William, stop!" Twisting she tried to avoid him causing William to throw a leg over her hips and watched the laughter in her bright blue eyes start to recede being replaced by desire. His touch turned to a caress as he captured her mouth for a breath-stealing kiss.

"William," she groaned, struggling to get her hands free as his other hand moved to envelop her breast. Releasing her hands, he pulled her closer.

"Cassandra," he murmured in a tight voice, "I need to go."

Breathing heavily, she met his gaze. "This wasn't such a good idea, huh?"

"Great idea, bad timing," he eased away to sit on the side of the bed and looked at her. He still saw fatigue in her eyes. "Take that nap. You'll feel better." As he stood to leave, Cassandra caught his hand rubbing her thumb across his knuckles. "What?"

She wanted to tell him to be safe, but it seemed silly. "Nothing," she let her hand drop. Making sure the door was secure, he headed to the Bridge.

∞ ∞ ∞ ∞ ∞

Several hours later Cassandra woke, looked at the time and jumped out of bed. Pausing, she realized all her symptoms were gone. "Wow, twenty-four hours; Grams was right again." In the shower she cleaned up, then headed out the door to get Tori.

∞ ∞ ∞ ∞ ∞

On the Bridge, the Admiral was discussing with Quinn the defensive strategy he wanted to use when docked at the Rodham space station.

"Admiral, an urgent call from Communications."

"Put it through. This is Zafar."

"Admiral, we've just decoded a Regulian ship-to-ship transmission."

"What does it say?"

"It doesn't say anything, Sir. It's just numbers."

"Give them to me NOW!" As the transmission was relayed, William started shouting orders.

"BATTLE STATIONS! ALERT STATUS ONE! ALL FIGHTERS TO THEIR PLANES! ALERT ALL BATTLESHIPS OF INCOMING FIRE!" The numbers were the coordinates of the Fleet's present location.

∞ ∞ ∞ ∞ ∞

"So how are you feeling?" Cassandra asked as she and Tori were heading back to their quarters.

"Not too bad. So can I go all day tomorrow?"

"I don't see why not. After all…"

"Battle Stations! Alert Status One! All Fighters to their planes! Incoming fire!" The page resounded through the Battle Star.

"Crap! Come on, Tori! Run!" Reaching their quarters, Cassandra secured the hatch.

"Aunt Cassie?"

"It's okay, Tori. The Admiral's in charge. We just need to stay out of the way." She hoped her voice was convincing. "What do you want to do while we wait for the all-clear? Should we practice our Regulian?"

"Okay." As they talked in Regulian, the battle raged.

∞ ∞ ∞ ∞ ∞

"Tell the Talon and Judgment to close in around the Sentinel, they are having trouble maneuvering," the Admiral ordered, bracing himself as the Retribution took a small hit.

"Damage."

"Minimal, Sir."

"Let's keep it that way," he ordered.

"Falco, I want the location of the Regulian's closest ship relayed to the Conviction. I want them to concentrate their fire on it. Take it out!"

"Yes, Sir!"

As the battle raged, William had to force himself to not think about Cassandra and Tori. He had to trust she would keep them safe. So would he.

Over an hour later it was over. William's strategy of concentrating fire on one of the Regulian ships had paid off with its destruction and the remaining ships withdrew.

"I want status reports on the entire Fleet. Quinn, I want Communications to go back over the last twenty-four hours of transmissions to see what they missed. Find out who missed it. How the fuck did they get our location? They know where we're going now! We stay on Alert Status One! DAMN!"

∞ ∞ ∞ ∞ ∞

Several hours later there was a knock on Cassandra's hatch door. It was Hutu with dinner.

"Hutu, thank you, we could have gone to the mess."

"No, ma'am. The Admiral wouldn't have liked that." As he checked the plates, he gave a smile to Victoria.

"So you're feeling better?"

"Yes, hopefully tomorrow I can go to class for the whole day. If there is class."

"Oh, there will be. There's been very little damage and the Regulians have left. Don't worry, little one, the Admiral knows how to protect what's his." This made Victoria smile as she sat down to eat. Cassandra walked with him to the door.

"What's the real status, Hutu?" she asked in a quiet voice. Hutu looked at Victoria.

"The Sentinel was badly hit and may have to be abandoned. The rest of the Fleet is fine."

"The Admiral?" she had to ask.

"Fine, going to have a long night," Hutu paused. "Might ease his mind if he heard the two of you were okay. He's on the Bridge." Turning, Hutu left and Cassandra secured the door.

"So how is your food tonight?"

"Good. Do you think Hutu knows how to make a grilled cheese?"

"I don't know. We'll have to figure out how to explain it to him. Then we'll see."

"Okay."

"Time for a shower," Cassandra told her after the meal.

"But it's early."

"I want you rested for tomorrow, otherwise half a day."

"Okay, okay." As Tori closed the bathroom door, Cassandra went to the communications console. Was Hutu right? Did William want to hear from her? If the situation were reversed…damn right, she would.

Putting on the headset she pushed the button to the Bridge.

"Get me the damage report on the Bounty, Quinn," William looked with irritation as his console rang again until he realized it was his private line. Putting on his headset he pushed the connecting button.

"Zafar."

"Hi, it's me, I know you're busy. I just wanted to let you know we're fine," he closed his eyes for a moment. That little fear in the back of his mind was relieved.

"Thanks. I needed to know that."

"You're okay?" she had to ask.

"Not a scratch."

"Good. I'll let you go then. See you tomorrow?"

"Count on it!" Removing the headset, William turned around to find Falco standing in his doorway.

"What is it, Falco?"

"Sir, the damage report on the Bounty."

He held out his hand with a raised eyebrow, "The report, Falco!"

"Sir? Oh sorry, Sir!" Handing him the report she left. That damn woman. Calling the Admiral like that, distracting him, and interfering with his command! She had to be stopped! Smiling, Falco knew just what to do.

Chapter Eleven

Hutu was right. There were classes the next morning and Tori was determined to go.

"You're sure?" Cassandra asked for the third time as they were walking to class.

"Yes, Aunt Cassandra! What else would we do? Sit in our quarters?"

"Good point. Okay, see you after class."

As Cassandra wondered what she was going to do with her day, she found herself in front of William's hatch. Deciding she could read one of William's books, she opened the hatch. Securing it she headed into his private quarters. Going through the connecting door she realized the shower was running. William's here. After a moment of indecision, she pulled off her boots then headed to the bathroom, stripping as she went.

Bracing his arms against the wall, William plunged his head into the brutally hot spray trying to wash away a night without sleep. The Fleet was secure, the Sentinel saved, but there was still the matter of how the Regulians discovered their location. As his tired muscles started to relax, he felt the caress of small hands moving slowly down his slick back, across his tensed flanks, and around to gently cup his manhood. "Cassandra…" he groaned. As her hands continued their exploration, they moved up his well-defined abdomen and massive chest, her mouth busily exploring his back. Turning in her arms, her mouth continued its quest across his chest to capture a taut, flat nipple while her hands flowed down exploring his haunches.

Any fatigue William had vanished. His life mate's obvious desire erasing it. Running his hands through her hair he tipped her head back stunned by the depth of desire he found in her eyes. It arrowed straight to his belly causing him to lift her for a kiss that she quickly controlled.

Cassandra was in flames. The feel of William beneath her hands and the knowledge that he was unharmed had released something within her, something basic and raw that she hadn't thought herself capable of. Her tongue plunged, sparring with his before entwining around it as her legs wrapped around his waist.

William was quickly losing control as she assaulted his senses from every angle; he soaked in the passion she was pouring over him. Using her hair, he pulled her mouth away to attack her neck. With a deep groan, she pulled him closer.

Bracing her against the wall, William angled her back farther allowing him a clear path to lick her breasts. Taking one into his mouth, he suckled fiercely and felt her legs start to tremble around him.

"William!" Cassandra cried out as he gave the same attention to her other breast. "Please, William, please," she begged as she felt him at her entrance.

William raised his head to find her desperate blue eyes flooded with passion and staring into his. He watched them widen, flash, then lose focus as he unhurriedly entered her, torturing them both.

She couldn't breathe as he slowly filled her. Here was what she'd needed her entire life. Him. The knowledge caused her to lose any remaining control she had. Her body tightened around William's as he set a frantic pace.

"Cassandra!" William exclaimed slapping an arm against the wall while wrapping the other around her hips to keep them upright, her need overtaking them both. Her scream echoed off the shower walls as a violent orgasm racked her body triggering William's own release.

Minutes passed with the only sounds being heavy breathing and running water. When Cassandra lowered her legs, William pushed off the wall letting her wet body slide down his until her feet reached the floor. Cupping her head with his hands, he watched her eyes start to focus again, knowing the second her mind reengaged. It was a powerful thing to know that he could make this woman unable to think.

"That was much better timing," he told her huskily.

Cassandra's eyes widened for a moment before she grinned at him, "I think I have to agree."

Shutting off the water he reached for the towels; handing her one she started to dry her hair. William, in the meantime, took it upon himself to dry her body, starting with her shoulders he worked his way down. When her breathing began to change, William looked up at her, a gleam in his eye.

"William…" was all she could manage as she placed a balancing hand on his shoulder. As he continued down her leg, she felt his muscles tense under her hand.

"Cassandra? What's this?" his tone was rigid.

"What?" Concerned at his tone, she looked down to where he was drying her right leg. "Oh that's just my birthmark," she said unconcernedly. Still holding her leg, he looked up at her.

"Your what?"

"Birthmark." When he didn't reply she tried to explain further. "It was there when I was born."

"I know what a birthmark is, Cassandra!" William rose testily, she was somewhat taken aback by his sudden change of mood. Taking the towel from his hands, she wrapped it around her body suddenly feeling the need to cover herself.

"I don't understand why you're so upset about it."

"Why haven't I seen it before now?" he demanded turning to get his own towel.

"I don't know!" His attitude was starting to irritate her. It was just a mark for God's sake. "Maybe you haven't looked?" Turning she left the bathroom, William followed close behind.

"Why didn't you tell me?"

"Why would I? Did you tell me about yours?" She picked up the trail of clothes she'd left on her way to the shower.

"Mine?" William's frown was puzzled.

"The one on your right forearm that looks like an arrow." William looked at his right arm, at the Imperial mark he'd always carried.

"I've never hidden mine," he shot back.

"Neither have I! It's hardly my fault you've never bothered to look!" Cassandra had had enough. She'd be damned if she were going to have an argument in only a towel. Dropping it, she pulled on her shirt.

"It's important, Cassandra," going to his closet William pulled on a pair of pants. "When did you first discover the birthmark?"

By this time, Cassandra had her pants on and was working on her socks. "There is no 'when did you first discover the birthmark,' William," she retorted giving him an exasperated look. "I was 'born' with it. All Qwes woman are born with it. It's just a fact of life!" With her boots on, she stood.

"Tori doesn't have one," William yanked on a shirt. He'd seen her legs in Medical when she'd been poisoned, a poison that had been meant for Cassandra.

"Of course she doesn't! She's not Qwes," Cassandra replied like he was a slow pupil.

"What do you mean she's not Qwes, she's your niece?"

"She's my brother's daughter," Cassandra responded as if it were perfectly clear. William was becoming worried, but he needed to hear her say it.

"So?"

She took a deep breath, "Qwes is the maternal side of the family, the women's side. I don't know what you call it on Carina. I have the mark, my mother had the mark, and her mother had the mark, and so on and so on. It only directly passes from mother to daughter. A son's daughter is not in the direct line."

"Your grandmother had this birthmark?" William persisted.

"Yes!" Cassandra suddenly realized William was in full Admiral-mode as he approached her, and for once she was a little intimidated.

"Sit down, Cassandra, we need to talk," he said as he led her to the couch.

"What is the big deal? It's just a birthmark!" she responded in exasperation.

"On Carina, birthmarks are a very 'big deal.' They denote lineage; which House you descend from; if you are in line to rule one day." William watched Cassandra closely to see if any of this was familiar to her.

"The birthmark on my arm denotes that I am from the House of Protection, the Arrow is our symbol. There is another 'marker' for descendants of the royal families, eye color. The House of Protection's is violet."

Cassandra was listening avidly trying to understand what William was telling her. "So you and Lucas descend from the Royal Family of the House of Protection. That seems fitting for who you are."

"That's not what I'm trying to tell you. There are four other Houses, each with their own symbols. One is the House of Knowledge," he paused watching her closely, "their birthmark is a tower on the inside of the right calf. They have a vast capacity to learn." Cassandra's eyes widened slightly. "The eye color of the Royal Family is sapphire blue." William could see Cassandra's mind racing.

"So you think that because of some birthmark and eye color that I'm a descendant of some Royal Family on Carina. That's ridiculous, William." Agitated, she surged off the couch to pace the room.

"The House of Protection is also called the Arm of Carina." Cassandra looked at him, waiting. "The House of Knowledge is known as the Light of Carina." Immediately, William saw the stricken look come into her eyes.

"The Glitter Man told Tori she wouldn't take his Light," she whispered. William decided he needed to tell her about the transmissions.

"Right after the destruction of Earth, we intercepted a Regulian transmission. It said:

`'Imperial Light still shining. Believe being protected. Will continue the search. If unable to obtain, will destroy. Agreement will then be honored.'`

"It was sent somewhere from deep within Carinian space. We haven't been able to pinpoint the location."

Cassandra's mind was racing, working through everything. There had been a thread implanted in Victoria, something they could track. Why hadn't they just taken her when they had her?

Tori said the Glitter Man checked her hands and feet. Looking for something, a birthmark, Tori didn't have one.

They were trying to find the one with the birthmark.

Her.

William watched as she assimilated all the information, running theories, drawing conclusions. He knew by her very stillness the minute she realized what it meant.

"They were looking for me," she said emotionlessly, "with Victoria, with the attack on Earth."

"That's what I believe."

"When they finally found me, you were there. So since they couldn't obtain, they destroyed," she continued, not moving from where she stood.

"Yes," he pressed wanting her to understand. "They want you, Cassandra. They are willing to sacrifice anyone and anything that gets in their way."

"The way they did Earth."

"Yes, the way they did Earth." Standing, he moved to take her in his arms. As he did, she moved out of reach walking toward the connecting door. With a deep sigh, he followed expecting to find her in his Ready Room. Entering all he found was an open hatch.

"Fuck!" Returning to his quarters, he pulled on his boots as he realized he'd made a major miscalculation. In his need to make her understand that she was in danger, he hadn't considered how she would take knowing an entire planet had been destroyed to get to her! Nearly her whole family! Fuck! He knew her capacity for caring, for believing she should be able to solve every problem. If he had stopped thinking like an Admiral for one fucking minute and thought like a life mate he'd have known she'd react this way.

Leaving his quarters, William hurried after her. The look on his face had everyone moving to the side. When the Admiral was on the war path, no one wanted to be in his way.

∞ ∞ ∞ ∞ ∞

Catching up with her as she approached her hatch, William found she'd already deactivated the lock and was starting to push the hatch open. He was not sure once she was in her quarters if she'd talk to him.

"Cassandra!" he barked out, harsher than he intended, causing the crewmen walking toward her to freeze.

With her hand on the hatch, she saw the crewmen freeze. She just wanted to get inside and shut everything out so she could be alone with her thoughts. But she couldn't bring herself to ignore William in front of his crew. Taking a deep breath, she stepped away from the now partially open hatch.

"Admiral," it was as far as she got before the world exploded throwing her into the dark.

William watched in horror as the corridor exploded sending shrapnel everywhere. Cassandra was thrown down the corridor and into the bulkhead where she fell unconscious to the floor. The crewmen were blown back down the corridor. Alarms sounded as he rushed to her side.

The seconds it took William to get to her felt like a lifetime. He knelt down and pressed unsteady fingers to her neck, closing his eyes in relief as he felt a pulse. The relief was short-lived as he saw blood seeping from under her head.

∞ ∞ ∞ ∞ ∞

"Admiral! Are you hurt?" Bliant rushed to his side.

"It's Cassandra, Bliant."

Bliant heard the fear in the Admiral's voice. He'd watched the relationship develop between them over the past few weeks. He knew there was a strong bond. "Admiral, you have to stand aside so I can check her." When he didn't immediately move Bliant tried again. "Admiral! I can't help her unless you move!"

William stood quickly and moved to the side watching as Bliant ran his skilled hands across Cassandra's body checking for injuries.

Over his shoulder, Bliant shouted to the approaching medical team, "I need a stretcher over here. Stat!" He looked up at the Admiral. "She's got numerous lacerations from shrapnel, some deeply embedded. Mostly on her left side, surprisingly though, no broken bones. The head injury seems superficial, but I won't know for sure until I get her back to Medical. She's stable." Bliant turned back to his patient. William stepped further back as the medical team moved in with the stretcher.

"Admiral!" William turned to find Quinn at his side.

"I want a security detail with the stretcher, Quinn."

"Yes, Sir."

"Get one sent to the class where Victoria is. Tell them to wait for Lucas. Contact Lucas. Tell him what's happened. He'll be in charge of Victoria's protection." He watched as the medical personnel carefully positioned Cassandra so as not to further aggravate the embedded shrapnel. When they started to move her, he turned back to Quinn.

"You're in charge here, Quinn. Get me some answers! I'm in Medical."

Cassandra's room filled with medical personnel as she was moved from the stretcher to a bed. Dozens of hands started checking and hooking up machines.

"Stop!" William ordered, freezing everyone.

"Admiral, we don't have time for this."

"Everyone OUT! NOW! Except you, Bliant," the personnel looked at Bliant. At his nod, they left the room.

"You are to remain outside this door," William ordered the security detail. "No one gets in here unless I clear them. Is that understood?"

"Yes, Sir!"

"Dismissed!"

"Admiral," Bliant tried again.

"This is the second attempt on her life, Bliant. You know that. Until I know who is to blame, no one touches her but you! Is that understood?"

Bliant finally realized the Admiral's concern. "Surely you don't suspect one of my people."

"I'm not taking any chances. You said she's stable. Can you handle her injuries?"

Bliant looked at the extent of the damage to Cassandra's left side. "Yes, I can handle it. But understand this, Admiral," Bliant turned fierce eyes to William, "if for any reason I feel she's in jeopardy, I will call in any personnel I deem necessary. Is that understood?"

"Yes."

"Okay then, since you've just become my assistant, lose the jacket. We need to cut these clothes off her so I can see the full extent of the damage. There is a blanket in the closet behind you, get it. We'll start at her feet and work our way up, covering her as we go. I don't want her going into shock." Working together, the two men started cutting off Cassandra's clothes.

∞ ∞ ∞ ∞ ∞

Lucas was stunned as he listened to Quinn. How the fuck had a bomb been planted in Cassandra and Victoria's quarters? What if Victoria had been there?

"You've sent a security team?" he demanded.

"Yes. They'll stand guard until you arrive," Quinn confirmed.

"Victoria is going to want to know how Cassandra is."

"All I know is Bliant said she's stable. From what I could see she took a lot of shrapnel to the left side and back. She had turned, taken a few steps away from the hatch before it blew. Otherwise…" Quinn trailed off.

"But she's stable," Lucas persisted.

"Yes. Your father is in Medical with her."

"Good. He'll have her secure. I'll do the same with Victoria. He put you in charge of the investigation?"

"Yes."

"Let me know what you find out," Lucas ordered as he disconnected. He sounded very much like the Admiral in Quinn's mind.

∞ ∞ ∞ ∞ ∞

All Cassandra saw was darkness. Were her eyes even open? She wasn't sure. She felt nothing. Was she supposed to be able to feel? What are feelings? The dark seemed to seep into her until she was the dark. There was something, something she needed to…she lost the thought. She was floating in the dark, it wasn't unpleasant. Maybe she'd just stay floating.

Something was trying to get her attention. Turning her head, she could see a very dim light. "So far away," she thought turning away. But something made her look back. The light was brighter and closer now. She was curious and stood up. Had she been sitting all this time? She walked toward the light.

The closer she got the brighter it was, but it didn't hurt her eyes. The dark started to fade. There was movement in the light, but she couldn't tell what it was. The closer it got, a shape seemed to be forming, emerging from the light. It looked so familiar, but why? Cassandra stopped and watched as the figure approached. "Grams?" she whispered.

"Hello, Cassie," the blue eyes that met hers were just as she remembered.

"Grams, I don't understand."

"We decided that I should be the one to talk to you."

"We?" Cassandra asked then realized other figures were emerging behind her grandmother. As she looked, she recognized them all, all the Qwes women, including her mother.

"Mom…" her mother smiled at her.

"Yes, she's here, but she had such a short time with you, she felt I should be the one."

"The one to what?" Cassandra returned her eyes to her Grams.

"Lead you from the dark. You are part of the Light, Cassandra…You don't belong in the dark. Now you must decide which light you will be a part of."

"Which one?" Cassandra looked around. "Grams this is the only light."

"That's the dark, trying to take it away. You have another light, Cassie. You need to decide whether to return to it or stay with us. It is your choice."

Cassandra looked from her grandmother and to all who came before her. One was standing slightly ahead of the others.

"Sabah," she whispered.

"Yes, Sabah is here, she was the First."

Sabah's beauty alone would make her stand out with her long black hair and deep, sapphire blue eyes. But she towered over the other women, easily 6'7". When their eyes met, Cassandra felt like she had forgotten something. It was there, just outside her grasp. The intensity in Sabah's eyes seemed to be telling her she needed to remember. When Sabah looked down, Cassandra's gaze followed stopping on Sabah's birthmark. It was a Tower of Light, the same as Cassandra's, but Sabah's glowed white with rays of color shooting out of it in blue, red, amber, green, and violet.

"Grams, tell me what to do," Cassandra looked into her grandmother's eyes, "I don't want to lose you again."

Grams reached into the gray to gently touch Cassandra's arm. "You've never lost me, Cassandra. I've always been there. All of us have in your dreams. But in this, only you can decide."

∞ ∞ ∞ ∞ ∞

"Something's wrong!" William told Bliant as he was removing the last of the shrapnel from Cassandra's back. All the color was draining out of her face, "She's not breathing!"

Bliant rolled Cassandra onto her back checking her pulse; rushing to the cabinet he retrieved the resuscitator.

William leaned over her, gripping her face. "Cassandra!" he called, "Damn it, Cassandra! Come back! I'm not letting go!" Bliant found him immovable as he tried to push him aside.

"Cassandra!"

∞ ∞ ∞ ∞ ∞

At Grams' touch, Cassandra could feel the love of all those who had come before. She shared their joys, sorrows, and life experiences. She'd come home. She smiled as she looked at her Grams, ready to go with her when something flashed behind her.

She saw another light. Small, dim at first, but it quickly grew so large and bright it hurt her eyes. There was something calling from the light. Something she could almost hear, straining she didn't realize she had pulled away from Grams' hand.

"I'm not letting go!"

"William!" It all came pouring back into her. William, how could she have forgotten William?

"Grams?" Cassandra turned to see their light was already fading.

"You've made your choice, Cassie. We'll see each other again," she said as they all faded away.

"Cassandra!"

She turned and ran to William's light.

∞ ∞ ∞ ∞ ∞

"Admiral," Bliant started to call for help when Cassandra's body suddenly arched off the bed; her body taking a long-deprived breath. Her eyes flew open searching until they found William.

"William," she whispered. Bliant stood rooted in place.

"I'm here, Cassandra," he rested his forehead against hers. "I'm here. Rest, I've got you."

As she drifted off to sleep, Bliant slowly returned the resuscitator to the cabinet. Returning to his patient, he realized he had just witnessed the real strength of love.

"Admiral, I would like to treat her head wound now." William was standing beside Cassandra holding her hand. "I need to get around you."

While William stepped aside, he refused to relinquish Cassandra's hand, reminding Bliant of Cassandra with Tori. Examining the wound, he was pleased to find it was only superficial and easily closed.

Bliant stepped back to allow the Admiral in and stretched the tired muscles of his back. It had been a long time since he'd done all the work himself. Going to the chart he wrote down what happened or at least what he could explain.

"What's her condition?" Bliant looked up to find himself under the Admiral's scrutiny.

"She's very lucky. The head wound was just a laceration. I don't expect her to have even a minor concussion. No broken bones, which is a testament to just how strong hers are. The shrapnel did some damage but hit no vital organs. She'll be bruised and sore for a while, and have a few small scars. She got off lucky."

"Lucky!" the Admiral snarled at him.

"Yes, Admiral, lucky!" Bliant stared him down. "If she'd been standing in the direct line of that blast we wouldn't have been bringing her to Medical!"

Paling, the Admiral looked back to Cassandra. "She isn't in any pain?"

"No. I'm giving her pain medication through her port," Bliant explained as he walked over to check her hand. "It might make her feel a little light-headed, but that should be all. Admiral," Bliant waited until their eyes met, "she's going to be fine." Bliant saw a flash of relief before it was gone. Pulling a gown out of a drawer, Bliant put it on her making her as comfortable as he could.

"When will she wake up again?"

"That I don't know." Bliant walked into his office and gave the Admiral some privacy.

∞ ∞ ∞ ∞ ∞

"Has anyone approached the hatch?" Lucas demanded of the guards.

"No, Sir, no one."

"Wait here," Lucas took a deep breath and relaxed his face into a smile. He didn't want to scare Tori. Opening the hatch, his eyes immediately searched for her. Finding her safe, he closed the hatch before walking to the Educator and explaining in a low voice there'd been an accident and that he was here to collect Victoria.

Turning, he found Victoria had gathered up her things and was walking toward the hatch. Once there she stopped, waiting for him.

She said nothing as Lucas opened the hatch and stepped out in front of her. Once in the corridor, Lucas scooped her up into his arms.

"Go!" he ordered. With a guard in front and back, they headed to the last place anyone would look for Victoria, Lucas' quarters.

Once inside, Lucas secured the hatch and put her down.

"What happened to Aunt Cassie?" she demanded. Surprise flashed through Lucas' eyes.

"Victoria… "

"Something's happened or you wouldn't have come to get me. If it weren't to her, then she would have come! Tell me!" Victoria was starting to become very upset.

"Calm down, baby."

"I'm not a BABY!" Lucas closed his eyes.

"I know you're not. Look there was an explosion," Lucas stared into Tori's eyes, "Cassandra was hurt. She's in Medical. She's stable."

"Where was the explosion?"

"Tori, it doesn't matter." Lucas didn't want to tell her.

"Where?"

"Your quarters," Lucas couldn't believe he was telling a nine-cycle all this.

"It's the same as the poison," Tori whispered.

"What?"

"The poison, it was meant for Aunt Cassie, not me. So was this, it's the same person." Lucas was shocked, he hadn't thought of that.

"I want to see Aunt Cassie," Tori demanded.

"I'm not sure that's such a good idea, Victoria." Tori moved to the hatch to disconnect the locks, "What do you think you're doing?"

"I'm going to go see my aunt!!! If you won't take me then, I'll go by myself!" Lucas caught a glimpse of the independent woman his life mate would become. He wasn't sure if he liked it or not.

"Fine, we'll go, but if I say we're gone for any reason, any reason at all, you will give me no argument! Is that understood?"

"FINE!" Tori shouted. Picking her up, Lucas opened the hatch. "I can walk you know."

"Not fast enough," Lucas shot back. "We're going to Medical, no one stops us, is that understood?" Lucas ordered the guards, "Let's go."

Chapter Twelve

William looked at the small bruised hand in his. Only three hours ago it had been holding him in the shower, caressing him, loving him. Now it was still, so still. He'd nearly lost her. He knew that. Here in this room she nearly slipped away, his life mate. He sat on the edge of the bed and gently kissed her palm, letting his tears fall.

Cassandra's eyes opened to the feel of William's tears silently falling into her palm. Gently she moved her thumb to wipe one away. His eyes shot to hers, "Cassandra... "

Looking around she was suddenly confused, "William?"

"Shhh…you're fine."

"What… "

"There was an explosion," it was all he could get out.

"Victoria?" trying to sit up she sucked in a quick breath.

"Fine! She's okay, Cassandra. She's with Lucas," William eased her back down.

"Bliant!" William yelled turning his head toward the doctor's door. Rushing in, Bliant saw she was awake.

"Well, look who's back," he efficiently checked her vitals. Pleased, he smiled down at her. "How are you feeling?"

Cassandra tried to take an inventory of her body. But she couldn't get her mind to focus. "I don't know," she said in a hoarse voice, "I feel like I'm floating."

"That's the pain medication. Let's get you some water." Bliant was about to call for it when he caught the Admiral's eye. "I'll be right back."

Cassandra looked at William. She could see the fatigue and worry in his eyes even if no one else could. Lifting her left hand to touch him she felt a sharp pain.

"Ouch!" Looking down she saw the port, "what?"

"Careful," William said gently putting her hand back on her stomach, "you don't want to rip it out."

"Says who?" she frowned at it.

"Me. You need it."

Trying to stop the floating feeling she focused on William. "How long?" she asked weakly.

"Just a couple hours."

"Hours..." Cassandra felt like she'd been gone days. "Do you know who?" She watched his face tighten.

"No."

Bliant reentered the room with the water.

"Here we go. Let's raise you up so you can take a sip." Moving the bed into more of a sitting position, Bliant put the cup to her mouth tipping it ever so slightly. As she drank, he looked at the Admiral acknowledging that he'd filled the glass himself. When she leaned back, some of the water spilled onto her front.

"You know I really need to introduce you guys to the concept of straws," she murmured as she closed her eyes. Turning her head, she looked at William trying to ask her question.

"Why are you here?"

Bliant quietly left them alone.

"What!?!" William was stunned by the question. "Cassandra…"

Hearing the hurt in his voice, seeing the pain in his eyes, she realized she hadn't said it right. Gripping his hand, she looked into his eyes.

"William…Shit, I can't get my thoughts straight! It's worse than the dark."

"Cassandra, you're not making sense."

"Do you think I don't know that!" she demanded then closed her eyes as the room started to tilt.

"I'm getting Bliant."

"No. Please, William…I need you to hear me." Her eyes stared into his, "The way I heard you…in the dark."

William went completely still.

"I heard you…I was…not lost…just nothing… I was nothing…then I heard you…calling my name…saying you weren't letting go…" Cassandra's eyes pleaded with his. "I wasn't about to leave you. You are my Light. When I was in the dark, your light showed me the way home."

Resting an elbow on either side of her head, William leaned down to capture her lips in a gentle kiss. "Cassandra," he rose up to look into her eyes, "you humble me. There is no light in my world if you're not in it. I'll never let go. You are mine and I am yours." Kissing her again, he pulled her as close as he dared.

"William?" she whispered.

"Yes?"

"Am I dying?"

"What! No!"

"So I'm going to be okay?"

"Yes! Cassandra, yes!"

"Then why are you here?"

"What?"

Putting a hand on his chest she continued, "You are Admiral William Hale Zafar, Commander of the Battle Star Retribution and five battleships. If I'm going to be fine, then the Fleet needs its Admiral."

"Cassandra…" he didn't know what to say.

"I'm safe, William," she rubbed her hand over his heart. "I'm not going anywhere. You were here when I needed you, now you're needed elsewhere. Go. Do what only you can do, be the Admiral."

After staring at her for a long moment, he gently kissed her. Rising from the bed, he found his jacket and pulled it on with all the responsibility that it carried. Cassandra watched the transformation, realizing it made her love him even more.

"There are guards posted outside the door," he told her buttoning up his jacket.

"I expected as much."

"No one comes in except Bliant, Cassandra."

"And Tori and Lucas," she countermanded.

"Yes, I'll let the guards know. I want you to rest," he was in full Admiral-mode now, causing Cassandra to give him a little grin.

"What!" he demanded.

"Have I ever told you…how sexy you look when you're in full Admiral-mode?"

William was speechless. Walking over his eyes blazed, leaning down he gave her the kiss he'd been desperate to give since she'd come back to him. "You will rest," he ordered huskily, "I'll be back later."

"I'll be here."

"Bliant!" the Admiral called out. Bliant came out of his office, "My orders still stand. No one other than you, Lucas and Victoria are allowed in this room. Understood?"

"Yes, Admiral."

Giving Cassandra one more long look the Admiral left the room. The doors had no more than closed when Cassandra turned her attention to Bliant.

"So, Doc, it's time to get this thing out of my hand."

"Cassandra, it is only pain medication."

"And I don't want it. I think I have the right to say what goes into my body!" She could feel the fogginess coming back.

"The Admiral wants it."

"Then stick it in him!" she fired back. Exasperated she started to try to remove it herself.

"Stop! You'll hurt yourself." Bliant pulling her hand away made her realize just how weak she was.

"Bliant, I'll make a deal with you."

"What?" he asked suspiciously.

"If you take that out of my hand, I promise to let you know if I feel I need something for the pain." Bliant raised an eyebrow. "I swear. I really don't like to be in pain but this stuff you're giving me, I like it even less. Oh and I'll deal with the Admiral too."

"Now that I can believe," Bliant said as he removed the port. "Now you will rest or I will give you something that will knock you out."

"That's not going to be a problem," Cassandra mumbled. She was already half asleep.

Stubborn woman, Bliant thought to himself. She and the Admiral were perfect for one another. He left her room to check on the other crewmen who had been injured in the explosion.

∞ ∞ ∞ ∞ ∞

"Put me down, Lucas," Tori demanded as they entered Medical. She'd seen the guards and knew where her aunt was, "Let me down!"

"In a minute, we need to make sure it's okay with Bliant." As they approached Bliant, Victoria wiggled out of Lucas' arms.

"Victoria!" he called. When she charged for the room, a guard grabbed her shoulder.

"Let go of me!" Tori yelled and kicked him in the shin. When the guard let go, she spun around him and ran through the door. The yell had Lucas rushing to her aid, only to find she'd taken care of it herself. When the guard turned to go after her, Lucas grabbed his arm.

"I wouldn't if I were you," his tone steely, "She's already beaten you once, don't go for twice." As the guard hesitated, Lucas continued, "The Admiral's already cleared us. You let her in, that's all you have to write up in your report." Slapping the guard on the back, Lucas followed her.

Once inside he wished he'd stayed out. Victoria was sobbing in Cassandra's arms. Lucas turned as Bliant entered the room. His pained expression made Lucas assume he didn't like crying little girls either.

"Shhh, baby, it's okay, I'm fine. Calm down," Cassandra put a hand under Victoria's chin raising her eyes to hers. "I wouldn't lie to you. I'm going to be fine. But if you keep crying like that then I have to assume I look pretty awful."

"No, not awful," Victoria sniffled, "but pretty banged up."

Hearing a snort from the door, Cassandra saw Lucas and Bliant.

"Out of the mouths of babes," Bliant said as he approached the two. "Hey, Victoria, do you mind if I have you sit on the bed beside your aunt?" When Victoria moved, Lucas noticed how pale Cassandra was, and that Bliant was worried about her.

"But I am fine. Dr. Bliant fixed me up just like he did you."

"Where's the Admiral?" Tori scanned the room.

"He had to get back to being the Admiral."

"He left you alone?"

"No, Tori, I wasn't alone. Dr. Bliant was here and there are guards outside. I'm fine even if I am 'pretty banged up.'"

"He was outside," Tori pointed her finger at Bliant.

"Just for a minute, there were other people hurt in the explosion, Tori. He has to help them too."

"You're sure you're okay?" Tori's voice was quivering.

"The Admiral wouldn't have left if I weren't. Would he?" she threw the question at her.

"No, he wouldn't leave you," she acknowledged.

"So there you have it," Cassandra changed the subject. "Lucas picked you up from class with no problems?"

"No problems," Lucas answered.

"Good," she could feel her energy draining and she needed to talk to Lucas, in private. "So, Tori, since you're here, I think Dr. Bliant should check your throat. You said it's been sore for the last few days."

"Aunt Cassie…" Victoria rolled her eyes.

"It shouldn't take him more than ten to fifteen minutes," Cassandra said as she stared down Bliant. "He can do it in his office, right over there," she pointed.

Bliant looked at Cassandra, understanding she wanted Victoria out of the room.

"Come on, young lady, let's take a look at that throat."

Cassandra looked at Lucas as the door closed.

"That was slick, really slick," Lucas said with admiration.

"Whatever," she said dismissively. "Tell me what you know. Do they know who's behind all this?"

"Cassandra, calm down. Last I knew the investigation was still in the preliminary stages. They won't know anything for a while."

She looked to the door then to Lucas. "I know who it is."

"What!"

"Keep it down! You heard me. These attacks are directed at me. You know that, William knows that. It's just taken me this long to figure that out. The poison was on my plate, the bomb in my quarters. That others got hurt by it didn't seem to matter to the person doing this. This was directed at me," Cassandra had to stop to catch her breath.

"Let me get Bliant," Lucas demanded concerned.

"No, I'm fine. There is only one person on this ship that hates me, Lucas, only one that would like to see me dead."

"Who?"

"Senior Chief Falco."

"Falco? Why the hell would Falco want you dead? How could you have pissed her off?"

Cassandra replied simply, "Your father."

"What?" Lucas had to sit down. "That's ridiculous, there's no basis for it." He saw her look, "The Admiral doesn't mess around on tour."

Cassandra raised an eyebrow.

"Present company excluded. And he especially doesn't with one of his crew!"

"What if it wasn't on tour and she wasn't one of his crew?"

Lucas surged out of the chair to pace. "You're telling me," he began...

"That she thinks she has a prior claim." She moved, trying to get comfortable. "We've had a couple run-ins."

"Dad knows about them?"

"The first one, yes, I didn't bother him after."

"Why?"

"Because he doesn't think it's possible, and I didn't realize I was the target until today. I was focused on the Regulians."

"We all were."

"Well I'm not now, and I know I'm right."

"Cassandra… "

"Don't believe me. I don't care, but check it out. Check it out, Lucas, because it could have been Victoria opening that hatch. Have you thought about that?" Cassandra knew she had played dirty but didn't care.

"I was supposed to get the poison, but Victoria did instead. Are you willing to give her a third shot? If I'm wrong then there's no harm done, but if I'm right…"

Bliant's office door opened and he frowned as he looked at Cassandra. Lucas turned to the two, a forced smile on his face.

"Come on, Victoria, time to go."

"But..."

"Victoria, Cassie's tired and needs her rest. Give her a kiss and we'll go."

Cassandra was somewhat shocked when Tori obeyed. Stretching across the bed, Tori gave her aunt a kiss.

"I'll see you tomorrow okay?" There was worry in her green eyes.

"You bet!"

Lucas picked Tori up then looked at Cassandra, "I'll look into it." Turning they left.

Bliant turned back to Cassandra intending to give her a piece of his mind only to discover she was asleep.

"Stubborn woman," he muttered.

∞ ∞ ∞ ∞ ∞

William surveyed the damage to Cassandra's quarters. The blast embedded metal shards into the wall across the hall but none within the room.

"A directional blast," William looked to Quinn for confirmation.

"Yes, directed out," toward Cassandra, it didn't need to be said. The interior of the room was blackened. The bed where just the day before he and Cassandra had had a playful moment was destroyed.

"DC-48?"

"That's what the preliminary tests show," Quinn replied.

"Do we know where it came from?"

"The Master at Arms is checking all inventories as we speak, Admiral."

"Good. It looks like you've got it under control. I'll be on the Bridge." William took one last look at the wall across from Cassandra's quarters, his jaw clenched, then headed to his Command Center on the Bridge.

Hours later that is where Quinn found him, reading communication reports. "Will, what are you still doing here? It's 2100. You're pushing 40 hours without sleep. Go get some."

"Engage the privacy screen, Colonel," Quinn raised an eyebrow as he lowered the screen. The Admiral never lowered the screen. It was his way of showing his trust in his crew.

"What do you have to report?" The Admiral demanded with tired but determined eyes.

"The Master at Arms can account for all DC-48 in all bunkers except one."

"Which one?"

"J 342. It was damaged in the battle at Earth. The Master can account for all DC-48 from there stored in other bunkers, but that amount doesn't total all that was in the bunker."

"By how much?"

"Two pounds," Quinn informed him and waited for the explosion, he wasn't disappointed.

"TWO FUCKING POUNDS OF DC-48 GO MISSING AND I'M NOT NOTIFIED!!" William was enraged.

"Admiral, there was a fire in the bunker. There was evidence some DC-48 burned. There was no reason to think any had been removed," Quinn waited.

DC-48 was an effective explosive, pliable and stable. Extremes of heat or cold caused it to break down into its base elements which were totally non-lethal. But add a detonator and it was deadly.

"How many detonators are we missing?" All detonators were stored in a separate location.

"Two from Bunker D 345, some of J 342's. DC-48 is stored there too," Quinn had anticipated the Admiral's question.

"Have you checked what personnel moved it?" The Admiral asked closing his eyes as he rubbed the back of his neck.

"Working on it as we speak. There's something else you should know, Admiral."

William waited.

"We were able to access the security log for Cassandra's door. We went back twenty-four hours from the explosion. It shows that at 1145 yesterday the hatch was opened internally."

"Hutu and myself with lunch."

"It was secured internally at 1150."

"Hutu leaving."

"Opened and secured, internally at 1230."

"Victoria leaving for class with Javiera."

"Opened and secured, internally 1250."

"Me leaving."

"Opened internally, secured externally, 1545."

"Cassandra going to get Victoria from class."

"Opened externally, secured internally 1615."

"Returning from class and the attack."

"Opened internally 1800, secured internally 1805.

"Hutu with dinner."

"Opened internally, closed externally at 0845 today."

"Cassandra taking Victoria to class."

"Opened externally 0915," Quinn looked at the Admiral and waited.

"That wasn't Cassandra."

"You're sure?"

"Yes, she arrived in my quarters shortly after 0900. Check my logs."

"I have," Quinn told him. "Her security code was used externally on your door at 0904, securing it internally at the same time. The door was opened internally with her code at 1007. The door wasn't secured until 1009 externally, your code. Cassandra's door was unsecured externally at 1013, with the explosion occurring less than a minute later."

William was silent as he thought about how close he had come to losing her, another minute in his quarters, him not calling out to her, small things.

"Will?" Quinn's concerned voice snapped him back.

"Why did you check my logs?"

Quinn looked at him then answered. "Her security was compromised. I needed to make sure yours wasn't."

"Her security is keyed entry. Mine is thumbprint-voice."

"I know, but I needed to verify it. Your quarters were externally secured yesterday at 0745, your code. It was unsecured, externally at 0855 today, secured internally, your code. No one else entered your quarters between those times. The door remained secured since you secured it at 1009 today. Your quarters are secure."

"Thank you, Quinn."

"Not a problem, Admiral. Now if I may suggest, again, go get some sleep. You're no good to anyone, including Cassandra, this way."

William looked at his longtime friend, "Colonel, I believe I'll retire for the night. Notify me if necessary."

"Yes, Sir."

Lifting the privacy shield, William exited the Bridge heading for Medical.

∞ ∞ ∞ ∞ ∞

Entering Medical, William saw the guards were at their posts.

"Report."

"Sir, with the exception of Dr. Bliant no one has entered or attempted to enter the room except Lt. Zafar and the girl."

"Victoria," the Admiral replied.

"Sir?"

"In your report, her name is Victoria Chamberlain," the Admiral told him.

"Sir, yes, Sir."

Entering the room he found the lights on low and Cassandra asleep. As the door closed, she opened her eyes. She saw him and gave him a soft smile. "There you are." As he approached, she could sense his fatigue. "You haven't slept," she accused as he leaned over giving her a gentle kiss.

"Busy being the Admiral," he murmured against her lips. Cassandra put a hand to his face, caressing his cheek with her thumb.

"Even an Admiral needs to sleep."

"I'll get some." Easing back he turned his head to kiss her palm. Pausing he looked at her hand.

"Where's your port," he demanded.

"Out," she retorted back.

William's tolerance was gone. Turning away from her he threw open the door to Medical and bellowed, "Bliant! Now!"

Bliant, who had been dealing with another patient, feared the worst. At a run, he entered Cassandra's room. Seeing her sitting up in bed he turned to the Admiral.

"What the hell's wrong?"

"Where's her port? Why aren't you giving her pain medication?"

Cassandra answered for Bliant, "Because I don't want it! It's my body. It's my choice," she swung her legs over the side of the bed.

"What do you think you're doing?" he demanded.

"If I'm going to have an argument with you then I'm at least going to be sitting up!" Twisting she continued, "None of this…" she couldn't finish as a shooting pain stole her breath. She braced herself against William's chest to stay upright. Seeing her pale, he grabbed her forearms.

"Bliant!" William started, but the doctor was already there turning the lights on full en route to the side of the bed to see her back.

"Cassandra, what is it," Bliant asked.

"I…I think you missed one," was all she could get out as she rested her head on William's chest.

Bliant opened the back of her gown…he could see what he had missed without the help of the scanner; the inflamed red line was easily visible.

"Cassandra, I want you to remain perfectly still." Bliant met William's eyes. William nodded understanding. Bliant went to a drawer and pulled out what he needed. Running the scanner above her skin, he found it was worse than he'd feared. Spraying the deadener on her skin he told her.

"I need you to stay still, Cassandra. I've numbed the area the best I can, but this is in deep. It's going to hurt, really hurt." Bliant looked at the Admiral.

"Just do it," she panted, "I can't catch my breath."

"Look at me, Cassandra, look at me," William ordered as Bliant started.

Looking up she saw the face of the man she loved, who she trusted more than anyone else. Suddenly it felt like a red-hot poker was being shoved in her back. She started to close her eyes.

"No, Cassandra, look at me. Come on, baby, there you go," he said as their eyes met, the pain in hers tearing him apart. "Breathe now, Cassandra, just small little breaths. Come on, you can do it."

The pain intensified, but she didn't move, her eyes locked with William's. He could feel her fingers digging into his chest, but she moved nothing else.

"William," she whispered when she couldn't take any more.

"Hang on, baby. Come on, just a few seconds more. Bliant!"

"Got it!" Bliant said, withdrawing a three-inch metal splinter from Cassandra's back. Cassandra sagged against William, her face damp with sweat. Cupping the back of her head, William kept her close as his expression bored into Bliant.

"What the hell is that? How did you miss that! If she'd been on the pain meds…"

Bliant cut him off, "I missed it, Admiral! I admit it. But if she'd still been on the pain medication, she wouldn't have felt it until it punctured her lung!" Bliant whirled away disgusted with himself.

"William?" Cassandra's weak voice was muffled against his chest.

"I'm here, baby."

"I want to go home."

"Cassandra, you're hurt," he started...

"There's nothing that can be done here that can't be done at home. Please, William? I want to sleep in our bed. I sleep better with you." William looked to Bliant.

"She's right, Admiral, what she needs now is rest. There are no more splinters, I ran a full scan. She'll rest better where she's most comfortable, I'd say that's with you."

William took a moment to think, "Cassandra, I'm going to lay you down here for just a minute okay? I need to arrange a few things." Laying her gently on her side, the Admiral went to the communications console.

"Marat, I want four more guards in Medical in five minutes, full gear." Turning to Bliant he continued, "You will give her something that will take the edge off of her pain. She's going to get bumped around. I won't have her hurting unnecessarily."

"She has the right to decide," Bliant stood firm.

"We'll ask her."

Cassandra had been quietly listening to the two men.

"Cassandra," Dr. Bliant started.

"I wouldn't mind some pain medication, Doc. I told you I'd tell you. But please not the stuff from before. I don't like floating. Just knock it back some."

"I can do that."

William waited as Bliant administered the medication. Quickly some of the pain eased from Cassandra's eyes, easing the grip around his heart.

"I'll need something to wrap her up in," the Admiral told Bliant. At the knock on the door, he leaned down, "I'll be right back."

Exiting the room, the Admiral addressed the six men. "You will be executing the Arrow of Protection. No one gets through! We will proceed from this room directly to my quarters. Two guards will be posted outside; arms on full stun. You have two minutes."

Reentering the room, Bliant had a large blanket ready for the Admiral.

"Cassandra," he gently whispered in her ear causing her to open her eyes, "let's get you up so we can go home."

"Really?"

"Yeah," wrapping the blanket around her shoulders, he helped her stand up letting the rest of it fall to the floor. Securing her in the blanket, William bent down to scoop her up in his arms.

"You okay?" he watched her carefully.

"As long as I'm with you," she leaned her head against his chest, closing her eyes.

"Let's go then."

Bliant opened the door. The security detail formed around the Admiral as he headed out.

The corridors of the Retribution were buzzing as the detail passed. The Admiral was carrying the Earth woman, with Arrow Protection. There had been some talk but now…Falco was one of the crew who saw the detail. She had to decide what she was going to do next.

∞ ∞ ∞ ∞ ∞

Quinn was just lying down in bed when his console rang. "Fuck!" he sat up to answer.

"Tar!"

"Colonel, this is Lucas Zafar."

"Do you know what time it is, Lieutenant?"

"Late. I had to be sure Tori was asleep."

"How is she?" Quinn was developing a soft spot for the girl.

"Holding up well, Sir. Sir, I think I have a very credible lead on who is doing this."

"What!" Quinn was out of bed.

"Sir…"

"Can the 'sir' stuff, Lucas, what have you got?" Filling Quinn in on Cassandra's suspicions, Quinn interrupted him.

"You're going on another woman's what? Intuition? Damn, Lucas…"

"I trust Cassie's intuition, Quinn, but I did some digging. Did you know that Falco has an E1 explosive rating?"

"What!"

"Specializing in directional blasts."

Quinn was quiet.

"I know it was a directional blast, Quinn. Hell, the entire ship knows. I've gone as far as I can, called in every IOU that I've got. Now I need help."

"Why me, why not your old man?" Quinn asked and was greeted by silence.

"Quinn, you've been my father's friend longer than I've been alive. Fuck, you're my Second Father! If this information is right, if all this is because Falco is jealous of Cassandra, and my father dismissed Cassandra's concerns, how is he going to react? We both know what will happen if he finds her first. Are you willing to take that chance?"

"Damn, Lucas, you argue like your old man. What do you need from me?"

Quinn listened, finding he agreed with what he wanted. "I'll let you know when I'm ready."

Chapter Thirteen

Entering their quarters, William secured the door before carrying Cassandra into their private quarters gently laying her on the bed.

"Cassandra, you're home," saying it out loud filled him with a satisfaction he couldn't explain. Opening exhausted eyes, she gave him a soft smile. "Sleep."

"What about you?" she started to sit up.

"No, lie back down. I have a few things I need to take care of. I'll just be in my Ready Room. It won't take long…Rest," kissing her he turned the lights low and left the room.

Cassandra watched him go with concerned eyes. He needed sleep too. Catching a smell, she wrinkled her nose.

"What is that?" Working her way out of the blanket she realized it was her. "Okay, time for a shower."

Carefully she put her feet on the floor. Standing slowly, she took an inventory. She felt a little like a human pin cushion, but it was more irritating than painful. Whether it was the medication or not, she didn't know. Her right arm was starting to show colorful bruising. Pulling her gown aside she found her entire right side blooming with bruises, "Just great," she mumbled quietly.

The thought of a hot shower had taken root, she really wanted one. Leaving the blanket behind she carefully walked into the bathroom, her abused muscles protested. With a shower the only thing on her mind, Cassandra entered and saw herself for the first time.

"Shit," raising a hand she touched her cheek where there was yet another bruise blooming. Her hair was a tangled mess with debris falling out as she tried to run her fingers through it. Her fingers came out smudged with soot.

"Oh, definitely in need of a shower." Slowly she worked the gown off, turned on the shower and stepped in.

∞ ∞ ∞ ∞ ∞

In his Ready Room, William leaned his head back on his chair. He'd gotten her home safely. Home. She'd called it home. With everything that had happened today, all the mistakes he'd made, she trusted him, felt he was her home. He needed to do a better job of taking care of her. Rubbing his eyes, he sat up, starting now. Turning to his communications console he started making calls.

"Tar."

"Quinn, I wanted to let you know that I've moved Cassandra from Medical to our quarters. I've also posted a security detail outside." The 'our quarters' wasn't missed by Quinn.

"She's doing okay then?"

"She's beaten to hell, Quinn!" William's rage was finally breaking free.

"Will…"

"She stopped breathing."

"But she's okay now," Quinn persisted. He knew his friend, knew he was blaming himself. Even without knowing what he and Lucas suspected.

"Yeah, she's sleeping."

"That's what you need to be doing. Get some rest, Will. There's nothing else you can do tonight. We'll get started on it again tomorrow."

"There's no new evidence?"

"No, Will. No new evidence. Go to bed," Quinn disconnected before William could ask anything else. He hadn't lied. He had no new evidence yet.

William knew Quinn was right, but he had one more call to make before he could sleep next to Cassandra. He waited as the call connected.

"Zafar."

William heard a hushed voice, "Lucas?"

"Dad? What's wrong?"

"Nothing, just checking in with you, is Victoria sleeping?"

"Yeah, she's been down a couple hours now. How's Cassie?"

"She's sleeping. That's what I wanted to tell you. I brought her home tonight."

"Home?" Lucas questioned before he thought about it.

"Yes. Home, with me, our quarters, because that's what it is now, Lucas, our quarters. After what happened today I'm not letting her stay anywhere else."

Lucas could tell he was building up a head of steam. "Dad, stop. You just caught me off guard. What about Victoria?"

"I'm working on that. I just wanted to let you know where to bring her tomorrow. Cassandra's going to want to see her. I don't know if going to class is advisable yet with us still unable to identify who's doing this."

"I agree," Lucas stated, trying to decide if he should tell him of Cassandra's suspensions. "Dad, there's something…"

"Fuck!" William interrupted him, he heard the shower turn on.

"What's wrong?"

"She's getting in the shower!" William disconnected.

Lucas took off his headset grinning. Yeah, Cassandra could handle his father.

William stormed into the bathroom ready to tear into Cassandra and stopped cold at what he saw. With her back to him, William got his first complete look at her injuries top to bottom. On one side, she was all scrapes and lacerations, closed by Bliant but still healing. On the other, one massive bruise. He took a deep breath, removed his clothes and joined his life mate in the shower, "Cassandra," he said quietly, "what are you doing?"

She wasn't surprised to hear William's voice. Deep down she'd known he would come when he heard the water. What did surprise her was that he wasn't angry. Turning slowly, she brought her hands up to his chest.

"I'm taking a shower."

"I can see that. Why aren't you in bed?"

"Because, not only am I filthy, I stink."

"Cassandra…" William could only sigh.

She raised a hand to his cheek. "William, yes I'm tired, yes I'm sore. I admit it. But I'm not going to lie down in our bed covered with whatever I'm covered in. My hair is full of soot and dirt. I just wanted to get clean." He found he couldn't argue with her.

"Come on then, let's get you cleaned up." Reaching behind her he filled a hand with shampoo and started massaging it into her scalp.

"William…I didn't mean…"

"Shhh…lean on me," as she did his hands worked their way through her hair, his touch soothing her. After rinsing her hair, he gently washed the rest of her body.

"You know," Cassandra told him as he washed her breasts, "if you were doing that any other time I'd be all over you."

"I'll hold you to that." Reaching her ankles, he stared at the birthmark that had started the argument this morning. It seemed darker. He'd have to ask her about it, but not now. Now he needed to get his mate to bed.

He turned off the water and reached for a towel to dry her hair, just as he'd done earlier that day. But things weren't the same now. Finishing, he leaned down to carry her to bed.

"William, I can walk," she protested in a weak voice, telling William just how far she'd pushed herself.

"Not tonight."

"I don't want to sleep unless you're with me."

"You couldn't keep me away." Turning off the lights he slid in next to her, making sure he was between her and the door. Secured or not he was taking no chances. Cassandra immediately found him in the dark, wrapping an arm around him.

"Easy, you don't want to lie on your side."

"You know you're right," she murmured in a sleepy voice. Pulling herself up onto his chest her body fell lax. Exhaustion caught up with William. He put his arms carefully around her and he followed her into sleep.

∞ ∞ ∞ ∞ ∞

Waking with Cassandra in his arms, William was content. The ringing of his console had him stretching trying not to wake her.

"Zafar."

"Dad, it's Lucas. Victoria had a dream last night. She said she needs to talk to you and Cassandra, something about understanding Regulian."

William ran a careful hand up and down Cassandra's back as he felt her waking. "Give us about twenty minutes then head over." Disconnecting, he looked down to find sleepy blue eyes watching him, "How are you feeling?"

"Who was on the comm?" she asked instead of answering.

"Lucas. He and Tori are coming over. She had the dream."

"What!" Cassandra winced as she leapt up without thinking, "Damn."

"Cassandra..."

"I'm okay, just stiff and sore." Looking into concerned eyes she leaned down, gave him a soft kiss, and said, "Good morning."

William wasn't that easily distracted. Easing her onto the bed he stood.

"I'm calling Bliant," he reached for his comm, "you need another shot." Ready for an argument she surprised him.

"That might not be a bad idea," she told him still lying on the bed.

After notifying Bliant, he called Hutu telling him to bring first meal for four, one being Tori.

"William," Cassandra slowly started to sit up.

"Take it easy," he gripped her elbows to help her.

"Trust me I am." Once she was sitting on the edge of the bed, William pulled the blanket around her. "William, I need something to wear."

"I'll find you something. You okay there?"

"Yeah," she admired his bare backside as he walked over to his closet to get her a shirt, pulling on pants he headed back. The man was built, she thought with a little smile. William raised a questioning eyebrow at the small smile on her face as he helped her into one of his shirts.

"Just admiring the view," she told him unable to meet his eyes as a blush crept up her neck. William found the blush captivating; that she could still be shy around him was amazing. Squatting down he tipped her chin up, looking into sheepish eyes.

"Glad you like it," he said causing her blush to deepen, but her eyes became mischievous.

"Oh trust me I did," a grin broke across her face. William rose at the buzzing at the hatch indicating Bliant's arrival. Going back to his closet, he pulled on a shirt.

"I'll be right back, stay put," he told her leaving the room.

Bliant entered the Admiral's Ready Room and waited as he secured the hatch. The Admiral appeared to have gotten some sleep.

"So how is she this morning?"

"Sore, she isn't even arguing about the medication," as he led him to the adjoining door.

"The day after is usually the worst. I'll check to make sure it's not anything more serious." Entering the private chambers, Bliant found Cassandra standing on the far side of the room next to the bed, wearing what was obviously one of the Admiral's shirts as it came down to her knees.

"You were supposed to stay sitting," William moved to her side.

"I'm not a damn dog." The look on his face told her he didn't understand. "Sorry, I just wanted to try to loosen up my muscles."

"Do you want to sit on the chair or couch?" Bliant broke the tension. Ignoring Bliant, Cassandra put a hand on William's forearm.

"Would you help me to the chair?" William's eyes locked on hers, "Please, William." Taking slow, small steps, he helped her to the closest chair. Easing down she breathed a sigh of relief.

"Thank you," she looked up at him with strained but grateful eyes. William stepped back, his jaw tense.

"She needs the shot, Bliant."

Bliant stepped around the Admiral. "So how are you feeling this morning?"

"Sore. More than I expected."

"You ready for another shot?"

"Yes, whatever you gave me last night. It helped without making me feel weird." Pulling out a pressure syringe he gave her the shot.

"I want to check your wounds." At the buzzing at the hatch, Cassandra looked at William.

"If that's Tori…"

"I'll keep her in the other room until Bliant is done." She flashed him a grateful smile. As he left, he closed the connecting door.

Checking to make sure there was no infection in the wounds Bliant continued to talk to her. "So you slept okay last night?"

"Yeah. I don't think I moved once I was asleep."

"You've had a shower."

"Yeah, it helped loosen up my muscles."

"No vision problems?"

"No."

Bliant checked her lungs. "Take a couple of deep breaths for me." When Cassandra obeyed, she winced. "Still really sore?"

"Yeah."

"Your right side absorbed the worst of the impact hitting the bulkhead. It's a deep contusion, and it's going to take time to heal. You need to not push yourself. When your body tells you it needs rest, take it. You'll heal faster."

"There's a lot going on right now…" she started only to be cut off.

"Right now you need to concentrate on getting better, let the Admiral handle the rest."

Cassandra just looked at Bliant, unsure of how to answer him, unaware he'd been contacted by Tar to dig into Falco's medical history.

"The Admiral's very good at his job, Cassandra. He'll find out who's doing this and it will be handled. But if he has to worry about you pushing yourself too hard it's going to distract him. Trust him."

"I've trusted him since the moment I met him. Nothing that's happened since has changed that." Looking at him she could see he was trying to make a point. "Why would you think it did?"

Bliant wasn't sure he should continue.

"You started this, Bliant, finish it," she ordered.

"You and Tori have both been injured while you've been under his protection, on his ship, by one of his crew. Some might start doubting his ability."

"A Carinian woman, you mean."

"Yes, especially with the Admiral being from the House of Protection. It will be a very serious concern for him." Bliant decided to get it all out there. "I've seen the two of you together. The bond you have. But you're still new to our ways and have ways of your own. I thought you should know how this is going to affect him." Listening to Bliant, Cassandra realized he knew of her suspicions.

"Lucas has talked to you."

"No, Tar. Lucas knows?"

"Yes."

"So everyone except the Admiral. He's not going to take that well."

"That's an understatement."

"He'll see it as me not trusting him that I went to Lucas instead of him, that's what you've been trying to tell me."

"Yes."

"Thanks for filling me in. You're right. There are things here I still don't understand." Moving to the edge of the chair she looked at Bliant, "Would you mind helping me up? I believe there is an impatient nine-year-old waiting for me." As she moved toward the door, Bliant was close by.

"How's the pain?"

"Better, I'm not as stiff."

"Good," Bliant opened the door, "remember what I said."

"I will." When Cassandra entered the Ready Room, William walked over to her, looking first at her then Bliant.

"She's healing well, just stiff and sore, she'll be that way for a while. You need to make sure she's not overdoing."

"She won't."

"Standing right here," Cassandra said looking at the two men. Stepping around them she saw Tori and Lucas sitting in front of William's desk. Smiling she moved toward her.

"Aunt Cassie!" Victoria started to get up when Lucas put a hand on her shoulder.

"Wait, Tori, let her sit down."

She sat in the chair next to her and opened her arms, "Come here, baby girl." Tori was immediately in her arms, William grimaced, knowing Cassandra's muscles were protesting.

"You're okay?" Victoria quizzed.

"Yes. Just a lot of bruises."

"Can I see?"

Cassandra smiled at her. "Maybe later."

At the buzzing at the hatch, Tori stood back up.

"That'll be Hutu with first meal," William told them.

∞ ∞ ∞ ∞ ∞

Hutu checked all the plates before turning to the Admiral. "Did you need anything else, Sir, something for the Doctor?"

"Nothing for me, Hutu, I need to get to Medical. Call if there are any problems," Bliant looked at Cassandra.

"Thanks, Bliant."

Picking up a couple of bowls, William gave one to Tori and the other to Cassandra.

"Eat," was all he said as Lucas brought one to him. William kept a close eye on Cassandra, making sure she ate all of it. When Lucas was finished, he removed the bowls then sat back down next to Tori.

"What's going on?" he asked.

"Victoria's been studying Regulian, so she might be able to remember what they were saying when they kidnapped her," the Admiral told Lucas. "Tori, what did you need to tell us?"

Tori looked first at William, then her aunt.

"I had the dream again last night, Aunt Cassie."

"Oh, Tori, I'm sorry I wasn't there," Cassandra started to move to her, but William's look kept her in her chair.

"It's okay, I wasn't scared this time. Well, maybe a little at first but then I remembered what you said. That I would know something they didn't want me to know, and you were right."

"What did you learn, Tori," the Admiral asked.

"The Glitter Man, he was mad! After he checked my hands and feet he told the ones I couldn't see that they were stupid, that I wasn't the Light. One in the dark argued back saying that they had followed his orders, that I was the one. That he would honor their agreement. The Glitter Man ordered them to get him the thread so he could put it in my arm telling them that this trip might not be a total loss. That maybe I could lead them to the Light. That's when he told me he would always be able to find me." As Tori said this to the Admiral, Cassandra realized that William had been right. The Regulians were looking for her. Meeting his eyes, she said nothing.

"They never called each other by name?" he asked.

Tori thought hard, "No."

William was disappointed that Tori hadn't discovered anything new but nothing was revealed on his face.

"You did well, Tori," the Admiral told her. "It's a very brave thing you did."

"It was?"

"Yes," he replied and Tori grinned at him.

Cassandra smiled at Tori. "The Admiral's right, Tori, you did a very brave thing. I'm really proud of you." Tori gave Cassandra a hug.

"Oh, there was this one other thing the Glitter Man said. He told the Regulians they would have to take me back because he needed to return to Messene before he was missed."

William, in the process of standing, froze.

"Messene? You're sure, Tori?" he demanded.

She nodded, "He said he couldn't go unseen much longer."

Sitting down, William leaned back in his chair to think.

"Tori, did I see your bag?" Cassandra distracted her.

"Yeah."

"Do you have some homework you need to do?"

"Some."

"Why don't you go into the other room and get started on it then." Tori looked at the three adults, then on a sigh agreed.

"Okay," picking up her bag she headed back.

"Oh, and close the door so we won't disturb you." As the connecting door closed, Cassandra turned to William.

"What's Messene?" she demanded.

"Dad, she couldn't have heard right."

"I think she did."

"Hello! Messene. What is it?" Cassandra demanded in a testy voice.

"It's a retreat on Goryn, used exclusively by the Royal Families and high-ranking officials, very private and secluded," Lucas informed her. William watched Cassandra.

"She got it wrong, Dad."

"I don't think she did," William said quietly watching Cassandra slowly rise and walk over to the painting of the setting suns. Lucas looked from his father to Cassandra.

"What's going on? What don't I know?" Before William could answer there was a buzzing at the hatch. Lucas opened it to Tar.

"Admiral…" Tar started. Seeing Cassandra, he paused.

"What is it, Quinn?"

"I have evidence on who I believe is attacking Cassandra."

Turning from the painting, she walked back to her chair and eased into it, watching Tar.

"Who," William demanded.

"Senior Chief Falco."

"What?" William looked to find Cassandra silently watching him. "What's your evidence, Colonel?"

"Falco has an E1 explosive rating specializing in directional blasts. While she moved out of the explosive branch six years ago, she's maintained her rating. Falco is also one of the crews who had access to bunker J 342. She helped move the explosive to D 345."

"What else?"

"I had Dr. Bliant look into her medical history. At first it looked clean, but he called a friend and discovered that she had been quietly removed from her last post, diagnosed with attachment issues," Quinn paused.

"Go on."

"She had 'attached' herself to Captain San during their last tour. She'd threatened his wife. San had her removed from his ship."

"Why was it kept quiet?" William demanded with a sinking feeling.

"It was believed that she and San had been intimate at one point. San didn't want his wife to know. She was quietly treated, prescribed Xyphrine."

William's jaw tightened, "How's she getting it?"

"It seems she was able to convince a doctor to let her have a two-year supply since she was going on tour."

"Idiot."

"Agreed."

"How'd you zero in on her?"

"After Lucas called…"

"Lucas?" Lucas found himself under the Admiral's intense stare. "Why would you be looking at Falco?"

Cassandra saved Lucas from answering, "I asked Lucas to look into Falco," she met his look head on. "Once I realized that I was the target, it was the only person who made sense."

"You went to Lucas."

Cassandra knew she was on tricky ground here, "I realized it yesterday in Medical. Lucas was there. I told him what I thought, asked him to look into it. If I was wrong, I didn't want to distract you from looking for the right person." Cassandra could tell William wasn't buying it.

"Why haven't you questioned her, Colonel?"

"Admiral, all the information we've gathered isn't proof. I want to get into her quarters, see what she's hiding. There's still some DC-48 unaccounted for and a detonator."

"Why haven't you?"

"During the investigation I discovered she has remote detection installed on her security panel."

"What's that?" Cassandra asked, feeling the sting of William's look.

Lucas finally answered, "It means she'll know as soon as anyone enters her quarters."

"Anywhere on the ship?" Cassandra's mind started to race.

"Yes."

"Would there be any reason she'd have to shut it off?"

Lucas looked at his father.

"She wouldn't chance it if my security screen were down on the Bridge. The security would trigger an alarm," the Admiral informed her.

"Then that's your answer," Cassandra stared William in the eye.

Quinn and Lucas looked at each other.

"It could work," Quinn finally broke the tense silence. "But she just came off a twelve-hour shift. She's off for the next twenty-four."

"I don't think we can wait that long," Lucas stated.

"What do you do if the on duty navigator gets sick?" Cassandra asked still looking at William.

"She still wouldn't be up," Quinn replied.

"Even if it's a personal request from the Admiral? That with all the crap going on he needs his most trusted navigator on duty?" The tension between William and Cassandra was growing. Both men noticed it.

"That could work. The Admiral only has to ask her to engage the security screen then we can go in," Quinn liked the plan.

"Anything else you'd like to add?" the Admiral asked in a cold voice.

"Many things, Admiral, but now isn't the time," Cassandra replied in a voice as cold as his.

"Get started making it happen, Colonel. Lucas, you need to take Victoria back to your quarters until this is over."

"No," Cassandra interrupted, "Victoria's safer here."

William said nothing for a moment. "Fine, Lucas you're with Quinn. Let me know when things are set. Dismissed."

As the two men left, William followed securing the hatch.

He turned and found Cassandra had risen to lean against the front of his desk. Saying nothing, he stopped in front of her, his violet eyes intense, staring into her unguarded blue ones, trying to find answers.

"You went to Lucas."

"I told you why."

"I can understand after everything that's happened."

"What is that supposed to mean?" William started to turn away, but Cassandra put a hand on his arm stopping him, both knowing he could have pulled away if he'd wanted to. "William…" Cassandra's eyes questioned.

"I haven't protected you very well. You had every right to turn to Lucas for help."

She realized Bliant was right.

"Why would you think that, William?" Cassandra framed his face with her hands. "You've done nothing but protect me. Me and Victoria."

"Right, she gets poisoned and you nearly get blown up."

"Neither of those is your fault! You couldn't have known they were going to happen. I've never doubted you!" she stretched to kiss him, but he pulled away.

"You didn't trust me, Cassandra, you should have told me about your concerns."

"I did!" she fired back. "That first night I told you. You didn't trust my instincts." She let her hands fall away at his rejection. "You didn't tell me you believed the poison was meant for me. You told Lucas, who else?" The shuttered look that came into Cassandra's eyes had William realizing he had hurt her. The fatigue in her voice reminding him that less than twenty-four hours ago she'd nearly died.

"Cassandra…"

"Who?" The sting of his rejection nearly stole her voice.

"Quinn, Hutu, Bliant."

"So everyone but me. You trusted everyone but me," her voice was flat and unemotional. "I'm not Salish, William. I haven't lied and deceived you. I've trusted you from the first moment on the Raptor. Everything that's happened since has only strengthened that trust for me, but then I'm just some stupid refugee," she used Falco's term as she turned to walk away.

William couldn't seem to move. Cassandra's words, what she said, as much as the tone told him how badly he'd hurt her.

He trusted her, still trusted her. His experience with his past wife wasn't influencing him.

Was it?

Didn't he keep looking for something she'd lied to him about? The way he did with her birthmark? Now Falco. Yesterday he'd nearly lost her. Today he was pushing her away. It was no wonder she told Lucas of her concerns.

Turning to follow her, he found she had stopped at the still closed connecting door. The pain revealed in her eyes staggered him.

"You should have let go, William. It would have been better for everyone." Entering what for less than a day she'd considered home, she closed the door.

On the other side, William couldn't breathe. It felt like his heart had been ripped out of his chest. Had he done that to her? Made her wish she hadn't returned to him? His life mate. Had his lack of trust in her destroyed what they were building? She'd accepted him from the very beginning. She'd been open and honest about what she felt even if it embarrassed her. Had he done the same without being pushed? He had to fix this.

Opening the connecting door, he found Tori sitting in a chair reading. She watched him with eyes much too old for such a young girl. Cassandra was lying on the couch with her eyes closed.

"Shhh..." Tori told him in a quiet voice, "Aunt Cassie's tired."

William squatted down next to the couch, taking in how pale her skin was, the bruising under her eyes that had nothing to do with the explosion. Caressing her cheek he tucked a strand behind her ear. Rising he went to the bed pulled off the blanket and gently covered her.

"Will you be okay here? I'm going to need to leave."

"Sure. Aunt Cassie and I, we take care of each other."

"You both do a good job too." Rising, William looked at the clock. "When you get hungry call Hutu, he'll bring you second meal."

"I'll have to wait until Aunt Cassie wakes up, I can't let him in."

He realized she was right and held out his hand, "Come on we'll take care of that." Leading her to his Ready Room console, William had her put her thumb on the security panel, "Say your full name."

"Victoria Lynn Chamberlain."

"There you go. Now you can let Hutu in. No one else, Tori."

"Okay," Tori watched him with those earnest eyes. "Admiral?"

"Yes."

"Aunt Cassie's hurt." Her voice wobbled. William sat down, setting her on his knees so he could look her in the eyes.

"I know she is, Tori. But she's going to get better. Her body just needs time to heal."

"That's not the only thing hurting her."

"I know that too."

"You're the Admiral. You're going to stop what's hurting her, aren't you? Aunt Cassie told me that's what you do. You make it safe so no one can hurt us, that I need to trust you like she does."

"You can trust me, Tori." William's voice was tight. "I'll make sure nothing else hurts her."

Tori's green eyes stared into his. "Okay," she put her arms around his neck and hugged him.

Hugging her back William closed his eyes. This was what Cassandra had given him, simple trust. No doubts, even when he'd given her cause. It was time he lived up to it. Setting Tori on her feet the Admiral stood up.

"You'd better go back to Cassandra. Remember what I said about only opening the hatch to Hutu. Okay?"

"Yes, Admiral."

Securing the hatch from the outside the Admiral nodded to the guards and headed to the Bridge. It was time to deal with this problem so he could come home and concentrate on the other one he'd created.

Entering the Bridge he found Falco at her post. Giving her a nod, he entered his Command Center and sat in his chair.

Quinn entered, "Here are today's reports, Admiral," Quinn stated. "We didn't contact you yet, Will," he said quietly.

"Did I ask your opinion, Colonel?" the Admiral announced in a loud voice. "When it's done, Quinn, get back here and get her out of my Command Center," William said in equally quiet voice. "If you don't have answers get off my Bridge!" the Admiral ordered.

"Yes, Sir!" Quinn left the Bridge.

"Falco!"

"Yes, Sir."

"My Command Center. Bring your charts!"

"Yes, Sir." Falco was feeling very smug. The Admiral had personally asked for her to come back on duty and now wanted her in the Command Center. Entering, she set down her charts.

"Engage the security screen, Falco," the Admiral ordered.

"Sir?"

"Engage the screen!" William turned away to allow her to disengage her remote detection device.

As the security system within the Admiral's Command Center recorded Falco's hand slipping into her pocket to disengage her detection system, Falco engaged the security screen.

The Admiral turned back around and while he was thinking, 'Let's play, bitch,' his face showed nothing.

"I want to see your charts for where the Fleet was twenty-four days ago. Where was the Regulian fleet?"

"Yes, Sir." As Falco arranged her charts, Tar and Lucas overrode her security.

"Ready, Sir." Falco showed the Admiral the locations moving closer to him. He didn't move away. Taking his time, William pretended to study the charts.

"Now twenty-two days ago," William allowed Falco to move even closer with her charts.

Chapter Fourteen

At first glance, Falco's quarters appeared normal. But closer inspection found nothing normal. A drawer in the bathroom revealed empty bottles labeled Xyphrine. Hidden under her pillow was the missing detonator. The DC-48 was found in her closet.

"None of this is hidden very well," Tar commented.

"I don't think she ever thought she'd be suspected," Lucas answered. "Let's go get the bitch!"

"Am I going to have a problem with you, Lucas?" Quinn asked. "I'm already contending with the Admiral."

"I'll be fine. But if he takes a swing at her I won't stop him."

"Then you're no help to me. Stay here. Make sure everything is done by the regs. We're going to nail this bitch to the wall."

The Colonel left taking several guards with him.

∞ ∞ ∞ ∞ ∞

"Admiral, here is the last set of charts you wanted. As you can see the Fleet was here," Falco pointed to a spot on the chart with one hand as she touched the Admiral with the other. There was a buzzing outside the security shield. Looking up, Falco saw Colonel Tar with several security guards outside the shield.

"Lower the shield, Falco."

"Excuse me, Sir?"

"Lower the shield."

"Yes, Sir."

"Quinn?"

"Senior Chief Falco, you are under arrest. You are charged with two counts of attempted murder and one count of sabotage of a Coalition vessel."

"What? William?" her eyes shot to him.

"Get her out of here," the Admiral's voice was icy.

As the guards tried to take her, she lunged for him. He simply stepped aside, letting her fall to the deck.

"You're mine! Mine! That bitch is dead!" she ranted as the guards picked her up.

Tar stiffened when the Admiral's eyes turned deadly. Stepping toward her, he told her in a dangerously quiet voice that had the guards stiffening,

"Come near my life mate again and you'll be the one dead. Tar! Get her out of here! NOW!"

"Yes, Sir." Relieved that the Admiral hadn't touched her, Quinn helped as the guards manhandled her out of the Command Center.

He turned to the Admiral, "You okay, Will?"

"I'll be in my quarters," the Admiral left without answering.

∞ ∞ ∞ ∞ ∞

Entering his Ready Room, William heard children's laughter. They had visitors. William took it as a good sign. Standing in the doorway he saw Tori and Amina sitting on the floor playing while Cassandra and Javiera sat on the couch talking. This was home. He was going to do whatever it took to keep it. Javiera was the first to see him.

"Admiral," she smiled.

Tori ran over to him. "So?"

William squatted down so they were at eye level. "Taken care of," he tapped her nose.

"Yes!" Tori said with a fist pump. "Did you hear, Aunt Cassie?"

William straightened to find Cassandra's flat blue eyes watching him.

"I sure did, sweetie, that's great," she forced herself to smile at Tori. Javiera was avidly watching the entire exchange. Cassandra's change in tone told her there was something major going on between the two.

"That is great," Javiera said. "How about if I take the girls to Deck F and let them run off some energy, then we'll have that makeup sleepover?" Both girls squealed as they hugged each other, jumping up and down.

"Javiera..." Cassandra started.

"You'll get more rest this way too," she pushed.

"That would be great, Javiera, thank you," William answered for Cassandra.

"Wonderful, so girls you ready?"

"Yes!"

Turning back to Cassandra, Javiera gave her a quick, careful hug. "Don't worry, everything will be okay. I'll get clothes for Tori to replace what was lost, it'll work out." Standing she looked at the Admiral, "I'll call before we come back."

"Bye, Aunt Cassie. I'll see you tomorrow." Tori gave her a quick hug and kiss.

"Bye, sweetie, have fun."

The room was silent once they were gone.

"Did you eat?" William asked breaking the silence.

"Yeah, Hutu already picked up the dishes," when Cassandra eased up from the couch William saw the bag.

"What's that?"

She looked down, "Javiera brought me some clothes."

William rubbed his neck in frustration. "I'm not doing many things right here, am I?" He watched her take a few stiff steps.

"You've had more important things to deal with than my clothes."

"Nothing's more important than you." William moved behind her. "Cassandra…"

"Is it safe for Tori to be without guards?" Cassandra turned, deciding it was time to face the situation. William looked into the deep sapphire blue eyes he loved that revealed none of her thoughts or feelings.

"Yes, I wouldn't have agreed if it wasn't."

She waited.

"You were right, from the very beginning, on everything. It was Falco, she had the empty Xyphrine bottles, the DC-48, the detonators. She's in the Brig. You don't have to worry about her. You and Victoria are safe."

"No one was hurt?" she couldn't help but ask.

"No, everyone is fine. Cassandra," William lifted a hand to her face, he needed to touch her. "Don't!" he exclaimed as she stepped back, causing her to freeze. "I am so sorry, Cassandra," William put his arms around her, gently pulling her stiff body close, kissing the top of her head, "I know I hurt you. That's the last thing I meant to do."

"It doesn't matter."

"Fuck that! It does! Please look at me," he tipped her chin up, the emotion he was finally able to see in her eyes tore him apart. "Cassandra, you're my life mate." Careful of her bruises he framed her face. "You are the most important thing in my life! I know I've been lousy showing it, in keeping you safe, you and Victoria. There's no excuse for it."

"William," she tried to stop him.

"No!" William's fingers tightened his eyes intense. "I need you to believe me, Cassandra, to believe *in* me again. I had no reason to attack you for going to Lucas. You had every right to protect yourself, I wasn't. Then to accuse you of not trusting me when I wasn't telling you everything you needed to know." Cassandra couldn't stand to see this proud, confident man doubting her belief in him, in himself. As her tears spilled onto his hands, his eyes filled with pain.

"Don't cry. Please don't cry," pulling her face into his chest he closed his eyes. How was he going to make this right?

Cassandra couldn't be this close to him, feeling his pain and not comfort him. No matter what had happened, what had been said, she loved him. She wrapped her arms around him and pulled him closer. Feeling her arms around him, William sucked in a sharp breath.

"Cassandra?" he whispered looking at her as she tipped her head up. Her eyes still flooded with tears, she carefully stretched up looking for his mouth. He lowered his head to find hers in a gentle meeting of lips.

"I've always believed in you, William, trusted you," her voice laced with tears as she eased out of his arms, "I've never stopped." Taking a few steps away she forced herself to finish, "But that's not enough, is it?" She looked him in the eye. "Life mate or not, you don't trust it, or me. Understandable when you think about it. It's not everyone who's responsible for the death of seven billion people."

"You're not responsible for that! Damn it, Cassandra! The Regulians are!"

"But you've never really trusted me, have you?" William could say nothing. "I didn't realize it until this morning. I was too wrapped up in you I guess," she shook her head. "I used to be smarter than that." Suddenly tired, she headed to the couch picking up the bag that Javiera brought.

"Is it okay if I use your shower?"

William found it hard to swallow, "Cassandra, it's our shower, you don't have to ask. This is your home."

"No," she gave him a sad look, "it's not." Walking into the bathroom she softly closed the door.

He was losing her…his life mate…She was right, he hadn't given her his full trust. Not like she'd given him. He'd allowed his experience with Salish to influence him. He'd never really forgiven her, Salish, for her lie or himself for not questioning her more before they'd joined. He loved his sons but had felt only responsibility for their mother.

Cassandra wouldn't tolerate being a responsibility. If anything that would piss her off. She was the strongest, most loving, demanding, opinionated, brave, and loyal woman he'd ever met. She was his life mate and despite her size, his equal. Was he really going to let another woman come between them? William was shocked to discover that that was exactly what he had done. First Salish, then Falco, protecting himself from being lied to again. Only Cassandra had never lied to him. 'Honesty, whether I like it or not.' That's what she wanted, but he'd never actually given it to her. It was time to start.

∞ ∞ ∞ ∞ ∞

Cassandra was tired; mind, body, and soul. Hoping the heat of the shower would give her some relief she stepped in. Closing her eyes, she let her mind go blank. Feeling William's gentle kiss on her shoulder, his large hands resting on her narrow hips she opened her eyes. The shower would provide no relief.

"I need you, Cassandra," William admitted next to her ear, "in every way possible, I need you." Turning her to face him he continued, "I need to ask something of you. Something I have no right to ask after everything I've done. But I'm asking just the same. Can you give me time? Time to show you that I believe in you, trust you, trust us? Everything has happened so fast. You wanted to talk, slow things down. Can you give us the time for that?" His eyes implored her. "Can you still believe in me, trust in me, and give me time to show you how much I love you? No doubts, no comparisons, just you and me. Honesty whether we like it or not?" William waited knowing the rest of his life depended on her answer.

Cassandra's turmoil was easy to read in her eyes. What was she supposed to do? Could she open herself back up to him? Risk being hurt by him again? Would she survive it? Would she survive without him? He said he loved her. Could she trust that? He only ever lied by omission. He wasn't the kind of man who would say I love you to a woman and not mean it.

She couldn't seem to resolve anything in her mind. She was battered and bruised, her senses too beaten to decide anything. Closing her eyes, she rested her forehead on his chest.

"I'm tired, so tired," with her voice quivering, William pulled her close finding it wasn't just her voice. Her entire body was starting to shake. She had pushed too far. Grabbing a towel, he quickly dried her before sweeping her up, carrying her to their bed.

"Rest, Cassandra," William covered her with a sheet. Pulling on a pair of bottoms he grabbed the blanket from the couch and wrapped it around her. As he sat next to her, he could see she was visibly shaking. Sliding in next to her he pulled her close trying to calm her.

"I'm here, Cassandra. I've got you. Rest, baby. Nothing has to be decided right now. I love you. Rest," William closed his eyes willing her to calm, ran a hand along her back and the shakes slowly ceased.

∞ ∞ ∞ ∞ ∞

Sitting on a cliff, Cassandra heard the crashing of the surf and watched in wonder at the setting of three suns and the brilliance of the colors. Turning her head, she saw Sabah sitting next to her.

"It's beautiful."

"Yes, it's one of the things I missed most about Carina."

"Do you regret it?"

Sabah turned away from the setting suns to look at her descendant. "Regret? Every important decision comes with some regret. Otherwise it wouldn't be important. The question you should be asking is, 'Did what I find make up for what I left behind?'"

"Did it?"

"I left behind my entire family. Everything I'd ever known. Everything I thought I was." Sabah looked into Cassandra's eyes, a reflection of her own. "What I found was myself. Who I really was. Who I was meant to be. The children I would never have had on Carina. With a man, I wouldn't have been allowed to love. He was my life mate. He sacrificed much because of me…for me. Many would say I gave more, but he gave all that he was. No one can give more than that."

"You didn't answer the question."

Sabah smiled at her, "We left behind what others demanded we be. What they tried to make us believe we must be. We found love, trust, and honesty even when we didn't like it. We listened to each other."

"So everything was perfect?"

"Hardly! We fought…We made up. My life mate was strong, opinionated, bull-headed, and would die for me…and I for him. But that didn't mean it was perfect. Perfect is…boring. We were imperfect, but we made a life together. A life I would and did sacrifice the setting suns for."

Cassandra looked back at the suns, "How did you know you were choosing the right path?"

"I didn't."

Cassandra's blue eyes pierced Sabah's.

"All I knew was I wouldn't give him up. He was worth any sacrifice, but I would never allow him to be one. They tried to convince me otherwise, including my life mate. Then one night I had a dream. I dreamed of the life I would have if I acquiesced. There was no joy, no laughter, not even pain. It was empty, dead like I would be without him even though I lived. So I rejected that life, choosing an uncertain one with him. I have no regrets. Will you be able to say the same?"

As the light from the setting suns began to fade, so did Sabah.

∞ ∞ ∞ ∞ ∞

Waking from the dream, Cassandra was still. What *did* she want? A perfect life…or one with William? A life full of joy, sacrifice, arguments, and trust? Where she knew he would never let go, would always be there for her? Would willingly die for her, as she would for him?

The mind that earlier couldn't think now saw everything clearly. There were still obstacles to overcome and discussions they needed to have. But her mind was clear. William was her Light and without him there was only darkness. He held on, she would do no less. She loved him and would sacrifice everything for him.

∞ ∞ ∞ ∞ ∞

The beating heart told her she was on William's chest; the warmth surrounding her, his arms. With her mind clear, she replayed what William asked her. That she give him time to prove he loved her. That she trust in him, believe in him until he proved he deserved it. Lifting her head she found him watching her intently.

"You need more rest, sleep."

"How long?"

"How long what?"

"Have I been asleep?"

"Eight hours," his eyes showed his concern. "You need more rest."

"I'm fine."

"You were shaking with exhaustion. It hasn't even been forty-eight hours since the bombing. You need more rest."

"You were trying to tell me something in the shower," she carefully pushed herself up on her elbows unconcerned about her nakedness.

"Asking…Asking you."

"Since when does the Admiral ask?" William's arms tensed around her but caused no pain.

"The Admiral wasn't in the shower with you."

"What were you asking me?"

William could sense something was different. He was not sure what it meant, but he'd promised honesty even if he didn't like the answer. "I was asking you to give me time to earn your trust, to show you your belief in me is justified, to show you just how much I love you."

"But those things aren't possible, William," he was told in a quiet voice and he felt his heart start to break. "You either trust someone or you don't. You either believe in them or you don't. You can't show someone you love them, you either do or you don't."

"I love you, Cassandra. I believe in you, I trust you with my life. But after everything I've done wrong, I don't expect you to believe or trust in me." He started to gently move her to his side.

"What have I done?" the pain in her voice stopped him, "to make you doubt me?"

"Nothing."

"To make you believe I'd lie to you."

"You never have."

"So why don't you trust my words?"

"Cassandra…"

With Sabah's words still echoing in her head, Cassandra went for what she wanted. "My mother died when I was nine. There was an accident. She survived for two weeks…I watched my dad suffer. Knowing he was losing his soul mate, trying to believe she would recover. I watched Grams, knowing she was losing her only daughter."

"Cassandra…"

"Please listen," she waited until he nodded. "As I watched them, I grieved." William saw the pain in her eyes. "But not for the reasons you think. I grieved that no man would ever love me like that. Would ever grieve for me like that; that I would never know the pain of losing a child. Because I'd never know the joy of having one. You see I knew then…at nine…that there was no soul mate for me on Earth. No one I'd want to have a child with. So I would have none."

"I'm your soul mate, Cassandra. I will give you all the children you want," William's voice was thick but firm.

"Why? You can't trust me. I could be like Salish…or Falco."

"No! Damn it, I know the difference…I know who and what you are."

"Are my words good enough for you, William? Or do you need me to prove myself to you?"

"You have nothing to prove to me."

"Then understand this, William. You have nothing to prove to me," she leaned forward to kiss him. "I love you," and she kissed him a little longer. "I have always trusted and believed in you." A longer kiss. "I'm not letting go," this time she sank into him, pressing her breasts against his chest and wrapping her arms around his neck.

Rolling her carefully onto her back, William broke off the kiss. Staring down into her incredibly blue eyes, he knew the gift he'd been given. He could see his future in her eyes…She was it.

"I love you, Cassandra. I will never break your trust. I believe in you, no matter what the odds. I'm never letting go." He leaned down and gave her a passionate but short kiss.

"I'm also going to make sure you take care of yourself, even if you don't like it." Rolling out of the bed, he headed to the comm center ordering up another meal.

"William, it's…What time is it?"

"Early. You'll eat then you'll sleep some more. I'm not having you all but collapse again." Sitting on the edge of the bed, he ran his fingers deep into her hair. "I love you. I will protect you even from yourself." As she opened her mouth to protest, William cut her off with a fierce kiss.

"Damn, you make it hard to argue."

"Good." While they waited for the food, they lay in their bed, talking about everything and nothing, learning those little things that only lovers know about each other.

As they were eating, the Admiral's comm rang. Ignoring the headset, William answered the call, "Zafar."

"Admiral, this is Tar. Falco is demanding she be interviewed to prove her innocence."

"She's in no position to demand anything."

"She has the right to request an interview within twenty-four hours of her arrest if she believes she's been falsely accused. It's in the regs, Admiral."

"Fuck," William looked at Cassandra who was listening.

"Totally agree, Admiral."

"Get it set up. I'll be there shortly," William disconnected.

"What kind of trouble can she cause for you?"

"None," he swung his legs to the floor.

"William…" she put her food aside.

"No real trouble." Caressing her bruised cheek, he continued, "She's going to try and justify what she's done and if that doesn't work, she'll lie."

"She is going to bring up your past relationship."

"Yes," he watched her closely.

"What?"

"I can make it go away." Cassandra gave him a confused look. "I have the power to do that."

"But why?" She moved closer as she rested a hand on his knee, "Why would you do that, William? She's guilty."

"Yes, but she's going to say things, things that might upset you. Things no one else has the right to know."

"So for *me*, you'd do what San did?"

"Yes."

"No," she framed his face in her hands. "William, I know you had a past relationship with her. But that was before our time. Others knowing isn't going to change anything between us. She's the past. We're the future. She needs to pay for what she's done; to you, Tori, me, and those crewmen she injured. You're the Admiral. You solve the problems, not push them off on someone else."

William carefully drew her close. "You continually amaze me, Cassandra." He rested his forehead against hers, "I love you."

"I love you too." Pulling back she smiled into his violet eyes, "You need to get dressed, Admiral."

"And you need to finish eating," he gave her a quick kiss, handed her back her plate, stood and headed for the closet.

Cassandra watched him as she finished her meal. With every piece of clothing he put on, he became more and more the Admiral, the jacket being the final piece. She loved watching the transformation; loved both men.

William felt her eyes on him as he dressed, but said nothing. Turning to her he pulled on his jacket. Seeing she'd finished eating, he leaned down to kiss her. "You'll rest while I'm gone. Hopefully, this won't take long."

"I'll be fine, go do what needs doing."

With one final kiss, the Admiral left their quarters securing the hatch on his way out.

∞ ∞ ∞ ∞ ∞

Entering the Brig, the Admiral was met by Tar. "I put her in the main interrogation room. It's all set for monitoring and recording." As they walked to the room, he continued. "Her counsel's in with her...Bayard. Chief Tibullus arrived from the Sentinel and is reviewing the evidence that was collected and reading the reports. He should be ready to start the interview in fifteen." Opening the observation room door, the Admiral entered.

"I need to speak with Tibullus before he goes into the interview."

Tar raised an eyebrow, "I'll get him."

While he waited for Tibullus, he watched Bayard talking intently to Falco. She just sat with a small smile on her lips.

Bayard finally turned away from her, disgusted with her lack of response. As he faced the window, he knew they were being watched even though he couldn't see them. He wished he hadn't drawn this case. It was going to be a mess. Word spread swiftly throughout the Fleet that the Admiral had claimed Cassandra. It was attempted murder on an Admiral's life mate. Shit.

∞ ∞ ∞ ∞ ∞

When the door opened, the Admiral turned to watch Tar and Tibullus enter.

"You needed to speak to me, Admiral?"

"There are some facts you need to be made aware of before you go in to the interview."

"I've read the reports, Admiral."

"This isn't in the reports. Nearly eight cycles ago, on Diomede for three days, Falco and I were involved. She was not under my command. It ended there. I've had no further contact with her until she was assigned to the Retribution six months ago." Silence greeted the Admiral's statement. "I believe she is going to claim it's been ongoing to justify her attack on Cassandra."

"You were never involved with her after Diomede?" Tibullus asked.

"No."

"And her assignment to the Retribution?"

"I had nothing to do with it. I didn't even recognize the name. It wasn't until we were on tour that I even remembered the leave."

"There has been nothing on this tour?"

"The Admiral already told you that, Tibullus!" Tar's voice was furious.

"It's okay, Quinn. No, there has been no personal involvement. I can think of only two times I've been alone with her. Once in my Ready Room eight days ago and then today in my Command Center with the security shield engaged."

"What happened eight days ago?"

"I reamed her ass for being in my Ready Room without authorization."

"You found her there?"

"No, Cassandra did."

"Cassandra has access to your quarters?"

"Yes, Cassandra and Victoria both have security access."

"So when she informed you she suspected Falco, what did you do?"

"She didn't inform me. She told Lucas."

Tibullus silently looked at the Admiral not wanting to ask his next question. "What's her relationship with your son, Admiral?"

William stiffened, his eyes blazing as he answered, "You're questioning the 'relationship' between my life mate and my son?"

"Will Falco?" Tibullus shot back.

While William didn't like it, he realized Tibullus was right. Falco was going to imply many things. "If you want to know Cassandra's relationship with Lucas you need to ask her."

"If you could get her to talk to me that would be helpful, Admiral." Tibullus knew there was no chance of this happening but threw it out there.

"Colonel," William turned to his longtime friend. "Would you go to my quarters, inform Cassandra that Chief Tibullus has some questions for her and see if she would be willing to answer them."

"Yes, Sir!" Quinn exited.

Tibullus was stunned. "Admiral…"

"We'll wait for Cassandra."

Chapter Fifteen

Hearing the hatch secure, Cassandra lay back down on the bed. It had been an eventful day already. She found her mind wasn't going to let her rest so she carefully got out of bed. Bliant's shot had worn off. A hot shower was in order.

Little aches started to vanish as the hot water worked its magic. Tipping her head to the side, Cassandra groaned softly as the pulsating water encountered a bruise.

Stepping out of the shower, she thought about what William had offered; 'to make Falco go away.' He'd been concerned about her reaction to the information getting out. Why?

Drying off, she left her hair down to cover her bruises, knowing they bothered William. Opening the bag of clothes Javiera brought her, she was surprised to find her own boots on top. She'd have to make sure to thank her for getting them. Would Javiera be able to explain it to her? Could she ask her?

Leaving the bathroom, she went to the comm center. Punching in Javiera's code she waited. If she didn't answer then, she didn't need to ask.

"Hello?"

"Javiera?"

"Cassandra! Is everything okay?" Javiera had heard the rumor the Admiral had claimed her.

"Everything's fine," Cassandra paused. "You remember when you told me I could come to you if I had questions?"

"Yes. What do you need to know?

"If you knew, that before you'd met Leander he'd had 'leave' with another woman and now people were talking about it, would you be upset by it?" The question wasn't what Javiera thought she was going to ask.

"Why would people talk about it?"

"Because the woman wants to start up with him again and is saying as much."

"Well… it would be embarrassing, people talking about his life before me," Javiera started.

"But why? You knew he had one, just like you did."

"I…I don't know…"

"I mean it's just talk. He isn't involved with her now, so why would it be a big deal?"

"It wouldn't bother you?"

"That it was in the past? No. That she was trying to rekindle it? Yes, if he were interested…Well, that would decide it, wouldn't it?"

Javiera was trying to figure out what was going on. "But if he wasn't interested, was committed to another, then it would be very upsetting…for Leander. Carinian males, especially from the Arm of Carina, take the protection of their life mate very seriously. That includes being embarrassed by something they might have done in the past."

"Really?"

"Really. Cassandra, what's going on?"

Cassandra debated with herself, but before she could decide the hatch buzzed.

"Javiera, I have to go. Someone's at the hatch. I'll fill you in later." She disconnected as she headed for the hatch. She opened it and found Tar on the other side.

"Colonel?" she stepped back and allowed him entry to the Ready Room.

"The Admiral asked me to see if you thought you would be able to answer some of Chief Tibullus' questions," Tar's tone was formal.

"What?" Cassandra was confused. "Who's Chief Tibullus? What questions?"

"Chief Tibullus is the investigator in the Falco matter. He will be interviewing her shortly. The Admiral felt he needed to inform him of his past relationship with Falco. Some questions came up that the Admiral believes you should answer."

"What questions?" The Colonel just stared at her. "Fine, don't answer. Sometimes you're a real asshole, Colonel." She spun around as she headed to the private quarters.

Quinn wasn't sure what stunned him more, being called an asshole by this small woman or the fact that she seemed to be willing to answer Tibullus' questions. He followed her and found her bent over trying to tie her boots.

"You're going?" Quinn asked as he knelt down to help her. Cassandra slowly stood, her muscles protesting.

"Of course I'm going. The Admiral asked, didn't he? Thank you." Heading into the bathroom, she pulled her hair up high. She would leave no doubt what Falco had done.

"Let's go."

Stares followed the pair as they walked toward the Brig. The extensive bruising on Cassandra's cheek that ran down her neck and disappeared under her shirt would be enough to draw attention. But with Falco's arrest, and the rumor that Cassandra was the Admiral's life mate, speculation was running rampant.

Quinn led her to the observation room. Opening the door, he allowed her to enter first. As she entered, her eyes found William's. She could tell he was furious about the situation he had put her in.

William took a visual inventory of his life mate as she entered the room. She'd pulled her hair back showing every bruise. The clothes she was wearing were obviously not hers, except for the boots that still showed smears of her blood. Looking in her eyes, William could tell she was on a mission. She turned her head as she zeroed in on Tibullus.

"You're the investigator for the Falco matter?" she was on the offensive.

"Yes." Tibullus wasn't sure what to make of this small woman who had obviously been injured, but was still standing in front of him.

"You have some questions for me?"

Chief Tibullus cleared his throat, "Are you aware that the Admiral and Senior Chief Falco are involved with each other?"

"*Were* involved, yes, nearly eight cycles ago," Cassandra corrected him.

"And you're aware of this because?"

"The Admiral felt I should know about it after Falco entered our quarters unauthorized."

"When was this?"

"I believe nine days ago, but that could be off a day or two; a lot has happened."

"You discovered her in the Admiral's Ready Room?"

"Yes."

"What happened?"

"When I discovered her there she demanded to know what I was doing there. Since it was none of her business, I refused to tell her. She threatened to call security. I told her to go ahead but that maybe she should check with the Admiral first. She called him in Communications. He ordered her to leave."

"Can anyone confirm that?"

"I can," Quinn told him. "I was in Communications with the Admiral nine days ago. Falco called requesting a secure line. The Admiral ordered her to leave immediately."

"What did she say to you then?"

"Nothing, she left the Ready Room."

"Then why suspect her?"

"She didn't verbally say anything, but I know hatred when I see it in someone's eyes. Just like I see doubt in yours, Chief."

"Are you sure they haven't been involved in the last eight cycles?"

She felt William stiffen behind her. "Yes."

"How?"

"Because that's what the Admiral told me."

"And you believe him."

"Yes."

"Why did you tell Lucas of your concerns about Falco and not the Admiral?"

"I told the Admiral I had 'concerns' as you put it the night she entered our quarters. The quarters are now always secured."

"And after the bombing?"

"You mean in Medical?" She couldn't see where this was going.

"Yes, why tell Lucas?"

Cassandra looked at William confused. "Once I realized that the poisoning of Victoria and the bombing were both aimed at me there was only one person I could think of who could be responsible. Lucas was there, I told him my concerns, asked him to look into it."

"What's your relationship with Lucas?" Tibullus asked.

"My relationship with..." she looked at William. "That's what this is all about?" She could tell William was furious with the question but was letting her answer. She turned back and Tibullus found himself pinned by a pair of blazing blue eyes.

"I met Lucas Zafar when he crashed his Blade on Earth twenty-seven days ago." Her voice was hard and pointed. "He was hurt. My family and I helped him. He was on Earth approximately three hours. A Raptor came to rescue him, on board were two pilots, Dodge, and Scratch, I believe, and the Admiral. While they were picking up Lucas, Strikers attacked setting off a nuclear bomb. The Raptor returned to the Retribution with Victoria and myself on board. The Earth was destroyed. Lucas made a point of checking on Victoria and me to see how we were settling in. I consider him a good friend. He's never been anything more to me than that, other than the Admiral's son. Does that answer your question on my *'relationship'* with Lucas, Chief Tibullus?"

Tibullus cleared his throat, "Yes, thank you."

"Any other questions?" Cassandra demanded in a frosty voice.

"No, no, ma'am. Thank you for your assistance," Tibullus found himself stuttering. "Admiral. May I have your permission to access your personnel file?"

William's eyes narrowed, "As Chief Investigator you don't need my permission."

"I know, Sir, but I'm asking."

"You have my permission."

"I believe I'm ready to start my interview."

"Dismissed then."

Quinn looked from Cassandra to the Admiral. "I'll be outside for a few minutes," he told them following Tibullus out.

William closed the distance separating them, gently caressing her bruised neck. Her eyes were still blazing.

"You handled that very well. I don't think I've ever heard Tibullus stutter before."

"That was bullshit, William. A *'relationship'* with Lucas? Please!" Her eyes questioned him, "You never thought…"

"I might have, in the very beginning." His eyes burned into hers. "He's closer to your age than I am. Then you were hurt," his thumb gently caressed her cheek where the new bruise was. "I had to see for myself you were okay. When you responded to me, then I knew."

"Knew what?"

"That you were mine, my life mate." Leaning down he kissed her. Cassandra wrapped her arms around his waist.

"I love you, William."

"I know."

At the discrete knock on the door, the two separated. Tar reentered the room. On the other side of the glass, Chief Tibullus entered the interview room.

"They can't see us?" Cassandra asked as she approached the window looking at Falco's smug face.

"No," William walked over to stand behind her. Quinn pushed a button so they could hear the interview.

"Let the log show this is Chief Tibullus in an interview with Senior Chief Delondra Falco and her counsel, Lieutenant Bayard. This interview is to determine if there is just cause to charge the Senior Chief with two counts of attempted murder and one count of sabotage of a Coalition vessel. Senior Chief, do you understand the charges filed against you?"

"Yes," Falco finally spoke.

"What is your answer to the charges?"

"Innocent of all charges."

"Senior Chief, explain to me how you believe you came to be accused of these crimes."

"It's that refugee bitch's fault!" The sudden venom in Falco's voice caught both men by surprise.

"Who would that be, Senior Chief?" Tibullus questioned.

"That Earth Bitch," Falco looked at the window.

"I need a name."

"Cassandra Chamberlain!" she spewed.

"Why would she be to blame for the charges against you?"

"Because she's jealous of me. She thinks she can take my place with the Admiral. She can't!"

While Tibullus had been prepared for this, Bayard was not. His shock was evident.

"What place is that?" Tibullus continued.

Falco got a very maniacal look on her face, "As his lover, of course. We've been lovers for over eight cycles, ever since Diomede. He's a very...inventive... lover," Falco said with a sly look at the window.

Feeling William stiffen behind her, Cassandra leaned against him just slightly, hoping he understood. Quinn caught the slight movement and was amazed to realize that she was trying to comfort Will, not find support from him.

"Where did you first meet the Admiral?" Tibullus brought her eyes back to him.

"I just told you when. On Diomede, when we were both on leave."

"You were serving under the Admiral then?"

"No, and he was a Captain."

"So that would be," Tibullus paused as he looked at his screen, "13 Marta 5245?"

"5246," Falco corrected.

"Where did you meet the next time?"

"What?"

"You just stated that you've been having a long-term relationship with Admiral Zafar. Where did you meet the second time?"

"We met at the Callao space station two months later."

"When?"

"30 Bealtaine."

Tibullus consulted his screen again. "Official records show that Captain Zafar was commanding the Battleship Babirusa on the Regulian border at that date."

"That's just what he put in the records."

"The Battle of Fayal took place during that time. Three Regulian battleships were destroyed, one captured. Captain Zafar was promoted to Vice-Admiral because of it. You're saying he wasn't there?"

Falco was silent.

"When was the next time?"

"There were too many over the cycles to remember exact times and places."

"What about your relationship with Captain San?"

"What relationship?"

"The one where you threatened his wife. You were removed from the ship, committed for treatment, and prescribed Xyphrine."

"That's a lie!" Falco exclaimed. "That bitch changed my records."

"And that would be…"

"The Earth Bitch."

"You're stating that someone who's been on the ship less than," Tibullus referenced his notes, "thirty days, would be able to alter secured Coalition files. Is that what you're claiming?"

"Yes."

"Empty Xyphrine bottles were found in your quarters. Xyphrine was used to poison Victoria Lynn Chamberlain."

"Bitch did that herself, to get rid of the little bitch, then planted the bottles in my quarters."

"Quarters that you secure with a remote detection system. How did she get in without you knowing?"

"She just did, she's tricky. Look how she's got the Admiral's private chef cooking her and the little bitch's meals, sending them to their quarters. Well they don't have any quarters now, do they?" Falco giggled.

Bayard and Tibullus looked at each other, both knowing Falco had lost her mind. In the observation room, William put a hand on Cassandra's waist as he felt her stiffen.

"Missing DC-48 and a detonator were also found in your quarters."

"Lucas planted them there," Falco told them.

"Why would the Admiral's son do that?"

"Because the two of them are lovers, have been since Earth. He's always sniffing around her."

Tibullus decided this needed to end.

"You know, whoever blew up those quarters was an idiot."

Falco's eyes flashed at him.

"I mean, *first* the bomb barely touched the target. All its shrapnel ended up in the wall. The timer didn't work, and it was pure luck that it didn't just blow a hole in the floor."

"Luck my ass!" Tibullus could easily see the hatred Cassandra saw in Falco's eyes. "That bomb was perfect! The timer was set so it wouldn't go off until the hatch opened sixty degrees. The shrapnel was arranged in a kill pattern and the DC-48 was formed into a perfect front-only blast for greatest impact. Hole in the floor, my ass! I have an E1 rating! I know how the hell to make a fucking directional bomb. Why that Bitch moved away, I don't know! She should be dead!"

"Lieutenant Bayard, I am ending this interview due to Senior Chief Falco's confession. Do you agree?"

"Yes, I do."

"Confession?!? What confession?" Falco demanded.

"Let the log show that this interview has ended. Senior Chief, you will be returned to your cube."

As Tibullus left the room, the Colonel shut off the speaker.

With Tibullus' departure, Falco seemed to have calmed. Bayard said something to her but got no response. She stood and walked to the door, waiting for it to open.

Cassandra turned to face the Admiral, the rage in her eyes banked, "He's good," she said of Tibullus.

"He's one of the best," the Admiral agreed.

"It'll hold?" she asked as the door opened.

"It'll hold," Tibullus answered for the Admiral.

"Then maybe you're not a complete jerk, Tibullus," Cassandra said before remembering she was with the Admiral. Glancing up, she saw William was amused though he was trying to frown.

"Thank you, I think," Tibullus replied, not sure what a jerk was.

"What else do you need?" the Admiral asked.

"Just a couple of things about the search of Falco's quarters and the deactivation of the remote sensor and we should be done."

"Admiral, if you or Tibullus don't need me here, I'd like to head back to quarters."

William turned concerned eyes to her and saw she was starting to fade. "Tibullus?"

"No, Sir, I have no questions for her." Even he could see the fatigue around Cassandra's eyes. Shit, this time two days ago she was in Medical, but still she came here and went toe-to-toe with him answering every question she was asked; standing by the Admiral. That alone earned his respect. The Admiral gave her a slight nod and she departed.

Turning down the hallway, all she was thinking about was how good that bed was going to feel. When the corridor widened, Cassandra heard a commotion behind her. Curious, she turned to see Falco escape her guards and barrel toward her.

Hearing the commotion, the Admiral opened the door of the observation room. He found the guards rushing by and heard…

"You Bitch!" and she entered the fray.

As Falco took a swing, Cassandra ducked, her hands raised, arms close to her sides. Falco spun around ready to attack again.

"I've had enough of *you*, bitch." Not realizing she'd spoken out loud, Cassandra ducked under Falco's next swing. Sinking her left into Falco's stomach, Falco doubled over. Cassandra came in with an uppercut that would have made her brother proud. The Admiral reached her just as Falco's eyes rolled back in her head and she slumped to the floor.

"Shit!" Cassandra exclaimed shaking out her hand.

"Guards!" the Admiral ordered, "get this piece of crap off my deck!"

Coming to as the guards drug her up by her arms, Falco glared at Cassandra. "This isn't over. You understand me, bitch? You and that little bitch are dead!"

Cassandra went very still, her blue eyes turning deadly. Slowly she advanced on Falco. The guards froze, uncertain what to do. "You ever come near me and mine again," Cassandra's tone had the blood draining from Falco's face, "and you won't be going to a nice little cube with a sore chin. You understand *ME*, bitch?"

Turning, she saw the look in William's eyes and realized she had the attention of the entire corridor. As her neck started to turn red, the Admiral stepped in.

"Get her out of here!" The guards holding Falco drug her out. "The rest of you get back to work!" The personnel in the corridor scattered leaving the Admiral, Cassandra, Tar, and Tibullus.

"Let me see your hand." Inspecting it, he found the knuckles scraped and bruised, but nothing broken.

"Sorry about that," she said quietly so only he could hear.

He raised his eyes to hers, "Where did you learn to fight like that?" Falco was a well-trained member of the Coalition. Cassandra had schooled her like a child.

"Big brother," at William's look she elaborated. "Peter, my brother…Peter, Victoria's father. He is…" William saw the quick flash of pain cross her face, "was a member of the Special Forces. He felt his baby sister should know how to protect herself."

"He did a good job," William told her.

"What are the Special Forces," Tibullus asked avidly listening. As the Admiral turned to him, he realized he should have kept his question to himself.

"It's a branch of the military," Cassandra answered not seeing the look Tibullus received. "Most men in my family served. Not all, but most. The Special Forces is…" she looked to William for help. "It's made up of small groups of highly trained men. Usually no more than six, they get sent in to solve specific problems then disappear."

"Shock Troops," Tar said quietly. Who the hell was this person? The Admiral's nod told Cassandra he agreed.

"So anyway he taught me how to defend myself." She shrugged her shoulders, "It's not a big deal." But the Admiral thought it was. Still holding her hand he felt the slight tremor in it.

Recognizing the signs, he turned to Tibullus. "The rest of the interview will have to wait. You have the tapes of this incident to review for your report."

"Wait! This," Cassandra circled her finger, "isn't going to mess up the investigation, is it?"

"No," the Admiral told her as he looked at Tibullus.

"No, it's not," Tibullus agreed. "It will show how out of control Falco is, and that she instigated the attacks. Admiral, Colonel," Tibullus nodded to both men, "Tomorrow?"

"Ten o'clock, my Ready Room."

Nodding, Tibullus turned to Cassandra. "Ma'am, it's been a real honor meeting you." Putting two fingers to the side of his head, he walked off leaving Cassandra confused.

William put a hand on the small of her back looking at Quinn, who fell in to flank her. Together the three left the Brig.

∞ ∞ ∞ ∞ ∞

Across the Retribution, word had quickly spread that the Admiral's life mate knocked out Falco with a single punch. Nearing the Admiral's quarters, Lucas joined them.

"I hear I missed all the fun," he started to joke stopping short at the look his father gave him. Entering the Ready Room, Cassandra sank into a chair. William opened a drawer and pulled out a chemical cold pack. Squatting down next to her he lifted her right hand.

"Here, this will help with the swelling," he gently applied the pack.

"Wow! You really did knock her out," Lucas exclaimed as he saw her knuckles.

Cassandra gave him a tired grin. "Thanks," she said looking into William's concerned eyes.

"You need to go lie down."

"I think I will."

Helping her up, he followed her out of the Ready Room closing the connecting door.

Lucas turned to Quinn, "What the fuck happened?"

Quinn wasn't sure where to start. "Falco demanded an interview." Quinn walked around the Admiral's desk pulling out a bottle and three glasses. He knew his friend, Will, was going to need a drink.

"Questions were raised about the Admiral's involvement with Falco." Pouring the Carinian ale, he carried two glasses around the desk and handed one to Lucas, "And Cassandra's relationship with you."

Lucas choked on the sip he'd just taken, "With me! What the fuck!"

"Tibullus was covering all his bases with what Falco might bring up."

"That's just crap!" Lucas shot out of his chair to pace.

"Oh trust me, Cassandra set him straight. She had Tibullus stuttering by the time she was done with him," Quinn smiled remembering.

"Cassandra…" Lucas turned to Quinn.

"Tibullus questioned her." Lucas was silent. "She stood, Lucas, stood strong. She left no doubt in her belief in William." Quinn looked down into his glass. "You should have told me everything about Falco and your father."

"Wasn't mine to tell." The two men's eyes met.

"Anyway, Cassandra was leaving when Falco saw her, broke away from her guards and went after her. Cassandra put her down… hard. I can't wait to see the record of it." He looked at Lucas. "Did you know Victoria's father was a member of a Shock Troop?"

"No." Lucas gave him a confused look. "I only saw him for a few minutes in the cabin. Cassie said something about him having a hurt shoulder, but that's all I remember."

"He taught her how to 'defend' herself. She's damn good." The two men turned as the connecting door opened.

∞ ∞ ∞ ∞ ∞

As William closed the door, Cassandra made it as far as the couch before she needed to sit down. With a deep sigh, she leaned back closing her eyes. Feeling William sit, she turned her head to look at him.

"You should be in bed," he told her, tucking a piece of hair behind her ear.

"I'll be fine here until you're done. I'm sorry, William."

"What could you possibly be sorry for?"

"Causing the scene with Falco in front of your crew."

"Falco caused the scene," William kissed her abused knuckles. "You just finished it, and quite well I might add. I believe every guard is going to be reviewing that recording and practicing that move."

"You're not upset?" her concerned eyes looked into his.

"At you? No."

"Not at yourself either. Right?" she questioned him.

"No, at the guards. It should never have happened."

"I agree, but William…" she hesitated.

"What?" He encouraged her.

"It felt damn good taking her out."

William looked at her then started to laugh. "I happen to have liked it myself." Cassandra grinned laying her head on his shoulder.

"You need some sleep." Easing her down he got a pillow and blanket from the bed and made sure she was comfortable then leaned down to kiss her and found she was already asleep.

"I love you, Cassandra Chamberlain," he whispered in her ear. Lowering the lights he returned to his Ready Room.

Chapter Sixteen

He approached his son and friend and saw they'd helped themselves to his ale. Sitting, he found one ready for him. Taking a sip, he leaned back and saw Lucas raise a questioning eyebrow.

"Asleep before her head even hit the pillow." William took another sip.

"Dad, what Tibullus said about Cassandra and me," Lucas started. William looked at his son knowing Quinn had told him.

"Lucas, it's fine. Don't worry about it." He saw his son was still concerned and he continued, "There was never any doubt for either of us." Relieved, Lucas nodded and leaned back.

"So things should settle down now," Lucas started.

"Oh sure, now all we have to do is deal with the Regulians," Quinn joked. But looking at William he could tell he wasn't amused.

"Anything new there?" he asked.

"No, long range sensors aren't picking them up. It looks like the misdirection worked. They still think we're heading to the Rodham space station."

"Rodham's been informed?"

"Yes."

"Tomorrow after we finish with Tibullus, I'm going to need a secure line to Valerian. I'm going to ask that he send the Dioscuri to replace us on this tour."

"What!" Lucas asked stunned, "What's going on?"

"You've figured it out," Quinn said quietly.

"Enough to know we need to put some space between us and the Regulians."

"Is this about Victoria?" Lucas demanded. "Where is she?"

"She's staying at Amina's. She's fine. Lucas, there are things you don't know, things I can't tell you right now, but Tori isn't the target."

"He said she wasn't the Light the Glitter Man wanted," Lucas said aloud. "So who is he looking for?"

"What are you talking about?" Quinn asked.

William brought Quinn up to speed on Tori learning Regulian, what she'd learned from her dream and Messene.

"Messene," Quinn said quietly. William looked at him. They all knew this went deep.

∞ ∞ ∞ ∞ ∞

Waking to William caressing her birthmark, Cassandra found she was naked in bed. The time was coming when they would need to discuss it again, but not now. Running a gentle hand down his back, she drew his attention to her. Turning to partially cover her, he pressed her into the bed, framed her face with his hands, and gave her a passionate kiss that he quickly broke off. It had been like this since the explosion, him pulling back. That would be ending soon too. But right now she needed to tell him what she wanted so he could decide.

"William," she looked up into the eyes she loved and he saw she had something on her mind.

"Hmmm?" his thumb caressed her cheek.

"I want to conceive your child." His utter stillness told her she'd surprised him. "Soon," she pressed.

William's gaze bored into hers. The thought of her conceiving his child touched a very fundamental place deep inside him. But she was more important to him.

"Cassandra, with everything that's happening, now might not be the best time."

"I want your child, William, a part of you, a part of me. The best time doesn't matter because it will be our time. I know you have concerns." She put a gentle hand to his mouth so she could finish. "I know you have a lot going on right now with Falco, the Regulians, and the Carinian traitor. But you need to know what I want and decide if it's what you want. That's your decision, mine is to have your child."

William rolled onto his back, pulling her over him, wrapping his arms around her, "Cassandra, I nearly lost you. If you'd been standing in front of that hatch when it blew…"

"But I wasn't!" she interrupted him. "I wasn't because of you. You're not going to lose me. I love you." Tightening her arms around him, Cassandra laid her head on his chest and fell asleep to the beat of his heart.

∞ ∞ ∞ ∞ ∞

The next morning, the Admiral put a plan in motion to convert his storage room into a bedroom for Victoria. Javiera agreed to have Tori spend another night so the room could be completed and be a surprise for Tori. She even had some suggestions about what needed to be done, telling the

Admiral she'd send Leander over with the items. When Cassandra awoke, everything was set.

∞ ∞ ∞ ∞ ∞

Waking up slowly, Cassandra knew she was alone. Seeing the time, she realized why; it was already 1030. Tibullus was supposed to be here at 1000 to finish the interview. Climbing out of bed with protesting muscles, she saw breakfast waiting for her on the table. Her stomach rumbled loudly as she took the cover off. Hutu made loblolly with thimbleberries. It was becoming one of her favorite breakfasts.

After devouring the bowl, she decided it was time for a shower before Tori came home. How were they going to work this? She didn't want to leave William's quarters, even if he'd let her, but Tori couldn't sleep on the couch either. Letting the hot water soothe her aches and pains, the only solution she could find was for them to find new quarters. Wrapped in a towel, she left the bathroom to find William entering their chambers.

As she came out of the bathroom, he was staggered by his love for her. She wanted to have his child; walking to her he sank his fingers into her still wet hair, framing her face as he leaned down for a kiss, "How are you feeling?"

"Pretty good."

"I'll call Bliant."

"No, William, really. I'm still stiff and sore but better." Leaning back she looked up at him, "How did the rest of the interview go?"

"Fine, everything was wrapped up. You don't need to worry."

"I wasn't, I knew you'd handle it. Now I need to get dressed before Tori gets back." She headed to the closet.

"She's not coming back today."

"What?" She stopped and turned to look at him.

"She's going to stay at Amina's one more night."

"Why?"

"One, so you can rest, and two, so we can get her room done."

"Room?" she raised an eyebrow.

"I have a crew coming to make the storage room into a bedroom for her."

"William," Cassandra rested her head on his chest.

"What's wrong?" he'd seen the tears in her eyes.

"Nothing's wrong. I was just in the shower trying to figure out how to tell you we'd need new quarters."

"You're home, Cassandra, this is where you stay," his voice was gruff.

"I know. I didn't say I wanted to. She's going to love it." Rising up on her toes, she gave him a kiss, "Thank you."

"You don't have to thank me. I want her here too. Now let's get you dressed before the workers arrive." Moving to the closet she found her clothes, what little she had, hanging up next to his.

"You've been busy."

"I want you here." As the hatch buzzed, he left to answer it.

Cassandra was dressed by the time William returned followed by Lucas. Pulling her hair back, she smiled at the two Zafar men.

"You're looking better," Lucas ran a quick eye over her.

"I'm feeling better. What's up?"

"I need to go to the Bridge for a while."

"Okay…" Puzzled she looked from William to Lucas realizing William meant for Lucas to stay with her. "I'll be fine alone."

"You won't be alone. There will be a crew in and out all day."

"I'll be fine."

"No," his eyes blazed telling her this was important to him. He needed to make sure she was protected even though the threat had passed. She couldn't fault him for it.

"If that's what you want," she turned. "Lucas, you're going to be bored out of your mind."

"Not me," smiling he walked to the couch. "I brought the deck. I thought I'd teach you how to play Five Square."

Cassandra looked at what he had in his hand, "Cards?"

"Lucas…" William gave him a warning.

"What? Just a friendly little game," his face was full of innocence.

"I take it he's somewhat good," Cassandra walked over to William.

"That would be an understatement." William saw the gleam come into her eyes. His life mate was competitive.

"Are you going to be all day?" she asked.

"A good part. I want you to rest when you need it," his eyes hardened. "I mean it, Cassandra."

"I will." Ignoring Lucas, she rose up to give him a kiss. After he left she walked over to Lucas, "so what's this game?"

∞ ∞ ∞ ∞ ∞

On the Bridge, the Admiral headed to his Command Center and found Quinn already there. "Engage the privacy screen. I need a secure, encoded line to High Admiral Valerian."

"I've arranged the line, Admiral. Will, are you really going to request the removal of the Retribution from this tour?" William said nothing waiting to be connected to the High Admiral.

"Zafar, what's going on?" demanded Valerian.

"Sir, I have a situation here that I believe requires immediate attention."

"I've read your reports, Admiral. While I agree something is going on, I don't agree with this need for secrecy."

"That's because I've intentionally left out many details from my reports, Sir. Not trusting that the Fleet wouldn't be compromised."

"You didn't report facts to me?" Valerian's rage was easy to hear.

"No, Sir."

"You suspect me?"

"No, Sir, but information has been leaked. Information that gave the Regulians the Fleet's coordinates in the last attack. It came from Carinian space on a Carinian channel in Regulian. It was our exact location, High Admiral." There was silence on the other end.

"What have I not been told?"

"Are your communications completely secured, High Admiral?" Quinn's eyebrows shot up at William's questioning of the High Admiral's security. William knew he was overstepping, but he was going to make sure his life mate was protected.

"You're pushing, Zafar."

"Yes, Sir, I'll be pushing more before this is done."

After several moments Valerian responded. "I've engaged all security. Now tell me what you've got, Admiral!"

William took the High Admiral through the Regulian attack on Earth, specifically the assault on the Chamberlains. Victoria's kidnapping. All the Regulian transmissions. Regulian attacks. The thread found in Victoria, the Carinian thread with Regulian technology. The High Admiral listened saying nothing.

"What you're suggesting…"

"I'm not suggesting anything. I'm point blank saying there is a high-ranked, Carinian traitor filtering classified information to the Regulians on our Fleet's locations!"

"Zafar! Stand down!"

"Damn it, Valerian!"

"Admiral! You should be reaching the Rodham space station shortly. I suggest you take some leave."

"No, we won't."

"No, you won't what, Admiral?" the High Admiral's voice was frigid.

"Be arriving at the Rodham space station. We are nowhere near it."

"Just where are you?"

He gave him their present location.

"You've falsified your Fleet's location to High Command!?!"

"Yes, Sir. I changed the Fleet's course after the last Regulian attack. So far they've been unable to locate us. The space station has been informed to be on Alert Status 1."

"I can bring you up on charges, Admiral."

William rubbed the back of his neck. "Do you remember in the Academy that once a month we'd have to play out a scenario of one kind or another?"

The High Admiral was listening, "Yes."

"We decided to give them code names, so the opposing team wouldn't know what we were doing."

"Yes."

"Do you remember PR25?"

"PR25? Fuck! You can't possibly think that's what this is!" Shock was apparent in Valerian's voice.

"It doesn't matter what I think. Someone high up thinks it. That's why the Earth was attacked, why the Regulians are so desperately attacking the Fleet. They've been promised something to make sure PR25 doesn't happen. I have two survivors from Earth on the Retribution; one had a thread in her arm that had been there for seven cycles. The Regulians continue to attack, targeting the Sentinel. The transmission said 'believed being protected.' The Sentinel is from the House of Protection." William was silently letting the High Admiral think.

"What do you want to do?"

"I want the Dioscuri to replace the Retribution on this tour, so we can head directly to Carina. That should draw the fire away from the Fleet and the Sentinel can then be repaired at Rodham."

"You realize what you're asking. If I grant this request, you'll never command another Fleet."

"Yes."

"You feel that strongly about this?"

"High Admiral, someone on Carina has conspired with the Regulians to murder seven billion people because *they* felt threatened. Who else are they willing to sacrifice?"

"Fuck. I'll authorize the Dioscuri to replace the Retribution. I'll let you know when to expect the Dioscuri."

"On a secure line."

"Yes, Admiral, a secure line. Stay in one piece until then."

"Yes, Sir."

As the call ended, Quinn looked at his longtime friend. "Are you going to tell me what PR25 is? Or am I a security risk too."

"If I'd thought you were a risk you wouldn't have been in this room, Quinn." William sat down in his chair.

"PR25 is a scenario for what we would do if the missing Princess of the House of Knowledge were ever to return. What we would do. What the possible fallout would be for the existing trustee's family and the procedures to follow for her protection. What would be needed to establish her legitimacy to the throne."

"But we've already established that Victoria isn't who they are looking for."

"She isn't."

"Then who…" Quinn trailed off, "you think it's Cassandra."

"I know it's Cassandra."

"Will, every member of the Royal Family has a birthmark. You have a birthmark. Victoria doesn't."

"Cassandra does. Her mother had it. Her grandmother had it. Her middle name is Qwes, Quinn. Every woman on the maternal side carries it. In the twenty-eight days she's been on this ship, she's not only learned how to fix our laser system, but she's also learned the Regulian language. She was the smartest person on Earth according to Victoria."

"If it's true, Will, you know what it means."

"Yes, I know."

Will looked his longtime friend in the eye. "Start getting all the Intel together the Dioscuri will need. Do it quietly. I'll be in quarters."

∞ ∞ ∞ ∞ ∞

Entering his Ready Room, William heard laughter; Cassandra's laughter. The sound made any sacrifice bearable. Following the sound, he found his life mate laughing and his son scowling.

"So how much is that you owe me?"

"I don't understand how you do it!" Lucas threw his cards down in disgust.

"Superior female mind, Lucas, superior female mind." She saw William and promptly forgot the card game. "You're home." Walking over she wrapped her arms around him. Hugging him she could tell something was off. "William?"

"Sounds like you're beating the boy's butt."

"Soundly," Lucas scowled. "I don't know how she did it, but after the first ten hands she's been beating me all day."

"Did you rest?" He scanned her face.

"Yes, Hutu brought a great second meal. They finished Victoria's room. She's going to be so excited." Cassandra let it go until they were alone.

"Good, so are you going to pay up or what Lucas?"

"Will you take a marker?"

William stared at the two. "How much does he owe you?" The figure Lucas stated amazed him. He looked at Cassandra, "Did you lose a hand?"

"A few."

"In six hours?"

"So?"

"Remind me to take you to Vargis."

Later that evening, Cassandra propped herself up on William's chest, running a hand along his cheek.

"What's wrong?"

"Nothing."

"William…"

"What could be wrong? You're safe in my arms. Victoria comes home tomorrow."

"But there's something."

"Just Fleet business. Nothing for you to worry about." At her doubtful look William continued, "Really, it's being handled."

Cassandra didn't know what to make of what he was telling her, but the Fleet was his business; she needed to trust he knew what he was doing.

"You're okay?"

"I'm all right. Go to sleep. Tomorrow Victoria comes home."

Chapter Seventeen

"Aunt Cassie!" Cassandra was just entering the Ready Room when Victoria came bursting through the hatch.

"Hey there," she caught Victoria in a hug ignoring William's look.

Javiera smiled, "How are you?"

"I'm good, getting better every day. Thank you, Javiera."

"No thanks needed. It was wonderful to have her. I need to get going. I'll talk to you later?"

"We will." As the hatch closed, she returned her attention to Victoria. "So you had fun?"

"Yeah, but I missed you."

"I missed you too. The Admiral has a surprise for you."

"He does?" she turned to him, "You do?"

"It's not just my surprise."

"Don't let him fool you, Tori, he did this himself."

"What is it?"

"Come on, we'll show you." Entering their private quarters. William put his hands on Victoria's shoulders pointing her toward what was once a storage room.

"What?"

"Turn the light on and look." The look that came over her face was something he wouldn't soon forget.

"It's a bedroom! Is it mine?" Hopeful eyes looked up at him.

"It's all yours."

"Aunt Cassie?"

"All yours. Just yours."

Victoria launched herself into William's arms. "Thank you! Thank you! This is awesome! Wait until I tell Amina!" Wiggling down she ran into the room.

Stepping into his now empty arms, Cassandra stretched up to give him a gentle kiss. "I think she likes it."

"I should have thought about it earlier."

"No. It would have been too soon."

"It would have kept you safe."

"William..." she rested her cheek against his chest.

"I need to get to the Bridge. You'll be okay here with Victoria?"

"We'll be fine."

"You'll rest," he tipped her face up letting her know it wasn't a question.

"I will." Giving her a hard kiss he headed for the hatch. Taking a calming breath, Cassandra turned to enter Tori's room.

∞ ∞ ∞ ∞ ∞

Over the next several days they developed a routine. The Admiral walked Victoria to class while Cassandra either rested or read from the library with Javiera walking her back. By the end of the seventh day, Cassandra was ready to go crazy. It was time to get things back to normal.

"You about ready, Tori?"

"Just about."

"Finish up while I tell the Admiral I'm walking you to class."

"You are?"

"I am."

Walking into the Ready Room, William was at his desk reading some documents, his face grim. Seeing her walk toward him he smiled.

"You're moving better."

"I'm moving fine. So fine that I'm going to walk Victoria to class."

"You need..."

"I don't need to rest. It's been over a week, William. I'm okay. I'm going to walk my niece to class."

William knew he was so cautious it was driving her crazy.

"Trust me."

"Okay, but…"

"I will rest if I need to." With a kiss goodbye, the Chamberlain women left the Admiral in his Ready Room.

∞ ∞ ∞ ∞ ∞

The corridors of the Retribution were buzzing that Cassandra was walking Victoria to class. Ignoring it, she concentrated on Victoria; they made it nearly to class before they met up with Javiera and Amina.

"You're moving!" Javiera hugged her.

"Yeah, I'm feeling really good."

"That's wonderful. Are you going to be heading back to Engineering soon?"

"I don't know. I hadn't really thought about that yet."

"No rush. You need to make a full recovery first." The girls gave each of them a hug before they entered their class. "Oh, I wish I could stay and talk. I promised Pakar I'd meet her on Deck J. Can we get together soon to catch up?"

"I'd really like that." Separating, the two friends walked in opposite directions.

∞ ∞ ∞ ∞ ∞

Cassandra let her mind wander as she headed back to quarters and enjoyed being mobile again. She stopped in front of their old quarters.

The damage from the bomb was still clearly evident. Shards of metal protruded from the wall directly across from a hatch that now sat half off its hinges. If she or Victoria had been entering the room…

Stepping inside she found it totally demolished. What the bomb hadn't destroyed, the fire had. The comm center where they'd learned Regulian, the couch where William had held her and the bed where she and Tori slept all destroyed. Turning to leave, she found Tibullus in the hatchway.

"Chief."

"Not a very pretty sight."

"No."

"What are you doing here?"

"Seems I needed to see it. What's new with Falco?"

"She's in the Brig and will stay there until she can be transported for trial." He looked at her for a moment. "You know, you're something of a legend down there."

"Me? Why?" Cassandra raised a shocked eyebrow at him.

"You took Falco down. She's a good six inches taller with fifty pounds on you."

"She pissed me off."

Tibullus' eyes widened slightly, "Remind me never to do so."

"You already have," Cassandra looked him in the eye, "but at least you were just doing your job. A job…according to the Admiral…you're very good at."

"I…thank you."

"Don't thank me, thank him. I've been learning about the Carinian justice system. She'll be tried on Carina by a Coalition jury?"

"Yes."

"Make sure it sticks, Tibullus."

"I will." With that, they parted ways.

∞ ∞ ∞ ∞ ∞

Entering their quarters, Cassandra found William just ending a call.

"I thought you'd be on the Bridge by now," she secured the hatch.

"I just have a few more calls to make then will be heading out. It took you a while to drop off Tori. Everything okay?"

"Yeah."

"You should still rest."

Cassandra's eyes flared into his, "I'm fine."

"It's been little more than a week." The anger in his voice surprised her.

"William…"

"I need to finish making these calls." Turning to the comm he pressed a button. Hearing the door to their quarters close he sighed. He knew he should have handled that better but the thought of how close he'd come to losing her made him want to protect her even more.

While he was on the com, hearing the connecting door open, he turned in his chair. He expected to see Cassandra walking out, just not in a robe.

"So what's the timeline for those repairs?" He raised an eyebrow as she walked toward him. While the report was given, Cassandra straddled his lap. Stunned, he lost focus. Working on his jacket, she ran her hands up his chest, softly kissing his lips.

"Could you repeat that last part, Captain?" William finally said as she released his lips.

As the Captain repeated himself, Cassandra's eyes never left his, her busy hands moving down to release him from his pants, her hands gentle but firm in their movements. Her robe fell to her waist revealing only skin.

"Captain, I'll have to get back to you." Quickly disconnecting the call, he groaned as she rose above him. "Cassandra!"

"I mean to have you, Admiral," she lowered herself onto his already thick shaft. Watching his eyes darken she took in more and more of him. "It's been so long, William." Leaning in, she took his mouth in a kiss that left them both breathless.

William didn't have time to control his passion. She had overwhelmed him. Encircling her hips with his hands, he thrust up into her, feeling her tightness close around him. He set a frantic pace, lost in the feel of her. As the pressure built, she wrapped her arms around him, pulling him even closer.

"William!" she cried as the orgasm ripped through her body on William's final thrust. Grinding her hips tightly against his, his body shuddered. With her forehead resting against his, she tried to catch her breath.

"Cassandra…"

"Don't you dare ask if I'm okay!" Her satisfied blue eyes had just a flicker of annoyance in them. "I love you, William. I understand your need to protect me. But I don't need protection from you."

"Ten days ago you nearly died!" If they weren't still joined, he would have stood.

"But I didn't! Because of you! I'm not going to let what Falco did change the way I live my life. Don't give her that power, William." Taking his face in her hands her eyes pleaded with him. "I love you. I would rather live a short life filled with you, then an eternity without. I've lived twenty-five years without you, I won't live one more." Leaning in she gave him an impassioned kiss.

William rubbed his hands up her back, pulling her closer as he returned the kiss. She was right about Falco, they would live a full life together, a long life, he would make sure of that. With the children she conceived with him, the thought caused him to stiffen inside her.

Gripping her hips he pulled her up against him. Releasing his mouth, Cassandra groaned gripping his shoulders. William's mouth began to work its way down her neck as he leaned her back for access to her breasts. Supporting her weight with one arm, his hand moved down to where they were joined, caressing her already sensitive nub with his thumb.

"William!" she gasped.

"I will protect you, Cassandra," William's eyes burned into hers as his thumb continued its gentle torment. Cassandra's hips moved against him. "You will have a child…soon." Her eyes widened. "But right now I just need you." As his thumb increased its pressure, Cassandra's body tightened around him. Her eyes lost focus. As the orgasm hit her, William found his own release.

With their breath still uneven, the comm center rang. William pushed the intercom.

"Zafar."

"Admiral, I have High Admiral Valerian on a secured line. Would you like it transferred to your Ready Room or come to the Bridge."

"I'll come to the Bridge. Tell the High Admiral five minutes." She had pulled her robe on as William answered Quinn and then stood.

"You have work, Admiral." Standing, William adjusted his clothing before pulling her close for one more kiss.

"I love you, Cassandra."

"I love you too."

∞ ∞ ∞ ∞ ∞

Arriving on the Bridge, the Admiral went directly to his Command Center where Tar was waiting. With the security screen engaged, he opened the comm to High Admiral Valerian.

"High Admiral, sorry for the wait."

"Admiral Carnot and the Dioscuri will be en route to you in 24 hours. They should reach your location in four days."

"Understood."

"You still want to handle it this way?"

"Yes."

"I will meet you once you dock in Carina."

"Yes, Sir."

"Good luck, Admiral." The High Admiral disconnected.

"Quinn, get Marat up here, I have a job for him."

∞ ∞ ∞ ∞ ∞

Stretching on a chair to reach the top shelf, Cassandra took down the last book. It was a very thin volume that seemed older than the others and with no title on the cover. Opening it she started to read. After several pages, she realized she was reading ancient Sumerian. Turning the book over in her hands, she studied it.

How could William have a book written in an ancient Earth language?

She continued to read and found the book related a history of ancient Carina. That nearly 2500 years ago, two houses were just about torn apart because of a relationship between a man from the House of Protection and a woman from the House of Knowledge. Neither was named. The book told of how one night they just disappeared.

The House of Knowledge lost a daughter that was to be Queen. She was their Brightest Light, a brilliant woman whose rule was much anticipated. With no direct heir, the Assembly appointed a distant family member to the throne, one who carried a faint birthmark but not the Imperial mark of the Queen. She would rule until the lost Princess or one of her descendants returned to Carina.

The House of Protection lost two sons. The Third Son, considered their Bravest Warrior unbeaten in battle, disappeared with the Princess. The First Son, who would be King, died suddenly. It was believed he was killed by the Third Son. The Second Son, Shesha, became King of the House of Protection. The Third Son's name was never spoken again, for he'd brought shame to his House.

Putting the book aside, Cassandra's mind was racing. William had been trying to tell her about her birthmark before the explosion. Were these the people he thought she descended from? That they left Carina and had somehow made it to Earth?

In her dream, Sabah had said they left behind what others demanded they be. That while everything hadn't been perfect, they found each other, trusted each other, had made a life together that they wouldn't have had on Carina.

Grams had always told her, listen to your dreams. When she'd been in the dark, they'd all been there, back to Sabah.

Sabah was the First, Grams had said, her birthmark blazing white with rays of color shooting out of it. Cassandra's wasn't like that.

She pulled up her pant leg and stilled. Her birthmark was changing. Its outline darkening and there was just a touch of white starting at the bottom.

Why was it suddenly changing? She needed William. Not letting herself think, she went to the comm center calling on his private line.

"Zafar."

"Can you clear a couple hours for me before I pick up Tori?"

"What's wrong?"

"I need to talk to you."

"Give me an hour."

"I'll be in your Ready Room." Carrying the book, Cassandra sat in the Admiral's chair to wait.

∞ ∞ ∞ ∞ ∞

Turning back to Chief Marat, the Admiral continued, "Your top ten men will make up a security detail for one of the Royals. I want them trained on all aspects of protection including attempted assassinations, hand-to-hand, and deadly force. They will have seven days to prepare. Anyone unable to make the grade will be cut. Understood?"

"Yes, Admiral."

"This information is classified, Marat. They are not to speak of it to anyone outside the group. Anyone who does will be severely dealt with."

"Yes, Admiral."

"Dismissed." The security shield was disengaged as Marat left.

"Quinn, I'll be in my Ready Room for the rest of the day. Unless we're under attack, I'm not to be disturbed until I notify you."

"Yes, Sir."

Leaving the bridge, William headed to their quarters to find out what Cassandra needed to talk about.

∞ ∞ ∞ ∞ ∞

Entering their quarters, he found Cassandra sitting behind his desk. The look in her eyes told him she was concerned.

"What's wrong?"

"Why do you have a book in Ancient Sumerian?"

"What?"

She handed him the book she'd been holding in her lap.

"Kyle gave me this nearly eight cycles ago." William turned it over in his hands. "He found it in the Archives about to be destroyed and knowing I had an interest in history, he acquired it for me. It's Ancient Carinian."

"Sumerian," she corrected. "It was the first written language on Earth. My fifth doctorate is in Sumerian. It's what I was studying when Tori was kidnapped."

"You can read this?" William's eyes widened.

"Yes. Can you? Do you know what it says?"

"Yes. It's a story about the missing Princess of the House of Knowledge."

"Before the explosion, you were trying to tell me about the House of Knowledge, about my birthmark, what you thought it meant. It's because of this book, isn't it?"

"Yes."

"Tell me." Leaving his chair, she walked to the painting of the setting suns.

William began to recount the story. "The Royal Family of the House of Knowledge is gifted with intelligence, but the missing Princess was exceptionally gifted. They have sapphire blue eyes and a birthmark on the inside of the right leg just above the ankle."

"Just like my birthmark?"

"No. All rulers' birthmarks change before they take their throne."

"There are two people in the story."

"The man is the third son of King Tibus. He disappeared with the Princess." Cassandra turned, seeing the judgment in William's eyes.

"You condemn him for leaving."

"He murdered his brother then ran away."

Walking back to him, she looked into his eyes. Did she dare to tell him? Would he believe her?

"Cassandra," William could see the hesitation in her eyes. "Tell me, whatever it is." Knowing he had the right to know she started.

"When I was in the dark, before I heard you, saw *your* light…there was another light." Taking a deep breath, she continued, "In that light, I saw all my ancestors. All the Qwes women who came before, and I knew them, William. I could look at each one and I knew their name, what happened in their life, everything." Seeing that he was listening, she continued.

"There was one; she was tall, head and shoulders above the others, standing slightly apart. She was beautiful, with long black hair, pale skin, and these brilliant blue eyes that seemed to glow."

Knowing she didn't realize she'd just described herself, William gently caressed her cheek bringing her incredible blue eyes back to him.

"Her name was Sabah. She was the First, the first Qwes woman. The look she gave me was like she was trying to tell me something that I should know or remember. Then she looked down at her leg at her birthmark."

"It was different than mine, William." She frowned slightly. "It was this glowing white tower of light and at the top there were rays of color coming out, violet, red, amber, green and blue. I was going to ask, but then I saw your light, heard your voice and suddenly I knew what Sabah had been trying to get me to remember…you. So I turned away from them and came to you."

Enfolding her in his arms, he pulled her close. William couldn't speak. This woman, this strong, amazing woman, his life mate, was the most precious gift he had ever received.

"William?" Easing slightly away she looked up at him, shadows in her eyes she asked, "Do you believe me?"

"Yes. Yes, Cassandra, I believe you. You had an encounter with your ancestors."

"Grams always said I should listen to my dreams that they'd tell me what I needed to know. I wasn't sure if you'd believe that." Here was one of the many subjects they hadn't had time to explore together.

"On Carina, some believe in dreams and visions, some don't," he told her. "The House of Protection believes strongly in them, I believe in them. I believe you, Cassandra."

"Tell me what it means. That Sabah's birthmark is different than mine."

"That she was the lost Princess. It is the birthmark of the Queen, Cassandra. You descend from the House of Knowledge or Light."

"How does that affect us?"

When he started to pull away, she tightened her arms. "You've had time to think about this, to pull it all together. You were the first to realize the Regulians were searching for something…me…that someone on Carina was involved, probably from the House of Knowledge. I need to understand, William. I can't help if I don't understand."

"I know," he gave her a quick kiss as he stepped out of her arms. Wondering how much he could tell her and still protect her. "Three days ago I contacted High Admiral Valerian and told him my belief in the Carinian traitor, its connection to the destruction of Earth, and the House of Knowledge. I requested that he send the Battle Star Dioscuri to replace the Retribution so that we could return to Carina and resolve the matter."

"Why replace the Retribution?"

"I believe the Regulians will cease attacking the Fleet if the Retribution is gone."

"They'll follow the Retribution, follow me."

"Yes."

"Because you'll make sure they know that the 'Imperial Light' is being protected here."

"Yes." He shouldn't have been surprised she'd put it together. She walked back to the painting.

"So what will happen when we get to Carina? What have you planned?"

"I'll meet with the High Admiral. Steps will be taken to ensure your safety until the Assembly can meet. They will decide between you and the reigning Queen, who has the most valid claim to the throne. Once they choose you, you'll be safe."

"But William...my safety isn't the issue," she turned to look at him.

"It's the only issue that matters."

"No. The murder of seven billion people is what matters. Justice for them is what matters."

"You can give them that once you're declared Queen by the Assembly."

"How would they decide that?"

"Since the death of Queen Gevira, Sabah's mother, the Assembly has appointed the Queen of the House of Knowledge. The current Queen is Queen Yakira, she's from the Nacar family; they have been the Royal Family for the last two hundred years."

"Why them? Why her?"

"She carries the most significant birthmark."

"Darker than mine?"

"No. You do realize yours has gotten darker recently."

"Yes. So a bunch of people will basically compare our legs then decide who will be Queen."

"Yes."

"You said the birthmark changes before they take the throne. Queen Yakira's didn't?"

"Only the true heir's will change, then there is never any doubt who is Queen."

Sitting in one of the chairs next to the Admiral's desk, Cassandra leaned back sorting through all this new information.

Waiting in his chair, William watched as her mind replayed everything she had just been told, processing it, organizing. He loved to see all the thoughts cross her face knowing her guard was only down for him.

Opening a drawer, he pulled out the bottle of Carinian ale, poured two glasses, put one in front of her and sat back to wait.

"Is there a way to get into the Archives so I can learn more about the Houses?" Cassandra picked up the glass, looked at it and took a sip, "Not bad."

"What do you want to know?"

"I don't know, that's the problem. There are too many things I don't know. I need information on the Houses, the Royals, the connections. You're already focused on the House of Knowledge. They have the most to gain, but there's got to be more."

"You want information that wouldn't be available to the common Carinian."

"It would be accessible to the Rulers, their families, and the military, wouldn't it?"

"Yes," William saw where she was going.

"So it should be available to me since someone thinks I could be Queen. Can it be done? From here without anyone knowing?"

"It'll be tricky. We can get so far on my security without raising any flags, but after that…"

"Then it will be up to me. What happens if the Royals find out your security code is being used?"

"It won't matter, you'll be Queen."

"Before that."

"It won't matter."

"William…"

"Cassandra, if you need the information you'll have it. But it will have to be either from this comm or the one in our sleeping quarters. They have the best security on the ship."

Cassandra's eyes narrowed, "Then why did you talk to the High Admiral on the Bridge?"

"Cassandra…"

"It was about the Dioscuri coming, wasn't it? You didn't want me to know."

"I didn't want anyone to know. Only Quinn knows. Cassandra, I know how to protect you."

"I've never doubted that, William, but protecting me and keeping me in the dark are two entirely different things."

"I told you about the Dioscuri when everything was set. You have to trust I know what I'm doing."

Standing she walked over to lean against the desk next to him. "I've always trusted you. I need to go get Tori, class is almost out. But there's something I want to show you, it's the real reason I wanted you to clear some time." Putting her foot on his thigh she lifted her pant leg.

Expecting to see her birthmark was darker, he was amazed to see it was starting to fill with color. Rubbing his thumb across it, he knew that anyone who saw it would have no doubt she was the lost Queen. Standing, he pulled her close, suddenly uncertain of their future.

"William?" Easing his hold he leaned down for a gentle kiss.

"You are the Queen, Cassandra."

"Maybe, but I'm also just me, your life mate."

"Yes, you are. I love you."

"I love you too."

"You need to make sure no one sees your birthmark until we reach the Assembly."

"All right, I need to get Tori."

∞ ∞ ∞ ∞ ∞

Walking Victoria to class several days later, Cassandra couldn't help but notice the unusual silence filling the Retribution. There were no yells, no shouts, no laughter, it was like a funeral. Even the kids were somber.

As Victoria entered the class, she saw Javiera and Amina coming down the corridor. They too were quiet with no smiles of greeting. Cassandra waited as Javiera hugged her daughter goodbye.

"Javiera, what's going on?"

"You should know," the accusation in Javiera's voice caused Cassandra to take a step back.

"What do you mean?" When she started to turn away, Cassandra grabbed her arm. "You told me that if I had any questions I could ask you. Well, I'm asking. What the fuck is going on? It's like someone died."

Javiera saw the honest confusion in Cassandra's eyes. "You really don't know, do you?" Javiera looked around the corridor. "Come on, we can't talk here."

Following her, Cassandra was suddenly aware of the eyes following them. Entering the Michelakakis' quarters, Javiera secured the door.

"You know the Dioscuri replaced the Retribution on this tour."

"Yes, it arrived yesterday."

"And that we're heading back to Carina."

"Yes."

"There are only two reasons for that to happen, Cassandra."

"What do you mean reasons…?" Cassandra started to get a sick feeling in her stomach.

"Either the Admiral has been ordered back because High Command has lost faith in his ability to command or the Admiral has requested it, because he no longer feels he can."

"Can what?"

"Command the Fleet."

"What!" Cassandra's eyes widened, "Javiera, that's just crazy. Why would anyone think that?"

"Cassandra! You don't just have a Battle Star replaced eight months into a tour! Especially one that has seen a lot of combat unless it is severely damaged or suffered heavy losses; the Retribution has had neither. It means there has been a loss of confidence in the commander at the highest levels."

"Why would anyone think that, especially on this ship?" Javiera just stared at her. "Because of me? Everyone thinks it's because I'm his life mate that he's lost his nerve to command?"

"Simply put, yes."

"But that's ridiculous. Javiera, you said you grew up on ships, you know the Admiral, you know there was a reason for this."

"And it has nothing to do with you?"

Turning away Cassandra ran a hand through her hair. "It does, but not in the way you think. Shit! Why didn't he tell me this would be what his crew would think?"

"I thought you didn't care what people would think. You didn't about Falco," Javiera accused.

"That was different. He was worried what everyone would think about or say about me. I could care less. But this…this is what his crew thinks about him! Are saying about him! Fuck! How could any of them doubt him? How could you?"

Javiera was somewhat taken aback by Cassandra's rage, "You really didn't know, did you?"

"If I'd have known I would have stopped it. There has to be another way."

"Another way to what?" At her silence, Javiera's mind started to race. "You're saying that there's another reason for this, one that justifies this."

"I can't tell you."

Javiera sat down on her couch. She'd known Cassandra only a short period of time, but in that time had come to trust her. Her gut told her to trust her now.

"Okay, don't tell me but there is something else you should know, and I doubt the Admiral will tell you. Even if there is another reason for returning to base, a major reason that High Command was aware of, the chances of the Admiral ever being put in command of another Battle Star, let alone another Fleet, are zero."

Cassandra's pale face told Javiera all she needed to know. While the Admiral had told her what was going on, he'd protected her from what it would do to him.

"They'll take away his command?" Cassandra's voice was faint.

"Yes."

The first change she noticed was Cassandra's eyes. Moments ago they'd been dazed and shocked to the point she'd thought of making her sit. But now, they blazed with fury, her cheeks filling with color.

"That son of a bitch! Damn him! What the hell gave him the right?"

Javiera was suddenly glad she was not the Admiral and not because of High Command. Cassandra pissed off was an unrivaled sight.

"I need to get back to quarters, but Javiera, don't doubt the Admiral. NEVER doubt him." As she strode the corridors of the Retribution, no one seeing her considered stopping her.

Chapter Eighteen

Entering the Ready Room all conversation stopped. Tar and Lucas were there making Cassandra realize she was the only one who didn't understand. Carefully shutting the hatch, she sat down in the chair to the left of the Admiral.

"Cassandra, we're having a meeting."

"Go ahead, it's not as if it concerns me anyway. Right? It was only my planet destroyed, only my family murdered. I mean, why should I give a damn? I'm just some stupid refugee that believes everything she's told. Isn't that right, Admiral?" Her eyes blazed into his.

"Lucas, Quinn, would you excuse us for a minute?"

"There's no need for that, Admiral, after all you keep them informed." Cassandra's eyes turned to the two men, the blazing cold froze them in their chairs. "While I, on the other hand, have been kept in the dark." Cassandra turned her attention back to the Admiral. "That ends now. So please continue on, I'd love to know how the three of you are handling my life!"

"You haven't been kept in the dark," the Admiral's own temper was rising.

"Really…so I've been told what the arrival of the Dioscuri means for you?" Quinn and Lucas looked at each other.

"You've been given all the relevant information."

"Relevant information…that's what you call it? You knew I wouldn't realize it would cost you your command!" She stood slamming her hand down on his desk, "you had no right to keep that from me!"

"It wasn't your decision!"

"No, it was yours! But it involved me! It's because of me! I should have been told!" Leaning over the desk, they were nearly nose-to-nose.

"You didn't need to know! There are more important things for you to concentrate on."

"More important? How are you not important? How is our life together not important?"

"Cassandra, once this is settled you'll be Queen, it won't matter." Hoping to distract her, he walked over to grip her shoulders. But Cassandra caught the look on Lucas' face, the looks he and Quinn exchanged. There was something else she wasn't being told.

"What don't I know?" Stepping around William, Cassandra advanced on the two men.

"Lucas," Cassandra's look bored into his, "What… don't… I… know?"

"Cassandra, this is between you and me." William gave his son a hard look.

"Bullshit! If it were I'd know about it, wouldn't I?"

"Dad, she has the right to know."

"No!"

"An heir to the throne cannot have a Union with anyone outside his or her House," Quinn told her earning a furious look from his friend. "A Queen has the right to know, William."

"What?"

Quinn saw the utter shock in her eyes.

"The Queen of the House of Knowledge must join with someone from her own House."

Cassandra's eyes shot from Quinn to Lucas, who nodded.

"You knew…" she turned to William. "All along, as soon as you saw my birthmark," William said nothing. "You knew that if I became Queen…and you didn't think that mattered!"

"Your safety is what matters! Damn it, Cassandra, they want you dead! I'm not going to let that happen!"

"So I can be Queen…have a life."

"Yes."

"One without you."

"If that's what it takes to keep you safe. Then yes."

"You've thought it all out, planned it, are willing to execute that plan," she slowly walked over to stand in front of William with eyes he couldn't read. She'd shut him out.

"Yes."

"So who have you picked?" she demanded.

"Picked? What are you talking about?"

"I'll have to marry, won't I? Produce an heir. So who is he?"

The tormented look on William's face almost made her stop, but the thought of him planning all this fueled her anger.

"Who's the man I'll sleep with every night, who I'll make love with, conceive with? Tell me, William, who will it be?"

Lucas stood up, "Cassandra, that's enough!"

"No, Lucas, it really isn't." Her eyes stared into his. "Because this is my life, my future. And no one, not even my life mate," she turned back to William, "has the right to make a decision like this for me!"

"That would be your decision, Cassandra," William finally replied in a tight voice.

"That's right, Admiral, *mine* not *yours*." Turning away from him, Cassandra went into the private quarters. The careful closing of the door louder than any slam.

William walked slowly to his desk, knowing he'd just lost any future he might have with his life mate. Sitting down he flexed his hands on the desk.

"We'll have to continue this meeting later."

"Dad…I'll go talk to her," Lucas started to rise.

"Leave her alone, Lucas," William's bleak eyes met his son's. "She'll work her way around to it, figure out it's the only way."

"The only way to what?"

"Keep her safe."

"Admiral," Quinn stood looking at his longtime friend, "I think you've misjudged her. She has hung out of a Raptor for her niece, climbed into an active array for the Retribution, and stood toe-to-toe with Tibullus, leaving him stuttering for you. She's not at all concerned about her safety. Come on, Lucas." Turning, both men left.

∞ ∞ ∞ ∞ ∞

Standing in the middle of the room, Cassandra didn't know what to do. How could he have done this? How could he believe she'd sacrifice him to be Queen? That she'd choose another to have children with? Had it all been a lie? Four days ago he'd promised her a child. 'Soon' he'd said. A lie or a wish?

She needed to sort this out, to come to a decision in her own mind and she couldn't do that in this room with all its memories. Turning, she entered the Ready Room, stopping when she found William there sitting behind his desk.

Hearing the door open he watched her enter. Her face was set, her stride determined, her sapphire eyes shuttered. When she stopped, he stood.

She was the most beautiful woman he'd ever seen. She was his life mate. How was he going to let her go? The thought of her sharing with another what they'd shared was tearing him apart. Starting toward her, he stopped as she turned, leaving him without a word.

∞ ∞ ∞ ∞ ∞

"Admiral, where's Aunt Cassie?"

"I'm right here, kiddo." Striding into the room she found them finishing their meals, a plate still covered next to William. Rounding the table, she pulled out the chair next to Tori.

"So how was school?" she asked.

"Good."

"Homework?"

"Some. Why didn't you pick me up?"

"I'm sorry. I asked Javiera to because I was worried I'd forget. You know how I get when I'm in the middle of a project," she forced a smile she wasn't feeling. "She picked you up, didn't she?"

"Yeah, she did."

"Good. You done?"

"Yup."

"Then let's hit that homework."

"I can do it." Leaving the table, Victoria went to her room and closed the door. Standing, Cassandra picked up the dirty dishes.

"You need to eat," William broke the silence, his eyes following her.

"Later." Picking up the bag she'd dropped by her chair, she headed over to the work area.

"Cassandra, we need to talk."

"No." With her fingers flying over the keys, she dove back into her research, shutting him out. Watching her, he sighed.

"I'll be at my desk if you need me." Receiving no reply he left after one last long look at her back.

Sagging in her chair, Cassandra put her head in her hands. This was going to be so much harder than she thought. To be this close to him and not touch him, not kiss him. But he needed to understand what his decision would cost; cost both of them. Looking at the screen she got back to work.

∞ ∞ ∞ ∞ ∞

Unable to put it off any longer, William went into their private quarters, hoping to find Cassandra already in bed asleep. Instead, he found her at the comm center, her plate untouched.

"You didn't eat."

"Hmmm…what?" she looked up to find him standing beside her. She'd been so consumed by what she had found she hadn't heard him enter.

"You need to eat." He got just a glimpse of the woman he loved before she shut him out.

"Later." Turning back to the screen she continued to scan the page.

"Cassandra…" As documents continued to scroll by, William rubbed his neck in frustration. Perhaps for the first time in his life he didn't know what to do. He was responsible for this *that* he knew, but there was no other way to secure her safety.

"If you want to sleep I'll go work in the other room."

"No, stay," he needed her close. "You're all set up." Turning to their closet he changed for bed.

Unable to stop herself Cassandra watched him. How could he possibly think she'd be willing to give him up? Dragging her eyes back to the screen she tried to concentrate.

Stopping on the way to bed, he waited for her to look at him. When she finally did, her eyes were unreadable.

"Don't stay up too late," he murmured raising a hand to touch her cheek. He froze as she jerked away. The pain her action caused clearly evident in his eyes. Dropping his hand, he turned to the empty bed.

Lying alone in the bed they should be sharing, he watched as she continued to work at the comm center. Her fingers flying over the keys digging out the information she needed. He knew she was searching for connections between the Royals and Regulians. They'd discussed it…before. He'd given her the codes she would need to access the records. He'd been willing to let her search, hoping it would keep her busy so she wouldn't realize what he was doing behind her back. He could admit it to himself. But he had the right to protect her, no matter the cost.

∞ ∞ ∞ ∞ ∞

The wind whipped his hair as the waves violently crashed against the cliffs. There would be no calming sunset for William. Storm clouds were building on the horizon, stealing the light of the suns. Sensing someone behind him, he braced for an attack.

"Wicked storm, wouldn't want to be caught in it alone."

Turning quickly he assessed the shorter man. What he lacked in height, he made up for in size. He would be a worthy opponent in battle. "Only an idiot would be out alone," William replied.

"Most men are, at one time or another, or so my life mate tells me." The man turned calm, violet eyes to William.

"You're Kayden."

"Yes."

"You murdered your brother then ran away."

"Did I?" His violet eyes hardened. "If I had, you would never be. You know nothing."

"You are the third son of King Tibus. You killed the First Son then ran away, taking the future Queen of the House of Knowledge with you."

"My brother lived. The King's First Son gave me his blessing. I left with my life mate."

"She was to be Queen," William fired at him.

"She was Queen!" Kayden shot back, "*My* Queen!"

"You stood in the way of what she was to be."

Kayden rounded on William. "You know nothing!" Rage filled his eyes. "Stand in her way? No one stands in my life mate's way once she's made up her mind including me!" Turning, Kayden stared at the gathering clouds, his chest heaving.

William watched the gathering storm and suddenly realized what Kayden had said. His brother lived. If he hadn't then William would never be. But William descended from the Fourth Son. He had said, 'King's First Son,' not his brother. There was something he didn't know. He was beginning to doubt what he had always believed.

"What don't I know?"

Kayden turned, staring at him as if he was trying to reach a decision. As William waited, there was a sudden break in the gathering clouds, a brilliant ray of light drove back the growing gloom.

It reminded him of Cassandra, his life mate, his Light. Of the decisions he'd made for her, all with good reasons. The clouds regrouped shutting out the light, William found Kayden watching him.

"I would have lost her, my life mate, if she'd done what I demanded. Followed the path I had decided was best for her. I was willing to make the sacrifice. She was not. She didn't care about winning the battle, she would win the war. She never lost sight of what was truly important. I did."

"What did she do?"

"She found another way; one unthinkable to me. She would leave Carina. She wanted no part of the darkness keeping us apart. She would go to Messene and from there disappear. Going somewhere she wouldn't be found. That was her decision. I would have to decide if she left alone. It was an easy choice to make. I couldn't protect her if I weren't with her."

William was shocked by what he heard. This was not what was believed in the House of Protection. Kayden had been labeled a murderer. His name was never spoken again.

"Your life together?"

"It was full, filled with children, love, arguments, respect and honesty. She was my Queen. I would willingly die for her and her for me."

"And *your* House?"

"We built our own. Letting in the light, fighting the dark, building the House we would never have been allowed on Carina. What I had to leave behind could never compete." As the storm began to rage, Kayden confronted William. "Will you make your own House with your life mate? Or live with the one you've been assigned? Will it be filled with light or darkness? It's always been your choice."

∞ ∞ ∞ ∞ ∞

Easing back from the comm center, Cassandra rubbed her tired eyes. Looking to William she found him asleep in the bed they'd shared, turned toward her as if he'd been watching her before sleep claimed him. She had to make him realize he was wrong. But words weren't going to work. She knew her life mate, he wouldn't change his mind when it came to protecting her. She understood. She felt the same way about him. It was how he would protect her that she had to convince him to change.

Walking toward the bed she quietly removed her clothes and turned off the light, time to show him what he would lose. Leaning over him, her mouth explored his chest while her hands lightly caressed his sides. Her mouth moved down with her hands, sliding under his sleep pants to caress his stiffening shaft.

Waking to darkness, fully aroused, William felt his life mate's hands holding him. Her mouth planting kisses across his abdomen he groaned, "Cassandra…"

Searching for her in the darkness he discovered she was naked. He gripped her waist and pulled her up for an urgent kiss. Straddling him she dove into the kiss, her breasts pressed against his chest, hands gripping his shoulders.

Breaking the kiss, she used her teeth along his jaw on her way to the sensitive spot behind his ear. Her hips were alive in his hands, telling him she was as aroused as he.

Her mouth continued its assault and William's control vanished. He pulled her under him, his mouth attacked her breasts while he removed his pants. Then he was deep inside her surrounded by her heat. He ran a hand down her thigh and pulled her knee up so they were even closer.

The pace was brutal, the desire unrestrained. Cassandra hooked her legs around his waist trying to get closer, her nails dug into his sweat-slicked back. Feeling her release approaching, she pulled his head up, her tongue mating with his as wildly as her body. Moments later they climaxed violently.

When sanity returned, William found himself still on top of Cassandra, pressing her into the bed. Easing away, he caressed her cheek and found it wet with tears.

"Cassandra, what..." her fingers on his lips silenced him. Curling into his side, she laid her head over his heart and slept.

In the dark, William was trying to figure out what just happened. She'd come to him, his life mate, after everything that had happened. She'd still come to him. But she hadn't spoken, he realized, hadn't said his name. The heart she slept on ached.

Waking up alone, William rose to find Cassandra back at the communications console as if the night had been a dream. Pulling on his sleeping pants he approached. "Cassandra…"

"Aunt Cassie?"

Both adults turned to the quivering voice, finding Victoria standing in her hatchway, cheeks wet. Cassandra was immediately out of her chair.

"What's wrong, Tori?" She was on her knees in front of her. "Bad dream?" The nightmares had stopped since the thread had been removed.

"No." Tori wrapped her arms around her burying her face in her neck.

"Then what? Come on, baby, tell me." Cassandra pulled her into her lap.

Raising her head, Victoria looked at the Admiral, who had squatted down next to them. "Are you in trouble because of me?" her eyes locked with his.

"What?" William was shocked.

"They said yesterday that you got in trouble because of the Regulians, that's why we're going back to Carina early. Is it because of me? Because of the thread?" William was appalled that Tori would blame herself for their return to Carina.

"Tori, that's not true! You're not to blame for any of this." He pulled both of them into his arms. "Neither of you are."

"Then why are you in trouble?"

William didn't know how to respond. The decision that he'd made to return to Carina to protect them had been easy to make. It should have only affected him. But it was affecting all of them; in ways he hadn't considered. Concentrating on the battle, he had lost sight of the war. It seems Kayden was right.

"It's not that I'm really in trouble, Tori." William looked to Cassandra for help, but her eyes told him he was on his own. He had caused this.

"Then what?"

"There are going to be people that are unhappy that the Retribution is back early. When High Admiral Valerian gets here, he's not going to like some of the things we have to tell them about what happened to Earth." Victoria studied the Admiral trying to see if he was telling her the truth then she moved to Cassandra.

"Aunt Cassie?"

"The Admiral wouldn't lie to you, Victoria, you know that." The conviction in her voice humbled him. He'd given her every reason to doubt him.

"So the kids are wrong? Wait until I tell them." Tori started to slide out of her aunt's arms.

"Tori, that's not such a good idea."

"Why?"

"Tori," Cassandra wasn't sure how to explain it so settled on the truth. "The things that happened to Earth and that happened to you, it's going to upset people. It will upset people on the Retribution. The Admiral needed to inform his boss first and he can't do that until we get to Carina. So you can't say anything."

"But others are."

"I know, but it has to be this way. Otherwise, the Admiral really will be in trouble."

William watched Tori processing it, thinking it through, just like her aunt.

"Okay, I won't say anything. I'll go get ready for class." Giving a quick kiss to both of them, she went into her room.

Standing, William helped Cassandra to her feet. Tipping her head up, he watched the shutters fall back over her eyes, shutting him out again. Refusing to let her pull away he kissed her. He knew he hurt her. That she was angry with him, but still, she'd told Tori he wouldn't lie to her. Pulling her close he rested his chin on her head.

"We need to talk. Cassandra, I need to speak with you."

"Will it change anything?" Cassandra's voice was quiet as she looked toward Victoria's room.

"I don't know…I honestly don't. I did what I thought was right."

"For who?"

William allowed her to ease away but wouldn't release her, "Everyone."

"It might have been right for you. But it was wrong for Tori and wrong for me. We have the right to decide what's good for us. As for you and me, there's no us. How can there be when you've decided my future?" She pushed against his bare chest, "If you wanted one without me in it, all you had to do was say so."

"How can you think that?" William demanded and gave her a hard shake, his voice low and urgent.

"Because it's what you've done," her voice broke as she looked away. "Let go, before Tori comes back…please."

Slowly he released her as she walked into the Ready Room, wiping her eyes.

∞ ∞ ∞ ∞ ∞

Returning she was followed by Hutu with first meal. Tori was out of her room, the Admiral dressed. Hutu checked the plates, giving Tori a smile.

"Thank you, Hutu," the Admiral dismissed him.

"You're welcome, Sir. Do you want second meal at the regular time, ma'am?" Hutu turned to Cassandra. Knowing she didn't eat her meal the night before.

"That would be fine, Hutu, thank you."

Smiling at her, he left the Admiral's quarters. Cassandra was finding it hard to eat as she sat next to William. Smiling at Victoria, she forced herself to take a bite of the loblolly Hutu had brought her. William noticed her lack of appetite; she should be starved after not eating the night before. When Victoria finished, she quickly picked up Victoria's plate and her own barely touched bowl.

"Why don't you go wash up and we'll head to class."

With Victoria out of the room, William walked up behind Cassandra, trapping her against the counter.

"You didn't eat." Saying nothing she gripped the counter, unable to turn and face him. The day was just starting and already she was struggling. William leaned in kissing her neck.

"Please…don't…" Cassandra begged, her voice wobbly.

"I'm done, Aunt Cassie."

William stepped away as Tori came out of the bathroom. Taking a deep breath, Cassandra pasted a smile on her face.

"Okay, grab your bag, and we're out of here."

"Bye, Admiral."

"Bye, Tori, have a good day at class." Watching them leave he realized that in a few days it would be forever. What he planned, what he put in motion would cause that. Walking to his desk he sat down. Was it really the only way?

Thinking back to the dream he'd had, Kayden had said he couldn't protect his life mate if he weren't there. Why hadn't he realized that? Why would he trust it to anyone else? Quinn was right. Cassandra would worry about everyone except herself. Someone had to worry about her and he would be that person.

Plans needed to be redrawn, strategies reworked. Cassandra needed to be included in every step. He had a lot of work to do, repairing the damage he'd caused. Getting on the comm he contacted Quinn and Lucas for a meeting in his Ready Room.

∞ ∞ ∞ ∞ ∞

Hugging Victoria goodbye, Cassandra turned to Javiera. She'd spent a lot of time the night before looking at angles, trying to figure out different scenarios. But the one thing she kept coming back to was that she couldn't do this alone, even if she and William were together, they'd need help. Help from people they could trust. For Cassandra, that meant Javiera and Leander. But they needed to know what they would be getting into.

"I need to talk to you, to you and Leander."

Javiera looked at her friend, seeing the seriousness in her eyes. "Leander was in quarters when we left. If we're lucky, we can still catch him." The two women walked in silence to the Michelakakis' quarters. Just as they rounded the corner, they saw Leander.

"Well, what do we have here? Hi, Cassandra," Leander's smile faded as he looked at them.

"Can I talk to you, both of you, in quarters?"

"Yeah, sure..." Turning he led the way unlocking the hatch. As they all entered, he secured it. "So what's wrong?"

Cassandra wasn't sure where to start or how to start.

"Cassandra, what's wrong?" Javiera asked. "I told you, you can ask me anything."

"I know, but this isn't so much asking you something, but telling you, both of you. You might want to sit." As they did, she started. "What do you know about the attack on Earth?"

"Know? That the Regulians attacked and destroyed it."

"But why?"

"Why?" Javiera looked at her husband, "Who knows with the Regulians?"

"They had a reason." Cassandra looked at Leander who had been quiet so far.

"What reason?" He wasn't sure he wanted to know.

"They believed the missing Princess of the House of Knowledge was there."

"What?" Both were stunned. "How would they know? Why would they care? Why destroy the planet?"

"I don't think they did know for a long time. I also don't think they would have cared one way or the other except someone on Carina found out and *they* cared, they cared very much."

"What are you saying?" Leander's voice was low and quiet.

"I'm saying that there is a traitor on Carina, one that's working with the Regulians because they care very much about the missing Princess."

"Cassandra, that's ridiculous. That legend is over 2000 cycles old...no one believed it was possible." Javiera was relieved this wasn't something serious. Leander looked at Cassandra.

"The Admiral believes this?"

"Yes."

"What? Leander this is crazy," Javiera's eyes became a little frantic.

"Is it? There was no reason for them to destroy the planet, Javiera. All they had to do was run, that's what they've always done. So why not this time?"

"I..."

"The poisoning of Tori...the bombing of your quarters...was Falco a part of this?"

"No, that had nothing to do with Earth. We thought it did at first, it fit but..." Cassandra trailed off.

"But what?"

"Falco had nothing to do with the Regulians. Both her attacks were directed at me, Tori got the poison by mistake. That's why we thought it was the Regulians."

"Why Tori?" Javiera whispered.

"Seven cycles ago, Tori was kidnapped; it was the Regulians. They implanted a thread in her arm. The Admiral discovered it after the second attack on the Fleet. Bliant removed it. The Regulians were tracking her. That's how they found the Fleet."

"But why do they care?"

"Someone on Carina has made a deal with them, Javiera, to either bring them the 'Light' as they called it or destroy it."

"Leander?" Javiera looked to her husband.

"The Admiral knew all this?"

"Yes, that's why he asked for the Dioscuri to replace the Retribution, to get back to Carina. Find the traitor."

"It would have to be someone high up, someone powerful."

"Who has a lot to lose."

"You're talking a Royal," Leander's eyes clashed with hers.

"Yes."

"Fuck, Cassandra, you're talking the House of Knowledge."

"Yes." Watching her two friends struggle with the information, she began to wonder if she was doing the right thing.

"Look, maybe I've made a mistake telling you this, but all I know is that in three days we'll be in Carina. The Assembly is going to be called to challenge Queen Yakira. And somewhere in that Assembly will be the person responsible for the death of seven billion people including my family. They need to be held accountable."

Leander had been watching Cassandra tell them what was going to happen, and what he saw stunned him. How had he missed it? "It's you..."

Cassandra said nothing.

"What? Leander, what are you talking about?"

"Cassandra, Cassandra's the returning Queen. You're going to challenge Yakira."

"Yes."

"Why are you telling us this?"

"Because we can't do it alone, we're going to need help. I'm going to need help from people I know and trust, but I need you to really think about it." Cassandra looked from Javiera to Leander. "It's going to be dangerous, Leander, and there's no guarantee it will work. It'll put your whole family at risk."

"Cassandra…" Javiera looked at Leander.

"I need you two to discuss it with each other, to decide what's best for your family. We have three days before we reach Carina. I'll need to know what you have decided by then. If you don't feel you can, I'll understand. It's a lot to ask." She looked at both of them not realizing she was looking like a Queen.

"And, Leander, the Admiral doesn't know I'm talking to you. I want you to know that this has nothing to do with the Coalition. There are no orders, no ramifications for your career if you decide you can't do this. It'll remain between us."

"Like there will be with the Admiral's."

"Yes," Cassandra whispered.

"He really didn't tell you what it would mean, did he?"

"No, he didn't. Look, I know I don't need to say this, but I have to anyway. You can't tell anyone what I've just told you. Not even Amina. Victoria doesn't even know everything."

"We won't tell anyone, Cassandra, whatever we decide."

"Okay, I need to get back…I still have a lot of things to learn before we reach Carina. I'll see you later."

As she left, Cassandra knew she'd done the right thing trusting the Michelakakis, she just wasn't sure it was going to be enough. She needed to start assembling her House. Surrounding herself and Victoria with people she could trust and depend on. Why hadn't she thought of this sooner? Heading back to quarters she had a plan to implement and a new possibility to look into. Time was running out.

Chapter Nineteen

Entering the Ready Room she found Lucas, Quinn and the Admiral leaning over a table looking at plans. All three heads turned as she entered. Straightening, William walked over to her.

"We're reworking some of the security procedures. We need your input." Putting a light hand at her lower back he guided her to the table. Standing so he brushed against her, the Admiral pointed, explaining what had been planned so far. Listening, Cassandra struggled to ignore him, unable to move away.

"When it comes to Victoria, we'll have a protection detail with her at all times. They will report directly to Marat."

"No, they'll report directly to Lucas." She saw the surprise in Lucas' eyes, "and you'll report to me."

"Are you sure that's what you want?" William's eyes revealed nothing. "Lucas hasn't had as much security training as Marat."

"Marat can be in charge of the guards, but he clears everything through Lucas regarding Victoria. You have the final word," Cassandra watched Lucas. "Do you have a problem being in charge of Victoria's protection?"

"No. No problem at all." He knew the trust she'd just given him…the responsibility. He looked at his father, he knew he realized it too.

"What else is there?"

"That should do it for now. Quinn, I'll be on the Bridge shortly."

"Yes, Admiral." With the meeting breaking up, Cassandra turned escaping William's touch, only to be stopped by Lucas as she entered the private chambers.

"Cassandra…Thank you, Marat's good, really good, but…"

"You need to be there. I get that, Lucas, but don't thank me." Looking to see that William was still talking to Quinn she continued, "Because if this all goes wrong, and you know as well as I do that it could, you have only one priority." Lucas recognized her look. He'd seen it before from the Admiral, only this time it was from a Queen. An order was about to be given.

"You get Victoria out! I don't care how, I don't want to know. You don't concern yourself with anyone else, is that understood? If you can't do that, then I'll find someone who can."

Lucas understood what she was telling him. He was not to worry about her, his father or his brother, only Tori. The thought of not helping them was unthinkable, but the idea of not protecting Victoria was worse. Sometimes you have to make hard decisions. His father had taught him that.

"I can do that, I won't like it, but I'll do it." Turning Lucas stopped her once again.

"He loves you, Cassandra." The eyes that met his flashed with pain before going blank. "Never doubt it."

"I never have, Lucas, which only makes it worse."

Finally escaping, Cassandra headed directly into the bathroom hoping for some privacy. She just needed a few minutes alone, away from William, his scent, his touch. Away from the demands, demands she was going to have to learn to handle on her own. She only needed a few minutes then she would start again.

She looked in the mirror. She saw she was beginning to pale. Lack of sleep was catching up with her, but there was still so much to do, to figure out. But she couldn't present an exhausted Queen to the Assembly. Another problem she would have to deal with.

She found William sitting on the couch with his head in his hands. It was the last thing she expected. He pulled his hands away as she appeared but didn't stand.

"Are you ever going to talk to me again?" his voice was tortured.

"I talk to you."

"No, you talk at me, not to me."

"I don't know what else you want."

"I want what we had before."

"Why?" she was worn out. "It doesn't matter. It was never anything but a dream. It's time to wake up." Starting across the room, she found her way blocked. She'd forgotten how fast he could move.

"It matters! Damn it, Cassandra! I know this is my fault…"

"No, it's mine. I should have realized when you promised…but then you didn't, did you? I just took it that way. I should have realized you were just distracting me, not wanting me to ask questions. You're able to do that to me, but soon that won't be a problem."

"What promise did I break?" William asked urgently, his mind racing.

"It doesn't matter."

"No!" He gripped her shoulders pulling her onto her toes. "Tell me!"

"A child. Remember? You said you'd give me one. But you had already made your plans for my life, hadn't you? You'd already talked to the High Admiral about returning to Carina. So I suppose it was a promise after all. I'd have a child, it just wouldn't be yours." She couldn't keep the pain out of her voice or the tears from falling down her face. The buzzing of the hatch broke the silence. Gently easing her down, William went to let Hutu in with lunch.

"I'll take it, Hutu, thank you." Securing the hatch, he returned to find Cassandra at the comm center. Setting the tray down, he approached her. He squatted down, put a tentative hand on her thigh, he needed the contact. She immediately stiffened.

"I love you, Cassandra. The thought of you not protected…again…" the unmistakable pain in his voice caused her to look down at him. "I can't tolerate it, I won't." Realizing he had her attention, he pressed on.

"Falco is on me, all me. You tried to tell me. I dismissed your instinct. You and Tori paid the price for that. I misjudged. Something I rarely do. As Admiral, you're not allowed to. But with you…you say I make you unable to think clearly...you do the same to me…I want you protected, no matter the cost. Please wait," William pleaded as she started to rise. Sitting back down, she watched him, her eyes unreadable.

"My head tells me I'm unreasonable, but my heart…Cassandra, I've been in the Coalition for over thirty cycles, in all that time I've always been able to make my decisions based on what needs to be done, not who it affects. Even with Lucas on board, I pick the best pilots and send them out. It's what I did on Earth. But with you, it's how can I protect you."

"I've never asked that of you."

"No, you never asked. You just trusted me, on the Raptor, when you had no reason to. Then you protected me, even as you knew your family was dying, you protected."

"What are you talking about?"

"When the alarm went off, you understood…horribly knew what it meant for your family. But as the blast hit, you covered my eyes, protecting them from the explosion. As your tears soaked my hands, you protected me."

"That's…"

"No one's ever tried to protect me before. I knew then, on that Raptor, that you would be significant in my life. I was right. You are my life." William moved his hands to her waist. A waist his hands could encircle. "I've always believed you had to be willing to sacrifice if something really mattered to you."

"Even if what you sacrifice *is* what matters?"

He momentarily buried his head in her lap. Her fingers itched to touch him. "See, that's what I couldn't see. I just knew I needed to protect. I needed you to show me what I was doing, but you couldn't because I didn't tell you. I'm used to keeping things close."

"Just not people."

"No, not people. Quinn is my oldest friend, and even with him I keep a distance. But you shattered all that. You were everywhere in my life, and I wanted you there. Needed you there. But old habits die hard," William raised a hand to gently caress her cheek. When she didn't pull away, he knew he had to give her the truth.

"I knew the Regulians wanted you. I knew if they couldn't get to you, they would try to kill you. I knew if I could get you to Carina you would be, if not safe, safer. So I did what I've always done, I made a decision. I would make the sacrifice, meaning my career. It was easy. Everything I've ever done has been leading me to this, to you. But you have to believe me," his eyes pleaded with hers, "I never meant for it to mean sacrificing you, our future, or our child. But once it started I couldn't see any way to stop it. If that were the cost, I'd pay it, not you, not Tori."

"Admiral to the Bridge. Admiral Zafar to the Bridge." The comm center announced.

"Fuck!" William stood to connect to the Bridge when Cassandra's hand stopped him.

"They want you there for a reason."

"We have more we need to talk about."

"You're needed on the Bridge, Admiral, you need to go." Cassandra looked into his eyes, the indecision there a testament to what she really did mean to him.

"Go do you job, William, we'll finish this later."

He was ready to argue until he heard her say his name. It seemed like cycles since he'd heard it.

"Cassandra…"

"Please, I need to think. And William," Cassandra waited until he looked at her, "you're the Admiral because you make the right decisions, military decisions. Tori and I will always be safe as long as you do." Leaning down he gave her a wrenching kiss, it told her he didn't want to leave.

"Please eat something," and the Admiral headed for the Bridge.

∞ ∞ ∞ ∞ ∞

"This had better be important, Quinn," the Admiral demanded entering the Bridge.

"The Regulians have attacked the Fleet, Admiral. They used nuclear devices. There was heavy damage on both sides."

"Casualties?"

"On all ships, the Sentinel is dead in space."

"The First Son?"

"Unknown at this time."

"Fuck! What happened?"

"It was the same as before, they had the direct coordinates."

"Who's feeding them the Intel? How are they getting it?"

"I don't know but, Admiral, the Dioscuri reports several ships broke off, after discovering the Retribution was gone. They're heading toward us."

"How much time?"

"If we make a run for it, we can get to Carina before they catch us."

William's first instinct was to heed Quinn's advice and run for Carina, keep Cassandra safe. But the Admiral knew it was wrong. To protect Cassandra, he needed to make the right military decision.

"No, go to Alert Status One. I want all fighters in their planes. The Regulians aren't reaching Carina. Navigation, plot an intercept course. Communications, contact the High Admiral. I want a secure line. NOW PEOPLE!!" The Admiral's furious voice had the entire Bridge jumping.

∞ ∞ ∞ ∞ ∞

Cassandra stared at the console, her fingers unmoving. She didn't know what to do. What to think. She didn't doubt William's sincerity. That was evident. He wasn't the type of man to lie. If he said something, he meant it. She'd always known that. It was the things he didn't say that kept causing problems. Could she trust that he would tell her what she needed to know, no matter what?

"Alert Status One! All pilots to their planes! Repeat Alert Status One!"

"Attention crew!" The Admiral's voice boomed over the comms. "The Regulians have attacked the Fleet. There have been massive casualties. Two Regulian ships are heading toward Carina, they are carrying nukes. We will intercept and stop them. All hands are to make ready for extreme combat."

Cassandra froze in her chair. How had the Regulians found the Fleet again? How had they found the Retribution? Something was very wrong. They were carrying nukes, they weren't taking any chances.

She had to get Victoria home. This wasn't going to be a regular attack. The Admiral made that clear.

∞ ∞ ∞ ∞ ∞

"Admiral, Valerian is on the comm, secure line."

"High Admiral."

"Zafar, what the fuck is going on?"

"We have a traitor, High Admiral."

"It isn't on my end! No one knew what was going on."

"At this point it doesn't matter. You've received the reports from the Dioscuri?"

"Yes."

"We are moving to intercept the two Regulian ships."

"You consider that wise, Admiral, with the cargo you're carrying?"

"It won't matter if Carina is destroyed, Sir."

"You're right."

"Sir, are there any other ships in the area to assist?"

"None that will get to you in time. I've ordered them to surround Carina in case you fail."

"Understood, Sir."

"Don't fail."

"I have no plans to."

The Admiral knew that while he was on a secure line to the High Admiral, the entire Bridge had heard the conversation. He wanted it that way. He wanted his crew to know they'd been betrayed. It would spread like wildfire throughout the ship. And if the person were on his ship, they would be flushed out.

"Navigator!"

"Yes, Sir."

"How long to intercept?"

"Sir, thirty minutes, Sir."

"Relay the information throughout the ship."

"Yes, Sir."

∞ ∞ ∞ ∞ ∞

Cassandra entered the classroom as the comms announced thirty minutes until they would intercept the Regulians. Seeing her aunt, Victoria started to pick up her bag then set it back down.

"Victoria? What are you doing? We need to get back to quarters."

"Aunt Cassie…I can't leave Amina."

"What? Amina, where's Javiera?"

"She has a post to man. She'll come get me when the battle is over." While the little girl was trying to be brave, Cassandra saw the fear in her eyes.

"Can you call her?"

"No."

"Well, you're not staying here. Come on. You're going with us. I'll let your dad know once we get back to quarters." As the girls picked up their things, the Educator approached.

"You can't just take her with you. A parent has to okay it."

"I will call Leander once we're back to our quarters."

"That's not the way it's done."

"Look. I really don't care how it's done. I am taking both these girls to the Admiral's quarters. If you have a problem with that, then I suggest you call the Admiral, he's on the Bridge. A little busy, but I'm sure he'd love to talk to you," Cassandra went toe-to-toe with the taller woman. "Are you going to call?" As the woman did nothing, Cassandra turned, "I didn't think so. Let's go girls we need to hustle."

∞ ∞ ∞ ∞ ∞

Back in their quarters, Cassandra turned to the girls.

"I want you to go into the other room, girls. I know you didn't get lunch, there's a plate of something on the table. Hutu brought it right before the announcement. Go ahead and eat it. I'll call your dad, Amina, and tell him where you are. He'll let your mom know, okay?"

"Okay."

As the girls left, Cassandra sat down in the Admiral's chair. Using his comm center, she punched in Leander's number.

"Michelakakis."

"Leander, Cassandra."

"A little busy here."

"I know, but you need to know that I brought Amina home with me from class."

"What?"

"Javiera needed to man a post. I wasn't leaving her in that classroom alone so I brought her home, to the Admiral's quarters, with Victoria and me. You need to let Javiera know."

"Cassandra…thank you…that's the safest place on the ship."

"So I've been told."

"She's okay?"

"A little scared, I think we all are. What am I supposed to do, Leander?"

"You stay put. Make sure the hatches are secured. Stay away from anything that can fall on you. Once it's over, there will be an announcement."

"Leander?" Cassandra had heard the break in his voice.

"Tell my little girl I love her, okay? Her mom and I love her very much." Cassandra heard the fear in his voice. "If something happens…"

"She'll be safe, Leander. I promise. She'll be protected, I'll see to it."

"Thank you. Gotta go."

Disconnecting, Cassandra leaned back in the Admiral's chair. Leander was worried they might not survive this attack. There had been casualties reported within the Fleet. The Retribution was alone. The Admiral had chosen to attack, to risk, with her on board.

He said she clouded his mind as much as he did hers, that his need to protect her had caused him to make some bad choices. He admitted that to her. A hard thing for a man used to keeping things close.

He was making the right decision, even if it put her in danger. If they went to Carina, the Regulians would follow. They'd nuke Carina, just like they had Earth. The Retribution was the only thing in the way.

Any doubts she may have had fell away. Yes, they still had a lot to work out, things weren't perfect. Wasn't that what Sabah had said, they'd had an imperfect life, but one together. They hadn't known what would happen, but they took the chance to live an uncertain life together with no regrets.

Was she strong enough to do the same?

Leander was worried they might not all live through this battle. If William died, with the way things currently were between them, could she live with herself not having told him one more time that she loved him? Before she could stop herself, she entered the code to the Admiral's private line to the Bridge.

∞ ∞ ∞ ∞ ∞

"Are all launch ports operational?"

"Yes, Admiral."

"Get them filled."

"Yes, Sir."

Turning to the ringing of his comm, he saw it was his private line. Picking up his headset he connected the call.

"Zafar."

"I brought Tori and Amina back to our quarters."

"Good. I need to go."

"I love you." Cassandra disconnected first. Pushing away from his desk, she went to see what the girls were doing.

∞ ∞ ∞ ∞ ∞

Removing his headset, the Admiral looked around the Bridge. She still loved him. He'd protect her by making sure the world they lived in was safe, safe for their children.

"Launch all fighters!" William ordered.

"Yes, Sir. Launch all fighters. Launch all fighters" the command went out throughout the ship.

∞ ∞ ∞ ∞ ∞

Back in their quarters, Cassandra found the girls had devoured her lunch. Good thing since nerves had her stomach rolling.

"So what are we going to do?"

"We were going to go play in my room if that's okay, Aunt Cassie."

"Go for it. Oh, Amina, I got hold of your dad. He'll let your mom know. He said to tell you he loves you and he'll see you soon."

"Okay."

As the girls left, she turned to the console. Should she work on it or wait? Time was running out. Just then the Retribution's guns started to fire.

Following Leander's advice, she began looking for things that could fall. Just like earthquake-proofing back on Earth. After she was done, she sat down to wait. She always sucked at waiting.

As the battle raged on it was hard to tell who was winning. Two against one were bad odds even when the one was a Battle Star. So far they'd managed to prevent any direct hits on the Retribution but that couldn't last forever.

∞ ∞ ∞ ∞ ∞

"Admiral, we have an inbound nuke. Starboard side."

"Rig for impact!"

As alarms sounded throughout the ship, the ship lurched to one side. The girls came running to Cassandra. She'd heard this signal before. With a child on each side, she pulled them close.

"Shhh now, it's going to be okay."

"But Aunt Cassie…"

"It will be okay, Tori. We're safe and we're together, right? Isn't that right, Amina? Soon this will be over and we'll all get to go to Carina. What's it like there? Where's your favorite spot?" As the alarms continued to sound, Amina told them about Carina.

Much later, after the alarms finally ceased, the comm center rang. Leaving the girls on the couch, Cassandra picked up the headset.

"Chamberlain."

"Ma'am, this is Hutu. Just checking to see what time you would like third meal."

"Hutu, we've just finished a major battle."

"Yes, ma'am, but you and Tori still need to eat." Cassandra was constantly amazed by his dedication.

"Well, we wouldn't refuse food but there are three of us. Amina is here."

"I'm sure the Michelakakis' greatly appreciate that, ma'am. I will plan accordingly. What time would you like it?" Looking at the clock, Cassandra realized it was already 1800.

"Whenever you can bring it would be fine, Hutu. Thank you."

∞ ∞ ∞ ∞ ∞

"Damage report!" the Admiral demanded.

"Sir, the worst damage is to Decks C, D, and E, sections 53-68. Those areas took the hit from the nuke. There was a moment of decompression before the shields kicked back in."

"Casualties?"

"Unknown at this time, Sir."

"Other damage?"

"All considered minor, Sir. We kicked ass! Sorry, Sir."

"Nothing to be sorry for, Ensign, we did. I want a secure line to the High Admiral and get me that casualty report!"

"Yes, Sir."

Looking at Quinn, the Admiral walked into his Command Center.

"Will, that section on Deck E is where the classroom was."

"I know."

"Victoria?"

"In our quarters, Cassandra got her and Amina out at the first sign of trouble."

"Thank the Ancestors!"

"Yes, hopefully, they are all safe." As his comm rang, the Admiral reported to the High Admiral.

∞ ∞ ∞ ∞ ∞

"Thanks, Hutu, this is awesome!" Victoria exclaimed as she saw a huge pile of chicken nuggets.

"I thought you and Amina might like this."

"You bet! Aunt Cassie, can we take it into my room? It would be like a sleepover!"

"Go ahead."

After the girls had left, Cassandra turned to Hutu, "Tell me."

"I don't know much, ma'am. The worst of the damage is on decks C, D, and E. They took a direct hit. There will be casualties, but no one knows how many yet. Both Regulian ships were destroyed. The threat is over."

"But you don't know much." She gave him a weak smile as she walked over to the couch to sit down, her legs suddenly weak. "Thank you, Hutu."

He saw how pale she was as he picked up the plate he had checked and brought it to her.

"You need to eat. The Admiral will be unhappy if he finds you passed out from hunger. Did you eat your lunch?"

"The girls needed it."

"You should have called."

"We were in the middle of a battle, Hutu. I couldn't have eaten anyway."

"You'll eat now."

Cassandra saw the determination in his face. "I will." At Hutu's look, she touched his hand, "I promise."

As Hutu left, she leaned her head back against the couch. What a day and it wasn't even over yet. It wouldn't be until William was home safe. Leaning forward, Cassandra looked at the plate Hutu had brought her. Picking up the forc, she made it through half before her stomach wouldn't take any more. She stood and headed for the console ready to start on the new possibility.

What if there was something else going on that had nothing to do with the House of Knowledge? Just like Falco's attacks on her had nothing to do with the Regulians. Falco hadn't even known the Regulians were looking for her, it had been a coincidence, and they'd assumed they were related.

What if some of these attacks on the Fleet were the same? If not her, then who and why?

There had been transmissions between someone in Carinian space and the Regulians. They talked about the Light. Did all of them? Had they found all of them? William had given her access codes to communications. She needed to come up with a way to search them. Something was being missed.

Going back to the first known transmission from the Regulians to Carina, she studied more than just what it said. They knew it came from the Regulian ship, Cimex, but not who it was sent to. They also knew it was about her. How did they know it came from the Cimex? There had to be some type of embedded coding. Cassandra quickly wrote a program comparing the first two transmissions looking for similar coding. As the program started, there was a buzzing at the hatch. Switching the console to privacy mode, Cassandra opened the door to Leander and Javiera.

"Hi."

"Cassandra…" tears filled Javiera's eyes.

"What? What's wrong?"

"If you hadn't taken Amina…"

"What…"

Leander put his arm around his wife. "Cassandra, the hit the ship took," she nodded at Leander. "It was a direct hit on the classroom. If Amina had been there…" he couldn't finish. Cassandra paled at the thought.

"We owe you more than we can say," Javiera embraced her.

"No, no you don't. You would have done the same for Tori."

"Mom? What's wrong?" Amina saw her mother crying.

"Nothing's wrong, honey, I'm happy everyone's okay, that's all."

"Hey, baby girl," Leander walked over to his daughter and picked her up, "give your old dad a hug." As all three embraced, Cassandra saw Tori in the doorway, a sad look on her face. Walking over to her, she squatted down pulling her into her arms.

"I love you, Victoria Lynn."

"I love you too."

After several minutes, the Michelakakis family left. Cassandra looked down at Tori. "So what would you like to do?"

"I'm tired. I think I'll just go to bed."

Cassandra looked at the clock and realized it was only 2000. "You're sure?"

"Yeah."

"All right then, let's get you ready for bed."

"I can do it myself, Aunt Cassie." Turning, Tori left the room.

"Oh." Cassandra was left wondering what was going on. Entering their private chambers, Tori's hatch was closed. Undecided on what to do, the comm beeped telling her that the search was done.

Reading the results, Cassandra began to smile. "Now we're on to something." Sitting down she started refining the search while adding more variables. "I'm on to you now, you son of a bitch!"

∞ ∞ ∞ ∞ ∞

"Casualty report, Sir."

"Eighteen, confirmed?" the Admiral scanned the list, grateful Lucas wasn't on it.

"Yes, Sir. Twenty-eight are in Medical with serious but not life-threatening injuries. All others are accounted for."

The Admiral knew it could have been worse. If the Regulians had made it to Carina, millions could have been lost. But he considered any loss of life on his tours an insult.

"Get me the names, Colonel. The families will need to be notified."

"Yes, Sir." Quinn knew the Admiral sent a personal letter to the families of all those he lost.

"Any news on The First Son?"

"No, Admiral. They're still scrambling to stabilize the ships."

"Get me the High Admiral back on a secure line."

"Yes, Sir."

∞ ∞ ∞ ∞ ∞

"That doesn't make any sense!" Cassandra argued with her console. "How can it have only one?" After peeling back layers of coding, she'd finally been able to isolate two strings of an identical series of numbers in the first three transmissions. They had to have some significance. But with the fourth transmission, the one giving the location of the Fleet, she could only match one string. How could that be?

Frustrated she started to pace. Seeing that Victoria's door was still closed she realized there'd been no goodnight hug, no goodnight kiss. Something was wrong.

Entering the room, she found her niece asleep with the tracks of her tears still visible. What had happened? She'd seemed okay when Amina was here. It wasn't until Leander and Javiera had come. Crap! Amina's parents had come to get her. Why hadn't Cassandra realized…as she was about to wake her, the outer hatch buzzed.

Opening it she found Lucas, still in his flight suit, somehow he'd known. Turning she left him to secure the hatch.

"Everything okay here?" When he got no response, he touched her shoulder.

"Cassie?"

"We're fine. Victoria's just a little down." Lucas looked toward the private chambers. "She's asleep," Cassandra told him.

"Oh."

"But it might do her some good to see you."

"What's wrong?"

"She's missing her parents. Leander and Javiera came to get Amina after the battle. It reminded her of what she'd lost. Seeing you might make her realize she's gained a few things too."

Turning the lights on low, Lucas saw the tracks the tears had left on Victoria's sleeping face. His heart ached at the thought of her crying herself to sleep.

"Victoria," gently rubbing her back Cassandra woke her. "Come on, Tori, wake up for a minute."

"No," came the crabby voice causing Cassandra to smile a little.

"Lucas is here to see you."

"Lucas?" Tori opened her swollen eyes.

"Yeah, right over there," she pointed to the hatch.

She watched her niece look at Lucas and realized missing her parents wasn't the only thing bothering her, she'd worried about Lucas too. The man she'd put in charge of her protection.

"I need to get some work done in the other room. Not too long," Cassandra gave a pointed look to Lucas. Receiving a nod she left the room.

∞ ∞ ∞ ∞ ∞

"What's your situation, Zafar?"

"We're good, High Admiral. Moderate damage, eighteen lost, twenty-eight in Medical, could have been worse."

"A lot worse, you did a fantastic job."

"I hear the Fleet is still scrambling to stabilize ships."

"Yes, they got caught looking."

"Someone gave them their location, there's a difference. The First Son?"

"No word."

"Fuck! How long until they are able to defend the border?"

"At least a week, maybe more."

"You're sending support?"

"Three more battleships."

"How long?"

"They'll be at the border in three days. Admiral..."

"We'll stay in place until the Fleet is secured unless you want us at the border."

"No, I want you right where you're at. If the Regulians try another attack, we'll need you to protect Carina. The other will have to wait."

"Understood, I would like to be kept apprised on The First Son."

"I know you're his Second Father. I'll let you know as soon as I do."

"Appreciate it."

∞ ∞ ∞ ∞ ∞

Lucas found Cassandra at the comm center as he quietly closed the hatch to Victoria's room.

"Sleeping?" she turned to him.

"Exhausted, I didn't know a little girl could cry that much. It about killed me."

"Seems you handled it or she'd still be crying."

"How do you deal with it? With everything you've lost?"

"By remembering we still have each other, remembering those we've lost and being grateful for those we've found." As the comm beeped, she turned back to it.

"What are you working on?"

"Trying to find connections between the Regulian transmissions."

"Any luck?"

"Not much." Cassandra saw the fatigue in Lucas' eyes, "Go home, Lucas, you look like crap." Grinning, she stood up to lead him to the outer hatch.

"You've been waiting to say that to me."

"I have. Thanks for helping with Tori."

"Anytime."

Securing the hatch, she returned to read the results of her latest search. There was still only the single series in common in all four communications. That had to mean it was either the same person sending the transmission or receiving it.

Which was it?

What about this latest attack? Was there a transmission before it? What did the coding mean? Was it a signature, security clearance? What? Wait… a security clearance.

How did a person send a transmission? What authorization would a person need? Was each person assigned their own? She'd have to ask William.

She leaned back in her chair and rubbed her eyes. She needed to take a break; checking on Tori she found she'd kicked her covers off. Tucking her back in, she leaned down to give her a light kiss and whisper, "I love you, Victoria Lynn, only good dreams."

Tears filled her eyes as she turned to leave and she discovered William just inside the room.

∞ ∞ ∞ ∞ ∞

Coming home William wasn't sure what he'd find. He hoped Cassandra would be sleeping. He'd given her a bad couple of days. He found her in Tori's room with tears in her eyes. It wasn't what he expected.

"She's okay?" he kept his voice low looking at Tori.

Nodding, she moved past him. Quietly he shut the door. Walking into their quarters she quickly wiped her eyes.

"What's wrong then?"

"Nothing," she couldn't seem to stop the tears. He was safe, Victoria was safe, Lucas and the Michelakakis' were safe. So why was she crying? William turned her around so she faced him.

"It's not nothing. You're crying." With his thumbs, he gently wiped her cheeks causing the tears to flow faster. "Please tell me."

Raising tear-drenched eyes, she looked at the man she loved. She never would have known him if the Regulians hadn't attacked Earth. If he hadn't saved her and Tori, but he hadn't been able to save them all. The pain swimming in her eyes staggered him.

"Cassandra…please…what's wrong?"

"Could you just hold me for a minute?" she whispered.

Wrapping her in his arms, William lifted her off her feet, carried her over to the couch, and pulled her across his lap. As she burrowed into him, sobs racked her body. He could do nothing but hold her, rubbing her back like she did with Victoria. He tucked her in close and rested his cheek on the top of her head. This was the strongest woman he'd ever known and she was devastated. What had happened? What didn't he know?

Was this how she felt when he kept things from her? Blind-sided, unsure of herself? It was something he'd never do again.

As the sobs subsided, he put a finger under her chin and tipped her face up to his. Searching, he found her beautiful blue eyes red-rimmed and exhausted. Leaning down to gently kiss her, he picked her up and carried her to their bed. Laying her down, he got her sleeping top and tucked her in. Turning away he walked back to the closet.

"William?" Cassandra finally found her voice while she watched him change into the matching bottoms.

"Sleep, Cassandra, you're exhausted," he slid in next to her and pulled her close, "we'll talk later." In the safety of his arms, she let herself fall asleep.

With her sleeping in his arms, William replayed the events of the day, starting with the most significant. He wasn't giving up his life mate. Together they would find a way. Even if it meant leaving Carina, they would have a life together, children. But to have that he first needed to find out who was trying to kill her. The traitor needed to be found. With his life mate in his arms, he slept.

∞ ∞ ∞ ∞ ∞

Opening heavy eyes, Cassandra discovered she was in William's arms, protected, safe. Turning her head, she softly kissed the place where his heart beat, his arms tightened. Looking up at him she found drowsy eyes full of love and concern looking back.

"You haven't slept long enough," he murmured rubbing a hand up and down her back. She looked at him, her life mate. He had held her while she cried Comforted and soothed her, without knowing what was wrong.

"What?" he asked when she continued to stare at him.

"Thank you."

"I didn't do anything."

"Yes, you did." Lifting herself up, she kissed him. "Yesterday was a difficult day."

"My fault."

"A great deal of it, yes." Honesty, whether you like it or not. "But not all. You aren't responsible for the Regulians attacking. You're not responsible for what happened after." William watched her, understanding she was searching to find the words.

"What happened after?" he asked.

"Leander and Javiera came to get Amina." William waited. "Leander wasn't sure how this battle would end. I could hear the fear in his voice, for his daughter. When it was over, Amina's parents came for her. They were still a family."

He began to understand, "Victoria's parents never came for her."

"No, it upset her, brought it all back; she cried herself to sleep."

"You comforted her, made it all right."

"No, I didn't; it got by me."

William saw guilt in her eyes.

"I didn't realize until later when she hadn't come out for a kiss goodnight. She had cried herself to sleep, William, and by the time I realized it, Lucas came. He made it right for her, comforted her."

"You think you failed her."

"I know I did. I should have realized she'd be upset."

"Maybe, but you didn't fail her. You kept her safe, her and Amina. If they'd been in that classroom..." He didn't like to think about it. "You've had to handle a great deal by yourself since the attack on Earth. You shouldn't have had to. I should have been helping instead of adding to it."

"William..." Gentle fingers silenced her lips.

"I've been very selfish. My need for you, desire for you, it added to the weight you've carried when it should have lightened it."

"You're not a weight, William," kissing his fingers she looked at him. "When Lucas was here he wanted to know how we dealt with it. I told him by knowing we had each other, by remembering what we lost but being grateful for what we'd found. I found you. It was a gift. It made what I lost bearable."

"You were sobbing. I couldn't help. I didn't know what was wrong," his heart twisted remembering.

"I know. But you did help. You held me, let me cry. Tori is safe, you're safe. Everyone I've come to care about is safe." She took a deep breath, "My family didn't survive, but I found you. I'd never have found you if the Regulians hadn't attacked Earth. They died and I found my soul mate."

"You had no control over any of that," his voice wouldn't let her take any blame.

"No, I didn't. But I know they'd want me to be happy. Sometimes, though..."

"It sneaks up on you."

"Yeah."

William rolled and pulled her under him to frame her face. "I'm here when it sneaks up on you. I'll hold you as you cry for what you've lost. I'm not letting go, Cassandra. I can't. We'll find a way, together. We'll have the life that we want with our children. I promise you," he sealed his promise with a kiss.

Returning his kiss, she slid her hands down his back under his waistband to pull him closer. She needed this man, needed him in every way possible. She brought her hands around and eased his pants past his rapidly thickening shaft. Lifting her hips, she pressed her entrance against his tip.

Releasing her lips, William slowly pressed into her, watching the passion build in her eyes as she took in more and more of him. As he moved to withdraw, she groaned and tipped her head back, hooked her ankles behind his legs and squeezed. His mouth attacked the neck she had exposed to him, causing a trembling to start deep inside her.

"William!" Something was different; she didn't know what, she just knew she wanted it.

Driving into her, William pinned her lower body to the bed with his. Lifting his head from her neck, he looked at her with his violet eyes more turbulent than any storm.

"I love you, Cassandra. With everything I am, I love you. Accept me, accept everything I am. Accept me as your life mate for you are mine." William watched as Cassandra's eyes widened then became an even darker blue as he made his request.

"I love you, William. With everything I am, I love you. You are my life mate, there will never be another." Pulling him to her she kissed him sealing her vow.

The trembling inside her was growing. William could feel it as he ground his hips against hers. It pulled at something very basic in him, the animal need to mate completely with her. Lifting her hips, he could feel the teeth of his desire demanding he take her, to make her his, and only his. Breaking off the kiss, William tried to regain some control. Looking into his life mate's eyes destroyed any chance he might have had.

Cassandra's eyes were ablaze, there was a need deep inside her fighting to break free. She needed to make this man hers and only hers. She needed him more than her next breath.

"Please, William," she cried out as her legs tried to pull him deeper, "I need you."

The animal broke free as he rammed himself into her deeper than ever before. Then withdrawing to do it again, her cries of passion captured in his mouth as his hands ripped open her shirt to claim her breasts, his fingers bruising, marking their territory.

Cassandra's legs wrapped around his waist. She must have more, must have all of him. Her nails dug into his back, marking him as her hips pistoned up to meet his.

Sweat poured off both of them as the passion grew, the need between them a living thing. Holding her hands over her head, William's mouth scorched a trail down her neck to furiously suckle from her breast, the actions causing her to viciously tighten around him. Exploding together, William emptied everything he was into his life mate and Cassandra accepted it all.

Minutes passed with heavy breathing the only sound. William finally managed to roll to his side, pulling her close. How had he ever thought he could give her up? Just thinking about it caused him to pull her even closer.

Lifting up on her elbow, Cassandra looked down at her life mate; his violet eyes satisfied, his handsome face relaxed. Reaching up, she caressed his cheek. Turning his head, he kissed her palm.

"You should get some more sleep," he started to tell her stopping when she smiled at him, "What?"

"You are always trying to get me to either eat or sleep. I think you want me fat and lazy."

"I want you to take care of yourself because you're always taking care of everyone but you." As she opened her mouth to argue, she stopped when she saw the look in William's eyes.

"How bad was the damage?" He let the subject drop, knowing she had other concerns right now, but it wouldn't be forgotten.

"We lost eighteen, all from the nuclear hit, twenty-eight serious in Medical. We were lucky."

Cassandra watched his eyes as he told her about his crew. An Admiral had to accept losses as part of the job; William did but didn't like it.

"I'm sorry, but I disagree. It was skill and training, not luck."

"We knew they were coming."

"They didn't know you knew. That's the skill. You took away their advantage."

"Possibly," looking at her he tucked a piece of hair behind her ear.

"How bad is your Fleet?"

"It's Carnot's Fleet."

"Bullshit, it's yours. Those were *your* men, *your* ships. How badly did Carnot mess it up?" she had no patience on this subject.

"He didn't mess up, they simply had no time. The Regulians shouldn't have attacked with the Retribution gone. But they did and they hit hard. The Sentinel is dead in space, no news on survivors. The rest of the Fleet took substantial damage. Not all ships are stabilized yet. Intel is spotty. At this point, the border is undefended."

"We're heading that way then?"

He should have realized she would expect that. Her protection instinct was strong. "No, Valerian is sending three battleships to the border. They'll be there in three days. Until then, we stand."

"The last line."

Again he shouldn't be surprised she understood, "Yes."

"Why didn't they have any time?"

"The Regulians had the Fleet's coordinates."

"Again?"

"Yes." Sliding out of bed, William started to pace. Cassandra saw the damage her nails had done to his back. "I don't know how they're getting the Intel."

Cassandra sat up. "There was another transmission?" As she went to button her shirt, she found she had no buttons.

"Yes." Watching her, William walked back, a self-satisfied smile on his face until he opened the ruined shirt to see the bruises he'd left on her. Gently he touched one. Seeing his expression, she rose to her knees, framed his face with her hands.

"I'm fine."

"I marked you."

"And I marked you.

"What?"

"Your back," William flexed his shoulders and felt a slight sting.

"That doesn't matter."

"And neither does this. William," she kissed him lightly, "do you regret what we experienced together?"

"Never."

"Then you can't regret this, it's part of it. I have no regrets, except you might have left me some buttons." Smiling, she kissed him again.

"I'll try to remember that next time." He pulled her up so her naked breasts were pressed against his chest, then he kissed her senseless.

Gripping his waist she tried to maintain her balance. He was always able to do this to her. Sliding the ruined shirt from her shoulders, his comm center rang, causing them to freeze. Resting his forehead on hers, he took a deep breath and pulled her shirt back up. With regret in his eyes, he walked over to the comm center.

"Zafar."

"Admiral, we've picked up another Regulian transmission."

"Translation?"

"We don't have it yet, the attack fried the translator, but it was sent from Carinian space." William looked at Cassandra, who nodded.

"Send the transmission to my Ready Room comm center, secured line."

"But, Sir. It isn't translated."

"I know that! Send it!" The Admiral was not happy. Walking to their closet, Cassandra pulled on pants and a shirt, giving William a slight smile as she buttoned it. Sitting on the bed she pulled on thick socks, deciding against her boots. Taking a moment she watched him dress. Feeling her eyes on him, William turned, putting on a shirt, his pants still unbuttoned.

"You're a beautiful man, William Zafar," she tried to control the blush she felt creeping up her neck. Tucking his shirt in his pants, William walked over to her, lightly touching her reddening neck.

"You're the most beautiful woman I've ever seen," his violet eyes solemn, "I will love you for eternity." Cupping her face, he softly kissed her. "Ready?"

"Yes." Together they walked into his Ready Room.

Chapter Twenty

As Cassandra listened, William played the transmission. Replaying it she began to translate.

"Where is the Light? It must be extinguished! The…."

"Replay that part," she leaned forward.

"The other is to be ignored. Find the Light…finish it."

She leaned back, "That's all it says."

"They don't know where you are."

"But they still attacked the Retribution."

"Only after they discovered we were gone. They were covering their bases. If they'd been sure, they would have sent all their ships. We wouldn't have stood a chance alone."

"Can you send this to the comm in our quarters?"

"Yes, why?"

"I want to show you something." Walking into their quarters, she turned the lights up. The day had started. At the comm center, she pulled up the results of the first three transmissions.

"It bothered me that you were unable to trace the transmissions. There had to be a way to know who sent and received them. So I worked out a program to search for identical coding in the known transmissions."

"Cassandra, do you realize what goes into sending a transmission, the layers of coding?"

"So I discovered, but while I can isolate a set of identical codes in the first three, the fourth only carries one. But I don't know what the coding means. I need a base to compare them to. This one I'm sure is Regulian."

"You were able to find common codes in the first three transmissions?" William wasn't sure why he was shocked. He held up his hand before she could answer. "Show me." While he studied the transmission coding, Cassandra put the bed in order, then sat and waited.

"This is the Regulians," he touched the screen.

"That's what I thought since it's also the coding in the Regulian ship-to-ship transmission that gave the Fleet's location. But what 'tells' you that?"

"Every ship has a particular transmission code. We've had the Regulians since the Battle of Fayal. Anyone sending had to know the code and have authorization to send to that specific ship. There are differing codes depending on the security level needed and the clearance level of the sender."

"So another string of coding would be included if the High Admiral were to send you a transmission whether it was urgent or just to tell you happy birthday."

"Yes."

"But if he wanted it secured…"

"There would be yet another layer."

"And somewhere in all that coding is not only the High Admiral's code…but yours."

"Yes, but to find it you first need to know the code."

"Not if you're comparing transmissions. I might not know whose codes they are, but I will know the codes. And somewhere in there it has to tell you where it originated and where it's going. Just like we know the second transmission that came from Carinian space was sent to the Regulian ship, Cimex, we have the ship's code."

Listening to her, she made it sound easy, but he knew it was not. It had always been a matter of pride that the Coalition's codes had never been broken.

"How does the personal coding work? Say for you. It would have to include some type of rank coding, then there's the name, security clearance, then I would guess something to make it distinctly your own. Something chosen by you, known only to you that must be entered to verify identity like a signature." Cassandra paced as she thought out loud. Standing, William stopped her. She'd just identified every single item needed to create a security code.

"What's the Magellan Award?"

"What?" She was baffled by the change in subject.

"The Magellan Award."

"It doesn't matter," she tried to pull away.

"I think it does. In Engineering you once said it's not like you don't have clearance. You wrote codes."

"I wrote some codes to protect military transmissions. Codes that would help keep my brother safe."

"And the Magellan Award?" Looking at him she realized he was not going to let this go and sighed.

"The Magellan Award is…was…given out once every ten years. It recognized a person's achievements in multiple fields of study. While the fields can vary, the person must be regarded as an expert by their peers in each area. If they don't find a worthy recipient, they wait another ten years. Satisfied?"

"How many fields?"

"William," giving in she answered, "four; Physics, Language, Communications, and Ancient Sumerian."

"You were considered an expert in all those fields."

"On Earth, it's not relevant here."

"I think it is. Cassandra, in the short time you've been here, you've learned not only our laser system, but a language very few understand, even after cycles of training. You read our ancient language and have basically summed up how we protect our communications. How can you think you're not relevant?"

"Because I still have so much to learn so I can fix the laser. How do I provide for Victoria? I understand Regulian, who speaks it? I can find you all the identical codes you want, but if I don't know what they mean how do I find the source?!?"

"Shhh," he pulled her into his arms, rubbed her back and kissed the top of her head. This woman of his had many layers, he'd always known that, but doubt in herself in her abilities was something he never thought she'd have. She always presented such a controlled front, something he of all people should know was just that, a front.

"We will work it out, Cassandra, together. We will provide for Victoria, she'll be safe and loved and have what she needs. I know you hate not knowing, especially the things we assume you do. You need to tell me when that happens otherwise how can I help? I won't think you stupid. Fuck, I believe you'll be the smartest woman on Carina too." Framing her face, he tipped her face up to look into her eyes, "Our children will be amazing."

"You're trying to distract me from feeling sorry for myself, and doing a really great job of it too." Rising up to her toes she gave him a soft kiss, "I'm sorry."

"For what?"

"Making the award into such a big mystery, it really doesn't matter, and not because it was on Earth." She stopped him before he could protest. "I wouldn't have won. That's the reason I didn't want to talk about it, ego over some stupid award."

"Why wouldn't you have won?"

"Honestly?" He nodded, "I don't have a dick." At his confused look, she started to laugh then gently caressed his. "One of these. No woman has ever been awarded the Magellan. I wasn't going to change that."

"That's wrong."

"Yes," looking into his eyes she saw he was still troubled. "It's good you asked. I needed to tell you. But now we have more important things to worry about."

"You need to understand the codes."

"If I'm going to track the Carinian source then yes. But I want to search on all Carinian communications. There's something missing, I can feel it."

"We've been recording all transmissions from all ships in the Fleet since the first transmission was found. They are here on the Retribution."

"Can I access them?"

"Cassandra, that's weeks worth of searching."

"No, it's not. It's not what the transmissions say it's how it was sent. That's just a blip on the transmission. I can find out if we've missed any." The gleam in her eye told him she was excited about the challenge.

"You'll have the transmissions. I'll work on the codes," both turned as they heard Tori's door open. A sleepy girl with red-rimmed eyes walked toward them, reminding William that all hadn't been right in her little world lately either.

"Hey, you're up early," Cassandra squatted down giving her a hug.

"I couldn't sleep."

"Still sad?" Little shoulders just shrugged. Cassandra looked up at William as she gave her another hug.

William squatted down next to her. He gently rubbed the small back. "Why don't I call Hutu and have him get first meal started," sad green eyes looked into his, pulling at his heart.

"Okay." Standing, he moved into his Ready Room, as much to make a special request as to give the two some privacy. At the comm, he connected to Hutu.

"Admiral, I hadn't realized you wanted an early meal."

"You're fine, Hutu, nothing was sent down. But I need to ask a favor."

"Admiral?" Hutu was stunned, the Admiral didn't ask.

"Victoria's a little down this morning. I was wondering if you could fix something special to cheer her up."

"She's not ill!?!"

"No, just a little homesick, missing her parents." The Admiral knew he had a soft spot for Tori.

"I'll come up with something special, Admiral. She's awake?"

"Yes, so whenever you're done is fine."

"Yes. Sir."

"Oh and, Hutu, whatever you bring Cassandra make sure it's a large portion, she's not eating enough."

"Yes, Sir," Hutu grinned on the other end.

Returning, the Admiral found Cassandra on the couch with Tori in her lap. Sitting beside them he put an arm around them both. While he had no experience with little girls, it was time he started easing some of Cassandra's burden. He'd promised that 'together' they would take care of her.

"Cassandra tells me you're missing your parents," taking Tori's hand he looked into her eyes.

"Yeah."

"Tell me about them."

"What do you mean?"

"Well, what did they look like?"

"You want to see? I have pictures."

"Tori…my iPod was destroyed in the explosion," William's eyes flashed to Cassandra.

"No, it wasn't, I took it to class that day to show Amina."

"You never told me."

"You never asked."

"So you have pictures?" William interrupted the growing argument.

"Yeah, I'll go get them," Tori hustled off the couch and into her room.

"Pictures?" he quickly asked.

"Similar to what you have on your desk of Kyle and Lucas."

He nodded as Tori climbed up into his lap with a hand-held device he assumed was an iPod. After touching the screen several times, an image appeared of a man and woman smiling out at him.

"See, this is my mom," she pointed to the woman. What he saw was a small woman, with blazing red hair and sparkling green eyes. She was the image of what Victoria would become.

"She's beautiful, Tori."

"Yeah, and this is my dad," her finger moved to the man. He stood head and shoulders over the small woman, his arms wrapped protectively around her. His hair was black like Cassandra's but cut short. His wide shoulders were a testament to his physical strength. While his eyes were brown, there was no mistaking he was related to Cassandra.

"That was taken last year on their ten-year anniversary," Cassandra told him in a soft voice. "Peter surprised Cyndy by getting home for it." Leaning her head on his shoulder, Cassandra watched as Victoria scrolled through pictures telling William about each one.

"That's Grandpa Jacob." William assessed Cassandra's father. An older version of Peter, he stood with a shoulder leaning against a post, arms crossed over his chest, looking out of the picture with serious eyes that seemed to return his assessment. While his body was aged, the strength it held was still evident as was the love he had for the one taking the picture.

"You took this," he looked at Cassandra.

"I did. How did you know?" she raised her head to look at him.

"By the love in his eyes." Leaning down he gave her a soft kiss.

Victoria continued to scroll through the pictures until the hatch buzzed, announcing Hutu and first meal.

∞ ∞ ∞ ∞ ∞

As he uncovered her plate, Victoria's eyes got big.

"Is that pancakes?"

"Well, I call them flatcakes. You'll have to tell me if they're what you know as pancakes. We put this on ours." Hutu poured a sauce over the cakes and waited for Victoria to try a bite. As she did, a grin stretched wide across what was once a sad face.

"These are awesome!" she exclaimed swallowing. Jumping up she gave him a big hug. "Thank you! Thank you! Thank you!"

"You're welcome, young lady." Smiling, he left. With Victoria digging into her flatcakes, William and Cassandra sat down. Lifting the lid off hers Cassandra looked at William.

"What?" he asked innocently.

"Hutu seems to have overfilled my plate. I wonder how that happened?" she raised an eyebrow at him.

"He must have made too much, you'd better eat it or he'll feel bad."

"Oh really?" Shaking her head she took a bite of the flatcakes filling her plate.

"Aunt Cassie?" Cassandra looked at Victoria with her mouth full, "Is there going to be class today?"

Swallowing so she could finally speak, "I don't think so, honey, the classroom was damaged in the attack yesterday."

"Oh."

"So what do you want to do today?"

"Can Amina come over?"

"I'll call and see, but maybe we should wait a little longer in case they're sleeping in."

"Okay."

As the three finished eating, the Admiral's comm rang. He picked up the headset.

"Zafar." Cassandra watched his eyes harden. "I'll be there shortly." Disconnecting he put down the headset.

"I need to head to the Bridge." Turning he walked to the closet and pulled out his jacket. "You have fun with Amina," he leaned down kissing the top of Tori's head.

"Bye, Admiral."

"Be right back," Cassandra rose and walked with William to the Ready Room.

"I'll work on getting you those codes, but it may take a while."

"The transmissions will keep me busy," she watched him.

"I'll have them sent once I get to the Bridge," he replied as he finished buttoning his jacket.

"What's wrong?"

"We lost the Talon."

"The Regulians attacked again?" Dread filled her.

"No, their shields failed. They hadn't finished hull repairs...rapid decompression. FUCK!" William could vent his frustration with Cassandra.

"How many?" she whispered.

"835 crewmen."

"Oh God, William," her eyes started to fill.

"Shhh…it will be okay," he pulled her close. "I want you to do something for me."

"What?"

"Stay in quarters today, you and Victoria. I need to know where you are." Looking at him she realized he was worried about the hit the Retribution took.

"If that's what you want, then we will, but can Amina come over?"

"That's fine," sinking his fingers into her loose hair he looked into her eyes, "I love you, Cassandra, with everything I am." He gave her a hard kiss that left her breathless and turned to the hatch, "Secure the door."

After securing the hatch, she returned to find Victoria had eaten every last bite of the flatcakes.

"I'd say you were hungry."

"It was so good."

"Do you want some of mine?"

"No, I'm stuffed."

"Okay, then why don't you go shower. By the time you're done we should be able to call Amina."

"Okay." As the shower started, she cleared the dishes from the table. Walking over to the couch she picked up the iPod. Scrolling back she found the picture of her father. Gently she touched his face.

"I love you, Dad. I miss you." With one last look, she shut off the iPod and took it into Tori's room.

∞ ∞ ∞ ∞ ∞

"Colonel, I want a status report on the hull repairs," the Admiral barked out as he entered the Bridge.

"Yes, Sir."

"Sensors, any contacts?"

"No, Sir."

At his Command Center, the Admiral picked up his headset punching in Communications.

"This is Zafar, I want all the recorded transmissions transferred to the comm in my quarters. Yes, ALL of them!" Disconnecting he looked at Quinn.

"Something I need to know?"

"Not at this time. Have you got the report?"

"Yes," Quinn handed it to him, "seventy-five percent complete."

"Tell them I want it 100 percent by 1100."

"Admiral..."

"The Talon's gone, Quinn. Rapid decompression. Their shields failed before repairs were completed. 100 percent by 1100!"

"Yes, Sir."

"Communications, open all comms."

"Yes, Sir."

"Attention crew. We will remain at Alert Status Two until further notice. The Coalition is sending three battleships to support the Fleet at the border. Until they arrive and the Fleet is fully operational, *WE* are the only defense between the Regulians and our homes. We will not fail. All posts will be manned at all times. All defenses *FULLY* operational. Make ready!"

"Quinn, go take your twelve."

"Yes, Sir."

∞ ∞ ∞ ∞ ∞

Listening to him, pride filled Cassandra. This was her man doing what he did best, leading his crew, protecting what he loved.

Walking over to the comm, she connected with Javiera arranging for Amina to come play. Ending the call, the recorded transmissions came in. William hadn't been wrong. It was going to take a while to search them.

"Time to get to it," she pulled her hair back then her fingers started to fly.

∞ ∞ ∞ ∞ ∞

"Aunt Cassie?" Cassandra raised an eyebrow as she chewed. "Can Amina stay here tonight?" Two pairs of eyes pleaded with hers.

"I don't see why not," she swallowed. The girls gave each other a fist bump. "But I need to check with your mom first." With arrangements made, second meal plates were cleared and two very excited girls headed into Victoria's room.

Reviewing the preliminary scan results, she found the majority of transmissions were in a group containing only sixteen lines of coding. "For now those can wait. They should be regular transmissions," Cassandra thought.

The codes she'd been able to isolate were all contained in transmissions with eighteen lines of coding. The scan produced several dozen transmissions with that many lines. Creating another query, she dug deeper into the transmissions, searching for transmissions with the two 'signatures,' and moved on to the next group.

Nineteen lines of coding, high security, these have to be between William and the High Admiral, there are only a handful. Running the query, Cassandra let the computer search.

The final group contained two transmissions, with twenty lines of coding each. Running the second query, she leaned back.

If she was right about the nineteen-line codes then who needed more security than a High Admiral? William would know.

∞ ∞ ∞ ∞ ∞

"Here's the casualty list you requested, Admiral."

"What are you doing here, Quinn," the Admiral took the report.

"I'm here to relieve you, Admiral, this is my twelve."

"What?" he looking at the clock and wondered where the day had gone.

"What do I need to know?" Bringing him up to date he picked up the list and headed to his quarters.

Entering his Ready Room, William heard the squeals of little girls' laughter. The sound lightened the weight of the list he carried. Leaving it on his desk, he followed the laughter to find mayhem.

"All right now, that's enough. Girls! I'm serious here!" Trying to fend off tickling fingers, Cassandra didn't see William enter the room. "I mean it! Victoria Lynn! Amina!"

"Looks like you're outnumbered." Three heads looked up from the couch where Cassandra was at the bottom of the pile.

"I am, help!"

Leaning over, William added his fingers to the tickling mix.

"William! Stop!" Laughing, Cassandra tried to wiggle away. "I give! I give!" Sitting up as the tickle attack finally ended she looked at William.

"Just remember. I believe in payback." She turned to the girls, "Why don't you two go get ready for bed." As they scampered off, William sat giving her a kiss.

"Looks like you've had a busy day."

"Not too bad. As you can tell, Amina's staying the night. I figured it was all right."

"It's fine."

"Did you eat?"

"On the Bridge," he pulled her close as she laid her head on his shoulder.

"Are you done for the night?"

"I have some paperwork I need to do." Thinking of the letters he needed to write he rose from the couch. "I'd better get to it." With one last kiss, he headed to his desk.

∞ ∞ ∞ ∞ ∞

With the girls settled for the night, Cassandra put the lights on low.

"Night, girls."

"Night, Aunt Cassie," two voices said in unison bringing a smile to her face. She now had two nieces.

Closing the bedroom door, she turned to look around their private quarters. It looked well lived in today. Walking around putting things right, she wondered if she should interrupt William with her questions. The paperwork he said he needed to do had brought a serious look to his eye. Sitting in front of her comm she studied the results of her searches.

All the known transmissions between the Regulians and the Carinian traitor had eighteen lines of coding. Her search identified two 'signatures,' one she knew was Regulian. The transmissions had been translated and not one of them gave the Regulians the Fleet's coordinates. So how did they get them? Could someone else have sent them? Was her search too specific? She needed to search for just the Regulian signature to see if they'd missed any. Initiating the search, she pushed back from the comm. It was time to ask William some questions.

∞ ∞ ∞ ∞ ∞

With his back to the door, William didn't hear her enter, just felt her touch as she hugged him from behind.

"Are you about done?"

"I have a while yet."

Reading over his shoulder her eyes widened. "You're writing the families of the men who died."

"Yes."

"It's your job to notify them?"

"No. The Coalition will handle that."

"But you're writing them too."

"They were mine."

She shouldn't have been surprised, this was who he was. He may keep people at a distance, but that didn't mean he didn't care. That he didn't take each loss personally. Taking his face in her hands, she gave him a long gentle kiss. Then left him to his work, her questions could wait.

Checking the comm she found some interesting results. There were two more eighteen-line transmissions sent to the Regulians, but from a different sender. Why hadn't Communications flagged them as Regulian? Opening the transmission, she discovered why. There were no words, just numbers. Here were the transmissions giving up the Fleet, both times. But how did they get the coordinates?

Using only the two new transmissions. she searched for the sender's 'signature.' Ten minutes later she had it. The same person sent both.

"Closer…getting closer." Sitting back she rubbed tired eyes. What's the next step? Who was this new person? How could she find him or her?

Knowing fatigue was starting to slow her down, she walked to the closet pulling out a sleep top with buttons and changed. Her mind was still on the latest results.

Walking back to the comm, she sat down cross-legged. There had to be more transmissions with the new signature. Reaching a decision she wrote a search to scan all transmissions for the new signature. Knowing it was going to be time-consuming, she decided it was time for bed. Hoping William wouldn't be much longer she climbed into their bed and was instantly asleep.

Finishing the last letter, William leaned back rubbing his eyes. Such a waste of life, someone would pay. Rising, he shut down his comm. He needed some sleep, he needed Cassandra.

∞ ∞ ∞ ∞ ∞

A new day started as he entered their quarters finding Cassandra asleep in their bed. Checking on the girls he found one at each end of the bed, sound asleep. Tucking the covers around each he quietly closed the door.

"They okay?" a sleepy voice asked as he moved across the room.

"They're fine," sitting on the edge of the bed he leaned down to kiss her, "you should be asleep."

"I will be once you're beside me."

Leaving her, he put on his sleeping pants, returned to pull her close.

"Did you finish?"

"Yes."

"You're a good man, William Zafar," she stretched up to give him a gentle kiss. "Those letters will mean a lot to their families." Laying her head over his heart she slept.

∞ ∞ ∞ ∞ ∞

An irritating buzz pulled Cassandra from sleep. Slowly she realized it was the comm with her search results. Easing across William, she rose to silence the buzz. Rubbing her eyes, she tried to focus on the search results.

"What have you got?" William sat on the edge of the bed.

"Just some search results, go back to sleep, you've got a long day ahead of you."

"We didn't get to talk about the transmissions yesterday."

"You had more important things to do."

"I don't now, tell me what you found."

She brought up the previous search results. "There are a total of four transmissions from the Carinian traitor to the Regulians. Both sets of signatures match."

"That includes yesterday's transmission?"

"Yes, but I couldn't match the signatures to the attacks where they had the Fleet's location. So I broadened the search to find any transmissions that contained the Regulian signature."

"Communications should have picked up anything in Regulian."

"They weren't in Regulian, just sent to the Regulians."

"They?"

"Two, each containing only numbers."

"The Fleet's location."

"Yes," Cassandra waited as he stood, pacing, then the Admiral's eyes pinned hers.

"It's not the same signature?" asked the Admiral.

"No."

"Someone else…it's the same in both transmissions?"

"Yes."

"There are two."

"It looks that way." Waiting, she watched as he ran all the different scenarios in his head. Pulling over a chair he sat next to her.

"What else?"

"All these transmissions have eighteen lines of coding. Which means some security, but not high level. The high level might cause someone to look, right?"

"Yes."

"I found transmissions with nineteen lines of coding. I'm assuming they are communications between you and the High Admiral."

"Assume?"

"I didn't open them," she looked at him.

"I gave you my codes."

"I know…"

"What?"

"Giving me your codes, you could get in serious trouble for it."

"That's not important."

"Don't start with that again, please. Your career is important, William. There's been enough damage to it because of me. I'm not going to knowingly cause more!"

"So you're going to protect me."

"Someone has to. You don't deserve to have people doubting you when all you're doing is your job."

He pulled her into his lap and just held her for a minute. "Thank you," his voice was low. Reaching around her, he entered his code playing the transmissions.

Cassandra listened hearing the Admiral blow up at the High Admiral, telling him of his suspicions, asking for the Dioscuri to replace the Retribution, knowing what it meant.

He felt her stiffen in his arms, but she said nothing. This would always be a sore point between them. Listening to the rest she could hear the High Admiral's frustration. But she also realized something else.

"You never told him we were involved." Sapphire eyes looked up at him.

"No."

"Because it would complicate things or because he wouldn't take you as seriously?"

"Both."

"So what's he going to do when you leave the Retribution with me?"

"He won't be able to do anything."

"William…"

"Once we arrive there will be a meeting. Here, I'll demand that. We've already arranged a security detail here on the ship, you know that. Since the return of the Retribution was already being questioned, my leaving the ship won't raise any eyebrows."

"But..."

"Let it go for now, we'll deal with it when the time comes."

"As long as we do."

William gave her a fierce kiss. "We're a unit, Cassandra, nothing separates us."

"Okay," she looked back at her data. "Who would have more security than the High Admiral?"

"What?"

"I found two transmissions with twenty lines of coding."

"Twenty? No one has twenty. The High Admiral has the highest security."

"But I have two transmissions. And William, they are both right before the transmissions to the Regulians with the Fleet's locations."

"There is no higher security. It has to be something else."

"So I need to compare the two to one of your transmissions to the High Admiral and find the differences. I can do that."

"I don't doubt it." Looking at the time, he lifted her to her feet. "I need to get cleaned up and relieve Quinn." As he headed to the shower, she sat down to write a new search.

Chapter Twenty-One

"The ships are a day and a half away from the Fleet, Admiral. All ships are stabilized but not yet fully operational. Communications are still spotty. There's been no contact on any sensors. It appears the Regulians have returned to the Relinquished Zone."

Nodding, the Admiral took the report from Quinn.

"Our repairs?"

"100 percent. All decks. All posts manned."

"Good. Dismissed, Colonel, get some down time."

"Yes, Sir."

Leaving the Bridge, Quinn headed for quarters passing the Admiral's quarters. He saw Cassandra opening the hatch for Hutu.

"Colonel."

"Cassandra."

"Could I speak to you for a minute?" Wondering what was up, Quinn entered the Ready Room.

"I'll just be a minute." Leaving him, she got the girls set up for first meal. Closing the connecting door, she walked Hutu to the hatch securing it. Turning she looked at him, William's friend, he returned her look.

"Look, Colonel, I know we haven't always gotten along," she started.

"I have no problem with you."

Cassandra gave him a little grin, "Oh we've had our moments, but that's beside the point. You are one of the Admiral's oldest friends, in addition to his Second-in-Command."

"Yes."

"You're willing to tell him when he's wrong."

"The Admiral is seldom wrong."

"Agreed," she ran a hand through her hair, not sure how to approach the subject.

"If you've got something to say just say it!"

The look he received told him he'd pissed her off. "Once the Fleet is up and running we will be proceeding to Carina," she waited.

"Yes."

"There is going to be some controversy over my arrival."

"That's an understatement."

"Yes. You've been involved in the planning, understand what's happening, and have a unique view of the situation."

"What do you want?" Tar was blunt.

"I want you to leave the Retribution with us. I want you to watch William's back."

The shock in Quinn's eyes was unmistakable. "He knows this?" he questioned.

"No."

"You want me to go behind his back and…"

"No! This is about me building my House. That's what it amounts to. You know there is no guarantee. Lucas will protect Victoria, William will protect me, but someone needs to protect him."

"Just how am I supposed to do that?"

"By being there, watching his back. I'm not the only one that's going to be attacked, is already being attacked. You know this."

"I know."

"It means risking your career, I know that too. That's why I asked you without the Admiral here. It's your decision. If you decide you can't, he'll never know."

"You think I wouldn't back the Admiral!?!?"

"You always have his back. But this is different. You know that. You also know he'd never ask it of you. So I am."

It was Quinn's turn to run a frustrated hand through his hair. She was asking a lot and she knew it. But she was not asking him to help her, she was asking him to help Will. She was right. The Admiral would never ask and they were going to need all the help they could get. From people, they could trust.

"I'm in," he made his decision.

"Thank you," she momentarily closed her eyes, another piece in place.

"I'm not doing it for you."

Her eyes flashed to his, "I know. Thank you anyway. He matters to me more than you can know."

"More than being Queen?" Quinn had to ask.

"I've never claimed I wanted to be Queen," she turned as the connecting door opened.

"Aunt Cassie, we're done." Tori entered the room. "Hi, Colonel," she gave him a brilliant smile.

"Hi, Tori."

"I'll be right there." She turned back to the Colonel. "Thank you, Colonel, I'd appreciate it if you'd keep this between us for now. The Admiral is dealing with enough."

"I can do that…for now."

When he left, Cassandra secured the hatch.

With the girls in the shower, Cassandra cleaned up the dishes. Realizing she never read the overnight search results she headed to the comm. Pulling them up she read.

"Shit!" The new signature she had been searching for was in both of the twenty line transmissions.

She needed to know if the same person received those transmissions. The search was quick. Not only were both transmissions received by the same person, but they were also nearly identical in every line of coding.

"Who is giving up the Fleet's location?"

∞ ∞ ∞ ∞ ∞

"Admiral, incoming transmission from High Admiral Valerian on a secure line."

"Zafar," the Admiral said into his headset.

"What's your status, Zafar?"

"100 percent."

"Good, still no news on The First Son. The communications out there are still sporadic."

"Crap, how hard can it be?"

"Look, I know you're frustrated not being there. But I need you right where you are."

"I know that. We've been doing long range scans. The only ships we're picking up are ours. We're staying at Alert Status Two until the border is secured."

"Understood. Once it is, we'll get back to the other matter."

"Understood. By then I might have some more Intel for you."

"What are you sniffing?"

"I'm not sure yet, but it's something."

"Dig it out, Admiral. I want this traitor!"

"So do I, Sir, so do I. Zafar out." Removing his headset, the Admiral leaned back in his chair, thinking about the transmissions Cassandra had found. Twenty fucking lines, what did that mean?"

∞ ∞ ∞ ∞ ∞

Opening the hatch, Cassandra found Leander and Javiera.

"Hi, come on in. The girls are in the back. They just got done with their showers." Securing the hatch, she found the Michelakakis' standing by the Admiral's desk.

"We wanted to talk to you alone first," Leander told her.

"You've reached a decision." Seeing them look at each other she knew they had.

"We leave the Retribution with you," Javiera announced.

"You're sure?" Her eyes jumped from Leander to Javiera. "Really sure? You've thought it through?"

"Yes, we have," Leander told her, "especially after this last attack. It really brought it home. Someone on Carina is helping the Regulians. They destroyed your planet. If the Retribution hadn't been here to stop them, they would have done the same to Carina. This isn't just your fight anymore, it's ours too. We need to find this traitor."

"Whoever it is?" she had to ask.

"Whoever it is."

Giving them both a hug, Cassandra took a deep breath, her eyes full of gratitude. "Thank you, both of you. I can't tell you what it means to me that…"

"Mommy! Daddy!" Amina came running out into the Ready Room. "I didn't know you were here! We've been having the best time!"

Hugging their daughter, they listened to her excited chatter knowing how close they'd come to losing her just days before.

"Do I have to go home now? Tori and I wanted to play more." Young eyes turned to Cassandra.

"She's welcome to stay. Especially since you both are on alert. I think it's good for both of them."

"I tell you what. Why don't we take them for a while and give you a break. Then if she could stay again, that would be great."

"Please, Aunt Cassie?!?" Tori pleaded.

"That's fine with me."

Leander turned as they were leaving, "We'll talk later."

"We will." Securing the hatch, Cassandra took a moment to be thankful for her new friends then headed back to the comm center.

"Time to find a traitor. So if I want to know where the twenty line transmission went, I need to compare them to the sixteen line. That will take too long…the nineteen I'm not opening without William…so that leaves the eighteen. I need to set it up to find any matches between the strings. Here goes." With the search running it was time for a shower.

Washing her hair, she let her mind wander. Lucas was in, he'd protect Victoria. Tar was in, he'd watch William's back. Leander, Javiera, and Amina were in. Leander would be with Lucas helping watch both girls. Javiera would help her understand Carina from a woman's viewpoint. She was going to need to know how to present herself, and that included dress plus all those little rules she didn't know.

It was starting to come together. She needed to talk to William, he'd know what was missing, but now wasn't the time. When they started back to Carina, off Alert Status Two, there would be time.

Turning off the shower, she leaned over wrapping a towel around her head. Standing up the room started to tilt. Grabbing the sink she steadied herself.

"What the hell was that?" Looking at her reflection she took a deep breath. "Time to see what Hutu has brought for breakfast." Wrapping a towel around herself, she left what had become an overheated room for the coolness of their chambers. Dressed, she headed to her covered plate.

Finding her favorite loblolly, she sat down managing to finish over half of the oversized portion. With her hunger satisfied, she put the bowl on the tray, turning as the comm buzzed.

The search had uncovered matches to different codes within the string. Pulling up the first match, she played the transmission and was surprised to hear the Admiral's voice.

"Admiral, this is Captain Procne."

"What the fuck are you doing over there, Procne! It takes you TWO WEEKS to send over Regulian traffic for translation?"

"Admiral, I can explain."

"It'd better be good!"

"Admiral, the transmission was recorded after the battle, but it wasn't on any of the normal Regulian channels. As you know, we took a serious hit during the attack losing a Communications Specialist."

Stopping the transmission, Cassandra realized it was the first transmission found in Regulian. But who is Captain Procne, Captain of what ship?

This was a transmission between the Retribution and another Coalition ship. Comparing this transmission to a nineteen-line one between the

Retribution and the High Admiral, Cassandra found the Retribution's code. And knew it meant no one on the Retribution revealed the Fleet's location. She hadn't realized she'd been worried the traitor was on board. But what ship did have the traitor?

Connecting to the Bridge she hoped William could tell her.

∞ ∞ ∞ ∞ ∞

"Sensors?"

"No contacts, Admiral."

Looking at his comm, he saw his private line was ringing. "Zafar," he answered putting on his headset.

"Question."

"Okay."

"Who's Captain Procne?" Silence answered her. "William?"

"He's the Captain of the Sentinel."

"The Sentinel? The ship that's dead in space?"

"Yes," he could hear her mind racing through the comm.

"That doesn't make any sense."

"What doesn't?"

"Admiral! I have long range sensor contacts!"

"Location!"

"Sir, they are still in the Relinquished Zone." Disconnecting, the Admiral removed his headset.

"Communications! Contact the Dioscuri. Make them aware of the situation."

"Yes, Sir!"

"Move us to Alert Status One!"

"Yes, Sir!"

"Communications, have you been able to raise the Dioscuri?"

"No, Admiral. I'm transmitting but have received no response."

"Keep trying! Get me a secure line to the High Admiral."

Picking up his headset, he suddenly realized he'd hung up on Cassandra.

"Zafar! What have you got?" Valerian demanded.

"Sir, at this time we're tracking multiple long-range contacts still in the Relinquished Zone. We've trying to raise the Dioscuri but get no response. We are at Alert Status One."

"Fuck!"

"Couldn't agree more, Sir."

"Stay on it. Keep me informed." The High Admiral disconnected.

∞ ∞ ∞ ∞ ∞

Cassandra was waiting at the hatch when Javiera came rushing up.

"Go! I've got them!" Securing the hatch, she ushered the girls back to the private quarters, closing that door too. Turning she found two frightened faces staring up at her.

"Hey, it's okay. Come on, let's go sit on the couch." Leading them over, one sat on each side of her.

"Are the Regulians attacking again?" Tori whispered.

"No, honey. I was talking to the Admiral just before the Alert. They are still in the Relinquished Zone. Nowhere near here. We're okay."

"So why the alarm?"

"Because the Admiral is doing his job, keeping us safe." The two girls looked at each other.

"Can we go play in my room then?"

"If you want." Watching them close Victoria's door, Cassandra took a deep breath.

What a morning it had turned out to be. Thinking about the Sentinel, she returned to her comm.

The traitor contacted the Sentinel twice, once before each attack. Who was he talking to? The Sentinel was being targeted. Why? Why would you target the ship your informant was on? What if they didn't know they were?

The Sentinel wasn't about the 'Light'…about her. This was something different, someone different, but who?

∞ ∞ ∞ ∞ ∞

As the day wore on the Retribution remained at Alert One.

"Sensors?"

"Sir, the Regulians have not crossed the border. They are maintaining their last coordinates."

"Sir! I have Admiral Carnot on the comm."

"Is it a secure line?"

"Yes, Sir."

"Ferran, what's your status?"

"The Fleet's at 75 percent. Communications are now fully operational on all remaining ships. Last casualty report was 1403 with another 500 in Medical."

"The First Son?"

"Unknown, his name isn't on the Medical list, we've only gotten numbers from the Sentinel, no names. But there's still crew on the Sentinel making repairs. Their communications are down."

"Reports were it was dead."

"They were able to maintain life systems. All Defensive, Sensor, Propulsion and Communications systems are down."

"The Regulians are sitting on the other side of the border."

"I see that."

"Your support will be there in twelve hours."

"Affirmative."

Another twelve hours until the border was reinforced. Would the Regulians wait that long to attack again? What were they waiting for? Another transmission? What was the 'other' to be ignored? The other person transmitting to them? Fuck, he had more questions than answers.

Putting on his headset, he connected to his quarters.

"Chamberlain."

Just hearing her voice eased some of his tension. "What's your status?" the Admiral demanded.

"The girls are in Victoria's room. I'm running searches. What's yours?" she retorted back.

Realizing he was treating her like a member of the crew, he rubbed his eyes.

"Are you okay?" she asked.

"Fine, it's going to be awhile."

"Anything I can do?"

"Just what you are. What were you talking about earlier about Procne?"

"You used his name in a transmission. I wanted to know what ship he was on."

"You isolated the code," William should have realized she would given time.

"Parts."

"Which?"

"William, I don't have it all yet, I don't know what it means."

"Tell me what you've got!" the Admiral demanded.

On the other end, Cassandra was a little shocked then realized she shouldn't be. If she were in his place, she'd want the information too. Lives were being lost.

"The twenty line transmissions were both sent to someone on the Sentinel. Fleet locations were sent to the Regulians shortly after by whoever initiated the transmissions."

The line was silent. Results from her latest search came up on her console. She'd isolated the extra line of coding sent to the Sentinel. It wasn't just code, it looked like…

"Cassandra," William's voice was low and urgent.

"What? Oh sorry, I was distracted. What were you saying?"

"What else?"

"I know that no one on the Retribution sent or received any transmissions from this sender."

William took a deep breath, his tension easing a little more.

"Thank you. Look, I…"

"Admiral, transmission from High Command."

"Transfer it to my comm. I have to go."

"I heard. I love you. See you later." Cassandra disconnected.

∞ ∞ ∞ ∞ ∞

Setting down her headset, she turned back to the console studying the search results. This line wasn't like any other coding in any other transmission. It seemed to carry little strings of codes, almost like a search.

"Oh fuck! It's a Trojan!" The person receiving the transmission didn't know it was there. He didn't know he was giving up his ship's location. The Sentinel was the specific target of these attacks. Why? There wasn't a traitor on the Sentinel, just a person someone else wanted dead. Who?

Entering the receiver's code into her query she waited for the results, hoping she could track it. Hoping they weren't already dead. Impatiently she started to pace.

"Aunt Cassie," turning to two little girls Cassandra tried to switch gears.

"Hey, girls, sorry I kind of got wrapped up here. Are you hungry?" At their nods, she called Hutu.

"I know we're still on Alert, but I've got two hungry little girls here."

"I'm just about done here, ma'am. Should be no more than fifteen minutes."

"Hutu, you're amazing! See you in a little bit." Turning to the girls, "It won't be long. What have you been doing all afternoon?"

"I've been showing Amina pictures of Earth, telling her about it. Carina's not that different."

"It's not?"

"No, I mean the creatures look different," Amina told her, "but otherwise a lot seems the same, especially when you compare what things are like."

"Give me an example."

"Well. Take baisteach. It's liquid that falls out of the sky."

"Rain?"

"Yes. See it's just a matter of finding out what's the same."

"You are a very smart little girl, Amina. So you've found lots in common between Earth and Carina?"

"Yeah, lots!"

"That's good to know."

With Hutu's arrival, the girls sat down to eat as Cassandra walked him out.

"Thank you again, Hutu. I don't know what we'd do without you."

"You're welcome, ma'am. Make sure you eat too. Otherwise, the Admiral won't be happy." Smiling at him, she just nodded.

"Oh, I put some extra treats on the tray for later. I thought the girls might like them."

"I'm sure they will. Has the Admiral eaten yet?" Hutu smiled at her concern.

"I'll be fixing his next. He insisted I prepare yours first."

"Good, you make sure he eats too."

"I'll do my best." Giving her a full blown grin, he headed back to get the Admiral's dinner.

Sitting down to eat, Cassandra enjoyed the girls' chatter. It was unbelievable how close the two had become in such a short time. That bond would become even more important once they reached Carina.

∞ ∞ ∞ ∞ ∞

Disconnecting from High Command, the Admiral leaned back in his chair. He hadn't told him anything he didn't already know. Actually he knew more than the High Admiral did thanks to Carnot's call. He hadn't relayed that information to Command. If they didn't know that there were survivors still on the Sentinel then neither did the traitor.

Hopefully, The First Son was among them. Seeing Hutu enter the Bridge he looked at the clock. 1900. Time to refuel for a long night.

Hutu set two plates on the Admiral's desk, one for the Colonel, and waited until he had the Admiral's attention.

"What is it, Hutu?"

"Sir." Looking around, he quickly leaned over to relay Cassandra's comments.

"Thank you, Hutu," as Quinn approached he saw a glimmer of humor in the Admiral's eyes. Picking up his plate, he started to eat.

"Hutu tell a joke or what?"

"No, just a bit of payback."

Realizing it must involve Cassandra, Quinn ate. Whatever it was, it eased some of the pressure the Admiral was under.

∞ ∞ ∞ ∞ ∞

While the pressure on the Admiral was easing, back in his quarters it was building. Results were coming in on the latest search. There were matches, in both eighteen and nineteen-line transmissions.

Leaning back from the console, Cassandra ran a shaky hand through her hair. Suddenly she was nervous. Why? Instinct? She wished William was here. Selecting the first eighteen-line transmission she closed her eyes and listened.

"Chief, you're to report to the Retribution."
"What for?"
"That will be explained to you once you get here."

The transmission ended.

Cassandra recognized the Colonel's voice but couldn't quite place the other. She should know it. Reviewing the codes, she isolated the Colonel's transmission code. Listening to the next transmission, Cassandra was no closer to the identity of the voice than she was before.

"SHIT!" Standing to pace, she grabbed the edge of the console as the room tilted. Taking a deep breath, she waited for it to right itself.

"Time to take a break," she thought on her way into Victoria's room and grabbed the treats Hutu had brought.

Chapter Twenty-Two

"Admiral, High Admiral Valerian is on the comm."

"Zafar."

"Admiral, support has arrived at the border. You can back down from Alert Status One; go to standby. You are to maintain your present position until the border is fully secured."

"Understood, they're early."

"Yes, I ordered them to maximum warp. No other news?"

"Not at this time, Sir."

"Tell your people good job."

"I will, Sir." Ending the transmission, the Admiral opened a comm.

"Attention, this is the Admiral. Support has arrived at the border. We are backing down from Alert Status One to Standby and will maintain our current position until the border is secured. Good job, people! That comes not only from me but from the High Admiral."

In quarters, two little girls jumped up and down on the bed.

"Aunt Cassie! Did you hear? It's all right!"

"I heard. I told you the Admiral would keep you safe. Now you both need to calm down before you fall off that bed, then we'd have to go to Medical."

Giggling, the girls plopped down on the bed.

"Hutu sent some extra snacks for you, ready for them?"

"YEAH!" as the girls devoured what appeared to be cookies, Cassandra just shook her head. Oh to be so young.

"It's late, you both need to get ready for bed."

"Oh, Aunt Cassie…"

"I mean it, it's late. You need to get to bed. You can talk for a little bit, but that's it."

"Okay." As the girls changed, she took the plate out to the counter. Returning they were in bed whispering.

"Well, that was quick." Leaning down, she gave Amina a kiss. "I love you, Amina. Sleep well."

"Night, Aunt Cassie, love you."

Reaching over she kissed Tori. "Goodnight, Tori, I love you."

"I love you too, Aunt Cassie."

"I'll see you in the morning." Putting the lights as low as they would go, she closed the hatch.

Cassandra couldn't bring herself to go work at the console. She wasn't sure why, she just knew she wanted to wait for William. She was very close. She could feel it. She just wasn't sure they were going to like what she found.

Changing for bed, she found she couldn't lie down. Entering the Ready Room, she walked over to William's desk, poured herself a glass of Carinian ale, and sat. Sipping the ale, she tipped her head back and let her mind wander. So much had happened in such a short time. What was connected, what wasn't? What didn't she know?

∞ ∞ ∞ ∞ ∞

The ruins of Kayseri in the moonlight had always appealed to Cassandra. The desert had reclaimed so much, but man was fighting back. In the quiet of the night, you could almost hear the ancient voices.

What would they tell you?

"What do you want to know?"

She should have been startled, but she wasn't. Turning she saw Sabah walking toward her, her long flowing gown not hiding the fact that she was heavily pregnant. Behind her, the ruins Cassandra knew returned to their former glory.

"Everything."

"That's too much."

"It's what I need."

"It's only what you think you need. Think smaller."

"Smaller? Okay, try this one. Why do I have to solve a problem you started?"

"I am the beginning; you are the end."

Her sudden anger surprised Cassandra. "Oh please…like that's an answer."

Sabah's eyes flashed, "It is the answer."

"The way I see it you took the easy way out. You left and I get to clean up the mess."

"Easy!" Sabah rubbed her distended belly. "Nothing about it was easy!"

"You decided it was too hard to stay and fight, fight for what you believed was right. So you left. You made a good life here. You made a difference here. But what you left behind…it eventually destroyed all this." Cassandra made a sweeping motion with her arms. "It destroyed all I loved and threw me into a world I barely understand. One that wants to destroy me and all I've come to love because of you!"

"It seems you understand it quite well."

"This is the world you ran away from. You had all the knowledge you needed to defeat them, I don't."

"You have all you need. You have your life mate. What you don't understand, he will. It will take both of you."

"That's a bunch of bullshit. You're just trying to justify running away! Seven billion people died because of you."

"No, because of you!"

"ENOUGH! BOTH OF YOU," a man strode toward them.

"Kayden," Cassandra whispered.

Sabah's eyes flashed, "Yes." She turned to him, "You shouldn't be here."

"She's mine as much as yours."

"This is mine to handle," Sabah lashed at him.

"And you're not!" They were nearly nose-to-nose, completely ignoring Cassandra.

"So you still get to fight when you're dead?" Angry blue and violet eyes whipped around to her.

"Yes," Sabah finally answered.

"And makeup?"

"Yes," Kayden grinned.

"Good to know," Cassandra couldn't help grinning back.

"It wasn't Sabah's fault." Her smile faded as Kayden moved to her. "It isn't yours. Others' decisions caused it. They took advantage when they should have protected."

"I want to change it," Cassandra whispered.

"To change it," Sabah interjected, "you'd have to sacrifice all you've found; your life mate, your child."

"I'd accepted I'd never have a life mate or child on Earth, so I wouldn't have known."

"But you do now," she argued back. "So you'd give up your life mate for seven billion people? Honorable. What about the child you carry? Will you sacrifice that as well?"

"What? What child?"

"Sabah!"

"What! I'm not telling her anything she doesn't already know in her heart."

Cassandra turned away from the bickering couple. Had she conceived? Was she carrying William's child? Putting both hands over her still flat stomach she closed her eyes.

Yes, a child nestled in her womb. William's child.

"Stop it! Both of you!"

A stunned silence greeted Cassandra as she turned back to the two Royals. It had been eons since anyone dared talk to them like that.

"How do I end it?" The life mates looked at each other.

"That's your decision," Kayden told her.

"Mine?"

"And that of your life mate," Sabah added. "You will always be stronger together than you ever will be apart."

"You already suspect," Kayden nodded. "You have good instincts. Your House of Protection is strong."

"She gets it from the House of Knowledge," Sabah argued back.

"Stop! Please," watching the moon hover over the horizon Cassandra was more confused than before. There was too much to understand.

"Cassandra," Kayden took her hands, "you have what you need. What you choose to do with it, only you can decide. Just remember, you're not alone. You have your life mate. He has great inner and outer strength. You'll need both before this is over."

"I would sacrifice everything for him, even our child," Cassandra looked into Kayden's blazing eyes so like William's.

"Find another way. If you sacrifice what you're fighting for…"

"Then you've lost," Sabah finished.

"Yes," Cassandra turned and walked to Sabah. "Which child is this?" Gently she put a hand on Sabah's belly and felt the baby kick.

"Our first son, we'll name him after Kayden's father." Sabah put a hand on Cassandra's flat stomach.

"You're son will be strong, like his father."

"Yes, he will."

As the moon touched the horizon, they faded.

∞ ∞ ∞ ∞ ∞

With all stations moved to Standby, the Admiral was finally willing to leave the Bridge in the hands of the Major of the Watch. He was going to get some much needed down time with Cassandra. Thinking about holding her in his arms, he opened the hatch to find her sleeping in his chair. Securing the hatch, he rounded his desk setting aside the nearly full glass of ale resting on her stomach.

The shadows under her eyes told him she'd been working too hard with the transmissions and taking care of the girls. She'd changed for bed and that was exactly where he was putting her.

Scooping her up, he carried her to their bed. When he laid her down, she opened sleepy eyes to his.

"William…"

"Shhh…sleep."

"Not without you…" she raised a hand to caress his cheek.

"You won't be." Kissing her palm, he moved to the closet. Moments later he was pulling her close.

"I love you, Cassandra," he murmured into her hair. In minutes, both were asleep.

∞ ∞ ∞ ∞ ∞

Waking with Cassandra in his arms was William's favorite way to start the day. Her thick ebony hair messy from sleep, long dark lashes fanning out on her cheek, full lips slightly parted, her head on his chest, arm around his waist, a leg thrown across him; perfection!

Running a hand along her bare thigh, he marveled that he had found her. They shouldn't have. Not with Earth so deep in the Relinquished Zone. Not with Earth's inability to travel to other planets. But here she was, sleeping in his arms, a gift from the ancestors. Whatever it took for them to be together, they would do it together.

Slipping his hand under her shirt, William followed the curve of her hip up to a narrow waist. So small, so soft, traveling up her ribcage he cupped her breast.

"Hmmm," Cassandra pressed her body closer to his. Waking up with him, his hands on her, was her favorite way to wake. Kissing the place where his heart beat, she looked into his eyes.

Forty days, he thought, looking into those deep sapphire blue eyes heavy from sleep, glowing with love. Just forty days ago he'd never seen those eyes, now he'd see them for the rest of his life.

Rolling her to her back he propped himself on his forearms looking into those beautiful eyes. Leaning down, he gave her a soft kiss filled with all the wonder, all the love he'd discovered since she'd entered his life.

Cassandra, breathless from the tenderness of William's kiss, ran gentle hands up his back and pulled him closer, returning the love-filled kiss.

Leaving her mouth, William worked his way down her neck, lavishing the same attention at each place his mouth stopped.

"William," she whispered, her body arched up as her hands traveled down to release him. Lifting his head, he watched her eyes widen as he slowly filled her, his eyes melding with hers.

When he slowly withdrew she let out a little gasp, her body tightening around him. He continued to slowly torture them both until those beautiful eyes started to lose focus.

"William…" dragging his head down Cassandra slowly wrapped her tongue around his, imitating their bodies.

Hooking an arm under her hips, William lifted her pressing deeply into her. Groaning she released his mouth, she could feel her body tightening around him. Her release was so close.

"Let go, Cassandra, I've got you," he softly demanded.

Cassandra's aroused eyes met darkening violet ones. Moving his hips as he watched her eyes darken and the blue deepen, he became driven as her body searched for its release. Pressing against her most sensitive part, William saw her eyes glaze over as pleasure took her. Her release triggered his and with one last deep thrust he joined her.

Knowing the moment her mind reengaged was humbling to William. For her to let go, to let her feelings rule…not intelligence…was something she gave only to him.

Running his fingers through her hair, he rested his forehead on hers. "I love you, Cassandra, with all that I am I love you."

Here he was, she thought. The man she loved, her life mate. He was her center and her strength to handle what lay ahead.

"I love you, William, never doubt it."

"I never will."

Lying in bed, they savored the time together, both knowing it would be a rare thing in the coming days. As they told the other what happened while they had been apart, their bond strengthened.

"How long until we head to Carina?" she asked propped up on William's chest.

"Three or four days," he answered running a hand down her arm.

"Then two more days to get there?"

"Yes." William waited, knowing she was thinking about something.

"Tell me about the Sentinel."

"The Sentinel? It's the pride of the House of Protection. Procne has been its Captain for three cycles, his service record impeccable." Sitting up he pulled her across his lap.

"What makes it special?"

"Special?"

"Why would someone target it?"

"What do you mean target?" Realizing he'd gone into Admiral-mode, Cassandra started to slide off his lap, only to have him stop her.

"Cassandra…"

"I need you to listen to something." Letting her up, he followed her to the console. Pulling up the last transmission, she waited as he listened.

"That's Quinn talking to Tibullus."

"Tibullus! That's who it is." William waited. "Tibullus is the one receiving the transmissions on the Sentinel."

"Cassandra, Tibullus wouldn't give up the Fleet's location. It's ridiculous to even consider it."

"Why?" Knowing Tibullus was innocent, Cassandra turned away finding she was hurt by William's doubt in her findings.

"Because he's The First Son!"

"What do you mean he's The First Son? Of what House?" Her head whipped around.

"The House of Protection." William was stunned she didn't know this. "You've been studying the Houses, Cassandra. How could you not know this?"

"The First Son of the House of Protection is Barek. He's King Jotham's son with his wife, Lata, who died in an accident when Barek was five." Cassandra strode to the closet, yanking out a pair of pants.

"That's right." He remembered the day well.

"I've read all the available information, William! And nowhere, in any of it, did it say that Barek is also called Tibullus!"

It was Cassandra's tone that brought him out of the past. Seeing her jerk on her pants, he realized he'd done what he promised he wouldn't. He made her feel stupid for not knowing something that was common knowledge. As she was changing shirts, he walked up behind her, kissing her now bare shoulder.

"I'm sorry. I didn't mean it the way it sounded." When she didn't respond, he turned her to face him, the shirt between them. Lacing his fingers behind her neck, he tipped her face up with his thumbs and saw the hurt in her eyes.

"Tibullus is the family name for the House of Protection. It's only used when they are serving in the Coalition." His thumbs gently caressed her jaw line, "I'm sorry."

Taking a deep breath, she closed her eyes. When they opened, they were clear with just a touch of humor. "So I called The First Son from the House of Protection a jerk?"

"You did."

"Nice."

"Cassandra, I'm also his Second Father." He watched to see if she understood.

"Second Father?"

"Jotham and I are not only related but longtime friends. We went to the Academy together. When Barek was born, he asked if I would make sure he was protected if anything ever happened to him."

"A Godparent, that's what it was on Earth. I'm Victoria's."

"Yes, you would be," he looked into her eyes, "We're okay?"

"Yes, I overreacted."

"No, you didn't. I did. Do you understand now why Tibullus would never give up our location?"

Walking away from him she pulled on her shirt. Tibullus was The First Son. He was on the Sentinel. The Sentinel was the target of at least two of the attacks. These are assassination attempts.

"Is he alive?" she turned.

"We don't know."

"He gave up the Fleet's location, William." She watched his eyes, saw him struggle with believing her and what he knew of Tibullus. "He didn't know he was."

"What don't I know?" Walking back to the console, she pulled up the coding she uncovered.

"The twentieth line of coding is a Trojan," stepping aside she let him sit.

"Trojan?"

"A series of codes that activate once the transmission is received. In this case, it searches for the location of the receiver then transmits the location back to the sender."

"You found this?"

"Yes, last night. Both transmissions were answered by Tibullus." Cassandra paused wondering if she should continue. "William…"

"It's an assassination attempt."

"Yes. These two attacks have nothing to do with me. They're all about Tibullus." Cassandra saw rage fill William's eyes.

"Who?"

Reaching around him, Cassandra pulled up the original transmission. "Can you access this?"

William entered his code to play the transmission and was denied.

"Why wouldn't you be able to access a transmission on your own ship?"

"Because of the royal coding."

"But you're a Royal."

"Not at this level."

"I've isolated the sender's code, but I can't tell you who it is. I'm sorry." William pulled her onto his lap, his arms encircling her.

"You have nothing to be sorry for. You found what no one else could."

"But not in time to help Tibullus."

"We don't know that. There are survivors on the Sentinel, they were able to maintain their life systems and are making repairs. Their communications are gone, so until someone physically goes over, no one is going to know."

"When will that be?"

"It's not a high priority."

"How can it not be?"

"Because the border isn't secure, the Regulians are sitting just on the other side, waiting."

"To see if they were successful."

"Yes."

"I'm sorry, William."

"Why, Cassandra?

"For Tibullus, you love him." Pulling her close, he allowed her concern to comfort him.

"I need to shower and change before the girls get up." Giving her a kiss, he stood.

"When do you need to be on the Bridge?" she watched him.

"Not until later. Why?"

"Go shower, I'll let Hutu know we're up."

"Cassandra…"

"I had another dream. I need to tell you about it." Walking back he framed her face, his eyes intense.

"You're okay?"

"I'm fine. I just need to tell you." After a long minute, he nodded and taking some clothes he headed for the shower.

Straightening the bed after calling Hutu, Cassandra wondered if she should tell William she had conceived. She had no actual proof, just a dream. Salish lied to him about conceiving. She needed to be sure before she told him.

How would William react when she told him she met Kayden, the ancestor he condemns? What is it that Sabah had said about her baby? It would be their first son, named after Kayden's father.

But Sabah and Kayden's first born son was named Barack, not Tibus. There'd been a scroll she'd studied while getting her doctorate. It told the story of how Kayden and Sabah had traveled a great distance from their homeland. That Kayden's father had given not only his blessing but the symbol to prove he was the King's son.

Cassandra never discovered what that symbol was. Answering the buzzing hatch, Cassandra let Hutu in.

"Hello, Hutu."

"Hello, ma'am.

"You can call me Cassandra, Hutu."

"No, ma'am. You're the Admiral's life mate. That wouldn't be right."

"Why?" she was honestly curious.

"Because he's the Admiral," Hutu seemed to think that explained all.

"The Admiral said you've been with him for over five cycles now."

"Yes, ma'am."

"You can set the tray on the Admiral's desk. We'll eat in here since the girls are still asleep." As he did, he checked both meals.

"What will you do once we return to Carina?"

"Ma'am?"

"Don't play dumb with me, Hutu. You are the most informed person on this ship. You know once we get to Carina all hell is going to break loose."

"I go with the Admiral, ma'am, no matter what. Who else knows what you and Tori like?" he watched Cassandra's eyes fill.

"Thank you, Hutu."

"You're welcome, ma'am," he shuffled his feet. "Let me know when the girls are ready for their meal." Turning, he returned to the kitchen. Securing the door, she turned to find William standing just inside the room.

"What did you say to fluster Hutu?"

"I asked him what he would do when we returned to Carina." She walked up to him.

"What did he say?" he looked at the secured hatch.

"That he goes with the Admiral, no matter what. You have a very loyal crew, Admiral."

William didn't know what to say. He hadn't considered that Hutu would go with him when they left the Retribution. He would never have asked.

"Eat, William." She saw she'd caught him unaware. He hadn't realized others were willing to sacrifice…for him…without him asking.

Sitting down, Cassandra handed him a plate. Picking up hers, she sat wondering if she would be able to eat, the smell had her stomach clenching. Pregnant?

"Tell me about your dream," he took his first bite.

"I'm not sure you'll like it," she took a small bite.

"Why?"

With her stomach holding, she took another. "I met Kayden."

William lowered the bite he'd been about to take. "What?"

"The ancestor you condemn. The one no one will speak of."

"I know who he is!"

Cassandra raised her eyes from her plate, "How if no one speaks his name?"

"I met him in a dream too."

Setting her plate aside, she leaned back in her chair, waiting.

Watching her, he realized he should have told her sooner. She'd been open with him about her dreams. Another area he needed to work on.

"It was the night you realized what the Dioscuri coming would mean to my career." He didn't want to think about how close he'd come to losing her. Forcing himself to remain seated, he looked at her. While her eyes darkened, she wasn't shutting him out.

"I was standing on the cliffs, there was a storm brewing, it blocked out the suns' light. When I turned he was there, I knew him, didn't have to be told, I just knew."

Cassandra nodded.

"I accused him of murdering his brother then running away. He told me that I knew nothing, that if he had, I would never be. He told me that his brother lived and that the King's First Son gave him his blessing." Finding he couldn't sit any longer, he walked toward Cassandra.

"He made me realize that I couldn't protect you if I weren't with you," William ran the back of his hand down her cheek, needing to touch. "I realized I'd made a mistake, that I would lose you. I wasn't willing to sacrifice you. Not you, not our future together."

"You believed him when he said he didn't kill his brother?"

"I…yes…I can't tell you why, but yes, I believed him."

"Wait here." Cassandra left him to go into their private chambers, returning with the iPod.

"When I was working on my doctorate I came across a scroll. Read this." Cassandra found what she was looking for then handed it to William. Looking at the device, William read the ancient Carinian.

"His father gave him his blessing," William read out loud.

"In my dream, Sabah was heavily pregnant." Seeing his look, she explained, "with child. I asked her which child it was and she told me it was their first son, that they would name him after Kayden's father."

"They named him Tibus."

"No. Read the rest of the scroll."

As he did, William went still, "Barack."

"Yes, that would mean Kayden was the First Son of the First Son."

Sitting down in his chair, William's mind was racing. If Cassandra was right, then the history of the House of Protection was false. Everything believed about Kayden was a lie.

Giving William time to think, she walked over to the painting of the setting suns. Kayden had said she had what she needed. So maybe it was time to stop gathering information and start putting it all together.

Barack was assassinated all those years ago. Why? The obvious answer was so he couldn't become King. The King's second son became King.

Tibullus had a brother, Dadrian, not from King Jotham's wife, Lata.

Coincidence? Possibly, but Cassandra's instinct told her no. This was what her dreams had been trying to tell her. That the past was repeating itself. Was she too late? Was Tibullus dead?

Hearing William, she turned. The man could make her catch her breath just by being; Sabah was right. Together they were more than they were apart. What she didn't know or understand he would. Just like with Tibullus.

"There's something I keep meaning to ask you."

"Ask," William wrapped his arms around her pulling her close.

"Is that painting," Cassandra pointed to the wall, "of the setting suns of Carina?"

William raised an eyebrow. "Yes."

Turning she looked at it again. "I thought so. I've sat on that cliff watching them set with Sabah in a dream. But I didn't really know."

William pulled her close; he knew better than anyone how important knowing was to her.

"I stood on those cliffs when I met Kayden."

"What do you think that means? That they both met us there." Waiting while William thought about it, Cassandra looked back at the painting.

"It must have been an important spot for them."

"Yes, and you just happened to have a painting of it."

"Coincidence."

"And the book?"

William said nothing.

"You descend from Kayden's brother, Walwyn. I descend from Sabah; House of Protection, House of Knowledge again."

"Too many coincidences."

"Yes, too many. Kayden told me I had what I needed, had all I needed. Sabah said that what I didn't understand you would. They're right."

"Yes, they're right."

"What do we do, William?" She turned in his arms and looked up at him.

"We'll put it together, together. Find out who is threatening you and Tibullus. We stop them."

"Together."

"Together." Leaning down William sealed the promise with a kiss.

"Aunt Cassie?" Both turned to see Victoria standing in the doorway.

"Hi, sweetie, you're awake."

"Yeah, we're hungry."

"I'll call Hutu," William picked up his comm.

"So Amina's up too?" Cassandra walked over to Tori.

"Yeah, she's in the bathroom."

"Well let's get the two of you dressed then Hutu should be here."

Left in his Ready Room, William sat. Assassination. While attempts were not unheard of, they were rare on Carina. Two traitors; one wanting Cassandra, one wanting Tibullus. Did it start out that way?

William's instincts told him no. This all started with Cassandra. Tibullus came later. Someone saw an opportunity with the Sentinel's original damage. Someone who found out about Cassandra and instead of reporting it used it to his own advantage. Who benefited? The obvious answer was Dadrian.

His gut told him Dadrian. But could he trust that? He'd never liked Dadrian. Something about him rubbed him wrong, but who else? Sometimes the most obvious was the answer.

If Dadrian was trying to gain the throne, that meant he discovered the plot against Cassandra and had done nothing. He knew the Regulians were involved and had done nothing. If the Regulians had gotten by the Retribution, they would have attacked Carina, and he'd have done nothing.

Rage began to build in William, the little foabhor! Who did he think he was? Standing by while his life mate was attacked! He'd destroy him! He didn't care who his father was!

The Admiral in him knew he had to bank the rage, not let it out, not until the time was right. But the man wanted to attack now!

The buzzing of the hatch brought William out of his thoughts. Hutu was here with first meal for the girls. People were depending on him. Cassandra was depending on him to keep them safe. He couldn't do that if he were bent on revenge. Pushing it aside, he let Hutu in and waited.

∞ ∞ ∞ ∞ ∞

Hutu found the Admiral waiting for him when he returned to the Ready Room.

"Sir?"

"Cassandra's informed me you plan on leaving the ship with me."

"Yes, Sir."

"It will jeopardize your career."

"With all due respect, Sir, you wouldn't risk yours unless you actually believed it was necessary. That's enough for me."

"Thank you, Hutu." Nodding, Hutu picked up Cassandra's plate then stopped.

"Sir."

"Yes."

"She didn't eat enough." The Admiral found himself grinning. Cassandra wouldn't appreciate others worrying about her.

"No, she didn't. Leave it, I'll make sure she eats."

"Thank you, Sir."

"No, Hutu, thank you. I won't forget this."

"Sir," with a nod Hutu left.

∞ ∞ ∞ ∞ ∞

As the girls ate, Cassandra wondered what William was thinking. His world had just changed. Would he believe it? Accept it?

Kayden told her what she decided to do was up to her. Was he telling her she had options? That they should leave if they wanted a life together? Could she do that to Victoria? Make her start all over again?

Chapter Twenty-Three

"Mama," Amina jumped out of her chair to hug her mother.

"Hello, baby, I missed you."

"I missed you too. Where's Daddy?"

"He's talking to the Admiral." Javiera gave Cassandra a pointed look. Nodding, Cassandra looked to the Ready Room.

∞ ∞ ∞ ∞ ∞

"Something on your mind, Chief?" Moving to sit behind his desk, the Admiral waited.

"Sir, I want to thank you for letting Amina stay here while we were on Alert."

"No thanks necessary. It was good for Victoria too."

"Yes, Sir. They've become good friends, as have Cassandra and Javiera."

"I know."

"Admiral, I've known you a long time."

"Since you were twelve."

"Yes, Sir. You were serving with my father."

"How is he?"

"He's fine. He and Mom have a place near Lake Baku."

"What's on your mind, Leander?"

"Your decision to return to Carina, Sir."

Hard eyes met Leander's. "My decision, Chief."

"Yes, Sir. The right decision to protect the Queen, to protect Cassandra."

"How have you come by this information, Chief?" But he already knew.

"Cassandra, Sir. She felt we had the right to know when she asked us to leave the ship with you."

"She what?" His voice was low and lethal.

"Asked us to leave the Retribution when the two of you do. She asked, explained what was going on. Made sure we understood it wasn't an order, wasn't coming from you. If we decided we couldn't, it wouldn't reflect on my service record."

"You've made your decision."

"Yes, Admiral, we told Cassandra yesterday. We're with you."

"Thank you, Leander."

"Not necessary, Admiral. I have family on Carina. This traitor has put them in jeopardy. He has to be stopped."

"Agreed."

∞ ∞ ∞ ∞ ∞

"Mama, can we go to F Deck? We haven't seen our friends in forever."

"I don't see why not if it's okay with Cassandra." Javiera turned. "It would give you a break. We could get together later, I've thought of some things you'll need to know."

"Works for me. What about you, Tori, you up for F Deck?"

"Oh yeah!"

"Let's go."

"Daddy!" Amina ran into her father's arms.

"Hi, squirt, you been good?"

"Yes, Daddy. Guess what?"

"What?"

"Mama's taking us to F Deck."

"Really?"

"Really. Are you going to come too?"

"I might for a little bit."

The Admiral got up as they walked to the hatch.

"Victoria," walking over to him she looked up. Squatting down, William gave her a hug. "You have fun, okay?"

"Okay, Admiral." With a big smile, she headed off. As Cassandra secured the hatch, the Admiral sat back down.

"You made her day." She saw he had something on his mind so she took a seat.

"Who else?" She didn't pretend to not understand.

"I wasn't keeping it from you. They only gave me their decision yesterday. I haven't had time to tell you."

"Who else?" The Admiral didn't break eye contact.

"Tar."

"What are you doing, Cassandra!?!" He ran a frustrated hand through his hair. "This could end their careers!"

"I know that! So do they! You didn't question my bringing Lucas in."

"That's different. You know he considers Victoria his life mate."

"So you understand why I asked him to be in charge of her protection."

"Yes, you couldn't have kept him away."

"She'll be his priority. I need her to be so I don't have to worry about her if this goes wrong."

"Cassandra…"

"I do not doubt you, William, I know you'll protect us. But I'm your priority. I need to know Victoria is someone's."

"Okay. Why Leander and Javiera?"

"They're my friends. I trust them. We're going to need people we trust, William."

"And Tar?"

"You trust him."

"What else?"

Cassandra knew that wouldn't satisfy him, "William…"

"Why Tar?"

"Because he'll watch your back!"

"Damn it, Cassandra! This is his career!"

"And it's your life!" Bracing her hands on his desk, she got in his face. "You're in as much danger as I am, because of me! I have as much right to protect my life mate as you do!" Pushing away she stormed into the other room.

Stunned, William remained seated. Protecting him. She's concerned about protecting *him*.

She was on the couch, head in her hands when he entered their quarters. Straddling her legs, he sat on the table. Kissing the top of her head, he rubbed her arms.

"I'm sorry. I've always protected, not been protected."

"You'll have to get used to it." Determined eyes looked into his. "I love you, and I will protect you. I am not losing anyone else. I am not losing you!" As her voice broke, he pulled her into his arms.

"Shhh…You're not going to lose me." With a hard kiss, he pulled her close. "I'm here. I'm here, Cassandra.

Her fingers dug into his jacket as she buried her face, tears suddenly flowing.

"It's okay, baby, it's okay."

Fighting to control her tears she took a deep breath, then another. "I'm sorry. I didn't mean to fall apart like that."

"You've had a lot going on."

"So have you. I didn't mean to add to it."

"You haven't." Holding her, he suddenly realized what she was doing.

"You're building your House." Why hadn't he seen it sooner?

"Our House," tilting her head up she looked at him, "with people we know. People we trust. People we love. Together, William."

Looking into her eyes he saw his future. In a House they built together. Kayden was right.

"Our House," he sealed their future with a hard kiss.

∞ ∞ ∞ ∞ ∞

In the days that followed, the Regulians remained in the Relinquished Zone. Repairs were completed on the Fleet and it was decided that the Judgment would return with the injured. The Retribution maintained its defensive position awaiting orders from the High Admiral.

Cassandra and Javiera finally had a chance to get together to discuss the upcoming changes.

"So now we need to discuss your wardrobe," Javiera pointed out.

"Wardrobe," Cassandra groaned shaking her head.

"Yes. Queen Yakira has sat on the throne for nearly fifteen years since she was eighteen."

"When her mother died."

"Yes. But there was a challenge from a cousin. Normally it's just a formality, but not this time. So they went through the entire challenge process, not just the presentation before the Assembly."

"Wait, what's the difference?"

"Well if it's just a formality, they are presented to the Assembly, birthmarks compared, and it's over."

"And in a Full Challenge?"

"Then it can be up to a two-week process."

"Two weeks?"

"Yes. It takes time to gather a Full Assembly. While they are waiting there are dinners and gatherings, so members of the Assembly can meet the candidates and form an opinion of them. It becomes about more than just the birthmark. At least for the House of Knowledge."

Cassandra mused, "They will basically be judging me."

"Yes," Javiera's look was sympathetic.

"So my birthmark will be the last thing that matters."

"Even if yours is darker than hers, they can decide to keep the current Queen if they feel she is a better choice."

"It's this way with all the Houses?"

"No. Those are obvious, the birthmark fills with color."

"They can't argue with that?"

"No."

Cassandra looked at Javiera, her mind racing. No one can see her birthmark. If she wants true justice for Earth, she could not present her birthmark.

"What will I need?"

"Everything," Javiera eyed her clothes. "A Queen is a symbol, especially for the House of Knowledge. She must not only be knowledgeable, but she must also look knowledgeable."

"Shit, you're telling me style matters."

"Yes."

"Our worlds really aren't that different. I hate fashion!"

"Is that clothes?"

"Yes."

"Well, you're in luck. My mother's younger sister and husband happen to make clothes. They can make you everything you need."

The look in Cassandra's eyes made Javiera laugh.

"Seriously. They're good. Let me show you." As she showed her pictures, Cassandra's stomach started to roll.

"Javiera, I really appreciate the thought, but I'm not sure…"

"What?"

She looked at a picture of a woman with hair piled three feet high, a blue face, and little else.

"Does that really look like me?"

"That! No. I was just showing off."

"What is usually worn to these things?"

As Javiera showed her pictures of the different types of events the Royals attended, she started to understand.

"They wear the colors of their House."

"Yes." The gowns, while different from Earth, were still gowns.

"Your aunt and uncle can make something like this?"

"My…"

"Mother's sister and husband."

"Yes."

"If I show them a picture, can they make it?"

"I would think so."

"How much would it cost?"

"Cost?"

"Javiera, it won't be free. They'll need to be paid."

"The Admiral…" She stopped as Cassandra surged to her feet.

"How much?"

"I don't know. It's for a Royal."

"I'm not a Royal yet."

"But Cassandra…"

"No!"

∞ ∞ ∞ ∞ ∞

Entering his Ready Room, William could hear women's voices. Javiera was here. The two had been planning for more than two days. He started to smile until he caught the tone of Cassandra's voice. Something was wrong.

"Hello, ladies." Smiling as he entered their quarters, he found the two by the comm center.

"Hello, Admiral." Cassandra was standing stiffly next to Javiera.

"Hello, Javiera. Are the girls with Leander?"

"Yes."

"Could Tori eat with you tonight?"

"That would be great. Why doesn't she spend the night?"

"Thank you."

"I'll see you tomorrow." Leaving, Javiera couldn't help but smile.

"Very smooth."

"I thought so," he gathered her into his arms.

"What's wrong?"

"That's my question. You were upset with Javiera." When she tried to pull away, he held her still. "Tell me."

"Did you know this wouldn't be just about comparing birthmarks?"

"What do you mean?"

"Javiera said if there's a serious challenge to the throne then there's a different set of rules."

William thought back to the last time the House of Knowledge was challenged, "Yes, I guess there is."

"Several weeks' worth."

"You can't be worried about that." Looking at her, he saw she was.

"It involves dinners, gatherings, being judged on how you look, dress, act."

"It won't matter."

"It will."

"Not once they see your birthmark it won't."

Looking at her life mate, she realized he didn't understand what she wanted.

"When will they see it?"

"As soon as we arrive. No one will be able to argue you are the Queen. You will be safe."

"Are we back to that?"

"Cassandra," William was honestly confused, "what do you want?"

"Justice. True justice for seven billion people." Her expression locked with his. "I want the one who murdered my family, who terrorized my niece, who was responsible for the deaths of your crew and who allowed the Sentinel to be attacked."

"You can have that once you're Queen."

"NO! I can't order justice, any more than you can order loyalty. It will be up to your Assembly to decide if the people of Earth deserved to die. If the offspring of Sabah and Kayden and Carinians from different Houses can finally find justice in the Carinian Assembly, with Carinian laws, when one of their own orders their deaths."

William gazed into his life mate's eyes and saw the determination, the rage. She of all people had the right to her anger. "It will make everything more difficult."

"I know, especially for you."

"Me?"

"I won't be safe. Not yet. But William, I need to know. I need to know if everything they brought to Earth, all the good, the Light that they considered the best of Carina, is real. Because if it's not, then I don't want to be there."

"You would be willing to leave? Start over again?"

"The only thing that matters to me here is you!"

He'd already considered stealing her away and taking no chances. But now, understanding what she wanted, he was unable to argue. He couldn't do it.

"What were you and Javiera arguing about?"

"Who said we were arguing?"

"I do. I know your tones. You were upset. Why?"

"There are dinners, gatherings, people judging, showing off."

He gave her a lost man's look. Exasperated, Cassandra looked at him.

"What are you going to wear?"

"Me? My uniform…" William suddenly replayed all the 'dinners' he'd been to and he felt himself shudder and grimace.

"Exactly."

"So we find you some clothes."

"Find me?" Knowing he was sinking, William grabbed the branch that was Javiera.

"What did Javiera say?"

"That she has family that can make me clothes."

"So there you go."

"Do you really think that I would go to a dinner that reflects on you, as much as me, wearing one of these things?" Cassandra gestured to the comm. Looking at it, William paled.

"That's not who you are."

"No, Javiera said these are bragging pictures."

"So they can make something you like?"

"Supposedly."

"So what's the problem?" As she stared at him, William was truly at a loss. "Cassandra, honesty whether we like it or not."

"This isn't about honesty! William, these are designer gowns."

"Okay…"

"Damn it! How do I pay for them!?!"

"How do you…" He lifted her to her toes, "*I pay for them*! You are my life mate! *My Queen*."

"William, I don't know what these cost. I don't know what you make. I have nothing of value to offer."

"Nothing of value," William's voice was lethal.

"Not on Carina."

"You think that matters to me?"

"No, I don't. I know it doesn't. But it matters to me!" Framing his face, she met the deadly look in his eye. "I told you about my mother's death. What I didn't tell you was that within six months, my father sent me to boarding school, a school far away from home," she explained seeing his confusion. "From the time I was ten I've been on my own."

William continued to stare at her.

"He loved me. I know he did, but I looked so much like my mom that it was hard for him to see me every day. I understand that now. I had my own money, knew what everything cost. Paid my own way." Looking at him, she saw his eyes calming. "I have a hard time not being able to pay for anything!"

"And not knowing if I can."

"Yes."

"Cassandra, I am an Admiral in the Coalition, a member of the Royal Family, this won't be a problem."

"Would you tell me if it was?"

"Yes. Honesty whether we like it or not."

"Okay," she replied stretching up to kiss his lips. "I'll tell Javiera to call her family."

"Good."

"So, Admiral," her eyes sparkled into his, "it seems it's just the two of us tonight, all night. What do you think we should do?" Looking into those eyes he couldn't help but be captivated.

"I plan on being very close to you. All night long."

"Really? Well, if you must." She sank into the kiss as he carried her to bed.

∞ ∞ ∞ ∞ ∞

Later, after Hutu had collected the last meal's dishes, Cassandra snuggled back into William's arms, lazily caressing his bare chest.

"Is there any news on Tibullus?"

"No," his voice was troubled.

"What's taking so long?" asked Cassandra.

"There's a support crew there now."

"You need to get him out of there, William. If the Regulians find out he's alive, they'll attack again."

"If he's alive."

"He is," Cassandra responded as William shifted to look down at her. "I refuse to believe we were meant to figure all this out only to have him die."

"If he is, I can't just order him back."

"Can you use me?" She pushed up from his chest.

"Use you?"

"The Challenge. As First Son, he would be required to be there, wouldn't he?" William raised an eyebrow. "Can't you get him on the Judgment without anyone knowing?"

Leaning back he considered what she was saying. "It might be possible. We'd need to make sure he's unable to communicate with anyone. We'd need to keep the information from not only the High Admiral but King Jotham." William frowned at the thought of not telling his friend that his son was alive.

"But it's only for a little while. He'd rather not know and have his son home alive than know and risk him," Cassandra told him knowing his concern.

"True, but it will take him time to see that. Especially if…"

"You think it's Dadrian too." Concerned eyes met his, "One son trying to kill another."

"I can't imagine what it would feel like to have your son betray you like that."

"He'll need his friend." Rising to her knees, she gave him a gentle kiss.

"I need to make some calls." He caressed her cheek with his knuckles.

"Go make them, we have all night." As he walked away in only his sleeping pants, she marveled at the man.

His broad shoulders, muscled back, trim waist, powerful hips and thighs, all perfectly proportioned on his over seven-foot frame. And his front wasn't bad either. He was comfortable with himself, confident in his abilities. He was a decorated Admiral in the Coalition of United Planets, a Royal from the House of Protection, and he loved her. He would sacrifice for her, as he'd already done, to make sure she was protected.

She had asked a lot of him, not wanting to show her birthmark when they arrived in Carina. He understood. He hadn't liked it, could have pressed, but he didn't. He would allow her to handle it her way while making sure she was protected.

She needed to make sure she didn't let him down. Gowns. Clothes. Shit! She knew they made a statement. They had on Earth. She just didn't like all the hassle and fuss that went into them. But William was a Royal. He might serve with women who were in uniform 24/7, but that didn't mean he didn't notice what women wore.

He had taken enough hits because of her. This wouldn't be one of them. But she wasn't going to dress like a Carinian. She would be true to herself, she knew what she liked.

Getting out of bed, she lifted their comm and called Javiera.

"Cassandra?"

"Call your family. See if they're willing to make my clothes."

"Oh, they will be."

"Javiera, you can't tell them anything. Not yet."

"I know, I was working on that. I can tell them it's a rush because you'll be leaving for Messene. That will give them the heads up they are important clothes but not for who or what."

"They'll accept that?"

"Yes."

"Okay. Also tell them they need to be making clothes for Victoria."

"I will. Boy, that will really drive them crazy!" Javiera laughed. "A woman and child going to Messene. They'll be racking their brains on every possible Royal."

"Javiera…"

"Don't worry, they won't think it's for someone on the Retribution."

"You're sure?"

"Positive. We're coming back from the border. There are no Royal children on a Battle Star."

"All right. I'm going to go through these pictures you pulled up. See if there's anything I like. How are the girls?"

"They're fine, playing in Amina's room."

"Give them both a kiss goodnight for me."

"I will. Goodnight, Cassandra.

"Night."

∞ ∞ ∞ ∞ ∞

In his Ready Room, the Admiral opened a secure line to Admiral Carnot. He was about to ask him to break all the rules.

"Carnot."

"Zafar. I need you on a secure line, Ferran."

"Secured."

"Are you on the Bridge?"

"Ready Room."

"Alone?"

"Yes."

"I need to relay some information to you, Ferran. Information High Command doesn't know and can't for a while."

"What the fuck's going on, Will?"

"We have a traitor that's giving the Fleet's location to the Regulians." He waited.

"And you don't think High Command needs to know this?"

"They know. What they don't know is that they are assassination attempts." There was silence on the other end.

"The Sentinel? Tibullus?"

"Yes."

"Why aren't you informing High Command?"

"There's a leak."

"What are you wanting?"

"First, you have to find out if he's still alive. If he's not, the rest won't matter. But if he is, keep him off all lists. Get him on the Judgment with the returning wounded with a full communications block. Once they're en route, I'll contact him, fill him in. But High Command can't be informed."

"The King will need to be told."

"No. If it leaks that he's alive, what ship he's on, it will be attacked. I guarantee it, Ferran. It's gone too far to be stopped."

"You want me to lie not only to High Command but to King Jotham?"

"No. All you have to tell them is he's not on any of your lists because he won't be. This won't come back on you, Ferran, it's all on me."

"This is why you took the Retribution back. Why not just take Tibullus with you?"

"At the time, all we knew was we had a traitor. Not that it was directed specifically at Tibullus." William leaned back in his chair waiting for Ferran's decision.

"If he's alive, I'll get him on the Judgment, keep his name off the lists. But if High Command or King Jotham asks me point blank if he's alive, I won't lie."

"Understood."

"I'll get back to you." Carnot disconnected.

Now he had to wait to see if Cassandra was right that Tibullus was alive. Because if he wasn't, and Dadrian was responsible, he wasn't sure what he would do.

"Zafar," he answered his comm.

"Admiral, your orders are to proceed to Carina," High Admiral Valerian told him.

"Understood, Sir."

"I'll see you in High Command two days from now."

"With all due respect, Sir, the meeting will be held in my Ready Room."

"Is that an order, Admiral?" the High Admiral's voice was icy.

"Security has already been established here, Sir."

"You're questioning the security at High Command?"

"No, Sir, but there are more risks involved going to High Command than in High Command coming here."

"We'll play this your way for a little longer, Admiral. But once you arrive you will be reminded just who is in charge!" the High Admiral disconnected.

Cassandra entered the Ready Room just as the High Admiral called. She hadn't meant to eavesdrop, but hearing the High Admiral's tone pissed her off.

"Why didn't you just tell him it's at my request?" William's shoulders were stiff under her hands.

Not answering, he connected to the Bridge. "Tar, we're to proceed to Carina."

"Yes, Admiral."

Turning in his chair, he tugged her into his arms. "It's my decision."

She scanned William's eyes. She'd gotten to know him well and could tell the High Admiral's tone had rubbed him wrong too.

"That you made because of me. He has no right to question it."

"Yes he does, he's the High Admiral."

"And if you were doing this for a real Carinian Queen?"

"You are a real Carinian Queen."

"Not until the Assembly says so."

"Your birthmark says so."

"You're not answering the question."

"Caught that did you?" Leaning down he gave his Queen a gentle kiss.

"Still not answering."

With a deep sigh he leaned back, his Queen could be stubborn. "No there would be no questions."

"So he's treating the situation, me, differently than if I'd been born on Carina."

"He doesn't believe there's a genuine challenge, just that we have a traitor. He doesn't have the information we have. I haven't told him."

"To keep me safe."

"Yes."

"Will you tell him?"

William raised an eyebrow.

"When we arrive, will you tell him everything? Do you trust him?"

"He's dedicated to the Coalition. He lost his family thirty cycles ago in a Regulian attack on Fortas, he's never forgotten. He wants this traitor."

"You didn't answer the question."

And she was tenacious. "No, I trust that he wants to find the traitor, he's just not going to care who he has to sacrifice to get him."

"William…"

"We're not doing it his way, Cassandra. We're not sacrificing anyone." Pulling her back, he tucked her under his chin. Settling in she closed her eyes, letting his strength and love surround her.

"Tell me how the meeting's going to go."

"With Valerian?"

"Yes. How's he going to approach it, approach me?"

"What do you mean?" Absently he rubbed a hand along her birthmark, a birthmark now in full color.

"He thinks Victoria and I are expendable. Two survivors from a planet he could care less about. He'll use us to find his traitor. He'll use you. He won't consider he's talking to a possible Queen of the House of Knowledge."

"No, he won't." His hand rested on her birthmark. "He's the High Admiral. People do what he tells them to. He'll expect no less."

"What's he going to tell me to do?"

"He won't realize you know about the traitor. He'll think you're only here to claim the throne."

"Because there would be no reason for you to tell me."

"Normally, no."

"What will happen when he discovers I know? That you and I are together?" Cassandra raised her eyes to his.

"It won't be pretty," he caressed her cheek.

"You've already thought this all through."

"Yes," he waited for the anger.

"Do I get to know?" Her eyes didn't change.

"Now that we're en route to Carina, I will contact King Jotham and request quarters for your 'House.' Once he agrees, I will then ask he send security to transport you to the House of Protection."

"You think he'll agree, with everything going on with Tibullus?"

"Jotham will agree."

"Valerian won't be happy."

"No, he won't. He'll want you under his control to lure out the traitor."

"Jerk. How should I act with him?"

"What do you mean?"

"Should I act intimidated, scared, grateful, or all Royal and look down my nose at him?"

"Look down your nose?"

Cassandra leaned back and gave him her best 'You are nothing. I will step on you like a bug' look.

"That's really good," William was truly impressed.

"So?"

"You act however you want."

"William…"

"Cassandra, he has no control here, over you, over me. You act however you want."

"Two days."

"Yes. I need to call Jotham and get things started."

"I'll be in bed," she gave him a hard kiss, "don't be too long." Getting up, she headed for the bedroom.

∞ ∞ ∞ ∞ ∞

"William! There's news?" Jotham didn't worry about formalities.

"No, Jotham, I just talked to Carnot. He's still not on any list." The silence on the other end was deafening.

"What did you need?" the King asked, the friend and father gone.

"A situation has arisen while on tour. I'm asking for security and quarters from the King of the House of Protection."

"Why?" The King's voice revealed nothing.

"Once the Retribution arrives, the Assembly will be called for a Challenge to the House of Knowledge."

"Why would the Challenger to the House of Knowledge request my protection?"

"She's not, I am," William waited.

"You have a lot to explain."

"Yes, but not this way."

"When?"

"We will arrive in two days. We will need security almost immediately. High Admiral Valerian is not going to be happy."

"He never is. I will see you when you arrive."

"Thank you, Jotham."

∞ ∞ ∞ ∞ ∞

Waiting for William, Cassandra thought about the day. Everything she'd learned, everything that still needed to be done. She needed to get her gown ideas to Javiera so her family could get started. She wasn't sure when she'd need the first gown, but would need clothes right away.

Valerian wasn't going to be a friend. His grudge against the Regulians will be more of a hindrance than a help. Once he realized William was protecting her and that they were involved, he would make sure he never held a command position again.

King Jotham. William's long-time friend. He's willing to risk that friendship for her, to keep her protected. How was the King going to react to his friend's life mate? What would he do when he found out he had been keeping information about his son from him? So many risks he was taking; for her.

"What are you thinking about?" William sat on the bed bringing Cassandra's attention to him.

"Hmmm?"

"You were lost in thought." Tucking a piece of hair behind her ear, he rested his hand on her neck.

"Just thinking. What did King Jotham say?" she asked as she sat up.

"We'll have security upon our arrival. They will escort us to our quarters in the House of Protection. What's bothering you?"

"He's one of your oldest friends."

"Yes."

"Is he going to treat you like Valerian, because of me?" Concerned eyes gazed into his.

"Protecting me again?"

"You don't deserve to be treated like that."

He should have realized she'd worry about him. He would if it were reversed. "Jotham will be suspicious," William wasn't going to lie to her. "He'll feel I'm acting out of character. That I've let you distract me and jeopardized my career for a much younger woman."

"Younger woman…What does age have to do with it?" Cassandra was honestly confused.

"A very beautiful, younger woman who believes she has a claim to the throne, who needs protection." With adept fingers, he unbuttoned the shirt she'd put on to eat.

"I'm using you because you're Royal. He'll believe I'm a conniving little bitch who's using you to get to the throne."

"It will be his first thought, yes," as he slid her shirt off, his mouth gained access to bare shoulders.

"William, what are you doing?"

"Hoping you'll use me," as his mouth continued its descent, she got to her knees pulling his head closer as he suckled.

All thought disappeared as he gave his attention to her other breast. Arching to give him more access, she moaned, need pooling between her legs.

Leaning her back, his mouth abandoned her breast to work its way down her torso leaving her quivering. Sliding his hands under her, lifting to find her most sensitive spot, he fed.

"William!" Cassandra's body bucked against his mouth, but he was unrelenting. Her taste, her smell, he must have more.

Her body vibrated under his hands, telling him her release was close. The knowledge drove him, he had to taste it. As he slid his tongue in, her world broke apart.

Her flavor drove him wild. Releasing himself, William surged into her pulsating heat, filling her to near bursting.

Still lost, William's renewed assault on her senses had Cassandra's body tightening around him. His kiss stole what little breath she had. Wrapping her limbs around him she joined him in the wildness. As her body imploded, she took him with her.

Long minutes passed with heavy breathing the only sound. Lifting his head, William stared into the face he loved. Her lips swollen, breathing ragged, eyes unfocused, knowing he put that look on her face was a powerful thing.

As her eyes started to focus, she brought her fingers up touching his lips. Gently he kissed them.

"William…"

"Yeah?"

"If that was me using you, I need to do it more often."

William grinned, rolled onto his back curling her close to his body.

"I think I can arrange that."

∞ ∞ ∞ ∞ ∞

The morning flew by as both the Admiral and Cassandra were consumed with the details of their arrival on Carina. Beyond the usual routine of bringing a Battle Star home, the Admiral needed to make sure Chief Marat was prepared to protect Cassandra and Victoria.

"Chief," the Admiral lowered the security screen.

"Admiral."

"Are your men ready?"

"Yes, Sir. Ten men trained to protect a Royal as ordered, Sir."

"Good. Tomorrow we arrive at Carina. You will have five men outside my Ready Room, the other five stationed outside the Michelakakis' quarters. A shuttle from the House of Protection will arrive. Once it does, your men are to escort the Michelakakis family, Hutu, Lucas, and Victoria onto the shuttle, is that understood?"

"Yes, Sir."

"Lucas has the final word on Victoria's security. Anything involving her is cleared through him."

"Yes, Sir."

"On board the shuttle there will be a security detail. They will be escorted to my Ready Room."

"Sir?"

"Listen, Marat."

"Yes, Sir."

"King Jotham's men will be in charge of getting Colonel Tar, Cassandra, and myself onto the shuttle. You and your men are in charge of our protection. You will take orders only from me."

"Yes, Sir."

"Understand this, Chief. No matter who else is on this ship, no orders penetrate the King's protection. The only orders you receive are from within the King's protection. Understood?"

Marat stood there for a moment, wondering what the hell was going on.

"Marat!"

"Yes, Sir! Understood!"

"Have your men ready. Dismissed." Raising the shield, Marat exited the Bridge.

"Tar!"

"Sir." When he approached the Admiral, the security shield lowered.

"Upon our arrival, the High Admiral will be coming aboard. He will be escorted to my Ready Room."

"Yes, Sir."

"You will remain."

"Yes, Sir."

"Once the meeting is over we will leave for the House of Protection."

"Yes, Sir."

"Make sure everything you want to take is in the hangar bay. It will be loaded onto the shuttle."

"Yes, Sir."

"And, Quinn, thank you."

"Not a problem, Will."

"You can still change your mind."

"And miss all the fun? No way," Tar grinned at him. As the Admiral raised the shield, he gave him a slight salute then left.

∞ ∞ ∞ ∞ ∞

"They need a scan of your measurements to make the clothes," Javiera told her.

"Okay."

"You need to be naked."

"Excuse me?"

"They need your real measurements, Cassandra. Then they can cut the clothes and get started."

Having sent Javiera the pictures and drawings of the gowns and clothes she liked to forward on to her family, Cassandra had thought her gown issues were done. But now they needed measurements.

"Give me a minute." Pulling out of the closet what she needed, she headed to the bathroom.

"Cassandra."

"Just a minute."

Closing the bathroom door, she changed into her sleeping shirt then covered her birthmark with a sock.

"Let's do this," Cassandra returned to Javiera.

"Cassandra?"

"No one sees my birthmark, Javiera. Not until the Assembly. The measurements will be okay with the covering. How long will this take?"

"A couple minutes. You'll need to stand with your arms out, legs slightly apart."

Taking off her shirt, Cassandra stood as instructed as Javiera walked around her with the scanner.

"Done."

"Are you packed?" Cassandra asked from the bathroom as she got dressed.

"Just about. We're telling Amina tonight."

"We'll be telling Victoria too." She looked at her friend, "There's still time to change your mind."

"Cassandra, we've been through this."

"I know. But if something happens to one of you…"

"We'll make sure nothing does. Stop worrying about us."

"All right, you'll get that to your family?" she nodded at the scanner.

"In a little bit."

"I have some other ideas…" Standing, Cassandra had to stop as the room started to tilt.

"Cassandra? What's wrong?" Javiera grabbed her arm to steady her.

"Nothing."

"Cassandra…"

Looking into the eyes of her friend, Cassandra couldn't decide what to do. Did she tell her she thought she had conceived before she told William? But if she hadn't and she told him, would he think she was like Salish?

"You've conceived."

"I don't know," she couldn't stop herself from replying. "It's only been twenty days since my cycle, I'm not late."

"When did the Admiral go off the Ollali juice?"

"I don't know if he has."

"Cassandra."

"We've been a little busy."

Javiera looked at her, thinking about everything she'd been through. Could her body just be reacting to all the changes?

"We could go to Bliant…"

"No, there's no time."

"There's a test you can do in the morning. Generally you take it after you're late, but…"

"Like a home pregnancy test."

"I don't know what you're talking about, but women generally take it before they go to the doctor."

"Can you get me one?"

Javiera looked at her, wondering how hard it would be to have everything going on that she did, and not know if she'd conceived. Could she handle it?

"I'll get you the test. But, Cassandra, you can't be worried about how the Admiral will react."

"If I've conceived, no, I know how he'll respond. But he doesn't need to wonder."

"But you're feeling okay?"

"Yes."

"Okay, I'll go send these to Pazel."

"Thank you."

Chapter Twenty-Four

With dinner finished, Cassandra looked at William then turned to Victoria.

"Victoria, I need to tell you something."

"What, Aunt Cassie."

"Tomorrow we'll be in Carina."

"I know, Amina told me," excited eyes met hers.

"Once we're there we have to leave the Retribution."

"What?"

"We're going to a place called the House of Protection."

"But we'll be coming back right?"

"No, baby, we won't."

"But my room!" Tears welled up in Victoria's eyes as she got up to run to her room.

"Victoria…" Standing, Cassandra followed her and found her crying on the bed.

"It's not fair, Aunt Cassie!"

"I know, baby, I know." Rubbing her back she tried to explain. "But we can't stay here. The Admiral has found us a better place."

"But we have to leave!"

"I know. But we'll be together. And how do you know it's not a better place?"

"But Amina won't be there!"

"Amina is coming with us." Victoria rolled over looking at her Aunt. "So are Lucas, Javiera, Leander, Hutu, Colonel Tar and the Admiral."

"Really?" Victoria looked over Cassandra's shoulder to the Admiral.

"Really," he told her. "Tomorrow we'll get on a shuttle, bigger than what brought you to the Retribution, and go to a special place on Carina."

"So you need to pack tonight so we're ready."

"What can I take?"

"Anything you want."

Sad eyes looked from Cassandra to the Admiral, "Okay."

William wrapped Cassandra in his arms once Victoria's door was closed.

"Shhh…. It's okay."

"Am I doing the right thing here, William? Should I just let it go?"

"You're doing what needs to be done. That's all you can do."

"But the look in her eyes…I never thought about how much her room meant to her."

"We'll get her another room. It's just a place, Cassandra. It's the people that make the difference."

"You're right. I know you're right but right now…"

"You're just tired. Come on, tomorrow will be a busy day. You need your sleep."

"And you don't?"

"We both need our sleep, but first we'll make sure Victoria's ready."

With Victoria packed and asleep, they climbed into bed together. Gathering her close to him she laid her head on his chest.

"What time tomorrow?"

"We'll get to Carina about 1000. Valerian will be waiting. King Jotham's security will arrive shortly after."

"You don't want him to know."

"Not until absolutely necessary. He won't take it well."

"Can he stop us from leaving?"

"Not with the King's protection."

"I love you, William."

"I love you too. Now sleep."

∞ ∞ ∞ ∞ ∞

The tentative touch on her hand had Cassandra jerking awake, William's arms tightening protectively around her.

"Aunt Cassie?" William's arms loosened so Cassandra could rise.

"Tori, what's wrong?"

"I'm scared. Will you sleep with me?"

Taking his arm from around her, William picked Victoria up and put her on the other side of her Aunt. With a grateful look, Cassandra rolled to her side, pulling her close.

"Did you have a nightmare?"

"No."

"What's wrong then?"

"I miss Mom and Dad."

"Oh, baby, so do I."

"Can the Retribution go kill all the Regulians?"

"What!?!" Cassandra was stunned.

"Payback, Daddy always said he believed in payback. So do you. Shouldn't we pay back the Regulians for killing everyone on Earth?"

"Victoria..." Cassandra was at a loss for what to say. Victoria wasn't wrong. She and Peter did say that. They both believed in it, but not like this. How was she going to explain it? William's hand on her hip told her she had his support.

"They all need to die. The Regulians, just like everyone on Earth."

"No, Victoria, no." Putting a hand on her niece's face, Cassandra looked her in the eye. "That's murder."

"It's what they did!" Victoria's eyes were fierce.

"Yes, I know but not all Regulians did it."

"I don't care!" Tears filled her young eyes.

"You do, I know you do." Taking a deep breath, she tried to explain so Victoria would understand. "Let's pretend that the Retribution did kill all the Regulians. What does that accomplish?"

"They wouldn't be able to hurt anyone else."

"True, but not all the Regulians did that. Regulians have families too; moms, dads, children. Should they all die for something they didn't do?"

"But that's payback."

"That's not what your dad meant. You know that. If you listened, or should I say eavesdropped, you know that's not all he said."

"He said he believed in payback," stubborn eyes met hers.

"What else?"

"That when someone hurts you, you hurt them back."

"That's not what he said, Victoria Lynn, and you know it. He believed that some people do bad things and that when they do, someone has to stop the person responsible. That's justice."

"That's what I said."

"He never said you kill everyone. Kill the innocent. He said you find the person responsible and stop them."

"But the Regulians are responsible!"

"All of them? Even the families that don't even know that it happened?"

"No, but..."

"If the Retribution killed all the Regulians, even the innocent ones that had nothing to do with Earth, what does that make us?"

"What?"

"If we do what the Regulians did, it makes us no better than them. And, Victoria," Cassandra's eyes focused on her niece's, "we are better."

"But I miss them!" Letting her cry, Cassandra rubbed her back.

"It will be okay, Victoria. It will," she murmured to her.

"But how? If the Regulians are still out there, how can there be justice?"

"Because we will find the person responsible."

Tori raised her eyes to Cassandra's, "The Glitter Man."

"That's right. He's responsible. We get payback, justice for everyone on Earth; for Grandpa Jacob, and your mom and dad by stopping the Glitter Man."

"That's why we're going to this special place?"

"Yes."

"I get to help?"

"You get to help. Now sleep, we have a lot to do tomorrow."

When Victoria rolled to her other side, Cassandra pulled her close, wrapping an arm around her. Behind her William did the same, covering Cassandra's hand with his own.

He'd listened to everything she'd said to Victoria. How she struggled to explain the difference between payback and revenge to a nine-cycle. That Victoria understood was a tribute to her parents. There were adults, like Valerian, that didn't understand the difference. Kissing her neck, he whispered in her ear, "You are an amazing woman, Cassandra. You'll make an amazing Queen."

"As long as I'm your Queen, I don't care."

"You'll always be my Queen, sleep."

∞ ∞ ∞ ∞ ∞

Waking to a ringing comm, the Admiral put on the headset hoping not to wake Cassandra and Victoria.

"Zafar," he answered walking away from the bed.

"Admiral, I've just arrived on the Bridge. We are an hour out of Carina," Colonel Tar informed him.

"What?"

"Sir, apparently orders came through overnight that we were to increase speed."

"Orders from who?" As if he didn't know.

"High Admiral Valerian, Sir."

"Why wasn't I notified?"

"The High Admiral requested it that way, Sir."

"Slow us back down, Quinn. I want two hours."

"Yes, Sir." Pulling off his headset, he turned to find Cassandra watching him from their bed.

"Valerian ordered an increase in speed overnight. We'll be in Carina in two hours."

"Go do what you need to do. I'll get Victoria to Javiera's." Nodding, William grabbed some clothes and headed to the shower.

Lying back in bed, Cassandra organized her thoughts. Valerian was trying a power play showing who was in charge. He was in for a surprise.

Dressed except for his jacket, the Admiral sat down on the bed.

"I want you back here, with the hatch secured, as soon as you take Victoria to Leander's. Understand?"

Cassandra nodded, putting a hand on his thigh.

"You do not open the hatch to anyone."

"I won't."

Giving her a hard kiss, he left their quarters pulling on his jacket.

∞ ∞ ∞ ∞ ∞

"Tar! Status!" The Admiral entered the Bridge.

"Admiral, we're ninety minutes out."

"Contact Marat. Tell him his men are to be at their stations in thirty."

"Yes, Sir."

Going to his comm, he contacted Leander.

"Chief, you have sixty minutes." Then Lucas, "Leander's in sixty." Disconnecting he turned to Quinn.

"You ready?"

"Yes, Sir."

"I need to contact King Jotham."

"I have a secure line ready for you, Sir."

"Connect me."

As the Admiral put on his headset, he looked around at his people on the Bridge. They knew something was up, their quick glances telling.

"Jotham."

"Your Majesty, we are less than ninety minutes out."

"Why the change?"

"High Command," he replied.

"Understand, Admiral, ninety minutes."

"Thank you, Majesty."

∞ ∞ ∞ ∞ ∞

"Wake up, Victoria, we need to get you to Javiera's."

"Aunt Cassie?"

"Yeah. Come on, wake up."

"What's wrong?"

"Nothing is wrong, it's just time to get you dressed and get to Javiera's. Time to find the Glitter Man."

"Really?"

"Really, a quick shower, change and we need to go."

"Okay."

With Victoria in the shower, Cassandra fixed the bed one last time. Taking a moment, she ran her hand across it, thinking about everything they'd shared there. Picking up a pillow she smelled William on it. She knew this wasn't the end, but Victoria was right, it was still hard to leave. Putting the pillow back down, she turned. Time to start their future.

"How you coming, Tori?"

"Just about ready."

Picking up the bag she put her and the Admiral's clothes in after her shower, she went to collect Victoria's. She found her brushing her hair and smiled at her.

"Aunt Cassie?"

"Yeah," leaning down she picked up the towel Tori dropped.

"Are you and the Admiral going to get married?" Freezing, Cassandra looked at her.

"I don't know. Why?"

"Well, if you get married, I could call him Uncle instead of Admiral. He'd be family."

"Yes, he would. But Victoria," she crouched down, "he's already family. Family isn't just related by blood, it's who you love."

"I know that!" she said in an exasperated voice.

"Then what?"

"Everyone calls him Admiral, even you sometimes. No one calls him Uncle."

"That would be special, wouldn't it?"

"Yeah."

"Well, I can't promise anything, but you never know. Now finish up, we need to go."

"Okay."

Leaving the heat of the bathroom, Cassandra leaned against the wall. She'd stood too quickly. As the room righted itself, she took a deep breath. She didn't have time for this.

"Ready."

"Let's go." Opening the hatch, Cassandra discovered guards.

"Ma'am," Marat nodded to her. He'd witnessed her take down Falco in the Brig. While he wasn't sure what was going on, he knew his job was to protect her.

"I'm sorry," Cassandra looked at the rank on his uniform, "Chief, I don't know your name."

"Marat, ma'am."

"Chief Marat, I need to take Victoria to the Michelakakis' quarters."

"Yes, ma'am, you will be escorted." Securing the Admiral's quarters, Cassandra turned. As she and Victoria started down the corridor, the security force closed around them.

Entering the Michelakakis' quarters, she found Lucas pacing the room. Seeing Victoria, he immediately calmed.

"Hi, Lucas!" Victoria ran over giving him a quick hug.

"Hi." Leaving him, she ran to Amina.

"Ready?" Cassandra looked from Leander to Javiera to Lucas.

"We're ready," Lucas answered for all of them. Walking over to the girls, Cassandra squatted down.

"Victoria, I need to go back to the Admiral's Ready Room. I'll meet up with you on the shuttle. Until then, Lucas is in charge. Do you understand me?" Tori looked from her aunt to Lucas and back with serious eyes.

"Yes, Aunt Cassie."

"Okay. Give me a hug, you too, Amina." As they did, she gave each a quick kiss and stood, "I'll see you at the shuttle."

Leaving, the security detail closed around her. Entering the Ready Room, she secured the hatch then sat to wait.

∞ ∞ ∞ ∞ ∞

"Navigator, put us into orbit."

"Yes, Admiral."

"Admiral, I have High Admiral Valerian on the comm."

"Put it on speaker. Zafar."

"Admiral, you're late."

"Actually we're early, Sir. We were scheduled to arrive at 1000, it's 0800."

"Don't tell me what time it is, Zafar!"

"Yes, High Admiral."

"My shuttle will be arriving in ten minutes, have your landing bay ready!"

"Yes, Sir."

Uneasy glances flashed around the Bridge. It was obvious to everyone that there was trouble brewing between their Admiral and the High Admiral.

"Communications, inform landing bay Alpha that the High Admiral's shuttle will be landing in ten minutes."

"Landing Bay Alpha, Sir?"

"Yes, Alpha. Navigation, send the landing instructions to the High Admiral's shuttle."

"Yes, Sir."

"Communications, inform Landing Bay Delta that a shuttle from King Jotham will be arriving in the next thirty minutes. They are to be given priority landing instructions."

"Yes, Sir!" Something was definitely going on.

"Colonel, you are to wait for the King's shuttle, then escort the detail to my quarters."

"Yes, Sir."

"Colonel, you have the Bridge until the King's shuttle is on approach." The Admiral was taking no chances that the High Admiral could change his orders. Going to his comm, the Admiral inserted a memory foil, entered a sequence of codes and waited. Once the foil was full, he removed it. He looked around the Bridge then turned to Quinn. "You have the Bridge, Colonel."

"Yes, Sir."

Leaving the Bridge of the Retribution for the last time, the Admiral headed to his quarters and his future.

∞ ∞ ∞ ∞ ∞

High Admiral Valerian raised an eyebrow as he and his staff approached Admiral Zafar's quarters. A security force of six lined the corridor.

"Chief."

"High Admiral," Marat saluted his superior officer.

"Why is there a security force outside the Admiral's quarters?"

"Sir, because the Admiral ordered it, Sir."

"Open his hatch, Chief. We'll wait inside."

"Sir, I am unable to do that, Sir."

"Excuse me?"

"Sir, I don't have the authorization codes to access the Admiral's quarters."

Moving to the security panel, the High Admiral entered his security code. When it was denied, he was enraged.

"High Admiral Valerian, nice to have you on board." Zafar approached from the opposite direction. "Marat," he nodded to the Chief.

"Sir."

"Zafar! You will explain the meaning of this."

"Of what, Sir?"

"Of my clearance not working on your hatch."

"Because the future Queen of the House of Knowledge requested it, High Admiral."

Marat froze at the Admiral's comment. The future Queen of the House of Knowledge; he was talking about Cassandra. His self-proclaimed life mate. Marat finally realized what they were facing. Looking at his men, he knew they realized it too.

Stepping up to the security panel, the Admiral entered his code. As the locks released, he gestured the High Admiral in.

"High Admiral."

Valerian passed, but the Admiral stopped his staff.

"Just the High Admiral."

"My staff is with me, Admiral."

"Yes, Sir, and they can wait in the corridor."

"You've overstepped your authority, Zafar!"

"It is my command until I leave the ship, High Admiral. I have the authority unless you wish to remove me from the command. To do so you will need to contact High Command, call a Commission, and explain your decision. Or you may enter my quarters alone and within the hour I will be off the Retribution."

The look in Valerian's eyes was deadly. Turning, he addressed his staff.

"You are to stay here. No one enters these quarters. Is that understood?"

"Yes, High Admiral."

Cassandra had been sitting when she heard the locks release on the hatch. Hearing the High Admiral, she stood and walked over to the painting of the setting suns. The man was disrespecting the Admiral on his own ship, in front of his crew. Something she was not going to tolerate. She'd dealt with self-important men before. Those who thought they knew more just because they were men. Apparently, Carinian men weren't that different than those on Earth.

William scanned the room as he entered, finding Cassandra in front of their favorite painting. The High Admiral glanced at her then took a seat.

"Explain, Admiral," his total disregard of Cassandra pissed William off.

"High Admiral Valerian, may I present Cassandra Qwes Chamberlain." Hearing the slight change in William's voice let her know he was no happier with the High Admiral than she was.

Turning, her eyes were cool and calm as they stared at Valerian. Turning her gaze to William she nodded, then retook her seat as the Admiral took his.

"So this is the Earth woman you think can challenge Queen Yakira?"

Saying nothing, Cassandra continued to meet the High Admiral's eyes. She had found through her years of study it really irritated some men.

"Will challenge and win," William answered, watching Cassandra watch Valerian.

"Show me the birthmark."

"No," she answered. Never breaking eye contact, she leaned back, crossing her right leg over her left. Her boots, socks, and pants covered her birthmark.

"Excuse me?" Valerian sat up higher in his chair.

"Hearing problem?" Cassandra challenged. "I...said...no."

"Zafar, what the hell is going on? You contacted me that there was a challenge to Queen Yakira!"

"I contacted you because we have a traitor who's killed seven billion people to stop the *possibility* that there was a challenger to Queen Yakira."

"She knows this?" Valerian jerked a thumb to Cassandra.

"Yes."

"Have you lost your mind? Why would you tell her? This is restricted Coalition information!"

"It is an assassination attempt on the future Queen."

"Oh please…She won't even show her birthmark to me."

"Are you a member of the Assembly?" Cassandra brought Valerian's eyes back to her. "A ruling King? A First Son?" she fired questions at him.

"No."

"Do you carry a Royal Birthmark?"

"No."

"Then why would I show you mine?"

"You obviously don't know who I am," Valerian started.

"You are High Admiral Ossie Valerian, only son of Oscar and Calla Valerian. You went to the Academy, where you were an average student, not really excelling in anything. You married and had a daughter. Your wife and daughter were both killed in a Regulian attack on Fortas. Since that time, you've moved up the chain-of-command by being single-minded in your hunting of all Regulians. Nine cycles ago, you were promoted to High Admiral by the Coalition Council, by one vote. Seems some of your tactics were questionable."

"I get results!" That this 'woman' thought she had the right to talk to him like this enraged him.

"You make sure there are never any Regulian survivors on any of your missions. That's not battle, that's revenge."

"How dare you!" Valerian surged toward Cassandra. The Admiral was immediately between them.

"I wouldn't," his voice deadly.

Looking from the Admiral to Cassandra, Valerian suddenly understood. "You're slamming her!"

Valerian didn't see the calming hand Cassandra placed on William's back. "Be very careful, High Admiral," William's voice was tense.

Removing her hand, she stepped around William.

"You have no understanding of the position *you're* in, Valerian," Cassandra stared him down. "You only became High Admiral by one vote. ONE! What do you think the High Council will do when they find out that for nearly eight cycles you've allowed a traitor free reign in the Coalition. That there have been easily found transmissions, in Regulian, on Carinian channels, that you've ignored. That this traitor has not only made a deal with the Regulians, but has traveled to and from the Relinquished Zone, and you allowed it. That this traitor was trying to assassinate a future Queen of Carina, and you've done nothing? How do you think they will vote? Do you have to guess how I will vote?" Cassandra's enraged eyes coldly bored into Valerian's.

"You have no proof," he fired back, refusing to acknowledge the possibility he was in the wrong.

"Don't I?" she raised an eyebrow.

As the Admiral's comm rang, Cassandra calmly walked to the side of his desk. The Admiral made no move to answer his comm until Valerian sat.

"Zafar," he put the call on speaker.

"Admiral, this is Tar, your detail is at the hatch."

"Understood." Disconnecting, he looked to Cassandra.

"What's going on, Zafar!" Valerian demanded.

"High Admiral Valerian, it is time for the future Queen to leave the Retribution."

"I have not given her that right."

"It's not yours to give." Making sure he was between them, he opened the hatch.

Immediately, eight very large males, dressed in black with purple jackets entered the room. They carried what Cassandra had come to know as stunners; their jackets bearing the insignia of King Jotham.

"Admiral Zafar, are you ready?"

"Yes."

As Marat and his men closed around William, Cassandra, and Tar, the King's men closed around them.

"Chief!" the High Admiral ordered, "You will stand down."

Inside the King's security, Marat ignored him.

"CHIEF, THAT'S AN ORDER!"

The Captain of the King's men turned to the High Admiral. "Are you trying to countermand the King's protection?" dark eyes gleamed at Valerian.

As he realized what was happening, that Zafar was now under King Jotham's personal protection, Valerian silently took a step back.

Turning, the group headed to the waiting shuttle.

Entering the shuttle, Cassandra immediately scanned the cabin and found Victoria sitting with Lucas. Everyone had made it safely. Some of her tension eased.

"Captain, we're ready whenever you are." William led her to a seat. In minutes, the shuttle was airborne.

∞ ∞ ∞ ∞ ∞

"I need to talk to Marat and his men," William leaned over to her. "To give them a choice."

As the shuttle hit some turbulence, Cassandra's stomach started to roll.

"Yes," seeing her pale, he turned her face to his, eyes concerned.

"I'm fine, go talk to your men," with a small smile she touched his leg. Nodding, he moved to the back of the shuttle. His seat was quickly taken by Javiera.

"Queasy?" she asked in a hushed voice.

With her eyes closed, Cassandra nodded.

"Did you eat this morning?"

Cassandra shook her head.

"Here, eat these, they'll help," Javiera said as she passed her what looked like crackers.

"I don't think they'll stay down," Cassandra confessed as she took them.

"They will," in a slightly louder voice, "shuttle turbulence always takes a little getting used to."

"Thanks, Javiera."

"No problem."

The Captain of the King's guards entered the compartment, eyes scanning, finally coming to rest on the Admiral, who was walking forward.

"Admiral, a message from Admiral Carnot." Taking the message, the Admiral read.

"Thank you, Captain. What's our arrival time?"

"Fifteen minutes, Sir. You and your party will be taken directly to the Royal Wing, where you can settle in. The King will see you at 2000 tonight."

"Understood. There will be several people arriving that will need to be escorted to the Royal Wing today. I will get you their names for security checks."

"I have not been authorized for that, Sir."

"They will be clothiers for the future Queen, they will be required."

"Get me the names, I will see if they can be cleared."

"Thank you, Captain."

As the Admiral walked back to Cassandra, Javiera returned to her seat. Seeing that his life mate was still pale, he frowned.

"It's just the turbulence and not eating this morning," she showed him the crackers Javiera had given her, "I'm fine. What did your men decide?"

"They're all staying."

"Even with the High Admiral?"

"Because of him." He reached into his pocket, handing her the message. Frowning, she scanned it.

'Not on any lists, sending you a going away gift on the Judgment, five days. Carnot.'

Handing it back to him, she smiled her understanding. Tibullus was on the Judgment, he was alive. In five days, he would be on Carina. She lost the smile as the shuttle hit more turbulence.

"Five more minutes," William told her.

"Okay, talk to me. Tell me what's going to happen next."

"We'll land and be escorted to our quarters in the Royal Wing. We'll be given the day to settle. We'll be meeting with the King tonight to explain."

"Okay."

"I need the names of Javiera's family for security clearance. They need to get started on your clothes."

"I'll need something for tonight."

"Yes."

She heard the concern in his voice. "I'll be fine, I promise. Go talk to Javiera."

Passing the information on to the Captain, the Admiral returned in time for the landing.

∞ ∞ ∞ ∞ ∞

"Welcome to Carina, Cassandra," William whispered in her ear. Squeezing his hand, she exited the shuttle.

"Aunt Cassie, look it's a castle!" Victoria came running up to her.

"I see," and what she saw amazed her.

The shuttle had landed inside what she gauged to be a thirty-foot wall; in a large, open, vividly green space with a walkway that led to the entrance of a four-story building that did resemble castles found on Earth. It seemed to be made of some type of gray stone that suddenly changed to purple as a ray of light struck it. Following that beam upward, Cassandra got her first look at the three suns she had only seen in her dreams and a painting. They tugged at something in her.

"Cassandra," William's voice pulled her eyes from the sky to his. "We need to go." He wished he could let her take her time but the guards needed to get them inside.

"Of course." Turning, she followed the others along the path.

The guards led them down wide corridors lined with portraits, art, and furniture. After several turns, they approached an enormous, closed door with guards stationed in front.

"Report, Sergeant," the Captain of the King's security demanded.

"Captain, no one has approached. Your seal remains intact." The Sergeant stepped aside so the Captain could inspect the seal. Satisfied, he removed a key from his pocket, unlocked the door breaking the seal, and stepped aside so the Admiral's party could enter.

"Admiral Zafar," the Captain turned, "the key to the Royal Wing." He handed the key to him.

"Thank you, Captain." William turned to find Cassandra had yet to enter.

She was looking at the Captain. Taking a step toward him, she stopped. "There are many rules that I am still unfamiliar with," she addressed the Captain. "Is it permissible to know your name?"

The Captain's eyes revealed none of his surprise, as they gazed down at the small, dark-haired woman who had acquired the protection of one of the most respected Admirals in the Coalition.

"Deffand, ma'am, Nicholas Deffand."

"I thank you, Captain Deffand, for all you and your men did today. Please pass that along to them."

"Ma'am," the Captain nodded.

Turning, Cassandra entered the Royal Wing.

∞ ∞ ∞ ∞ ∞

The Royal Wing was set up as a private residence for guests in need of high security and their staff. The first floor contained the only entrance to the wing; it opened into a formal foyer. As Cassandra passed through, she entered a mid-sized formal reception room, obviously set up for entertaining with couches and chairs. What would be considered her staff waited for her direction. Unsure what her next move needed to be, she turned to William.

"Marat, two of your men need to be stationed outside the door at all times. No one gets in unannounced. All are scanned except the King. *All,* is that understood?" The Admiral stared at each man.

"Yes, Sir." Marat motioned to two of his men to guard the door.

"Hutu, the kitchen is that way," he pointed. "It is fully stocked and has been inspected by the King's personal chef. Get everyone something to eat."

"Yes, Sir," Hutu hustled out knowing no one had eaten yet.

"The third floor consists of rooms for guards and staff. You'll need to assign those rooms, Marat."

"Yes, Sir."

"Lucas, take Cassandra, Victoria and the Michelakakis' to the second floor. There you'll find the other living quarters. Get everyone settled while the Colonel and I show the guards the perimeter."

"Yes, Sir." Turning, Lucas headed farther into the first floor, obviously he knew his way. Knowing this was the way it had to be, Cassandra followed Lucas into yet another foyer. This one was round and contained a curved staircase in its center. As Lucas led them to the second level, the stairs continued on to the third.

"This level is divided into two separate areas." Opening a door, he led them to the front half of the second level. "Leander, this is the largest suite, it has a private living area, bath, and second bedroom for Amina that can only be accessed through this door. I'll take the first room across the hall, the Colonel the second. There is a common living area down the hall that we can set up for the girls."

As he spoke, Tori and Amina ran into the suite to look at the room.

"It's set up to be easily defendable," Leander said to Lucas.

"Yes, on the small chance someone could get this far." Lucas turned to look at Cassandra.

"Cassandra, Victoria's and your quarters are this way."

"Go ahead. We'll bring the girls over after they're done exploring," said Javiera.

Turning, Cassandra let Lucas lead the way to the door that opened to the other half of the level.

It opened into a large living area, not as formal as the first level, but still not what Cassandra would consider homey.

"This is your public area. Back this way," Lucas crossed the room to open another door that led down a wide hallway, "is the private living area; a small suite for Victoria, and your suite."

"Mine and your father's. Is that going to be a problem?" she asked as she entered the suite. The room was huge.

"No, not for me."

"Then who?"

"Cassie…"

"Lucas, if there's something I need to know, tell me."

"There's going to be talk."

"We're both aware of that."

"Kyle's going to have a problem with all this."

"All this?"

"The talk, you, what's going to be said and whispered about the two of you."

"That I'm a much younger woman, using your father to get to the throne."

"Yes," his eyes shot to hers. "You're aware of what's going to be said."

"Yes, William thought I should be prepared. Anyone who believes your father could be used is an idiot." Cassandra's eyes flashed. "Kyle's problem is going to be me."

"Yes. He likes to believe that Dad and Mom would have eventually gotten back together if she hadn't been killed."

"They wouldn't have."

"No, they wouldn't. But Kyle's never had the idea challenged before."

"So I'll be the scapegoat."

"The what?"

"The one he blames."

"Yes."

"Aunt Cassie!"

"Coming. We'll talk later but, Lucas, he'll just have to deal with it."

"Is this my room?!?" she was in the smaller suite.

"It is for as long as we're here."

"Awesome! Amina come look!" As the two girls went in to explore, Javiera entered.

"Sorry, they got away from me."

"Not a problem. Where's Leander."

"He went to see if the bags have arrived yet."

"I'll go help him," Lucas headed out. Sitting on a couch, Cassandra leaned her head back, closing her eyes.

"How are you doing?"

"Better, but there's a lot of day yet to go. I'm going to need an outfit for tonight."

"Tonight?"

"Audience with King Jotham, 2000."

"I don't know if any of the gowns will be done."

"I was hoping for one of the pant outfits."

"That might be possible. They didn't need as exacting measurements for those."

"Well, that will be the priority when they get here."

"Okay. I was able to get a test before leaving the ship. Once we get settled, I'll get it to you."

"Thank you."

"Aunt Cassie!" She sat up. "There's an enormous tub in here!"

"Is there?" Cassandra smiled.

"Yeah, come see."

"On my way."

∞ ∞ ∞ ∞ ∞

"The King's men patrol the other side of the garden wall. Marat, I still want one man patrolling inside."

"Yes, Sir."

"That should cover everything for now. Get your men settled and gear organized. Once you have your duties assigned, turn it over to Colonel Tar for approval. Dismissed."

As Marat and his men left, the Admiral turned to Quinn.

"What do you think?"

"The place is a fortress, well designed, easily defendable if anyone could even get in the Palace."

"It's not people getting into the Palace I'm concerned about. It's the ones already inside."

"You're thinking one of the King's people?"

"It's a possibility."

"Will, you got her here. She's safe."

"There's still the traitor to deal with. He's not giving up. It's gone too far."

"It's one thing to attack some unknown woman on some unknown planet, Will. But to attack a Challenger to the throne, under the protection of King Jotham, that's suicide."

"Maybe, but this is the situation he's been trying to avoid. Now it's in his face. It could make him more dangerous than the Regulians."

"Admiral."

"Yes, Hutu."

"Where do you want the meals served?"

"Where is everyone?"

"Lucas and Leander are transporting bags, I believe the women and children are in the Royal Suite."

"Send the meals to the Royal Suite and the guards' meals to the third floor. Tell Marat to make sure the men at the door are relieved to eat."

"Yes, Sir."

∞ ∞ ∞ ∞ ∞

Entering the Royal Suite, the Admiral and Tar found Hutu had set up a table in the large living area. Everyone was eating except Cassandra. She wasn't in the room.

"Where's Cassandra?"

"Back in your suite," Lucas said after swallowing.

"Eat, Quinn."

Going to find her, he passed through the empty living area and entered the sleeping chamber.

"Cassandra." She turned from the window. Walking over to her, he rubbed her arms. "You need to eat."

"I will, I just needed a minute." She looked back out the window. "The gardens are beautiful." Pulling her back against his chest, he looked at the gardens thinking about security, not flowers.

"Tell me what's bothering you."

"The day started so fast, I'm just trying to catch up. Understand everything that's happened, prepare for what's coming."

"Not everyone will be like Valerian."

"No? Most will be thinking everything Valerian said."

"Let them think what they like. The people that matter to us know the truth."

"All of them? What about King Jotham?" William turned her around, tipped her chin up.

"He'll come around. Once he gets to know you and understands us, he'll be your biggest supporter."

"Even when he finds out about Tibullus?"

"That's on me, not you."

"I'm not sure he'll see it that way."

"I am," a hard kiss stopped any response. "Now you're going to go sit down and eat." With an arm around her waist, he led her to the outer living room.

Chapter Twenty-Five

"Admiral?"

"Yes, Marat," William answered the portable comm they were carrying now.

"Door security reports that the Juruas' are here."

"Have them scanned then escorted to the Royal Suite."

"Yes, Sir."

"Finish." His look stopped Cassandra from rising. "They'll be a little while."

Giving him an exasperated look, she took another bite. When she'd finished nearly the entire plate, she pushed it away.

"I plan on using the private living room for the fittings. Any concerns with that?"

"That should be fine."

"Aunt Cassie, can Amina and I watch?"

"I don't see why not. Why don't you two go on back?"

"Okay." The knock on the door announced the Juruas'. The Admiral answered the door himself.

"The private living space, Marat." He stepped back, allowing the two to enter followed by several guards carrying boxes.

"Sir," Marat led the guards back.

"Kia! Pazel!" Javiera rushed across the room to give her aunt and uncle a hug.

"Javiera!"

"Javiera…" Leander nudged his wife.

"What? Oh, sorry," she looked at the Admiral. "Kia, Pazel, I'd like you to meet Admiral Zafar."

"Admiral," they said in unison.

"And this is Cassandra," Javiera turned to find her crossing the room.

"Hello," Cassandra stopped in front of the two.

"Look, Pazel, she really is that tiny. I was sure Javiera misused the scanner."

"And I told you she wouldn't do such a thing," Pazel replied.

"Javiera, would you take them back to the other room. I'll be there in a minute."

"Of course," As Javiera led them to the other room, the men headed for the door.

"Admiral, a minute please."

"I'll meet you downstairs." Closing the door, he waited.

Walking over, Cassandra pulled his head down for a smoldering kiss that caught him unprepared. Wrapping his arms around her, he lifted her off her feet and crushed her against the door.

Pulling his mouth away, William tried to control his desire. The look in Cassandra's eyes was not helping.

"Cassandra..."

Her eyes started to focus. "I know. We both have things we need to do." As her feet touched the ground, she put a hand on the side of his face. "I just needed you for a minute."

"You have me forever."

"William..." A knock on the door startled them both. "I'd better get these fittings started. See you at third meal?"

"Yes. Are you all right?"

"I'm fine." Sliding out of his arms, she walked across the room.

"I love you, Cassandra."

Turning, she gave him a brilliant smile. "I love you too." Then she disappeared down the hallway.

∞ ∞ ∞ ∞ ∞

"Sorry to keep you waiting," Cassandra entered the room.

"Not a problem, Your..." Pazel trailed off.

"It's Cassandra. Is it all right if I call you Pazel and Kia?"

"Yes, of course."

"Good. Next I need to let you know that I don't need you to make clothes for Messene."

The two looked at Javiera.

"Don't blame, Javiera, she was under orders." Cassandra waited until their eyes came back to her. "I need you to make clothes for the Challenger to Queen Yakira."

"What?!"

"I am challenging Yakira to be the Queen of the House of Knowledge." She gave it a minute to sink in. "Javiera highly recommended your work and felt you'd be up to the task of making gowns for Royal events along with more casual clothing."

"Yes..." Pazel stuttered, realizing what was being offered to them. "Of course we can!"

"Good because we don't have a lot of time. I need something for tonight. Not a gown." She saw the panic in the pair's eyes. "But something… I have an audience with King Jotham. Javiera sent you my measurements. You said you'd have some things ready when we arrived."

"Yes, some…but they will need finishing."

"Then let's get at it, we have…" Cassandra looked at a clock. "Seven hours until I meet the King."

The two whirled into action; opening boxes, pulling out gadgets.

"You must remove your clothes for the fitting."

"Look, I'm not going to stand here naked."

"No…no…in your eadai," Kia looked to Javiera for help.

"Underwear, Aunt Cassie," Victoria chirped in.

"Oh, well, you see…" Cassandra was slightly embarrassed. "Since the explosion…"

"Oh shit, Cassandra, I didn't even think about that!" Javiera looked to her aunt and uncle. "There was a…well forget why, all her eadai were destroyed."

"Then we start there," Kia said going to a different box to pull out some items. "Go into the other room and see if these fit. Then we'll get started.

In the bedroom, Cassandra looked at what the Juruas' had brought her. Underwear, to have underwear again excited her more than the clothes. She never said anything to William about the lack; it seemed unimportant with everything going on, but these were beautiful. She couldn't wait to get them on.

After several minutes of trying things on, she decided on a set of black, high cut bottoms and a bra very similar to what she was used to, just a little more revealing. Pulling on the matching robe, she returned to the room.

"Good?" Pazel asked.

"Very good, thank you."

"Then come, we'll start. Stand here, take this off." Pazel took the robe off Cassandra tossing it to Javiera. "What is this? It must come off!" As Pazel reached for the material covering her birthmark, Cassandra gripped his wrist.

"No. It stays covered until the Assembly. No one sees it. That includes you. It will be covered at all times, with all outfits."

"What? How? Kia! How can I make gowns without showing legs," Pazel was a temperamental artist.

"My legs can show, but they will be covered with pants, leggings, hose, or footwear. No exceptions. If you can't do that, I'll find someone who can."

"No, no, we can do that," Kia chimed in soothing Pazel.

"Good, let's get started."

With clothes being pulled on and off and alterations marked, the afternoon flew by.

∞ ∞ ∞ ∞ ∞

"Pazel, I must go if I'm to be back in time!"

"Go then, go! I will finish."

"Cassandra, which one for tonight?" Kia asked.

"The black pants and jacket," Cassandra turned for Pazel. "Blue cami, but I want all the detailing done in the violet."

"Violet?"

"Yes."

"But..." Kia shot concerned eyes to Pazel.

"Go, Kia, do what she wants! Turn!" he ordered.

With Kia hustling out, Cassandra stepped down to have Pazel and Javiera help her out of yet another outfit.

"Cassandra..." Javiera hesitated.

"Yeah?" She stepped out of the skirt.

"What Kia is worried about is violet is the color for the House of Protection."

"I know."

"You're challenging for the House of Knowledge."

"Know that."

"Normally you only wear your own House colors."

"Know that too. But it's not a law."

"I don't understand."

"You don't have to, Javiera, or you, Pazel, it's all on me." She turned suddenly tired, "What else?"

"That is all we had done. Now we talk about gowns."

"We can sit for that, right?"

"Yes."

"Javiera, would you mind seeing if Hutu could send something up. Some type of snack and a drink? I'm sure the girls would like something too." The girls had long since gotten bored and gone into Tori's room to play.

"Sure."

"Ready to argue about gowns?" Cassandra turned to Pazel.

"Argue?"

"I have some very set ideas, Pazel. I know what I like. Many will be different than what you're used to."

"I've looked at the visuals you sent."

"Can you make them?"

"Yes, they are…unique."

"They will be considered your designs here on Carina."

"No, that can't be."

"Pazel, these designs," she wasn't sure what to tell him, "they're from a planet that no longer exists. And with the changes I want you to make, from things I like from *your* designs, they *will* be Juruas originals."

"Why would you do this?" What she was offering was generous, the designs she'd shown him stirred his imagination. Most Royal's own the designs they wear. It was the cost of dressing a Royal.

"Because I'm going to be very demanding in what I want. It isn't going to follow any Carinian rules, but my rules. It might hurt your business, making my clothes. You need to think about it."

A Queen, even a possible queen, concerned about her clothier. It was unheard of. This was a very unusual woman. The designs she'd sent him were unique in their simplicity. Royals, especially the women, were always trying to outdo the other. Juruas designs would stand out, it was worth the chance.

"We will make your clothes. You will shine like no other Queen."

"All right then, let's get down to it."

As designs were brought up on Patel's design board, Cassandra dictated the changes she wanted, colors, and embellishments.

"That back is not possible!"

"Yes it is!" she argued back. "You use these beads, draped across like this and it will hold it together."

"I…it would work," Pazel was amazed.

"Sapphire and violet beads."

It was a reoccurring theme in her clothes, Pazel found. There was always a combination of sapphire and violet on every piece of clothing whether it was buttons, trim or beads.

"All right," he'd stopped arguing with her about it. She had an agenda.

It was nearly 1800 when William returned to the suite, fully expecting to find the clothiers gone. But what he found was Cassandra arguing with the man called Pazel, over something on his screen, wearing a short black robe.

"Admiral," Javiera was the first to see him.

"Javiera, Hutu is bringing up the meal."

"I'll get the girls."

"Meal," Cassandra gave him a confused look.

"It's nearly 1800."

"Already!"

"No, it cannot be…" Pazel looked at the clock. "I must call Kia, see where your clothes are!"

"Use the front room."

The Admiral waited until everyone had left before moving to Cassandra. As she stood, he saw he was right. A very short robe revealing long, well-toned legs, and a concealed birthmark. The material was silky beneath his fingers.

"Nice." His eyes telling her he wasn't just talking about the robe.

"If you think this is nice, you should see what's under it." Her eyes sparkled into his.

William's eyes flared as she walked into their bedroom. Following, he shut the door. Reaching out, he slowly untied her belt allowing the robe to fall open. The glimpse he got of black lace against pale skin started a fire.

Sliding his hands under, caressing soft shoulders, the robe fell away and what was revealed fueled the fire.

"Cassandra," was all he could say before his mouth captured hers, his hands running down her back under the slip of material covering her. Her arms wrapped around him, pulling his mouth closer and changing the angle of the scorching kiss.

"William…" she gasped against his mouth.

"Aunt Cassie?" Tori called from the other side of the door.

"Yeah?" Cassandra dropped her head to William's chest, hoping her voice sounded normal.

"Time to eat."

"Okay, we'll be there in a minute." Leaning back, she looked into William's eyes, humor cooling the desire.

"We'll finish this later," William framed her face for a gentle kiss. "Go get dressed." Turning, he left the room.

Picking up the forgotten robe, Cassandra indulged herself in a small smile. Apparently, Carinian men liked lingerie. At least hers did. Something to keep in mind when talking to Pazel. Pulling on her pants and shirt, she joined her family for a meal.

"Pazel is downstairs waiting for Kia," Javiera told Cassandra as she sat next to the Admiral.

"Did he get something to eat?"

"I…I guess I don't know," Javiera answered.

The Admiral took out his comm. "Hutu, Cassandra would like you to make sure Pazel gets something to eat."

"Yes, Admiral."

Giving Cassandra a pointed look, the Admiral started to eat. Understanding, she started in on her own plate. The conversation was light around the table. The long day had taken its toll. Even Victoria and Amina were quiet.

∞ ∞ ∞ ∞ ∞

Pazel paced the formal living area waiting on Kia. They had so much work to do, so little time. The impact of these clothes on Carinian society would be unmatched. They needed to get material chosen, fittings completed. Where was Kia?!?

"Sir."

Pazel turned finding the Admiral's personal chef standing at the entrance to the dining room.

"There is a meal on the table for you."

"Meal?" Pazel walked into the dining room to discover the table was set for him.

"Yes, Cassandra wanted to make sure you were provided a meal."

"Cassandra did?" Pazel was amazed she would worry about it.

"Yes." Hutu went back to his kitchen kingdom.

"What an unusual woman," Pazel sat down.

∞ ∞ ∞ ∞ ∞

"So what did you and Amina do in your new room today?" Cassandra asked as they walked down the hallway.

"Not much, just checked everything out, unpacked."

"You unpacked?"

"Yeah, there wasn't that much."

Cassandra swallowed hard. "Show me what you did."

William watched the two head into Victoria's suite. They needed some together time. He knew she was worried about Tori. Going into their suite, he realized neither had thought to unpack their things.

Walking across the room, William noticed the multi-colored pile on the bed. Picking up the scraps of the material reminded him of the black lace Cassandra was currently wearing. Smiling, he picked up the items, enjoyed inspecting each one as he put them in a drawer.

With that enjoyable job done, he turned to their bags. Organizing his uniforms, he inspected them for any needed repairs or cleaning, especially his dress ones. Opening the last bag, he found Cassandra's things; shirts and pants, two shirts, two pants, nothing else.

Looking at the drawer he'd just filled with her eadai he looked back to what he'd hung up.

How had he not realized she was doing without? He was with her every day. She'd never said a word, never worried about having clothing made. He was going to have to do a better job of taking care of her.

∞ ∞ ∞ ∞ ∞

"You did a good job, Tori."

"Amina helped. Tonight, when you're gone, I'm going to help her unpack."

"That's good. When the Admiral and I get back, we'll come get you."

"Okay," Cassandra looked at Tori being so brave.

"You know what I thought?"

"What?" Green eyes looked at her.

"I thought that after Pazel and Kia got done with me, they could scan you. Make you some new clothes."

"Really!"

"Yeah. It might take them a couple of days. But I think they'll have the time, something for Amina and Javiera too."

"I can tell them what I want like you do?"

"Within reason."

"Okay," Victoria's smile brightened Cassandra's heart.

"All right then. Well, I suppose I should go take a shower and get ready to meet the King."

"Is it okay if I go to Amina's?"

"I'll walk you over."

"I know the way."

"Victoria," Cassandra knelt in front of her. "Someone, an adult, needs to be with you at all times now. You don't just go to Amina's, not without someone."

"Aunt Cassie?"

"Tori, the person responsible for the destruction of Earth is on this planet. Until he is caught, we have to be careful. Do you understand?"

"Yes, but we're in the King's castle."

"Tori, I can't leave you, go do what I need to do unless I know you are safe. None of it will matter if something happens to you. I have to be able to trust that you'll listen and obey what I, the Admiral, and Lucas say. We're only trying to keep you safe."

"For how long?"

Cassandra leaned back looking at her niece, realizing she felt the same way about being kept 'safe' as she did with the Admiral.

"Not for long, just until we catch the traitor. Then you can go out and play whenever you want, just like at home."

"Okay."

"I love you, Tori."

"I love you, Aunt Cassie."

Entering their suite, Cassandra found William just coming out of the bathroom a towel around his neck and another one riding low around his waist, hair still damp from the shower. The sight of him had her heart beating faster. Walking over, she gripped the towel pulling him down for a long kiss.

"Thank you."

"For what?"

"Giving me time with Victoria."

"She's a priority for me too."

"I know. I told her that Pazel and Kia would scan her and Amina for some new clothes." Cassandra looked at him.

"That's good, whatever she needs. Cassandra," he framed her face, "why didn't you tell me you needed clothes?"

"What?" she frowned, "I did, now we're getting some made."

"I don't mean here for the Challenge. Why didn't you tell me on the Retribution? You have a total of three outfits! Including what you're wearing."

"So?"

"Cassandra…"

"William, when we arrived on the Retribution we only had what we *were* wearing. I'd say three outfits is an improvement."

"How many does Victoria have?"

"Six, thanks to Javiera."

William rested his forehead against hers. "That will be corrected."

"William."

"Damn it, Cassandra! You didn't even have any eadai and I never noticed!"

"It's been a little busy lately, what with traitors and Regulian attacks."

"That's beside the point."

"It's not, and…" she cut him off, "it's not a problem anymore. I have lots of eadai," pointing to the bed she frowned, "well I did."

"I put them in the top drawer."

Cassandra looked up at him, "You did?"

"Yes," William couldn't help but smile at the memory, "very nice."

"Really?" Cassandra smiled back, "so you liked."

"Oh yeah. I'm really going to enjoy thinking about what you've got under your clothes from now on." His hands slid under her waistband caressing the black lace.

"Good, I like you thinking about me." Her hands slid under the towel covering his firm backside, eyes teasing.

Eyes darkening, William picked her up as his comm buzzed. With a deep breath, he released her, walking over to the table to pick up his comm.

"Zafar."

"Admiral, Kia has arrived," Marat told him.

"Have them escorted up to the outer living room."

"I'll go shower." Taking a moment, William watched her leave then turned to dress.

∞ ∞ ∞ ∞ ∞

Pazel and Kia were sitting on a couch with Marat standing by the door as the Admiral entered the room in a dress uniform. Both stood.

"Cassandra will be a few minutes. Kia, if you'd go on back, I need a few moments with Pazel. Marat, would you help her with the cases?"

"Yes, Admiral." Shooting a quick glance at her husband, Kia picked up a case.

"Yes, Admiral."

William waited until they were alone. "Victoria, Amina, and Javiera all need to have clothes made too."

"What?"

"You can get your scans after you are done here tonight. I will let Lucas know."

"Admiral, what kind of clothes are you talking about?"

"Whatever is needed, especially for Victoria. I'm sure there will be some formal clothes necessary, but mostly daily wear. Speak with Javiera about it. If she has any questions, she will talk to Cassandra."

"All right."

"I will have a hundred thousand credits transferred to your treasury tomorrow, as soon as I receive the necessary information."

"Admiral," Pazel's shocked eyes met the Admiral.

"They are to have what they need, is that understood?"

"Yes, Admiral."

"Good. Marat!"

"Yes, Admiral."

"Pazel, you can go back now."

Nodding he left.

"After Cassandra and I leave, the Juruas' will be scanning Victoria, Amina, and Javiera. You and Lucas will need to coordinate that."

"Yes, Admiral."

"Your security detail is ready to escort us to the King?"

"Yes, Admiral. They are waiting for you at the door."

"That door will be secured until our return."

"Understood, Sir."

"Dismissed."

∞ ∞ ∞ ∞ ∞

Leaving the bathroom, Cassandra found the room empty. Walking across the room, she saw William had laid out violet eadai for her and a robe. Smiling she dropped her towel, putting on what William wanted her to wear. Violet, his House color under her clothing next to her skin. With her birthmark covered, she put on the robe and headed to the private living area.

∞ ∞ ∞ ∞ ∞

Entering the private living area, William found Pazel furiously whispering in Kia's ear, her eyes large.

"Where's Cassandra?" he demanded.

"She went into the bedroom," Kia told him.

"Lucas is waiting for you down the hall." Striding across the room, William entered the bedroom.

An ornate free-standing floor length mirror reflected back an image Cassandra could barely recognize. A tall, pale-skinned woman whose black hair was clipped back low on her neck. Her vivid blue eyes were made more intense by the matching blue material in her form-fitting scoop-necked camisole, the violet thread gathering the bodice created almost an arrow pattern that was duplicated on the straps.

Covering it was a black, three-quarter sleeve, cardigan-style jacket ending several inches below the waist band of matching pants. Both were made of a silky material that seemed to kiss her skin as it floated away from her body. Toes strapped into four-inch heels barely peeked out of the wide-legged pants.

Staring into her own eyes, she wondered who this person was. She looked…Royal…where had she come from?

Her eyes locked with William's as his reflection joined hers in the mirror, the strength and depth of his love easily seen.

"You're beautiful."

Her eyes reflected her gratitude, "Kia did a wonderful job."

"I'm not referring to the clothes."

Turning away from the mirror, Cassandra caressed his cheek needing to touch him.

William frowned as he looked down at her. "You're taller."

Cassandra pulled up a pant leg showing him her shoes. "Levels the playing field a little."

"You don't need to be taller for that."

"Maybe, but it can't hurt."

"Cassandra," he framed her face, "you just need to be you. It's more than enough."

Looking into his eyes, she saw his belief in her. It calmed the nerves she hadn't realized she had. Reaching up she gave him a gentle kiss.

"Thank you."

"Just being honest," he looked at the time. "We need to go." Putting a hand on her lower back, they left the room.

∞ ∞ ∞ ∞ ∞

Marat opened the exterior doors of the Royal Wing as they approached. Passing through, the security detail closed around them. Marat secured the door then took the lead.

The closer the detail got to the King's Wing, the more guards were present in the corridors. At the King's door, they were met by Captain Deffand and his men.

"Admiral, your men are to remain here. We will escort you the rest of the way."

"Marat," the Chief turned to the Admiral, "you and your men are to stand here until we return."

"Yes, Admiral." Marat and his men stepped aside and Deffand's men replaced them. The doors to the King's Wing opened and were secured once they passed through.

With eight, enormous, Carinian males surrounding them in full dress uniform and fully armed, Cassandra could see little of her surroundings.

Arriving at what she believed to be the King's private chambers, Deffand opened the door. Guards parted, allowing them to enter an empty room. Deffand followed them in.

"King Jotham will be with you shortly." Deffand left the room, closing the door.

William frowned at the room they'd been escorted to. Jotham only used this room for formal meetings.

Seeing the frown, Cassandra could tell this wasn't what William expected from his friend and King. Before she could comment, a door across the room opened.

Cassandra assessed the man entering the room. While tall, he was shorter than William. While fit, he appeared softer. His dark hair contained a great deal more gray, his violet eyes hard and shuttered. What might have been a handsome face was unsmiling and unwelcoming.

"King Jotham," the Admiral nodded to the King, who nodded back. "May I present Cassandra Qwes Chamberlain."

The King's eyes hardened as he looked at Cassandra.

"Majesty," she nodded, her eyes never breaking contact. She could tell the King had already formed an opinion. She could guess who she had to thank for that.

The King nodded to her then sat in the single chair facing them, obviously meant for the King.

"Sit," the King gestured to the two chairs before him.

"Admiral Zafar," the King turned his hard eyes to him. "I granted you protection with the understanding that you would explain why a Challenger to the House of Knowledge would need it. You will explain now."

William had planned on explaining to his friend and King in great detail everything that had happened. But obviously he'd already decided many things, one being his opinion of Cassandra. William's blood began to boil at his judgment.

"King Jotham, there are Carinians conspiring with the Regulians." The coldness in the Admiral's voice had Cassandra's head turning to him.

"Excuse me?"

William was silent.

"What is your proof?" Jotham demanded.

"I have recorded transmissions from Carina to the Regulians, transmissions from the Regulians to Carina."

"Why would someone do that, Admiral?"

"To stop the return of the true Queen of the House of Knowledge."

The King gave Cassandra the Imperial once-over.

"And you think this woman is that person?" he almost sneered.

"One of your people was willing to murder seven billion people to not take that chance," Cassandra answered, her tone matching his look.

The King sucked in a sharp breath, his eyes shooting back to the Admiral, and what he saw there shocked him. William had been his friend and confidante since the Academy. They'd been through triumphs and tragedies together. He was his son's Second Father. And in all that time, he'd never seen such a coldly-contained rage on his face.

"There is proof of this allegation?"

"The Fleet entered the Relinquished Zone forty-eight days ago, after discovering a Regulian warp signature in an uncharted solar system. En route to the system, the Regulians began a nuclear attack on the planet. A battle ensued in which the Regulians were able to destroy part of an orbiting moon. The resulting debris decimated the planet. It's on record."

"If the planet was decimated how is she here?" The King nodded to Cassandra.

William's tone became even icier, "Cassandra and her niece, Victoria, were on the Retribution at the time."

"Why, Admiral?"

"Because they'd just gotten done saving Lucas' life, Majesty!"

"What happened to Lucas?"

"His Blade was shot down on Earth. Cassandra's family helped him, got him to the recovery spot. When the Raptor arrived, the Regulians attacked. Cassandra and Victoria were the only survivors."

The King leaned back in his chair. Obviously, information had been withheld from him.

"How is Lucas?" Jotham had to ask.

"Recovered fully in three days."

"Good."

Cassandra remained quiet during the exchange. The King obviously cared about Lucas, a point in his favor.

"And you believe they destroyed this planet to kill a possible Queen?"

"If they were unable to acquire her they were to destroy her so she couldn't return."

"All this you got from intercepted transmissions?"

"Yes."

"And Cassandra claims to be the lost Queen."

"I've never claimed anything."

The King's eyes shot to her as she interrupted the conversation. "Forty-eight days ago I didn't know you even existed. You mattered to me as much as I matter to you. We should never have had any contact. But one of your people made contact. One of your people decided that the Earth posed a threat, a threat to him. He claimed the true Queen to the House of Knowledge was on Earth, not me. Until a few days ago, I'd never heard of it!" Cassandra's eyes shot back to the King.

"Yet you've been able to obtain the protection of a Coalition Admiral, convincing him you need mine. How?" And there it was, what Valerian had been telling him.

"You tell me," Cassandra challenged him, "you seem to think you're so well informed."

"Cassandra didn't ask for your protection!" the Admiral let his fury show, "I did!"

"I wasn't speaking to you, Admiral." The King's own anger was starting to show.

"No, you were speaking to me." Cassandra brought the King's focus back to her. "You've obviously been in contact with Valerian. I'm surprised a King would make a decision without having all the facts, especially one involving a long-time, trusted friend." Her tone was the same she'd use on a disappointing student.

"People are dying because Valerian has a personal agenda. An agenda that's allowed a traitor to operate in Carina for nearly eight cycles. He can't accept that, so he attacks the one who discovered the traitor. The Admiral. That you would doubt the Admiral because of something Valerian said amazes me. I would have thought you would have more loyalty. As for the relationship between the Admiral and myself…It's none of the King's damn business!" Her eyes blazed into Jotham's.

Jotham was stunned that this woman would speak to him in such a way. No one talked to the King like that, especially one needing his protection. Her total defense of his friend also surprised him. It didn't agree with Valerian's opinion of her using the Admiral.

"Cassandra," the Admiral drew her blazing gaze from the King. His look told her she'd said enough. Staring into his eyes, seeing his strength, she calmed.

Jotham watched the silent exchange, surprised at how the two seemed to communicate with just a look. It reminded him of himself and Lata. There was more going on here than what he'd been told.

This woman, Cassandra, was right. As much as he hated to admit it. He hadn't waited for all the facts before he made his decision. Something, as King, he shouldn't do. But he hadn't been thinking like a King, but a friend who knew someone had to be to blame for the damage to William's career. Cassandra had to be the one to blame.

But that's not what he saw here. William was obviously not being controlled by this woman…if anything he was controlling her. William was a decorated Admiral in the Coalition, a Royal member of the House of Protection, and a trusted friend. If he took the obvious personal relationship out of the equation and looked just at the facts William presented, then everything the Admiral had done made perfect, logical sense. He needed to talk to his friend.

"Cassandra, would you mind excusing us. I'd like to speak to the Admiral alone."

Cassandra said nothing.

"Deffand will escort you back to your detail."

"No," the Admiral told the King. "Either I escort her to her security or they come here."

Jotham raised his eyebrow at the Admiral's demand. That William felt the need to protect her, even within the King's guards, was telling to Jotham. The King pressed a button. Deffand entered the room.

"Deffand, the Admiral will accompany you as you escort Cassandra back to her security detail. Then he will return here."

"Yes, Majesty," Deffand waited at the door.

Realizing she was being dismissed by the King and that William wanted her out of here, she stood.

"Majesty," she nodded to the King then turned to the Admiral. William put a hand at the small of her back, saying nothing as he guided her to the door.

"Marat," the Admiral barked as they exited the King's Wing.

"Admiral," the security detail closed around them.

"Cassandra is to be escorted back to the Royal Wing."

"Yes, Sir. Are we to return, Sir?"

"No, secure the Wing."

"Yes, Sir."

He turned to Cassandra, saw her eyes full of concern, concern for him. He put a gentle hand to her cheek, soothing her.

"It will be fine," he stepped away. "Marat." He waited until the detail was out of sight before turning back to Deffand.

Chapter Twenty-Six

The room was empty when William returned, but the door to the private area was open. Passing through, he found Jotham sitting with a glass in his hand. Seeing William, he motioned to the chair across from him. Sitting on the table was a glass filled with ale. William sat and picked up the waiting glass.

"What's going on, Will?" William looked and saw his friend.

"We have a traitor, Jotham." He took a sip.

"You honestly believe she's in danger?" Jotham thought of him not trusting the King's guards in the King's Wing to escort her.

"I know she is and she'll be protected whether she likes it or not." The steel in his voice was unmistakable.

"She doesn't think there is a danger?"

"Oh, she knows there's danger. She'll just make sure everyone else is protected. Her safety will be the last thing on her mind. It's the first on mine. She's first." William watched his friend over his glass.

"Why? I realize she's young and beautiful, but you can find that anywhere."

"Did you? After Lata, did you find it?" Jotham paled at the mention of his Queen, Tibullus' mother.

"No one can replace my Queen," Jotham's voice was rough with emotion.

"No one can replace mine," William fired back.

Jotham stiffened in his chair, "What are you saying, Will?"

"Cassandra's my life mate, Jotham. I will protect her from whoever the traitor is. I will not lose her."

"William…" Jotham had to stand. This wasn't what he'd thought, what he'd been led to believe. William actually thought this woman was his life mate.

"You don't know her, Jotham. I do. You know me. Believe me, not Valerian," William watched his friend struggle. He knew Jotham would have his doubts; if it were reversed, he would too.

"You can't be sure of her. That it means the same to her."

"I can and it does."

Jotham really looked at his friend, seeing the conviction in his eyes. "I owe you an apology." William raised an eyebrow. "For listening to Valerian, I know better. But for you to ask to return, because of a woman…even if she is your life mate."

"I asked to return because there is a traitor. One who has made promises to the Regulians. One who is trying to kill the true Queen of the House of Knowledge. A Queen, who was on my ship, who needed my protection. Being my life mate had nothing to do with it."

"Yet you're letting everyone believe differently."

"No one needed to know who Cassandra was until she was safe on Carina, safe from the Regulians."

"Valerian doesn't know you've claimed her."

"If he had, he'd never have allowed the Retribution to return. He doesn't care about Cassandra or the House of Knowledge, only the traitor."

"His hate runs deep."

"Yes. It makes him willing to sacrifice the innocent to catch the guilty. Something I won't allow."

"There will be talk. There already is. You may never command again."

"Do you remember what you said to me after Lata died?" William saw the pain in his friend's eyes. "You told me that if I ever found my life mate that I was to do whatever was necessary to protect her. To keep her safe, because to lose her was to lose everything that truly mattered."

"I remember. It's still true."

"Well, I've found her, Jotham. I nearly lost her. I won't let that happen again. I will do what's necessary to keep her safe and protected! Everything else is secondary."

"Including your command?"

"Including my command," William finished his drink. "Give her a chance, Jotham. Don't judge what you don't know. That's all I ask. I need to get back." Turning to leave, he saw the question in his friend's eyes and stopped.

"She worries about me," William left slightly embarrassed.

To have a woman worry about you, it had been a long time, but he remembered how it felt. Jotham swallowed hard.

∞ ∞ ∞ ∞ ∞

"Thank you, Marat, gentlemen." Cassandra entered the Royal Wing.

"Ma'am."

"Aunt Cassie!" Seeing Tori and Amina at the top of the stairs, she smiled. Time to switch gears.

"Hey you," Cassandra started up the stairs, "what are you two up to?"

"We just got done with Pazel and Kia. Javiera is talking to them in their quarters."

"Let's go there then." Entering Javiera and Leander's suite, she found the three laughing.

"Cassandra, come sit down." Javiera moved over on the couch.

"I don't want to interrupt."

"You're not. Sit. You've been going hard all day." She looked at her with a critical eye, seeing she was slightly paler than normal.

"Hutu sent up some snacks, eat." Passing her the plate, she waited until Cassandra took one.

"I've been talking to Pazel and Kia about the clothes Victoria will need. They've scanned everyone, that wasn't necessary."

"Yes, it was. Tell me what's been decided."

Pazel pulled up his screen showing her the designs. Most were very basic, day-to-day clothing. But there were several that were more formal.

"Those look fine. Will you have time?" She looked at Kia, she seemed to be doing the actual work.

"We will have extra hands," Kia replied."But it would be helpful if you, all of you, could come to the shop; to pick out material, have fittings there instead of us bringing it all to you. It would save time."

"Kia!" Pazel exclaimed, "I'm sorry."

"Why would it save time?" Cassandra asked, Kia biting into what seemed to be some type of bar.

"You could pick your material. We would then be able to cut, fit and start construction of the garment almost immediately. Instead of bringing you the material, leaving to cut it, returning to fit it, leaving to construct it, and then returning for the final fitting."

"It would be more efficient." Cassandra thought about it. "You could get everyone done at the same time?"

"Yes."

"With all but the final fittings done in one day?"

"Yes," Kia saw Cassandra was considering her request.

"I will discuss it with the Admiral. If he is agreeable and security can be arranged, we will be at your shop tomorrow."

"Yes, ma'am."

"I'll let you get back to your stories." Standing, she held her hand out to Victoria, "Time to go."

"Bye, Amina. Bye, Javiera," Tori slipped her hand into her aunt's.

∞ ∞ ∞ ∞ ∞

"Javiera…what's her story?" Pazel asked.

Javiera turned to her daughter, "Amina, go get changed for bed." She waited until her daughter left the room before turning back to Pazel.

"Story?"

"She's challenging Yakira for the House of Knowledge. But who is she?"

"She is the Challenger to the House of Knowledge."

"Javiera, where's she from? How is she related to the House? She's different from the other Royals."

"How?"

"Well, she's concerned, considerate, and even kind. She made sure I was served a meal!"

"Those are good things."

"No Royal worries about their clothier. She has given me the rights to her dress designs!"

"You would prefer she didn't?"

"Of course not! But it's unheard of!"

"Pazel, Cassandra isn't like any other Royal. She'll make a wonderful Queen."

∞ ∞ ∞ ∞ ∞

"So, do you want to try out that big tub?" Cassandra looked down at Tori.

"Can I?"

"I don't see why not. Why don't you get it started while I change?"

"Okay."

Entering their suite, she groaned as she slid her shoes off. Her feet were killing her. She'd have to remember to tell Pazel and Kia to lower the heel. Picking them up, she walked into the closet. Changing back into her clothes from the Retribution, she hung up Kia's beautiful outfit.

It amazed her, the difference in the feel of the material. Leaving her feet bare, she returned to Victoria.

"Wow! You were fast." Cassandra found Tori already in the filling tub.

"Aunt Cassie, I could almost swim in here."

"I can see that. It's not too hot?"

"No, it's perfect!"

Cassandra smiled at her niece. It was nice to see her happy and excited. Looking around the bathroom, she found the shampoo and soap.

"Here you go, time to get clean."

"Okay," bubbles filled the tub.

Shaking her head, she leaned down picking up Victoria's clothes. As she stood, the room tilted. Bracing herself against the wall she waited until it righted itself. Taking a deep breath, she quickly glanced over. Thankfully Tori hadn't noticed. Continuing into the bedroom she put the clothes away before sitting on the edge of the bed.

Closing her eyes, she put a hand on her flat stomach. William's son rested here. She knew it. But she would wait to tell him, wait until she had proof. He deserved that after what Salish did.

"Aunt Cassie, I'm done!"

"Be right there." Standing, she returned to the bathroom.

∞ ∞ ∞ ∞ ∞

"Goodnight, sweetie. I love you," she hugged Tori.

"I love you, Aunt Cassie. See you in the morning."

Snuggling down into the fluffy pillows she was instantly asleep.

At the door, Cassandra lowered the lights. Turning, she saw William entering the room. Without a word she walked into his arms, sighing as he held her close.

"Asleep?"

"Just went down." Closing her eyes, she soaked up some of his strength.

"You need to do the same." With her still in his arms, he led her to the bedroom.

"We both do. What time is it anyway?"

"2200."

"Not so late," she looked up. "Tomorrow Tori, Amina, Javiera and I need to go to Pazel and Kia's shop."

"No."

"William, it makes sense for us to go to them instead of them bringing everything to us. I can see all the material, they can cut the gowns, and get the first fittings all done for all of us."

"Cassandra, there are security issues in going into Pechora."

"I know. But this needs to be done. Otherwise, there will be people in and out of here for a week."

"Let me think about it."

"That's all I ask. How'd it go with Jotham?"

He stopped beside the bed. "He'll be opened-minded."

"Really…"

"He knows he was wrong to listen to Valerian. But that wasn't about you."

"It was for Valerian. He wants the King to doubt you, to attack me for causing him to doubt you. He knows you'll defend me like you did on the Retribution. If you did that to the King…he could withdraw his protection. In Valerian's mind, if the King does that then you would stop thinking with your 'dick' and not protect me. That would leave me vulnerable to attack from the traitor and then Valerian could catch him."

Listening to her, William realized she was right. He shouldn't be surprised. That was exactly the way Valerian would think.

"You're right about Valerian," he rubbed her shoulders. "Jotham realized it too, that Valerian was trying to use him. He won't let it happen again. He'll keep an open mind."

Saying nothing, Cassandra turned to the bed and started pulling down the covers.

"Cassandra…"

"What did you tell him?"

"I told him the truth. You're my life mate." William watched her.

She looked at him over her shoulder. "He believed you?"

"Yes."

"But he doesn't believe you're mine." Straightening, she looked at him.

"He doesn't think you understand what it means. He doesn't know you yet," he gently caressed her cheek.

"And you still think he'll keep an open-mind?" her eyes questioned him.

"I know he hasn't given you a reason to believe in him. But I do," he framed her face, "believe in me."

"I'll always believe in you," gripping his wrists she used them to stretch up to seal her vow.

Holding her tighter, he changed the angle of the kiss, his tongue sweeping into her mouth igniting the passion they'd had to keep at bay all day.

"William…" her nimble fingers pulled at his jacket and shirt, her hands sliding down his front to caress him.

Breaking away from her mouth, William's eyes blazed into hers. Gripping her shirt, he tore it down the front, revealing heaving breasts covered by scraps of violet lace. The sight incinerated his control.

Stripping her, she fell across their bed, eyes burning into his. Naked, he pulled her up wrapping her legs around his waist as he plunged into her wet heat.

"William!" Cassandra wrapped her arms around his neck pulling his mouth down for a soul-searing kiss as her hips pumped against his. She couldn't think, couldn't breathe. Her body tightened around him and her heart pounded.

William would have her, all of her. His tongue plunged into her mouth. He would drive her mad, he must! This was his life mate. Capturing her hips, he held them still as he continued to drive into her, his thumbs torturing her nub.

Her body tightened like a vice. Unable to move, to find relief, she imploded around him. William exploded within her.

Minutes passed with heavy breathing the only sound. Cassandra found she was on her back, William's head on her chest, not sure how he got there.

Lifting a heavy hand, she ran her fingers through his damp hair, cradling him against her. This was her man, her life mate. It didn't matter what Jotham thought, it didn't matter what anyone thought.

William rested on his elbows, her hand falling to his shoulder. Staring into her eyes he saw everything he'd ever wanted. Leaning down he gently kissed her.

"I love you, Cassandra."

"I know," she caressed his cheek, "I love you too." She started to smile.

A thought passed through her eyes followed by the smile William loved as he raised an eyebrow.

"I'll need to let Kia know that I'm going to need a lot of eadai." William's eyes flashed at the memory of the lace against her skin.

"You will, especially the violet." After a hard kiss, he stood, picked up their clothing and carried them to the closet. As she watched, she saw him finger the lace that had been her eadai.

Oh yes, she would definitely need more. Before she could get up, he returned. He lifted her legs, slid them under the covers then lay down next to her. Dimming the lights he pulled her close.

"Sleep." With his arms around her, she laid her head on his chest and the beat of his heart lulled her to sleep.

∞ ∞ ∞ ∞ ∞

As William slid away, it woke her.

"William?"

"Shhh, go back to sleep."

Sleepy eyes saw the light outside the bedroom windows. "What time is it?" she sat up.

"Early, it's just first sunrise."

"First sunrise?"

"Carina has three sunrises." William leaned over kissing her as he eased her back to the pillows. "Sleep some more," he could still see fatigue in her eyes.

"You're up."

"I need to see about security for Juruas' shop."

"You won't let me sleep too late?" her eyes were closing.

"I won't."

"Okay," she mumbled. He watched her for a few minutes more as he dressed for the day.

∞ ∞ ∞ ∞ ∞

With the third sun rising, so did Cassandra. Searching for a clock she found it was 0700. Time to start the day. Entering the bathroom, she headed straight for the walk-in shower. Last night she hadn't been able to enjoy the multi-head experience that it offered. She'd been too nervous about meeting the King. But this morning she would allow herself the luxury of trying all it had to offer.

Thirty minutes later she emerged, deciding the waterfall effect was her favorite and wondered how soon she could get William under it with her. Wrapping a towel around herself, she found him entering the bedroom.

"You're up," he quickly assessed her.

"Just a little bit ago."

"You could have slept longer."

"I'm fine." Stretching, she turned to give him a gentle kiss. "Good morning. I missed you."

William's arms wrapped around her, pulling her closer for another kiss, his hands sliding under the towel. As her head started to spin, he eased back, resting his forehead against hers.

"I missed you too." His portable comm beeped. Releasing her he answered, "Zafar."

Turning away, Cassandra walked to the drawer where William had put her eadai. Opening it she found he had arranged them by color. The thought of this large man taking the time to organize her underwear for her brought a soft smile to her face. Selecting a blue set, she moved to the closet. Once inside she dressed in one of the outfits from the Retribution.

"Juruas' shop has been cleared," William told her entering the bedroom.

"Good. What time?"

"Security will be ready to transport you at 0830."

"What! I need to get Tori moving, let Javiera know. Have Hutu get breakfast."

"Slow down," he stopped her from rushing past. "I'll let Hutu and Javiera know. You finish getting ready and wake up Tori. There's time."

She looked into his eyes and calmed. He was right. There was time.

∞ ∞ ∞ ∞ ∞

"Time to wake up, Victoria," Cassandra turned on the light after having finished getting herself ready. "We have things to do."

Victoria rolled over in the mound of pillows to look at her aunt with sleepy eyes.

"What are we going to do?"

"We're going to the Juruas' store to get fitted for our clothes. We need to leave in about forty-five minutes so we need to hustle."

"Really? Is Amina coming too?"

"Yes. Now get up and get ready."

With Tori dressed, they entered the private living room to find Hutu setting up breakfast.

"Thank you, Hutu, I know it is short notice."

"Not a problem, ma'am. I will prepare a meal for all of you and deliver it to the shop."

"I…thank you, Hutu."

"You're welcome." Smiling at Tori, he headed back to his new-to-him kitchen.

∞ ∞ ∞ ∞ ∞

Tori dug into the plate of flatcakes like it was her last meal. Shaking her head, Cassandra started in on her own.

If she closed her eyes, she could almost see herself sitting in her father's kitchen eating pancakes with him. He always managed to burn them. Her father had been a lousy cook. Smiling at the memory, she took another bite of Hutu's perfect flatcakes.

The Admiral entered the room as they were finishing.

"Morning, Admiral," Victoria ran over to give him a hug.

"Good morning, Tori." The Admiral dropped down to return the hug. "How was sleeping in that big bed?"

"Good. Did you know we're going to the Juruas' shop to get new clothes?"

"I did."

"Everyone's going."

"Just about."

"Victoria, why don't you go wash your hands and face before we go."

"Okay." As Victoria headed to her room, Cassandra asked William, "Did you eat?"

"Yes, with Tar and Marat."

"Tell me what's going on."

"Marat, Leander, Lucas and four guards will go with you to Juruas'. You'll be traveling in two limisins that the King has provided. Hutu will make you a meal and deliver it to the shop." William's eyes locked with hers, "You will go nowhere else."

"Where else would I go?" Walking over she put a hand on his chest, understanding his concern. "You're not going?"

"No." Taking a deep breath, William hugged her close. "There are things to arrange here. There are no events scheduled for tonight, but tomorrow Jotham has a small dinner planned here with about twenty members of the Assembly of the House of Protection."

"That's small?"

"Yes."

"I'll make sure Kia knows I'll need a gown for tomorrow. What else?"

"There will be some gatherings during the day, a chance to meet smaller groups around the Palace."

"Okay, several outfits."

"Yes."

"Have you heard from the Judgment?"

"They're still four days out," he gently caressed her cheek.

"But safe," she scanned his eyes.

"Yes."

She knew William was concerned about how Jotham was going to react when Tibullus got to Carina so she let it drop.

"I assume I'm not getting my goodbye kiss in front of everyone."

William raised an eyebrow.

"So I'll take it now." Going to her toes she pulled him down to her and gave him a heart-stopping kiss. "That ought to hold me until I get back."

"It won't hold me." He swept her back into a kiss that had them both breathless. "That might do," he said watching her eyes come back into focus.

"It just might," she agreed.

"I'm ready," Victoria came skipping into the room.

"Then let's go." The Admiral escorted his two ladies downstairs.

∞ ∞ ∞ ∞ ∞

Entering the formal foyer, they found everyone assembled. "Marat, we're ready."

"Yes, Admiral." Marat opened the exterior doors, his guards closing around the group, Cassandra and Victoria in the middle. After they passed through, Colonel Tar secured the door before rejoining the group.

To Cassandra's surprise, they didn't travel far before they turned into a garage of some sort. Waiting there were what appeared to be two white cigar-shaped vehicles except they had no wheels. They seemed to float above the ground. As they approached, one of the King's guards lifted the door open.

Marat's men parted allowing the group to enter the first vehicle. Cassandra turned to look at the Admiral knowing they were being watched.

"Remember what I said," the Admiral's voice was brusque.

Nodding her understanding, Cassandra turned and entered the vehicle. As the door shut, she looked at the interior. Leander, Amina, and Lucas sat facing her while Javiera and Victoria sat beside her.

"Aunt Cassie, this is like a limo at home."

"Pretty close, I'd say. What's it called here?" Cassandra asked. After several seconds, Lucas answered her.

"A limisin," he looked at Cassandra then slightly nodded his head toward Javiera and Leander.

She looked at her two friends and realized something was wrong. The tension between the two was palpable. As the limisin started to move, she raised an eyebrow to Lucas.

"So Amina, Tori, what should we have Kia make for you first?" Cassandra asked and the two little girls started talking like magpies.

∞ ∞ ∞ ∞ ∞

The Admiral watched the limisins pull away, his gut tightening. She was away from his protection. Even knowing she had five guards didn't lessen the feeling. Nothing would until she was back with him.

"She's protected, Will," Tar reassured his friend.

"I know." Turning he looked at his long-time friend. Leaving the now empty transfer room, the two headed for their meeting with Deffand to discuss tomorrow's security.

∞ ∞ ∞ ∞ ∞

Arriving at Juruas' shop, Cassandra reached for the door handle.

"Cassandra, no," Lucas stopped her.

"What?"

"You need to wait for the guards to open the door and then I get out first. You wait until I give you the okay."

"Is this really necessary?"

"It's either this way or we take you back to the Palace," he gave her a hard look, reminding her of his father.

"Fine, but let's get moving."

Once Marat and Lucas decided it was clear, they were allowed to exit the limisin, with guards on the sides and Leander brought up the rear. Pazel and Kia were waiting to open the doors.

"Welcome!" As they entered the shop, the guards spread out covering all exits, checking all rooms.

"Hello, Pazel, Kia," Cassandra walked up to them. "I want to start with the girls first. Get the material picked out and the first fittings, then we can get to Javiera and me."

"But…" Kia looked at Pazel.

"That will be fine," Pazel gave Kia a hard look. "While we're doing that, you can look at the gown designs and decide in what order you want them made."

"That's fine," she turned and found Javiera lost in thought, "Javiera?"

"Hmmm...What?"

"Are you okay?"

"I'm okay. What were you saying?"

"We're going to start with the girls. We need to decide on materials." Javiera frowned at her.

"Okay," she turned and focused on the task at hand.

The hours flew by quickly. Materials were selected, designs chosen. While the girls' clothing was cut, Pazel turned to Cassandra.

"Have you decided your priority?"

"Tomorrow I need several day outfits and a gown for a formal meal. These two pant outfits for day wear. This gown for tomorrow," Cassandra showed him the design they'd argued about with the open-beaded back. "I want it in this material." She held up a satiny material the color of topaz, "the beads in the strings in all the royal colors, sapphire and violet at the top."

"All the colors…" Pazel gasped.

"All. Now the pants…" As Cassandra continued, Pazel and Kia were frantically taking notes. They had thought they would have to lead her through the process, but once she got started, she knew exactly what she wanted.

"Javiera, any thoughts?"

"No, I think you've covered everything."

"Oh, and for the day wear no heels taller than two inches, for evening no more than three."

"But…"

"Kia, there is no way you can make me as tall as your average Carinian female, so I'm not going to try. Besides that, my feet were killing me last night. Have we got the materials for Javiera's clothes?"

"All done," she was informed.

"Good, so are we ready to fit the girls?"

"The first cuttings are coming out now."

"Good." As Cassandra was led to another room, a bolt of material caught her eye. "Pazel, what's that?"

Pazel brought the thin, sleek material to her. It was the deepest most vibrant violet color she had ever seen.

"This is silke. It's made in the Trudor region."

"I want some things made out of it." Cassandra fingered the silky material knowing exactly what she wanted. "You'll need your design board. Javiera, can you handle the girls for a few minutes?"

"Not a problem."

"Aunt Cassie?" Victoria looked at her.

"I just need ten minutes, Tori, then I'll be right there."

"Okay," she followed Javiera.

"What are you thinking?" Pazel's mind was flying. This was full House of Protection color, for her to wear this...

"It will be very simple." Cassandra drew a loose gown, spaghetti straps with a modest V-neck front, and a plunging one in back. The gown ended just above the floor. "It's a single layer."

"This can't be worn in public!"

"No, it's for private, to sleep in. Does this come in other colors?"

"Yes, sapphire, black, white."

"I want a robe, long-sleeved, belted, two inches longer in length in the sapphire to go with this."

"I can design that."

"Good, then variations of this in the white and the black. Can you do that?"

"Yes."

"Okay, here's the tough one."

Pazel wasn't sure if he was excited or afraid of what she wanted next.

The gown she drew was strapless, form-fitting, and widened just above the knees. "It will be done with this as the lining and matching lace over it.

"But..."

"I want it done this way, Pazel, the beading will be in violet."

"I will see if I can match it."

"Thank you. Now I need to see about Victoria."

∞ ∞ ∞ ∞ ∞

"Aunt Cassie, these clothes are awesome!"

"Good, Amina?"

"They're great!"

"Cassandra, Hutu is here with the meal." She turned to Javiera.

"Meal?" She looked at the time to find it was 1230. Where had the morning gone?

"You girls hungry?"

"YES!"

"Of course you are." The smile Cassandra shot Javiera faded at the look on her face. Cassandra walked over to her.

"Javiera, what's wrong?"

Javiera looked quickly at Leander then away. "It's nothing. Let's get the girls fed."

Not wanting to push in front of the girls she let it drop, for now.

"Aunt Cassie?"

Cassandra looked at her as she chewed.

"How much longer will we be here?"

"What? Bored already?"

"No, but if we're done…"

"What do you think, Javiera?"

"There's really no reason for them to stay." Rising from the table, Cassandra walked into the outer room where the men were.

"Lucas."

"What's up?"

"The girls are done. They need to be escorted back to the Palace."

"We stay together."

"No. They need to go back. You and Leander can take two guards and go back to the Palace then send the guards back. Javiera and I have a lot left to do."

Marat had been listening. He knew Lucas had the final word on Victoria's protection, but he had final on Cassandra's.

"He can take one guard. That's three guards for two girls."

"And four for two women," Cassandra fired back.

"One or they stay." Marat wouldn't budge on that, he had his orders too. He turned to Lucas waiting.

"We'll be okay with one guard," Lucas interjected, "I'll notify the driver."

Chapter Twenty-Seven

"Victoria!" The Admiral's head whipped around at Lucas' voice to see Tori running down the corridor toward him. Deffand stepped out, meaning to stop the small girl. One minute he was gripping her shoulder the next he was being kicked in the shin and she spun out of his hands and continued on her way to the Admiral. The King held up a hand, stopping the guards.

"Hi, Admiral," Victoria smiled up at him.

The Admiral frowned at her as he dropped down to her level so he didn't smile. "Victoria Lynn, you know you're not to run away from Lucas."

"But I wasn't running from Lucas, I was running to you," Tori told him with simple logic.

"Really?"

"Uh huh."

"Is Cassandra going to see it that way?" Victoria looked at her feet then raised hopeful eyes to his.

"You don't have to tell her." The Admiral's eyes stared into hers. "Okay, okay, I won't do it again."

"Good. Now," lifting her up with one arm. "King Jotham, may I introduce to you, Victoria Lynn Chamberlain. Victoria, King Jotham."

Victoria's eyes widened slightly as she looked at the King. She'd never met one before, but Grandpa Jacob had always said that people were just people and this one had nice eyes.

"I really like my room, thank you," she looked trustingly into those eyes.

Jotham raised an eyebrow at the little girl in his friend's arms. She was a tiny little thing, flame red hair, bright emerald-green eyes that currently stared trustingly into his. He couldn't help but be charmed.

"You're welcome."

"You look like Tibullus when you do that."

The King went still. "You know my son?"

"I met him once, on the Retribution, he came to talk to Lucas." She looked over at Lucas, who nodded, "after Aunt Cassie was hurt. You remember, Admiral?" She looked up at him.

"I remember, Tori." The King caught the change in his friend's voice.

"This is all very nice. Can we get rid of the girl so we can get back to the matter at hand?" Valerian didn't appreciate the interruption.

All heads turned toward Valerian. Victoria shrank into the Admiral's arms.

"Are you giving me orders, High Admiral?" The King's voice was cold.

Realizing his mistake, Valerian backtracked, "No, Majesty."

"I didn't think so. As for the matter at hand, we're done discussing it. I will let you know my decision."

"Yes, Majesty," Valerian knew he'd been dismissed and walked away.

"He has eyes like the Glitter Man," Victoria whispered to the Admiral.

"What?" the Admiral looked down sharply.

"They're mean like the Glitter Man's." William looked at Lucas.

"Who's the Glitter Man?" the King asked.

"He's the big Carinian man that had the Regulians kidnap me when I was two," Victoria told the King matter-of-factly.

King and guards alike stared at the little girl.

"Victoria, I need to talk to King Jotham. Go to the Royal Wing with Lucas," the look in the Admiral's eyes told her not to argue.

"Okay," she hugged him as he put her on her feet. Walking toward Lucas, she stopped then walked over to Deffand. She waited until he looked down at her.

"I'm sorry I kicked you. You were in my way. I didn't know you were protecting the King."

Deffand's eyes shot to the King, who nodded. Deffand squatted down to the little girl. "Don't try it again, you could be hurt." Victoria gave him a large disarming smile that melted the big man's heart.

"You'd have to catch me first," and turning she slipped her hand into Lucas' then walked away.

"Pretty confident little girl," Jotham told William.

"Her father was a member of a Shock Troop," the Admiral watched Deffand rise. "So was her grandfather, Cassandra's father. They made sure their women knew how to defend themselves," he saw the understanding in Deffand's eyes.

"So the rumor was true."

William looked at Jotham, "Rumor?"

"That Cassandra took down a member of your crew with one punch."

"Two, if you ask her, but yes. Falco attacked her, she took her out. Came out of the whole thing with only a couple of bruised knuckles." The Admiral frowned at the memory.

"You need to fill me in on this Glitter Man," the King turned toward his wing knowing the Admiral would follow.

∞ ∞ ∞ ∞ ∞

"That's the last one," Kia said helping Cassandra out of the final fitting.

"When do you think you'll have them all done?" Cassandra slipped on her borrowed clothes.

"The ones you need for tomorrow can be taken with you now. The rest we will deliver tomorrow."

"And shoes?"

"The same."

"Javiera's and the girls'?

"Some will go with you tonight, the rest tomorrow."

"Wonderful. Thank you, Kia and Pazel."

"You're welcome."

As she entered the outer room, Cassandra saw the suns were setting.

"What time is it?" she looked at Marat.

"1830, ma'am."

"What! Javiera we need to get back, I didn't realize it was so late."

"I'll have the limisin brought around," Marat told her. As they waited, the finished clothes were loaded.

"We're ready for you." The security detail surrounded the women escorting them to the waiting limisin. Once they were alone, Cassandra turned to Javiera.

"Tell me what's wrong."

Javiera's eyes filled with tears as she looked at Cassandra, "Leander found the test."

"Okay…"

"We fought about it."

"Why?"

"He…he thinks…he accused me of…"

"Of…?"

"Of being with someone else since he's taking the Ollali juice."

"Javiera, why didn't you just tell him it was for me?" She was aghast that this had happened because of her.

"He should have trusted me, believed in me! How could he think…?"

"This is my fault."

"No, it's Leander's!" As Javiera broke down, Cassandra wrapped her arms around her. She was going to have to fix this if she could. When they came to a stop, Cassandra saw they were back at the Palace.

"Javiera, we're back."

"What?" Looking up she quickly wiped her eyes. Her cheeks were dry when the door opened.

Exiting the limisin, Cassandra found William waiting, his eyes going from her to Javiera.

"Marat, let's get them into the Royal Wing."

"Yes, Sir. Vetter, you're to remain on guard here."

Security enclosed the group leading them to the Royal Wing. As they approached, security unlocked the door allowing them entrance.

"I'll go check on the girls," Javiera quickly left. William watched Cassandra's concerned eyes following her.

"Is there a problem?" he gently touched her cheek, bringing her attention to him.

"I need to speak to Leander."

"Can it wait? He's in a security meeting with Quinn."

"I need him for five minutes." Cassandra wouldn't budge on what she wanted. This needed to be settled.

"Go to our suite, I'll send him up. Then we'll eat," William's eyes told her not to argue with him.

"I can do that." Tugging on his arm, she gave him a soft kiss, "I missed you today."

"I won't be long."

Nodding, she headed up the stairs. William waited until she entered the suite then went to find Leander.

"Cassandra's in our suite. She needs to speak with you." The Admiral entered the room they had converted into their Ready Room. He saw Leander's eyes flash.

"I'll talk to her when we're done here."

"You'll go now," the Admiral's voice was icy, making Leander realize he'd not only questioned an order from the Admiral but from the future Queen.

"Yes, Sir." He left the room.

"Problem?" Quinn asked.

"I don't know. What have you got?" The Admiral looked at the plans on the table.

∞ ∞ ∞ ∞ ∞

Knocking on the suite's door, Leander waited, fuming that he'd been summoned for what he considered a private matter. Cassandra opened the door and stepped back as she allowed Leander to enter.

"Look, Cassandra," he turned as she shut the door. "I know you and Javiera are friends, but this is none of your business."

"The test was for me," she got straight to the point.

"What?!?"

Cassandra stayed silent. Leander was stunned.

"The test was for you?" he ran a shaky hand through his hair. "Why didn't she just tell me?"

"Maybe you should have trusted her," Cassandra's voice was as hard as the Admiral's had been cold.

"I need to talk to her," he headed to the door.

"You need to apologize to her."

Leander stopped, turning to look at her. "Does the Admiral know?"

"That's none of your business," Cassandra shot back to him. Leander stared at her and realized he had more than one bridge to mend, but his wife came first.

∞ ∞ ∞ ∞ ∞

Cassandra walked out of the bedroom as William entered the private area. She walked into his arms, resting her head on his chest.

"I told Hutu to send third meal up," William said into her hair, feeling her nod. "Is everything okay?"

"I think so," she looked up at him. "Who'd have thought standing still could be so tiring."

"You were gone a long time."

"Yeah, I'm sorry. I hadn't realized it was so late. At least we got it all done. The rest of the clothes should be here sometime tomorrow."

"For all of you?" William hadn't thought that would be possible.

"Yep, Victoria is going to be thrilled. Thank you." Stretching up she pressed a gentle kiss to his mouth.

"Don't thank me. I should have realized it when you first got on the Retribution." Knowing this would be an issue they'd never agree on she let it go.

"So what happened around here today?" Before he could answer, third meal arrived. While Hutu was checking the plates, William pulled out a chair for Cassandra.

"Eat," William said as he sat next to her. He needed to tell her about Victoria but not until she ate.

Eating in a comfortable silence, Cassandra thought back over the day. They'd accomplished a lot in a short amount of time. Now came the hard part, catching the traitors. William was risking everything for her, for her to try and find some justice for her planet. Then there were the assassination attempts on Tibullus and his keeping it from his friend and King. So many things could go wrong if they didn't work together. Now Javiera and Leander…because of her…she needed to confirm she had conceived so she could tell William. He had the right to know.

William watched as her thoughts showed on her face, knowing she was only this open with him. "Serious thoughts." He thought worry and fatigue were in the eyes she turned to him. The fatigue seemed to be happening more often. He'd have to look into lightening her load.

"Just thinking," she pushed her plate aside. "So what do I need to know?"

"About?"

"Today. You never answered me then told me to eat." He raised an eyebrow at her. "Which means there's something that I need to know and I'm not going to like it. I've eaten so…"

Both turned as Lucas and Victoria entered the room.

"Uh, hi, Aunt Cassie."

Cassandra raised an eyebrow at her niece's lack of enthusiasm.

"Hi." Her eyes flicked from Lucas to William then back to Victoria. Something was definitely up.

"Did the Admiral tell you?" Tori looked at her with nervous eyes.

"No. Why don't you." She so knew she was really not going to like this.

"It's not like I really did anything wrong."

"Victoria, tell your aunt," the Admiral's voice brooked no argument.

"I sort of ran away from Lucas," Victoria looked at her feet.

"You what?" Cassandra's voice was quiet.

"I saw the Admiral in the corridor," Victoria pleaded her case, "and I wanted to tell him about all the clothes, so I ran down to him. It wasn't like I was running away from Lucas, I was running to the Admiral."

"Tell her the rest, Tori."

"There's more?" Cassandra saw William nod.

"I uh…sort of…uh…"

"Victoria Lynn! Spit it out!" Her sharp tone had Tori's eyes shooting to hers.

"I had to get through the King's guards to get to the Admiral."

"You were with King Jotham?" Cassandra's eyes sought William's.

"Yes."

"You broke through the King's security?" she looked back to her niece.

"They were in my way," Victoria told her defiantly.

"Go to your room, Victoria." The total lack of emotion in Cassandra's voice had Victoria looking uncertain. She'd expected her aunt to be angry. She wasn't sure what this was.

"But…"

"Victoria Lynn Chamberlain, now!" While she didn't raise her voice, Cassandra's eyes hardened as she looked at her niece.

Victoria knew she wasn't going to get any help from Lucas or the Admiral, so she went into her room and shut the door.

With the door closed, Cassandra launched herself out of her chair. Running a hand through her hair she turned to Lucas.

"What happened?"

"We came in an entrance further away from the Royal Wing so the guard could get back quicker. We'd just turned a corner. I was saying something to Leander, the girls in between us when suddenly Tori started running. The next thing you know she put a move on Deffand and is standing in front of Dad."

"Deffand?" Her eyes widened, "Captain of the King's Security Deffand?"

"Yes," William answered her.

"Great."

"She apologized, all on her own when we were leaving."

"Well that makes it all okay then, doesn't it?" she fired at Lucas, her eyes starting to blaze. "She's lucky she wasn't hurt! That one of the guards didn't fire at her! Damn it!"

William was up pulling her into his arms as her voice broke. "But they didn't. She's okay, Cassandra." Feeling her tremble he tipped her face up to his, "She's safe." Seeing the strength in William's eyes she calmed.

Lucas knew that his father and Cassandra were life mates and that they had a strong bond. But he'd never witnessed just how strong until now.

Seeing how they responded to each other made him feel like he was intruding on a private moment.

"How did the King react?"

"She charmed him," William couldn't help but smile at the memory. "She thanked him for her room then told him he looked like Tibullus."

"Tibullus? When did she meet Tibullus?"

"On the Retribution," Cassandra looked at Lucas as he spoke. "He came to see me after Falco attacked you. Victoria was with me."

Cassandra gave William a concerned look. "He was nice to her?"

He realized she was worried Jotham had treated Tori like he'd treated her.

"The King was fine. Valerian was the ass," Lucas informed her.

"Valerian…" her hands clenched on William's chest.

"He never got near her," William reassured her, his eyes flashing at Lucas. "He never touched her."

"Why are you worried about the High Admiral?" Lucas demanded. "He wants to catch the traitor as much as we do."

Cassandra backed out of William's arms. She needed to think.

"Dad…"

"He wants the traitor," William watched Cassandra, "he just doesn't care who he has to sacrifice to get him."

"What are you saying?" Lucas' stomach sank.

"He'd use Victoria as bait with no regard for her safety if it gets him his traitor."

"This can't happen again, Lucas," Cassandra turned facing him, her eyes serious. "If it does, I'll put Marat in charge of Victoria."

"You can't do that!"

"I can and will," she stared him down. "If this had happened with Marat in charge you would have been enraged."

"I…" Lucas found he couldn't argue with her; she was right.

"She needs to be protected at all times, Lucas."

William read his son's look. "We don't know who this traitor is, where he is, or who else is involved. Everyone is suspect."

"King Jotham?"

"No, not Jotham, but everyone else and I mean everyone, Lucas. If you actually want to protect Victoria, you have to suspect everyone outside this House."

"This House?"

"The one Cassandra's building for her House as Queen."

Looking from his father to Cassandra, Lucas suddenly realized that's exactly what was happening. Cassandra was choosing those she trusted, keeping them close, creating her own House. He also realized she was giving him a second chance, to protect not only his life mate but the only family she had left.

"She'll be protected, even from herself." Hearing his own words out of his son's mouth, William knew his son had finally realized what it meant to protect a life mate. The weight of it.

"All right then," Cassandra heard it too and knew he was still the best protection for Victoria. The ringing of William's portable comm ended the conversation.

"Zafar."

"Admiral, there is a transmission for you from the Captain of the Judgment. Would you like me to transfer it to your portable?"

"No. I will come to you. Tell Huerta two minutes," the Admiral disconnected.

"Go."

"I won't be long."

Cassandra gave him a soft smile. "You'll be as long as you need to be." Stretching up, she gave him a quick kiss goodbye.

"Lucas, with me," the Admiral headed for the door.

∞ ∞ ∞ ∞ ∞

Cassandra entered Victoria's room and found the little girl lying face down on her bed. "Victoria," moving to the far side of the bed she sat. "Come on, Victoria, we need to talk."

"You're mad at me," Victoria rolled over revealing red-rimmed eyes.

"Upset, I'm upset with you. I have every right to be."

"I just wanted to see the Admiral."

"What did we talk about yesterday? About you always being with someone."

"But I was."

"Who?"

"Well…"

"Victoria, if I can't trust you then we might as well stop all this right now."

"But we have to catch the Glitter Man!"

"How? How can I do that if I have to worry about you all the time?"

"You said I get to help."

"And you will. Victoria, you're the only one who knows what the Glitter Man looks like. What do you think he'll do if he sees you first? If he finds you alone?"

"He'll take me again," Victoria whispered.

"That's right." Cassandra knew she was scaring Victoria, but she had to make her understand. "He'd take you again. That's why you can't run away from Lucas."

"Are we safe here?" Victoria crawled into her aunt's lap.

"Yes, we're safe here," Cassandra hugged her. "Victoria, I want you to understand. The Admiral is protecting us, he's very good at it. But he can't do it by himself, we have to help him."

"How?"

"By listening to him, not going where he says we can't, and by staying with our guards. They are there to protect us."

"Just like King Jotham's."

"Yes, just like King Jotham's. They keep him safe." Her eyes captured her niece's. "You could have been hurt today."

"But I wasn't trying to hurt the King."

"They didn't know that. Their job is to protect first, ask questions later. You're lucky the Admiral was there."

"I'm sorry, Aunt Cassie," Victoria's eyes were earnest.

"I know you are, baby. Do you understand now why when you're out of this Wing you have to stay with your guards?"

"Yes. I'll stay with Lucas, no matter what."

"Good."

"Are you still upset with me?" Cassandra decided she needed to be honest with Tori.

"A little, you scared me."

"I didn't mean to."

"I know, and I'll get over it, as long as you don't do it again. Promise me."

"I promise," Victoria gave her a big hug.

"That's good enough for me," she hugged her back. "Now let's get you ready for bed."

∞ ∞ ∞ ∞ ∞

Sitting in a window seat, Cassandra looked out at the moonlit garden. Sighing she rested her head against the wall. The gardens were beautiful, full of flowers she'd never seen before.

There were so many beautiful things here. Would she ever get to just enjoy them without worrying about the danger? Would she ever get to sit on that cliff with William and watch the suns set?

Everything changed tomorrow. She would no longer be just Cassandra Qwes Chamberlain, in love with William Zafar, aunt to Victoria. She would be the Queen's Challenger, a genuine threat to someone. It was no longer just a possibility. Would that make the Glitter Man disappear or become bolder? Could she find justice for the people of Earth?

∞ ∞ ∞ ∞ ∞

Picking up his headset, the Admiral opened the secure line.

"Zafar."

"Admiral, Captain Huerta."

"Captain."

"I have someone who would like to speak with you."

"Are your communications secured?"

"Yes, Admiral."

"Put him on."

"Admiral, what the FUCK is going on?!? I'm pulled off my ship, put on a communications block, with no explanation?!!"

"Since when does an Admiral need to explain things to a Chief?" he fired back.

"This isn't about me being Chief!"

"No, it isn't."

"Then what? Is it my father?"

"No, the King is fine."

"What's happened?"

"There is a Challenger to the House of Knowledge."

"What?" Tibullus' mind was racing. A Challenger. That meant a full assembly, the King must be present. But not The First Son. There had to be more.

"There's been an assassination attempt made on the Challenger," William had decided to give Tibullus as much information as possible without telling him he too was a target.

"That still doesn't explain why I've been recalled."

"The attempt was made by the Regulians. You needed to be removed."

"By the Regulians? That makes no sense, how could they attack someone on Carina?" Tibullus demanded.

"They didn't," the Admiral waited.

"It was out here, the attacks on the Fleet."

"Were assassination attempts, they were trying to keep the Challenger from reaching Carina."

"Why would they care? There's no way they could know unless…" Tibullus faltered, hoping he was wrong, "You think we have a traitor?"

"I know we do," his utter conviction stunned Tibullus.

"Helping the Regulians attack the Fleet? Helping them kill thousands?"

"Billions," the Admiral corrected.

"Billions? Earth? This all goes back to the attack on Earth? That would mean the Challenger was on Earth."

"Now she's on Carina."

"Cassandra?" Tibullus was staggered. The Admiral's life mate, challenging Queen Yakira? Was it really possible that she was the lost Queen? Did the Admiral know what it would cost him if she were? What it had already cost him?

"You needed to be recalled with no one knowing to stop another possible attempt on a Royal. The situation with the Sentinel provided the opportunity; no one knows where you are. It has to stay that way."

"I need to notify my father."

"Your father's being kept informed. You can't contact him until you're safely back on Carina. You would jeopardize the lives of everyone on board the Judgment. You're four days out with no protection. If the Regulians locate you, they'll attack."

"Why would they risk that?"

"To delay the Challenge, your death would do that. It would give the traitor time to eliminate the Challenger." The Admiral waited, letting Tibullus process everything he'd been told.

"I'll accept the communications block. But once I'm back I expect to be fully briefed on what's going on." Tibullus didn't realize he'd just given an order to the Admiral. An order only a King can give.

"Once you arrive at the Palace I'll give you all the information I have," the Admiral agreed, knowing that information would forever change Tibullus' world.

"About Cassandra…" Tibullus hesitated.

"What about her?"

"Are you sure, really sure, she's the lost Queen?"

"Yes."

"But you've claimed her as your life mate. If she becomes Queen…"

"Let me worry about that, Barek, you worry about getting yourself home with no one finding out."

"I can do that. See you in four days," Tibullus disconnected.

Chapter Twenty-Eight

Entering their room, William found an empty bed. A quick scan of the dimly lit room found Cassandra in one of the window seats overlooking the garden.

The sound of the door shutting had Cassandra turning her head. The soft smile on her lips couldn't hide the worry in her eyes. Removing his jacket, he lifted her into his arms before taking her spot. Sighing, she sank into his embrace. The steady beat of his heart soothing her.

They both knew there were things they needed to discuss, decisions to be made. But right now they needed this time together, to just be together.

Closing his eyes, William let the feel of her in his arms settle his thoughts. Here was what mattered, what was important. He'd unknowingly searched for her his entire life. Every decision he'd ever made, right or wrong, led him to her, to their life together. Absently he caressed her bare leg, enjoying her softness under his fingers.

The caress of William's fingers along her leg, the love in the touch, was something she had come to depend on. For a man who claimed he always kept a distance, he never did with her. He was always touching her in some way. Giving her his support, his strength or just to let her know he was there. He let her in, not only into his world but into his heart. A heart she would always protect.

As his breathing slowed, his fingers stopped moving, letting Cassandra know he has slipped into sleep. Lifting her head she looked into the face she loved. The moonlight revealed the sharp angles of his cheekbones, the fullness of his mouth. Sabah told her that her son would be strong like his father. If he had half his heart, he would be a great man.

Unable to resist, she reached up to trace the arch of his brow, the angles of his cheeks, his lips that were able to command men, or give her the greatest of pleasures.

"I love you, Cassandra," he kissed her fingers as he slowly opened entirely unguarded eyes, the depth of his love undeniable. "I will always be yours, no matter where we are." Lifting her, he carried her to their bed. "You need to sleep."

"In a little bit. What happened with Tibullus?"

Knowing 'their time' was over he sat beside her. "I told him what he needed to know. That we have a traitor, that there were assassination attempts being made, that he needed to be recalled to Carina to make sure the Regulians didn't attack another Royal."

"He accepted that?"

"He'll accept it until he reaches Carina in four days. Then he'll question everything and everyone."

"And when he finds out you only told him half the truth? That he was a target and that his brother was trying to assassinate him?"

"We won't know that for sure until he decodes the transmission."

Cassandra knew he was hoping it wasn't Dadrian, that there was a possibility they were overlooking. For his sake she hoped it was true.

"Come to bed, you need to sleep," she slid over pulling back the covers. Stripping down he pulled her close.

"Victoria?"

"Won't run away from her guards again."

"Good, sleep."

Secure in each other's arms they did.

∞ ∞ ∞ ∞ ∞

With the rising of the first sun, William woke to Cassandra sleeping in his arms her head on his chest. Today was the start of her Challenge. From now on she would be in constant danger. The thought of her threatened had his arms tightening.

Turning her head, Cassandra kissed where his heart beat before raising sleep-filled eyes to his, her love easily seen.

"Morning." Leaning down William kissed her gently.

"Morning," he responded. "You can sleep longer, it's only first sunrise."

"We didn't get to talk about today yet," she lifted herself up on her elbow to lie across his chest.

"You have your first gathering in the Public Wing at 1100. There will be approximately ten people there for you to meet."

"You have the names?"

"Yes, I have the data on each one compiled for you. It's on the comm in the other room."

She gave him a grateful look. "You know me well."

"I know you," he tucked a piece of hair behind her ear. "You want to be prepared before you meet them."

"I do, thank you."

"You'll spend about two hours with them then you'll return here. At 1430, you'll have another gathering with the other ten people who will be at tonight's meal."

"Another two hours?"

"Yes, then you'll return here to rest before the meal at 1900."

"Are you with me at these gatherings?"

"I'm at your side," nothing could keep him from it. "Marat's men will escort us to and from each."

"The meal with the King?"

"Will be in the King's Wing, with the King, Dadrian, the members you met earlier, and anyone else the King selects. It will be formal with at least a dozen courses."

"A dozen?" she gave him a worried look.

Understanding her concern about unfamiliar foods, William ran a supportive hand down her arm.

"Watch me if it's unfamiliar to you, I'll show you how to eat it. Take small bites. If you don't like it, it'll be easier to swallow. Then you can just cut it up, and move it around your plate."

Cassandra had to smile at him. "Sounds like you have experience with this."

He smiled back. "Royal meals tend to lean toward the absurd, every House trying to show off their foods and creativity. It doesn't always eat well."

"How long does it take to eat twelve courses?"

"It will last nearly three hours."

"Really, to eat?"

"There will be conversation, amusing stories…"

"And more questions for me."

"Yes."

"Dadrian will be there?"

"Yes," he saw her eyes change.

"What are you thinking?"

"Would the King have talked to him about the traitor?"

"Not necessarily. Why?"

"I'd like to see his reaction to the traitor being common knowledge. To have people wondering, questioning."

William understood what she was looking for. "Dadrian may be the Second Son, but he's had all the Royal training. It will be hard to get a reaction from him," he warned her.

"Perhaps," Cassandra ran her fingers lightly over his chest, "but it's something to think about."

"What else is bothering you?" Picking up her hand he kissed her palm.

"What do you mean?" her eyes softened at the touch of his lips.

"I know you. Something's been on your mind for the last few days," he waited patiently.

Sighing, she cupped his cheek. "There is something. I just need another day or two to sort it out. Then I'll tell you about it. Can you give me that?"

William looked into his life mate's eyes. She had always been open and honest with him, trusted him. Now she was asking him to trust her, how could he do any less?

"You're okay?"

"I promise."

"Then I can wait." Pulling her up his body he gently kissed her.

Knowing what he'd just given her, she sank into the kiss. The feel of his thickening shaft between them had her spreading her legs to take him in.

William gripped her hips setting a slow, steady rhythm that within minutes had her gasping for breath.

"William!" as her body tightened, he emptied himself into her with one last thrust. Wrapping his arms around her, he kept her close as they caught their breath.

∞ ∞ ∞ ∞ ∞

He found the bedroom empty after his shower. Shaking his head, he headed to the closet. He found three hanging bags and he smiled, soon she would be wearing clothes provided by him and only him. Dressed, he headed off to find her.

Sitting cross-legged at the comm, she was reading the information he had compiled for her; Assemblymen, wives, children, their status in the House of Protection and the Assembly. Hobbies, interests, dislikes, basically a full biography. She heard the bedroom door open and looked up.

"How were you able to get all this so fast?"

"Most of it is part of their Assembly package, the rest Quinn and I compiled."

"I'll have to thank him." Her heart beat a little faster seeing him in his uniform.

"You don't need to thank him for doing his job, Cassandra."

"I really don't think this is a Colonel's 'job.'"

"It's recon, that's why it is part of a Colonel's job," he looked at the screen she was on, "It's one of his specialties."

"Really?" Cassandra wondered if she could get him to look into something for her.

"Really. Assemblyman Terwilliger has been in the Assembly over fifty cycles. His wife considers herself the 'Queen' of the Assembly, since Lata's death, and expects all others to follow her lead."

"And do they?"

"Enough. She has influence. She respects strength and conviction. She can't tolerate fools."

"Good to know."

Over the next hour, they sat going over the Intel that had been compiled. William told her little things about each that wasn't included in the reports. A knock at the outer door interrupted them.

"You'd better go change," he said looking at her birthmark that she hadn't yet covered.

Returning, she found Hutu alone in the room.

"The Admiral got called to the door, ma'am. He said you were to eat without him." While disappointed William hadn't told her himself, she realized it was going to happen.

"Thank you, Hutu. What have you got for me today?"

"I thought flatcakes would be filling for you since you'll be in a gathering over second meal. I will have something waiting for you here between gatherings."

"Thank you, Hutu, you take very good care of us."

"It's a pleasure, ma'am," he told her then with a slight nod left the room.

∞ ∞ ∞ ∞ ∞

"Kyle." Entering the foyer the Admiral hugged his second son, keeping it brief. "What are you doing here? Thank you, Marat," he dismissed him.

"Sir."

The Admiral led Kyle into the formal reception area.

"Wanting to know what you're doing here. Why aren't you with the Fleet? And why did I have to find out about it from Dadrian?" Kyle demanded.

Closing the doors, the Admiral turned to look at his son. "Since when do I consult with you about military decisions?"

"From what I hear there isn't anything military about this decision. It's about you letting some woman use you!" Kyle's tone clearly reflected his opinion of the woman.

"Be careful, Kyle," the Admiral's voice was cold, "be very careful."

"What? I can't tell my father when he's being used. Fuck, Dad, she's claiming to be the lost Queen like that's even a possibility! You're ruining your career over some piece of…"

"KYLE!!!!" Lucas cut his brother off and stepped between the two men. When Marat told him his brother was here, he'd thought they'd get to catch up, not walk into him insulting Cassie.

"Kyle, you don't know what you're talking about!" Lucas shot a worried look over his shoulder to their father. While William's face was impassive, his eyes were blazing, his fists clenching and unclenching.

"Get him out of here, Lucas."

"Dad, he just doesn't know what's going on."

"Let Dadrian fill him in," the Admiral looked at his son. "Don't come back, Kyle." He turned and left his sons.

"What the fuck were you thinking, Kyle?" Lucas ran a hand through his hair.

"What are you thinking? This woman is ruining our father and you're just standing there letting it happen!"

"Cassandra isn't doing any such thing."

"Cassandra? Don't you call her Your Highness? Fuck! She's gotten to you too," Kyle turned away disgusted.

"She saved my life, Kyle." Kyle's eyes shot to his brother's, "And it cost her family theirs."

"That doesn't change anything," but doubt flickered through his eyes.

"You don't know everything."

"And whose fault is that!?!"

"It was Dad's call," Lucas stared down his brother.

"Right, like she had nothing to do with it."

"I don't know what Dadrian's been telling you. Actually, I don't understand why you even listen to him. But he doesn't know anything. He's just repeating rumors he's heard, stirring things up. It's something he's always been good at."

"At least he had the courtesy to let me know my father and brother were staying at the Palace. I didn't even know you were back on the planet."

"We've been here less than two days!"

"I should have been told!" Turning, Kyle left the wing.

∞ ∞ ∞ ∞ ∞

Entering their suite, William heard Cassandra and Victoria laughing over first meal. The sound made him pause. He didn't want to bring Kyle's ugly allegations into that room. He took a deep breath, forced back his rage then walked down the hallway.

"Admiral!" Victoria was out of her chair, a wide smile on her face.

"Good morning," he swung her up into his arms. "You seem pretty happy this morning."

"I am! Look!" She pulled at her shirt. "I'm wearing my new clothes!"

"You look very nice," he set her back in her chair. "Sorry I had to leave," he leaned over to give Cassandra a quick kiss.

"That's okay," looking into his eyes she could tell he was upset. "You need to eat."

Sitting down between the two, he lifted the cover off his plate. "So what are you going to do today?" he asked Victoria.

"Amina and I are going to play until Kia and Pazel get here. Then we get to look at the rest of our clothes."

"That will be fun."

"Yeah, you two have to be in gatherings all day."

"That's right. Then we have a meal with the King," Cassandra turned to Tori. "So you're not going anywhere without Javiera or Lucas. Right?"

"Right," Tori nodded.

"That's good, Tori," the Admiral told her. "We don't want you to get hurt."

"I know," Tori looked to her aunt. "I'm done. Can I go over to Amina's?"

"Let me call over, see if they're up yet." After talking to Javiera, Cassandra turned to Tori. "Go wash up and I'll walk you over, I need to talk to Javiera."

"Okay."

Sitting down, Cassandra put a hand on William's arm. She felt the need to touch him, "What's wrong?"

He should have known he couldn't fool her, "Kyle was downstairs."

"Kyle? Your Kyle?"

"Yes."

"And this is a problem because…" she waited hoping she was wrong.

"He's upset that he wasn't informed we were on planet."

"He should have been, I'm sorry, I should have realized." She'd forgotten about Kyle with everything else going on. To forget about William's family was inexcusable.

"No, this isn't on you."

"He should have been included. If all he hears are Valerian's rumors, he'll be upset."

"He's getting his information from Dadrian."

"Dadrian…"

"I'm ready," Tori came skipping out of her room. Cassandra looked at William knowing the conversation was over for now. She gave him a hard kiss and got up.

"Let's go, kiddo."

"Bye, Admiral."

"Bye, Tori."

Javiera was opening the door to their suite as Cassandra closed the exterior one.

"Amina's back in her room," she told Tori, and she was gone. Javiera closed the door.

"Javiera?" Cassandra followed her as she walked down to the common area. "Is everything okay?"

"It's better, thank you for telling Leander."

"It was my fault."

"No, it's something that Leander and I have been avoiding," As Javiera sat on one of the couches rubbing her hands together she continued. "I've wanted to have another child for a while now. Leander doesn't." Javiera looked into Cassandra's eyes. "I had problems with Amina. It was recommended that I not conceive again."

"He's worried he'll lose you," she gripped her friend's hand.

"I know but, Cassandra, I have this need. To have just one more, to give Leander a son. I know he says it doesn't matter to him. That he loves Amina. But still…"

"There's a different connection between a father and son," Cassandra finished.

"Yes, you understand," Javiera's shoulders sagged in relief.

"I do. I'm a second child, Javiera. My brother was nine years older. There were things he and Dad could talk about, shared experiences that only they understood. It never meant he loved me less it was just a 'man' thing. It was special for both of them."

"I want Leander to have that."

"But he wants you more," she squeezed her hand. "After my mom died, my father couldn't look at me." Javiera's eyes widened. "I looked too much like her. It reminded him of everything he'd lost," Cassandra's eyes saddened. "He had to send me to boarding school so he could heal. I understand that now, I didn't at nine. I just knew I'd lost my mother and then my father."

"I never knew…"

"We worked it out. It took time, but when it's family, you work it out. That's what you and Leander have to do. He loves you, Javiera. He's scared of losing you."

"I know but, Cassandra, I want this so badly."

"Then you need to tell him that, and if you do decide to conceive again, then you need the best doctor on the planet because, Javiera, I don't want to lose you either." They hugged and both wiped their eyes.

"Okay, enough of that," Javiera leaned back to pull the test out of her pocket. "You'll get the best results if it's done first thing in the morning," and went on to explain what she needed to do.

"Okay, so tomorrow I'll know," Cassandra gave her a wobbly smile.

"It'll be okay, either way. The Admiral loves you."

"I know. I'd better get back. I need to get ready for the gatherings," Cassandra stood.

"Do you need help?"

"Maybe tonight, I'll let you know."

∞ ∞ ∞ ∞ ∞

Finding their suite empty she sighed. She'd hoped to finish talking about Kyle. He was family, family stood together. William was going to suffer over this, his son and his life mate. She didn't want him put in the position where he had to choose. Realizing she needed to get ready for the first gathering she headed for the shower.

∞ ∞ ∞ ∞ ∞

Lucas entered the Ready Room to find his father, Marat, and Quinn deep in a conversation about the day's security.

"That should cover it, Chief. Have your men in the foyer by 1045."

"Yes, Admiral."

Lucas waited until Marat left. "Dad about Kyle…" The look in the Admiral's eyes had Lucas pausing.

"Not now."

"Dad…"

"NOT NOW!" The rage the Admiral had been trying to control slipped out. "Quinn, I'll be in my suite if you need me." Quinn and Lucas watched him leave.

"What was that all about?" Quinn looked at Lucas.

"Kyle was here earlier. Dadrian's been filling him in on how Dad is being 'used.'"

"Kyle listened to that little foabhor?"

"Agreed, but yeah he did. Especially since none of us bothered to fill him in." Lucas rubbed his neck. "Fuck, Quinn, I think they'd have come to blows if I hadn't shown up. The things Kyle was saying. Dad told him not to come back."

"Fuck, no wonder the old man was so pissed."

"Yeah, just what he needed before these gatherings."

"It could have been planned that way," Quinn sat down to think. "Dadrian has never cared for your father, or you for that matter, too many comparisons. He's probably sitting back enjoying all these rumors about how the mighty Admiral has fallen, and over a woman. Fuck, he knew exactly what he was doing talking to Kyle!"

Lucas looked at Quinn, "What are we going to do about it?"

"Nothing, at least not right now. Right now we concentrate on finding the traitor. That will go a long way in explaining things."

∞ ∞ ∞ ∞ ∞

Discovering Cassandra wearing only white eadai turned William's remaining anger into desire. "That isn't appropriate for gatherings." Walking over he kissed a bare shoulder while his hands caressed her sides.

"No?" Cassandra was more than willing to play if it kept that earlier look from his eyes, "I thought it would make an impression."

"Oh, it would, believe me." He ran a finger over the swell of breast her eadai had pushed up. "But I want to be the only one you leave this kind of impression on."

"I heartily agree." Putting a hand behind his neck, she pulled his head down for a deep kiss. As their tongues sparred, his hands slid under her eadai gripping her bare bottom pulling her up against him, his desire evident.

"William," she gasped tearing her mouth from his. Wrapping her legs around him she dove back into the kiss.

William was on fire, this passion igniting too quickly for him to control. Pinning her against a wall he released himself, gripped her hips and thrust. She was hot, wet, already tightening around him and he wanted more, he wanted it all.

Tearing his mouth away, he looked into her face. It was flushed, her lips swollen, breathing rapid, but it was her eyes that sent him over the edge. They were blazing into his, full of passion, desire, love, and just starting to lose focus.

The orgasm suddenly caught both of them off guard. Cassandra's head dropped to William's shoulder as he braced an arm against the wall to keep them upright.

When they were finally able to move again, Cassandra looked up at him, a slight blush staining her cheeks.

"What?" he had to know what caused her to blush.

"I really like my new eadai," her blush deepened.

William laughed a rich, full laugh that relieved the last of the pent-up rage, "So do I."

Chapter Twenty-Nine

Cassandra checked herself in the mirror; Kia had done a fantastic job on the white pantsuit. It was just the look she'd been wanting. A beaded, sleeveless tank just covered the top of the straight-legged pants that hugged her hips and skimmed her toes enclosed in white heeled boots. Covering it all was a sheer, long-sleeved jacket that stopped at her knees. As she turned, the beadwork of the jacket shimmered and flickered like a flame in the wind.

She loosely pulled her hair up, exposing her neck, securing it with matching clips Kia had provided. It gave her a soft windblown look. Satisfied, she walked into the private area. She needed to get hold of Quinn.

William found the bedroom empty after his shower and moved to the closet to dress. One of the bags was hanging empty; he wondered what she was wearing. He pulled out a more formal uniform, not dress, but not every day. He checked himself in the mirror and turned to see Cassandra at the comm center.

"Tar," the Colonel answered the comm in the Ready Room.

"Colonel, this is Cassandra. I want to thank you for the Intel you compiled for me on the gatherings."

"No thanks necessary, ma'am."

"Well I'm thanking you anyway and want to know if you could look into something else for me," she waited.

"What are you looking for?"

The Admiral was right, Quinn loved this stuff, "The Battle of Fayal."

"What about it?" Quinn couldn't help but be interested.

"The captured Regulian ship, what happened to it? The Admiral said that you got their ship identification codes because of its capture. What else was learned from the ship? Who was in charge of translating the Intel? Who did he report to? And where is he now?" Cassandra fired off what she needed.

"What do you need to know all this for?"

"Because it's connected. I can't prove it yet, but I know it is."

Quinn heard the conviction in her voice and believed her. "I'll get started on it for you."

"Thank you, Colonel."

She disconnected. Her heart skipped a beat as William walked into the room in a uniform she'd never seen. Its gray color reflected the hints of gray at his temples while deepening his eyes. On his chest was the array of medals he'd earned during his distinguished career, a career he was jeopardizing for her.

She walked around the comm center and stopped in front of him. "You're a handsome man, William Zafar." And all mine, she thought with a smile on her lips as she rested her hands on his decorated chest.

"And you're my life mate, the most beautiful thing in my life," William gently rested his hands on her shoulders as he softly kissed her. "Let me look at you."

Cassandra stepped back, slowly turned for him, and waited. "The white tower, the tower of the House of Knowledge, that's what you look like," William could see what she was doing. She was planting the seeds.

"Is it too obvious?" she had her first doubts.

"No, it's perfect," his eyes reassured her. "It will start them thinking, without knowing why. You truly are a genius." Cassandra gave him a grateful smile.

"Ready?" William looked into her beautiful sapphire eyes that had suddenly turned serious, "What?"

Cassandra rested a hand over his heart, "I love you, William. No matter what happens with this Challenge, I am yours."

He covered her hand as he caressed his life mate's cheek, "And I am yours. I'll always love you." They shared one last look as they turned to start their future.

∞ ∞ ∞ ∞ ∞

Marat watched the pair approach. The Admiral in his grays, evidence of a stellar career on his chest, walking beside a small woman dressed in white that shimmered and shone as she moved. Together they made a striking couple.

"Ready, Marat?"

"Yes, Admiral." Marat turned, opened the doors of the Royal Wing as the Admiral and Cassandra stepped out and advanced to the security detail that closed around them.

The Public Wing of the Palace was the farthest from the Royal Wing. As the detail approached, Royal Guards opened the closed door leading to another corridor. Cassandra looked up at William. She'd never seen this door closed before.

"Whenever there are guests in the Palace or gatherings in the Public Wing, the King's Wing and the Royal Wings have extra security measures," the Admiral quietly let her know. "There will be extra guards posted at each entrance." Nodding her understanding, Cassandra moved into the next corridor.

As they approached the last door, Cassandra raised her internal defenses. She was used to being scrutinized; all those years of study, the defense of her doctorates, the sometimes harsh criticisms of professors. Professors who didn't appreciate being surpassed by someone her age; because of them she'd learned how to keep her thoughts and reactions to herself, to stay calm with pointed questions. They'd all prepared her for this, the ultimate examination.

The Admiral sensed the change as he looked down at his life mate. As he watched, her eyes changed from open to shuttered and he knew she was pulling herself in; not allowing others to see what she was thinking or feeling. He hated her ability to close herself off from him, but now he was grateful for it. She was going to need it in the days to come.

The detail paused before the last door, waiting. Marat turned and looked at Cassandra. She realized he was waiting for her, the Challenger, to give the final order that will start her Challenge. She calmly looked him in the eye, "Chief Marat, please open the doors." Marat nodded.

"Yes, your ladyship." Marat opened the doors.

∞ ∞ ∞ ∞ ∞

"Evander," Evadne Terwilliger softly spoke to her husband, "What have you heard? No one I've spoken to knows anything."

"I know as much as you, my darling." Assemblyman Terwilliger knew how his wife disliked not knowing more than others. The absolute secrecy in all areas concerning this Challenger was unprecedented. As were the rumors flying about Admiral Zafar.

"We should be finding out soon enough, its 1100."

"Maybe she's changed her mind," but as she spoke the doors to the Wing opened.

Evadne ran a critical eye over the couple entering the room. Admiral Zafar was as handsome as ever, his gray uniform impeccable, his stride confident. At his side was the woman they had all come to inspect. She was a tiny little thing, hardly more than six foot, dark hair pulled back, sheathed in shimmering white, and young, she couldn't be more than twenty-five cycles. Her brilliant sapphire eyes calmly scanned the room with confidence that surprised Evadne.

Assemblyman Terwilliger touched his wife's arm as he moved to approach the couple now stopped several feet inside the room. A smart move, he knew, he'd used it himself making them come to her.

"Admiral Zafar, a pleasure to see you again."

"Assemblyman Terwilliger, Madame Terwilliger, may I present to you Cassandra Qwes Chamberlain of Earth, Challenger to Queen Yakira," the Admiral took a slight step back.

"Assemblyman Terwilliger, Madame Terwilliger," Cassandra nodded to the couple, "a pleasure to meet you." Her voice was fuller than they'd expected and while she didn't speak loudly, her words were easily heard by all in the room.

"The pleasure is ours, your," the Assemblyman stumbled for a moment, "ladyship. Won't you sit?" He gestured to an arranged seating area where the rest of those present were hovering. "We'll get to know one another."

Nodding her head, Cassandra and the Admiral walked toward the waiting group. Seeing there were only three empty chairs, one obviously meant for her as it faced the others, she looked at Terwilliger.

"My apologies, Admiral, I hadn't realized you were staying," Terwilliger was beginning to wonder how much of the rumors were true.

"I'll stand." Escorting her to the chair, their eyes met briefly before she sat, turning her attention to the people before her. The Admiral moved to stand slightly behind her chair.

"That is a beautiful outfit," Madame Terwilliger began, "I don't believe I recognize the clothier."

"It's from Pazel and Kia Juruas."

"I don't think I've ever heard of them."

Cassandra said nothing.

"Why should we consider you a Challenger?" A voice from farther back asked.

Cassandra moved her head slightly to find the source of the voice. "Assemblyman Umbarger, you don't have the right not to consider any Challenger presented to the Assembly," her voice was calm.

"You are correct, your ladyship," Terwilliger was impressed not only by the Challenger's knowledge of the process but her calm at Umbarger's attempt to fluster her.

"Your home planet is called Earth?"

Cassandra looked at the man addressing her, "That's correct, Assemblyman Hartshorn."

"I am not familiar with that planet. Where is it located?" he asked.

"It was located approximately 5000 light years inside the Relinquished Zone."

"Was?"

"The Regulians attacked Earth 50 days ago, decimating the planet." Hartshorn saw the shadow flicker through her eyes.

"Why would they do that?" Terwilliger inquired.

"To stop the return of the rightful Queen of the House of Knowledge. What they called the 'Imperial Light.'" Cassandra's statement caused a rush of voices, each trying to be heard. Sitting back in her chair, Cassandra waited. The Admiral's fingers briefly touched her shoulder.

"Quiet! Quiet!" Terwilliger commanded the group.

"Why would you reach such a conclusion?" Terwilliger demanded. If what she said was true, the implications would be far reaching and would go a long way to explaining not only the need for secrecy but the Admiral's actions.

"From transmissions intercepted by the Retribution after the destruction of Earth," Cassandra replied calmly.

"You have these transmissions?" Terwilliger demanded of the Admiral.

"The transmissions are not the concern of this gathering."

"We have the right to know what was in those transmissions, Admiral."

"Military communications do not fall under the jurisdiction of the Assembly. This gathering is for you to meet the Challenger." The Admiral's voice carried the authority of his rank.

"There was enough information in the transmissions to convince the Admiral there was a viable threat against me as Challenger. If that doesn't satisfy you, you'll have to contact High Admiral Valerian." Cassandra took back control of the conversation.

"The High Admiral was in agreement with this?"

"He wouldn't have replaced the Retribution, in the middle of a tour, had he not been. Your laws are very clear. 'If there is a viable threat directed at a Royal in a combat situation in an effort to change succession, that Royal must be removed from harm's way in a manner that will guarantee the Royal's safety.'" Cassandra's eyes moved around the group as she quoted Carinian Law word-for-word, her voice carrying the authority of a Queen.

Silence greeted her statement. Many of the Assemblymen were completely unaware of the law she had just quoted. They looked to a frowning Terwilliger for confirmation.

"You are correct, your ladyship," Terwilliger nodded to her.

"Thank you, Assemblyman Terwilliger. Now if we could get back to the matter at hand. Were there more questions regarding my Challenge?"

As the gathering proceeded, Cassandra was able to answer the questions knowledgeably and concisely, making contact with each Assemblyman and spouse. All felt they had received her attention and consideration, a remarkable feat.

At Marat's signal, the Admiral put a hand on Cassandra's shoulder, drawing her attention. "Five minutes," he announced. Nodding, she turned her attention back to the gathering.

"One last question," Assemblyman Umbarger spoke, "Who are you claiming to descend from?"

Cassandra wasn't surprised by the question only that it had taken someone this long to ask it.

"My father was Jacob Chamberlain, my mother was Cassidy Qwes Chamberlain. My mother's parents were James Golliday and Lysandra Qwes Golliday." Cassandra waited, knowing this wasn't the information Umbarger was asking for but wanted him to pointedly ask the question.

"Who do you claim to descend from on Carina?" Umbarger demanded.

"I don't 'claim' anything. I am the direct female descendant of the First Queen of Sumeria. You know her as Sabah."

"That's not possible," Umbarger whispered.

"This gathering is at an end," the Admiral stepped up next to Cassandra as she stood.

"I look forward to seeing you again at the King's dinner tonight." Cassandra's look had encompassed all those in the room before she and the Admiral turned to leave the room.

The Admiral and Cassandra did not speak on their return to the Royal Wing. "Chief, have your men get a meal then be back here by 1415."

"Yes, Sir."

The Admiral put a hand on Cassandra's back to lead her to the stairs. "Go on up, I need to check in with Quinn."

"Then you'll be up?" He lifted a hand to gently caress her cheek. The shuttered look in her eyes finally falling away, letting him see the woman he loved.

"Yes, I won't be long." Nodding, she headed up the stairs. He watched her enter their suite before turning to the Ready Room.

"Quinn, report."

"There have been no changes to the second gathering list. The King's meal is still at 1900. The Juruas' arrived at 1130 with multiple packages. All were scanned and cleared. Javiera and the girls helped put them away."

"They were in our private quarters?"

"No, Sir. Javiera hung Cassandra's bags in your closet, the rest she left for Cassandra."

"Thank you, Quinn. Did you get a meal?"

"Yes."

"Good, I'll be in our suite if you need me."

"Yes, Sir."

∞ ∞ ∞ ∞ ∞

He entered their private quarters and found Cassandra sitting in front of the comm, eating from a small plate of mixed berries that Hutu had come to know she liked.

"You need more than that."

She looked up from the screen, "I'm fine. I've never eaten much before an interview."

He walked over to see what she was studying and he shook his head, "You know this." He took her hand and urged her out of the chair, picked up her plate, led her to a couch, and then sat down with her.

"You were amazing at the gathering." Feeding her a thimbleberry his finger caressed her bottom lip. "You never let Umbarger fluster you and he tried."

"None of the questions were unexpected," she swallowed the berry.

"But some of yours answers were."

"Really? Like what?"

"Like, telling the Assemblymen they don't choose the Challenger only the Queen."

"It's the truth."

"I know it is, but you putting them in their place was surprising for them," he selected another berry.

"They need to know I'm not going to let them push me around, politely of course."

"Of course," William smiled.

"So what other answers surprised you?" Cassandra fed him a thimbleberry.

"Your knowledge of a little known Carinian law, one that justified the return of the Retribution," he tipped her face up to his. "How did you know that law?"

"I'm a good student."

"Cassandra, you can't be worrying about my career while you're involved in this Challenge," William's expression bored into hers.

"Yes I can, and don't try that 'Admiral' look on me," Cassandra pointed a finger in his face. "It's a Carinian law. And while it wasn't the reason for bringing the Retribution back, it didn't make it any less true. As for your career, you've already sacrificed that for me. You will not sacrifice your reputation, not for doing the right thing and not when I can prevent it."

William pulled her back into his lap as she surged off the couch, "Protecting me again?"

"It's my right!"

"It is," Cassandra relaxed in William's arms at his agreement. "I guess I'll have to get used to it."

"Yes you will," she allowed herself a few moments to enjoy the feel of his arms around her. Home. That's what her heart told her. He was home.

∞ ∞ ∞ ∞ ∞

The second gathering was similar to the first only with less powerful Assemblymen. There were no new questions asked, which surprised Cassandra. She'd have thought Terwilliger would have sent instructions for information he wanted.

"You need to go up and rest," William told her as they approached the staircase. Frowning, he looked at the open doors to the garden and the guard standing there. "Kocourek, report!"

"Sir, Lieutenant Zafar, Chief Michelakakis, his wife, and the girls are in the garden."

"What are you doing?" the Admiral asked as Cassandra headed to the open doors.

"I am going to go see everyone and get outside for a little while," she retorted over her shoulder and nodded at Kocourek as she passed.

Several steps into the garden, Cassandra stopped to let her senses take in the sights and smells. It had been over fifty days since she'd actually just stood outside breathing fresh air. Lifting her face, she closed her eyes and let the warmth of the Carinian suns warm her skin.

As he watched, William came to realize this was one of the small things she had been missing, like her eadai. To be outside feeling the sun on her face, such a small thing. He stepped close as he gently wrapped his arms around her, supporting her as she relaxed against him.

"I'd forgotten how good the warmth of the sun could feel."

"I should have realized," his arms tightened around her.

"Stop."

"You and Victoria aren't used to being shut up in a Battle Star, traveling in space for months at a time."

"It's not like you had a choice in the matter, William. We're fine and we're outside now."

"Admiral," Marat stood in the doorway. Gently touching his hand, she eased out of his arms. Turning to face Marat, he was back in Admiral-mode.

"Colonel Tar would like to see you when it's convenient, Sir."

"Tell him I'll be right there."

"Yes, Sir," Marat retreated.

"You need to rest before tonight," William stroked her cheek.

"I will, but I want to touch base with everyone first." Nodding, he gave her a soft kiss then headed to the house.

Following the sound of the girls' laughter, Cassandra found them all in an open area at the center of the garden.

"Aunt Cassie!" Victoria ran over and hugged her around her waist.

"Hi, kiddo," she smiled and hugged her back.

"Doesn't the sun feel good?"

"It sure does. Have you been outside long?" she asked as they walked back toward the others.

"A little while."

"Hi," Javiera moved over to give Cassandra room to sit on the bench. "How'd the second gathering go?"

"Fine. Thank you for hanging up my gowns."

"Not a problem."

"These gardens are beautiful," Cassandra looked at all the unusual plants. She would have to study up on what they all were.

"Queen Lata had a great love for flowers. It was her personal mission to make sure the gardens were always in bloom. King Jotham continued it in her memory."

"He's done an incredible job."

"Mom, can we go find Hutu and get a snack?" Amina asked.

"No, but I can take you." Standing, Javiera turned to Cassandra. "Do you want me to have him bring you something?"

"No, I'm good, thanks."

As the men started to follow Cassandra stood, "Lucas, could I have a few minutes?"

"I'll stick with them," Leander said to Lucas and followed the ladies.

Waiting for the group to get out of earshot, Cassandra leaned over to smell a flower, its scent was similar to roses on Earth. Watching her, Lucas wondered what was on her mind.

Straightening she turned to him, "What happened this morning?"

"What do you mean?" Lucas hoped he was wrong.

"Don't play dumb with me, Lucas!" Cassandra hadn't realized she was mad, "Kyle."

"Cassie, that is between Dad and Kyle. If you want to know about it, you need to ask one of them."

"Oh really, so the information Dadrian has been feeding him has nothing to do with me?"

"Dad told you?"

"That Kyle was here, that he was upset that he wasn't informed you two were on planet," Lucas said nothing. "I know there's more. I know it concerns me, it wouldn't have upset him so if it didn't."

"Cassie… "

"You already told me Kyle was going to have a problem with me no matter what. So I'm the one he should be talking to. Not your father."

"It's more than that. You know what's being said about Dad, about your relationship with him."

"About 'why' I have a relationship with him," Cassandra corrected Lucas.

"Yeah."

"What did Kyle say?"

"That he had the right to tell our father when he was being used, especially by someone who couldn't possibly be the lost queen."

"I bet that went over well, what else?"

"That he was ruining his career because of you."

Her expression locked with his. "I'm sure that's not how he worded it."

"He never got to finish it."

"It didn't come to blows, did it?"

"No, but almost. Dad told him not to come back." Lucas ran a frustrated hand through his hair. "Look, Cassie, Dad and Kyle have always had a difficult relationship. Kyle was always closer to Mom and when she died...I don't even know how to explain it. Kyle isn't military, he's a thinker, a learner."

"More like me," she interjected.

"Yeah, I guess. He tries..."

"He knows you and your father have a lot in common, you've chosen the same careers, both of you excel at them and are recognized for them. And there he is the Second Son, trying to fit in, trying to gain his father's attention and approval. Knowing he can never really compete with you, the First Son."

"That's not fair. Dad's never played us against one another."

"Of course he didn't, that's not the kind of man he is. But Lucas, this isn't about being 'fair;' it's about the truth. You and your father have a special bond that Kyle isn't a part of, he knows that. My guess is he had that bond with your mother. Her death left a hole."

Lucas just stared at Cassandra stunned. "How can you possibly know he and Mom had such a special bond?"

Cassandra gave him a sad look, "Because my mom and I did, I'm a second child too, and while part of it was mother/daughter it was also because we were so alike. When she died," Cassandra had to swallow hard to continue. "I tried to find that same connection with my father, it wasn't there. It wasn't his fault and it didn't mean he loved Peter more, he just loved me differently. It took me a long time to figure out that that was okay. It doesn't sound like Kyle's figured it out yet. And my coming into the picture, taking his 'mother's place' with your father, causing people to question him, isn't helping matters."

"He doesn't know what's going on."

"And whose fault is that? Not Kyle's. We should have told him, not Dadrian. We should have trusted and included him. He's family, Lucas."

"I'm not sure Dad sees it that way anymore."

"He does, Lucas, Kyle's his son. He'll always love him. So they had a fight, big deal, families fight. They makeup, they stick together. Peter and I used to fight all the time, didn't mean I didn't love the big jerk."

"Kyle may not see it that way, may never see you as part of his 'family,'" he felt he needed to warn her.

"Maybe not, but he will be a member of our family, a part of this House we're building. If it takes me not being there when he's with you and your father, then so be it. William isn't going to be made to choose between Kyle and me. It would break his heart, and that I won't allow. He's mine to protect, Lucas. No one hurts him."

Lucas had to grin picturing 6'1" Cassandra protecting his 7'1" father. "Does he know this?" Lucas chuckled.

"Yes and stop laughing at me, you big jerk. I took down Falco, didn't I?"

"Yes…Yes you did," but he was still grinning.

"Family, Lucas, there's the one you're born with and the one you make filled with the people you love. You protect it, because in the end when everything else explodes around you, it's all that matters."

The humor drained from Lucas' eyes at Cassandra's words. He knew she was talking about the meadow, how she and Victoria's world exploded around them, leaving them only each other.

"We need to get him back here. Tell him what's really going on. Let him choose what he believes."

"Dad will never go for that, it puts you at risk."

"How could he put me at risk? He won't know about the traitor until we tell him. He doesn't know who he is. The only thing at risk is Kyle's relationship with his father."

"I'll talk to Kyle, see what I can do. But Dad's up to you."

"That's all I ask." As they walked back to the wing, Cassandra paused. Turning, Lucas was shocked to see the honest worry in her eyes.

"How bad is it?" her eyes locked with his. "Honestly. How big are the hits William is taking because of me?"

Lucas wanted to reassure her, but couldn't lie. "Pretty big. Rumors are running rampant and Valerian isn't doing anything to stop them. If anything, he's feeding them."

"To make your father look weak so the traitor will strike at me."

"That would be my take, yes."

∞ ∞ ∞ ∞ ∞

"What is it, Quinn," the Admiral entered the Ready Room.

"There have been several additions to the King's dinner," Quinn watched his friend's eyes harden as he read the two additional names.

"What do you want me to do, Will? It's within your rights to challenge these additions."

"Challenge the addition of the High Admiral and my son? That only makes us look like we have something to hide. Why would Jotham do this?"

"My guess?" The Admiral nodded. "The High Admiral requested to be included. Jotham couldn't refuse without making it look like he was keeping him from the Assemblymen. And Kyle is just to keep the numbers even, a friendly face for you. Jotham doesn't know about this morning's incident."

"Incident?" the Admiral's voice frigid.

"Fuck, Will, I've known you close to thirty cycles. You love that boy."

"Leave it alone, Quinn. Is there anything else?"

"No, Admiral."

"I'll be in my suite."

∞ ∞ ∞ ∞ ∞

Silence greeted William as he entered the suite. An empty silence, telling him Victoria and Cassandra weren't there. As he walked through the suite, William stopped to look in Victoria's room. The bed was made, somewhat haphazardly but made, obviously done by Victoria herself. A pair of shoes, one tipped on its side beside a chair with a towel thrown over its back. Picking up the towel, he took it into the bathroom and hung it up where it belonged.

He was fifty cycles; he had his sons. He never considered having more children. But that was before Cassandra. She wants a child, his child. The thought filled him with longing and terror. She was such a little thing, she didn't think so, but she was. For her to bear his child, would she survive it? She mattered to him more than any child yet to be conceived. But if she chooses to become Queen, she'll have to have a daughter.

That thought brought him back to thinking about a daughter. How different would it be from a son? Victoria had already captured his heart. He couldn't love her more if she were his own. How would it feel to hold his own in his arms knowing someday he'd have to let another man protect her?

Deep in thought he entered their bedroom to find Cassandra putting away the clothes Javiera left on the bed. She had changed out of her white outfit into a long black robe, belted at the waist and pooling at her feet. The silky material clung to her curves making his fingers itch to touch.

"How long have you been back?" He walked across the room and he saw the surprise in her eyes.

"I didn't hear you come in."

"You left the door open," he reminded her.

"Only the bedroom door, not the suite." She knew better than to leave the suite open.

"I was in Victoria's room."

"There's a problem?!?" Cassandra's eyes instantly filled with worry.

"No, no problem. I just hadn't seen it yet. I thought I should." While the anxiety eased, it didn't fully leave her eyes. "I promise, there's no problem," his promise erased the last of her worry.

"And?" she raised an eyebrow.

"It looks like a little girl lives there. Smells like a little girl. I didn't realize there was a difference."

"Boys are stinky." William's shocked look made her laugh. "They are. They're sweaty and dirty while girls are perfect and clean."

"Oh really?"

"Yes. Now men are an entirely different animal." Standing on her tiptoes, her sleeves fell down her arms as her hands rested on his broad shoulders. Stretching, she gently kissed his lips.

The robe slid under William's hands as they rested on her hips. "You need to rest before the King's dinner," he murmured against her lips.

"I know, I was going to after I finished here. Rest with me." Unbuttoning his jacket she slid it off his shoulders. "Did I happen to tell you how handsome you looked in this, Admiral?" She walked over to the closet as she hung it up.

"I believe you did."

She returned to him, took his hand, and led him to their bed.

"Good, I'd hate to forget such an important thing." Sliding across the bed, she waited for him to join her. After slipping off his shoes and pants he did, pulling her into his arms.

"You never forget. Now rest," and the beat of his heart lulled her to sleep.

Chapter Thirty

"Cassandra..." William's voice whispered in her ear. "Cassandra, you need to wake up."

"Umm...what?" she opened heavy eyes.

"It's time for you to get ready for the King's dinner." William sat on the bed, gently rubbing her arm.

"The King's dinner?" Cassandra shot up and discovered William had already showered and changed, "What time is it?"

"It's only 1730, you have time." William enjoyed her robe opening to expose a naked breast. Unable to resist, he caressed her. Leaning into his touch, Cassandra's eyes began to lose focus.

"William," she whispered.

Regretfully, he closed her robe, "But we don't have time for that."

"Oh really?" Cassandra's eyes looked into his.

"Tonight after the dinner, we'll have all the time we need." He gave her a hard kiss and got up from the bed. Taking her hand, he helped her.

"Go shower, we have things we need to discuss before the dinner."

"Things?"

"Change first, then we'll talk." He ran the back of his hand down her cheek, turned and left the room.

Cassandra took her time in the shower as she organized her thoughts. Tonight's meal was one more step. A formal meal with the King and Assemblymen she'd met during the day. Including Dadrian. Dadrian...the Second Son...who wanted to be King. She knew he was behind the attempts on Tibullus, knew it the same way she knew William was her life mate. But William still hoped there was another explanation, for Jotham's sake.

And now Dadrian had filled Kyle's head with half-truths. Kyle, William's Second Son, yet another connection. He struck at William through his son, as he attempted to distract the Admiral so that he wouldn't see what he was doing. Well, she'd see about that.

In the bedroom, she put on the bronze eadai that matched her gown. Along with the eadai, she slid her legs into the bronze leggings Kia had made. In the closet, she stepped into her gown.

It was a simple sleeveless dress with the front draping to show just a hint of cleavage. The back repeating the drape except it extended to the small of her back. Five strings of beads, representing the Royal Houses of Carina, accented the drape and helped keep the dress together. She slid her feet into the matching three-inch heels as she checked her reflection in the mirror.

The gown hugged her hips, the amber embroidery accenting the color of the gown. Taking a few steps, the train flowed gracefully behind her. Lifting her hair up, she secured it with the matching clip Kia had provided, allowing it to fall freely. She checked herself one last time before she went in search of William.

∞ ∞ ∞ ∞ ∞

Staring out a window of the private living area, William wondered how he was going to tell Cassandra about the added names for dinner. Valerian she would handle, she'd already shown she could. But Kyle, how was he going to explain Kyle to her? Explain how she needed to handle him.

His son, fuck, he hadn't wanted Kyle anywhere near this until after the Assembly. It was one of the reasons he hadn't contacted him. He hadn't forgotten. But Dadrian had made it a point to fill his head with rumors and half-truths, the little foabhar. Now Cassandra would have to deal with being attacked by someone she considered family, his family. Lost in thought, he didn't hear Cassandra enter the room. Her scent reached him a moment before her touch.

∞ ∞ ∞ ∞ ∞

She watched William as she approached, Cassandra could tell he was troubled. The incident with Kyle troubled him, she knew that just as she knew he loved his second son. Kyle was going to have to become a priority; she wouldn't have William upset if she could help it. But for now all she could do was support him. Reaching out she touched the man she loved.

Turning, William looked down into the brilliant sapphire blue eyes he loved. In them, he saw her love for him, her trust in him, her belief in him, and just a hint of worry for him. He ran his hands up her bare arms, trailed them across her collar bones, before cradling her face. Leaning down he gently kissed her. Here was his priority. He knew she needed to be told so she would have time to think. William started to lead her to the couch only to stop when his hand touched bare skin.

He took a step back and looked at her. The dark topaz of the gown made her skin glow. The gown was unadorned, the detailing of the material more than enough; until you looked at the back, which wasn't there. Five strings of beads held the dress together before the material rejoined at her lower back, accentuating her backside as it cascaded to the floor to pool behind her as she walked.

"Cassandra…it's beautiful. You look stunning." He couldn't resist running his fingers down her exposed back. She turned in his arms as she tipped her head for a kiss.

"Thank you," she whispered against his lips.

"We need to talk." Regretfully he led her to the couch. Tonight, after dinner, he would explore the rest of this dress. "There have been two additions to the King's dinner."

"Okay," she waited.

"Valerian," William watched as her eyes darkened but said nothing, "and Kyle."

"Your Kyle?" her voice revealed her surprise.

"Yes."

"Well it's not how I'd planned on first meeting him, but I don't see a problem."

"Kyle is the problem. Cassandra…he's not going to be…friendly to you."

"I know. I'm sorry." She put her hand on his.

"What do you know?" William demanded.

Cassandra was slightly shocked at his tone. "I know that Kyle would've had a problem with me no matter what."

"What are you talking about?"

"You…me…Salish. Kyle doesn't want someone taking his mother's place, her place with you."

"That's ridiculous. Salish and I concluded our union over fifteen cycles ago. Kyle knew that."

"Yes, he knew, but that doesn't mean he wanted someone to take her place."

"Why would you think that?"

"Lucas told me. He thought I should know Kyle would have a problem with me, with me being with you."

"When did he tell you this?" William surged up to stride across the room.

"Right after we arrived on Carina," she watched him.

"There was no reason for him to tell you that. There are more important things for you to concentrate on."

"What's more important than the relationship between you and your son?" Cassandra knew she had to be misunderstanding him. "You intentionally didn't tell him we were here. You didn't just forget with everything going on." Rising from the couch she wasn't sure she liked where this was going.

"I'd never forget, Kyle. I didn't want him here, didn't want him involved in this. This isn't something he's equipped for. Fuck!"

"But now he is, because of Dadrian. Now he is and he doesn't know the truth, the full truth because we didn't tell him. Now he's on the wrong side because he's trying to protect you."

"That's ridiculous!"

"Is it? Why, because he's not military? Because he's a thinker, a learner? Because of that you think he can't protect the people he loves from harm. Is that what you really think, William?" Cassandra's eyes burned into his.

"You're not understanding. Kyle isn't like Lucas, he's..."

"Like me."

"What?"

"He's like me; a thinker, a learner, someone who's not military; someone who's much happier with a book than ordering people around."

As he listened to her, William realized she understood Kyle perfectly. Saw him more clearly, having never met him, than his own father did.

"That would be Kyle," he mused as he walked over to her to put his arms around her.

"He loves his family, he loves you. He's lost his mother, he's not willing to lose anyone else, not without a fight," Cassandra looked into his eyes. "I fully understand."

"Cassandra, Kyle isn't like you."

"Like me?"

"You stand. For what you believe in, for who you believe. For those you love. You're willing to risk everything for those you love."

"And Kyle didn't do that? Coming here this morning, risking your anger, to tell you what he believed? William," she laid a hand over his heart, "I haven't done anything heroic, anything special. I was there the day Victoria was born. I watched her take her first breath. If we hadn't been able to get her out of that fire…"

"We didn't, you did."

"No, it took all of us, together. You underestimate him, William," Cassandra's eyes looked into his.

"Cassandra, you haven't even met him."

"I don't have to, to know he loves you. His coming here this morning proves it. It also proved he'll stand. He'll protect his family. In this case, *you*, from the enemy, *me*. For that alone I like him."

"That's what I'm afraid of." William lifted her hand, kissing her palm.

"Why? Why are you afraid I'll like him?"

"Because that means he can hurt you. Cassandra…what he is saying, repeating, you open your heart to family. That means he can hurt you, badly. I won't tolerate that. No one hurts you, not even my son." William's eyes began to blaze.

"Trust me, William, he may be your son, but that doesn't mean I trust him. He'll have to earn that, because in his trying to protect you, he hurt you, and I won't tolerate that. No one hurts you, not even your son." Cassandra threw his words back at him.

"I trust you," his eyes calmed. As his portable comm rang, he reached into his pocket.

"Zafar."

"Admiral, your detail is waiting at the door."

"Thank you, Marat, we'll be right down."

"Ready?" Pulling his head down, Cassandra gave him a deep kiss.

"I am now." Turning they left the suite. As they started down the stairs, Cassandra smiled at William.

"Aunt Cassie!"

Turning to Victoria, Cassandra caught her heel on the stair runner. One minute she was turning, the next falling.

"Cassandra!" William reached for her, pulling her into the safety of his arms. Resting her head on his chest, she tried to catch her breath. Her heart was racing, she thought she was going down.

"Cassandra, are you okay?" William's voice was in her ear.

"Yeah, my heel just caught." Looking up she saw she had scared him. "I'm fine, thanks to you." She gave him a quick, reassuring kiss.

"Aunt Cassie?" At the quivering voice, her eyes looked to the top of the stairs.

"Hey, baby, I'm okay." She walked back up the stairs.

"You started to fall."

"Yeah, good thing the Admiral was there, huh?"

"Yeah, I wanted to tell you goodnight."

"We didn't get to see much of each other today, did we?" Ignoring her dress, she knelt in front of her niece.

"Uh uh."

"We'll have to see if we can't do something about it tomorrow then, okay?"

"Okay."

"So when we get back tonight, do you want me to come get you or are you staying at Amina's?"

"I want to sleep in my bed."

"Okay then that's what we'll do. But if Javiera tells you bedtime you go, understood?"

"Yes, Aunt Cassie."

"All right, I need to go." She gave her a kiss and stood up.

"Night, Admiral."

"Good night, Victoria."

Looking at Javiera, Cassandra saw the worry in her eyes. "I'm fine." Watching them enter the suite she turned back to William.

"Shall we try this again?"

∞ ∞ ∞ ∞ ∞

Approaching the King's Wing, the detail slowed.

"William?"

"The King's men will escort us the rest of the way." William nodded to Marat, who stepped aside allowing them to advance into the King's Wing. Four guards, two on each side took their place.

"Deffand."

"Admiral?" Deffand turned to William.

"There is a step in the Royal Wing that requires attention. You'll need to clear someone to repair it."

"A stair, Sir?"

"The runner is loose. Cassandra nearly fell down the stairs because of it," the Admiral's eyes locked with his.

"Yes, Sir," Deffand's eyes flashed to Cassandra, "I'll contact the proper personnel."

Nodding, the Admiral started to advance only to feel Cassandra's gentle touch.

"Captain Deffand," Cassandra addressed him, "I would like to personally apologize for the incident yesterday involving my niece, and to thank you for making sure she wasn't hurt." Deffand stared at her for a moment.

"She's a child, who would hurt a child?"

"You'd be surprised. But I have talked to her, she won't do it again."

"That would be best."

Nodding, Cassandra turned back to William.

∞ ∞ ∞ ∞ ∞

Kyle watched his father enter the room, the woman at his side not at all what he had expected. She was tiny, barely coming up to his father's shoulder in heels. Her brilliant blue eyes scanned the room, stopped on him for a moment, before turning to the approaching Assemblyman with a polite smile on her lips.

"Interesting looking, isn't she?" Dadrian commented, his eyes scanning the woman at the Admiral's side. He would definitely have to get to know her. "Easy to see how the Admiral's become...distracted," Dadrian dug at Kyle.

∞ ∞ ∞ ∞ ∞

Scanning the room, Cassandra recognized the Assemblymen and their wives from earlier in the day. Valerian was there, as were two men, standing together across the room. One was Dadrian, the other was obviously William's son, Kyle. The resemblance was evident even though Kyle's features were more delicate, more like those of Salish she assumed. But his eyes were all Zafar. Moving her gaze from him, Cassandra turned her attention to Assemblyman Terwilliger.

"Assemblyman Terwilliger, Madame Terwilliger, a pleasure to see you again," Cassandra politely smiled at them.

They moved around the room, making small talk before proceeding on. Approaching Kyle and Dadrian, Cassandra could feel William's fingers tense on her back. She wasn't sure if it was because of Kyle or Dadrian.

"Cassandra, my son, Kyle Zafar," William introduced them. "Kyle, Cassandra Qwes Chamberlain."

"It's nice to finally meet you, Kyle. I've heard a great deal about you from Lucas and your father," she offered the branch.

"While I've heard nothing about you from either of them," Kyle's voice was just barely polite.

Dadrian's lips quirked.

"Unfortunately that's true. The need for security has created a great many problems, including allowing groundless rumors to flourish. Now that the Challenge has begun, those can be laid to rest."

"And how will that be accomplished?" Dadrian could no longer take being ignored.

Cassandra's sharp blue eyes turned to him, "By the truth coming out. And you are?"

Dadrian stiffened.

"Cassandra, His Royal Highness Prince Dadrian. Prince Dadrian, Cassandra Qwes Chamberlain, Challenger to Queen Yakira."

"Prince Dadrian?" Cassandra shot William a confused look.

"King Jotham's Second Son." William leaned down to tell her so only she saw the quick sparkle in his eyes at her jab.

"Of course," Cassandra's gaze returned to Dadrian. "Your Highness," she offered no apology. Dadrian was infuriated, as Cassandra wanted. Before he could respond, King Jotham's arrival was announced.

"His Majesty King Jotham." All heads turned to the doorway. Nodding to the Assemblymen and spouses as he passed, the King walked over to his son and friend.

"Admiral Zafar, Princess Cassandra," the King acknowledged the couple.

"Majesty," William and Cassandra nodded to the King, their expressions unchanging at Cassandra's sudden title. The same couldn't be said for Dadrian.

"Kyle, it's good to see you again," the King smiled at him.

"You too, Majesty," Kyle smiled back as he nodded and Cassandra noticed he had the Zafar smile.

"Dadrian," while the King continued to smile his tone was cooler.

"Sir," Dadrian nodded to his father, unsmiling.

"Majesty," all eyes turned to find Valerian had approached.

"High Admiral?"

"Might I have a moment of your time before the meal is served? It's regarding The First Son." Cassandra could tell Valerian had pushed the right button.

"Excuse me." King Jotham led the High Admiral, who had an air of self-satisfaction around him, out of the room. Cassandra looked up to William, wondering if Valerian had discovered where Tibullus was.

The conversation had barely resumed in the room when the King returned, his face an unreadable mask. Valerian had lost his self-satisfied look.

"Majesty," a servant entered the room, "The meal is ready."

Nodding his permission, the servant opened the doors to the dining room.

Placing a hand on Cassandra's lower back, William guided her into the room. As the Guest of Honor, she would be seated closest to the King. As they walked to their seats, his thumb absently caressed her soft skin. Servants pulled out the chairs and everyone waited for King Jotham. Once he sat, everyone else was allowed to.

With the King at the head of the table and William to her left, Cassandra looked across to find Dadrian directly across from her, Kyle across from his father. Next to Kyle sat High Admiral Valerian, who was currently staring intently at Cassandra. Raising an eyebrow, she coolly stared back, letting the High Admiral know he didn't intimidate her. Kyle watched the silent exchange with interest.

"Ladies and gentlemen, tonight's meal is the conclusion of the first day of the Challenge to Queen Yakira's throne. You, as the Assemblymen for the House of Protection, have all been invited to meet the Challenger so you will be able to make an informed decision on what is best for Carina." The King looked at each of them. "With that said, I believe we should have some words from the Challenger before we eat." King Jotham gave her a pointed look.

Cassandra's eyes were calm as she listened to Jotham. She realized he had not given the Assemblymen his opinion of her Challenge. William's friend or not, he was not going to publicly support her. Realizing this, his next comment didn't surprise her. He was testing her, seeing how she'd stand. So she would.

As she started to slide her chair back, a servant stepped up to assist her. Nodding her thanks, she stood. She first addressed the King.

"I'd like to thank King Jotham for this opportunity. His understanding of the uniqueness of the situation is appreciated." Nodding to him, she turned her attention down the table.

"While I have met with each of you today, I realize that small amount of time isn't enough for you to make an informed decision about my Challenge. It is my hope that in the following days, we will be able to spend more time getting to know one another. So you, as King Jotham so eloquently put it, will be able to make the best decision for Carina." As she turned to sit, the servant pushed her chair back in for her.

Silence greeted Cassandra's statement until Evadne Terwilliger began to clap her hands together. The Admiral and Assemblyman Terwilliger were quick to follow. As the King clapped, the others followed. After a nod to Madame Terwilliger, Cassandra turned her attention to King Jotham. Her eyes stared directly into his, waiting for his next move. When he stopped clapping, the servants began to serve.

The first plate was small. It contained what looked to Cassandra to be a pasta dish even though it was black in color. Reaching for her glass filled with what she knew was water she took a sip, waiting for William to take his first bite. Following his example she took a small bite, finding that while the texture was pasta-like, the flavor was more like black licorice. Chewing she tried to make sense of the contrasts.

William discretely watched as she took her first bite, chewed and swallowed. She was a constant amazement to him. She hadn't known Jotham would ask her to speak but acted as if it had been a well thought out plan. Now she was eating things she'd never seen before without complaint. When did she ever complain?

The conversation was light during the first course, all knowing they would be there a long time. As the plates were removed and replaced, King Jotham turned his attention to Cassandra. He was impressed with how she'd handled his thrusting her into making a speech, she hadn't faltered.

"Have you been able to see much since your arrival?" the King asked politely, knowing she hadn't.

"Unfortunately no," Cassandra replied to him. "There will be time after the Challenge is completed," her confidence apparent. "However, I was able to spend some time in the Royal Garden today. Queen Lata had an excellent eye for color and contrast." She watched the quick flash in his eyes at the mention of his late wife.

"She redesigned that garden herself. She wanted you to be able to stroll through it, to be surprised."

"She certainly accomplished that, the center is unexpected and welcoming. The girls particularly liked having an open area to play in."

"I'm glad they enjoyed it."

"I hope they were better behaved than when they returned to the Palace yesterday," High Admiral Valerian criticized.

King Jotham watched Cassandra's eyes turn icy before she slowly turned to the High Admiral.

William, along with the rest of the table, had been following Cassandra and the King's conversation with interest. Valerian's interruption, and his comment about the children, had a jarring effect on all present. It also told William that the High Admiral had a spy within the Palace.

"Why would you think they'd been out of the Palace?" the Admiral's eyes were rock hard as they looked at the High Admiral, his voice revealing nothing.

"It was obvious," the High Admiral replied. In his attempt to undermine Cassandra, he hadn't yet realized what he had revealed. The King had.

"How so?" William pressed.

"I don't need to explain myself to you, Admiral," Valerian barely contained his sneer.

"You do to me, High Admiral," Jotham's voice carried the authority of his position. He'd been aware of the animosity between William and Valerian, but to hear the High Admiral so openly disrespect him, in a public setting, Jotham would not tolerate the lack of respect. "I was there yesterday and saw no indication of an outing."

"They were coming from the Public Wing, Majesty," Valerian had to respond to the King.

"That indicates nothing, High Admiral," Jotham's tone hardened.

"The child must have said something then," he tried to cover his tracks.

"Victoria said nothing to indicate she'd been out of the Palace. Her only comments were about her room and Barek."

"Then I must have heard it somewhere, Majesty."

"You're implying that someone from *my* House would inform you about the movements of my guests?"

"No, Majesty," Valerian began to sweat. "I must have misunderstood the situation." He was forced to admit he was wrong or tell the King he had eyes in the Palace.

"Yes, High Admiral, you did," Jotham drove home his point.

Cassandra watched Valerian as the King stepped in. She too realized what he had revealed. He'd been watching Victoria, watching all of them. He had a spy in the House of Protection. Her fingers clenched under the table. Feeling William's gentle touch, she looked to him. What she saw calmed her fears. He wasn't going to let anything happen to Victoria. Lacing his fingers with hers, he gave her a reassuring squeeze before returning his hand to the table. Picking up his forc, his look let her know she should do the same.

"Barek?" Dadrian lowered his forc. He'd been enjoying the High Admiral's belittling of the Admiral until his father's intervention, and now Barek was the subject.

"Victoria met him when she was on the Retribution," Jotham told his second son.

"Why wasn't he on the Sentinel?"

Cassandra sat back as plates were exchanged. Watching Dadrian she could almost see his thoughts. Where had Barek been during the Regulian attack on the Sentinel?

"Your brother's position has him traveling throughout the Fleet," King Jotham informed Dadrian.

"I realize that. I meant, why was he on the Retribution?" Dadrian picked up a goblet.

"Because of an assassination attempt," Cassandra informed him, watching as wine sloshed onto Dadrian's hand.

A servant was immediately there mopping up the spill. The King looked questioningly at his second son.

"Assassination attempt!?!" The table had gone silent.

"Yes," Cassandra let it hang there for a minute, "He needed to interview me." Dadrian stared at her.

"There was an attempt against you?" Kyle hadn't heard this. Cassandra's eyes turned to Kyle.

"Several, Victoria was hurt during the first, several of the Retribution's crew members during the second."

"But you were unharmed," Dadrian pressed her.

"The Princess was badly hurt in the second attack." While the Admiral's tone and expression were cool and unreadable, both Cassandra and Jotham knew better. Jotham realized this was where William had nearly lost his life mate.

"It was what convinced the Admiral, and then High Admiral Valerian," Cassandra made sure everyone understood that Valerian was in full agreement with the decision, "that the Retribution should return to Carina."

"The Succession Protection Law," the Admiral gave his son a surprised look.

"Yes," Cassandra nodded to Kyle.

"Why wasn't this made public, High Admiral?" Terwilliger demanded. "Rumors of all sorts have been flying about Admiral Zafar and the return of the Retribution." Murmurs of agreement filtered around the table.

"Making it public would have put the Princess and her remaining family at risk. It's what we were trying to avoid," Admiral Zafar spoke for the High Admiral, earning himself a glare.

"And the rumors?" Umbarger demanded.

"Were helpful in diverting attention away from the Princess."

"Not all diverted attention away from Cassandra," Dadrian couldn't help but comment. Things were going too much the Admiral's way.

His comment and use of her first name earned him a cool look from Cassandra, but the Admiral eyes flared before cooling, telling him he'd scored a hit. He'd have to remember that. But his enjoyment was short-lived as he met his father's eyes. The King was not happy with him.

"I've never put much stock in rumors or those who spread them, Prince Dadrian," Cassandra put the subtlest of emphasis on his title, scoring a hit of her own.

Leaning back, William allowed the servant to remove his plate and his temper to cool. Cassandra had handled Dadrian perfectly, making her opinion of him known without actually referring to him. When the next plate appeared, he discovered it was Zebu. Remembering the first time they'd shared it, William looked to Cassandra. The slight smile she gave him let him see she remembered too. The shared moment went unnoticed by all except Dadrian.

What could she possibly see in that old man! He silently raged. She must absolutely hate sharing a bed with him. He'd show her what a real Carinian male could do in bed. Then she'd talk to him with more respect!

Sitting next to Dadrian, Kyle was silently chewing his Zebu. He'd come here tonight having made up his mind about Cassandra. He'd listened to Dadrian, to the rumors of his father being controlled by a conniving woman.

But what he'd found was that his father had indeed made a military decision, following the law, in the protection of the heirs to the throne. That he'd knowingly allowed the rumors to further that protection. Dadrian was apparently one of the people Cassandra didn't put much stock in.

Valerian fumed as he ate. How dare this…woman imply that he believed she was a Royal entitled to protection under Carinian law! But arguing would only make him have to explain why he really wanted the Retribution back. He needed that child to flush out the traitor, and he'd almost said too much when he'd commented on them leaving the Palace. If the King found out he had eyes in the Palace…but he wouldn't…now he just needed to bide his time.

"So you spoke with my son," King Jotham commented as another course was served. It appeared to be some sort of soup.

"Yes, twice actually," Cassandra stirred it with her spoon missing William's raised eyebrow. It seemed thick for such a clear soup.

"What was your impression?"

"Impression, Majesty?" Cassandra slowly let go of her spoon. Looking at the King she wondered how honest she should be.

"Yes."

Valerian sat back. He was going to enjoy this.

"I found Tibullus to be mildly conceited, somewhat irritating, and totally intrusive." The King couldn't keep the shock off his face. No one in the room moved. Cassandra felt William's hand gently touch hers under the table. "That being said, he was also thorough, competent and damn good at his job."

Jotham was silent, Dadrian was not.

"You will not speak about my brother that way!" He pounded a fist on the table causing the crystal to ring, "Especially when he may be dead!" He'd given Cassandra her in.

"Why would you think he's dead?" she was cool and questioning.

"His ship was lost!" Dadrian's voice carried just the right amount of anguish.

"The Sentinel wasn't lost, the Talon was. The Sentinel is dead in space."

"It's the same thing."

"No, it's not. The Talon experienced rapid decompression after the Regulian attack. The ship was destroyed, the entire crew, eight hundred and thirty-five to be exact, died." Cassandra's tone was that of a teacher to a dim student. "The Sentinel is dead in space. That means it has no defenses, no propulsion system, and no ability to communicate. But it has life support. Its crew is still alive. That means there is a good chance Tibullus is alive."

"He's not on any list," Dadrian fired back, enraged that he was being talked down to.

"You did serve, didn't you?" she questioned Dadrian, knowing very well that he had but only for the minimum of one year. "The military never puts a name on a list unless they can back it up. It makes them look incompetent." Cassandra shifted her focus to Valerian. "Isn't that right, High Admiral?"

Valerian sat up straight as suddenly all the eyes in the room were on him, including the King's. "No name goes on a list without verification," Valerian reluctantly agreed with her.

"What does that prove?" Dadrian demanded.

"That there is no proof he's dead. So unless you know something no one else does, there's no reason to assume he is." Cassandra's voice was cool as she watched Dadrian.

"You haven't explained to me why you think my son is alive." While King Jotham's voice was steady, Cassandra could hear the pain that not knowing was causing him. She was going to give him what she could.

"Because of everything I said before, Majesty. Tibullus is smart, he knows his job, how to handle things. I can't see him allowing a Regulian attack to get the better of him."

King Jotham said nothing as he stared at Cassandra. Leaning back he allowed the servant to remove this course.

The meal continued with others asking questions of Cassandra ranging from simple to complex. The King listened but did not participate. Cassandra managed several bites of each course, some she forced down. William leaned over occasionally to tell her something.

"Why do you call him Tibullus?"

Cassandra glanced at the King as she gladly put down her forc. This course didn't agree with her. "I call him Tibullus because that's how he was introduced to me, as Chief Tibullus. It wasn't until, I believe, nine days ago that I discovered he was The First Son of the House of Protection."

"You seem to have acquired a great deal of knowledge since your arrival on the Retribution. How is it you didn't know Tibullus was the family name?"

"I have learned a great deal, Your Majesty. Mostly from books and memory foils on the Retribution. I'd challenge you to find a book that states the family name for any of the Royal Houses." Cassandra's eyes were steady. "It is considered common knowledge, for a Carinian. You were never called King Tibullus, it's always King Jotham and 'Tibullus' is referred to as Prince Barek.

"So your opinion of my son?" she saw Dadrian tensing out of the corner of her eye.

"Was formed before I knew he was First Son."

"And once you knew?"

Cassandra raised an eyebrow to the King. "It changed nothing, if anything it reinforced it. I would think all the traits I described would be necessary for being First Son and eventual King."

While the King said nothing, the look he gave William was full of humor, before he leaned back so the last course could be presented.

What was placed in front of Cassandra could only be described as a masterpiece. If it was what she thought it was, she was going to enjoy it, but she was not getting her hopes up. Picking up her forc she took a small piece of what appeared to be a four-layer chocolate cake, with a cream filling, chocolate frosting, and chocolate sauce. Her taste buds said that her eyes hadn't been deceived.

William watched as her eyes half-closed at her first bite of the dessert. The look in her eyes said she more than liked this course. He'd have to let Hutu know.

"Admiral Zafar?" Madame Terwilliger set her forc aside, wanting information more than dessert.

"Madame Terwilliger," the Admiral watched her carefully, she'd been married to an Assemblyman for nearly fifty cycles. She wasn't as harmless as she looked.

"During the gathering today it was suggested that Earth was destroyed to keep Princess Cassandra from challenging Queen Yakira."

"Yes."

The High Admiral's eyes widened. He hadn't been informed this had been discussed at the gatherings.

"And that you have proof of this."

"Yes.

"Can you explain further what that means?"

"Admiral Zafar, you will not answer," Valerian ordered. As the two men's eyes clashed, Cassandra put down her own forc.

"It means someone on Carina is working with the Regulians and has been for nearly eight cycles," Cassandra replied to Madame Terwilliger.

"I said you will not answer!" Valerian's eyes stabbed into Cassandra's.

"You have no authority over what I can and cannot say, High Admiral," Cassandra's eyes were as frosty as her tone.

"You know nothing," the High Admiral lied.

"I know that for the last eight cycles, a traitor has gone undetected under your command. I know that this traitor has been sending and receiving transmissions, in Regulian, on Carinian channels. I also know that if it hadn't been for Admiral Zafar and his crew, you still wouldn't know anything about it." Cassandra was unaware of the power her voice carried, the power of a Queen.

William watched her as she tore the High Admiral apart. Her conviction was absolute, her power undeniable. His Queen was a sight to see when she was righting what she saw as a wrong.

Jotham could also see it. He saw a beautiful young woman who will make a remarkable Queen if she's given a chance. He saw his friend's pride in his life mate. He saw her total commitment to him, something he hadn't believed, in her subtle and not so subtle defense of him. He wondered if they knew what they were up against.

The sound of the High Admiral's chair being shoved back had the Admiral tensing, turning to protect Cassandra from possible attack. Seeing this, the King's eyes shot to Valerian.

"Is there a problem, High Admiral?" the King asked in a calm voice.

"Your Majesty," Valerian nodded slightly. "Forgive me, I am not feeling well. I need to retire for the night."

"I will call for the Doctor, High Admiral."

"No, Majesty, thank you, that's not necessary. I believe I have just over-indulged in tonight's delicious meal. I will be fine by morning."

"If you're sure, High Admiral."

"I am."

"Then I will have Captain Deffand escort you to your transport to assure you reach it without interruption," Jotham spoke briefly to a servant.

"Thank you, Majesty," Valerian said through clenched teeth. As the High Admiral left the table, Deffand waited in the doorway.

With the exit of the High Admiral, conversation resumed at the table. When Cassandra picked up her forc, she found her stomach wanting to revolt. Carefully she reached for her water hoping it would settle her.

William sensed the change. Watching closely he saw the slight tremor of her hand as she reached for the goblet. It was 2200, she'd been observed, assessed, attacked and criticized for nearly eleven hours and she'd held, but she was starting to tire. Looking to Jotham, William saw his friend had also noticed. Jotham remembered when his Queen had been pushed too far.

Standing, King Jotham addressed the table. "I want to thank you all for coming tonight. I would like to personally thank Princess Cassandra for her open and candid remarks on some serious issues. I believe her life experiences have given her a unique opinion and outlook not only on Carinian life but life in general." Cassandra returned the slight bow he gave her. "You will be escorted back to the Guest Wing." Turning back to the others, "I look forward to seeing you all tomorrow night at the Royal Ball in the Public Wing." With the King's dismissal, everyone stood up.

"Princess Cassandra, if you'd join me? Dadrian." Looking at William, Cassandra joined the King discovering he was forming some sort of receiving line.

Standing between the King and Dadrian, Cassandra thanked the Assemblymen and their spouses for attending tonight's dinner. With each couple, Dadrian moved closer to Cassandra. Not quite touching but invading her space.

"Is there a problem, Prince Dadrian?" Cassandra turned her head to find him within inches of her.

"No, Princess Cassandra," Dadrian had been watching the Admiral as he moved in on Cassandra. He could tell he was displeased but could do nothing about it. Watching the Admiral, he missed the slight movement of Cassandra's heel. As it pierced his instep, he let out a girlish squeal.

"Oh I'm so sorry, Prince Dadrian, I hadn't realized you were there."

William watched Dadrian move closer to Cassandra. He could do nothing unless he wanted to cause a scene. Just as he was reaching his breaking point, Cassandra drove her heel into his instep. William found the resulting squeal very satisfying.

Kyle had been watching too. Watching his father's reaction to Dadrian and Cassandra. She had him worried, about Dadrian? Obviously his father didn't trust the woman. At Dadrian's squeal, Kyle looked back to the group.

"Dadrian, what's wrong?" Cassandra noticed the King didn't ask if he was okay.

"Nothing, Father, just a misstep."

"My apologies, Majesty, I hadn't realized Prince Dadrian was so close when I moved."

"I'm sure it was unintentional, Princess."

With the last of the Assemblymen gone, Cassandra walked over to Kyle, "Will you be at the Royal Ball tomorrow?"

"I plan to be, yes," Kyle responded to her.

"Do you have a place to stay tonight?"

"Kyle is staying in my suite," Dadrian stood beside Kyle.

"Really, I'm sure your family will be disappointed to hear that."

"I sincerely doubt that," Kyle watched his father approach.

"Your security detail is on its way, Princess," the Admiral informed her as he looked at his son.

"I don't," Cassandra waited until Kyle looked back at her before she turned to the Admiral. "I just need to thank the King," she told him. "I'm glad to finally get to meet you, Kyle. I hope that soon we'll all be able to get together in a less formal setting. Prince Dadrian." Cassandra nodded to him. Turning, she allowed William to guide her to the King.

"Princess Cassandra, it has been a pleasure sharing a meal with you," King Jotham nodded to her.

"And with you, Majesty, it was truly an interesting meal."

"Yes, it was," the King turned to his friend, "Admiral."

"Majesty."

"The High Admiral is now a threat."

"I know."

"You will take the necessary precautions."

"Yes, Majesty."

"As will I," the King turned back to Cassandra. "I look forward to dancing with you tomorrow night." Nodding he left the couple.

"Dancing?" Cassandra shot William a stricken look.

"Admiral, your detail is here," Deffand stood just inside the door.

"Thank you, Captain." Giving his youngest son one last look, William put a hand on Cassandra's back guiding her from the room.

Chapter Thirty-One

Entering the Royal Wing, the Admiral turned to Marat. "Deffand will be clearing someone to repair the runner on the step." Marat had been standing at the base of the stairs when Cassandra had tripped.

"Yes, Admiral."

Cassandra continued walking as William stopped to talk to Marat. She was tired, she knew she needed to rest, but she found herself at the garden doors.

"Cassandra?"

"Can we walk in the garden for a little bit?"

"You're tired," he tipped her face up looking into her eyes.

"I am, but I'd like to walk in the moonlight with you."

William's heart was touched, a walk in the moonlight with his life mate, how could he say no? Opening the doors, he took her hand. Stepping into the garden they paused allowing their eyes to adjust to the darkness. The air was crisp and fresh, scented with night-blooming flowers. They strolled along the path Lata created arm-in-arm. Reaching the center she looked up at the stars.

"Is this what you looked at when you were growing up?" she asked and William looked up.

"Yes. I used to lie on my back and stare at them for hours on end. Wondering what was out there? Who was out there?"

"They look so different."

"Different?"

"None of them are where they should be," she leaned back against William's chest and sighed. "Maybe they're trying to tell me something."

"You're right where you should be; in my arms, looking at the stars. I used to dream that someday I'd find this," he kissed the top of her head.

"What? To stand in the dark with a woman someone wants dead? Who's not only responsible for the death of seven billion people, but who has made your son and best friend doubt you?"

"Stop!" William turned her to face him, giving her a little shake. "To stand here with my life mate. The woman I love and who loves me. You've caused none of those things, Cassandra. You're dealing with what others have caused."

"What about Kyle?"

"It will work out. Give it time, Cassandra, we've only been here three days."

"Is that all? It seems longer." She looked up into his eyes, "Would you know… "

"What? What do you want to know?" he saw the glimmer of tears in her eyes.

"Where Earth was? Could you even see it from here?"

William's heart ached for her. Turning her around, he hugged her close to his chest. Taking her hand, he pointed her finger to a very dark spot in the Carinian sky.

"Wait for it. There. Did you see that faint sparkle?" He felt her nod. "That's your sun. It likes to tease the eye, make you think it's not there. But it is. It's still there." William felt her relax against him.

"I don't know why…all I wanted was to stroll in the garden with you. But when I looked up…it was so different. I don't know why I hadn't realized it would be."

"Why would you think of it? You've never traveled to a place where the stars changed. In your world they're constant, never changing. There are many on Carina the same way. You have to travel a considerable distance for that to happen. You have."

"In so many ways," she turned to face him.

"Yes."

"You make it bearable you know, just you." She touched his cheek. "All the differences, the changes, the challenges, I can handle them with you at my side. You're not like the Earth's sun, teasing me that you're there. You are the Carinian suns. Strong, steady, constantly pulling at my soul in ways I never knew were possible, letting me know you'll be there for me." Stretching up she kissed his lips.

"I will always be here for you," William promised as he deepened the kiss. Pulling her close, he ran his hands up her bare back molding her to him. Sliding her arms around his neck, Cassandra sank into the kiss letting his love flow over her.

William could feel her love, her trust, and commitment to him in her response. He also felt her fatigue. Easing her down he looked into her eyes. Fatigue and love gazed back at him. Kneeling before her he gripped her ankle.

"William?" She looked down confused, putting a hand on his shoulder as he lifted her foot.

Sliding her shoe off, William turned his attention to the other one. As her feet touched the cool grass, she let out a sigh of relief. Standing, William looked down. She was back to her natural height. Pulling her close she fit perfectly in his arms.

"That's better," he kissed the top of her head.

"Yes, it is."

With one arm around her, the other carrying her shoes, he led her back through the garden and up the stairs.

"We need to get Tori," she lifted her head that had been resting on his chest.

"We'll get her." Together they approached the Michelakakis' suite. Leander answered their knock.

"She's asleep in Amina's room." Leading the couple back, they found the two sleeping friends sharing a bed. Handing Cassandra her shoes, William leaned down to scoop Victoria up holding her protectively in his arms. Silently they headed back to their suite. As Cassandra pulled back the bedding, he carefully laid the sleeping child down.

"Aunt Cassie?" sleepy eyes opened.

"Right here, kiddo," she tucked the covers around her.

"You're back," Tori looked to see the Admiral.

"We are and you're in your own bed, go back to sleep."

"Okay," and with the ability of the innocent, she was back asleep. Leaving her suite, William quietly shut the door.

They entered their suite and Cassandra could feel the remaining weight from the day disappear. Here she was just Cassandra, in love with William. Looking at him over her shoulder, she gave him a soft smile. Seeing it he ran the back of his hand along her cheek.

"Go change, you need to sleep," he said softly. Nodding she headed to the closet. Inside she slipped her dress off her shoulders. Hanging it up, she took off the leggings and eadai. Sliding on the violet nightgown Kia had made, she sighed. The silky feel of the material against her bare skin was unbelievable. Adding the sapphire blue robe she walked out of the closet.

William had taken off his jacket and was talking on his portable comm when she returned. Picking it up, she returned to the closet hanging it up. Listening to Marat he watched her, his eyes enjoying the way the robe clung to her figure.

"Yes, that will be fine." Disconnecting he followed her into the closet.

"I can do that," he touched her shoulder.

"I know," she turned to him. "I wanted to. You were busy. Is everything okay?"

"Yes," William turned her, "Marat was just informing me the Wing is secure." He ran his hands up her arms. "Go to bed. I'll be there in a minute." With a gentle kiss, he moved her along.

As she left, William unbuttoned his shirt. It had been a long night. But a lot had been learned. Whether he liked it or not Dadrian was involved with the attacks on Barek. His control had slipped just long enough to convince him. Cassandra played him perfectly with her comment about the assassination attempts.

He'd also seen Dadrian's interest in Cassandra, an interest that was partly because of him, but more Cassandra's beauty. There had been incidents in Dadrian's past regarding beautiful women that had been hushed up. While Cassandra had handled him during the reception line, he'd have to make sure she was never alone with him. Pulling on his sleeping pants, he entered the bedroom only to stop short.

Cassandra was pulling back the covers, her robe lying at the foot of the bed. Thin straps held up a simple floor length gown. Her back was partially exposed while the front showed only modest cleavage. But it was the color that stopped him. Violet, deep violet. It always pulled at something basic in him seeing her in his House color.

∞ ∞ ∞ ∞ ∞

Cassandra started pulling back the covers on the bed. It had been a long day and she was tired. But she'd learned a lot. The High Admiral had been trying to discredit William by spreading half truths, some of which were addressed tonight. He was attempting to keep the knowledge that there was a traitor secret so it wouldn't reflect badly on him, at least until the traitor was caught. Then he could have the glory. That wasn't going to happen. He also had a spy in the House of Protection telling him Victoria's movements. Lucas would need to be informed and security tightened around her. Nothing was happening to her niece.

She had also learned a great deal about Dadrian. He was a cocky little shit, her pretending not to know who he was proved that. As Second Son, he felt entitled, not only to respect but to attention. He was also involved in the attacks on the Sentinel. When she'd said assassination attempts, he'd immediately thought of Tibullus. It was telling. He also didn't like William. He took particular pleasure in the High Admiral trying to discredit him. He also very much wanted to be King.

Now Kyle, she hadn't learned nearly as much as she'd wanted to about him. He didn't seem to fit with Dadrian. And while both were second sons, Kyle was quiet and reserved, thinking before he spoke. He'd known about the Succession Protection Law, surprising his father. He loved his father, he hadn't liked the way Valerian had spoken to him and while he wasn't sure he should believe the rumors, he still didn't trust or like her. He wasn't sure if she hadn't turned his family against him. William was right, she needed to give it time.

"Let it rest for a while." Turning her to him, William let his hands flow down her back, molding her to him. Looking up she saw he knew she had been replaying the night in her head.

"You know me well." She rested her hands on his chest.

"Yes, I do." Leaning down he captured her lips, letting her know he had other things for her to think about. His hands caressed her backside, the silky material sliding under his fingers.

Stretching up on her toes, she wrapped her arms around his neck. Lifting her, William laid her down. Lying on his side, William fingered the delicate purple strap of her nightgown tracing it down to the swell of her breast. The gentle caress had her nipples tightening under the thin material. Need began to rage through William; she was his, this vision in violet.

Cassandra saw his eyes start to smolder at her body's reaction to his touch. Her breath caught as he leaned over sucking her through the material. Instinctively she arched up offering him more, her fingers sinking into his hair.

Skimming a hand down the silky material he pulled her gown up, gaining access to the even softer skin underneath. Intimately he caressed her and found her wet and ready.

"William…" She couldn't hold back her moan.

Using his hair, she pulled his head up latching her mouth onto his. The kiss was deep and intimate letting him know her need. Twisting, she hooked a leg over him pulling him closer.

Releasing himself, he slowly entered her heat. Resting on his elbows, he framed her face, watching her as he filled her. Her body accepted all of him, her passion-filled eyes began to lose focus causing him to harden even more. Slowly withdrawing, he tortured them both.

"William!" Cassandra's hands slid down his sweat-slick back trying to pull him closer. She was even tighter and with his second slow thrust his arms started to tremble with restraint. As he began to withdraw again, Cassandra wrapped her legs around him.

"No!" She had to have him. Her hips surged up bringing him back home, she would have him. Now! William's control snapped at her demand. Surging into her he set a frantic pace that had them both gasping as they climaxed together.

Catching his breath, William rested his forehead against Cassandra's, his elbows keeping him from crushing her. How had he ever lived without this woman? She touched his soul, made him whole. She loved him and desired him, only him. She made him a better man. All that just by existing.

Feeling her loving touch on his back, he raised his head, looking into satisfied blue eyes. Did she know what it did to him, knowing he put that look in her eyes?

Cassandra looked up into her life mate's eyes. Here was the man she'd dreamed of all her life but never thought she'd find. He loved her, protected her, and believed in her. When he was at her side, she could face anything.

"I love you, William."

"You are my life." He gave her a hard kiss as he moved out of her arms. Turning off the lights, he returned pulling her back into his arms, "Sleep." And closing her eyes she let the beat of his heart lull her to sleep.

∞ ∞ ∞ ∞ ∞

The third sun was up before Cassandra woke. Reaching out, she found William's side of the bed cool. Sweeping her hair out of her face she opened her eyes. The room was filled with light, but no William. Sitting up she looked at the time, 0900. Sliding out of bed, she pulled on her robe and headed for Victoria's room. Finding it empty she panicked, turning she rushed straight into William's arms.

"Whoa! What's wrong?" William's arms went around her.

"Where's Victoria?" Voice shaking, her panicked eyes met his.

"She's with Amina in their suite." Understanding her fear, he pulled her close. "She's fine. We just wanted to let you sleep."

"Oh God, I'm sorry," she took a shuddering breath. "I should have realized when I slept so late…"

"Enough," he gave her a slight shake. "After Valerian's comments last night you have every reason to worry. I should have left you a note."

"She doesn't know?"

"No. I've informed Lucas, Marat, Quinn and Leander. With instructions they are not to tell anyone else. Until we find out who's working for Valerian, everyone else is under suspicion.

"Not Javiera, not Hutu," Cassandra insisted.

"No, but they aren't part of security."

"William, you can't possibly think it's one of the guards."

"I'm not ruling them out. Someone is feeding Valerian Intel." The Admiral's eyes were hard. "It has to be someone from Jotham's house." Looking in his eyes, Cassandra realized this was what made him such a good Admiral. He'd look at every angle, every possibility, whether he liked them or not. Just like Dadrian. If she wanted to keep Victoria safe she needed to think like he did.

"Okay. I may not like it but okay." Resting her head on his chest she took a moment. "So do we bring in more security?" She looked up trustingly to him.

Her trust in him was humbling. "I'm working on it. There are some people I could call that I trust if I need to."

"Okay." If William trusted them so would she. "What do I have for today?"

"Nothing until tonight."

"Really? I thought there'd be more gatherings?"

"Tonight will be the Ball. The Assemblymen from yesterday will be there along with whatever others have been able to attend on such short notice," William paused.

"What?"

"Queen Yakira will be there tonight. Along with her husband and whatever Assemblymen they bring."

Cassandra was silent, her mind working through everything. "You intentionally kept that from me," her eyes cleared as they met his.

"Yes. You had enough to focus on yesterday."

Stepping out of his arms, she walked over to a window. She didn't like what he'd done but understood it. He was right, she wouldn't have given her full attention to the Assemblymen at last night's dinner if she'd been worrying about Queen Yakira.

"Where will they stay?" Her question surprised him. He'd expected anger.

"They will return to the House of Knowledge after the Ball."

"The House of Knowledge is on the other side of Carina. How can that be possible?"

"Cassandra," he came to stand behind her as she looked out at the gardens they'd walked in the night before. "The House of Knowledge is the wealthiest of all the Houses. It has the fastest ships, traveling here will only take them a few hours."

"The wealthiest?" she turned to look at him.

William realized this was another one of the things he assumed she knew. She hadn't realized Jotham had thought she was after wealth.

"Yes. You've always known knowledge was power. On Carina, it is also wealth. Past Queens have used their knowledge to secure their wealth."

"They've profited from their knowledge? They haven't shared it?"

"Each House profits from its specialty. That's the way it is."

"You're telling me the House of Healing would not share something that would save lives? That the House of Growth would not share food?"

"No, that's different."

"How?"

"All Houses share, it's just that whoever has it first profits the most."

"Knowledge is for everyone. Health is for everyone. Everyone deserves Protection and everyone deserves to be fed." Cassandra's eyes stared pointedly into his.

"I agree, unfortunately, that's not the way it is."

"So I'm not only a conniving little bitch, I'm one who is money hungry."

"Money hungry?" he raised an eyebrow.

"I want wealth."

"That's the way it would be seen."

"So this traitor isn't only worried about losing power, he's worried about losing wealth."

"Yes. When you are declared Queen, you receive everything that goes with it. Yakira is only the trustee until the real Queen arrives."

"That's a lot to lose."

"Yes," William realized this new information bothered her. She worried about paying for her clothes when she was challenging for the wealthiest house in the Coalition. She didn't yet realize the power and wealth she would have as Queen.

Wrapping her arms around him she sighed, "You have something I can study on them?"

"It'll be ready shortly."

"Okay. William…" He felt the sudden tension in her.

"What's wrong?"

"Dancing?" His eyes widened before he started to laugh. Cassandra frowned up at him.

"You amaze me," he continued to chuckle. "With everything going on what worries you most is dancing?"

"Stop laughing at me!" she slugged him playfully in the arm. "Everyone is going to be watching, especially when I'm dancing with Jotham. I assume I can't refuse."

"Not Jotham, he's your host." William frowned. He hadn't considered her dancing with anyone other than himself and Jotham.

"William?"

"We'll work on it after second meal. You'll be fine." He gave her a quick kiss.

"Okay, I'll go shower and get dressed."

"And eat."

"And eat." She turned mischievous eyes to him. "Unless you'd like to join me in the shower."

Pulling her close he let her know just how much he'd like to join her when his portable comm rang. Sighing he pulled it out of his jacket.

"Zafar."

"Admiral, I have the new plans ready for you."

"I'll be down shortly."

"Time to be Admiral," Cassandra kissed him lightly. "Are you going to be bringing or sending the data?"

"I'll send it. I'm not sure how long I'll be."

"Okay. I want to spend some time with Victoria today."

"That shouldn't be a problem."

"Second meal?"

"I'll be here." Giving him one last kiss, she turned and headed back to their bedroom.

∞ ∞ ∞ ∞ ∞

Going over to the bureau, Cassandra opened her eadai drawer thinking about what William had told her.

The wealthiest of all Houses, wasn't that just perfect. Like they weren't contending with enough. Power AND wealth. Someone wanted to keep it, was willing to kill for it, and had killed for it. Reaching into the drawer her hand touched a small box.

Looking at it, Cassandra realized she'd forgotten. Today she was going to take the test to verify she was carrying William's son. What would William's reaction be? With everything that's happening, will he welcome this child? In the bathroom, she turned on the shower. With a deep breath, she sat and took the test, then set it aside to process. Stepping into the shower, she let the warmth of the water relax her suddenly tense muscles. Taking her time, she washed first her hair then her body, her hands pausing over her still flat stomach.

A child, William's son, was there. She knew it as surely as she knew William was her life mate. As surely as she knew he would love their child, but he would worry about her. Turning off the water, she wrapped a towel around her head then one around her body. Walking over to the counter she picked up the test.

Positive.

With suddenly weak knees, Cassandra sat. When should she tell him? At second meal? After the ball? Will he think of Salish, of her lies?

"Aunt Cassie?"

Cassandra looked up to see Victoria standing in the doorway. "Hi, sweetie."

"Are you okay?"

"I'm fine." Pulling on her robe, she slipped the test into a pocket. "Sorry, I slept so long. Did you get first meal?"

"Yeah with Amina." Victoria looked at Cassandra's pocket saying nothing. She remembered when her mom had had one of those tests.

"Good. Why don't I get dressed and then we can go out in the garden?" Cassandra walked over and gave her niece a hug.

"Can Amina come?"

"Sure. Why don't you call over and see if she wants to go."

"Okay." Walking over to the bedroom comm she picked up the headset.

Shaking her head, Cassandra walked over to the bureau. Victoria had quickly adjusted to all the changes in their lives. How was she going to react to a baby? Choosing an outfit suitable for the garden, she quickly dressed. She towel-dried her hair and then pulled it back.

"Ready?"

"Javiera said to go ahead without them, they'd be down later."

"Oh, okay." Cassandra frowned as they walked down the hallway. "How'd you get over here?"

"I brought her over," Lucas said as they entered the formal living room.

"Oh," she stared at Lucas. How was he going to react to having another brother?

"Cassie, you okay?"

"What? Oh, yeah I'm fine, just thinking," she smiled. "We're going down to walk in the gardens, you want to come too?"

"Sure," but the look in his eyes told Cassandra he wasn't satisfied with her answer. "Have you eaten yet?"

"It's late enough I'll just wait for second meal," Cassandra told him as she walked to the door.

"Dad's not going to be happy about that," Lucas pulled out his portable comm.

"It's only a couple more hours. Let's go, Tori."

∞ ∞ ∞ ∞ ∞

Walking in the garden, Cassandra and Victoria caught up with each other's recent activities. Lucas followed a little bit behind, giving them some privacy.

"So some of the food was icky?"

"Some was, but some was excellent. The dessert was chocolate cake."

"Chocolate cake! Like Earth chocolate cake?" Victoria stopped, looking up at Cassandra, her eyes wide.

"Just like, with chocolate frosting and chocolate sauce."

"Oh…" Victoria groaned. Cassandra smiled down at her, she knew her niece was a chocoholic.

"What's wrong?" Lucas hustled up at Tori's groan.

"Nothing," Cassandra smiled.

"Nothing! How can you say it's nothing when you got chocolate cake and I didn't!"

"What?" Lucas was confused.

"Dessert at dinner last night, on Earth it's called chocolate cake. It happens to be one of Victoria's favorite foods."

"And I didn't get any."

Cassandra laughed at Tori's put out expression. "Sorry, kiddo, I couldn't sneak any out for you." As they continued walking, they reached the center of the garden. "Maybe you can sweet talk Hutu into making you some."

"You think?" The gleam in Victoria's eye told Lucas they would be making a trip to the kitchen.

"It's possible," Cassandra stared at the basket sitting on the bench. "Lucas…" she pulled Victoria behind her. Following her gaze, he quickly understood her concern.

"Its fine, I called Hutu to bring something out for you to eat."

"Oh," Cassandra released Victoria.

"Aunt Cassie?"

"Sorry, baby, it's okay. Should we go see what Hutu left us?"

"Sure," but her eyes went from one adult to the other.

The rest of the morning passed without incident. Javiera and Amina joined them. As the girls played and Lucas used his comm, Javiera turned to Cassandra. Saying nothing, Cassandra just smiled at Javiera and squeezed her hand.

∞ ∞ ∞ ∞ ∞

Entering their suite, Cassandra found Hutu just checking the plates, two plates. Looking at him she waited.

"The Admiral said you should eat, he'll be awhile yet."

"Oh," Cassandra hadn't realized how much she'd wanted to see him, to talk to him. "Well, kiddo," Cassandra looked down at Victoria, "looks like we're on our own."

"Hutu…" Victoria's voice was sugar sweet.

"Yes?" he asked suspiciously.

"Can you make a chocolate cake?"

Cassandra started to laugh.

"Chocolate cake?" Hutu gave them a confused look.

"At the King's dinner last night, the dessert course was what on Earth was chocolate cake. I don't know what it's called here. It's a favorite of Victoria's."

"You mean Fudge Torta," Hutu removed the covers from the plates, showing a slice of chocolate cake on each.

"Hutu!!!" Victoria was jumping up and down with excitement. Cassandra just looked at him questioningly.

"The Admiral noticed you enjoyed it last night."

"Thank you, Hutu."

"You're welcome. If you need anything else let me know." As Hutu left, Victoria was already seated eating her cake.

"That's supposed to be dessert, young lady."

"I know," she mumbled her mouth full, "but it's so good."

There had been little since the Earth was destroyed that had made Victoria's eyes sparkle the way they were. Cassandra couldn't bring herself to dim it.

"Just this once. Next time we have it, you have to eat everything else first. Deal?"

"Deal."

Picking up her forc, Cassandra couldn't help but take a bite of the cake herself. Closing her eyes, she let herself enjoy its taste on her tongue.

∞ ∞ ∞ ∞ ∞

After walking Victoria to Javiera's, Cassandra returned to start reading the research William had compiled on the Assemblymen from the House of Knowledge. Hours passed unnoticed as she digested the material. It was as in-depth as yesterday's, but without William's insider knowledge. Damn, she wished he were here.

Rubbing her eyes she stood, only to grip the edge of the table due to dizziness. Breathing slowly she waited for the room to right itself.

"New rule, always rise slowly," she muttered to herself.

Chapter Thirty-Two

"Anything else, Quinn?" William looked at the time, 1400; six hours until the Ball.

"Only this," he held up a memory foil. "Cassandra asked for some information on the Battle of Fayal."

"Fayal?" He wondered what she was thinking. "I'll give it to her." Taking the foil, he put it in his pocket.

"Then that's it."

"Go get some down time, Quinn, I'll see you at the door at 1945."

"Yes, Sir."

∞ ∞ ∞ ∞ ∞

Entering their suite he found Cassandra standing at a window, lost in thought. Walking over he tucked a piece of hair behind her ear, bringing her eyes to him.

"Hi."

"Hi, did you eat?"

She smiled at him. "Yes, thank you for the Fudge Torta. You made Tori's day."

"Good."

"I hadn't realized you'd noticed."

"That you all but moaned at the first bite?" he teased her.

"I did not."

"Pretty close."

"Well, it was good." Smiling at him she stepped into his arms. "Did you eat?"

"With Quinn. We were working out some changes in security for tonight."

"What changes?"

"Quinn and Marat will be attending the Ball with us."

"Why?"

"It's common for there to be extra security for the Royals."

"I didn't have 'extra' last night."

"That was a controlled area, everyone always in sight. There will be more movement tonight, people coming and going from the Ball Room and gardens." William's arms tightened around her, "You go nowhere without security."

"That will make it a little hard to dance."

"You dance with no one but Jotham or me."

Cassandra touched his cheek, "I have no problem with that. But what excuse do I give?"

"Royal's only dance with their spouses, family members and trusted members of their Houses. It won't be a problem."

"So why am I dancing with Jotham?"

"As your host, it's his choice."

She gave him a serious look. "If he has a choice then why? Won't it be perceived that he supports my Challenge?"

"It will. You've impressed him. I never doubted it."

"William?"

"Jotham knows what he's doing." He gave her a quick kiss. "Now for your dance lesson."

"Oh God, I'm a lousy dancer."

"Nice to know there's something you're not good at." Stepping away he put a foil in the comm. "Quinn gave me this for you." Pulling out the second foil he put in on the table. "Why are you interested in the Battle of Fayal?"

"It's not so much the battle as the Regulian ship. Something's there, I just don't know what."

As the music started, he pulled her into his arms. While it was different from Earth music, it still had a rhythm; it was almost classical.

"This is what will be playing tonight?" Cassandra put her arms around his neck as he brought her closer rubbing his hands up her back.

"Or something similar, it will be very formal music."

"And this is formal dancing?" she stroked his neck.

"No, this is me wanting to hold you dancing." He leaned down as he captured her lips. He needed to hold her, just for a while. Running through all the possibilities with Quinn and Marat brought home just how vulnerable she was going to be tonight. Even with extra security. Here in his arms she was safe.

Giggles had him lifting his head to find Victoria and Lucas in the doorway. Victoria smiling, Lucas looking faintly embarrassed.

"Hi, Admiral, whatcha doing?" Victoria plopped down on the couch.

"Teaching your aunt how to dance," William heard Lucas' snicker.

"Good luck," Tori giggled again.

"Hey! I'm not that bad," Cassandra complained.

"Yes, you are."

"Then we'd better get serious here," he smiled at Cassandra as he moved her arm's distance away. "One hand here," he put one on his shoulder, "the other in my hand. My hand goes right here," he put it on her waist. "Now follow me."

Watching his feet, Cassandra followed, frowning in concentration.

"There's no frowning while dancing," William tipped her chin up, "look at me." With the hand at her waist, he guided her around the room, moving around furniture to circle back.

"It's a waltz!" Cassandra suddenly realized.

"It's called a valsa," William corrected her.

"Valsa," she committed it to memory.

"I think you were teasing me, Tori. Your aunt dances just fine."

"Well yeah, this kind of dancing, but she looks silly when she dances for real."

"I'd say it was the partner," Cassandra smiled at him. As the music stopped, he leaned down for a kiss. "This is just with me too," he said against her lips.

"Good to know," her eyes smiled at him.

"Now me, Admiral," Victoria jumped up off the couch.

"You?" They both looked down at her. "I thought this wasn't real dancing."

"I'll have to learn it sometime, won't I?"

"Yes. Yes, you will, so…" William looked at Cassandra a little at a loss as how to start.

"Have her stand on your feet." Cassandra backed away, enjoying watching them.

"So, Cassie, shall we?" Lucas held out his hand. Sliding hers into his, he waltzed her around the room. While Lucas wasn't as smooth as his father, he was good.

"So who taught you to dance?" Cassandra asked.

"Mom, she really liked to dance. When Dad was away, Kyle and I filled in." Lucas looked at her suddenly worried he'd said too much. But Cassandra's eyes remained clear.

"She did a good job. It's a good memory."

"Yeah it is."

"My turn to dance with Lucas," Victoria demanded.

Lucas stepped back from Cassandra, gave her a slight bow then turned to Tori. Smiling, Cassandra walked into William's arms.

"I told Hutu to send up third meal at 1730. That'll give you time to eat before you need to change."

"Will there be any Fudge Torta?" Cassandra couldn't stop herself from asking.

"I'll see what he can do." He smiled at her. "You need to rest until then."

"I will but first I…" She was interrupted by his portable comm.

"Zafar."

"Admiral, I have King Jotham on the comm for you."

"I'll be right down." Gently he touched Cassandra's cheek. "Lucas, you're with me." Together the two Zafar men left.

"Well, Victoria, what do you want to do?"

"Can I go to Amina's? I want to tell her I learned to valsa."

"I'll walk you over," and she held out her hand.

Returning to an empty suite Cassandra paused. She didn't feel like resting, not without William. She hadn't told him about their child. Hoping he would be back soon, she went to the comm and put in Quinn's memory foil.

∞ ∞ ∞ ∞ ∞

"Princess?"

Cassandra looked up to find Hutu had entered the suite.

"Hutu? What is it?"

"I've brought up third meal."

"What?" She looked at the clock, the time had slipped away from her. Looking back to Hutu she saw he was carrying only one plate. "The Admiral's been detained?"

"Yes, Princess. He said to eat without him."

"Of course." She'd arranged for Victoria to eat with the Michelakakis' so she and William could talk. Trying to hide her disappointment, she smiled at Hutu. "Is there any Fudge Torta left?" Hutu lifted the cover to show her the slice of cake.

"Thank you, Hutu. Is there enough for the Michelakakis'?"

"Yes, Princess."

"Would you make sure they get some with third meal?"

"Yes, Princess."

"Thank you, Hutu." As he left, she walked over to look at the meal Hutu had prepared. It smelled and looked delicious. Sitting down Cassandra found she had no appetite. She wanted to share this meal with William, to tell him he was going to be a father again. Knowing she needed to eat, not just for her but for the baby she picked up the forc. After several bites, her stomach began to revolt. Taking slow deep breaths, she tried to calm her stomach.

"No, that's not going to work," and on a dead run she hit the bathroom. After several minutes, she was able to stand. Looking in the mirror she saw she was still slightly green.

"Crap." Still shaky she took a sip of water, waiting to see what happened. When it didn't immediately come back up, she forced herself to move. Walking through the bedroom her stomach started to settle until the smell of food hit her. Quickly crossing the room, she covered the plate and carried it to the formal living area.

"No more of that." Returning to the private area she looked at the clock, 1815. She needed to start getting ready, especially if she had to move slowly.

∞ ∞ ∞ ∞ ∞

William checked the time, 1845. He needed to get upstairs and change.

"You understand the changes Jotham made?" He looked at Lucas.

"Yes, I'll handle it. You need to go."

Giving Lucas one last look he headed upstairs. In the bedroom, he found Cassandra in a black robe brushing damp hair. Seeing him she gave him a gentle smile.

"Hi," he leaned down as he kissed her.

"Hi, yourself."

"I need to get cleaned up."

"It's all yours." After another quick kiss, he headed for the shower.

"Cassandra?" Turning to the sound of Javiera's voice, Cassandra walked out to the private area.

"Javiera, what's wrong?"

"It's Victoria."

"What? What's happened?"

"I don't know. One minute we're all talking and the next she wanted to come home. She's near tears. She's in her room." Javiera gestured toward her suite.

"Okay, I'll handle it."

"Cassandra, you need to be gone in less than an hour." But Javiera was talking to an empty room.

"Tori?" She found the bed empty and quickly scanned the room. Victoria was sitting in the window seat, hugging her knees to her chest.

"Tori? What's wrong?" Cassandra sat across from her. Sad green eyes looked at her.

"Tell me. Maybe I can make it better."

"You can't," her sad voice told her.

"Tell me anyway," she took her hands in hers.

"Do you know what today is?"

"Today?"

"Yeah, on Earth, do you know what today is?"

Mind racing, Cassandra thought. It had been fifty-one days since the Earth was destroyed. That had been early March.

"It's Mother's Day," Victoria whispered. "I only remembered because Amina was talking about all the different holidays they have here on Carina. How could I forget about Mom?" Huge tears ran silently down her cheeks.

"Oh, sweetie," Cassandra tugged her into her arms. "I'm sorry…I didn't think…" She was at a loss. She hadn't celebrated Mother's Day since her own had died. It always made her sad, thinking about what she no longer had. But for Victoria it was different.

"They were going to tell me the big secret today," Victoria burrowed into Cassandra.

"Big secret?" Cassandra's stomach sunk, could Victoria have known?

"Yeah, I was going to have a baby brother."

Cassandra closed her eyes pulling the trembling little body closer to her. "I know," tears seeped out as she bowed her head to Victoria's.

∞ ∞ ∞ ∞ ∞

William was surprised to walk into an empty bedroom. He hadn't been that long, Cassandra shouldn't be ready yet. Walking into the closet he put on pants and a shirt before realizing the dress bag hanging open still had the dress in it. Something was wrong.

In the private living quarters he found Javiera.

"Where's Cassandra?"

"In Victoria's room," she pointed to the partially closed door and William's stomach clenched.

Entering the room, he found them wrapped together in the window seat. Walking over he heard Victoria say something about a big secret. But what she said next froze him in his tracks.

"I was going to have a baby brother."

"I know." William saw the tears running down Cassandra's cheeks as she comforted her niece for the brother she'd never know.

It was easy to forget all these two had lost. They stood so well, adapted to all the changes. They made it easy on everyone else to not think about what they no longer had. Closing the distance between them, he knelt down wrapping his arms around them both, pulling them close. Cassandra looked at him with sad eyes.

"Snuck up on you?"

"Yeah, both of us, you heard?"

"Yeah."

Watery green eyes turned to him. "Hi, Admiral." The voice had none of the life in it from earlier in the day.

"Hi, Tori, tough one huh?" She only nodded. "I'm sorry."

"It's not your fault. Did you know I was supposed to have a baby brother?"

"No, I didn't," William let her talk.

"It was a secret. Mommy and Daddy were going to tell me today. It's Mother's Day on Earth. I wasn't supposed to know, but I accidentally heard them talking."

"Accidentally?" Cassandra questioned with a slight smile.

"It wasn't my fault they didn't know I wasn't in bed," Victoria's voice lost some sadness.

"Of course not, they should have realized you were up."

"Yeah." She was quiet for a moment. "Anyway, Mom told Dad it was a boy and that I would be a great big sister."

"You would have been," William told her.

"I would have liked that." The three were silent. "Aunt Cassie?"

"Yeah?"

"Aren't you supposed to be somewhere?"

"It can wait." Cassandra looked at William and saw he was in agreement.

"But you'll be late."

"So?"

"So you hate to be late," shocked green eyes looked into hers.

"Some things are more important than being on time."

"Like me?"

"Like you. I love you, Victoria Lynn."

"I love you too." Green eyes turned to William. "I love you too, Admiral." Tori wrapped her arms around his neck.

"I love you, Victoria." William hugged her tightly.

"Aunt Cassie?"

"Yeah?" She had to swallow the lump in her throat.

"I left my Fudge Torta over at Amina's."

"Oh really?" she raised an eyebrow.

"Yeah. Do you think I could go back over and eat it?"

"Oh, I don't know. Maybe we should just throw it away."

"NO!!! Admiral, don't let her!" Things were back to normal.

"I think your aunt's teasing you." William realized it too.

"So can I go back?" her eyes pleaded.

"Let's go." William stood up and helped them both stand. Walking out of the bedroom, they found Javiera waiting.

"Victoria's hoping to go back with you and eat her dessert," Cassandra told Javiera.

"Then we'd better hurry before Leander gets to it. He has a terrible sweet tooth," Javiera looked at Cassandra then took Victoria's hand.

∞ ∞ ∞ ∞ ∞

"What time is it?" Cassandra asked as she hustled back to the bedroom.

"1930," William informed her.

"Shit! How bad is it going to be showing up late?"

"It couldn't be helped. I'll contact Jotham, let him know. After that, it's his call." He watched as Cassandra shed her robe on the way to the closet. She was wearing black eadai with black leggings.

"His call?" She hadn't noticed William's distraction.

"On whether to start without you or wait," he followed her into the closet.

"Start what?"

"The Ball. You and he will have the first dance."

"What?" she turned into his arms.

"First Dance, you, Jotham."

"Oh, crap!"

"It'll be fine." Pulling out his portable comm he contacted the King.

"Jotham."

"We're going to be late," William told his friend and King.

"Excuse me?"

"There was a situation here that had to be resolved. We should be there by 2030." William ran his fingers over Cassandra's collar bone.

"I hope it was important."

"It was." William disconnected as his mouth swooped down to capture hers.

"William," she gasped as he let her up for air. "We have to get ready."

"We will, in a minute." Lifting her, her legs wrapped around him. Trusting him to support her, Cassandra's hands released him taking him in. Pressing her against the wall, William drove into her.

"Yes!" Cassandra exclaimed as he filled her. Already trembling she pulled his mouth to hers, losing herself in his taste. Moments later the world exploded.

Holding her close, William rested his forehead against hers. She was his world. Holding her in his arms he held everything.

"William," raising his head he looked into beautiful sapphire blue eyes. Eyes full of love for him, "We're going to be late…er." Those eyes smiled into his.

"Yes we are," reluctantly he released her.

∞ ∞ ∞ ∞ ∞

"Dad?" William was putting on his jacket when he heard his son's voice.

"I'll take care of it."

"You're late. You told Marat 1945, its 2000."

"There was a problem with Victoria."

"Victoria! Why wasn't I told?" Lucas turned to leave.

"Wait!" The authority in his father's voice stopped him. "It wasn't something you could help with. It involved her mom and dad."

"Oh."

"Lucas, Victoria's mom was going to have a baby, a baby boy."

"Oh, shit."

"She just needed her aunt."

"Okay," he looked at his father. "How's she doing?"

"Bouncing back, she's a tough little girl." Both turned as Cassandra entered the room.

Tonight she was in black from neck to toe. The material clung to her curves until just below the top of her thighs then it separated into panels that teased the eye. Making you think you would see a bare leg. Instead you got black leggings. Her forearms were wrapped in the same material with strings of colored crystals connected to shoulder cuffs providing sparkle to the satiny material. Her hair was left down, just grazing those shoulders.

Cassandra looked at William. He was in a different uniform, the pants deep violet with a black stripe down the leg. His jacket, snowy white, making all his decorations stand out and sparkle. He was a handsome sight.

"Crap, Cassandra, you're going to put Yakira to shame." It was the first time Lucas had seen her in her 'Royal' clothes.

"What?" She turned her gaze away from William.

"He thinks you look beautiful." William gave his son a hard look.

"That's exactly what I meant."

"We need to go." William held out his arm and she slipped her hand into it.

"Victoria," Cassandra looked at Lucas.

"Dad filled me in, I'll head straight over. It'll be fine."

"She'll want to go to bed early. It's her way, her bed."

"I'll keep her safe."

"Cassandra," William waited.

"Okay, let's go."

∞ ∞ ∞ ∞ ∞

The arrival of the Challenger didn't go unnoticed. Her escorts were all dressed in the formal white Coalition jackets, the pants indicating their House. The violet color a perfect foil for the black of the Challenger's dress, the crystal sleeves sparkling.

As Cassandra and the Admiral moved into the room, Marat and Tar stayed a step behind, eyes scanning the crowd. A servant approached offering a tray of drinks in crystal glasses.

Taking a small sip, Cassandra found it similar to champagne as her eyes scanned the gathering. Many faces were familiar from yesterday's meetings, she nodded to several. Others she recognized from studying the comm today.

It appeared the House of Knowledge brought their entire Assembly. Across the room, her eyes met Queen Yakira's. She was tall, easily 6'8" without the extra foot her coil of black hair added. Her dress was brilliant sapphire, multi-layered, each billowing out further than the last. In her hair, around her neck, and on her arms was what on Earth would have been called bling, lots of bling. The entire effect reminded Cassandra of a giant sparkling ball. Giving her a slight nod, Cassandra turned her attention to the man standing beside Yakira.

Prince Audric, Yakira's husband. He was shorter than the Queen, dressed in the white uniform of the Coalition, his pants the blue of the House of Knowledge. Across his chest were medals Cassandra knew to be honorary, granted to him by the Queen. He'd only served the minimum time required by Carinian Law. Audric had no Royal ties, carried no birthmark. The marriage between him and Yakira had been arranged by her parents after the death of her intended in an accident on Messene. While his expression was neutral, she could feel the anger in his stare. He was not happy with this Challenge. Keeping eye contact, Cassandra acted like she was taking a sip from her glass. Audric's eyes narrowed.

The music changed as King Jotham entered the room. Everyone turned at the entrance of their host. He too was wearing Coalition white and Cassandra knew the medals on his chest were earned. He looked distinguished and not at all concerned about arriving thirty minutes late. Two of Deffand's men were a step behind the King. A servant offered him a glass. Picking it up, he proceeded into the room.

"I was kind of hoping he would have already started the Ball," Cassandra said quietly to William.

"I believe he was looking forward to dancing with you," William replied. "You'll be fine." The Admiral raised his head as the Terwilligers approached.

"Admiral Zafar, Princess Cassandra," Evander greeted them.

"Assemblyman Terwilliger, Madame Terwilliger," Cassandra acknowledged them.

"Interesting evening last night," Evander fished.

"Quite interesting," her tone let William know she knew what Terwilliger was doing.

"That is another gorgeous gown. Juruas' again?"

"Yes."

"Assemblyman Terwilliger, Madame Terwilliger," King Jotham nodded to the group.

"Majesty."

"Princess Cassandra, would you honor me with the first dance?" The King held out his hand.

While William knew she was nervous, none of it showed as Cassandra placed her hand in the King's, a relaxed smile on her face.

"The honor is mine, Majesty." All eyes watched as Jotham led her to the dance floor. As the music started, the King guided her around the room.

"You valsa quite well, Princess," Jotham made small talk.

"It is similar to a dance called the waltz on Earth, Majesty." She wasn't yet sure she trusted Jotham's change of heart.

"You danced it often there?"

"No, only on formal occasions, mostly weddings."

"Weddings?"

"I believe you call them Unions here."

"Ah, I see. You attended many?"

"No, the last was my brother's. Eleven years…cycles ago," she corrected herself.

"You are adapting quickly to our world, learning the similarities and differences."

"There really wasn't any choice in the matter…Majesty," Cassandra remembered at the last minute to tack on his title.

"No, I guess there wasn't. How is your niece, Victoria, handling it all?"

Cassandra's eyes sharpened on his, trying to decide if he was just making polite conversation or if he really cared. William trusted him, she trusted William. "She has her moments. Tonight was especially hard for her. I feel I need to apologize to you for our lateness," she continued to look him in the eye.

"William said there was a situation. He didn't say it involved Victoria," Jotham frowned slightly. Cassandra knew what he'd thought.

"He knows I'm very protective of her. I'm what you would call her Second Mother. I take her well-being very seriously. She took priority over being on time."

While her expression never changed, Jotham could see her honest commitment and love for the child in her eyes and tone.

"A child should always be a priority," he told her.

"On that, Majesty, we are in total agreement."

When the music ended Jotham stepped back giving her a slight bow before leading her back to his friend.

∞ ∞ ∞ ∞ ∞

Audric watched King Jotham dance with the Earth woman, his rage simmering. How dare he support her! Does he know who he's dealing with? Just because he's a real Royal he thinks he can do whatever he pleases. He will pay for this slight once this Challenge is over.

∞ ∞ ∞ ∞ ∞

Dadrian's eyes followed Cassandra as she danced with his father. While she was a little thing, she had all the right curves. He wondered if she was small everywhere, the thought causing him to shift his stance. He'd have to find out soon.

∞ ∞ ∞ ∞ ∞

"Thank you for the dance, Majesty," Cassandra gave him a slight bow as he returned her to William.

"My pleasure. Admiral." Nodding to William, the King walked away making his way across the room to Queen Yakira. Time to do his Royal duty.

"That wasn't so bad was it?" William leaned down as he handed her a fresh goblet of wine. He had watched them dance, his friend and life mate. She never faltered. She confidently allowed Jotham to guide her around the room, all the while carrying on a conversation. He never doubted her ability, his eyes telling her just that.

"You're a better dancer," Cassandra raised the glass to her lips but didn't drink, her eyes saying she wished she'd been dancing with him. His eyes flashed as he straightened.

As the music started again, the Terwilligers moved to the dance floor, other couples following. Mingling, William subtly led her to those she needed to either speak to or meet. He had a few contacts within the House of Knowledge, most from his Academy days. He started with them.

"Assemblyman Bevington, may I present Princess Cassandra Qwes Chamberlain. Princess Cassandra, Assemblyman Nestor Bevington."

"Assemblyman Bevington, a pleasure," she nodded to the man she knew was an old friend of William's. They'd gone to the Academy together. He'd been at the Battle of Fayal. He'd left the service when his wife became ill.

"Princess, may I present my daughter, Kira," Bevington touched the elbow of the young woman next to him. Cassandra knew her to be at the head of her class in what on Carina was a university. She was twenty.

"This is Kira?" The Admiral allowed the shock to show in his voice. "Last I saw you, you were this tall," he put a hand on his waist.

Kira gave him an open smile. "That was nearly seven cycles ago, Admiral. I've grown up."

"Yes, you have."

"Kira is in her final year at Montreux." The pride in Nestor's voice was unmistakable. Cassandra knew Montreux was the top university on Carina, very exclusive.

"What are you studying?" she asked knowing the answer.

"I'm specializing in Ancient Carinian, Princess." While she spoke confidently, nerves were in her voice.

"Really, I've also found it very interesting. The Admiral's son, Kyle, specializes in it. Have you met?"

"No, Princess." There was interest in the younger woman's eyes.

"We should make sure you're introduced." Cassandra looked up at the Admiral.

"That can be arranged," he agreed.

Bevington watched the interaction between the Admiral and Princess. Rumors had been flying about the two of them; her unfounded claim to the throne, the Admiral's loss of nerve, her manipulation of the Admiral, the Admiral's total captivation of the woman. He had known the Admiral longer then Queen Yakira had sat on the throne, he'd withhold judgment.

"There has been a great deal of speculation at your arrival, Princess," Bevington went to the heart of the matter. Looking at him with cool eyes, Cassandra found she liked that.

"How so?"

"You have taken refuge in the House of Protection while challenging the House of Knowledge."

"I've taken refuge where the Admiral felt I could be best protected. There have been several attempts by the Regulians to stop my Challenge to Queen Yakira. Innocent lives have been lost. The Admiral thought it best not to give the assassin any more opportunities. I trust the Admiral's judgment."

"The Regulians!?!" Bevington's eyes shot to his friend.

"They attacked the Princess's homeworld and destroyed it in an attempt to stop her return. They killed all but one member of her family." The Admiral met Bevington's startled look. "They continued to attack the Fleet trying to stop the Challenge."

"That makes no sense, Will…Admiral. The Regulians have never shown an interest in the Houses."

"Someone has given them cause."

Bevington sucked in a quick breath. His eyes shot to Cassandra instantly understanding what the Admiral was implying. "And you felt the House of Knowledge wouldn't be safe?"

"No," the Admiral's implication was clear.

Bevington knew exactly who benefited from Queen Yakira staying on the throne. Looking at the Admiral, he understood that he did too.

"Admiral Zafar." A guard dressed in House of Knowledge colors addressed the Admiral. Turning, he gave him a cold look.

"Captain."

"Prince Audric requests your presence."

"Really?" Raising his eyebrow, he expressed his opinion of Prince Audric's request.

"Assemblyman Bevington, Kira, would you excuse us?" Cassandra paused, looking at the Captain from the House of Knowledge. "The Admiral owes me a valsa." Turning, she looked up to him. Taking her hand, William led her to the floor, leaving the Captain gasping.

"That was very smooth," William held her closer than King Jotham had, moving her around the floor. It was immediately apparent they knew each other well.

"I'll be damned if I'll be summoned," she politely smiled up at him.

"Totally agree," William's face was set.

"I liked Bevington." Cassandra enjoyed the freedom dancing was giving her to talk to him.

"He's a good man." His fingers squeezed her waist.

"You trust him." Her fingertips grazed his neck.

"Yes."

"Good to know." When the music stopped, they approached Queen Yakira.

∞ ∞ ∞ ∞ ∞

Yakira watched the Admiral and small woman move around the floor. They looked as if they'd danced together for cycles. While their expressions never changed they were obviously carrying on a conversation. She knew Audric was fuming at what he saw as a slight. What she saw was a confident couple who refused to be summoned.

When the music ended they approached. A guard stepped up to stop them. Audric had given them orders to search the Challenger. The Admiral stepped in front of Cassandra as the guard's hands moved toward her.

"I wouldn't if I were you," the Admiral's voice was low but deadly. Marat and Tar enclosed Cassandra.

The guard looked to Audric.

"It's fine, Captain," Queen Yakira told him. Nodding to her, he stepped away.

"Queen Yakira, I present to you Cassandra Qwes Chamberlain, Challenger to the House of Knowledge. Princess Cassandra, Queen Yakira, Trustee of the House of Knowledge, appointed by the Assembly."

"Queen Yakira, a pleasure to finally meet you," Cassandra gave her a slight bow.

"Princess Cassandra, I would like to know why I had to travel to the House of Protection to meet the Challenger to my throne," Yakira went straight to it.

'Fine,' Cassandra thought, 'let's get straight to it.' "You didn't have to do anything, Majesty. You could have waited for the full Assembly. You chose to come here."

Audric sucked in his breath. "The Challenger must come to the House of Knowledge," Audric's tone was acid.

"Exactly where is that written?" Cassandra fired back. Silence greeted her.

"It's the way it is done. If you had any knowledge…" Cassandra cut Audric off.

"It is the way it's been done since Nacars have tended the throne because there hasn't been a non-Nacar Challenge for two hundred cycles." She put just a touch of haughtiness in her tone. "Prior to that, the Challenger always stayed outside the House of Knowledge, ensuring her protection. It seems some would do just about anything to maintain control over the House of Knowledge."

"You believe you would be threatened if you were in the House of Knowledge?" the Queen raised an eyebrow.

"I see no reason to risk it. Not when attempts have already been made. Innocent lives lost because of it. Admiral Zafar feels I am best protected within his House. I trust the Admiral's judgment, implicitly." Cassandra's sapphire blue eyes never flinched from the Queen's light blue.

"You feel there is a valid threat," Yakira turned her attention to the Admiral.

"I know there is, Majesty."

Yakira held out her hand, "Audric, we'll valsa."

As the couple moved around the dance floor, Cassandra realized her first impression was correct, a giant bouncing ball. Finding it hard to control her smile, she drank from the glass William had placed in her hand.

"An interesting couple," Cassandra's tone was neutral as she looked to William.

"Admiral, Princess Cassandra," both turned at Kyle's voice.

"Kyle," the Admiral nodded to his son.

"Kyle," Cassandra's voice was much warmer, "You look very handsome tonight."

"Thank you, Princess."

Kyle had been watching the two since they'd entered the room. From Cassandra's confident first dance with King Jotham to her dance with his father; a dance of two people perfectly in tune with one another, to their short conversation with Queen Yakira. They showed a united front.

"Do you happen to know Assemblyman Bevington?" Cassandra looked to William as he discretely put in his earpiece.

"I believe he once served with my father," Kyle had also noticed.

"Yes. He's here tonight with his daughter. She's in her last year of study at Montreux specializing in Ancient Carinian."

"Really." She saw she'd piqued his interest. "That's interesting."

William touched her arm. "I need to step out for a moment." He leaned down whispering to her.

"Victoria?"

He saw the fear in her eyes, felt it in the sudden tension in her body. "No, she's fine." His eyes reassured her.

"All right."

"Kyle," nodding he walked out the nearest door. Cassandra watched him go before returning her attention to Kyle. She saw he'd noticed her distraction. She gave him a slight smile.

"Shall we valsa?" she held out her hand to him.

"Princess?" Marat stepped up.

"The Admiral's son and I are going to dance, Captain Marat." She allowed Kyle to lead her to the floor. There was silence for the first few turns.

"How did you know I could dance the valsa?" Kyle finally asked.

"Lucas told me, this afternoon when your father was teaching me."

"You learned it this afternoon?"

"It's similar to a dance on Earth called the waltz. Lucas said your mother taught you when your father was gone on tour. She did a good job."

Kyle missed a step at the mention of his mother. "You know nothing about her."

"I don't," Cassandra agreed with him, seeing the conflict in his eyes. "Not really. I do know you had yours longer than I had mine. My mother died when I was nine. They are hard people to lose. You never really get over it."

Kyle saw the cloud that passed through her eyes. He wondered if it was real or if she was just trying to trick him. Dadrian said she was a deceiver, she was deceiving his father, that he could prove it if he could get her alone.

"I'm not trying to take her place," she brought his attention back to her.

"You never could."

"No, mothers are irreplaceable." She thought of Victoria earlier, of how soon she herself would be a mother. As Kyle led her through a turn, the room continued to spin.

"Kyle," she whispered her fingers tightly gripping his shoulder.

Kyle glanced down sharply at her sudden change in tone, seeing her go pale.

"Could we step outside for some air? Please, I need some air." Taking her arm, he led her off the floor and into the gardens.

Chapter Thirty-Three

"Where's the Princess," the Admiral demanded returning to Tar and Marat.

"Dancing with Kyle," Tar nodded to the dance floor. As he watched, William saw Kyle leading her from the dance floor and into the gardens.

Dadrian had been watching the pair with great interest and as they headed into the garden, he made his move. Slipping out another garden door he followed them.

"Are you all right?" Kyle hated that he felt he needed to ask.

"I'll be fine." He led her to a secluded area. "I just need a minute."

"What's wrong?" Looking up at him she saw William's intensity in his eyes.

"There are just a lot of things to adjust to," she'd give him that much. William would be the first she told she'd conceived.

Kyle watched her, her color was returning. He hadn't thought about all she'd had to endure. He hadn't let himself. He'd been all consumed with protecting his father. He let himself believe the rumors, wanted to believe them. He wanted to be the one to get his father's command back. To do something no one else could for him. For once. Dadrian said he could help him.

"Kyle, is there a problem?" Dadrian approached the pair.

"The Princess just needed some air." He was surprised at Dadrian's arrival.

"Really? Are you okay, Cassandra?" Dadrian moved closer. "Kyle would you give us a few minutes? I think I can resolve this situation for you tonight."

While he understood what Dadrian was telling him, he was suddenly unsure of leaving Cassandra alone with him.

"Go, Kyle," Dadrian commanded. Cassandra watched as Kyle left her with Dadrian.

∞ ∞ ∞ ∞ ∞

Kyle got no more than a few steps into the ballroom when he was confronted by his father.

"Where is Cassandra?" While his voice was quiet, the urgency was undeniable.

"Dadrian wanted to speak to her alone." Kyle had never seen his father's eyes so hard before.

"You will take us to exactly where you left them!" The Admiral grabbed his son's arm forcing him out of the room, his heart pounding, hoping he was not too late.

∞ ∞ ∞ ∞ ∞

"What situation do you think you're going to resolve, Dadrian?" Cassandra's tone was icy as she moved out of his reach. She'd been taught better than to allow herself to be boxed in.

"Kyle thinks I'm going to help his father get his command back." He liked the way she moved. "But I'm going to help you get the throne you so desire."

"And how would you do that?" She side-stepped again.

"By making sure you have the support of the King of the House of Protection." Dadrian blocked her way to the rest of the garden.

"What would I have to do to accomplish that?"

"First, you will lose the old man. He's going down." Dadrian stepped forward believing he had her. "Then you and I will…get together."

"How would that give me the support of the King?"

"My father won't be around much longer," Dadrian was getting angry as once again she stepped out of reach. "You need to be nicer to me."

"You will never be anything but a Second Son," Cassandra felt her head start to spin. She needed to end this. "An insignificant one at that. Your father and brother outshine you the way the Carinian suns outshine the Earth's." She saw an opening to the garden path, but as she moved she faltered.

Dadrian grabbed her upper arms in a bruising grip. That this tiny woman would even think about refusing him was enraging. He'd show her what a real Carinian man was. Yanking her off her feet, he slammed her against him.

"You'll regret that."

"Get your hands off me!" she demanded trying to aim a knee at his groin.

"I'd do what she says if you want to live."

Dadrian froze at William's voice.

Ripping her arms out of his hold, her dress tearing, Cassandra moved to him. The look in William's eyes scared her more than Dadrian.

"Admiral, nice to see you. I was just having a very interesting conversation with your…what exactly are the two of you?"

When William took a step toward him, Cassandra put a hand on his chest. "I want to go. Please, William, get me out of here." Looking down at her he saw the bruises forming on her arms. His eyes flared. "Please," she whispered.

"Admiral," Deffand came up behind them. "We'll handle this. My men will lead you to your security detail so your party can return to the Royal Wing." Deffand waited, hoping he wouldn't have to stop the Admiral from striking Dadrian. No matter how much he deserved it, Deffand couldn't allow it.

It was the trembling of Cassandra's hand on his chest that changed William's focus. Looking down he saw her eyes pleading with his.

"You'll inform Jotham?" The Admiral's eyes were deadly as they met Deffand's.

"Yes, Sir."

Drawing her close, he turned and Kyle got his first look at Cassandra. She was pale, her dress torn with dark bruises already forming on her arms. He raised stricken eyes to his father's, knowing he was to blame for this. He should never have left her alone.

"Move, Kyle," the Admiral ordered coldly. Kyle turned, following Marat and Tar as Deffand's men led them across the garden.

With his hand on Cassandra's waist, William kept her close, his rage barely controlled. The thought of Dadrian's hands on her, her struggling against him, had him pulling her even closer. That his own son would put her in such danger gave him a sick feeling. If he hadn't gotten there when he had…he couldn't let himself think about what would have happened. If he did, he'd turn around and kill Dadrian.

Cassandra could feel William's rage. This was her fault. She should have never left the ballroom. She should have asked Kyle to stay. She'd underestimated Dadrian and William was paying the price.

Reaching the Palace, the guards opened an unseen door. On the other side, Marat's men stood ready. The walk to the Royal Wing was tense, the guards shooting concerned looks at Cassandra knowing something had happened. No one spoke.

Entering the Wing, William didn't slow down.

"Marat. Quinn."

"We'll double-check security, Admiral," Quinn answered the unsaid orders watching as Cassandra was taken directly to their suite.

"What the fuck happened, Kyle?" Quinn rounded on the Admiral's son.

"She got pale all of a sudden on the dance floor, wanted some air. So I took her out into the gardens. After a few minutes, she seemed okay. Dadrian was suddenly there and wanted to talk to her in private."

"And you just left her? When you already knew she wasn't feeling well?"

"It was Dadrian. How was I supposed to know?" But he had, he'd known something wasn't right, he just ignored the feeling. "She didn't stop me."

"No, she wouldn't." Quinn looked at the closed door, "She'd handle it on her own. She always does. I need to secure the Wing. If you know what's good for you, you'll get your ass upstairs and explain it to your father."

∞ ∞ ∞ ∞ ∞

As the door shut, Cassandra turned into his arms, "I'm sorry. God, I'm sorry." It was all she could say as she burrowed into his chest; William's arms wrapped around her, still feeling her tremors. She'd scared him badly.

"You were not to leave your protection!" William's voice was rough, full of rage and relief.

"I know. It's my fault," Cassandra raised dark eyes to his.

"What happened?"

Before Cassandra could answer there was a knock at the door. When Cassandra started to move out of his arms, he pulled her back. He wasn't ready to let go yet.

"They can wait." Leaning down, he captured her lips in a kiss that conveyed all his anger, fear and relief. She wrapped her arms around him, gripping his back, sinking into the kiss. They both needed this to erase Dadrian.

∞ ∞ ∞ ∞ ∞

Hearing the knocking on the outer door, Lucas entered the room to find his father and Cassandra in each other's arms. Clearing his throat, he looked at his feet. As they started to separate, he noticed her torn sleeves and the bruised arms.

"What the fuck happened?" he demanded as the knocking on the door started again.

"Get the door, Lucas." William held a still trembling Cassandra.

"Kyle." Hearing Lucas, William's head whipped around, his eyes hardening.

"You don't want to be here right now, Kyle."

Lucas was shocked at the rage in his father's voice.

"It's not his fault, William," she stepped out of his arms to walk across the room. She needed to get herself under control. "Let him in, Lucas, close the door."

"He left you unprotected!" William raged.

"Which was my fault," she fired back. She wasn't going to let this come between father and son. "I knew better. I could have said something. I thought I could handle it."

Kyle watched in amazement as Cassandra argued with his father, defending him.

"Would someone please tell me what's going on?" Lucas demanded.

"Your brother left Cassandra alone with Dadrian," William's eyes were like broken glass.

"With Dadrian…" Lucas looked again at Cassandra's torn dress. "Fuck, Kyle, what were you thinking?"

"He was thinking about getting his father's command back."

Kyle's shocked eyes looked at her.

"What the fuck are you talking about?" William found himself shouting at her.

"I'm talking about your son, trying to get your command back," Cassandra shouted back. "He was attempting to help you, William!"

"That's ridiculous! Dadrian doesn't have that kind of power, never will! And since when do I need help?"

"How can you possibly know that?" Kyle asked quietly.

"Because Dadrian told me," she fired first at Kyle, then jabbed William in the chest, "and we need all the help we can get, you big idiot!"

"Aunt Cassie?" Cassandra spun around at the sound of Victoria's voice.

"Victoria's here?"

Her eyes flew to Lucas. "In her room."

"William..." Even Kyle could hear the panic in her voice. His father was already removing his jacket, helping her slide her bruised arms into the sleeves. Pulling the lapels together, he gave her a reassuring kiss.

Kyle wasn't sure what astonished him more; that one minute they were arguing and the next working together, that never happened between his parents, or the little girl walking into the room. She was tiny, no more than five foot, dressed in what he would assume little girls slept in. Her flame red hair was messy from sleep.

"Hey, kiddo, did we wake you up?" Cassandra forced a smile onto her face and into her voice as she knelt in front of her niece.

"Yeah, you were yelling." She looked into her aunt's eyes demanding the truth. It was the one thing she'd tried to give her since the Earth was destroyed.

"Yeah, yeah I was. Sorry about that."

"Why are you wearing the Admiral's jacket?" Her little eyes missed nothing.

"The Admiral thought I should cover up. We were in the garden." While Cassandra wasn't lying to her niece, she was stretching the facts.

"Oh. Why were you arguing?"

"Who says we were?"

"Oh please..." Victoria rolled her eyes. "You used to yell like that at Daddy." Victoria looked to the Admiral. "She usually won. It used to make Daddy soooo mad." She gave Cassandra a half happy, half sad look at the memory.

"Not always," Cassandra rubbed her cheek.

"Is it because you didn't eat third meal?"

"What?!?" The Admiral's eyes narrowed as he looked at Cassandra's back.

"Why would you think that?" She tried to put an innocent look on her face.

"Because it's right over there." Victoria pointed to the table where earlier she'd put her meal.

Turning, she saw Hutu hadn't picked it up. She wasn't so sure he didn't do it on purpose.

Walking over, William took the cover off the plate discovering it full. The look he gave her let her know his displeasure.

"Busted," Lucas commented.

"Shut up, Lucas," they said in unison.

Victoria giggled. "See I told you, you were arguing."

"You're right, we were," Cassandra stood paling slightly. William immediately took a step toward her. She shook her head. "And we still have things to settle. But first, I need to get out of this dress. Want to do me a favor?"

"What?" Victoria looked at her.

"You think you can handle these three until I get back?" she nodded her head at the men.

"Three?" Victoria looked around her aunt to see Kyle.

"That's Kyle."

She walked toward him, "You're Lucas' brother, the Admiral's son."

Kyle wasn't sure what to make of her, "Yes I am."

"Lucas says you're the smart one in the family," her eyes serious.

"Does he really?" Kyle looked to his brother who gave him a careless shrug.

"Yup, he says you're a great little brother." Kyle watched her eyes go sad. "I was supposed to have a little brother."

Kyle's eyes shot from Victoria to his father. How was he supposed to handle this?

It was Lucas who stepped in. "They can also be a pain in the butt." He drew Victoria's attention to him. "When I was ten he 'borrowed' my favorite air shoes and tried to use them to cross the lake. Totally ruined them."

"I was six!" Kyle played along. "You can't still be mad about that!"

Lucas just raised an eyebrow.

"So do you think you can handle them? Keep them from arguing until I get back?"

"Aunt Cassie, all families argue. It's what they do afterward that matters." The wisdom out of the child's mouth had the three men sucking in their breaths.

"You're absolutely right, Victoria." Cassandra eyed each man. Holding out her fist, Victoria gave her a fist bump. "You're in charge." Turning she headed back to their suite.

∞ ∞ ∞ ∞ ∞

Walking into the closet, Cassandra carefully hung up William's jacket. Sitting on the bench she put her head in her hands. Oh God. He'd attacked her. He wouldn't have stopped if William hadn't gotten there. How could she have been so stupid, so arrogant, thinking she'd handle Dadrian all by herself?

She needed to get this dress off her body. Stripping down, she knew exactly what she wanted next to her skin. Going to the bureau, she pulled out the violet nightgown Kia had made her. As William's color caressed her skin she sighed. It was like having his arms around her. Pulling on the black robe she headed back out to confront the Zafar men.

∞ ∞ ∞ ∞ ∞

Watching her leave, William frowned. There was something going on, something she wasn't telling him. She was tiring too quickly. He'd promised her that in a few days it would be over.

Turning he looked at his sons, two grown men both unique in their own way. But right now he wasn't happy with Kyle. Kyle looked him in the eye, never flinching, but William could see the regret in his eyes. Kyle had never been good at covering his emotions.

"Sit down, Kyle. You too, Lucas."

"What happened to Aunt Cassie?" Victoria faced the Admiral. "Her dress was torn."

William should have realized Victoria missed nothing, she was too much like her aunt. Walking over he squatted down so they were eye-to-eye. "She tore it in the garden. She didn't want you to worry. She's okay. I promise."

She stared into his eyes for several moments then nodded. "Okay, if you promise." The Admiral nodded to her.

Kyle watched the exchange, puzzled. Looking to Lucas he saw his brother wasn't at all surprised. What is going on? His father was talking to this child as an adult. Suddenly he found he was the focus of bright green eyes.

"You were at the Ball," Victoria eyed his clothes.

"Yes."

"Did you dance?" she walked over to him.

"Yes, with your aunt."

"Really? How are your toes?"

"What?"

"Aunt Cassie is a terrible dancer. Even Grandpa Jacob said so, well not to her, he used to say she danced on his toes more than her own."

"Her valsa was fine." Kyle, while confused at the conversation couldn't help but be charmed.

"Are you going to help us catch the Glitter Man?" she demanded.

"What? Who? What's she talking about!"

"Victoria, it's time for you to get back to bed," Cassandra swept into the room just in time to hear her last comment.

She was wearing a long black robe, but it was what was underneath that had William's breath catching. Violet, House of Protection violet, even after Dadrian.

"Aunt Cassie…" and suddenly she sounded like a little girl to Kyle.

"Victoria Lynn, it's late. You need to get back to sleep."

"But I want to help. How can I help if I don't know what's going on?"

Cassandra looked at William. This was what they'd just been arguing about. "There are some things you don't need to know, Victoria." William stepped in.

"Why?" Victoria looked at the Admiral with stubborn eyes.

"Because you're nine. Some things you need to let us handle."

"But the Glitter Man…"

"When the time comes you get to help with that. I've told you that." Cassandra knelt down to her, "I promise."

"Okay. But do I have to go to bed?"

"Yes."

"Well…"

Even Kyle could see she was up to something.

"What?" Cassandra wasn't sure what was going on in her niece's mind.

"Can I have your piece of Fudge Torta?" Victoria looked longingly at the plate the Admiral left uncovered.

"That would be your third piece today." Trying to keep a serious face, Cassandra started to stand, finding William there to help her.

"Yeah, but if you're not going to eat it…"

"If you go straight to bed you can have it."

"Yes! Night, Lucas. Night, Kyle. Night, Admiral." Victoria hustled over to pick up the cake before her aunt could change her mind. "Night, Aunt Cassie."

"Night, Tori," Cassandra walked over to the hallway. "And I want your door closed! No 'accidental' hearing!" she yelled after her.

"Oh, man…" was her only reply.

Cassandra turned to face the Zafar men. They were quite a sight. All tall, broad-shouldered and handsome, but William was her Light.

"Cassie…" raising a hand she cut Lucas off.

She turned, walked over to a table and poured three glasses of Carinian Ale. Silently she handed one to each man. Hearing the door finally shut, she sat down on the couch, tucking her legs under her.

Cassandra looked to William, "Kyle needs to know, William. I know you were trying to keep him safe by keeping him out of it. But Dadrian has brought him in, he has the right to know the whole truth," she paused, "so does Lucas."

"Damn it, Cassandra, we don't even know if we're right."

"You know we are, especially after tonight. We just can't prove it, yet."

"What's going on?" Lucas leaned forward frowning. "What don't I know?"

William looked from the woman he loved and trusted to his sons. Two men he couldn't be prouder of. She was right, he'd had time to cool down, think through what she'd said. Things would have been different tonight if Kyle had known what was going on.

Sitting down next to her, William started to fill Kyle in on what had been happening over the last fifty days. The attack on Earth, the thread, the decision to return to Carina, the transmissions, and the translations.

"You learned how to speak Regulian in four days?" Kyle was stunned.

"Languages have always come easy for me."

"But Regulian…Victoria can speak it too?" He looked to the bedroom.

"Yes."

"You broke the Coalition's transmission codes? Do you know the amount of time that went into creating those?" Lucas demanded.

"Not enough. They could be better. But the good news is the Regulians will never crack them…" Cassandra's eyes widened as she looked to William. He saw what she was thinking. Could that be it? What the traitor was offering?

"If you have the transmission codes you know who the traitor is," Kyle accused.

"It doesn't work that way. I can tell you what personal code sent what transmission and what code received it. But I can't tell you whose code it is, not without hearing the transmission and even then you'd need to recognize the voice."

"High Command would know," Lucas looked to his father.

"High Command doesn't know Cassandra's broken the codes. No one does." William gave his sons a hard look telling them he wanted to keep it that way.

"You didn't recognize the voice?" Lucas looked to his father.

"It was run through a Regulian translator."

"What does all this have to do with Dadrian?" Kyle looked from Cassandra to his father. While they'd been talking, William put an arm around her pulling her close. Now he stood, walked across the room and looked out the window.

Cassandra's eyes followed him, saying nothing. This was William's call. Kyie and Lucas exchanged looks, both realizing this was something big. But what could be bigger than a traitor trying to kill Cassandra?

Turning back, she saw he had reached a decision, a hard one. One an Admiral makes.

"There are two traitors."

"What?" Both boys stood.

"Cassandra found two distinct signatures on the transmissions to the Regulians."

"Both through translators?"

"No, one only contained numbers," the Admiral watched Lucas.

"Numbers? Like coordinates? Fleet coordinates?" Cassandra could see Lucas was starting to put it together.

"What are you talking about?" Kyle demanded.

"Speed attacks against the Fleet. The first one, the Regulians were able to locate us because of the thread in Victoria's arm. But that wasn't the exact location. There were two more after, they didn't come out of warp until they were firing."

"Someone was giving them the Fleet's location to stop Cassandra?" Kyle didn't realize it was the first time he'd called her by name. William did.

"No. I thought they were. Cassandra found the transmissions giving up the Fleet's location. She was able to isolate the signature and tied it back to two other transmissions. Transmissions sent prior to the attacks." William paused. "Transmissions sent to the Sentinel."

"The Sentinel?" Lucas' mind was racing. The Sentinel was severely damaged in the first attack that the Regulians had the Fleet's coordinates. It was dead in space after the second. The Regulians had been sitting just inside the Relinquished Zone as if waiting for confirmation.

"Barek," Lucas said quietly, thinking about his friend and future King.

"Yes," William acknowledged.

"Why?" Kyle's mind was racing, trying to sort it all out.

"You know the answer to that, Kyle," Cassandra told him.

"No." He stared hard into Cassandra's eyes. He didn't want to believe it. Didn't want to think he'd had any part in it.

"It's the only logical conclusion. Whether you like it or not, you can't deny that." Her eyes while firm were sympathetic.

"You think it is Dadrian," Lucas finally said it out loud, finding he needed to sit down. William walked over, picked up the bottle of ale and refilled his sons' glasses. "Dad, I know Dadrian is a foabhor. Tonight especially proves that, but he's not smart enough for something like this. Let alone patient enough, the Glitter Man was on Earth over seven cycles ago."

"I don't believe Dadrian's been involved that long. The Regulians only started getting Fleet locations about thirty days ago. That's when Dadrian got involved."

"Got involved," Kyle looked at his father. "You're saying Dadrian somehow discovered there was a traitor, one that was responsible for the murder of everyone on Earth, and instead of reporting it decided to take advantage of it?"

"That pretty much covers it." William realized he'd underestimated his youngest son. Cassandra was right again, just because he wasn't military didn't mean he didn't understand or wasn't able to help. He owed him an apology.

"But that doesn't make him King unless..." No one said anything. "Dad, it's bad enough that he'd go after his brother, but his father?"

"He wants to be King, he thinks it's his right," Cassandra's voice was firm. "He all but admitted it tonight. He said he could make sure I had the support of the King of the House of Protection."

"He can't promise Jotham's support," William told her.

"It wasn't Jotham's support he promised," she looked at William knowing he realized what Dadrian wanted in return by the hardening of his eyes. His sons realized it too.

"You made a point of saying he wasn't on any list." Kyle looked at Cassandra, things falling into place. "At dinner, when you 'explained' military procedure to Dadrian, you said he wasn't on any list." Kyle's eyes turned to his father. "You've made sure his name stayed off. Barek is alive." William's respect for his son grew.

"He's not on any list and won't be until he's on planet."

"He knows?"

"Only that there had been assassination attempts made on Cassandra by the Regulians. That because of them, all Royals needed to be removed from combat situations to curb more attempts."

"You said you can't prove it yet," Kyle looked to Cassandra.

"The transmissions have royal coding. Until they are played, we can't prove anything."

"So Dadrian sent a transmission to Barek. Barek wouldn't give up the Fleet's location especially to Dadrian," Lucas argued.

"There were two transmissions sent to the Sentinel, each with twenty lines of coding."

"No one has twenty lines, not even Royals," Kyle interrupted.

"The twentieth line is what on Earth we called a Trojan, a program that activates when the transmission is answered. It finds the location of the receiver and transmits it back to the sender. It took two minutes. Each transmission was two minutes ten seconds. Ten minutes later there was a transmission sent to the Regulians containing only numbers."

"Barek never knew," Kyle whispered.

"No."

"Dadrian wasn't smart enough to write a 'Trojan,'" Kyle informed her.

"No," she waited. "I believe he got the program from the original traitor."

"But you have to have knowledge of the codes to do that and the only ones who do are the Coalition, High Command and…" Kyle trailed off.

"Those who write them, the House of Knowledge."

"It's back to stopping you from returning."

"Yes," Cassandra rubbed her temple. William saw her fatigue.

"Now you know what's going on, what's at stake."

"Why was Dadrian so intent on getting me involved?" Kyle asked.

"It distracted your father," Cassandra answered for him. "He wanted him concerned about you, not him, just in case."

"Fuck, he used me."

"Yes, yes he did." Cassandra stood. She needed to let these men have some time alone. William was there helping her, a concerned look in his eyes. "I think we've covered everything. I'm going to bed." She touched William's cheek. "Kyle, there's an open room in the other suite, you're welcome to it. I hope you'll stay, but it's your choice. Goodnight."

Three pairs of eyes followed her exit, each with their own concerns.

"Dad, is she okay?" Lucas drew his father's attention.

"She just needs more rest. She's had a lot to adjust to in a very short time." He hoped that's all it was.

"That's what she said earlier," Kyle told him.

"When," William demanded.

"When we were in the garden. I'm sorry, Dad," Kyle rushed on. "I shouldn't have left her, even without knowing what was going on. You taught us better than that."

William stared at his youngest son seeing the honest remorse. "Why did you go into the garden?"

"We were dancing. One minute she was fine, the next she's pale and asking if I'd take her to get some air."

"Knowing that you left her?" Lucas demanded.

"After a few minutes she was fine, and then Dadrian showed up. The rest you know," Kyle continued to look at his father, "I'm sorry."

William walked up to his youngest, looked at him then pulled him into his arms for a hug. "Cassandra's right, this isn't your fault, even though you know better." William stepped back. "There's something you need to understand, Kyle. Cassandra's my life mate. You may not like it, but it's not going to change."

"Life mate?" Kyle looked at Lucas, who nodded. "And she understands what that means?"

"She understands Regulian, you think she doesn't understand life mates? On Earth, they called it soul mates."

"And you didn't kill Dadrian?"

"She needed me to get her out of there more. Her needs took priority."

"Even over your career?" He was still having trouble with that.

"Everything I've ever done, right or wrong, has been leading me to her. I won't give her up especially not for a career. I did that with your mother." The commitment in his father's voice amazed Kyle.

"And after the Challenge?" Kyle couldn't help but ask.

"After she's Queen, we'll work it out."

"Dad…"

"Kyle, she is the Queen, never doubt it."

"Then why the Challenge?" Kyle had to believe his father.

William rubbed a hand through his hair. "Cassandra wants justice, for the people of Earth, for her family. I can't blame her."

"The Houses deal with their own 'Royal' problems unless it affects all, then it is up to the Assembly. You have to have a full Assembly like one for a Challenge," Kyle saw what she was doing.

"Yes."

"It puts her in greater danger."

"She knows that, so do I."

Kyle could tell his father had already thought of all this. "Okay. Is it all right with you if I stay?"

William closed his eyes for a moment, "Yes, of course, it's okay. Kyle, I owe you an apology. I should have contacted you as soon as we arrived."

"You've had a lot going on and it's not like I'm going to be a lot of help."

"I think you are. You knew about the Succession Protection Law and what it takes to accuse a Royal. I'm sure there will be more things you know that will help." William looked to Lucas, "You'll get him set up next door?"

"Not a problem."

"Good, then I'll see you in the morning. We'll go over our next steps concerning Dadrian."

∞ ∞ ∞ ∞ ∞

Victoria was sound asleep when Cassandra checked on her. Smiling she tucked her feet in and pulled the covers up. Leaning over she gave her a kiss. "Love you, kiddo." Back in their room, she opened a bureau drawer pulling out the test. Looking at it, she walked over to the window seat and waited.

Chapter Thirty-Four

Walking into the private area, William first checked Victoria then headed to Cassandra. Entering their suite, he found the lights dimmed and the bed empty. Scanning the room he found her in the window seat.

"Why aren't you in bed?" Sitting across from her he gently rubbed her leg.

"I was waiting for you."

"I'm here. Come on, you're tired." He moved to rise, but Cassandra's hand stopped him.

"We need to talk." She squeezed his arm, her eyes serious.

"Whatever it is it can wait until tomorrow. You've been through enough today."

"So have you, but it's waited all day, that's long enough." She handed him the test.

"What?" William was confused as he looked down, not sure what she handed him. Staring at it for several moments he suddenly froze, his eyes shot to hers, "You've conceived."

"Yes," she watched him closely, not sure what she was seeing.

Standing, he walked across the room. She'd conceived. She was carrying his child. Dadrian attacked her while she was carrying his child.

"How long have you known?"

"I took the test this morning." She didn't move from the window seat.

"That's not what I asked."

"William, I wasn't sure until this morning."

"But you suspected."

"Yes, for about ten days."

While they'd still been on the Retribution, he realized. "Why didn't you tell me?" He started to pace.

"Because I didn't know," Cassandra stressed to him.

"You knew or you won't have gotten the test!" William looked at her. "Where did you get the test?"

"Javiera got it for me."

"That's why you needed to talk to Leander, he knew."

"He found it, thought it was Javiera's. It caused…problems."

"He knew you'd conceived."

"NO! You are the first person I've told," she wasn't sure what was happening, this wasn't how she'd thought he'd react.

"You've been tiring easily, suddenly paling. You promised me you were okay!"

"I am."

"Fuck that! You got dizzy on the dance floor, that's why Kyle took you into the garden. That's why Dadrian was able to attack you! Damn it, Cassandra! You should have told me as soon as you suspected!"

"And if I was wrong?" Cassandra found she couldn't sit any longer. "If it really was just all the changes, space travel, food, stress. If that's all it was, and I'd told you, what would your first thought have been?" she demanded.

"What are you talking about?" he glared at her.

"You would have thought of Salish, and how she deceived you." Cassandra's eyes met his hard look. "I'm not Salish. I wasn't going to make a mistake." Feeling her eyes start to fill, she turned away.

William was stunned. She thought he wouldn't believe her, not without proof? That he'd compare her to Salish? She was nothing like Salish.

"Cassandra…" as he approached her, she suddenly bolted for the bathroom.

Thinking she was shutting him out, he raced after her only to find her on her knees vomiting. Kneeling down he put a tentative hand on her back.

"Cassandra…"

"Go away," she demanded in a weak voice.

"No." Standing he wet a cloth and brought it back to wipe her pale, sweaty face. It hurt his heart to see her like this. "Breathe, Cassandra."

Concentrating on her breathing, she tried to get her body back under control. There was nothing left in her stomach. With closed eyes, she slowly eased back to see how her stomach reacted. When it stayed steady, she opened them and started to stand.

"Easy," he murmured to her. Gripping her waist he helped her up.

"I'm fine." She tried to move out of his grip.

"I'm not letting go, Cassandra." William locked eyes with her. "Never."

Closing her eyes, she sighed. She hadn't realized how much she'd needed to hear that.

"Drink this." He handed her a glass of water.

"No."

"Drink." William raised the glass to her lips.

"Stop, William." She pushed his hand away. "I'm not a child."

"No, you're having one. You need to drink."

"It'll just come back up. Just let me rinse out my mouth. It will be enough for now." Taking the glass from him she did just that. With a slightly shaky hand, she put the glass down. Looking in the mirror she saw the concern in his eyes.

"I'm fine."

Saying nothing he guided her to the bed. Untying her robe he tossed it to the end of the bed.

"Get in."

"William…"

"Do it, Cassandra, or I'll put you there." Knowing he was serious and not sure how her stomach would take it, she slid into the bed.

Pulling the sheets up, much like she'd done for Victoria, he leaned down to give her a hard kiss. "I love you." Standing, he headed to the closet to change.

∞ ∞ ∞ ∞ ∞

She had conceived. It was like a drum in his head. His life mate was going to have his child. Ripping off his shirt he was about to throw it down when he saw her dress, her ripped dress, ripped by Dadrian. She'd gotten light-headed because she'd conceived. She hadn't eaten her third meal because she couldn't keep it down. She hadn't told him until she had proof because of his past. Closing his eyes, he took a deep breath. Pulling on his sleeping pants he headed back to her.

Cassandra watched him as he crossed the room, her eyes concerned. She knew he loved her, had no doubt, but something wasn't right.

William saw the concern as he darkened the room. Sliding in next to her, he propped himself up on an elbow, the other hand resting on their child. Looking into her eyes he gave her a gentle kiss. Putting a hand behind his head she held him there changing the angle, increasing the pressure. Slipping her tongue between his lips she teased his mouth open to twine around his.

Breaking off the kiss, his eyes burned into hers, his breathing ragged. She could see his desire, watched him pull it back.

"You need rest," and rolling onto his back he enclosed her in his arms.

"William…"

"Sleep, Cassandra, you need to sleep."

Suddenly she realized what he was doing. It was just like when she'd been hurt in the explosion. He was holding back, worried he'd hurt her, her and their child. That carrying his child would hurt her. Sliding over she straddled him.

"I need you," sliding the straps of her nightgown down, she let it pool at her waist, leaning down to kiss him, her breasts caressed his naked chest.

William gripped her arms meaning to lift her away, but her sharp gasp had him freezing. Looking at his hands he realized he was clutching her bruises. Immediately he released her, "Fuck, Cassandra, I'm sorry," his voice full of regret.

"Stop," she rested her hands on his chest, looking into his eyes.

"I hurt you."

"No, Dadrian did, and he would have done worse if you hadn't been there." She watched his eyes flare. "You have never hurt me, not like that. You never would," she caressed his cheek, "but it hurts me when you pull away because you're worried you might. You did it after the explosion. You're doing it now."

"Cassandra, you are my love, my life, and now you're having my child. I can't *not* protect you."

Staring into his eyes, she saw his love, his conflict. "I know, but I don't need protection from you." She lifted his hands to her breasts, "I just need you." Sliding her hands down, she released him.

"Cassandra..." he groaned as she took him in.

"I need you, William," she whispered against his lips, "I'll always need you." As she slowly rotated her hips, his hands moved to hold them still, thrusting into her to the hilt.

"Ahh..." she moaned into his mouth. She hadn't realized how much she needed this. To be close to him like this after Dadrian. Locking her mouth onto his, she sank into him to the feelings only he could arouse.

Feeling her accept all of him, demand all of him, made William realize just how much he'd needed her too. He had been pulling back to protect her, because he hadn't. Dadrian made him fear that his size, his strength, would hurt her. Her total belief and trust in him washed away the fear.

Rolling her onto her back he positioned himself above her. Gripping her hands, he watched her eyes as he increased his pace. He watched them losing focus as she tightened around him, as he drove her higher.

"Let go, Cassandra," his voice was thick with demand, "Let me watch you let go."

"William!" she cried as the orgasm ripped through her, her eyes locked with his. It shredded his control and with one final thrust he emptied himself into her.

Resting his forehead against hers, he tried to regain his breath. Lifting his head he watched her eyes, seeing her mind reengage. The love they held was undeniable, but he also saw the fatigue.

He gave her a gentle kiss as he moved to his back. Reaching for the covers he pulled them up as she settled in next to him. With his arms encircling her, they both fell asleep.

∞ ∞ ∞ ∞ ∞

First sunrise was just beginning when Cassandra felt his touch, William's hand gingerly caressing her still flat stomach. Staying still she enjoyed his touch, knowing he was thinking about their child. Should she tell him it's a boy? She had no proof, except Sabah in a dream. Turning her head, she gently kissed his chest before looking up at him. The love glowing in his eyes flowed around her.

"Morning," she said softly. He answered her by kissing her gently, his hand still on her stomach.

"You'll sleep longer," he ordered still seeing fatigue in her eyes.

"You won't let me sleep too late?"

"I'll wake you if it gets late. You don't have anything until 1300." He tucked a piece of hair behind her ear.

"Okay," she let him slide away. "I love you."

Pulling the covers back over her, he said, "I love you too. Now sleep." With one last kiss, he headed for the shower.

∞ ∞ ∞ ∞ ∞

William worked from the comm in the private quarters. He was staying close to Cassandra today. He needed to for himself. The stakes had just gone up. She'd conceived, extra precautions would be required at every level. The gatherings would need to be spread further out so she could rest and eat properly. A doctor would be necessary to make sure she was okay.

A baby…he leaned back from the comm. He was fifty cycles…to be a father again…for Cassandra to give him a child…would it be a son or daughter? A daughter would be the heir to the House of Knowledge. He let that thought settle in his mind. His daughter would one day be Queen of the House of Knowledge…as her mother will be…he'd never fully considered that. Hearing a door open, he saw Victoria walking sleepily to him. Lifting her into his lap, she burrowed in.

"What are you doing up so early?" he rubbed her back.

"I'm hungry," she said, still half asleep.

"What would you like Hutu to make?"

"Flatcakes."

He picked up the headset and connected to Hutu. "Hutu, Victoria would like flatcakes this morning," he listened, "just for two right now. I'll let you know when Cassandra is ready to eat." Taking off the headset, William looked down at Victoria.

"It'll be here in a little bit."

"Okay." Victoria looked at him now with alert eyes. "Admiral?"

"What?"

"Are you and Aunt Cassie getting married?"

William stilled. "What?"

"You and Aunt Cassie, are you getting…it's not married here it's called…"

"A Union."

"Yeah, that. So are you?" She watched him with curious eyes.

"I think that's something for your aunt and me to decide."

"That's what Aunt Cassie said too."

"Why are you asking, Victoria?" He watched her, saw she was trying to decide what to say.

"Well if you married Aunt Cassie, I wouldn't have to call you Admiral anymore." She raised hopeful eyes to him, "Everyone calls you Admiral. I could call you Uncle. I'd have Aunt Cassie and Uncle William."

He was surprised at what she wanted. She wanted to have an exclusive claim to him, to be able to call him something no one else did. Uncle. For it to be a special relationship just between them, for him to truly be part of her family, for her to be part of his. Touched, he pulled her closer.

"I would like that, Victoria, to be your Uncle William. But Cassandra and I have to decide that."

Avid green eyes looked into his, "But you'll think about it?" she raised a disarming eyebrow to him.

Oh, she's going to be a handful as she grew up. He was going to enjoy being a part of it. "Yes."

"Good. Why isn't Aunt Cassie eating with us?"

"She's going to sleep awhile longer. She had a busy day yesterday."

"You promised she was okay."

"She is. She's just going to sleep a little longer." A knock on the suite's door stopped Victoria from questioning further. "That's Hutu with first meal. Should we go let him in?"

"Yeah." Sliding off his lap she led the way.

∞ ∞ ∞ ∞ ∞

"Cassandra…" Feeling William's touch on her cheek, she rolled toward him. "Cassandra, you need to wake up."

"Don't want to."

William smiled, she sounded like Victoria. "But you need to its 0900. I promised I wouldn't let you sleep too long." He rubbed a hand down her arm.

"0900?" Heavy eyes opened to his.

"Yes, I've called Hutu, he's bringing up flatcakes for you." He gave her a hard look. "You'll eat."

"I can do that," sitting up she kissed him. "Good morning."

"Good morning." He returned the kiss. "You have time for a shower. Victoria's already eaten and is over at Amina's."

"Really? Sounds like you've had a busy morning."

"Not really. I enjoyed it." He helped her out of bed. "Go get in the shower." Steering her toward the bathroom, he kissed the back of her head.

"You're not joining me?" She gave him a playful look over her shoulder. William's eyes flared at the thought of joining her in the shower. Whipping her around, he gave her a long hard kiss.

"Later," he promised then turning he left her breathless.

∞ ∞ ∞ ∞ ∞

The shower felt wonderful. Lathering up her hair, Cassandra let the heat cascade down her. It would have to do in place of William's hands. She felt fantastic this morning. No queasiness, no light-headiness. Maybe on Carina it's evening sickness when you're pregnant. She'd have to ask Javiera.

As she finished up, she stepped out of the shower to wrap a soft towel around her and drying her hair she looked in the mirror. Her eyes were clear and bright. She looked rested and happy. She was going to have William's baby, his son. Grinning at herself she strolled off to get dressed for the day.

∞ ∞ ∞ ∞ ∞

"Thank you, Hutu." The Admiral watched as he lifted the cover to check the plate of flatcakes he'd brought up for Cassandra. "She's going to enjoy them."

"I hope so, Sir. She didn't eat last night."

"I know. She will today. She's going to start taking better care of herself." Hutu saw the Admiral's eyes harden.

"Yes, Sir."

"Also, the Fudge Torta…" the Admiral smiled. "She really likes it, so does Victoria."

"I'll make sure to have some on hand, Sir."

"Maybe just for one meal. Victoria had three pieces yesterday."

"Three…"

"Yes."

"I'll keep an eye on it, Sir.

"Thank you, Hutu." As his portable comm rang, Hutu left.

∞ ∞ ∞ ∞ ∞

Standing in the closet, Cassandra tried to decide what to wear. It needed to be something with sleeves. The bruises on her arms were even darker today. Choosing the black pant outfit with the sapphire camisole she'd worn to meet Jotham, she dressed. Deciding against the shoes and jacket just yet, she walked out to the mirror to fix her hair. Pulling it back, she heard raised voices in the outer room.

∞ ∞ ∞ ∞ ∞

"Zafar."

"Admiral, King Jotham and Barek are on their way up," Marat told him.

"What?"

"Sir, I couldn't stop them."

"Is Deffand with them?"

"They were alone, Sir."

"Contact him and make sure the King's security is allowed in."

"Yes, Sir."

Disconnecting, he headed for the suite door knowing this wasn't going to be a pleasant meeting. He was still in the hallway when he heard them.

"Zafar!" Jotham stormed down the hallway toward him. "What the fuck is going on!"

"Majesty, Barek," the Admiral nodded. "Won't you have a seat?" He gestured back to the private area.

"You will explain!" Jotham's eyes were blazing. "Explain why you lied to me! To ME!"

"I never lied to you, Majesty."

"Then you did to me," Barek's eyes were just as angry. "You told me my father was being kept informed."

"He was. He was given all the information he needed."

"He didn't know if I was dead or alive!"

Cassandra entered the room, her eyes widening as she saw Tibullus. He wasn't supposed to be here for another two days. Hearing his last comment, she quickly assessed the situation.

"But you are. Alive that is. You can thank the Admiral for that. Now!" Her eyes were hard as she stopped next to William, looking at both Barek and Jotham. She wasn't going to let them talk to him like this. Both men sucked in a breath at her tone.

"You may leave, Princess, this doesn't concern you," Jotham dismissed her, turning his attention back to his friend. In doing so, he missed the cold fury in her eyes. Barek didn't.

"I think not, Majesty, and it does concern me. When my life mate put himself on the line, called in favors, all to keep a promise he made to you, it concerns me."

"He kept my son's condition from me!" Jotham turned toward her. William tensed.

"He kept him alive!" Cassandra moved just a step. "I must have misjudged you, Majesty. I thought you cared about your son. That having him alive would be more important to you than knowing he was alive."

Jotham sucked in a sharp breath at her accusation. "You know nothing!"

"I know that nearly twenty-nine cycles ago you asked William to protect your son if you couldn't. That's what he's done, whether you like the way he did it or not!"

"Cassandra," William put a gentle hand on her back telling her she'd said enough.

"There was no reason to keep his status secret," Jotham fired back but with less heat.

"Everything you told me," Barek looked at his Second Father, "was true, to a point. The Regulians were trying to stop Cassandra from reaching Carina, but not only her."

"Correct," William answered. Cassandra watched Tibullus' mind work.

"There were assassination attempts."

"Yes."

"Not only against Cassandra."

"No, not only against her."

Jotham followed the conversation between his first born and the man he'd asked to be his second father. A sick feeling grew in his stomach.

"There were attempts made against Barek? The Regulians were trying to kill my son?" Jotham stared at William. "And you didn't tell me?" William stared at his friend saying nothing. Cassandra knew how he struggled with this.

"Majesty, Tibullus, sorry, Prince Barek, let's sit down. There's a lot you need to know," she gestured to the sitting area.

As they sat, she poured four glasses of Carinian Ale. They were all going to need it before this was done. Setting them on the table, she sat next to William.

"You believe this Glitter Man, this Carinian traitor who is trying to stop Cassandra's Challenge, is also attempting to kill my son?" Jotham asked William.

William looked at his longtime friend. How does he do this to him? How does he tell him? Cassandra gently touched his leg.

"No, no he's not."

"Then who?" Jotham demanded.

"You think there's a second traitor," Barek's mind was racing.

"Yes."

"One interested in the House of Protection."

"In who will be King, yes," William confirmed.

"If you knew this why didn't you bring Barek back with you on the Retribution?"

"Because at the time, I believed all the attacks were aimed at Cassandra. She's the one who uncovered the transmissions, discovered the attacks against Barek, against the Sentinel."

"You have transmissions?"

"The Retribution has been recording all transmissions since the first one was found from the Regulians to Carina concerning Cassandra."

"That's weeks' worth of transmissions."

"Yes."

"No one person could listen to them all," Jotham accused.

"You don't have to listen to them," Cassandra spoke up. "You just have to find similar senders and receivers." William was amazed at how simple she always made it sound.

"That's impossible. You would have had to break Coalition coding." She just raised an eyebrow to the King. "You broke the codes?"

"Depends on your definition of breaking. I understand what the codes are saying. They really weren't that difficult."

"What do you mean?" Jotham demanded. Cassandra looked to William wondering how much she should reveal. With his nod, she turned back to Jotham.

"Coalition transmission codes have basically three levels. The first is comprised of sixteen lines of coding. It's your basic transmissions; Ship-to-ship, news reports, nothing of major importance. The next is eighteen lines of coding. This is your more secure information; orders from High Command, standard Fleet locations, etc. Then there are your nineteen lines of coding, highest security. Used during battle and for the highest ranking members of the Coalition and Royal Families. At the second and third levels of security, either the sender or receiver must enter a code to open the transmission." Cassandra paused to see if Barek and Jotham were following her.

"Go on."

"I can tell you what personal code was sent to another and how many. In some cases, I can even tell you who one or the other is."

"But not all?" Barek asked.

"No. Once you hit nineteen lines, you have to have the personal code." Cassandra looked at Barek. "And then there are the twenty line transmissions." She let that hang.

"What! There's no such thing," Jotham said.

"There were two recorded by the Retribution, sent from Carina to the Sentinel, each lasting just over two minutes. Within ten minutes of each, the Regulians received a transmission that contained only numbers."

"The Fleet's location," Barek's eyes were hard.

"Yes," the Admiral confirmed.

"Who?" Barek wanted to know who was responsible for the death of his friends.

"You tell us," Cassandra spoke so William wouldn't have to.

"What do you mean?" Barek demanded.

"You received both transmissions," she stared back at him.

"Fuck that!" Barek surged out of his chair. William put himself between him and Cassandra. After last night, he was taking no chances.

"That's impossible!" Jotham agreed watching William's defensive move.

"Prove me wrong," Cassandra stood, touching William's arm. Stepping around him, she walked to the comm center. Typing in a series of commands she brought up the search results she wanted. "This is your personal transmission code, is it not?" She turned the screen so it faced Barek and Jotham.

Barek's eyes widened as he saw his code. "How did you know this was mine?"

"I compared the twenty line transmission signatures to all other signatures the Retribution had recorded. Colonel Tar contacted you to transfer to the Retribution regarding the Falco matter. The signatures matched."

"How did you listen to it?"

"It was initiated by a sixteen line transmission. No personal codes are needed to listen to it. The Admiral verified you were the receiver." She slid the keyboard over. "If you want to know who wants you dead, who is responsible for the destruction of the Talon, enter your code."

Barek looked her in the eye. She saw his rage that people died because of him. That someone wanted him dead that badly. She, of all people, understood. But she also knew for him it wasn't a stranger.

Walking over to her, Barek looked at the keyboard and entered his code. There was silence for several moments then…

"Tibullus."

"How's life on the border, big brother." She gripped Barek's arm as he paled, hearing his brother's voice. William watched Jotham, wishing they'd been wrong.

"It's going fine. What do you need, Dadrian."

"Can't I just call to see how you are?"

"Sure, you just never do."

"Look, I know we've had our differences, but you're still my brother." Silence greeted his statement. "Okay, yes I do need something. You see there's this girl."

"Fuck, Dadrian, what did you do?"

"She was a piece of work, Barek. Built. She led me on then acted all outraged when I took it to the logical conclusion." Barek looked at Cassandra's arms.

"I don't want to know this, Dadrian. I'm done bailing you out. I've told you that. You're on your own."

"Wait! How do I tell Dad? What do I say?"

"That's up to you, leave me out of it."

The transmission ended.

"No," was all Jotham said.

Cassandra looked up at Barek, knowing she had to finish. "That makes this," she pointed to the screen, "Dadrian's signature."

"That doesn't prove anything," Barek was grasping.

"This," she pointed, "is the twentieth line of coding. It's what on Earth we call a Trojan. It's a program that activates when the transmission is opened. It takes two minutes for the program to gather data on the receiver's location and transmit it back to the sender. That transmission lasted two minutes and ten seconds." Cassandra pushed on. "Ten minutes later the Regulians received a sixteen line transmission containing only numbers. This is the signature." Cassandra brought them up side by side. They were identical.

"It's a coincidence," Jotham looked at William.

"He contacted Barek again, Jotham, right before the last Regulian attack, the one that destroyed the Talon." He looked to Barek for confirmation.

"He did." Barek looked to Cassandra, "you have that one too?"

"Yes."

Barek walked over to the window staring at the garden. Picking up Barek's glass, her eyes met William's conflicted ones. Touching his leg, she gave him all the support she could then picked up her own glass and walked over to Barek.

"Your mother designed a beautiful garden." As Barek looked at her, she handed him a glass. "The girls have especially enjoyed it."

"Girls?"

"The Michelakakis' are with us. They have a daughter, Amina. She's Victoria's age."

"Why are you telling me this?" Barek's eyes were angry.

"To give you something else to think about, if only for a minute. When your world suddenly changes it's the small, insignificant things that help you through. Like knowing two little girls like to play in your mother's garden." Cassandra's eyes let him know she'd been there.

"It's not the same."

"No, it's not. I don't know who wants me dead. You do. Over fourteen hundred people died because of you," she saw the pain that caused him. "Nearly seven billion died because of me. It's not at all the same."

Looking at her, Barek saw she understood like no one else could. He took a sip from his glass.

"Will, I know Dadrian has problems. Always has. But this…"

"Jotham…" William didn't know how to help his friend, to help him when one son wants the other one dead. And they hadn't even told them about Dadrian wanting to be King. Suddenly they heard the outer door to the suite burst open, hitting the wall.

"Father!" William stiffened at Dadrian's voice. He immediately went to stand between him and Cassandra.

Storming down the hallway, Dadrian entered the private area. "There you are. Look I don't know what the Admiral's telling you about last night, but I can promise you it's not true."

"Last night…" Jotham suddenly realized where the bruises on Cassandra's arms had come from, why his friend stood between his second son and his life mate.

"All I was trying to do was stop her from embarrassing herself. I wasn't interested in what she was offering."

"And just what was that, Dadrian?" Jotham asked in a neutral voice, watching his son.

"Herself in exchange for my influence on you in support of her Challenge. She has tired of the Admiral and is ready to move on." There was a gleam in Dadrian's eyes as he looked at William.

William wanted to wipe the floor with Dadrian's face. The little foabhar stood there, insulting his life mate after he attacked her last night, the woman who carried his child.

Cassandra could feel William's rage building. That Dadrian would slander her, to his face, how much is a man supposed to take?

William knew what Dadrian was doing, and he was not going to give him the satisfaction. The Admiral stared him down.

When he realized he was not going to get a rise out of the Admiral, Dadrian turned his attention to Cassandra. The little bitch was going to pay for last night. He'd ruin her. Suddenly he realized it wasn't only Cassandra standing behind the Admiral.

Barek turned away from the window to stand at the Admiral's side.

"Barek..." A myriad of emotions crossed Dadrian's face, "You're alive! You're here! Why wasn't I told?" Dadrian demanded of his father.

Barek walked to the comm. Watching his brother, he replayed the transmission. Dadrian paled as he listened, his eyes flying from his brother to his father.

"What is this?" Dadrian turned on the Admiral. "What lies have you been telling them? What is that bitch telling you, you stupid old man?" Dadrian was starting to lose control. "They're making this up, Father."

"What are they making up?"

"That I would try and kill Barek!"

"Who said you were?" William asked quietly.

Suddenly, Dadrian realized what he'd admitted. He saw that everyone in the room knew it too. Turning he fled from the suite.

Jotham hurried after his son, William following close behind. He would protect his friend, his King, even from his own son.

"Dadrian!" Jotham's voice boomed through the stairway.

Everyone who heard the King came running, Lucas and Kyle from the other suite, Marat, Deffand, and the King's guards from downstairs. On the stairs, Dadrian froze. Turning he looked up at his father then to Barek. Spinning back, his foot caught on the runner.

"No!" Jotham tried to grab Dadrian but it was too late. In horror, they watched as he tumbled down the stairs, his neck making a sickening crack. For a moment no one moved, then chaos.

"Aunt Cassie!"

"Victoria!" Cassandra turned to see her staring at the bottom of the steps. "Lucas!" Quickly he grabbed her, taking her back to the suite.

"Stay here," William ordered her.
"Maybe I can help," she looked at him.
"There's nothing to help with. Stay here."
Nodding, she stepped back.

Chapter Thirty-Five

Dadrian was dead. The Second Son of King Jotham was dead. The Palace was in shock. The planet was in shock. He died in a senseless accident while visiting the Royal Suite. It was witnessed not only by the Challenger but the King himself. All Royal functions had been canceled, the Challenge postponed.

Cassandra sat in Lata's garden, watching Victoria and Amina play as William approached. Standing, she walked into his arms.

"How is he?"

"Royal."

"William…"

"He'll do what he has to do."

"And Barek?"

"Blaming himself, knowing it's not his fault, but still blaming himself."

"I understand."

"Yes, you do." He gave her a hard look, "Have you eaten?"

She gave him a slightly guilty look.

"Cassandra."

"I did," she looked him straight in the eye. "You just won't think it's enough."

"You will take care of yourself."

"William," she looked at the girls, "it doesn't do me any good if I can't keep it down." Her eyes pleaded with him, "I ate as much as I could." She put a hand on his cheek, "I promise you, I'll eat. I'll take care of myself. I'll protect your son."

"What?" his arms tightened around her.

"What?" she looked at him.

"You said son. You can't possibly know. Not yet." His eyes searched hers.

"You're right," she found herself backtracking.

"Cassandra…" he gripped her chin. "Tell me."

"I…William I have no proof, just what I've been told by my Grams."

"Tell me," his thumb caressed her cheek.

She looked back to the girls. He understood her concern. "Wait here." Minutes later he returned with Lucas and Javiera.

"Hey girls, I hear Hutu made Fudge Torta, anyone want to go get some?" In seconds, the garden was clear.

"Very smooth."

"I have my moments," he watched her walk away from him. "Tell me."

"William…"

"Cassandra, I trust your instincts more than I trust other people's facts."

Sighing she told him, "In my dream, the one where Sabah is pregnant, she told me my son would be strong like his father." She looked up seeing the flare in his eyes, "There's more."

"Tell me."

"Sabah had nine sons before she had a daughter," William paled. "I've never found a Qwes woman that had just one child. But once they have a girl they never have another."

"You're saying we'll have more than one child," his arms embraced her.

"Yes," she scanned his face.

"Cassandra…as long as you're okay, I have no problem with having multiple children with you. You can't think I would."

"We haven't talked about it. With everything that's happened with Dadrian…"

"Enough! Every child we have together will be loved. A part of you and me that goes on. But only if you are safe. I won't risk you. Not even for our child."

"I'll be fine. I promise," she rested her head against his chest.

∞ ∞ ∞ ∞ ∞

The next few days were quiet in the Royal Suite. Preparations were being made throughout the Palace for Prince Dadrian's funeral or sochraide as it was called on Carina. Members from all the Royal Houses would be attending along with Assemblymen and everyday citizens. Security inside the Palace, as well as the City of Pechora, had been increased to accommodate the arrivals.

"Tell me what's happening." With Victoria asleep, Cassandra sat on a couch in the private quarters. She looked at William, who had been talking to Kyle and Lucas. Walking over he sat down drawing her close.

"The Royals have begun to arrive. They will be staying in their House's Consul in Pechora."

"House's Consul?" she gave William a rare lost look.

"Yes," he thought how to explain it to her.

"Every House has an Emissary stationed in the city of a Royal House," Kyle spoke up. "They will basically have a small Palace there. It's considered the same as the Royal House. The Emissary is the go between for their House and the House where they are," Kyle watched to see if Cassandra was following. "When a Royal visits, that's where they stay. It's equipped for their needs."

"So it's an Embassy, got it," she nodded to Kyle. "What about the sochraide? How does that work?"

"It will be held at the temple in Pechora. The ceremony for the dead will be presented along with the remembrance of the ancestors." William picked up her hand as he spoke, "There will then be a procession from the temple back to the House of Protection. Dadrian will be placed in the family temple until the private ceremony the next day. Then he will be interred in the family tomb."

"All right...." She looked at Kyle and, Lucas then back to William. "What am I missing?"

"After Dadrian is placed in the family temple there will be a gathering in the Public Wing."

"And?"

"It will be an enormous gathering; all the Royals, the Assemblymen, and citizens of the House of Protection."

"You're worried about my security," she could see she was right.

"Yes, it would be safer for you not to attend."

Getting up, Cassandra walked over to the window, thinking about what William was saying. Knowing he had every right to be concerned. The Glitter Man, if it were who she believed it was, would be there. Victoria would be in danger.

"If I were the Queen of the House of Knowledge, my not being there would be seen as a slight, an insult." She turned back to see the Zafar men watching her. No one answered her question.

"Kyle?" she stared at him. Kyle looked first to his father then back. If she truly was the Queen, as his father was convinced she was, she needed this information.

"Yes, it would be seen as an insult."

She looked at William, "You, Kyle, and Lucas will all need to be there not only because Jotham is your King, but you are also all Royals."

"Yes."

"When we arrived, the Royal Suite was locked and sealed."

"Yes, there is only one key." William knew what she was leading up to.

"So if, after the procession, Victoria, the Michelakakis', Tar, Marat and the guards return to the Suite and seal the door, Victoria will be protected."

"You left yourself out," he told her.

"I'll be at the gathering protected by the Zafar men. I'll be perfectly safe."

"Damn it, Cassandra!" William moved off the couch.

"If I were Queen, we wouldn't even be having this discussion. I'll be damned if I'm going to hide away while this fucking traitor is at the gathering making all nice! He's nothing but a coward hiding behind the Regulians and terrorizing children. He's not going to try anything tomorrow."

"Then why all the security for Victoria?" The two were almost nose-to-nose. Kyle and Lucas looked at each other.

"Because I could be wrong," the fire went out of her eyes. "He could think it's the perfect time to go after Victoria."

"No one's going to touch her," William stroked her cheek.

"I'm staying back with her," Lucas looked at the pair.

"You need to be there to show your support for Barek and your King," Cassandra informed him.

"That doesn't come before Victoria!" Kyle was shocked at his brother's tone and, his attachment to the little girl.

"Do you think it does for me!?!" Her eyes flashed at Lucas, "But this needs to be done. If she's ever going to be safe, if she's ever going to get to grow up, have a life, then the Glitter Man needs to be caught."

"You think he'll be there," Lucas paled at the thought of him anywhere near Tori.

"I know he will," she looked back to William. "Nothing could keep him away. The one person who knew who he was, what he has done, is dead. He's safe again. Or at least he thinks he is. Now he can concentrate on me."

"Then you need more than the three of us," Kyle stood, "I'm not going to be much help."

"You want to bait him," William's frown said he didn't like the idea.

"Not so much bait as…irritate. And you sell yourself short, Kyle," Cassandra watched William.

"He'll watch you arrive with no professional security. He'll see it as you having no fear, no fear of him. It will infuriate him."

"Yes, he'll make a mistake."

"Maybe, he'll try to talk to you."

"He will, to test the waters, to look for weaknesses. He will see you as one, Kyle, but he'll be wrong. He's not abducting a little girl, on a distant planet this time. He's dealing with three men from the House of Protection, something he's not. He doesn't protect, he destroys."

William had told her he trusted her instincts more than other people's facts and while he didn't like it, he thought she was right. This would be an opportunity for the Glitter Man to observe her, to judge her strengths, her weaknesses. Seeing her 'unprotected' at a very public gathering will do more than irritate, he'll see it as a challenge.

"If we do this…IF, you will not leave my side. If I say we leave, we leave. Understood?" he gripped her chin as his eyes locked with hers.

"Yes," Cassandra knew when to concede.

"I need to contact a few people. Fill in Marat and Quinn." Giving her a hard kiss, he headed to the Ready Room. Kyle and Lucas watched him go then looked at Cassandra, amazement in both their eyes.

"What?" she asked looking at the two, a faint blush on her cheeks. "It's not like you've never seen us kiss."

"It's not that," Lucas told her.

"Then what?"

"It's like you know what the other one is thinking; like you've been together for cycles, not weeks. You understand each other."

"We have our moments."

"Even when you fight," Kyle said quietly. "I've never seen anyone stand up to him like that. You'll go toe-to-toe with him, argue your point, tell him he's wrong. You get angry but not…mean, not hurtful."

"Why would I want to hurt him?" she gave them both a confused look.

"When he and Mom used to fight…he would just go silent, Mom would say some…hurtful things," Kyle had to look away.

"Kyle you don't have to tell me this. Every relationship is different."

"This is right," he looked back at her. "This relationship is good; for Dad and, for you. I didn't want to admit that before. What they had wasn't right, it wasn't right for either of them."

Cassandra said the only thing she could, "I love him."

"And he loves you. It shows," it was Kyle's turn to blush.

∞ ∞ ∞ ∞ ∞

In the Ready Room, the Admiral finished up his last transmission. He'd contacted all those he could trust. Cassandra would have all the protection he could give her without Marat and his men.

"What's up, Will?" Quinn entered the room.

"Sit down, Quinn, we need to talk." As Will filled in his longtime friend on the plans for tomorrow, Quinn said nothing. "I know it's a lot to ask."

"No, it's not. I would only be there out of respect for the King. You and your family need to be there, you're Royals." Quinn leaned back, looking at Will.

"What's on your mind, Quinn?"

"High Command."

"What about it?"

"Word's out about there being a traitor. That there's been one for over seven cycles and that Valerian was oblivious until you brought it to his attention."

William leaned back saying nothing.

"Now Tibullus is on Carina when Valerian couldn't tell Jotham if he was dead or alive, a neat trick by the way." Quinn watched his friend. Will had always kept things to himself. "Valerian's losing support. Command doubts his abilities to lead. Rumors are flying that they're going to make you High Admiral."

William's eyebrows shot up, "That's ridiculous."

"You have the support of the other Admirals and Captains in the Fleet. They trust and respect you. Especially now. You're willing to risk everything to catch this traitor, including your career."

William found himself slightly embarrassed by what Quinn was telling him, "I'm only doing my job."

"You're doing more than that, and you know it. It also means you have a big problem."

"What's that?"

"Valerian."

"'He's hearing this?" William rested his elbows on his desk his chin on his knuckles.

"Yes. It's also known that Cassandra tore him apart, in front of King Jotham and the House of Protection Assemblymen. She's getting quite a reputation within the Fleet."

"What do you mean 'reputation'?" William's tone was icy.

"Easy," Quinn said. "She entered an active array, possibly saving the Retribution. Falco, she schooled her like she was a child. She's a Challenger to Queen Yakira of the House of Knowledge. And she's willing to go head-to-head with the High Admiral in your defense. Oh, and then there's just that little thing of you claiming her as your life mate."

"Fuck."

"Will…they stand behind her." Shocked eyes looked at Quinn, who gave him a wry grin. "She's won them over with her honesty, courage, and commitment to you. She has their support as much as you do."

"Valerian will be rabid."

"Already is."

"Thanks for the heads up."

∞ ∞ ∞ ∞ ∞

"William?" Cassandra lifted her head from his chest to look at him.

"Yeah?" he ran a hand up and down her back.

"On Earth, when there is a funeral…sochraide, people tend to wear black. Is it that way here?"

"Black?"

"Yes. Should I ask Javiera?"

William thought, this was one of those things he'd never worried about before. He always wore his uniform. But for women…

"I've never noticed a consistent color, except uniforms. Black does represent death, the ceremony for the dead. But white is the color of the ancestors, of redemption if you like," he could see she was thinking.

"It's that way with all the Houses?"

"Yes, it's a unifying point." He tucked a loose piece of hair behind her ear, letting his fingers caress her neck.

"Redemption…a nice thought," she gave him a soft smile.

∞ ∞ ∞ ∞ ∞

The day dawned bright and beautiful. The first sun was high in the sky as the Challenger's cortege entered the Temple of Pechora. Heads turned as the group passed, guards blocking a clear view of the Challenger. They were led to the front of the Temple.

Victoria's eyes avidly scanned the Temple, taking in everything at once. Turning, she looked up at her aunt sitting next to her. Cassandra looked down at her giving her a slight wink.

They talked earlier about this, that if Victoria had questions she would wait until they were back in the limisins. This was a solemn event and they would give it the respect it deserved.

As the music changed, all in the temple stood at the entrance of the King and his remaining son, Barek. They followed the funeral coffin of Dadrian as it was placed in front of the altar and then the King and Prince sat.

The ceremony, full of rituals that Cassandra only partly understood, was long, and performed by a Guide, the Carinian equivalent to a Priest. Part way through Victoria slid her hand into hers. Looking down, she saw tears in her niece's eyes. Squeezing the little hand, she let her know she understood that the tears weren't only for Dadrian.

William watched the two. He'd been concerned it might be too much for them. There had been no sochraide for their family. He put his hand on her free one, offering what comfort he could. Cassandra raised sad but grateful eyes to him.

When the ceremony ended, all stood allowing Jotham and Barek to leave first, following Dadrian. When it came time for them to leave, the guards closed back around them.

∞ ∞ ∞ ∞ ∞

Back in the limisins Victoria climbed into Cassandra's lap. Wrapping her arms around her, Cassandra held her close.

"Hey, it's okay," she rubbed her back. William put an arm around Cassandra holding them both close. Victoria looked up at him with subdued eyes so unlike the little girl. The ride back to the Palace was quiet.

"Victoria," the Admiral rubbed her back as the limisins entered the Palace. She looked at him. "Do you want me to carry you?"

"We're back already?"

"Yes."

"You have a gathering to go to." They'd told her what would be happening today.

"Yes."

"I can walk." When the limisins stopped, guards opened the door.

∞ ∞ ∞ ∞ ∞

Entering the Royal Suite they were greeted by Hutu.

"Sir, I took the liberty of preparing a snack for the girls. It is in the formal dining room." Hutu saw the sadness in Victoria's eyes. "If it's all right with you, I'll take them in."

"That would be fine."

"Thank you, Hutu." Cassandra knelt down to Victoria, "I'll see you later okay?"

"Okay."

William helped her up as she watched Tori leave. Suddenly they heard both girls exclaim, "TORTA!" Smiling at William, she shook her head.

"You're going to have your hands full once they're done," Cassandra told Javiera.

"They may be in a fudge coma. It's a good idea," Javiera smiled at Cassandra.

"Marat," William turned as he entered.

"The Wing is secure, Admiral."

"Cassandra..." William touched her back, letting her know it was time.

"We'll keep her safe," Leander reassured her.

Nodding she turned to William, "Ready."

∞ ∞ ∞ ∞ ∞

Cassandra had taken this walk before, from the Royal Wing to the Public Wing. She thought there'd been a lot of guards then, but today there were triple the number. She looked at the guard standing in front of the hidden door they'd used after Dadrian's attack. William noticed and gently touched her arm.

"We can still go back."

"No. But thank you," she covered his hand with hers, "I'll be fine."

"Remember what I said," he gave her a hard look.

"I'm not leaving your side."

Six guards were at the doors of the Public Wing. They watched the four approaching, three males and one female. While the Sergeant recognized the Admiral, he still consulted his list, making a notation of the time they arrived.

"Admiral, Princess," he gave them a nod then turned to the guards, ordering them to open the doors.

Entering the Public Wing, Cassandra was amazed at the number of people contained there. She'd been in several rooms and of course the ball room before, but all the doors had been opened, connecting all the rooms and gardens, and still it was full. With William's hand on the small of her back, she allowed him to guide her to a spot where he felt she would be secure.

Queen Yakira noticed her Challenger enter the room, along with everyone else. It wasn't that she was simply dressed in white, looking like a beacon, a tribute to the ancestors; it was that she had no security, just the Admiral, and his two sons.

Prince Audric also noticed. He'd been having a hard time disguising his glee at the death of Dadrian. Now he had no problems. She arrived with no security? Did she have no fear of him? He destroyed her planet. He would destroy her.

Cassandra could feel the rage directed at her. Scanning the room, her eyes settled on Audric. She knew she'd been right, she allowed her eyes to move past him, dismissing him.

"What are you doing?" William leaned down to whisper, he'd felt her tense.

"Irritating," she whispered back. Kyle and Lucas exchanged glances.

"Assemblyman Bevington, nice to see you again, you too, Kira," Cassandra addressed William's friend.

"Princess, Admiral." Bevington gave them a slight bow.

"Nestor, you remember my sons, Lucas and Kyle."

"Of course. Lucas, I hear you're quite the pilot."

"Thank you, Sir."

"And Kyle, in the Hall of Records, it must be very interesting."

"I enjoy it, Sir."

"Kira is hoping for such a position when she graduates."

"Really?" Kyle looked at the beautiful girl currently blushing at her father's side. "You'll have to let me know when you are ready to apply, maybe I can help."

"That would be wonderful, thank you," Kira's voice was subdued, but Cassandra could see the sparkle in her eyes. Looking at Kyle, she saw it wasn't one-sided. Hiding her smile, she looked and saw William had also noticed.

While they talked, servants circulated with trays of drinks. William selected one then handed it to her.

"Thank you," her eyes widened slightly as she looked past him. Turning, he watched Dr. Bliant approach.

"Admiral, Princess Cassandra," Bliant nodded. "May I present Assemblyman Ugolsky of the House of Healing."

"Assemblyman Ugolsky," Cassandra nodded.

"Princess, I apologize presenting myself to you at such a time. I took advantage of my nephew's relationship with the Admiral."

"Your nephew?" Cassandra raised an eyebrow to Bliant.

"My mother's sister's husband, Princess," Bliant informed her.

"I see. No apology necessary, Assemblyman Ugolsky." She turned her attention back to him, "At times like these, meeting new people helps take one's mind off senseless tragedies."

"I couldn't agree more, Princess, and since the formal gatherings have been canceled…"

"With all due respect, Assemblyman Ugolsky, I don't feel this is the proper setting for that type of discussion. It would be disrespectful not only to the deceased but to King Jotham and Prince Barek." Her eyes said she would brook no argument on this subject.

"Of course, Princess," Ugolsky nodded, his esteem for the woman increased. He'd wondered if she'd take advantage of the situation.

"How is Victoria?" Bliant asked changing the subject.

"She's adjusting," Cassandra gave him a warm smile. "She's discovered Fudge Torta."

"Oh really," Bliant smiled at her.

"She'd eat it at every meal if she could."

"Wouldn't we all."

"Princess Cassandra."

"Assemblyman Terwilliger, Madame Terwilliger," Cassandra acknowledged. "I'm sure you know Assemblyman Bevington, his daughter Kira, Assemblyman Ugolsky, Dr. Bliant, and the Admiral's sons, Lucas and Kyle." Greetings were made.

William watched as Cassandra made small talk with some of the most influential people in the Assembly, if not on the planet, making it look easy. Across the room, he saw King Jotham and Barek enter. They stopped and spoke to several on their way to them. As they approached, people stepped aside. There was much speculation about the Prince dying in the Royal Wing.

"Majesty, Prince Barek," the Admiral spoke first. Nodding to them, Cassandra did the same.

"Admiral, Princess," the King acknowledged. "Kyle, Lucas, your presence is appreciated."

"We would be nowhere else but at your side, Majesty," William replied looking his friend in the eye.

"Princess, your presence is especially noted, I'm sure you had misgivings."

"Majesty?" Cassandra shot a look to William then back to the King. Suddenly all ears were listening.

"With all you've been through because of…"

She cut him off, "It has been difficult, Majesty, senseless death always is." Cassandra wasn't sure what she should say, so she spoke from the heart. "I am truly sorry for the loss of your son, Majesty. A parent should never outlive a child. My grandmother told me it was the most devastating moment of her life, the day my mother died. She never truly recovered. She always believed there should have been something she could have done to prevent it. But the truth is, we are all responsible for our own decisions." She continued to look at Jotham, "Remember the happy times you had with your son, Majesty. Be grateful for what you still have, it will help ease the pain, I know."

Silence greeted Cassandra's comments to the King. She suddenly realized the room was silent, and that she may have revealed too much of herself.

"Thank you, Princess," the King's voice was gruff. Turning, he continued on his way. Barek stayed a moment longer, she met his look.

"My father tells me you think I'm conceited, irritating, and intrusive," he said in a dry voice.

"You've forgotten competent and a jerk," she replied in the same tone, receiving a quirk of his lips.

"Yes. Admiral, Lucas, Kyle," he nodded to them then followed his father.

William removed the glass from Cassandra's hand, replacing it with another. Looking into her eyes he saw her doubt. Her doubt, that she may have said too much and revealed too much of herself. Leaning down he whispered so only she could hear, "It was fine."

Cassandra nodded. His hand at her waist gave her a reassuring squeeze.

Audric was furious. The little bitch, thinking she could console the King, that she had any right to even speak to him. And the Admiral, standing there touching her, never leaving her side, thinking he can catch him. What a fool to let a woman turn his head, even one that looked like that. He knew that Dadrian attacked her the night of the ball, yet there wasn't even a whisper of it.

"Audric!" Queen Yakira hissed at him.

"Yes?" He realized he'd been ignoring her.

"I wish to speak to the Challenger."

"I will send word," Audric motioned to a guard.

"No," Yakira stopped the guard. "We will go to her, on our way to give our regrets to King Jotham." She started to move across the room, her guards clearing a path, Audric followed.

William watched the group approach, his eyes flashed to Lucas and Kyle. They both immediately understood. As did Bevington, Ugolsky, and Bliant. William put a hand on Cassandra's waist as she talked with Madame Terwilliger. With a slight nod, she continued the conversation until Madame Terwilliger noticed the approaching Queen.

Cassandra's eyes were politely blank as they met the Queen's. She waited.

"Princess Cassandra," Yakira finally spoke.

"Queen Yakira," Cassandra gave her a slight nod. "Have you been introduced to Admiral Zafar's sons, Lucas and Kyle?"

Yakira must acknowledge them or appear rude, "Gentlemen," she gave them a slight nod.

"Majesty," they nodded back.

"I was disappointed at your early departure from the Ball," the Queen's eyes were hard. "There were many disappointed," her tone accusing.

"If I owe apologies, Majesty, I will give it to those in question, not to you. You chose to leave the conversation when you didn't like the answers."

"How dare you!" Audric took a step toward her, Kyle stepped in front of him.

"I don't believe I was speaking to you, Prince Audric," Cassandra's eyes were as icy as her tone.

"Princess, you will give my spouse the respect he deserves," Yakira demanded.

"Respect is earned, not given, Majesty," Cassandra countered.

"You judge me when you stand with this man!" Audric was infuriated at her slight. Everyone within hearing distance stiffened. Yakira watched as Cassandra's entire being froze in a cold rage. Except her eyes, they were blazing.

"The man I stand with has earned every medal on his chest. None was given to him to make him feel more like one. He is Royal by blood, by birthmark. He doesn't need to be given a title. You will show him the respect he has earned, Prince Audric."

"Queen Yakira," Deffand interrupted before Audric could respond. "King Jotham would like you to join him in the other room. At your convenience of course." Deffand gave her a slight bow. His eyes shot to the Princess whose eyes were still locked with Audric's.

Yakira was still watching Cassandra. Her defense of the Admiral, given in a cold even tone, revealed no emotion. But none hearing it doubted the rage. She actually believed in the Admiral, cared for him, she wasn't using him.

"Of course, Captain," Yakira acknowledged the King's guard. "Audric," she held out her hand. When it was not immediately taken, her eyes shot to her spouse. She saw his were still locked with Cassandra's. "Audric!"

∞ ∞ ∞ ∞ ∞

Who did this little bitch think she was! He'd destroyed her entire planet; he'd destroy her, and the man who she thinks he should respect. He'd do it slow, starting with the child, watch her suffer knowing she'd caused it.

"Audric!"

He looked to his spouse. She'd only given him a token defense, allowing this Challenger to humiliate him. Seeing her hand, he realized everyone was watching him, waiting. Pulling himself back in, he put a slight smile on his face, not realizing it made him look feral.

"Of course, my dear," Audric took her hand, leading her away.

Everyone watched Cassandra take a calm drink from her glass. Her eyes met the Admiral's at the slight touch of his hand on her back. She turned back to Madame Terwilliger to continue their conversation.

Ugolsky was impressed, beyond impressed. He hadn't believed his nephew. He'd described the Challenger as beautiful, confident, loyal, and one who stood. He assumed he'd exaggerated. He hadn't.

Her total belief in the Admiral was undeniable, as was his commitment to her. They were glaring opposites of Queen Yakira and Prince Audric. A union arranged by her family after the death of her intended.

Ugolsky wasn't the only one to notice. Admiral Zafar was respected throughout the Houses. He had commanded many of their children, doing his best to make sure they got home; and when they didn't, would write a personal note. He was the hero of the Battle of Fayal. His capture of the Regulian battleship, the Rappen, resulted in vital information being obtained, saving thousands of Carinian lives. Audric's disrespect had not gone over well.

The Admiral stood by, as more and more people approached, wanting introductions to the Challenger. He knew this wasn't the time or place. Cassandra didn't want it to appear she was using it that way.

"Princess," he leaned close. She turned her head slightly and he saw the first hints of fatigue. "We need to return to the Royal Wing." He saw the slight flare in her eyes and realized she believed there was a problem. He gave her waist a reassuring squeeze, her eyes settled.

"Of course," Cassandra's eyes swept the group surrounding them, "If you'll excuse us."

It wasn't a question. She turned to the Admiral, waiting. With his hand on her lower back, he guided her through the crowd, Lucas on one side, Kyle behind. At the doors, the guards made a note of their leaving. Walking down the corridor, Kyle moved to his father's side.

"I assume it's okay to leave without saying goodbye to Jotham and Barek."

"He won't expect it if you've spoken to him once." Approaching the Royal Wing, William removed the key from his pocket.

"Report."

"No one has approached the Wing, Admiral." Nodding he unlocked the door. Once inside he secured the door. Marat approached.

"The Wing is secure Admiral, there have been no intrusions."

"Good. Initiate Eagle's Nest."

"Yes, Sir. Princess, Victoria is in the Michelakakis' suite."

"Thank you, Chief." Marat nodded then left the room.

"Eagle's Nest?" she asked.

"Let's some of the guards rotate out."

"How are they holding up?" she asked as they headed for the stairs.

"Fine, why?"

"There's only ten of them, William, we've been running them pretty hard."

"That's their job."

"For the Coalition maybe, this isn't Coalition business." She stood on the first step, eye level with William.

"They're fine." Giving him a quick kiss she let the subject drop and, headed up to find Victoria.

∞ ∞ ∞ ∞ ∞

William watched until she was safely upstairs, then he turned to his sons.

"We need to talk." He led them to the Ready Room. Once there he sat behind the desk, looking at his sons. "Opinions."

"Cassandra handled herself like a real Queen. She was controlled, respectful, not letting anyone push her around," Kyle commented first.

"She won over Ugolsky. But Audric, he'd like to see her dead," Lucas stared at his father. "That's who she's 'irritating.'"

"Prince Audric?" Kyle leaned back thinking. "She knew he had no Royal affiliation, no birthmark."

"Cassandra does her research."

"That's how she knew he didn't 'earn' any of his medals?"

"Yes."

"Did you know he was going to take a shot at you?" Lucas asked.

"No, but I'm not surprised."

"Yakira didn't defend him," Kyle looked at his father.

"What?" William gave his attention to his youngest.

"When Audric took a shot at you, Cassandra tore him apart. Yakira didn't defend him, just let it go. He was pissed about it."

"It was more than that," Lucas looked at his father. "Everyone saw. Saw the difference between them as a couple and you. You and Cassandra stand together, they stand apart. It gave everyone a good look at what the House of Knowledge could be, especially their Assemblymen."

"There have been rumors," Kyle looked from Lucas to his father, "from the very beginning. Yakira's intended, Vane, was killed in a freak accident on

Messene. Less than two months later, she was joined in a Union with Audric. Their son was born less than seven months later. He was 'early.'" Kyle watched his father. "It is rumored Audric can't stand the boy. He's fifteen now. Yakira lives her life around him."

"Not all rumors are true," William stated, but it raised some interesting questions.

"There's more. They've kept separate quarters since they were joined. Yakira consulted with a doctor that guaranteed her a daughter for her second child, an heir."

"How can you possibly know that?" Lucas demanded.

"I'm the 'smart' one, remember?" Kyle grinned at him.

"Vane died on Messene?" William stood to walk to look out the window.

"Yes," Kyle watched him, " A climbing accident."

"Audric was originally from Messene. The Glitter Man needed to get back to Messene. It's not a coincidence."

"You think he killed Vane so he could marry Yakira and become Prince?" Lucas frowned.

"It's possible," William looked to Kyle. "Can you get me all the Intel on the 'accident' quietly?"

"Shouldn't be a problem."

"Do it."

"Dad, you really think it matters?" Lucas asked.

"I don't know, Cassandra's been working on something concerning the Battle of Fayal. She's sniffing out something, this might help."

"Fayal?"

"Something to do with who translated the Intel."

"Scholar Olah." William and Lucas stared at Kyle. "What? I did a thesis on him. He was in charge of all data translations from the Regulian ship. He died over seven cycles ago."

"How?" William demanded.

"That transport accident in Kisurri."

"The 'freak' one? Where only the last transport rolled?"

"Yes…" Kyle paled at the thought, "he couldn't have…"

"Why not? That was only one hundred people, compare that to seven billion," William's eyes were hard. "Get me the Intel, Kyle, on all that. I want to know who he'd been in contact with before he died. Go back a month."

"Yes, Sir. Are the comms upstairs on full security?"

"Yes, if you need more let Quinn or me know, and Kyle, don't let anyone know you're sniffing."

"Not a problem," Kyle headed upstairs.

"Dad…you think it goes that far back?"

"It started somewhere. If he killed to get Yakira, he'd kill to stay there. After killing seven billion people, what's a few more." William walked up to his first son, "Stay on your toes."

Chapter Thirty-Six

"Aunt Cassie, you're back."

"Sure am. What are you up to?" She sat down next to her.

"Javiera has us catching up on homework."

"Really," Cassandra looked at Javiera.

"I thought it would keep them busy."

"It's a good idea. You have what you need?"

"Yeah, I've just been pulling it up on the comm," Javiera gave Cassandra the once over. They hadn't talked about the baby yet. She could wait until Cassandra was ready to talk. But that didn't mean she wouldn't keep an eye on her friend.

"Why don't you go eat, I think the girls left you some Fudge Torta."

"We did," Victoria piped up.

"I've got enough to keep them busy for a couple hours. Eat, rest, it's been a trying day," Javiera shooed her out.

"Have you been talking to William?" Cassandra accused laughing.

"No, but I will if that's what it takes."

"The Admiral always makes her eat," Victoria chimed in.

"Then she must, he's the Admiral."

Smiling, Cassandra left them. It felt good to smile. Finding the suite empty she slipped off her shoes.

"Ahh, that's heaven." Picking them up, she headed to the closet. Hanging up her white outfit she turned to the bureau. Kia had made her a pair of jeans. She'd protested the whole time but once Cassandra had discovered a material similar to denim she'd insisted and, had drawn a very detailed sketch. Getting them out she looked at them. Smiling as she put them on, the fit was perfect. As she buttoned them, she realized she'd better enjoy them while she could. Soon William's son would make them impossible to wear. The thought made her laugh. Donning a shirt she headed out to find food, barefoot.

Walking down the steps she thought about what William had told her. Tomorrow there would be a private ceremony for Dadrian. But William hadn't said anything about going. Would he and his sons normally have gone? Was there a reason they weren't?

"Chief Marat," Cassandra saw him at the bottom of the stairs wondering if he'd know.

"Princess," Marat watched as she approached. No one seeing her now would think she would soon be Queen. She was wearing some kind of blue pants he'd never seen before, a very casual shirt, loose hair and bare feet. Bare feet!

"I have a question I'm hoping you can answer."

"I'll try."

"Tomorrow there will be a private family burial of Dadrian."

"Yes."

"Under ordinary circumstances, would the Zafars attend?"

Marat thought for a moment. The Admiral was not only related but a good friend of King Jotham, he was Barek's Second Father, and their sons were friends.

"In my opinion, yes, Princess."

"Could you contact Deffand for me and find out if he feels it would be a problem for them to attend?"

"Princess?"

"I think it will do them all good to be there together, privately. Victoria and I will not be attending. If you could do that?"

"I'll do what I can, Princess. It might be awhile, the gathering is ongoing."

"Thank you, Chief." She turned, heading to the kitchen.

∞ ∞ ∞ ∞ ∞

"Princess!" Hutu was shocked to find her in his kitchen.

"Hutu, hello. I thought I'd come down and see if I couldn't beg a meal from you."

"You only had to call."

"I know, but I felt like coming down for a visit. Anything you have is fine. Is that soup?"

"Yes, Princess." Hutu filled a bowl. Setting it down, he handed her a spoon.

"Thank you." She took her first sip. "This is wonderful, Hutu." He smiled and set down what she'd come to know as Carinian bread. Tearing off a piece, she dipped it in the soup.

"How are you adjusting here?"

"Princess?" Hutu gave her a confused look.

"I've never asked. Where are you originally from, Hutu?"

"I'm from the Latakia Region of the House of Growth, Princess."

"Well, that explains why you're such a good cook. Do you have family there?"

"I have several brothers and one sister. They've all married and had children. They work together on the family acreage."

"It's large enough to support them all?"

"Yes, Princess."

"So where are you in the mix?"

"Princess?"

"Oldest, youngest?"

"Youngest son, only my sister is younger."

"And your parents?"

"They've gone to be with the ancestors, Princess." Hutu's look was somewhat sad.

"I'm sorry."

"Don't be, they are together, that's how they would want to be."

Cassandra nodded her understanding. "So you didn't wish to stay on the farm…acreage?"

"No, I used to look at the stars and wonder what it was like, really like to go there, not just in a simulation. So since there were enough to work the acreage, I left."

"It would have been hard on your parents."

"Yes, it was, but they also understood." Hutu turned to work at the counter.

Cassandra thought back to her father and, how he understood her need to study. "They tend to do that when they love you."

"Yes, Princess," Hutu set a piece of Fudge Torta in front of her.

Looking down, she found her bowl empty. Grinning at him, she took the forc he was holding out.

"You're going to make me fat if you keep making this." She closed her eyes taking her first bite, "Yum!"

"Good," the Admiral came up behind her, placing a kiss on her head.

"Admiral, would you like some soup?"

"Thank you, Hutu."

Turning away Hutu rushed to fill a bowl. An Admiral and a Princess sitting in his kitchen eating soup, who'd believe it? He had been telling a Princess about his family. He set the bowl in front of the Admiral.

"So how many nieces and nephews do you have?" Cassandra continued her conversation with him.

"Hmm, at last count seven nephews, six nieces."

"Really?!?" Her eyes widened. "Do you get to see them much?"

"I get home when I can. It depends on the length of the Admiral's tour."

Saying nothing, she enjoyed another bite. Hutu couldn't help but grin at her enjoyment.

"I should make my mother's special fudge chip wafers for you," Hutu realized he had spoken out loud.

"Wafer?" Cassandra frowned, "Wafer…you mean like a cookie? Round." She showed him with her hands. Hutu nodded. "With 'fudge chips?' If you're talking chocolate chip cookies, I may have to kiss you."

"Uhhh…" Hutu's eyes flashed to the Admiral, relaxing when he saw his grin.

"You'd better make some, Hutu. If it's what she's thinking, you will be a very lucky man."

"Yes, Admiral."

"Are you done with that?" William looked at her empty plate.

She blushed, "Yeah, thank you, Hutu."

"You're very welcome, Princess."

Standing, William helped her off the stool. Looking down he saw her bare feet. She wiggled her toes at him. Shaking his head, he smiled.

"Where are your shoes?"

"In the closet where they belong."

"And here I thought we could walk in the garden."

"Sounds good to me." Wrapping an arm around his waist she let him lead her out the kitchen's garden door.

"You're going to hurt your feet," William said as they walked along the path.

"If I do, you'll just have to carry me," she teased. "Might hurt your back after all that torta I ate." William laughed at the thought of her being that heavy. They needed this, a few moments of carefree together. Wandering Lata's garden, they found a little peace.

"William?"

"Hmmm."

"Why aren't either of your sons named after you?"

"What?" he looked down at her.

"Lucas and Kyle, why wasn't one of them named after you? Is that not done on Carina?"

"It can be," he walked her over to a bench and sat down. "Salish named the boys."

"What?"

"I was gone when they were born. She chose their names."

"You had no say?" Cassandra frowned.

"I made suggestions, but all the paperwork was done by the time I got there."

"So Lucas?"

"Lucas Matthew. Lucas for her father, Matthew for mine."

"Kyle?"

"Kyle Weddell. She liked the name Kyle, and Weddell for her grandfather." She looked into his eyes. Smiling softly, she touched his cheek.

"So what do you want for this one?"

"I…" He realized he hadn't thought about it. He'd thought she'd want to choose.

"You'll need to give it some thought, but we have time." She rubbed her thumb across his lips.

"What are you thinking?"

"Oh, I've had some thoughts, but nothing seemed right. My mom liked to tell the story of how Peter was supposed to be George Jacob or Jacob Robert, after my dad and then my grandfathers. But once he was born they looked at each other and knew he had to be Peter."

"Why Peter?"

"They didn't know, but his name was to be Peter and Dad refused to let his middle name be Jacob because he didn't want him called PJ. Something about the names you military types make up."

William laughed, "So what was his middle name?"

"Matthew." William's eyes widened. "Interesting huh?"

"Yeah."

"Pardon me, Admiral," Marat approached the couple.

"What is it, Chief?"

"I have a message for the Princess." William frowned looking at Cassandra. "Deffand said it would be greatly appreciated, Princess."

"Thank you, Chief. I appreciate you taking the time."

"Princess." Nodding, Marat left.

"What was that about?"

"It's about you and your sons attending the private burial tomorrow."

"Cassandra…"

"He's a friend that's just lost his son. It doesn't matter why. He's your King. You're his surviving son's Second Father. You're related by blood. You're family, he needs his family."

"There are security issues that will intrude."

"No there's not. Victoria and I will stay in the Royal Wing, inside the Wing. You can seal it yourself. We won't leave." Cassandra put a hand to his cheek, "I promise. You need to go."

William looked at her, realizing he should have discussed it with her. She would have understood.

"Okay, I'll let the boys know." He gave her a gentle kiss, "You are amazing."

"Oh really. Remember that the next time I piss you off," she grinned at him. Her smile slowly faded, her eyes became serious, "I love you, William."

"I know. That makes me a very lucky man." Standing he helped her up. "Kyle's working on compiling some information for you." He tucked her under his arm as they started back to the doors of the Wing.

"Kyle is?"

"On Fayal and who translated the Regulian data."

"Really?" Her eyes flashed at the thought.

William shook his head. Some women liked jewels, his woman liked data. His woman…his mate…someday his wife.

"William?"

"What? Sorry, just thinking. He should have it for you tomorrow."

"All right."

Entering the Wing, he led her up the stairs. "You should rest for a while."

"If I sleep now, I won't tonight. Go talk to your boys, I'll find something to do on the comm."

"That scares me," William gave her a hard kiss.

"Liar, nothing scares you." Smiling at him she turned into the Royal Suite.

"Just losing you," he said quietly and turned to find his sons.

∞ ∞ ∞ ∞ ∞

"William?" Cassandra woke up and felt him pulling away.

"Sleep," he kissed the top of her head as he slid out of bed. "I need to get ready for Dadrian's entombment." She watched him head to the shower. He explained last night what would happen today.

At first sunrise, a transition ceremony would be performed, in the King's private temple, preparing Dadrian to meet the ancestors. At second sunrise, his funeral coffin would be transported to the family tomb, in a valley a short distance from the Palace. With the rising of the third sun, Dadrian would be placed in the tomb. Then his journey to the ancestors would begin with the burning of Daktar, the resulting white smoke rising to show him the way. After the smoke disappeared, they would return to the Palace and have a meal to celebrate his safe arrival.

William walked out of the bathroom, a towel low on his hips, his chest still wet. Watching, Cassandra's eyes flared. God, he was beautiful, and he was all hers. Smiling, she watched as he entered the closet. Several minutes later he walked out fully dressed except for his jacket. Seeing she was still awake, he walked to the bed.

"You're supposed to be sleeping." He sat down next to her.

"After you leave, right now I'm enjoying the view."

"Really?"

"Oh yeah." Rising up she kissed him deeply. He pressed her back into the bed.

"I need to go," he murmured against her lips.

"I know. That should hold me until you get back."

Attacking her lips he left her breathless, "That will have to hold me." Rising while he still could, he left the room.

Watching him, she tried to catch her breath. What that man could do to her…touching her lips she smiled, the man could kiss. Rolling to her side she closed her eyes. After several minutes she sighed, sleep wouldn't come. Suddenly a thought entered her head.

"Fudge Torta," her stomach growled. Sitting up, she suddenly realized she 'needed' Fudge Torta, her first craving. Getting up she pulled on her jeans and a shirt and headed to the kitchen.

∞ ∞ ∞ ∞ ∞

There it was…entering Hutu's kitchen with the light of first sunrise showing the way. She spied the Fudge Torta in a far corner. Taking a large knife out of a drawer, she moved to cut a slice.

"No, High Admiral, if I'd known sooner I would have informed you." Freezing, she turned toward the garden door.

"All security is in the Wing, only the Zafars left." She watched as Ensign Paa entered the kitchen talking on a portable comm. She turned the knife in her hand, gripping it defensively.

"There are no plans to leave the Wing. Everyone else is sleeping." Paa listened to Valerian. "Yes, High Admiral. I will notify you as soon as there is any change. I must get back to my post." Ending the communication, Paa slipped the portable comm inside his jacket then left the kitchen, never seeing Cassandra.

Sagging against the counter, she sucked in a much-needed breath. There were Valerian's eyes within their own security. What if he had seen her?"

"Princess?" Cassandra raised the knife then realized it was Hutu.

"Princess, what's wrong?" He looked at the knife in her hand.

"Hutu, it's you."

"Yes, what's wrong?"

She put the knife on the counter. "Would you contact Colonel Tar and Chief Marat. Tell them to meet me in the Admiral's Ready Room, please."

Hutu looked at the knife, looked at her, "Yes, Princess, of course."

"Thank you," she glanced at the knife and left the kitchen.

∞ ∞ ∞ ∞ ∞

Tar was the first to arrive. Entering the Ready Room, he found Cassandra sitting behind the Admiral's desk. Seconds later, Marat arrived.

"Cassandra, what's going on?"

"Chief Marat, would you have Ensign Paa report here, please."

"Princess?"

"Ensign Paa, please."

"Yes, Princess." Marat looked at Tar then called on his portable comm. Tar watched Cassandra carefully. Minutes later, Paa entered the Ready Room.

"Colonel Tar," she looked him in the eye, "would you please relieve Ensign Paa of his weapon?"

"What?" Paa asked. Tar looked at her then took the weapon.

Standing, she walked around the desk stopping in front of Paa. She held out her hand, "Your portable comm."

"What?"

"Your comm, Ensign Paa."

Paa looked at Marat. "Give her your comm, Ensign." Reaching into his pocket, Paa removed his comm and handed it to Cassandra.

Putting it on the desk behind her she held out her hand again, "Now the other one." She saw his eyes widen.

"Princess?"

"The one inside your jacket pocket." When he didn't move, Cassandra looked at Tar, "Colonel."

Tar realized what was happening. He stepped in front of Paa, ripped open his jacket, and pulled out a second portable comm. With hard eyes, he handed it to her.

"Thank you, Colonel." Walking around the desk she sat, watching Paa she pushed a few buttons.

"Paa, what do you have for me?" High Admiral Valerian's voice came over the comm. Marat and Tar sucked in their breath.

"He has nothing for you, High Admiral," Cassandra told him. There was no sound on the other end. "You've lost your eyes."

"I have no idea what you're talking about, Princess," the High Admiral sneered.

"That's okay, High Admiral," Cassandra sneered back. "I expected no less from a man who has allowed a traitor to exist for over seven cycles." She disconnected before Valerian could answer.

Turning her attention to Paa she waited. Paa started to sweat in the silence.

"I've done nothing wrong," Paa finally broke.

"Really?" Her eyes were hard. "Sneaking around the Royal Wing, reporting to Valerian who's coming and going, where security is, you see nothing wrong with that?"

"He is the High Admiral. I took an oath to defend the Coalition, to obey orders," Paa fired back.

She leaned back in the Admiral's chair. "On Earth, men in the military take a similar oath, to defend against any enemy, foreign or domestic. Do you understand what that means, Ensign Paa?"

"Yes."

"Yet you've chosen to not defend against a traitor."

"There is no traitor. That's just a rumor you made up to get the Admiral to help you," Ensign Paa fired at her.

"And who told you that?"

"High Admiral Valerian, Commander of the Coalition."

"When?"

Paa was silent.

"You will answer, Ensign," Colonel Tar commanded.

"The day we arrived on Carina."

"After the Admiral gave you a choice."

"Yes."

"So you're a spy for the High Admiral."

"I am protecting the Coalition," his voice was stiff.

"From what, Ensign? A little girl?"

"No, from you."

"Me. How is my Challenge to the House of Knowledge a threat to the Coalition?"

"The High Admiral said it was. I didn't question his judgment."

"But you feel you can question the Admiral's?" Cassandra's voice was cold. "Valerian is using you, Paa, to protect himself. I am a threat to him."

"I followed orders," Paa justified himself.

"Colonel Tar."

"Princess."

"I would like Ensign Paa restrained until the Admiral's return, kept isolated.

"Restrained?" Paa was shocked.

"You put my niece in jeopardy, Ensign, with your blind following of Valerian's orders." She walked around the desk to stand in front of the younger man. "No one threatens my family, Ensign. But you are right about one thing. This is a military matter and will be handled by the Admiral. He'll decide what happens to you." Cassandra looked to Marat.

"You will make sure his patrol is covered?"

"Yes, Princess."

"Thank you, gentlemen." she said as she left the room.

∞ ∞ ∞ ∞ ∞

It was nearly 1000 when the Zafars returned to the Royal Wing. As they approached, the Admiral noticed the looks the guards were giving each other. They were tense. Something's not right. Entering the Wing they found Marat waiting for them.

"Report," he demanded.

"The Royal Wing is secure, Sir," he reported. "There is a situation that needs your immediate attention in your Ready Room, Sir." While Marat's eyes remained steady with the Admiral's, he could see guilt in them.

"The Princess?"

"Is secure, Sir, as is Victoria. They are upstairs, they never left the Wing."

"Kyle, get that Intel to Cassandra, Lucas with me. Where is Colonel Tar?"

"In your Ready Room, Admiral," Marat responded. Turning he followed them.

∞ ∞ ∞ ∞ ∞

Kyle entered the guest suite to find Cassandra, Victoria, Amina, and Javiera in the common area.

"Hi, Kyle," Victoria saw him first.

"You're back. All of you?" Cassandra asked.

"Yeah, Dad and Lucas are down in the Ready Room. I've got some Intel for you."

"Javiera?" Cassandra looked at her.

"I've got them, go."

"I'll get it from you later," Cassandra told Kyle, then turned and left the room.

∞ ∞ ∞ ∞ ∞

Entering his Ready Room, the Admiral found Colonel Tar sitting across from Ensign Paa, who was in restraints. His expression unreadable, he walked around his desk and sat.

"ATTENTION, Ensign Paa." His voice hard and cold, Paa jumped to his feet. "Explain."

"Sir, I was following orders, Sir." Paa couldn't look the Admiral in the eye.

"Whose orders, Ensign Paa?"

"High Admiral Valerian's, Sir."

William saw Cassandra slip into the room. "And what were those exact orders, Ensign Paa?"

"That I was to report all movement in and out of the Royal Wing, so he could properly defend the Coalition against unfounded rumors that were causing a disruption in the effectiveness of the Fleet."

"You were informing High Admiral Valerian on the locations of the Royals within the House of Protection?" the Admiral's tone was deadly.

"NO SIR, only the locations of the two refugees from Earth."

"The returning QUEEN of the House of Knowledge and her family?"

"The High Admiral guaranteed me her claims were false."

"And you believed him?"

"Sir, he's the High Admiral."

Cassandra looked at William. She could hear the youth and innocence in Paa's voice. He honestly believed that the High Admiral wouldn't lie to him, wouldn't use him.

The Admiral put his comm on speaker then entered the High Admiral's code.

"High Admiral Valerian's office," Valerian's assistant answered.

"This is Zafar, put me through."

"I'm sorry, the High Admiral is not receiving your calls."

"Put me through, Lanier, or your nephew will be facing Royal treason."

"What?"

"You got him into this, Lanier, let's see if the High Admiral will get him out." Seconds later, Valerian came on the line.

"What is it, Zafar!" Valerian demanded.

"I'm calling to see what you want me to do with your spy, High Admiral."

"Excuse me?"

"Ensign Paa, the one you ordered to report to you the movements of the Royals in the House of Protection."

"I have no idea what you're talking about, Zafar. That would be treason. Palaces are sovereign ground. The Coalition has no power there unless asked by the Monarchs themselves."

The Admiral watched Paa pale.

"So you're saying you didn't order Ensign Paa to report the movements of Princess Cassandra and her niece to you? That you didn't give him a personal comm," he picked up the second comm on his desk. "Didn't receive reports from him?" He scrolled through the comm seeing transmission times.

"That's exactly what I'm saying. If you insinuate anything else, I'll destroy you." The High Admiral was furious that he had been found out.

"Paa is your problem, do with him whatever you want." Valerian ended the transmission.

"There seems to be some discrepancy, Ensign."

"Sir, I swear to you, Sir. The High Admiral gave me orders."

"He explicitly said, 'I order,' to you," William hammered him.

"I… no…he said he wanted my help…that it would help save lives."

"And he gave you the personal comm."

"No, my Uncle did. He came to the Palace, the day we arrived and gave it to me."

"All this after I gave you the option to not be involved."

"The High Admiral said I would be more useful here."

"I'm sure he did," William looked at Cassandra.

She'd been listening. While no one else in the room was surprised that Valerian had denied everything, Paa was shocked and devastated. Valerian had just destroyed the young man's belief in his commander. He was no longer the innocent young man he'd been just a short time ago. While her expression didn't change, William could see the sadness in her eyes.

"Princess," the Admiral brought all eyes to her, "Your opinion." Paa's head whipped around and she saw she was not wrong. He was pale with a lost look on his face and looking at her like she was his executioner. She walked forward to stand beside the Admiral.

"The High Admiral is an asshole."

"Agreed," the Admiral's eyes flashed at her, "but with regard to Ensign Paa." Cassandra gave him a considering look then turned her attention to Marat.

"Chief Marat," his eyes locked on hers, she could see the guilt. "Would you explain to me why you chose Ensign Paa to be part of the security force?"

"Princess, Ensign Paa, while young, was at the head of his class at the Academy. He showed a natural ability in security and defense. He excelled on the Retribution and with his heritage was an obvious choice."

"His heritage?"

"Paa's grandfather was High Admiral before Valerian, Princess," Colonel Tar answered for Marat.

"You knew him, Colonel?"

"Yes, Princess. He led by example. He was killed in battle saving multiple crew members." There was no doubt of Tar's respect for Paa's grandfather.

"So Ensign Paa's subterfuge was totally unexpected."

"Yes, Princess."

"Lieutenant Zafar, your opinion."

"Princess, I'd never met Ensign Paa until our arrival on Carina. I'd heard good things about him on the Retribution, from people whose opinions I trust."

"So you finding out he's been reporting to Valerian on the movement of me and Victoria surprises you?"

"Definitely."

She turned her gaze to Paa. It was obvious to her that the High Admiral had chosen his patsy well. A young, still idealistic male, who was trying to follow in his grandfather's footsteps. Who, up until a few minutes ago, believed the current High Admiral was like his grandfather, honest and sincere. One no one would ever suspect.

"Admiral."

"Yes, Princess."

"Paa's uncle?"

"He is not blood. Ensign Paa's father was High Admiral Paa's only son. Lanier married Hargrove's third daughter."

"You knew the High Admiral personally."

"Yes, Princess, he was a good High Admiral, a better man."

Cassandra heard the respect in William's voice for the late High Admiral, had heard it in all their voices. Yes, Valerian had chosen well, the fucking jerk.

Ensign Paa saw the Princess' eyes harden and knew he was finished. He deserved to be, he had shamed his grandfather's memory.

"Ensign Paa," Cassandra waited until he made eye contact. "I said it earlier. The decision regarding you is a military one. Admiral Zafar will make that decision. That being said," she turned to look at William, "if it's your decision that Ensign Paa stay as part of the security force I will not oppose it. But he will have no contact with Victoria."

"Understood, Princess," he gave her a slight nod. Nodding back, she gave Paa one last look then left the room.

Paa stood shocked at the Princess' comments and exit. Turning his eyes to the Admiral's he realized he was not clear yet.

"Sit, Ensign," the Admiral ordered. "Marat, remove the restraints." As he did, Paa rubbed his wrists.

"Can you work the schedule so Paa's never alone?"

"The only place for that is exterior door security, Admiral," Marat answered.

"He will be issued no comm, no weapon."

"Yes, Admiral." Paa's eyes widened. He didn't understand what was happening.

The Admiral looked at Tar, "Colonel?"

"I agree, Admiral."

"Lucas?" William realized his son was going to have a hard time with this.

"He stays away from Victoria." Paa saw the deadly look in Lucas' eyes.

"Yes, and Cassandra." The Admiral allowed Paa to understand the closeness of his relationship with the Princess. "I would like a few minutes alone with Ensign Paa." The Admiral looked at the three men in the room.

"Shut the door, Quinn." The Admiral stared down at Paa as the door closed. "Does Valerian have anyone else in the security force?"

"No, Sir, I'm sure of it."

"Why?"

"Because the High Admiral told me I was vital in the protection of the Coalition." The Admiral nodded.

"Understand me, Ensign, if you endanger my family again, I won't care who your grandfather was. Your family will never find your body. Do you understand?"

"Yes, Admiral."

"Report to Marat."

"Yes, Sir." Paa rose quickly heading for the door, then stopped and turned back to William.

"Why?"

"You're questioning your good fortune, Ensign?" the Admiral raised an eyebrow.

"Yes, Sir," Paa stood at attention. "I gave you my loyalty then betrayed it. I reported locations of Royals. The Princess knows this. Why am I not being arrested?"

The Admiral leaned back in his chair. It took a great deal of inner strength for Paa to stand there, after Valerian's betrayal, and question him. It showed he had already learned that to accept blindly is to be blind.

"You're not being arrested because the Princess sees something in you. She understands that Valerian used you then abandoned you. She realized he chose you because of who your grandfather was. That you would believe what he told you because of that. He used your youth and inexperience against you," the Admiral stood.

"She's not that much older than I am, Admiral, that was one of the High Admiral's reasons for her using you."

"Cassandra uses no one," he stared at Paa. "I'll tell you something that not many know, Paa. Cassandra's father and brother were both members of Shock Troops. She understands how the military works, knows that not all those in command should be there. She's giving you a second chance, but she's not trusting you." William gave him a hard look. "Chances are you'll never be trusted by her again. But she's not going to destroy you for doing what you honestly believed was right. She could, but she won't. She believes in justice; that the innocent shouldn't pay for the guilty. Dismissed."

"Yes, Sir."

Chapter Thirty-Seven

William found Cassandra alone in their suite.

"Tell me." He walked up behind her, his arms going around her as she stared out the window.

"What did you decide?" she countered.

"He'll be standing guard with no comm, no weapon. You didn't have to give him a second chance."

"Neither did you," she turned in his arms. "Fuck Valerian. Paa was an innocent."

"Yes he was, now tell me."

Cassandra looked up at him. "After you left, I couldn't get back to sleep. Someone was a hell of a kisser," she gave him a slight smile.

"Thank you," he smiled back at her.

"But suddenly I had this need for Fudge Torta. Your son is somewhat demanding."

"You had a craving?"

"Oh, just a really big one. So I went down to the kitchen to get a slice. I overheard Paa talking to Valerian. He didn't see me."

"You were in the kitchen alone?"

"Just me and the Fudge Torta."

"You should have called Hutu," William's eyes were hard.

"It was early. There was no reason to bother him."

"There became one."

"William…"

"You could have been hurt," he held her arms.

"That kid wasn't going to hurt me," her voice was dismissive.

"Kid? He's a highly trained member of the Coalition," William gave her a slight shake.

"That may be, but he's still a child, at least he was until Valerian betrayed him."

"He's only four cycles younger than you."

"I haven't been that young and naive since my mother died," Cassandra rested her hands on his chest, letting the beat of his heart comfort her.

"Did you ever get your Fudge Torta?" He held her close knowing it still hurt her, her father sending her away.

"No," she looked up at him, pouting slightly. "By the time everything settled Victoria was up. I didn't think it would set a very good example to have it for breakfast. I got loblolly instead."

William couldn't help but smile at her, "I suppose I could be convinced to have Hutu send you up a piece."

Her eyes sparkled into his, "Really?" Sliding her arms up his chest, she put her hands around his neck to bring his head down. "What would it take to convince you?"

William crushed her to him. Things could have gone very differently in the kitchen, he could have lost her. Her and their son. Breaking the kiss he framed her face with his hands.

"You'll rest."

"What?" Cassandra's mind wasn't fully engaged yet.

"After the Fudge Torta, you'll rest."

"That's blackmail," she frowned at him.

"Yes, it is," he was not the least apologetic.

"I still need to get through Kyle's Intel," she argued back.

"Fudge Torta…" he dangled the temptation.

"Sometimes you are just mean," she smiled to soften her words. "Get me the torta and I'll lie down for a while."

"Until 1300."

"William!"

"That's the deal."

"And hard-headed," but she knew she'd lost.

∞ ∞ ∞ ∞ ∞

Kyle had been able to compile a great deal of information in a short period of time. She was impressed; it was thorough and well-presented. Standing, she walked over to the window letting her mind filter through it, not noticing the darkening skies.

So long ago…it started so long ago…all because of a birthmark. Sabah's birthmark that she'd passed on to her daughter and granddaughters. That the Regulians had documented when her grandmother had been abducted over fifty years ago. That Olah discovered when he was translating the data from the Regulian ship captured by William during the Battle of Fayal. Data that Olah passed on to Prince Audric.

Prince Audric, born on Messene, the planet where Royals went to get away. Audric was born to commoners, both his parents working as servants. For some reason Queen Hestia, Yakira's mother, had taken a liking to him. She'd paid for him to be educated and trained. During that time he became friends with Vane, Yakira's intended. He'd been climbing with Vane when he'd had his 'accident.' It had been blamed on faulty equipment. The man in charge of the climb had sworn that the equipment was brand new and in perfect condition, he'd inspected it himself. Several weeks later he was found dead, an apparent suicide, the note he'd left stating he could no longer live knowing he'd been responsible for Vane's death.

But the most interesting thing she'd learned was that Audric had a genetic condition. A very rare condition found only in those born on Messene. It affected his eyes. In certain lighting, they would seem to 'sparkle,' or 'glitter,' especially to a two-year-old.

Turning from the window, she walked back to the comm pulling up a picture of Audric. He was standing beside Queen Yakira, their son next to his mother, their daughter in front. A very stiff formal picture with no one touching. While there was no doubt the children were brother and sister neither child resembled Audric. Interesting. Would Victoria recognize him? Did she dare put her through it?

She had done so much better since the thread was removed. No more nightmares about the Glitter Man. She'd gotten a little slice of her childhood back. She could run and laugh with Amina. Even with the destruction of Earth, and the death of her parents, she was finding joy. Was it necessary that she be put through it?

"You're thinking awfully hard." William walked over to see what she was staring at on the screen. "The Royal family?"

"Hmmm."

"What are you thinking?"

"Do I show Victoria?" she turned troubled eyes to him. "She has been doing so much better."

"You promised her she could help," he reminded her.

"I know." He heard the indecision in her voice.

"Cassandra," William caressed her cheek, "how would you feel, if after I had promised you we'd do this your way, I changed my mind and settled it without you?"

Her eyes flared, "I would be very upset." Closing her eyes, she sighed. "I know, I get it. I just want to protect her." She looked into his eyes, knowing that's what he wanted to do for her. "It's two entirely different things."

"Yes, it is. She is always protected, you…you like to 'irritate' the man you believe responsible for the destruction of your planet…you go alone into a dark kitchen for a piece of torta and discover a spy."

"I have you," Cassandra rested a hand over his heart. "You understand me, allow me to be me, tell me when I'm wrong, protect me, and love me. I couldn't do any of this without you."

"And Victoria has us. She needs to be part of this, to know she has some control."

"And if the nightmares return?"

"Then we'll help her through them."

Cassandra looked at him and nodded. "Okay, but when? When do we show her Audric?" William just looked at her. "Now?"

He saw the fear in her eyes. "The sooner it's done, the better you'll feel." Knowing he was right, she nodded. He leaned down pushing a button on the comm.

"Zafar."

"Lucas, bring Victoria over to our suite." He disconnected before Lucas could ask anything.

∞ ∞ ∞ ∞ ∞

Minutes later, Lucas and Victoria entered the private area, Victoria chattering away. Looking at her aunt, she went quiet.

"What's wrong, Aunt Cassie?" She moved closer to Lucas, seeking support.

"There's nothing wrong, Victoria," William said. "We want you to look at something on the screen." He held out his hand.

"On the screen?" Victoria walked to take his hand, trusting him.

Lucas looked first at his father then Cassandra. Cassandra was concerned; his stomach tightened.

Cassandra sat down in the chair, she needed to be strong. "Yeah, baby, come sit on my lap." Once she was in her arms, she turned her to the screen. To Audric.

Immediately, Victoria stiffened. Lucas saw her pale.

"No…no…no…he's found me."

"No, baby, no. It's just a picture. He isn't here."

"It's the Glitter Man!" Cassandra closed her eyes.

"Are you sure, Victoria?" William demanded. The frantic, fear-filled eyes that shot to him broke his heart.

"Yes," she whispered.

"What the fuck is going on?" Lucas rushed toward Victoria, William blocked him.

"It's all right, baby," Cassandra softly told her as she buried her face in her neck, her little body quivering. "I'm here. You're safe. I promise."

"Why would you do that?!?" Lucas demanded of his father, his face furious.

"Calm down," William pulled him away from the comm.

"Don't tell me to calm down! That wasn't necessary! Since when do you get off scaring little girls?"

"Enough!" There was no doubting the authority or the anger in his father's voice.

"Stop it! Both of you!" Cassandra's voice was commanding, her eyes hard as she looked at them. They softened as she looked into her niece's eyes, seeing the fear, the shock, and the trust. "We promised you that when the time came you could help. That you were the only one who'd ever seen the Glitter Man, would ever recognize him. Is that him?"

"Yes," she whispered.

"Okay then," she took a deep breath. "Now we know. Now we move on." She looked at the Zafar men, seeing that both had calmed down. Leaning down she whispered in Victoria's ear, "I think Lucas could use a hug." The eyes that met Cassandra's were older than her nine years.

Victoria slid out of her aunt's arms to walk over to Lucas. Lifting her arms, she waited for him to lift her up so she could wrap her arms around his neck.

"I'm okay, Lucas, I helped."

"You did," he held her tightly.

"Aunt Cassie?" Victoria looked at her, "Who is he?"

"Prince Audric, husband to Queen Yakira."

"He's a bad man."

"Yes he is, and now we can stop him." She walked over to William slipping her arms around him. "Victoria, you can't tell anyone, not yet, not even Amina."

"Why?"

"Tori, you've done your part, now you have to let us do ours," the Admiral said.

"How long?" she demanded.

"Not very."

Victoria looked from the Admiral to her aunt. "Okay." Suddenly there was an enormous boom from outside, causing both women to jump.

"Hey, it's just tuono," William's arms tightened around her.

"A what?" Cassandra raised slightly shaken eyes to him.

"Thunder, Aunt Cassie."

"Thunder?" Cassandra looked at the darkened windows, it was only 1600. "A storm?"

"Stoirme," William corrected her.

"Stoirme," she repeated as she walked over to the window. This time she noticed the dark rolling clouds, heavy with moisture. "A tuono stoirme and this is baisteach." Cassandra's finger followed the trail of water on the outside of the window.

"Yes," William watched her take in the information.

"Do you have lightning too?" She looked to William, seeing his confusion, then looked at Victoria.

"I don't know. I never asked Amina," Victoria said.

"It sounds like you're learning a lot about Carina," Cassandra smiled at her.

"Yeah, Javiera has been letting us use the screen and Amina's showing me lots of stuff," Victoria smiled back.

"That's good. Soon you'll be teaching me," Cassandra smiled and winked.

Victoria laughed rolling her eyes, "Like that would ever happen."

It was good to hear her laugh. There was a flash of very bright light outside, two heads turned to William.

"Tintreach," he told them. "It can be deadly. You don't want it to hit you."

"Just like lightning. Same rules, Tori," she looked to make sure she understood.

"Got it. Can I go back to Amina's until third meal?"

"If you want… " she gave her a considering look.

"I'm okay, Aunt Cassie," Victoria's look was steady.

"All right then, I'll see you at third meal."

As Lucas and Victoria left, Cassandra turned to William. "What now?"

"Now," William walked over to rub her arms, "we wait. Nothing can be done until they resume the Challenge."

∞ ∞ ∞ ∞ ∞

The storm continued during third meal.

Cassandra turned from the window, "Does it usually baisteach this much?"

"It can, especially during this part of the cycle," William replied.

"Is it like this where the House of Knowledge is?"

William turned to her, "In Kisurri? No, it's quite a bit drier there, hotter."

"It has a lot of deserts, Aunt Cassie."

"Really, so it's like Kayseri on Earth."

"Yeah."

Cassandra chewed her food, thinking of Sabah. "Has it always been called Kisurri?"

"I don't know. Kyle would, why?" William asked.

"The city where Kayden and Sabah's Palace was used to be called Kaisaria, now it is…was called Kayseri. It would make sense that arriving on Earth they would choose a place with a climate that was similar to what they knew. At least Sabah would."

"It wouldn't have been that different for Kayden, there are areas in the House of Protection's realm that are similar to Kisurri."

"Aunt Cassie," Victoria whispered looking over Cassandra's shoulder.

Cassandra froze, the bite she was about to take forgotten. Her eyes flew to William. "What?"

"Look," Victoria pointed out the window.

Turning Cassandra looked out the window, William saw her jaw drop.

"Cassandra? What is it?" He looked out the window seeing nothing strange.

"The rain, baisteach, it's different colors."

"Yeah," he looked from Victoria's amazed eyes to Cassandra's. "I take it rain wasn't like this on Earth?"

"No," there was awe in Cassandra's voice.

"Aunt Cassie, can we go outside?" Cassandra looked to Victoria, finding she wanted to go too.

"William?" He saw the desire in her eyes.

"It's safe." As soon as the words were out of his mouth both women were out of their chairs, headed for the stairs. "Careful!" William held his breath as the two flew down them, his tone bringing people running. He held up his hand to Marat.

Kyle and Lucas came running from the guest suite, "Dad?" Kyle watched the two.

"The baisteach, it's different than on Earth."

"Different how?" Kyle wanted to know.

"I don't know." Heading down the steps, they followed them into the garden.

Cassandra was looking up watching jewels fall from the sky while Victoria was trying to catch them in her hand. William smiled remembering when Lucas and Kyle used to try.

"It's," Cassandra looked at William, "incredible."

"What was it like on Earth?" Kyle asked.

"Clear, always clear."

"Really?" he was astounded.

When Cassandra looked to William, he saw the wonder in her eyes. Walking over he curled his arms around her. "Happy?" he whispered so only she could hear.

"Yes, it's like watching jewels falling from the sky. It has something to do with the suns, doesn't it?"

"Stop thinking, enjoy it." He didn't know if he'd ever seen this much wonder before in someone's eyes. Little things, he needed to remember it was the little things that matter.

"Aunt Cassie, they go clear when you catch them."

William looked up. "The story goes that the Loki drop their treasures from the sky to watch them sparkle. If you can catch them before they disappear, you will be allowed to keep them. If not they return to them. It is also believed it happens when the ancestors are welcoming someone home."

"Dadrian."

"Yes, it will help Jotham."

"I'm glad." Cassandra watched as the skies cleared and the 'jewels' disappeared.

"Aunt Cassie, there's no rainbow," Victoria gave her a confused look.

"There wasn't always one on Earth."

"I know, but I thought there would be…"

"What's a rainbow?"

"After a storm, stoirme, when the sun would break through we'd sometimes get a rainbow in the sky. It's an arch in the sky," Cassandra motioned with her hand, "that had ribbons of color in it. The same colors as your baisteach."

"If you reached the end of the rainbow before it disappeared there was a pot of gold, and you were rich," Victoria informed the Admiral.

"Really?" the Admiral said. Victoria nodded.

"It was also believed by many to be a promise, a promise that the Earth would survive any storm. I always liked to think it was my mom, watching out for me."

"Similar beliefs for similar things," Kyle frowned slightly as he commented.

"Beliefs brought by Kayden and Sabah? That survived this long? It's possible."

"Admiral," Marat stepped out. "You have a call."

"I'll be right there. Lucas," William looked at him to see he understood he wanted him to stay with Cassandra and Victoria. "I'll see you later." He looked down at Cassandra.

"Okay." Smiling she stepped out of his arms.

"What do you think, Victoria? Should we go in and get you dry?"

"Yeah I suppose," Victoria hedged.

"What?"

"Can I take a bath?" her eyes were hopeful.

Cassandra knew she loved that tub. "Sure, but then you get ready for bed."

"All right."

∞ ∞ ∞ ∞ ∞

Later with the bathroom put back in order, Cassandra ran a brush through Tori's damp hair.

"Aunt Cassie…"

"What?" Victoria turned around to look at her. "What?" she asked again, she could tell there was something on her mind. "Is it about Prince Audric?"

"No."

"Then what?"

"I saw the test," Victoria watched her aunt's eyes widen.

"What?"

"When you were in the bathroom, the day of the Ball, you had a test like Mom did when she was pregnant."

"I..." Cassandra knew what Victoria was talking about. She just didn't know what to say. She had made a point of trying to be honest with Victoria.

"So are you?"

"Yes." She watched Victoria closely, worried it would make her sad. Instead, Victoria gave her a big grin.

"That's awesome!"

"You think?"

"Yeah," Victoria gave her a questioning look. "The Admiral knows doesn't he?"

"Yes, Victoria, William knows," she smiled at her.

"What about Lucas and Kyle?" Tori frowned at the thought.

"No, they don't know. We haven't told anyone. We've been getting used to the idea ourselves first."

"So I know something they don't?" Her eyes sparkled mischievously.

"Victoria Lynn, you will not say anything. It's for the Admiral to tell them. When he's ready."

"But why are you waiting?"

"Victoria, you and I, we've had a lot of changes to deal with lately. A lot to adjust to. It hasn't been easy has it?" she saw the sparkle go out of her niece's eyes.

"No."

"We aren't the only ones adjusting. The Admiral, Lucas, Kyle, the Michelakakis'; they have all had to adjust too. We're just waiting until things calm down a bit, letting everyone get used to those changes before there's another one. Can you understand that?"

"I guess, but it's such good news. It's like I'm still getting a baby brother or sister. It will be like that, won't it?"

"Yeah, baby, it will. You'll be a great big sister." Cassandra brushed her cheek.

"So I have to keep the secret, even from Amina?" Victoria didn't like that thought, she told Amina everything!

"For a while. Think how you'd feel if Amina told you about it because she'd heard it from Lucas or Kyle."

"I'd be upset."

"So Kyle and Lucas need to hear it from their father, when he's ready to tell them, not from you."

"Okay, I won't tell."

"Promise?"

"Promise."

"Okay let's finish this hair."

∞ ∞ ∞ ∞ ∞

With Victoria in bed, Cassandra found she was at loose ends. William had yet to return and she didn't feel like going to bed without him. Getting a glass of ale she looked at the tub, it was even larger than the one in Tori's bathroom.

'Might feel good to just relax,' she thought. Walking over, she turned on the water. Around the tub were different jars. Opening one she sniffed. Throwing a handful of crystals in she watched it immediately bubble, filling the room with a wonderful vanilla scent. Stripping down she stepped into the steaming water, leaning back she closed her eyes and sighed. As the water enveloped her, muscles she didn't even know were tense started to unwind. She should have done this days ago; as she relaxed, her mind drifted.

Chapter Thirty-Eight

The suns were high in the sky, their dry heat warming her. It felt familiar, as did the Palace. Following the path, she wandered into a private courtyard with benches and small groupings of plants that were able to take the heat. Some were even blooming. Walking over she sniffed. Yes, vanilla, how strange.

"Not really," Cassandra turned to find Sabah, a much younger Sabah. "I've always loved that scent. When I left, I took seeds with me."

"You planned it all out?" Cassandra raised an eyebrow.

"Not all, but enough. I took with me what I thought I would most want. What does a girl of eighteen cycles know?"

"Enough to start a new civilization."

Sabah gave her a smile, "You give me too much credit. That was Kayden."

"It was both of you, together."

"Yes, together, what I didn't know he did. What he couldn't do, I could." Sabah leaned over to smell the flower. "We were always so much more together."

"Where are we?" Cassandra looked up seeing the three suns. "This isn't Earth."

"No, it's the House of Knowledge. The Queen's garden." Sabah sat. "Your garden."

"Perhaps," Cassandra wasn't agreeing to anything.

Sabah's eyes hardened, "What do you mean perhaps? You carry the birthmark, it's already changed. You are the Queen."

"That will be my decision, William's and mine together. If I choose to become Queen, it will be on my terms."

"You will have no choice," Sabah told her.

"There is always a choice. You made yours, I will make mine."

"The House of Knowledge will not survive without you."

"It has survived 2500 cycles without the real Queen. It will survive without me if it has to."

"Not this time. Not once the traitor is revealed. It will never recover, not without the leadership of the true Queen!"

"That's not my problem. I will not lose anyone else I love. Not for anything as unimportant as being the Queen."

"Unimportant! It is an honor to be Queen," Sabah's eyes flashed at her.

"If it's such an honor you should have stayed!"

"That was different! I was just the heir. It would be cycles before I would be Queen. I wasn't willing to wait or, to sacrifice Kayden for it."

"And I'm not willing to sacrifice William!"

"You don't have to! You are the Queen!"

"What are you talking about?"

∞ ∞ ∞ ∞ ∞

"Cassandra, Cassandra," William touched her cheek. When he first entered, she seemed so peaceful and relaxed, but now something was wrong.

"Cassandra, wake up," William ordered.

"What?" she opened confused eyes to his, "William?"

"Yeah, you were sleeping in the bath."

"I was?" Sitting up she realized the water had cooled. She must have dozed off. He watched as her breasts rose from the water. Seeing his eyes darken, her breath caught.

"Come out," he held out his hand.

Taking it, she watched him as she stood. His eyes followed the water streaming down her body. Circling her waist he lifted her over the edge, holding her wet body against his.

"William," she rested her hands on his shoulders.

"Shhh." Leaning down he took her lips in a reverent kiss as his hand slid over her slick skin. His fingers ignited fires wherever they touched. Groaning she slipped her tongue past his lips to tease his mouth open, caressing his tongue. Holding his shoulders, she pulled herself closer to him, needing him.

Here she was. The one he had searched for his whole life, the one he would sacrifice his life for. She was his life mate, he was hers. She carried his son. She was everything. Tearing his mouth from hers, he looked into her eyes. Those eyes of deepest, clearest blue that let him see her soul. They let him in, only him. Right now they were starting to lose focus, letting him know her desire for him, only him.

"I need you," she whispered.

Sweeping her up into his arms, William carried her to their bed. Laying her down, her fingers started on his shirt. With it open, she slipped her hands in to caress his massive chest only to slip around to his wide back as he pressed her into the bed, skin to skin.

"Oh, William," Cassandra arched to feel more of him.

Kissing his way down her neck, William gave his attention to her breast, her full and beautiful breast, teasing it until it was a taut hard peak before turning his attention to its twin.

She was lost, the sensations he could arouse in her left her breathless. How had she ever survived without him? Her release was so close and he'd hardly touched her. He was the only one who could do this to her, make it so she could give everything while still being protected.

Moving her hands downward, she worked on his pants and found him hard and heavy. Releasing him she guided him to her entrance. Lifting his head he watched her as he entered.

She was hot, wet, tight and welcoming. Her eyes blazed into his letting him know she wanted more, more of him. As her eyes flared, she wrapped her legs around his hips pulling him home. That was what this was, home. Forever she would be his home.

Arching above her, he slid an arm under her hips setting her at just the right angle to pleasure them both, the rhythm long and deep. This would not be a quick mating, it would be one of pleasure, tenderness, desire and commitment. Commitment each to the other on the deepest level until desire finally took over and they found pleasure together. Breathless, William collapsed beside her shuddering.

Cassandra couldn't move. Her entire body was trembling, her mind nonfunctional. How did he do this to her? She would never know, didn't want to, she would just enjoy it. With a satisfied smile on her face, she managed to turn her head. His eyes were closed, hair spiked, breathing uneven. It made her smile grow that she was able to do that to this beautiful, strong man; make him breathless.

His eyes opened, violet eyes meeting sapphire, honest and open and what she saw there caused her heart to flutter. Love for eternity for her, commitment to her, no matter what anyone else thought or believed. She felt her eyes fill.

"Cassandra? What's wrong?" he framed her face.

"Nothing, there is not one thing wrong." Touching his hand she turned to kiss his palm, "I love you. Only you. Forever.

William's eyes were calm. He leaned down and gently kissed her, "Forever."

∞ ∞ ∞ ∞ ∞

The comm beside the bed woke William. Easing away from Cassandra, he reached for it.

"Zafar."

"Admiral, King Jotham is at the door requesting entrance."

"What?!? Granted! Show him in immediately. I'll be right down."

"William? What is it?" Cassandra sat up holding a sheet over her breasts.

"Jotham is at the door."

"What? What time is it?" Finding the clock she saw it was 0330.

"I have to go."

"Of course," she put a hand on his arm as he rose. "Bring him up. You need privacy."

Nodding, he pulled on pants and a shirt. As he left, Cassandra got on the comm. Rising, she put on a nightgown and robe before heading to Victoria's room.

∞ ∞ ∞ ∞ ∞

"William, I wasn't thinking, I shouldn't have come."

"Jotham, it is fine. This is exactly where you should have come." William saw Marat enter. "Does your security know where you are?"

"What? Oh, I'm sure they do." Marat nodded to the Admiral as he left the room.

"Let's go upstairs, Jotham, we'll talk."

"No, it's late. I should go."

"No, Jotham, you need to come upstairs with me." William took his friend's arm, leading him. Something that hadn't been done for him since he had become King.

Jotham paused at the top of the stairs and, looked back down, down to where his son had died.

"Could I have prevented it, Will?"

"No." Both men turned as the door to the Royal Suite opened. Cassandra walked out carrying a sleeping Victoria.

"Majesty," she gave him a slight nod then continued on her way to the guest suite. William moved to open the door wanting to take Victoria from her.

"I'm fine," she whispered, "take care of your friend."

"Will, she shouldn't be carrying that child."

"Cassandra is somewhat stubborn on what she can and cannot do, especially when it comes to her niece. Come on, Jotham."

As he led his friend into the Royal Suite, Leander was taking Victoria from Cassandra's arms.

"I'm sorry, I know it's late." She looked at her two friends.

"Cassandra, it's fine. Is everything all right?" Javiera asked.

"Jotham is here. He needs to talk to William."

"Oh."

"I need to get back," she hesitated. "She's been okay, but we had some new Intel on the Glitter Man today. She might have a nightmare."

"If she does, I'll contact you right away."

Cassandra took a deep breath, knowing she couldn't do it all by herself. "Okay," and turning she left.

On the landing between suites, Cassandra saw Hutu start up the stairs carrying the tray she ordered. Suddenly there was a commotion behind him. She watched as Deffand and Marat struggled with each other, as each moved for their weapons she spoke up.

"ENOUGH!" Both men froze. "You will both stand down!" Lifting her robe and gown she started down the stairs. Both men watched her.

"Princess, you shouldn't be here," Hutu told her.

"This is exactly where I should be."

"Marat, report."

"Princess, Captain Deffand forced his way into the Royal Wing. I was about to subdue him."

"I could see that," she turned to Deffand. "Captain Deffand, you feel you have the right to enter the Royal Suite not only unannounced but carrying a weapon?"

"I am here for my King's protection!" Deffand's uniform was unbuttoned, his hair disheveled. He'd obviously been in a hurry.

"The King you lost?"

"Excuse me?"

"If it hadn't been for the Admiral having Chief Marat inform you, you would still be sleeping not knowing where your King was."

Deffand found he couldn't argue with her, she was right.

"Do you feel there is a threat to King Jotham here?" She waited.

"No, Princess," Deffand was forced to admit.

"I understand your sense of duty to your King, Captain, but he came here tonight to see a friend, his oldest friend. He came as a man, not a King.

Chief Marat would have done the same thing." Cassandra's comment allowed Marat to know she put no blame on him. "I assume the rest of the King's security force will be arriving soon?"

"Yes."

"So you have a choice, Captain. The Admiral has made it clear. No one is allowed into the Royal Wing with a weapon." She saw his eyes flare. "Either you and your men, will be allowed in, unarmed, to wait in the outer room until the King is ready to leave. Or, you may remain with your weapon. My call, Chief," Cassandra silenced Marat with a look, "And your men will stand down, outside the Royal Suite. It's your call."

"You feel you have the right to negotiate with me, Princess?"

"I know King Jotham's well-being is your primary concern. You know there is no threat here. If King Jotham had wanted you in the room with him, he would have put you there himself."

Deffand found he was unable to argue, "I will remain, with my weapon."

"Fine. Marat," she turned her attention to the Chief. "You will stay with Deffand. Hutu, if you'd carry the tray up for me, I'd appreciate it." Turning, she headed up the stairs.

∞ ∞ ∞ ∞ ∞

"Jotham, sit." William led his friend back to the private area.

"Will, I shouldn't have come."

"Yes, you should have, Jotham. You've been my best friend for over forty cycles, this is exactly where you should be."

"You have enough to deal with. The Challenge, Valerian, the threat against your life mate, the attack on her by my own son."

"Jotham," he didn't know what to say.

"Majesty," Cassandra swept into the room carrying a tray laden with cups and refreshments. William immediately stood taking it from her, setting it on a table. Leaning forward she poured a cup of Hutu's coffee, handing it to Jotham.

"Princess," Jotham didn't know what to say. Cassandra looked to William.

"Majesty, if you'll excuse me I'll let you men talk." She got up only to be stopped by Jotham's hand on her wrist.

"Stay, please."

Cassandra sent William a confused look. "Majesty, I think you'd be more comfortable talking to William alone."

"Are you his life mate?" The King had yet to let go of her wrist.

"Yes," she answered him with no hesitation, her eyes steady as she met his.

"Then stay, he'll tell you anyway."

"Majesty," Cassandra slowly sat, "While William is my life mate, he'd never break your confidence, not even to me."

Jotham gave her a half-smile, "I know that, Cassandra, but I also remember what it was like, to have a life mate, to need to share with her." She found she could say nothing. The King's use of her first name had shocked her.

"Tomorrow, no today, I will go before the Assembly informing them my son was a traitor," Jotham looked into the cup in his hands.

"Jotham," William paled at the thought. This would destroy Jotham's reign and, the House of Protection.

"Why would you do that, Majesty?" Cassandra asked honestly puzzled.

Jotham looked at her, "You know why. My son was responsible for deaths, thousands of deaths. He used when he should have protected."

"What I know, Majesty, is that Dadrian contacted Barek on board the Sentinel to ask his brother for advice on a problem he was having. That I can prove. That's all I can prove."

"You know there's more, the Regulians…"

"Attacked the Fleet as they always have," Cassandra rose and put a memory foil into the comm and after a few keystrokes removed it. Walking back to William she held it out to him.

What was she doing? William looked at her then, looked at the foil. He raised concerned eyes to her. Does she really want to do this? Looking into her eyes, he saw she did. He took the foil from her.

"It wasn't a standard attack, it was caused by Dadrian," Jotham watched them.

"Prove it," she turned back to Jotham.

"What?"

"Prove it. Where is your proof?" she demanded.

"He admitted to it, he ran."

"He admitted nothing and he fell. What proof can you produce that says anything different?" Cassandra pounded at him.

"You have the transmissions." Jotham watched as William snapped the memory foil in two.

"What transmissions, Jotham?" he asked.

"You can't do that! There must be justice!" Jotham surged to his feet.

"I couldn't agree more, Majesty, but that wouldn't be justice. It would bring no better good. It would only cause the innocent to suffer and that isn't justice, or at least not what I consider justice."

Jotham looked at his friend, "William, make her understand."

"I can't, Jotham, I agree with her." William stood looking from his life mate to his friend and King. "The only one who would benefit from that is the original traitor. It would put the House of Protection in a position that it may never recover from. Loss of trust, you know what that means, Jotham. It won't affect just you but Barek and his children. He doesn't deserve that."

"We don't always get what we deserve," Jotham walked to the window, looking out into the dark.

"No, Majesty, we don't. We deal with what life gives us," Cassandra looked at him and saw a man, a father, struggling with his son's decisions. "May I speak freely, Majesty?"

Jotham turned, "You haven't been?" Her eyes didn't change. "Speak."

She looked to William, he nodded. "You don't know me, Majesty. Don't know my beliefs. You've found reasons to doubt. I don't hold that against you. But everything I've just said I can say about you." She saw Jotham's eyes change. "The difference is William. He believes in you, I believe in him. Therefore if I trust his judgment, and I do, I must believe in you."

She looked at William drawing strength, "Things happen within families. Some good, some bad. You can hurt each other. If you're lucky, you have time to make it right. Dadrian didn't have that time. That doesn't mean he wouldn't have if he had. Grant him the benefit of the doubt, Majesty. It's the least any of us can do."

Jotham looked at the two, seeing the unit they made, a solid unit. She should be out for blood, after what Dadrian did to her. But she wasn't.

"Others will find the transmissions."

"Why would they look?"

"What?"

"They aren't in Regulian," she stared at Jotham. "There's nothing there to cause someone to take a second look."

"You took a second look."

"Jotham," William looked at his friend, "when Cassandra explained to you how she found the transmissions, she made it sound easy. It wasn't. She's the only one to ever break the codes; to link them, no one else will."

"And justice?"

"I will have it," Cassandra's hard eyes met his. "But I will have it from the one who started it. The one that is still alive. He is responsible, Majesty, for all of it. He started this. He killed seven billion people to stop me from getting to this point. He's the reason Dadrian even thought about doing the unthinkable. Justice will be served when he is revealed, not Dadrian."

Jotham looked at her considering.

"Jotham, she's right. Let it go."

"Can you, after he attacked your life mate? Can you let it go?" Jotham watched William tense, knowing it needed to be said. "Can you?" He turned his eyes to Cassandra.

She also had felt William tense. Wishing Jotham would have just let it go, left it unsaid. But that would have been the easy way, and neither of these men would ever take it.

"Yes," Cassandra's eyes were steady as they met Jotham's. She was not going to let her mistake come between them.

"William?" Jotham looked at his friend.

William looked to Cassandra, his life mate, she was the one Dadrian attacked. She was willing to let it go. Was he?

Cassandra saw the struggle in his eyes. He raised a hand to gently caress her cheek. She was here, Dadrian was not.

"Yes, I can let it go." William's eyes were open and honest as they looked at his friend.

Jotham straightened. A weight he didn't know he was carrying had lifted. He scrubbed his face with his hands. Dadrian's actions hadn't cost him his friend.

"Thank you, thank you both." Jotham looked over to see they had sat back down.

"Not necessary, Jotham."

"Yes, it is and it's a lot to forgive. I'm in your debt."

"No."

"Don't argue with me, William, I'm your King." Jotham smiled at him, the first real smile he'd had in days.

"You were his friend first," Cassandra corrected him.

"Yes, yes I was, and still am." Jotham was still smiling as he looked at Cassandra then back to William. "Do you ever win an argument with her?"

"Not when she believes she's right," William smiled back.

"Now wait a minute, this is two against one." William wrapped an arm around her pulling her into a hug.

"Am I wrong?" He looked down at her.

She looked up at him, understanding. "Trick question. No matter how I answer you're right."

Jotham laughed. Yes, these two were truly life mates. They understood each other. They would need it. His smile faded. "Queen Yakira has convinced the other Royals and Assemblymen to forego the rest of the gatherings and call the Challenge." Jotham watched the humor leave William's eyes.

"When," he demanded.

"Tomorrow, 1300."

"Fuck!" William stood.

Cassandra watched him with concerned eyes. "William..."

"She's trying to control the Challenge." He ran a hand through his hair as he paced. "She thinks if the Assembly is called now they will vote in her favor." Jotham nodded his agreement.

"So?"

"So? Cassandra, it might work."

"William," she walked over to him. "That doesn't matter. Not to me. You know that."

"What do you mean, it doesn't matter?!!!" Jotham stood. "It's what the Challenge is all about."

"No it's not, not for me," Cassandra fired over her shoulder, her eyes never leaving William's.

"Would someone explain to me what's going on?" Jotham demanded. "The whole point of the Challenge is for you to be declared Queen. It's why you're here."

"No, it's not," Cassandra's voice was angry. "There are more important things."

"William," Jotham looked at his friend.

"The point of Cassandra's Challenge was to have a full Assembly." He finally looked from Cassandra to his friend and King. "You have to have a full Assembly if you are going to accuse a Royal of treason."

"A Royal? Another Royal?"

"Yes."

"You were never truly challenging Yakira, that's why you wouldn't show your birthmark."

"I never cared about being Queen, just justice. And my birthmark is my business."

"Jotham, she is the Queen, there is no doubt."

"William," she was cut off by his comm ringing.

"Zafar."

"Dad, it's Victoria." Through the line, all three could hear Victoria's terrified screams. Cassandra was halfway down the hall before either man moved.

∞ ∞ ∞ ∞ ∞

"No! No! Let me go!" Victoria was struggling in Lucas' arms.

"Calm down, Victoria!" Lucas was getting desperate.

"Give her to me," Cassandra ordered entering the room. "I'm here, baby, I'm here. She wrapped her arms around her, holding on tight, rocking her. "Shhh, you're safe. Look at me, Victoria."

Cassandra tipped her head up. "Open your eyes and look at me," her voice firm, finally Victoria did. "I'm here, you're safe."

"The Glitter Man…"

"Isn't here. Look, look who's in the room," she eased her hold so she could see Lucas, Kyle, Leander, Jotham, and William sitting right next to her. "See no Glitter Man."

Jotham had followed William as he raced across the hall. The feisty, charming, little girl he'd met before was now a terrified child, clinging to her aunt as if her world was ending. And it had. He'd forgotten. It had for both of them. Because of this traitor. This traitor she was worried he would interfere with her exposing.

"You were falling," Victoria whispered to Cassandra. "The Glitter Man made you fall and the Admiral couldn't get to you."

"Shhh, just a dream," Cassandra hugged her close, her eyes meeting William's. "It was just a bad dream."

"Promise?"

"I promise." She gave her a quick hug then eased back. "Let's get you back in your own bed. Okay?"

"Okay."

William stood taking Victoria from Cassandra's arms. "Hey, kiddo, let me carry you." With Victoria's arms around his neck, he lifted her with one arm while helping Cassandra up with the other. As a family, they turned to leave the room.

"Lucas," Cassandra looked at him.

"Later. Take care of her first."

She nodded.

∞ ∞ ∞ ∞ ∞

The first sun was rising as they laid Victoria down in her own bed. Exhausted, she fell quickly to sleep. Returning to the private area, Cassandra stopped short finding Jotham still there.

He saw her fatigue and her strength as she straightened her shoulders ready to stand. Stand for what she believed in. Stand for who she loved. In this case, his most trusted friend, William. She was willing to trust him because she trusted William. Maybe it was time for him to follow suit.

"It's easy to forget," Jotham spoke first, looking from his friend to Cassandra.

"What is?" her voice was calm, her eyes steady.

"What you've been through, what you've both survived. She was clinging to you as if her world was falling apart because it did, for both of you. Everything and everyone you knew are gone."

"Yes," Cassandra's voice was tight but steady. William put a hand at her back giving her his support.

"Yet you fit. Here. You make it look easy as if this was where you were always meant to be."

"Maybe she was," William told his friend.

"Nothing about this is easy, Majesty," Cassandra walked away from William, pacing. "Having a nine-year-old, little girl terrorized isn't easy. Having the man I love and trust doubted by his closest friend isn't easy. But I'll be damned if I'm going to let that son of a bitch get away with it! With murdering seven billion people on the chance, that I could be Queen."

Jotham finally saw her true fury and it was incredible. "You want revenge?"

"I want justice. There's a difference."

"Yes, there is. And the Challenge? Why not be declared Queen then go after the traitor?"

"Can you decree justice, Majesty? And have it be true justice?"

"No."

"So tomorrow we will find out if there is justice on Carina, after that we can worry about whether or not I take the throne."

"Cassandra," William walked over to her, rubbing her arms. He felt the slight tremor.

"William claims you are the Queen."

"She is!" William's voice was angry. He was tired of Jotham's doubts.

"Then why is there a question about the throne?" Jotham would not give up.

"Because of me!" William's eyes were blazing as he looked at his friend. Cassandra had pushed too far, again. "Come on, you need to lie down."

"I'm fine."

William had had enough. He swept her up into his arms, carried her into their bedroom, and laid her down in the middle of the bed.

"You will stay here and you will rest!"

"Damn it, William."

"I mean it, you're trembling. I won't have it!" Leaning down he kissed her, letting her know the extent of his anger, his concern. Framing his face, she returned the kiss, trying to comfort him.

"All right, I could lie down for a while. But what will Jotham think?"

"I'll handle Jotham." He gave her another hard kiss as he got up, shutting the door on his way out.

∞ ∞ ∞ ∞ ∞

He found Jotham looking at Lata's garden as the second sunrise started. He turned when he heard the door shut.

"Is she okay?"

"Just worn out." William walked over pouring them both a glass of Carinian Ale.

"She stands so strong."

"Until she breaks," he handed his friend a glass.

"She'd sacrifice the throne for you."

William looked deep into his glass, "She wouldn't see it as a sacrifice." He took a deep drink.

"That says something. It says she loves you, truly loves you," Jotham finally believed.

"I already knew that."

"And if she doesn't take the throne?" Jotham suspected, knowing his friend, but had to ask.

"Then we leave. Together. She'll never be safe otherwise."

Jotham sighed, "You have it planned?"

"Yes. I won't lose her."

"If you need my help you have it."

"Thank you, Jotham," Nodding, Jotham finished his drink and left the suite.

∞ ∞ ∞ ∞ ∞

Entering their room he slid into bed, drawing her into his arms. He needed to hold her. Tomorrow, this would be done. She'd either be Queen or they'd be gone, forever. He'd already chosen their escape route, had everything in place. The thought of leaving his sons and Carina, hurt. But not having Cassandra would be unbearable.

"You're thinking awfully hard," she rubbed a hand across his chest.

"You're supposed to be sleeping," his arms tightened around her.

"I was thinking," she murmured.

"You're always thinking, sleep."

"William…"

"Shhh, later."

"No, it won't wait. You've given up a lot to get us this far," she raised up leaning on his chest.

"I've given up nothing that truly matters."

She gave him a soft smile, "Things could go wrong at the Assembly."

"They won't."

"But they could. You've already thought of that, thought of how to get us out," she met his eyes.

"Yes," he saw the acceptance and trust.

"There's something I want to ask of you before I'm presented to the Assembly."

"Cassandra, what do you need?" He tucked a loose piece of hair behind her ear. He saw nerves in her eyes, "Ask."

"When I'm presented to the Assembly, I want to be presented as Cassandra Qwes Zafar." She watched his eyes widen before he sat straight up.

"What!?!" he whispered gripping her arms.

"I want you to be my husband when I'm presented to the Assembly."

"Cassandra," William was shocked. He hadn't expected this. Looking into her eyes he could tell she had been thinking about it for a while. He didn't know what to say.

"William?" Cassandra had been so sure, now she wasn't. "Honesty even if I don't like it."

He saw the doubt enter her eyes. "You would take my name?" his voice was hoarse.

"I…yes, unless you don't want me to. I thought…" William kissed her deeply. Twisting he pressed her into the bed, framing her face with his hands.

"I very much do, Cassandra Qwes Zafar." She could see how saying it pleased him.

"Yes, I very much want to be able to call you my husband." She put a hand on his cheek, her thumb caressing his lips, "To be Admiral William Zafar's wife."

She had given him yet another gift. Did she even realize it? For her to take his name, she was Qwes. It was unheard of for the heir to change her name. The husband did. Salish hadn't even taken his name, wanting to keep her 'identity.'

"William?" Cassandra saw his mind had wandered.

"You humble me, Cassandra, it would be an honor to have you carry my name."

"William, the honor is mine," she kissed him. As the kiss started to deepen, he broke it off.

"No," he said roughly.

"What?" Confused eyes met his.

"The next time I make love to you, I want you to be my wife."

"William," her eyes filled.

"You will rest while I get things arranged."

"But…"

"No buts, Cassandra, you're not getting enough rest." His eyes were challenging.

"I'm getting as much as you are."

"I'm not carrying a child," he replied as he gently touched the place where their son rested.

"We're fine," she covered his hand with one of hers.

"And I'll make sure you stay that way."

"William…" Cassandra looked into his eyes, "Victoria knows."

"What?"

"About the baby, she recognized the test, from the one her mother had."

"And she hasn't said anything?"

"No, she just told me last night. When she asked, I couldn't lie to her," she looked at him hoping he'd understand.

"Of course you couldn't," he looked at her. "She's okay with it?" he frowned, thinking about the little brother she'd lost.

"She thinks it's awesome."

"Really?" he had to grin. "That's good. I need to tell the boys." He saw the concern in her eyes. "It will be fine. So you'll rest." William wouldn't be distracted, his expression locked with hers. "Then you'll eat."

"William," she started to disagree.

"Then we'll have our Union."

She closed her mouth, "And you say I always win an argument."

William gave her a quick kiss, "I think we both won."

"So do I." She smiled as he rolled out of bed before he changed his mind.

"Sleep," he ordered then headed to the shower. Smiling he thought of all he had to do.

∞ ∞ ∞ ∞ ∞

"Lucas?" William walked into his Ready Room.

"What? Oh, Dad, hi."

"What's wrong?"

"Wrong? Nothing, what could be wrong? Victoria's having nightmares, I can't help her but hey, nothing's wrong."

William could see the frustration in his son's eyes. "You want to, feel like you should be able to, because she's your life mate."

"Yes."

"Lucas, she may be, someday, but not today. Today she is a nine-cycle, little girl who needs her aunt, someone to guide and protect her."

"I can do that," Lucas interrupted.

"To be a parent," William finished. "You can't be both, Lucas. You can't be a parent and a life mate. It doesn't work that way. You have to choose."

"What do you mean?"

"If you want to someday claim her as yours when she's old enough to understand, then right now you have to step back. Let her become that person."

"That leaves her unprotected!"

"I'll protect her. Cassandra and I will, she's ours to raise," he looked into his son's eyes. "When she's old enough she'll make her own decision."

"How do I step back? How do I take that risk?" Lucas sat down.

"By trusting me, trusting Cassandra, and mostly trusting Victoria. If there's no trust, then there is no relationship."

"Like you and Mom."

"What?" William froze.

"You didn't trust each other, not after what she did," he met his father's eyes. "I know you tried to make it work after she lied to you about having conceived."

"Lucas..."

"I've known for a long time. But when she did conceive you, you stayed."

"You're my son, of course, I stayed."

"But you didn't trust her again. And she never really believed you'd stay."

"We both made mistakes."

"Yeah, I don't want to make one with Victoria."

"She needs the chance to grow up, to find her way. Find her way to you, if that's her choice. You have to give her that opportunity, Lucas."

"It scares the fuck out of me, Dad. What if she chooses someone else?"

"Her choice, Lucas," William put a hand on his son's shoulder. "But I promise you. If she's given the choice and chooses you, you'll be the luckiest man on the planet."

"You're speaking of Cassandra."

"Yes. Is your brother awake?" William stood to walk around the desk.

"I don't know."

"Would you go find him for me, bring him down here, I need to talk to both of you."

"Dad, what's going on?" Lucas frowned at him, something was up.

"Please, get your brother."

"Okay."

"Shut the door." With one last look, Lucas left closing the door.

∞ ∞ ∞ ∞ ∞

Picking up the headset, William pushed a button and waited.

"Jotham."

"Jotham, it's Will. I need a favor."

"Ask."

"I would like you to perform Cassandra's and my Union this afternoon."

"Excuse me?" William was silent. "Will, you're serious?"

"Definitely."

"If she becomes Queen…"

"We'll deal with that when the time comes."

"Why now, Will?"

"Jotham, I want her for my wife. She wants me for her husband. She wants to be Cassandra Qwes Zafar."

"What?" Jotham was stunned.

"I want it too. I hadn't realized how badly I wanted it until she said it." He leaned back in his chair. "I'm asking my friend and King for his help."

"What time?"

William released a breath he hadn't realized he'd been holding, "1500."

"I'll be there by 1430."

"Thanks. And Jotham, bring Barek."

"I'll let him know," the King disconnected.

∞ ∞ ∞ ∞ ∞

William was just taking off the headset when there was a knock on the door. "Enter."

Lucas and Kyle walked in. "Close the door, sit down."

William watched his sons as they sat. They were two grown men he was very proud of, soon he'd have a third. The thought filled him with pride and terrified him.

"Dad, what is it," Kyle asked.

"Queen Yakira has called for and been granted a full Assembly to finish the Challenge tomorrow at 1300."

"What!" Kyle sat forward. "There haven't been all the gatherings."

"And there won't be. It's done." William looked at his sons. "Today at 1500, King Jotham will be here to perform a Union, a Union between myself and Cassandra."

"Today?" Kyle looked at Lucas. "Why?"

"It's what I want, it's what Cassandra wants." Time to tell them everything. "There's more."

"What?" Lucas asked.

"Cassandra's conceived." Both his sons sat back stunned. William waited.

"You're sure, she's sure?" Lucas asked.

"Yes."

"It could be all the adjustments she's gone through," Kyle told him.

"That was Cassandra's first thought. It's why she waited so long to tell me. She wanted to be sure."

"Are you?" Lucas had to ask knowing why his mother and father got married.

"Lucas, I haven't done anything to prevent it."

"But..."

"I wanted her to conceive, selfish of me, but there it is."

"It's why she was light-headed at the Ball," Kyle said.

"Yes."

"It's why she seems to be tiring easier."

"Yes. She's pushing too hard. Trying to handle too much on her own, she's stubborn that way."

"Oh, she is?" Lucas challenged with a smile. William smiled back.

"So now you know. Are either of you going to have a problem with this?"

"Dad, what do you want us to say?"

"Congratulations would be nice," William's face hardened.

"This is what you want, what you really want?" Kyle asked.

"I want Cassandra as my wife more than I've wanted anything in my life." The conviction in his voice had Kyle hesitating.

"And the baby?"

"Scares the hell out of me, she's so little. Once this Challenge is over, she's going to the best doctor on the planet if I have to tie her up to get her there."

The brothers grinned at each other. It was rare to see their father express his emotions this way. Cassandra had had a good effect on him.

"If you're good with it so am I," Kyle replied first.

"Me too," Lucas said.

"Thank you. Both of you, it means a lot. You know it doesn't change anything, between the three of us."

"Yes it does," Kyle was not going to lie to his father. "But that's okay, it'll just get better. I'll finally get to be a big brother. Oh, crap!" Kyle paled.

"What!"

"What if it's a girl? What do we do with a girl?"

William laughed at the stricken look on both his sons' faces. "I personally happen to like women," William chuckled.

"Women, yeah, but little girls; they're terrifying. Look at Victoria last night. She nearly scared me to death. I've never felt so helpless in my entire life," Kyle shuddered remembering. "She's okay, isn't she?"

"Yes. Still sleeping and I'll let you off the hook. It's a boy."

"What! How can you know that?" Lucas demanded.

"According to Cassandra, a Qwes woman always has a son first."

"Really, she's got that documented?" Kyle's eyes sparkled.

"God, sometimes you're just like her, all excited about data." Kyle just smiled at him.

"So, 1430 we meet down here with Jotham and Barek."

Chapter Thirty-Nine

Getting up, Cassandra couldn't help but smile. She'd gotten a good three hours of sleep, now it was time to get ready for her Union with William.

"Aunt Cassie?" Pulling on her robe, she turned to find Victoria in the doorway.

"Hi, how are you this morning?" she walked over to kneel down in front of her niece.

"Okay, sorry about last night."

"Hey, there's nothing to be sorry about." She gathered her into her arms, "We all have bad dreams."

"Do you?"

"Yes."

"You never tell me."

"I guess it's because I tell William."

"And he makes them go away like you do for me?"

"Yes."

Victoria thought about it, "I guess that's okay then as long as you tell someone."

Cassandra gave her a quick hug, "Are you just getting up too?"

"Yeah."

"Good then we can eat together and talk. I'm thinking flatcakes. What about you?"

"That sounds good."

"Do you want to call Hutu or me?"

"I will," Victoria ran to the comm.

"Victoria Lynn, no Fudge Torta," though her mouth watered at the thought.

"Oh, man."

Smiling she watched her niece talk to Hutu. She was okay.

Cassandra wasn't sure she'd ever had flatcakes that tasted this good. Finishing her plate, she saw Victoria's eyes were wide.

"Sorry," she swallowed the bite in her mouth. "We were supposed to be talking."

"That's okay. I've never seen you eat like that. It must be the baby," Victoria said in a knowing voice. "Did you know that when Amina was born she weighed ten hectic…pounds?"

"Ten?" Cassandra paled just a little. She was going to have to talk to Javiera.

"Yeah, I was only eight."

"I know, I was there," Cassandra smiled at her.

"So what's up, Aunt Cassie?"

"Well…I was wondering if you'd like to go to a wedding this afternoon."

"A wedding? Who's getting married?" Victoria's eyes widened as she stared at her aunt, "You? You and the Admiral?"

"Yes."

"Really? Really, really, really?" Victoria was out of her chair, jumping up and down.

"Really," she had to laugh at her excitement.

"I'll have an Uncle William!"

"Yes, you will," William entered the room, hearing Victoria. Leaning over he gave Cassandra a hard kiss, "Good morning."

"It is," she touched the side of his face, enjoying the look in his eyes.

"This is better than the baby! Oops," Victoria stopped jumping. "Sorry, Aunt Cassie."

"That's okay, honey. I told William you knew."

"But I promised not to say anything."

"I think we can forgive you," he picked her up smiling. "I see you got your aunt to eat," he looked at the empty plate.

"She was really hungry. I told her it was the baby."

"You may be right."

"Do Lucas and Kyle know yet?" Victoria questioned.

"I just got done telling them."

"About the baby too?"

"Yes," he watched her.

"Can I go over now then? I can tell Amina, can't I?"

William looked at Cassandra to see what she thought, "Yes, that's fine."

"Awesome!" She wiggled out of William's arms. "Bye!"

"Wait," the Admiral's voice stopped her cold, "you can't just run across."

"I forgot, sorry."

"I'll walk you over. I'll be right back," he told Cassandra as he followed Victoria.

Waiting, Cassandra looked out the window to Lata's garden. It was a beautiful day.

"What are you thinking?" William's arms went around her.

"Just that it's a beautiful day." She turned in his arms, "So tell me, Admiral, what have you been doing today?"

"Oh a little of this, a little of that," he caressed her cheek. "Planning a Union."

"Really…anything I can help with?"

"That depends. I thought we'd have it in Lata's garden."

"Sounds perfect."

"I need to know what you want. I don't know how it was done on Earth."

"All I need is you. You, your sons and Victoria, but I'd like everyone else there if possible, including Jotham and Barek."

"I've taken care of that, Jotham's agreed to perform the ceremony."

"Jotham? The King performs Unions?" she frowned.

"He can, it's not common, but it can be done."

"How is it normally done?" William hesitated. "William?"

"A Guide usually performs the ceremony."

"Like the one from the Temple."

"Yes."

"And we're not having one because…"

"A Guide wouldn't perform the ceremony," he watched the sparkle go out of her eyes.

"Why?" she asked softly.

"There are protocols, things that must be determined before a Guide will perform a Union."

"You had one with Salish."

"Yes."

"So it has nothing to do with my having conceived."

"No! Cassandra, it's a formality. Not everyone has a Guide perform the ceremony. There are others who perform it, it's still recognized."

"But you didn't want to tell me. Why?"

William ran a hand through his hair, his frustration showing, "I didn't want you upset about it." She waited. "Some will consider it void when you become Queen."

"But why?"

"Because we're from two different Houses."

"Let them try and void my Union," Cassandra's eyes blazed, "and we're not from two separate Houses!"

"You're Qwes, Cassandra, that's House of Knowledge."

"I also descend from Kayden, that's House of Protection."

"They won't see it that way."

"I don't care how they see it. That's the way it is."

William pulled her close for a quick kiss. That was all he was allowing himself. "Let's worry about it if it happens. Right now I need to know what you want for the ceremony."

"William, I don't know how it's done here. All I know is I want to be your wife," she put a hand over his heart.

"Go change. I'll have Javiera come over, you two can talk, find out what you want. Jotham won't be here until 1430." He nudged her toward the bedroom.

"But William…"

"Cassandra, I'm going to be no help here. This is something women talk about." The lost look on his face made her smile.

"Well, at least that's the same as on Earth. You men get all flustered with wedding details." She gave him a teasing look, "Are you sure you don't want to join me? We are all alone…"

William's eyes flared at her, "You're a tease sometimes." He hugged her against his chest, kissing her until she was limp in his arms. Finally, he released her lips. "That will have to hold me until tonight." He smiled as he watched Cassandra's eyes start to focus again.

"I'm not the only tease around here," she was breathless looking at him.

"That wasn't a tease, it was a promise." He stroked his hands down her back one last time before stepping away.

"I'll hold you to it." She watched him leave before turning to get dressed.

∞ ∞ ∞ ∞ ∞

"Cassandra!" Javiera called from the private area.

"Be right there." Pulling her hair up, she headed for the door. "Hi!" She had a big grin on her face.

"Hi… Hi? What do you mean, Hi? Get over here!" Javiera swept her into a big hug, "A baby and a Union! This is great!"

Cassandra hugged Javiera back suddenly tearing up. It seemed like a lifetime since she'd just been able to sit down and talk to her when in reality it had only been nine days. She hadn't realized how much she needed to talk to a woman. William had.

"Hey, are you okay?" Javiera leaned back giving her a worried look.

"I'm fine. I just missed you. So much has been going on."

"You're telling me, gatherings, dinner with the King, Balls, Dadrian's death. Now a Union, and a baby."

"I know and I've barely been able to talk to you."

"So we'll talk now," Javiera led her to the couch, sitting down. "Leander and Lucas are with the girls under orders to keep them occupied. No interruptions."

"That would be nice, better than nice," Cassandra sighed.

"What do you need to know?"

"There's the problem, I don't know." She gave her a lost look. "Let's start with the Union ceremony. Tell me how it's normally done on Carina. How was yours and Leander's?"

"Well let's see. We had it in the Temple at Nias, just family and friends, a small union."

"A Guide performed the ceremony?"

"Of course," she saw Cassandra's frown. "What's wrong?"

"Why would someone not have a Guide perform the ceremony?"

"Not? Well, there could be some conflict between the families, as in one not supporting the Union. In that case, a Guide would not perform the ceremony. Or it could be the couple doesn't want to wait for the formalities. There is a mandatory waiting period to see if one or the other changes their mind."

"Or if they are considered from different Houses?"

"Yes. But Cassandra they are still recognized, just not in the Temple."

"And how does that reflect on someone, say an Admiral," Cassandra's eyes were steady as they met Javiera's. "The truth."

"Some of the very traditional members of the Coalition would look unfavorably on it. But Cassandra, you can't possibly think that matters to the Admiral."

"No, I know it doesn't. He could care less what some small-minded person thinks of him. But I need to know if it could be a problem for him, because of me."

"So who's performing the ceremony?"

"King Jotham."

"Really!!" Javiera was amazed and realized she shouldn't be. "Cassandra, for the King to perform the ceremony means he supports the Union. That is huge! It will go a long way with the traditionalists. King Jotham is very highly thought of."

"What else?"

"What do you mean?"

"At your Union, what did you wear?"

"A Union dress. It's a special dress a woman picks on her own, usually only worn on that day. I still have it," Javiera smiled.

"Color?"

"Traditionally it's the House color but any color can be chosen," Javiera frowned. "We don't have time for Pazel and Kia to make you something special."

"I already have something in mind." Smiling she thought about the violet dress she'd demanded to be made. "Javiera, you did take Leander's name didn't you? I've always assumed you did, but…"

"Yes, I know it isn't very modern of me, but I wanted to. But, Cassandra, that's not something you need to worry about."

"Why?"

"Why? Because you're Qwes. You'll be Queen Cassandra Qwes."

"I'm Cassandra Qwes Chamberlain. I'll be Cassandra Qwes Zafar whether I'm Queen or not," Cassandra's tone was firm.

"Cassandra, really?" Javiera was shocked.

"Why is it such a big deal?" She was genuinely puzzled.

"You're Qwes."

"Chamberlain," she argued back.

"But you carry the Qwes name."

"And still will. Every woman in my line has carried the name, but we change our last name to our husband's."

"I…I guess I just never considered it. It's not how it's ever been done." That had Cassandra smiling at Javiera.

"And everything I've done so far has been the way it's been done?"

Javiera looked at her and started to laugh, "No, not one thing. The House of Knowledge is in for a surprise."

"Yes, they are." She thought about Audric; about what he'd done then put it away. That was for tomorrow. "So anything else I need to know about the ceremony?"

"I can't think of anything else."

"We're going to have it in the garden."

"That will be beautiful."

"On Earth the groom would be with the…Guide, the bride would walk up to him, usually escorted by her father." She had to stop. It caught her off guard. She hadn't thought about it…her dad, he wouldn't be there to give her away. Neither would Peter or Cyndy. She stood as she walked to the window blindly looking out.

"Cassandra…"

She held up her hand, indicating she needed a minute.

"I'm going to call the Admiral." Javiera stood.

"No," Cassandra's voice was tight but firm. "Is it done that way on Carina?" She turned to look a Javiera.

"No. Well maybe a thousand years ago, but not today. The woman walks to her intended by herself, showing she's willing to be his wife."

"Then that's how it will be done," she sat back down.

"But Cassandra…"

"Javiera, there's no one here to walk me down the aisle even if I wanted them to. We're on Carina, we do it the Carinian way. William doesn't need to know any different."

"If that's the way you want it," Javiera wasn't convinced.

"I do, which brings me to what's said during the ceremony."

"King Jotham will lead you through the ceremony. He'll tell you what to say. You just repeat it."

"I can do that." Cassandra took a deep breath and looked at her friend. "Now tell me about babies."

"What?" Javiera laughed.

"William seems to be overly concerned about me, about my conceiving. Why?"

"Because he loves you."

"I know that. But what else?"

"Well, Cassandra, I know you don't consider it an issue but you are rather tiny," she saw Cassandra's eyes flare, "for a Carinian woman." Javiera quickly added. "And the Admiral is rather large even for a Carinian male. It does raise some issues whether you would be able to carry his child full course."

"Full course, you mean term. What is a full course on Carina?"

"Nine moon cycles."

"Moon cycles?"

"Umm, it's been close to two moon cycles since the Earth was destroyed."

"And all moon cycles are the same length?"

"Within a day or two, yes."

"So a month, nine months, same as Earth."

"It's the same?"

"Yes, but from talking to Victoria, there may be a size difference at birth. Amina was really ten hectic?"

"Ten hectic even. She was early. I told you I had problems."

"How early?"

"One moon cycle," Javiera frowned thinking back. "I thought I could do anything and then I fell. It was so stupid. I was rushing, it had been a long day, and I missed a step and fell. I was in my sixth cycle, I started to bleed." Javiera had to take a deep breath. "They kept me in Medical, hoping I could make it the full nine cycles, but I only made it to eight. I started to bleed internally. There had been damage from the fall they couldn't repair while I was carrying Amina. Once I delivered, there was a lot of scar tissue. So they thought it would be dangerous for me to conceive again."

"I'm so sorry, Javiera." Javiera just nodded. "So she was ten hectics at eight cycles. What should she have been?

"Oh, eleven or twelve easily."

"Really?"

"What are they on Earth?"

"Ten is a large baby."

"Really," Javiera looked at her. Now *she* was concerned. "Cassandra…"

"But they can be bigger, depends on the parents."

"You need to find out how big Lucas and Kyle were. It should give you an idea."

"I believe Salish was somewhat larger than I am, so that would have to be considered."

"Still," Javiera watched her friend.

Cassandra leaned back thinking. William had valid reasons to be concerned. Every pregnancy had its own risks, but she honestly didn't believe there would be a problem. Most of it was instinct, the rest was Sabah's reassurance that her son would be strong.

"We'll just have to see what happens."

"Cassandra…"

"Javiera, I'll take precautions. I've conceived, nothing is going to change that," she took her friend's hand, "it's a happy thing."

"Yes, yes it is. And it's a happy day."

"Yes." Javiera saw the sparkle in Cassandra's eyes. "So are you going to help me get ready today?"

"You couldn't stop me. 1500?"

"1500." The two women grinned at each other.

∞ ∞ ∞ ∞ ∞

As the time drew near, William found he was nervous. He'd dressed earlier, wanting Cassandra to have the suite to herself. Now Javiera was with her doing all those mysterious things women do before a Union.

Lucas and Kyle entered followed by Quinn. Quinn walked over and started to pour them all a drink as Barek and Jotham entered the room.

"Majesty," William nodded.

"Colonel, are you going to stand there or hand out those drinks?"

"Majesty," Quinn started around the room.

"I'll propose the first toast," the King raised his glass. "May your Union be long and joyful." They all took a sip and the toasts continued.

∞ ∞ ∞ ∞ ∞

"Cassandra..." Javiera was at a loss for words.

"Aunt Cassie, you're going to knock his socks off!" Victoria was never at a loss for words.

Cassandra turned from the mirror. The violet-colored dress had turned out just has she'd envisioned it. Strapless with a heart shaped neckline, the dress hugged her curves until it reached about mid-thigh and then it flared out. Pazel had found the perfect lace to complement the color and Kia's accenting with crystals made the dress sparkle and shimmer elegantly. Turning she found the train followed nicely behind her. They'd even made a shawl and trimmed it with the same lace and crystals. With her hair pulled up, her neck looked long and lovely.

"So?" she turned to them.

"It's beautiful, Cassandra. The Admiral will love it nearly as much as he loves you."

"Aunt Cassie, it's great!"

"What about you, Amina?" Cassandra looked at the little girl who'd been very quiet.

"You look like a Princess," she whispered.

Cassandra walked over and sat down next to Amina. "Thank you, Amina, but can I still be your Aunt Cassie?" Amina nodded then gave her a big hug.

"You know, I think you look very pretty too, both of you." She looked over at Victoria. They'd each picked their favorite dresses for the ceremony. "You too, Javiera."

"Thank you but you will be the only one anyone will notice," Javiera smiled at her. "Now it's almost time."

"Already?" Cassandra looked at the clock.

"Yes. Girls, why don't I walk you to the door? Leander's waiting to take you down."

"Okay," Victoria walked over to her aunt, "I love you, Aunt Cassie."

"I love you too, Victoria."

"Look what I'm wearing." Victoria pulled the necklace with Cassandra's 'lucky' ring on it out from under her dress.

Cassandra touched it, remembering. "That's good, baby."

"It's yours, maybe you should wear it."

"No, you wear it."

"Victoria," Javiera called from the other room.

"I'll see you in a little bit okay? You keep those Zafar men under control."

Victoria smiled like she knew she would, "I can do that."

Standing, Cassandra walked over to the mirror taking one last look. "I wish you were here, Daddy," she whispered. Taking a deep breath, she turned and walked toward her future.

∞ ∞ ∞ ∞ ∞

"Fuck, Will, you're nervous!" Jotham exclaimed so only William could hear. He hadn't seen him like this since they were sixteen and trying to peek in the female cadets' bathroom.

"Where is she?"

"Getting ready. Are you sure you want to do this?"

The eyes boring into his were deadly, "Yes, absolutely."

"Then calm down. Crap, Will, you're making *me* nervous. She'll be here when…" Jotham trailed off as he saw Cassandra enter the garden.

William slowly turned. There she was. Praise the Ancestors, there she was. As she walked toward him, he finally realized what she was wearing; violet, pure violet. Moving, he met her halfway.

"I thought I was supposed to come to you," she whispered up to him.

"We come to each other." Taking her hand, he placed it on his arm and escorted her to Jotham.

"Family and friends, we are here this day to witness the Union of this man and this woman..." Cassandra listened to Jotham finding many similarities between the ceremony here and on Earth.

"Do you, William Hale Zafar, accept this woman, Cassandra Qwes Chamberlain, as your wife? To love, honor and protect until you meet the ancestors?"

"I do and beyond."

Jotham raised an eyebrow. "And do you, Cassandra Qwes Chamberlain, accept this man, William Hale Zafar, as your husband? To love, honor and obey until you meet the ancestors?"

Cassandra raised an eyebrow at the King. "I, Cassandra Qwes Chamberlain, vow to love, honor and protect William Hale Zafar until I meet the ancestors and beyond."

William smiled into Cassandra's eyes. He'd forgotten that part of the vows. Leave it to his life mate to make sure she didn't promise anything she didn't mean. Jotham cleared his throat.

"Yes, well I'll take that as I do." There was soft laughter behind them. "The ring…"

William saw the shock in Cassandra's eyes, "I know it's very old-fashioned, but I want you to wear my ring." Another thing he hadn't asked. Jotham watched her slowly nod. William slipped the ring he'd always worn off his smallest finger.

"With this ring," William slipped it on Cassandra's index finger, already knowing it would fit, "I make you my wife." He saw the tears start to fill her eyes. Lifting her hand, he kissed where he'd just placed his ring.

"Ladies and…"

"Wait!" Cassandra looked at William, then turned, walked to Victoria, and knelt down. "What do you think?" Cassandra asked.

Victoria looked at the Admiral and nodded pulling the necklace over her head and handed it to her aunt. Removing the ring, she gave the chain back to Victoria.

Standing, she walked back to William. Back at his side she showed him what she had. William's eyes widened. Cassandra looked at Jotham, who frowning nodded.

"With this ring," Cassandra slipped it on William's index finger, a perfect fit, "I make you my husband." This time the tears slipped out. William gently wiped them away.

"Kiss your wife, Will," Jotham told him.

Framing her face, William leaned down giving her a hard, reverent kiss.

"Ladies and gentleman, I announce the Union of William and Cassandra Zafar."

∞ ∞ ∞ ∞ ∞

Hutu had arranged refreshments and small bites for after the ceremony. As everyone mingled talking, William held up a plate to Cassandra, a devilish look in his eye. Watching her look down, he saw her eyes widen. Slowly she picked up a wafer, taking a small bite.

"William, these are so good!" She quickly took a bigger bite.

"Chocolate chip cookies?" He enjoyed the pleasure in his wife's eyes.

"Yeah," her eyes closed as she finished the wafer.

"You know what you told Hutu," he teased.

"I know. Where is he?" William turned her to see Hutu refilling the refreshments. Cassandra walked over, William following behind. This would be interesting.

"Hutu…"

"Yes, Princess?" he turned.

She reached up to pull his face down to hers and gave him a firm kiss, right on the lips. The room went silent.

Releasing him she smiled, "Thank you." Hutu was bright red. Looking at the Admiral, he saw no anger and smiled back.

"Aunt Cassie? What's going on?" Victoria was never afraid to ask the question.

Cassandra took a wafer from the plate William still held. Everyone watched the little girl's eyes widen. Reverently she took the wafer from her aunt then took a bite.

"Chocolate chip cookies!"

"Yep, Hutu made them."

"Really!?! Hutu you're the BEST!" Victoria jumped at him, he instinctively caught her. Victoria imitated her aunt by kissing him, "Thank you, Hutu!"

"You're very welcome," Hutu set her back down.

"Thank you, Hutu," the Admiral nodded.

"Sir," he nodded at him then left the room.

William held the plate back up to Cassandra. Smiling she took a bite of another wafer.

"Uncle William, can I have another one?" Tori looked at him hopefully. William looked down enjoying his new title.

"Why don't you take the plate and share with Amina," he smiled at her.

"Okay," Victoria hurried off with her prize.

Still smiling, William handed Cassandra a glass. "What if I wanted another cookie?" Cassandra smiled at him.

"Then I guess you'll have to ask Hutu," William teased. "But give the man some time to recover. I thought he was going to drop when you kissed him."

"Oh please," Cassandra laughed.

"You don't realize the effect you have on others. That kiss will ruin him for all other women. I speak from experience," he gently caressed her cheek.

"Will," they both turned to Jotham, "We have to go, meetings."

Jotham was not going to tell Will they had to do with him. They already had enough going on.

"Thank you, Jotham." Will shook his friend's hand.

"Yes, Majesty, thank you." Cassandra stepped forward, resting her hands on his shoulders and kissed him lightly on the cheek.

"You're welcome," Jotham said slightly pink.

"Barek, thank you for attending."

"Wouldn't have been anywhere else, Admiral." Barek smiled at the two, with just a hint of sadness in his eyes, "Congratulations."

"Thank you, Barek." Cassandra smiled at him.

Turning, Barek followed his father.

Over the next several minutes, people began to filter out, each giving their best wishes until it was just the immediate family.

"Aunt Cassie, can I stay at Amina's tonight?" Cassandra gave William a concerned look.

"You don't want to sleep in your own bed tonight?"

"I want to stay with Amina, it's been forever!"

"Well, I don't see a problem if it's okay with Leander and Javiera."

"It is," William told her, Cassandra raised an eyebrow.

"If there's a problem you'll call?" Cassandra looked at Lucas.

"Yes."

"I'll be fine, Aunt Cassie," Victoria reassured her.

She nodded.

Kyle walked over, carrying a tray of glasses. One for each, including Victoria. He raised his. "A toast, to Cassandra and Victoria," he winked at Tori. "Welcome to the family, I hope you know what you're getting into." Touching his glass to Tori's, she giggled and they all took a sip.

"To Dad and Cassandra, and the little one on the way. May he be as smart as his mother," Lucas nodded to Cassandra, "and as good looking as me."

William couldn't help but laugh.

"To my wife," there was no doubting the pride in his voice, "and niece," or the love, "beautiful additions to our family."

"To the Zafar men, each and every one of you is a gift in our lives. Isn't that right, Victoria?"

"Right," she agreed.

"Admiral," William turned to Hutu, who seemed to have recovered from Cassandra's kiss.

"Yes, Hutu?" Lucas and Kyle left the room with Victoria.

"Sir, the suite has been prepared per your instructions."

"Thank you, Hutu."

"Sir, Princess," Hutu nodded then left.

Cassandra looked up at William, "What was that all about?"

"Hutu has prepared a meal for us. It's up in our suite." He wrapped his arms around her, around his wife.

"That was nice of him," she leaned into her husband.

"Should we go enjoy it?"

"I could eat." With his arm around her, he led her out of the room and up the stairs to their suite.

∞ ∞ ∞ ∞ ∞

Entering the private living area, Cassandra stopped. This wasn't the room she'd left to get married. Candlelight filled the room. Furniture had been moved so there was a lone table in the middle of the room, set with china and crystal, silver domes covering the food. Music played softly over the comm.

"William," she turned wonder-filled eyes to his. Reaching up she gave him an emotion-filled kiss, "It's beautiful."

"I wanted our first meal as husband and wife to be special," he cupped her face, his thumbs caressing her cheekbones.

"It is."

The love in his eyes took her breath away. Guiding her to the table, he pulled out her chair, seating her. He lifted the covers and poured a golden liquid into their glasses. She watched him, unable to speak. He went to all this trouble, for her. He truly was an exceptional man.

Smiling at him she looked down at her plate, Zebu. The first meal they'd ever had together, after the first time they'd made love. It touched her heart that he remembered.

"Eat before it cools," he told her.

As they ate, they talked. William told her stories about Kyle and Lucas growing up, things they'd done. She told him more about her family.

"You have a cabin in the mountains?"

"My great grandfather built it. Every generation adds something."

"Really? Do you get there often?"

"Only between tours. Kyle uses it a lot, though."

"Can we go sometime?"

"You'd want to? It's pretty remote," William leaned back looking at her.

"I'd love to."

"I'll arrange it then." Standing, he walked around helping her up. Drawing her into his arms, he slowly moved her around the room to the music. Sighing, Cassandra laid her head over his heart, her arms wrapped around his waist.

Lowering his head, William's mouth started at her temple before continuing its journey down to nuzzle her ear.

"Hmmm," her hands gripped his back as she turned her head allowing him better access to her neck. William took advantage by exploiting all the sensitive spots he knew so well.

"William," Cassandra groaned as his mouth moved down her neck. Raising his head, he looked down to see her desire, his wife's desire. It was a potent thing. Leaning down he swept her up into his arms, carrying her into their bedroom.

Cassandra was trying to catch her breath. This man, her husband, had done so much to make this a perfect day, from beginning to end. A memory to hold on to that would get them through the hard times. And she had no doubt they would have them, that's life. But it was what you did in between that would sustain you.

"I love you, William," she looked into his eyes as he let her legs slide down his body.

"I will always love you, wife," William sealed his vow with a kiss. "Did I tell you how beautiful you looked?" His fingers tunneled through her hair, gently removing the pins holding it up. "When you entered the garden, Cassandra, I have never seen anything so beautiful, you took my breath away. You are my heart, my soul, all that matters in my life, you're my wife." The emotion in his voice had her eyes filling.

"When I entered the garden, all I saw was you," Cassandra touched his cheek. "You were standing there, my Light, my love, the only one I'll ever have. You're my husband. All I'll ever need is you." Kissing him, her fingers moved down to work on his jacket sliding it off his massive shoulders. "You always look so handsome in your uniform," she turned to carefully place the jacket on the back of a chair. William leaned down to kiss her bare shoulder, his fingers working the buttons on the back of her dress. Freeing her, it slid down her body as his hands slid around her to cup her breasts.

Groaning, she leaned back letting him support her as her body began to ache. "William..."

He released one breast as his fingers teased their way down her side to slip under the scrap of violet eadai covering her. Finding her hot and wet, he slid a finger into her.

"William!" her body moved against his hand, he could already feel her starting to tremble. As his thumb caressed her nub the trembling increased.

"Let go, Cassandra," he whispered into her ear, gently biting her lobe, increasing the pressure of his thumb, "let go for me."

She couldn't breathe. The pleasure he was giving her coming so fast. Reaching behind her she wrapped one arm around his neck the other gripping his thigh as her hips moved against his hand.

"William!" she gasped as her body exploded.

Holding her trembling body against his, William kissed her shoulder. Did she know what it did for him, her response to his touch? That she allowed herself to lose control with him. Bending, he swept her into his arms carrying her to their bed. Laying her down he saw her eyes begin to focus. Removing the remainder of his uniform, he joined her.

Cassandra watched him undress, her breath still not steady. He was such a large man in every way. Strong, tough, sometimes gruff, but he'd never hurt her. She had known that since the first day on the Raptor. He put her needs first, her need for understanding, her need for justice. Even when it made things harder for him, she was first. He protected her, even from herself. He was her life mate, her love, her lover, and now her husband. As he joined her in their bed, he let her roll him onto his back.

Laying across his chest, her fingers gently caressed his lips as her eyes looked into his. Slowly her lips replaced her fingers, her eyes never leaving his. The kiss she gave him was soft, full of all the love she had for him. Her tongue played with his as her hand moved down his chest, fluttering across his well-defined abdomen to his thick shaft.

As her fingers danced across him, teased him, William felt his control slip. He gripped her hips and lifted her so she straddled him.

Breaking off the kiss, she watched him as she slowly took him in, inch by glorious inch. His eyes flared as she took all of him, only to slowly reverse the process. Sweat broke out on his chest, his fingers clenching as he tried to maintain control.

"Let go, William," Cassandra's voice was husky with passion, "let go for me." She watched as his eyes darkened and turned just a little wild.

Pulling her mouth down, his hips drove home. Rolling her, he crushed her into the bed, his thrusts long and deep. Locking his hands with hers, he held them above her head bracing himself above her as his mouth continued its assault.

Cassandra wrapped her legs around him as she ripped her mouth from his desperate for air. "More," she panted as she started to tighten around him. "Please, William, more."

William growled at her demand. Attacking her mouth, he lost the last vestiges of control, and blind desire took over. He barely heard her cry of release as she tightened around him. He would have more. He would take more.

"More!" he demanded releasing her mouth, "give me more!"

Her eyes widened at his demand, she didn't think she could, but her body was already starting to tighten. William was giving her no recourse as he fed on her breasts, using his teeth to tease her already throbbing nipples.

As the orgasm exploded through her body, Cassandra screamed. He captured it with his mouth as he emptied himself into her with one last powerful thrust.

Cassandra was limp beneath him. With great effort he lifted his head, his breathing still irregular. He found her eyes closed and her lips swollen. Releasing her hands, he caressed a flushed cheek.

Lifting heavy eyelids, glazed eyes met his. "Are we alive?" she whispered.

Easing to her side, he leaned down to gently kiss her lips. "I think so," he murmured his hand wandering down her body, resting over their son.

"Good, that's good."

He enjoyed her barely formed words. A testament to just how far he'd taken her, how far they'd taken each other.

Cassandra couldn't get her mind to function, it was shut off. How did this man, her husband, she couldn't help but smile, do that to her? Covering his hand she laced their fingers.

"Do you know what I like more than my eadai?" she asked when she finally caught her breath.

"What?" he loved to hear her desires.

"Being your wife."

He watched her eyes sharpen, her mind reengage, "being Cassandra Qwes Zafar, Admiral Zafar's wife." William's heart tightened, hearing her say it. He'd never get tired of hearing it.

"My wife," he lifted her hand to kiss the ring he'd placed there only a short while ago.

"Tell me about the ring," she rolled onto her side facing him.

"It was my first House ring, given to me by King Kado, Jotham's father, before I went to the Academy."

"How old were you?"

"Thirteen."

"And you've worn it ever since?"

"I couldn't seem to part with it. So as I grew I just switched fingers instead of getting a new one."

"William..."

"I know it's out of style, the giving of rings, and even when it was in style, it wasn't an old House ring. I can get you something more appropriate."

"Just try and get it back," she closed her hand around his. "That you would give me a ring you cherish matters more to me then some fancy thing that's only there to show off."

"It's a symbol of the House of Protection, Cassandra." He wanted to make sure she understood.

"My husband is from the House of Protection, it's appropriate." She saw the concern in his eyes, "What do I not understand?"

"It's not that, people will ask questions. Question your commitment to the House of Knowledge if you wear a ring from the House of Protection."

"The ring is about my commitment to you. How I express that commitment is up to me. It has nothing to do with the House of Knowledge."

"But you need to know it could be brought up tomorrow." She looked at him understanding what he was telling her.

"Thank you," leaning over she kissed him.

"Tell me about mine," William looked at the thick, wide band on his finger. It's mellow golden color, the edges softened. A large square-cut black gem filled the face; frowning as the light hit it he realized it was violet, not black, the deepest violet he'd ever seen. Sitting up he looked at the sides. One had a crest, the other a single arrow. It was a First Son's ring.

"Cassandra, where did you get this?"

"I found it in Sabah's tomb, the last time I left Kayseri."

William's eyes flew to hers. "When?"

"After Victoria."

"And you never went back?"

"There was nothing to go back to. The tomb collapsed the day I left."

"After the ring was removed."

"Yes." Sitting up Cassandra touched the ring.

"You've had the ring ever since?"

"Yeah," she gave him a slightly guilty look. "I know I should have turned it over, but I couldn't part with it. Victoria likes to call it my lucky ring."

"Why?" he watched her closely.

"Because of my dad. I showed it to him. He told me to keep it, that it was meant to be mine and would always keep me safe. It kind of became the family talisman; if you wore it, you'd be protected." He saw the touch of sadness in her eyes, talking about her father.

"If it's yours, why was Victoria wearing it?" He saw her eyes darken.

"After the poisoning she was scared, she didn't want to admit it, but she was. I gave it to her to wear."

"So she'd feel safe."

"That and it made her feel closer to Peter. He'd wear it when he was away." Cassandra looked into his eyes and saw he understood she meant when he was on missions, dangerous missions.

"But she gave it up." William's throat tightened as he looked at the ring. "Today, both of you gave it up, to give to me," his eyes locked on hers.

"We don't need the ring to protect us anymore. We have you." She touched his cheek letting him see the belief, the trust they had in him.

What had he ever done to deserve this? The trust of not only his life mate but of Victoria. They'd given him the one thing they had left, something special to each of them.

"Cassandra," he rested his forehead against hers. "I don't know what to say."

"William, I can't prove it, but I believe I was meant to find this ring, Kayden's ring. I was supposed to bring it back to Carina, to you, it's back where it belongs, on the hand of a man from the House of Protection. I believe that's why Sabah hid it, instead of giving it to their son. The ring needed to be returned to Carina, to one of Kayden's descendants, to you."

"I don't descend from Kayden."

"You descend from Walwyn, his brother. You are family. The ring needs to be returned to the family," she touched his cheek.

"The way Sabah needed you to find it, to return it, to have a Qwes woman return to the throne of the House of Knowledge." He touched her birthmark which by now was not only blazing white, but all the rays coming out of it were colored; the five House colors.

"Maybe."

"Cassandra," William's voice was aggravated.

"William," her eyes were serious as they looked into his. He could tell she had thought this out. "I understand what you're saying, and yes I even believe it. There are too many coincidences for it not to be. But I'm not going to let that dictate my life, my life with you, Victoria and our son. That will be our decision. Not the Assembly's, not the ancestors, ours."

William listened, really listened to her, and she was right. He had to smile, she usually was. Pulling her to him he gave her a long kiss.

"What was that for?" her eyes sparkled into his.

"For being right; you usually are. We will decide our future."

Chapter Forty

The first sun was barely rising as Cassandra felt William sliding away from her.

"Where are you going?" her voice was heavy with sleep.

"Shower. Sleep, there's time." Kissing her softly, he tucked the covers around her. Watching her eyes close, he left her. He hadn't allowed her much rest; his need for her, for his wife, had surprised him. They had loved fast, hard, slow, and soft. Even now he wanted her. Turning on the shower he stepped in.

Sleepy eyes watched his firm bare backside move away from her. He had marks on his back from her nails. They'd loved long into the night, exhausting each other, to have only a touch, a look, rekindle the passion. Just the thought had her body starting to tingle. Hearing the shower, she smiled.

"You missed a spot," William froze, his head whipping around to see the water flow over his wife as she stepped into the shower. Tipping her head back, her hair streamed away from her face as sapphire eyes met his. "Let me get it for you," she ran her hands down his magnificent flanks as she turned to gently but firmly stroke him.

"Cassandra." What she could do to him, this small woman, his wife. As her inventive hands continued to glide over him, he found himself bracing his hands against the wall.

"Do you know how many fantasies I've had about you and this shower?" she whispered, kissing the marks on his back.

The feel of her hands on him, her lips and tongue on his back, water everywhere; how much is a man supposed to take? Pushing away from the wall, he turned and held her face with both hands.

"Show me," he demanded as his lips captured hers.

She couldn't believe how badly she needed this man, would always need him. As her tongue dueled with his, he backed her into the wall. His arm swept under her, lifting so she could wrap her legs around him.

Poised at her entrance, he ripped his mouth from hers, "Tell me!"

"I am yours! Only yours!" Tightening her legs around him she pulled him in.

"Yes!" Pounding into her he pulled her closer. This wouldn't take long. Her hands had devastated his control. "I am yours, Cassandra! Only yours!" As he thrust one last time, she shattered around him.

With the water still pouring over them, they tried to breath. Cassandra's arms were locked around his neck, and her legs around his waist just to keep her from melting into a puddle at his feet.

"You and I are going to have a long discussion about your fantasies," William straightened, a wicked gleam in his eye.

"I have lots and lots of them."

William found he could only grin at the thought. Turning off the water, he eased her feet to the floor. Reaching for a towel he began the enjoyable task of drying her. "Do you realize how precious you are to me?" Cassandra's eyes darkened as he tenderly wiped the moisture from her hair. "I thought I knew my place. What my life was to be, where it was going, was content with it. Then you entered my life. And I discovered I'd been living only half a life. You gave me love, honesty, trust and asked for nothing in return. You stand. For what you believe, against any who disagree, even me. And you protect; the innocent and those you love, including me. You are my love, my life mate, my wife. You make me a better man."

"William…"

"Shhh…I'm winning this one so be quiet," kissing her he gathered her close. "Now, since you won't rest, you will eat." Turning her, he guided her out of the bathroom.

∞ ∞ ∞ ∞ ∞

Sliding her half-eaten meal away, she saw William frown. "I'm fine. If I get hungry later, I'll ask Hutu for something." Reaching she touched his hand. "I promise."

"It's going to be a long day."

"I know. Before you walk me through it, Lucas is set? For Victoria? Everyone has been covered?"

"It's taken care of, do you want to know?"

"No. I'm sorry. I'm not doubting you."

"You just needed it verified." Squeezing her hand, he let her know he understood.

"Yes, now I can forget about it. So walk me through today."

"We'll need to leave for the Assembly by 1200. Jotham has made limisins available for us."

"We all go?"

"Hutu will remain behind, he knows what to do. All guards go. Deffand's men will guard the Wing."

"Including Ensign Paa?"

"Unless you object." Watching her, he waited.

"No, I don't object. He'll need his weapon and communicator."

"You trust him?"

"You do, that's good enough for me."

"We will be one of the last to arrive. Assembly guards will escort us to our places on one side of the speaking platform. Queen Yakira's entourage will be seated on the other side."

"She'll make sure she arrives after us."

"Yes, so she can make her grand entrance."

"Do you think she'll be a giant blue ball again?" Her eyes sparkled at him.

He couldn't stop himself from laughing at the image. "I doubt it. She'll be wearing full Royal attire, a gown of some sort that reveals her birthmark, but her royal robe and crown will be prominent. She'll want to show she is the Queen."

"Smart move." Standing she walked to the window.

"It will play with those who don't know you." Watching her, he wondered what she was thinking.

"They will be making a visual comparison, something to consider. What's next?"

"The Head of the Assembly, Terwilliger, will call the Assembly to order and present you as the Challenger."

"Will I need to stand and approach? Or just stand?"

"You will need to approach, acknowledge the Assembly, and you present your Challenge to the Assembly."

"No."

"No? What do you mean no?" William stiffened.

"Yakira will have to defend her throne first."

"Cassandra, a very strict procedure is followed in a Challenge."

"I know and if the gatherings had been completed, then the Challenger must present first. But if the Challenge is called, for any reason, then the defending Queen must speak first. The rule was established to prevent just what Yakira is attempting."

"You're sure of this?" William wondered why he was even questioning.

"Yes, and I'll bet you all the credits Lucas owes me that neither Audric nor Yakira realize it. There is no reason for them to. The Challenge has never been called before."

Leaning back, William thought about what she was telling him. "Yakira won't be expecting it. The Assembly can't just vote to deny your Challenge."

"No, and that's what Audric was counting on. They had enough supporters to call the Challenge. He'll assume this was all a formality." Walking over she settled into his lap.

Cuddling her against his chest, he finished her thought. "She'll appear unprepared and uninformed at an Assembly she called. That won't go over well." Absently he rubbed his ring on her finger.

"Is Terwilliger going to give me any trouble when I call him on it?" With her head on his shoulder, she burrowed in, letting her arms settle around his waist.

"You know exactly where this procedure is, page, code?"

"Of course," she sent him an insulted look.

"Of course you do." He kissed her nose smiling. "Terwilliger will look it up, if he doesn't already know it and will concede you're correct. He'll enjoy doing it too. He can't stand Audric."

"I hadn't realized that."

"Terwilliger's been in the game a long time. He knows better than to say anything publicly." The silence between them was comfortable, each thinking about what needed to be done while enjoying the other's closeness.

∞ ∞ ∞ ∞ ∞

"Aunt Cassie! Uncle William!" They both looked toward the hallway as they heard Victoria.

"Tori, they may still be sleeping."

"Huťu said he brought them breakfast ages ago."

"We're up, come on back."

"See!" Victoria rushed into the room. "Hi!"

"Good morning, sweetie. I take it you had fun at Amina's." Cassandra slid out of William's lap, tightening her robe.

"It was good. No nightmares."

"That's good. Have you eaten?"

"With Amina, flatcakes and chocolate chip cookies," Tori's mischievous smile warmed Cassandra's heart and gave her a craving.

"Chocolate chip cookies? You got cookies with your breakfast?" William received a seriously putout look from his wife.

"I'll have Hutu send some up." Smiling at Lucas he turned his attention to Victoria.

"Just how did you convince Hutu to bring you cookies with your breakfast, young lady?"

Innocent green eyes meet his. "I'll never tell."

William looked to Lucas, "You have your work cut out for you."

∞ ∞ ∞ ∞ ∞

Brushing Victoria's hair, Cassandra thought about the day ahead. "Victoria," putting the brush aside she turned her niece around to face her. "Today we go before the Assembly. Today we get the Glitter Man."

"Really!?!" Victoria's eyes lost their innocence, breaking Cassandra's heart.

"Yes. So now you have to listen to me." She gripped Victoria's chin, "You stay with Lucas today, right at his side. Do you understand me?"

"Yes, Aunt Cassie."

"You do exactly what he tells you, he'll keep you safe."

"I know, Aunt Cassie," Victoria rolled her eyes.

"No, Victoria, you don't. Listen to me." Cassandra waited until Tori's eyes settled. "If Lucas tells you you're leaving, you leave, whether William and I do or not. Do you understand me?"

"Aunt Cassie?" Victoria finally looked scared.

"It's been arranged, Victoria. Do you want to get the Glitter Man?"

"Yes," she whispered.

"Then you have to promise me. Promise me, you'll do this. I can't do what I need to do, neither can the Admiral, if we have to worry about you; about you not listening to Lucas."

"I'll listen, Aunt Cassie, I promise."

"All right, we leave at 1200. Let's finish your hair then you can decide what you want to wear."

∞ ∞ ∞ ∞ ∞

"How's she doing?" Watching Cassandra enter their room he could tell she was troubled.

"Good, picking out what she wants to wear." Walking over to the dresser she picked out black eadai. Leaning back on it, she looked at him. "Am I doing the right thing? Putting her through this?"

"You're doing what you have to do to keep her safe."

"If we left now she'd be safe."

"What kind of life would she have, Cassandra?" Framing her face, he told her what she already knew. "Always hiding, worrying about Audric finding her. It's time to finish this."

"You're right, I know you are." Looking into his steady eyes, she drew strength, "I just needed to hear it."

"You're tired." William was concerned. She never doubted herself unless she was tired.

"I'll be fine, I have you." Stretching up, she gave him a reassuring kiss. "But I could sure use a cookie."

Her request eased some of his tension. "I'll get you some. Now get in the shower," he turned her to the bathroom.

"Alone?" She looked over her shoulder realizing she was only half teasing as her husband's eyes flared.

"Yes. We'll have time for that later." But he indulged himself with one hard kiss. "Now go, I'll have cookies waiting for you when you get out."

"Cookies, as in multiple?"

"Yes, multiple," with a gentle shove he sent her on her way.

∞ ∞ ∞ ∞ ∞

Biting into a cookie, Cassandra looked at the clothes Pazel and Kia had made for her. They were beautifully done, elegant. Hopefully, she'd get to wear all of them. Wiping the crumbs from her fingers, she reached for the black pant outfit she had yet to wear. Letting her robe fall to the ground she put on the pants first. They were tailored to fit her form perfectly until they widened at mid-thigh. Kia had placed inserts in the legs allowing them to drape as they widened. Pulling each leg to the side, the hidden slit on the inside of each leg opened, easily revealing her birthmark.

Satisfied, she donned a simple camisole style top that was covered with simple black lace accented with a few clear crystals. Wide straps, unadorned, finished the top. Leaving the matching long-sleeved jacket hanging, she turned for footwear.

Heeled boots, not too high in case she needed to move quickly, but high enough for the pants to just brush the floor. Zipping them tight she checked; with the tops ending just below her knee, her birthmark was completely covered. Smiling she walked into the bedroom.

Munching on another cookie she looked at her reflection in the mirror. Where at Dadrian's sochraide she'd been a tower of white, today she would be dark, not for darkness but in remembrance of those she'd lost. Today there would be no redemption. Not for Audric.

Holding the cookie in her mouth, she pulled her hair up high looking at the results. Shaking her head, she let it fall. Running her fingers through the dark mass she let it fall naturally onto her shoulders. Yes, that's what she wanted, an outward sign she wouldn't be controlled or confined.

Finishing the cookie, she turned to find William leaning against the door frame, watching.

∞ ∞ ∞ ∞ ∞

William had found her dressed in elegant black, deciding how to wear her hair and a half eaten cookie between her lips as he watched from the door. He could see her mind working, up, back or down. What was the image she wanted to present? As she ran her fingers through her hair letting it fall free and natural, he knew she had found it. Finishing the cookie she turned and saw him.

"How many?" he asked.

"What?" Walking toward him she frowned.

"Cookies."

"Oh, uh, just three, so far," she gave him a guilty smile.

"Really?"

"I'm not done yet." Smiling, she gently kissed him. Drawing her closer, he deepened it.

"It's almost time to leave," his lips continued to brush hers.

"I know," her arms were wrapped around his waist and she frowned.

"What?" Easing back she looked at him. She hadn't seen him wear this jacket since their arrival. It contained none of the medals she'd grown accustomed to seeing on his chest and had a large bump.

"You're carrying a weapon."

"Yes." The thoughts running through her mind were written on her face. She voiced none of them, just nodded.

"Let me get my jacket and I'll be ready."

∞ ∞ ∞ ∞ ∞

"Marat, report."

"Sir, King Jotham, and his security have left the Palace. Four limisins are waiting at the private garage. All the men are ready, weapons and communicators checked. Waiting for your orders, Sir."

"Cassandra?" William turned to her. She was standing at the doors to the garden, listening as she looked out. The garden where, just yesterday she'd married William. It was time to block it out, to focus on what she had to do.

Turning he saw she had pulled herself in, her eyes flat, shutting everyone out. While he understood it, he despised it. "I'm ready."

Entering the garage, Tar and the Michelakakis' got into the second limisin while William led his family to the third. Once everyone was secured, guards filled the first and last limisin, surrounding them with protection.

"Aunt Cassie?" Victoria was sitting between Kyle and Lucas, watching her aunt.

"What, baby?" she saw the flicker of fear in her eyes. "Come over here." She held out her hand, sliding over so she could sit between her and William. "Tell me."

Closing her eyes, she burrowed into her aunt. Leaning down, Cassandra kissed the top of her head. "Hey, it's going to be okay. We've got three big, strong, Zafar men here that are going to help and protect us."

"I know," Tori's voice was muffled.

Cassandra knew her niece, she hated having to sit still, had an active mind, always wanting to learn. "Tori," she tipped her chin up. "I need you to do something else for me."

"I already promised I'd listen to Lucas."

"I know and I still need you to do that, but there's something else. Something I need you to do. That only you can do."

"Besides say who the Glitter Man is?"

Cassandra had captured her attention just like she'd hoped. "Yes, besides that. I need you to watch him for me, the whole time. Watch his reactions to what I'm saying. Tori, he doesn't know you've remembered, that you've told us. He thinks of you as a scared little girl. He doesn't know that you're the bravest girl on any planet, that you know what he did, that you understand what he said, and more important that you know who he is."

"He doesn't?" Cassandra watched as Victoria began to understand.

"He doesn't. So he's going to be very surprised at some of the things I say. I need to know when he gets mad. Because when he does…"

"His eyes will glitter. But how will I tell you?"

"Well, I was thinking. If I'm sitting, listening to Yakira, then vous pouvez parler français pour moi, but in a whisper. I will nod if I hear you."

The Zafar men looked at each other trying to follow the women's conversation. "Cassandra…" Her hand on William's arm stopped him.

"And when I'm on the platform speaking and you think I need to know something," moving her hands Cassandra signed, 'you do this.' "Okay? Can you do that? Be my second set of eyes?"

"I can do that." Fear left Tori's eyes replaced by determination. Holding up her fist, Cassandra gave her a bump. She went back to sit next to Lucas.

"What did you say to her?" William asked.

"To speak French to me, it was a language on Earth. No one will know what she's saying."

"And the hand thing?"

"Sign language, a way to speak to each other without saying a word."

"And again, no one will know what you're saying." William gripped her face, "You are truly brilliant!"

Cassandra's smile faded as she looked out the window of the limisin. Following her gaze, William saw they were approaching the Assembly Hall. Turning back, he saw the shutters fall, but not before he saw the nerves. Leaning over so only she could hear, he touched her cheek.

"Take a deep breath. You are in control here. Whatever you want to do we'll do." Looking into her husband's eyes, Cassandra could feel herself settling, her nerves disappearing. As the limisin stopped, she kissed his lips.

"I'm ready."

∞ ∞ ∞ ∞ ∞

Guards exited their limisins, surrounding the second limisin first. Once everyone was out, as one, they moved to the third, to the Challenger. Kyle was the first to exit when Lucas moved to follow, Cassandra grabbed his wrist.

"Lucas…" her eyes locked with his.

"With my life." Nodding she released him. With one last look at his father, he got out. Holding out his hand for Victoria, he helped her out.

Saying nothing, William looked at Cassandra. At her nod, he stepped out of the limisin. His eyes scanned the crowd gathered outside the Assembly Hall. Assembly security was holding them back. They all wanted a look at the Challenger, at his wife. None of them was getting close to her.

Seeing the Assembly security approach he stepped forward. Cassandra knew she was not to get out of the limisin until he assisted her.

"Admiral, we are here to escort you to your places in the Hall."

"Your security will flank ours."

"Yes, Admiral."

Returning to the limisin, he extended his hand to his wife.

∞ ∞ ∞ ∞ ∞

While she waited, Cassandra organized her thoughts. Everyone in this building was here to judge her, to decide if she was worthy of being Queen. They thought she'd used a good man to get to this point. That all she wanted was the throne. They were wrong. They didn't know what she did. They didn't know her and that was her advantage. When William extended his hand, she slid hers in to his. Time to reveal a traitor.

∞ ∞ ∞ ∞ ∞

The noise level of the Assembly Hall was high. As the group entered and crossed the platform to their seats, it quieted. They all wanted to see the Challenger, this woman from another planet claiming to be the lost Princess. Rumors had been flying. She had gained the protection of the most respected Admiral in the Fleet, a hero to many, and was said to be using him. When security stepped aside, they finally got their first look.

She was tiny, really tiny, hardly over six feet. Dressed in black, her dark hair moved freely around her shoulders and face. But it was her blue eyes that gave them the most pause. They were brilliant sapphire blue and currently scanned the room seemingly taking everything in at once.

Cassandra was prepared for the size of the Assembly. The main floor that was divided into five sections, one for each House. Each section contained seating for the twenty Assemblymen and their Royals, all of whom would be present today. It was the balconies that had her raising an eyebrow. There were three of them, each progressively higher wrapping around the front half of the room and filled to overflowing. Glancing at Victoria, she saw her eyes were dancing with wonder, trying to see everything at once.

William watched her take it all in. He'd been prepared for the mass of people wanting to see his wife and still the sheer number was impressive. Cassandra would have not just the ears of the Assembly but of the people of Carina. The raising of her eyebrow was the only indication she gave that she was surprised.

Looking into the Assembly she found familiar faces. Terwilliger was the Head of the Assembly. Therefore, the House of Protection occupied the center section. He was seated in front, next to the podium he would speak from, the other House of Protection Assemblymen around him. Jotham and Barek were seated behind them, along with the other Royals of the House. It was where William, Lucas, and Kyle would have been sitting if not for her.

To the left, sat the House of Knowledge's Assemblymen. Bevington was there watching. The Queen's seats were empty, but Royals had filled the remaining ones. As she took in the remaining Assembly, William touched her elbow.

Turning her attention to him she saw his strength and commitment to her. "You can sit," he leaned down to tell her, "You don't need to stand until her arrival."

"But I'm not going to rise for her entrance," Cassandra turned her face to his, their lips nearly touching. "She won't be much longer, she wants this over."

Many watched the interplay between them with interest until their attention was drawn away by the entrance of Queen Yakira.

Yakira entered first. As William predicted, her gown was simple, white in color coming only to her knees. When she walked, the outline of a tower could be seen on the inside of her right calf. Her hair was piled high on her head, an open crown keeping it in place. Across her chest, a chain of heavy gold secured a robe on her shoulders, the sapphire velvet trailing six feet behind her.

Cassandra leaned toward William, her eyes never leaving Yakira. "That's her birthmark?"

"Now you understand my reaction to yours." Cassandra's had been twice as dark when he had first noticed it over thirty days ago.

As Yakira crossed the platform, there was clapping and hollering from her supporters in the Assembly. Acknowledging them, she waited for Audric and her children to come and stand behind her.

Cassandra heard Victoria's quick breath. "Are you okay?" She asked in French, her eyes never leaving Yakira.

"Yes," she replied in the same language.

Turning, Yakira assumed her position on the other side of the platform, her staff having to arrange her robe. As she watched, Cassandra wondered how she was going to move when she had to defend her appointment to the throne.

Yakira finally looked across the platform to her, with a slight nod Cassandra acknowledged her then took her seat first. The rest of the Challenger's group followed.

Yakira's eyes widened at the move, the Assembly filled with whispers. Ignoring it all, Cassandra turned her attention to Terwilliger.

Terwilliger was as amazed as the rest of the Assembly at the Challenger's move. In his fifty cycles in the Assembly, he thought he had seen and heard everything, that nothing could surprise him anymore. But watching the Challenger, a young woman he only recently met, he felt that not only he but all of Carina was in for a tremendous surprise. Standing, he approached the podium. It was time.

"Citizens of Carina, Assemblymen, Royals, we come here today to witness the Challenge by Cassandra Qwes Chamberlain to Queen Yakira, trustee to the throne of the House of Knowledge." Terwilliger paused allowing the supporters of Yakira to quiet.

"We will begin with the presentation of the Challenger. She will then present her Challenge to the throne."

While Terwilliger spoke, Cassandra looked down at Victoria sitting to her left. Moving her hand slightly, she made a fist. Victoria gave her a little bump. Going to stand, she found William there, holding out his hand to assist her. Taking his hand, her expression didn't change. Only William saw the flash of love in her eyes, only he felt her thumb caress the ring he wore. When she stepped away from him, his heart tightened. Resuming his seat, his eyes followed her.

Everyone watched her walk across the platform. Her stride smooth and confident, eyes steady, face calm.

"Assemblyman Terwilliger, thank you for the introduction, but I'm afraid you've been misinformed," she calmly looked around the Assembly.

"My name is Cassandra Qwes Zafar." The Assembly was shocked into silence. "Now that my correct name is entered into the record I will return to my seat so Queen Yakira may defend her appointment as Trustee to the throne of the House of Knowledge." Turning away the Assembly erupted.

Terwilliger pounded his gavel on the podium. "Quiet! I will have quiet in this hall! Princess Cassandra," stopping she turned back to him. "I know you are new to our ways, but there are specific procedures that must be followed in a Challenge."

"I know," her voice was steady as her eyes met his.

"Then you must know that one of those procedures is that the Challenger must..."

"'Present first, explain why she would make a better Trustee to the throne until the return of the true Queen.' Article Two, page one-thirty-one, of the Carinian Assembly Procedure Book." She saw Terwilliger's eyebrows raise as she interrupted him. "That is the proper procedure in the normal course of a Challenge," she walked back toward the Assembly.

"A normal Challenge, as outlined in the same Procedure Book, is when the Challenger attends a day of gatherings with each House's Assemblymen and Royal family so all have a chance to meet the Challenger, and ask questions so an informed decision can be made as to who would be the best Trustee for the House of Knowledge, until the true Queen returns," Cassandra looked to the balconies.

"After that is completed, the Assembly is called and the Challenger presents to not only the Assemblymen and Royals, but to the citizens of Carina themselves, why she thinks she would be a better trustee. At that point, the current Trustee, in this case, Queen Yakira," she turned to look at Yakira, "can call for an immediate vote to deny the credibility of the Challenger, thus ending the Challenge." Before Terwilliger could speak, Cassandra continued.

"This is not a normal Challenge," she returned her gaze to the Assembly. "Queen Yakira has called the Challenge. By doing so, Article 152, page five-sixty-five of the Procedure Book goes into effect."

Terwilliger's eyes widened. He immediately opened the official Procedure Book that always sat on the podium as Cassandra continued.

"It states that, 'If the residing Trustee calls the Challenge for any reason, then that Trustee must speak first. She must defend her reign as current Trustee and explain why she should be allowed to remain. The Challenger can then call for an immediate vote from the Assembly ending said Trustee's term, making herself the new Trustee; or the Challenger may speak, allowing the Challenge to run its course.' This Article prevented the residing Trustee from improperly using the power entrusted to her until the return of the true Queen."

After a moment of stunned silence, the hall erupted. Leading Assemblymen from each House stormed the podium. Stepping back Terwilliger allowed each to read Article 152, it was on the exact page quoted. After a quick conference, all returned to their seats. Terwilliger stepped up to the podium.

Cassandra calmly stood there while the Assemblymen conferred. The raised voices from the balconies and members on the floor seemingly had no effect. Terwilliger pounded the gavel to quiet the hall.

"Princess Cassandra, you are correct. Queen Yakira will speak first." The room gasped.

"Thank you, Assemblymen Terwilliger." Cassandra nodded to him. "I apologize for having to bring it to your attention in such a way. As you stated, I am new to your ways and thought Queen Yakira would have informed you earlier to avoid this unnecessary confusion. An oversight I'm sure. No one would call a Challenge without knowing the consequences."

Turning, Cassandra met Yakira's eyes. While Yakira's expression hadn't changed, Cassandra could tell her mind was racing. Ignoring Audric, Cassandra continued on to her seat. William rose as she approached. She saw the pride in his eyes, seating her he retook his.

"He's mad, Aunt Cassie," Victoria whispered.

"Are his eyes glittering yet?"

"No."

"Let me know when they are."

William listened to their quiet conversation, not understanding a word of it. Looking to Lucas next to Victoria, he saw him give a very subtle shake of his head. Telling William, he didn't know either.

∞ ∞ ∞ ∞ ∞

What does this little bitch think she's doing! Audric was enraged, spouting off Articles and page numbers as if she knew anything. And Terwilliger, the old fuck, deferred to her. He was probably slamming her too. He'd pay for that insult! When this was over, they'd all pay!

This was what she got for listening to Audric. Yakira couldn't believe she'd let herself get into this position. It was like being eighteen all over again. Having to stand in front of the Assembly and justify herself, allowing them to judge her, her and her children, judge their lives. She looked at her children seated to her right. They were both so beautiful they were her reason for existing. She would do this for them, to protect them. Fuck Audric.

∞ ∞ ∞ ∞ ∞

"Queen Yakira," Terwilliger felt he had waited long enough. "Your defense please, of your Trusteeship of the throne of the House of Knowledge."

Cassandra watched as Yakira looked at her children. They were both beautiful. The boy fifteen was in his third cycle Academy uniform, the girl thirteen was dressed in Knowledge blue. Neither bore any resemblance to Audric.

Standing, Yakira realized she'd forgotten about her robe. It was long, heavy and hard to maneuver in without assistance. She wore it for what it represented; knowledge, the House of Knowledge. To remove it to defend herself, would be equated with her not knowing what calling the Challenge meant. That would undermine her position. When her staff rose to assist her, she waved them off. This was for her to do.

Slowly, steadily, Yakira approached the Assembly, her eyes scanned those on the main floor, those who mattered, who voted. She ignored the balconies.

"Assemblymen, fellow Royals. I will not keep you long. I come before you today as the humble Trustee of the House of Knowledge. A responsibility you charged me with over fifteen cycles ago. Since that time, I have faithfully performed all the duties required of the Queen of the House of Knowledge. I have not faltered."

"During my reign as Queen, Carina has become much safer, due in no small part to the House of Knowledge scholars. Ships designed by them fill the skies. They are safer, faster, and more maneuverable than any that have come before. They have assisted the Coalition with capturing Regulian Intel securing the safety of all Carinians."

"You know me. Know my family, which I descended from, where I come from. You know my values, my beliefs. We have shared experiences.

To entrust such an important position to someone unknown puts us all at risk." Giving the Assembly a slight bow she turned. Her supporters erupted in their seats.

It took Yakira several long moments to complete her turn. She negotiated around the six-foot velvet train. Once she finally reached her seat, she allowed her staff to assist in seating her. Audric never moved.

∞ ∞ ∞ ∞ ∞

Listening to Yakira's defense of her throne, William couldn't help but be angered. That she would use something he had done, the Regulian Intel, against Cassandra. He hadn't thought about it.

"Its fine," Cassandra's voice was low, for his ears only, her lips barely moving. "It's actually perfect." Her eyes never left Yakira. She spoke directly to those whose votes she needed, ignoring all others. Something she'd done her entire reign. Played to their fears of the Regulians, of the unknown, of her. It would be a smart move, usually. Change was a hard thing, it scared many, but a traitor will scare them more.

Terwilliger, who resumed his seat during Yakira's defense, now stood. Waiting until Yakira was seated, he approached the podium, dreading what he must now do.

"Princess Cassandra, as per procedure, you now have the right to call for an immediate vote on ending the current Trustee's term." Angry voices rose from the House of Knowledge section. Terwilliger watched as Admiral Zafar stood, his back to the Assembly.

"Are you ready, Victoria?" Cassandra looked down to her niece.

"Yes."

"Remember what you promised."

"I will."

"I love you."

Putting her hand in William's she stood, switching back to a language he understood, "I love you too." William squeezed her hand then turned so she could reply to Terwilliger.

Chapter Forty-One

"Assemblyman Terwilliger, I see no reason to call the vote." A hush fell over the Assembly. "Queen Yakira has raised some very important questions, questions concerning myself and the protection of Carina. Questions that I, for one, believe deserve to be answered. So following Carinian procedures, I will speak."

"Princess Cassandra, you have the Assembly." Terwilliger sat knowing Carina would never ever be the same after this Challenge.

Letting her mind settle, she approached the Assembly. "Queen Yakira stated that you should allow her to remain Trustee because you know where she comes from. Let me tell you where I come from."

"A planet called Earth, a great distance from here, even by Carinian standards. A small planet, half the size of Carina, with one sun, one moon, and an abundance of life hard to imagine. It was similar to Carina in many ways, with land, water, heat, and cold. It supported seven billion people; men, women, and children. People with lives, hopes, and dreams, just like here on Carina."

William watched as his wife moved around the platform making eye contact, not only with Royals and Assemblymen but with the people of Carina, allowing them to see her, her world.

"But unlike Carina, we hadn't yet advanced to long distance space travel. We were looking at the stars knowing there would be planets like Carina out there. We were developing the technology so that one day our civilizations would meet. But a little over two of your moon cycles ago we were no threat; not to you, not to anyone."

"But the Regulians attacked and destroyed the Earth anyway. They murdered seven billion people. They had their orders: 'Find the Imperial Light or destroy it.'" She ignored the gasp from the Assembly.

"An unusual phrase, 'Imperial Light.' It meant nothing on Earth, it meant nothing to the Regulians. The only place that phrase means anything was here on Carina. It is the phrase used to describe the Imperial House of Knowledge, of the heir to the throne; she was always described as the Light of Carina. But why would the Regulians care?"

Cassandra answered her own question. "They cared because they had been promised something. They had an agreement with someone who very much cared about the very possibility that the lost Princess, the true heir to the House of Knowledge, was on Earth; and might return to claim her throne." She paused letting what she had said sink in.

"What it means is that Carina has a traitor. For nearly eight cycles, someone has been willing to not only deal with the Regulians but make promises to them, promises that threaten Carina." Cassandra finally turned to look at the group from the House of Knowledge. She saw the shock in Yakira's eyes. In nearly everyone's eyes, except Audric, in Audric's there was rage.

"Princess Cassandra!!! Princess Cassandra!!!" Terwilliger drew Cassandra's attention. "You must explain this to the Assembly. How you've come to reach such a conclusion."

"Gladly, Assemblyman Terwilliger." Cassandra looked at Victoria, who brought her first two fingers down to her thumb, signing 'No.'

"Nearly eight cycles ago there was a great battle, a battle between the Regulians and the Coalition Fleet. It was long and bloody with many lives lost on both sides. Many in this room fought in that battle; Admiral Zafar, Assemblyman Bevington. Many more lost sons, daughters, husbands, and wives. In the end, the Coalition was victorious. You know this, Queen Yakira has referred to it. It was the Battle of Fayal. It was the turning point. For Carina, for Earth, all because of the Rappen, of the information it contained."

"Queen Yakira was correct," she gestured back to her. "The scholars from the House of Knowledge were able to translate the data the Rappen carried. They translated the data about their weapons systems, tactics, and communication systems, all vital to the Coalition. That information was turned over to High Admiral Valerian." Cassandra met Valerian's hard eyes seated in the House of Knowledge section.

"But the scholars found more. Specifically, Scholar Olah found more, in the databases of the Rappen, he found research files. The Regulians had been studying a distant planet, a planet occupied by a humanoid species genetically similar to Carinians. They abducted people from the planet. Men, women, and children. They scanned them, studied them, to see if there was a weakness they could find that they could use against the people of Carina."

"A particular young girl they kept longer than the others, nearly a week, because they found something interesting. A mark on the inside of her right leg. They studied it, imaged it, tried to figure out what caused it. And what they found was this girl was different than all the others. Her genetics were nearly identical to those on Carina. Because of that they implanted a thread in her arm so they could find her when they returned."

"The Regulians had no idea what they'd found, what it meant, but Olah did. He immediately contacted High Admiral Valerian. To tell him he'd found the Lost Princess."

"You can't possibly know that!" Valerian was out of his chair. William tensed as Cassandra walked toward him.

"I can," her eyes were hard as she stared at Valerian. "Scholar Olah kept a meticulous journal of all the data he'd found and who he reported it to. It's procedure. On 20 Nallag 5247 he contacted HAV, the same abbreviation he used in his journal when he gave progress reports on the Regulian systems; High Admiral Valerian. He also made notations about the conversation. Beside this entry, he wrote 'Not interested.'" Valerian's face turned bright red, but he remained seated.

"But Olah knew this was vital information to end the mystery of where the Lost Queen went to. That there might be a true heir to the House of Knowledge on a planet deep in the Relinquished Zone, so he decided to contact someone he knew would be interested in this information, Queen Yakira." Cassandra turned to face Yakira.

"What!" The shock was easily read by all on Yakira's face.

"Olah's same journal 20 Nallag, he made an appointment to meet with QY regarding the LP data at 1400 25 Nallag." Cassandra took several steps to Yakira as she spoke.

"This is an outrage!" Audric stood. As he did, so did William. "For this… person… to accuse my wife of treason is intolerable."

Cassandra gave Audric a look of pure disdain. "Assemblyman Terwilliger," she turned her back on Audric and walked back to the Assembly, "this is my time to answer questions Queen Yakira has raised. Is it not?"

Terwilliger rose, "Yes, Princess, it is."

"Then would you kindly tell Prince Audric to sit down and be quiet?" The Assembly gasped in unison at her request. Cassandra waited.

Clearing his throat, Terwilliger looked at Audric. "Prince Audric, would you please resume your seat so the Challenger's response can continue."

"This is outrageous!"

"Audric," Yakira's voice was cold. "Sit!" He did so slowly, and William resumed his seat, but he didn't relax."

"As I was saying before I was interrupted, Scholar Olah scheduled an appointment with Queen Yakira on 25 Nallag. He copied all his data and took the transport to the Royal Palace in Kisurri, sitting in the last coach. It was well known that Scholar Olah always sat in the last coach of the transport. Upon his arrival, he was told Queen Yakira was unavailable."

Cassandra turned looking at Yakira. "Earlier in the day her son, Prince Vance, had been involved in a 'freak' riding accident. She was at his side, where any parent would be." Giving Yakira a slight nod, Cassandra turned her attention to Audric.

"Because of this, Prince Audric took the Queen's appointments." A murmur started within the Assembly, eyes turning to Audric, including Yakira's. "Scholar Olah, while disappointed not to be speaking with the Queen herself told Prince Audric what he'd discovered, what he believed." She turned her back on Audric, knowing her speaking about him in such away would 'irritate' him.

"Olah wrote in his notes he was disappointed in Prince Audric's lack of interest. He felt the Prince didn't understand what he was saying. But Prince Audric took the data copies he'd brought, said he would present them to the Queen and get back to him on her decision. Taking the transit home, Olah could do nothing but wait."

"He didn't have to wait long. Two days later he received a communication from PA. Prince Audric stated that Queen Yakira requested he bring all the original data to the House of Knowledge so it could be studied in more depth. She would like him there the next day, 28 Nallag at 1500. Olah complied and arrived on time only to find that Queen Yakira was again unavailable."

Cassandra turned back to Yakira. "He didn't know she was traveling with her son to Moncton for medical treatment for his earlier injury. Had, in fact, left the day before. I find it interesting that an appointment can be made in the Queen's name when the Queen wasn't even in residence." She could see Yakira's mind racing. Turning back to the Assembly, she continued.

"So Olah gave the requested data to Prince Audric and left. He got on the transport along with hundreds of others, sat in the last coach and ten minutes later was dead. He and a hundred others, as the last coach of the transport uncoupled and plunged into a ravine. It was considered a 'freak' accident." She gave the Assembly a moment to consider.

"Two months later on Earth, the Regulians began their search for the young girl. I'm sure as many of you know, Regulian technology while more advanced than Earth's, was inferior to Carinian. They had to be within a hundred feet of the girl for the thread to transmit. Because of this, their search took time, but they got lucky, and within a month were able to locate the transmission. In a city called Kayseri, in an arid region of the Earth, a place where my grandmother, sister-in-law, niece, and I happened to be visiting."

"Early one morning my niece was abducted from the home we were staying in. From a high-walled garden, she was taken." No one in the Assembly doubted the rage behind Cassandra's voice. "Queen Yakira has questioned what some of my beliefs are so I'll tell you what I believe."

"I believe a child is a precious gift that should always be protected. That a child has the right to not be abducted from her home, from her family. To not be examined by a strange man, to be threatened and terrorized, to not have a thread implanted in her arm and be told she will always be found! That is what I believe, but maybe on Carina your beliefs are different."

Turning, Cassandra walked toward Audric. "You traveled to Earth, abducted my niece and terrorized her, all because you thought she might have a birthmark."

Audric responded, "You can make up whatever stories you want, no one here believes you. You are nothing but a refugee from a dead planet."

The Assembly was shocked as Cassandra laughed, genuinely laughed at Audric. William prepared to move to defend his wife. "You were born in Messene on Goryn, the son of servants, would have been one yourself if it hadn't been for the 'charity,'" Cassandra stated, "of Queen Hestia. She took pity on you after the mysterious deaths of your parents, rumored a murder-suicide."

"Queen Hestia had you educated, taught manners, included you in many Royal functions. She let you see what it was like to be the one served, not serving. You actually came to believe it was your right to be a Royal when you were nothing and still are nothing. You can claim no House, carry no birthmark, have no family."

"You know nothing!" Audric told her.

"I know that it was all ending for you, with Yakira's upcoming Union to Prince Vane. You were being ignored, becoming unimportant. You'd been unimportant before, you weren't going back. So you arranged for a vacation, sort of the last boys trip for you and Vane, a climbing trip on Messene. Vane was an excellent climber. He was excellent at everything he did, unlike you."

"Vane's death was caused by equipment failure. It was a…" Audric hesitated.

"Freak accident?" Cassandra raised an eyebrow at him. "That happens a lot around you. Your parents, Vane, Scholar Olah, even Prince Vance." Cassandra heard Yakira suck in her breath. Yakira looked at her spouse, her eyes flat.

"This is outrageous! You will pay for slandering me this way!" Audric stood.

"No. You will pay, for what you did to my niece, to my family, to my planet, to your own. You murdered seven billion people because of a possibility. A possibility that the true Queen was on Earth, you didn't even know."

"You will never prove it."

"You're right." A gasp went up from the Assembly. "I won't." Turning Cassandra looked at Victoria.

Everyone watched as the tiny little girl with long red hair crossed the platform in unusual blue pants. She stopped beside her aunt.

"What is this?" Audric demanded his eyes glaring at Cassandra.

"This is Victoria Lynn Chamberlain, my niece."

"You really expect anyone to take the word of this child?"

"I'm not scared of you anymore," Victoria stared into his eyes. Her voice, while young, was firm. "I used to be. I'd have nightmares of you coming back, of finding me again, but not anymore."

"You took me in the morning and put me on a table so I couldn't move. It was bright, so bright it hurt my eyes but just outside the light it was dark. And in the dark there were voices, lots of voices. Then you were there, staring at me, touching me." The mood in the Assembly was turning, Audric could feel it.

"You can't possibly believe a hysterical child," Audric yelled at the Assembly.

"Hysterical?" Cassandra looked at Victoria then back to Audric.

"She's a child, she couldn't possibly remember anything!" Audric didn't realize what he had just admitted. Cassandra did and saw that Yakira did too.

"You were angry, angry at the Regulians." Victoria switched to Regulian. "You called them stupid. Told them that I wasn't the Light, that you wouldn't honor the agreement." Audric paled at what Victoria was saying.

"That's impossible."

"What is?" Cassandra asked. "That Victoria not only speaks but understands Regulian? I am Qwes, she is my niece. It took her four days."

"Not possible."

"Not for you, but then you've never excelled at anything. Have you, Audric, except death; death and deception."

"What did she say?" Prince Vance asked looking at his mother. Cassandra looked at the boy, soon to be a man.

"'You called them stupid, told them that I wasn't the Light, that you wouldn't honor the agreement,'" Queen Yakira translated.

"Yes," Cassandra nodded to Yakira.

"She's just repeating what you've told her, what you've been schooling her on. The child was terrified, she remembers nothing!"

"Do you remember what else you said?" Victoria asked taking a step toward him.

"I wasn't there. I said nothing."

"It was you. You told the Regulians they'd have to 'return me' because you needed to get back to Messene before you were missed. You couldn't go 'unseen' much longer."

As the Assembly gasped, Audric's eyes started to 'glitter.'

"I never told anyone what you said, 'That you'd find me no matter where I went. That you'd hear me, find me, that I wouldn't take your Light.' I was too scared. Scared of the Glitter Man. But that was before. Before the Admiral and the Retribution. The Admiral knew what it meant when I told him. And he made it right. Dr. Bliant took the thread out of my arm so you couldn't find me. Me or Aunt Cassie, because she's the one you really wanted. You don't scare me anymore."

Cassandra put herself between her niece and Audric as he took a step. "It's an interesting name isn't it, 'Glitter Man.' Tori always called you that, because your eyes 'glittered' at her. Eyes on Earth don't do that. Eyes on Carina don't either for that matter."

"But on Goryn," she took a step toward him, "one-tenth of one percent of all men have a genetic condition called Oculus Spangle. When you get angry, your eyes 'glitter' just like they're doing right now. Victoria couldn't have known that unless she'd seen it, seven cycles ago."

"You are nothing! You and that little bitch you call a niece! I should have killed her when I had the chance!" As Audric lunged for them, the room erupted. Cassandra and Victoria moved as one taking a quick side step their fathers had taught them. When Audric flew past he faced a wall of angry Zafar men. Before he could turn, he found his arms restrained.

"Get your hands off me! I am Prince Audric! Guards!" Yakira raised her hand, stopping the House of Knowledge guards.

"Cassandra?" William's voice was gruff as he looked at his wife. He had let her handle this her way, knowing it was the only way she could heal, that both of them could heal, but it was taking its toll.

"We're fine."

"She'd better have been the best slam in the universe, Zafar, because you're a dead man; you and your entire family. I will destroy you." The Admiral's only response was to twist Audric's arms tighter. The hall started to quiet, all wanting to hear what was being said.

"You will destroy nothing else, you pathetic little man," Cassandra nudged Victoria to Lucas as she took a step toward Audric. "You have just confessed to the murder of nearly seven billion people. Including those previously mentioned, you are responsible for the attacks on the Fleet, that's nearly another fifteen hundred Carinian lives."

"You have no power here! You can't try me!"

"No, I can't," Cassandra turned to walk to the front of the Assembly. It was in chaos, some stood, some sat. Standing there looking at the Royals, the Assemblymen, to the balconies and the citizens of Carina, she raised her voice to be heard.

"Audric is correct, I have no power here, in this place." The Assembly quieted. "He is Royal by his wife's declaration at their Union. No common court can try him. He has murdered many from the House of Knowledge making it an 'internal' problem. He has murdered seven billion people on a distant planet, in doing so he conspired with the Regulians, that makes it a Coalition problem." Cassandra looked at Valerian. "But we all know Valerian will do nothing. Those lives meant nothing to him. All he cared about was using Audric to kill more Regulians, making him no better than Audric." She gave him a disdainful look.

"But with that conspiracy came a threat to all Houses, to all Carinians. And that makes these crimes the jurisdiction of this Assembly. I ask for a vote from the Full Assembly, present here today, on the guilt of Prince Audric for High Treason."

"You can't do that!" Audric struggled against William's hold.

"Princess Cassandra," Terwilliger began.

"Guilty," Cassandra turned, surprised to hear Queen Yakira cast the first vote.

"Guilty," King Jotham stood casting his vote.

"Guilty."

"Guilty."

"Guilty."

Cassandra closed her eyes as she heard the vote. Turning she looked at her husband, at her family.

Terwilliger pounded his gavel on the podium. "Assembly Guards, Prince Audric has been found guilty of High Treason." Terwilliger couldn't believe he was saying this, "Secure him while the Assembly decides his punishment."

As guards moved to take control of Audric, a chant began in the balconies. "Death, death, death."

As William moved toward Cassandra, his eyes scanned the crowd. This could get ugly fast.

"Stay close," he put an arm around her as she nodded.

"No!" Both turned at the sound of Victoria's voice. "No, Aunt Cassie, they can't!"

"Can't what?" She knelt down to look into frantic eyes.

"They can't kill him."

"Victoria, I don't think we have any say in that."

"Uncle William! Make them listen to me." Looking into crystal green eyes, William saw someone older than she should be.

"Assemblyman Terwilliger," the Admiral's voice boomed through the Hall cutting through the maelstrom of noise.

"Admiral Zafar," Terwilliger acknowledged him.

"There is someone who would like to speak, I think we should listen." Looking to Victoria, he stepped back.

"My name is Victoria Lynn Chamberlain." Tori stepped forward undaunted by the crowd in front of her. "That man," she pointed, "Prince Audric, kidnapped me when I was little, killed my grandfather, my father, my mother, and my unborn baby brother. I think that gives me the right to say what his punishment should be. Is that not Carinian Law? That a victim can suggest punishment?"

Terwilliger found himself caught in that clear green gaze. "It is."

"Then I choose Seleucia, on Niue." A shocked silence greeted her statement. "Where he will be clothed, fed, and work from sunrise to sunset the rest of his life." Turning, Victoria looked at Audric. "I hope it is a long, long life." With one last look, she turned away from Audric and walked to her aunt and uncle.

"Victoria?" Cassandra asked. "What is Seleucia?"

"It's a prison," Tori told her.

"It's a very hard prison, cold, and dark. They do mining mostly. I think you chose well, Tori. I'm very proud of you." William leaned down hugging his niece.

As the Assemblymen pondered and debated Audric's fate, the Admiral led his family back to their seats.

"How did you learn about Seleucia?" Cassandra looked at Victoria.

"I happened to hear one of the guards mention it so I looked it up on the comm."

"Happened to overhear?" William quizzed.

"The door wasn't shut tight, is that my fault?" Those bright green eyes, so old minutes ago were young and mischievous again.

"No, not your fault. I'll have to speak with Marat on that." Looking over his shoulder, he saw Marat had heard.

"But if you do that, how will I learn anything?"

"The old-fashioned way," Cassandra told her, "you'll have to ask."

"Where's the fun in that?"

The pounding of the gavel ended their conversation.

"Royals, Assemblymen, Citizens of Carina. The Assemblymen have voted on the punishment to be given to Prince Audric for High Treason. The vote was unanimous. Seleucia, for life."

"No, you can't do that! I am a PRINCE!" Audric shouted as guards forced him out of the Assembly Hall.

"Princess Cassandra, would you rise?" Cassandra looked to William. Only he saw the question in her eyes as she stood.

"This Assembly, indeed all of Carina, is in your debt for you bringing this matter to our attention," Terwilliger gave her a slight bow.

"With all due respect, Assemblyman Terwilliger, I… We'd much rather have our family back than be in your debt. But that isn't possible, so we'll accept in the spirit it is given."

"Thank you. Are you prepared to continue your Challenge?" Cassandra looked at Yakira for a moment then walked to the center of the platform.

"Assemblyman Terwilliger, I don't believe I have anything else to say concerning the Challenge."

"Then, Princess Cassandra, the only thing left is for you to reveal your birthmark." Everyone in the Assembly sat forward as Cassandra's hand moved to her boot.

"She must dissolve her Union first!" Cassandra's hand froze. Her eyes cold as she found the voice, Assemblyman Oschofield of the House of Knowledge.

"Excuse me?" her voice was frigid stabbing Oschofield.

"The heir to the throne must marry within her House. Admiral Zafar is of the House of Protection." Cassandra said nothing just looked at Terwilliger.

"I'm sorry, Princess. It is the law."

"Just so we are all clear," Cassandra looked from Terwilliger to the Royals, seeing the regret in Jotham's eyes, to the Assemblymen, then to the people in the balconies. "You are saying I must choose between my husband and the throne?"

"Yes, your Union must be dissolved."

Turning from the Assembly, she walked to William, who stood at her approach.

"I'm ready to go." Ignoring those watching, William framed her face with his hands, looking deep into her eyes, seeing the truth.

"You're sure?"

"Yes."

"Guards!" The Admiral's voice commanded. Security immediately surrounded them. "Marat, you have point."

As the group started to move out Yakira stood, "What are you doing!?!" she demanded. Cassandra put a hand on William's arm.

"Marat," he halted Marat as Cassandra walked to Queen Yakira.

"The throne is yours, this Challenge is ended. I will not sacrifice my husband for it." She looked to the Assembly and knew she had something that must be said. Walking forward she started.

"Twenty-five hundred cycles ago, a man and a woman fell in love, a Prince and a Princess. But because they were from different Houses, a Union was denied. They were ordered to marry others. Instead of submitting to a life of misery, they left together. Your own text called them Carina's Brightest Light and it's Bravest Warrior, Sabah and Kayden, my ancestors."

"They took what they believed to be the best of Carina, leaving behind what they saw as injustice. And they built their own House on a planet that was named Earth. They brought the first written language and skills never before seen on the planet. They built, created, lived and protected each other and the family they had."

"Nine sons and one daughter. All went on to become Kings and a Queen on their own; creating dynasties. Building a civilization based on the freedom of choice and that there must be more than just laws but justice because, without justice, your laws, your rules, and procedures mean nothing."

"Today, you as an Assembly, as a people, stood for the people of Earth, against one of your own and found them justice. For myself, Victoria, and the family we lost on Earth I thank you for that." A tear ran down Cassandra's cheek before her voice became pointed.

"But if you think, for one minute, that I would choose a throne, a crown, a House, over my husband, then you've learned nothing from Sabah and Kayden's leaving. And just to make sure we are perfectly clear. I choose Admiral William Zafar. It's my privilege to be his wife." Turning she walked to her future.

William watched his wife turn her back on the Assembly. On what was rightfully hers, by birth, for him. Her eyes, while clear, still contained the fire of what she considered a slight against him. Walking out to meet her he saw Valerian charge the platform drawing his weapon. "Cassandra!"

Cassandra spun around just in time to see Valerian fire his weapon, at William. In horror, she watched as both Paa and William went down, hard.

"No!" she screamed.

"You will not take my command!" Valerian ranted as he advanced on her.

On the floor, William was struggling to move the injured Paa off him. The stupid kid dove in front of him, taking the full blast from Valerian's weapon. He had to get to Cassandra.

"And you!" Valerian pointed his weapon at Cassandra, "You will never be a High Admiral's wife."

Seeing William moving, she knew he was alive, Valerian didn't. If he did, he'd fire at him again. She needed to keep his focus on her.

"What the fuck are you talking about?" Cassandra challenged moving to the side making Valerian move his head.

"Do you think I'm stupid, that I don't know they voted yesterday to make Zafar High Admiral. To retire me! After all I've done for them, all the cycles I've given."

"Like letting a traitor have free reign for over seven cycles?"

"You with your fake challenge to the throne! All you care about was catching Audric so Zafar could become High Admiral! That's what this is all about!"

"So it has nothing to do with the murder of billions of people, people that might have been saved if you'd done your job!"

"Who cares about them, you used them to get what Zafar wanted and now you won't show your birthmark. Proof that this was all a hoax, a hoax to discredit me." As William was finally getting free of Paa, Valerian's eye caught the movement.

"You want to see my birthmark?" Cassandra's sharp question distracted him from the motion. "You want proof? So everyone here knows once and for all just what kind of man the Admiral is?"

"Yes!"

"Fine!" Pulling her pant leg aside, Cassandra unfastened her boot, grabbed the heel and flung it aside. "There, is that what you needed to see!"

No one in the Assembly moved as for the first time in nearly twenty-five hundred years the birthmark of the true Queen was seen.

"No, that can't be." Valerian staggered back, shocked, his weapon lowering slightly.

"It can be, you sorry excuse for a leader. It filled with color while on the Retribution, still two days from Carina."

Valerian's eyes went wild as he realized what he had done. He had threatened and insulted the true Queen. Threatened and spied on her family, in an attempt to kidnap a Royal. He was finished. But he wouldn't go down alone.

"You will never take the throne," he brought his weapon up and fired.

∞ ∞ ∞ ∞ ∞

William was the only one moving as Cassandra revealed her birthmark. Valerian was insane and his wife was in the line of fire. He tackled her moments before Valerian fired. Tar shot at the same time, followed by every weapon from Cassandra's House. Valerian was dead before he hit the floor.

"Cassandra," William looked down at her pale face, "Cassandra!"

Opening her eyes at William's demand, she found her husband frantically searching her face. She had scared him.

"I'm fine," she wheezed, "Just got the wind knocked out of me." As William sat them both up, she wrapped her arms around him, burying her face in his chest. Her guards surrounded them, weapons drawn.

"Come on." Kissing the top of her head, he stood, lifting her with him. "Let's get you out of here."

"Victoria!" Her eyes searched for her but couldn't see past the guards. "William!"

"She's in Lucas' arms, she's safe." Cassandra gave herself a second to sag against him, to draw from his strength.

"You're not hurt?" Her hands started to fly over him.

"No, Paa took the full hit." With his arm around her, he helped her hobble on one heel toward Victoria.

"How is he?" She looked at Paa being tended by Bliant.

"Kid's lucky," Bliant answered the Queen's question "He wore his blast jacket. Otherwise, he'd be dead. Still, he'll be hurting for a while."

She looked at the unconscious young man. She owed him more than she could ever repay. He'd saved her husband. His grandfather would be proud.

"He's to receive the best care, Bliant."

"He'll get it, Majesty." Bliant gave her a slight bow then turned back to his patient.

"Aunt Cassie!" Lucas continued to hold Victoria until guards enclosed them all, then released her into her aunt's arms.

"You're okay? All of you?" Cassandra scanned Leander, Javiera, and Amina.

"Fine, we're all fine," they reassured her.

"Cassandra…your birthmark. It colored while you were still on the Retribution?" Kyle gripped her arm.

"What?" She frowned at him, "Yes, before we arrived."

"Cassandra, it's important. You're sure?" Kyle tightened his grip.

"Kyle, she's sure." William frowned at his son. "Now we're leaving. Guards!"

"No! Dad, Cassandra, wait, just wait! Please?" It was his son's insistence that had William pausing. He looked at Cassandra, she nodded.

Kyle pushed his way through the guards to the front of the Assembly, walking around Valerian's now covered body.

"Assemblyman Terwilliger! Assemblyman Terwilliger! I need to be heard!" When he was ignored, he turned. "King Jotham!" Kyle sent Jotham a pleading look.

"Terwilliger! Recognize Kyle Zafar!" King Jotham's eyes would brook no argument.

Not sure any of them could take much more, Terwilliger pounded his gavel on the podium until some semblance of order was reestablished.

"Quiet! I will have order or I will have this hall cleared! The Assembly recognizes Scholar Kyle Zafar."

"Assemblyman Terwilliger, there can no longer be any doubt that the true Queen has returned. Cassandra bears the full birthmark, she is the Queen."

"Scholar Zafar," Terwilliger rubbed his neck. "While no one here argues with you, that she carries the Queen's birthmark, the fact remains she has married outside her House. If she refuses to dissolve her Union, our hands are tied."

"Why?"

"Why?" Terwilliger was becoming angry. "As stated earlier the heir to the throne must marry within her own House!"

"Of course he or she must," Kyle agreed.

"Then what are you arguing about?!?"

"King Jotham, when did you become King?" Jotham raised an eyebrow at the question, not sure where Kyle was going.

"I was crowned King of the House of Protection 10 Iuil 5252."

"No, when did you *become* King?"

"I became King twenty days earlier when my birthmark colored," Jotham began to see where Kyle was going.

"Assemblyman Terwilliger, do you accept that an heir to a throne becomes King or Queen when their birthmark fills in, not when they are crowned?"

"Of course but…"

"And do you believe the statement made by Cassandra that her birthmark filled in when she was still on the Retribution?"

"I see no reason to doubt her word."

"Does anyone in this Assembly question her word?" Kyle challenged and silence greeted him.

"Then I charge that this Assembly has no say over *Queen* Cassandra's Union. The law applies only to the heir to the throne, not the current Ruler. She was Queen before her Union. Therefore, the Union Law does not apply."

Terwilliger looked from Kyle to Cassandra and the Admiral, who had stepped out of their security to listen to Kyle. There was nothing he'd like to do more than agree but...

"Agreed." All heads turned to Yakira. "Once a birthmark fills, the heir is the Queen and the Queen may choose anyone she wishes for her Union."

"William..." Cassandra looked at him not sure what she was hearing.

"You are Queen. Cassandra, it's your birthright, your destiny."

"Only with you at my side, you are my destiny." William lifted her hand to kiss the ring on her finger.

"I will always be at your side. I told you, I'm not letting go."

"Okay. Then here we go." Turning, Cassandra walked alone to the center of the platform and became Queen Cassandra Qwes Zafar of the House of Knowledge.

Chapter Forty-Two

Returning to the Royal Wing, they found Hutu had arranged a celebration in the formal living room. Taking the glass William handed her, she waited until everyone had one, including the guards.

"I would like to personally thank each and every one of you. Each of you played a vital role in making my reign possible. To Chief Marat and his men," Cassandra named each one, "you've kept us all safe and secure during some trying times."

"Colonel Tar, your knowledge, skills, and loyalty were invaluable. Hutu, for keeping us all fed, for finding those special things like Fudge Torta, and chocolate chip cookies. Leander, your support here and on the Retribution. Amina, my new niece, you have been a joy to know. Javiera, your support, understanding, and friendship has made difficult times easier."

"Lucas, while there are many times I'd like to beat you, you've been a good friend and someone I trust implicitly.

"Kyle, you once said you wouldn't be much help. You were wrong. If it weren't for your knowledge, I wouldn't be Queen."

"Victoria, you are the bravest little girl. Your parents and grandfather would be very proud of you."

"And to the Admiral," she turned to her husband, eyes full of love, "For protecting us. For knowing what needed to be done and being willing to do it. For being my life mate and husband, I love you."

William listened with pride to his wife, to her making sure everyone knew they had a hand in what happened today. That each was vital. It was her way, and would make her a beloved Queen, always recognizing the contributions of others. But he hadn't expected her to include him. Her words, full of love humbled him.

"You are my life, my wife, and my Queen. I love you." Leaning down he kissed his wife, long and hard, much to the enjoyment of those present.

"To Queen Cassandra and Admiral Zafar," Quinn proposed the toast. With glasses raised the toast was repeated. With her husband's arm around her waist, Cassandra's eyes sparkled as she sipped the Carinian champagne.

Looking around the room she saw their House, filled with family and friends. The one, she and William had built together, on their own terms.

"And what are you two whispering about over there?" She'd been watching Victoria and Amina, they were plotting something.

"Who us?" Victoria's voice was sugary innocent, her eyes mischievous.

"Yes, you."

"We just thought that maybe someone should eat some Fudge Torta before it goes bad."

"Goes bad?" Cassandra looked to see Hutu covering his mouth.

"Well it might, and that would be a very bad thing."

"I couldn't agree more. Why don't you and Amina make sure everyone gets a piece, then you two can have what's left."

"Really?" The girls exchanged excited looks.

"Really. Let Hutu cut it, though, we might want more than just a bite."

"Oh, man!" Victoria knew she had been caught but with a smile headed to Hutu.

"What's she going to be like at eighteen?" William leaned over to ask, smiling.

"Trouble, lots of trouble. Won't it be fun?" Cassandra smiled back.

"Admiral," Marat walked to the couple's side, "Majesty, King Jotham and Queen... Princess Yakira are at the door."

"Show them in," William looked at his wife knowing this was their life now. As they entered, the room quieted.

"My apologies for intruding at this time, Majesty," Jotham gave Cassandra a slight bow. "I know it's been a trying day. I need to speak with the Admiral and Princess Yakira was hoping for a few minutes of your time."

"No apologies necessary," Cassandra spoke first. "Let's go to a quieter spot." All eyes followed them as they left the room.

"Admiral, if I could speak with you alone?" Will raised an eyebrow to his friend.

"We'll use my Ready Room."

"Princess Yakira, it's a lovely day out. Would you mind if we walked in the garden? I'd like to stretch my legs."

"Cassandra," William frowned.

"I assume the King's guards are still on patrol?" Jotham nodded. "Would you prefer I get Marat?" she waited for William's decision.

"I'll let him know where you are. Where both of you are." With a nod to Princess Yakira, he led Jotham to the Ready Room.

∞ ∞ ∞ ∞ ∞

Opening the garden doors, she allowed Yakira to go first. Following, she left the doors open.

"You really would have waited for Marat if Admiral Zafar had wanted you to?" Yakira wasn't sure why she was amazed, not after all that happened today.

"Of course, his only concern is for my safety." Cassandra walked along one of the paths.

"And yet he allowed you to go through the Challenge, knowing you were the true Queen. Knowing you would be at risk. Why?"

"Because I asked him to." Cassandra turned to look at Yakira. And she realized it was as simple as that.

"What do you want, Yakira?"

"To know what you're going to do. So I can prepare and, prepare my family."

"You mean your children."

"Yes, this is going to be difficult for them."

"They're beautiful children. Their resemblance to their father is remarkable."

"They look nothing like Audric!" Yakira found herself having to take a deep breath.

"I said their father, Prince Vane, not your husband."

Yakira's eyes were wide with shock at Cassandra's statement. No one knew, only her and Audric. "How could you tell?"

"They are obviously brother and sister. They look nothing like Audric. Vance was born seven months after the Union. And Audric despises both of them."

"Yes, yes he does."

"Once things have calmed down, settled, and you've had time to confer with your children, I would not oppose getting the correct father listed on their proofs of birth."

"What?" Yakira was stunned at the thought, that she would be willing.

"You chose to marry Audric, that's no reason to punish your children."

"I…thank you. They already know, they will be grateful."

Cassandra nodded. "Now down to business." She walked into the center of the garden. "I would like Assemblyman Bevington to accompany you back to Kisurri, if he's willing to be my intermediary during this transition. Will you have a problem with that?"

"No."

"As it's been over two hundred cycles since such a transition has occurred, there will be questions. For you, for me, for the citizens of the House of Knowledge. Hopefully, together we will be able to do this with the least amount of turmoil. There's been enough of that lately."

"Agreed."

"I'm hoping two weeks will be long enough for everyone to settle and get used to the idea. Have you given any thought to where you'd like to relocate to?"

"No, all the buildings are owned by the House of Knowledge."

"I believe you had one built, in the Neva area."

"Yes, it's near Vane's parents," Yakira refused to let herself hope.

"Would that be suitable for your family? Big enough for your needs?"

"I...yes."

Cassandra nodded. "Then it will be part of your compensation for tending to the House during my family's absence. Other arrangements will also be made. You and your children will not be discarded."

"Why? Why are you doing this?" Yakira had to know. "It isn't required, no one expects it."

"Why?" Cassandra leaned down to smell a rose. "Why did you cast the first 'guilty' vote? He's your spouse." She stood confronting Yakira. "Why did you agree with Kyle on my Union? You could still be Queen."

"Audric was guilty, he used me, my position, the power of the House of Knowledge to murder. Not because he loved me but because he wanted the power being my spouse gave him." Yakira saw the sympathy in Cassandra's eyes. "Not like you. You were willing to abandon the throne of the most powerful House on Carina for your spouse. And he would have let you."

"He loves me." Cassandra let the simple statement say it all.

"And you love him, it's obvious to everyone. You stand. For each other, for what you believe in. The House of Knowledge will need that, need both of you, to recover from the damage Audric has caused. Your Union is valid, its right, that's why I agreed."

∞ ∞ ∞ ∞ ∞

Jotham waited while Will contacted his chief of security, informing him of the Queen's location. "She'll have to get used to that." William raised an eyebrow. Jotham continued, "Having someone always knowing where she is."

"She'll handle it. There's little she can't, given time."

"And that's what makes her perfect, for you. You're the same way. Something I've always admired."

"What's up, Jotham?"

"Valerian was right."

William leaned back in his chair. "About?"

"There was a High Council called yesterday to discuss Valerian's recent behavior; the rumors of the traitor, his comments about the Challenger, about you." Silence greeted Jotham's comment. He smiled. His friend, Will, hadn't changed. Standing, Jotham walked over to pour them each a glass of ale, handing one to Will.

"A preliminary vote was taken. You were chosen to be High Admiral. But it was decided that the final vote would be made after the Challenge was completed."

"They wanted to judge Cassandra first."

"She would be the High Admiral's wife. It's a powerful position."

"As opposed to being Queen," William commented wryly.

Jotham smiled at his friend, "Yes, as opposed to being Queen." Jotham's smile faded looking into his friend's eyes, "The final vote was made after you left the Assembly."

"Carnot will make a fine High Admiral." Taking a sip of his ale, William looked at his friend and King.

"Will, the vote was unanimous. We want you." Jotham saw the shock in William's eyes. "You've more than earned the position."

"Jotham..." He had to move. As he paced, he thought, High Admiral. He'd never considered it, never considered the possibility of it. Even after what Quinn had said. His wife was Queen, a powerful Queen. He turned, "I'm not giving up Cassandra." His eyes locked with Jotham's.

"No one's asking you to. Will, she was and is the Queen and your wife. She made that quite clear." Jotham smiled slightly at just how clear she'd made it. "You were the choice before the Challenge; Cassandra's actions only reinforced that. She stands, Will. For you, for Carina, for what she believes in."

It was Jotham's turn to lean back. "You realize the two of you are becoming something of a legend. Apparently when she presented herself as Cassandra Qwes Zafar, the Fleet went wild."

"What?" William sat back down. "They couldn't have gotten reports that quickly."

"Will, the Challenge was transmitted, real time throughout the Coalition. Every planet, every ship, voice and image. The Admiral's Queen, that's what they're calling her."

"She's her own Queen."

"True, but you're her Admiral. She stands at your side." Jotham wondered if he realized how rare that was.

"Jotham, I'm honored, but I need to discuss it with Cassandra first. You and I know what it means to be High Admiral. She doesn't."

"I expected no less. Tomorrow?"

"I'll let you know once a decision is made." Jotham nodded.

∞ ∞ ∞ ∞ ∞

He found her sitting on a bench in the garden, her face raised to the lowering suns, eyes closed, boots off, a gentle smile on her lips. Hearing his approach, she opened those incredible eyes to look at him.

"I knew you'd find me," smiling she started to stand.

"Sit."

"What's wrong?" her smile faded.

"Nothing's wrong."

"William," she knew him, "what did Jotham say?"

Looking at his wife he realized she was thinking the worst. After the day she had, he should have realized. He needed to just tell her.

"Valerian was apparently right."

"Right about what, the man was insane."

"The High Council voted to remove him."

"What? William," he watched her eyes start to sparkle, "tell me…."

"They voted unanimously for me to become High Admiral. Whoa!" He laughed as she launched herself into his arms.

"William, that's wonderful! You deserve it. You'll make a great High Admiral!"

"Cassandra," he kissed her to quiet her, "I haven't accepted."

"What? Why?" Leaning back she looked at him, "Because of me?"

"Cassandra, you are about to assume the most powerful throne on the planet. There are going to be thousands of decisions that need to be made."

"And you don't think I can make them?"

"Of course you can! That's not what I'm saying."

"So what are you saying?" She slipped out of his hands as she stood and walked away from him.

"That I don't think this is the right time."

"It probably isn't the right time for me to have conceived either. But I have. You've been offered the most prominent position in the Fleet. A chance to make High Admiral means something again, how can you say no?"

"You would have given up your throne for me!" William rose along with his voice.

"That was entirely different. It meant nothing to me. This, you've worked your whole life for this!"

"And it means nothing without you!"

"What are you saying?" Cassandra paled. "They asked you to dissolve our Union?"

"No! No," William rubbed her arms and found her chilled. "I'm not doing this right. Give me a minute." Taking off his jacket he wrapped it around her, drawing her close.

"I told Jotham I needed to speak with you first, let me finish." She nodded. "The High Admiral…it's every hour of every day."

"24/7 got it," Cassandra smiled.

William raised an eyebrow at the term, finding he liked it. "I can be called away at a moment's notice. Not be able to keep appointments. Be gone for days at a time."

That got a frown from Cassandra. "Why gone?"

"If there's a battle I need to be available."

"Of course you do. But why can't you come home after?"

"Cassandra, it took nearly two hours for us to get here from the Retribution."

"It did? I hadn't realized. I just thought it was my trying not to vomit that made it seem so long." William rested his forehead against hers. Thanking the Ancestors for her.

"That's four hours round trip."

"William, being Queen is going to be a 24/7 job too. I can be called away at any time. Be needed anywhere. Am I right?"

"Yes."

"So all that is a wash, it doesn't matter," she explained. "Now not having you next to me every night, I'm not going to like that. Really not going to like that." Touching his cheek she already missed him. "But it won't be every night."

"Cassandra...."

"And if you play your cards right, you might be able to convince the Queen of the House of Knowledge to give her husband, the High Admiral, one of those fast little ships of hers," she said as she stretched to give him a kiss. "Totally outfitted for a High Admiral's needs, of course. To get him to and from in the fastest possible time," she gave him another soft kiss.

"You're serious," William leaned back to stare at her.

"It's time you start using your wife instead of her using you." Smiling she let him know she was joking.

"Take the position, William. It's what you were born to do. It's your destiny. I'll be at your side. I'm not letting go either. We'll work the rest out, it won't be a perfect life, but it will be our life."

"Our life," leaning down to seal his promise with a kiss, the star that was Earth's sun sparkled just a little brighter for a moment.

∞ ∞ ∞ ∞ ∞

Michelle has always loved to read and writing is just a natural extension of this for her. Growing up, she always loved to extend the stories of books she'd read just to see where the characters went. Happily married for over twenty five years she is the proud mother of two grown children and with the house empty has found time to write again. You can reach her at m.k.eidem@live.com or her website at http://www.mkeidem.com she'd love to hear your comments.

∞ ∞ ∞ ∞ ∞

57929673R00376

Made in the USA
Columbia, SC
15 May 2019